MW01132302

Draven's Afterlife

King of Kings

Book 1

By Stephanie Hudson

Copyright

This book is a work of fiction. Names, characters, places and incidents are either a product of the author's imagination or are used fictitiously. Any resemblance to actual people living or dead, events or locales is entirely coincidental.

Warning:
This book contains explicit sexual content, some graphic language and a highly addictive Alpha Males.

Cover design by: © Blake Hudson Designs

DEDICATION

I dedicate this book to an eighty-year-old love story...

A man named Noel Close once met a woman named Joan Tickle. They met as friends back in a time when people left their doors unlocked, and kids played on the streets without fear of what dangers this new modern world held. It may have been a time of war, but at the best of times, I am told, it was all about the dances.

And Joan and Noel loved nothing more than to dance. They started dating at the age of fifteen, and soon after he married the woman he loved. They travelled the world together and took many pictures of all their adventures. But then, as is only deemed natural but cruel in life, age slowed them down and soon Joan became very ill after suffering a stroke. She swiftly became bedridden for the last five years of her life, where Noel, at aged 92, looked after her every need until the day she died.

I was told that day that when she passed, he had been holding her hand when suddenly the light blew above them. He got up to try and fix it, getting a new bulb but when he came back...*she was gone.*

The light of his life had suddenly vanished, in what seemed like a mere flicker of time.

My Grandparents were married for 71 years.

The moral of my story is that time is precious, and we need to live each day, not like it's our last but as though our last breath is worth our time.

'Put your hand on a hot stove for a minute, and it seems like an hour. Sit with a pretty girl for an hour, and it seems like a minute.'

Albert Einstein.

Afterlife Saga

About the Author

Stephanie Hudson has dreamed of being a writer ever since her obsession with reading books at an early age. What first became a quest to overcome the boundaries set against her in the form of dyslexia has turned into a life's dream. She first started writing in the form of poetry and soon found a taste for horror and romance. Afterlife is her first book in the series of twelve, with the story of Keira and Draven becoming ever more complicated in a world that sets them miles apart.

When not writing, Stephanie enjoys spending time with her loving family and friends, chatting for hours with her biggest fan, her sister Cathy who is utterly obsessed with one gorgeous Dominic Draven. And of course, spending as much time with her supportive partner and personal muse Blake who is there for her no matter what.

Authors words...

My Love and devotion is to all my wonderful fans that keep me going into the wee hours of the night but foremost to my wonderful daughter Ava...who yes, is named after a cool, kick ass, demonic bird and my son Jack, who is a little hero. I am also happy to say that we are expecting our next little bundle of madness to our family in July 2019.

WARNING!

This book contains explicit sexual content, some graphic language and a highly addictive Alpha Male.

This book has been written by a UK Author with a mad sense of humour. Which means the following story contains a mixture of Northern English slang, dialect, regional colloquialisms and other quirky spellings that have been intentionally included to make the story and dialogue more realistic for modern day characters.

Thanks for reading x

Contents

Keira

PROLOGUE

"Why are we afraid of the darkness when the light shows us more of the land of nightmares?"

I listened overhead as the footsteps grew nearer. My body convulsed as a natural reflex took over. Every fibre in my being was screaming as every sense told me danger was near. The smell of the damp space was flooding my nostrils as though a rotting corpse was sat in the corner. The palms of my hands bled from the nails I was imbedding into them, knuckles bone white until every finger ached.

I heard him now. The boots he always wore were like the drums of Hell dragging him closer to me, and the sound was my very own personal mental torture. They were thick soled like biker's boots, only every time he came to me I never heard the heavy roar of a bike's engine. I knew I didn't have long now until the foul breath of a true monster was breathing down my ear, explaining to me how the things Hell created could feel... *Could love.*

I didn't believe his lies, for who could?

My breath caught in my chest as I had counted the time in heartbeats I had left. Was this the end? My end? Was this the time, my final time, in which the darkness would drag me under?

The black space flooded with unnatural light and a figure emerged like death's silhouette. No matter how many times he had come to me I still couldn't prevent the gasp that escaped my bitten lips, already swollen and bloody. Fear gripped at them making them quiver uncontrollably, the way they always did every time I saw something I couldn't explain. I wanted to be strong enough. I needed to be, or I would never be freed from this curse.

The time was now.

His time was at an end.

The sharp edges I wouldn't let go of dug into my hands making them slick with blood. I heard that first footstep descend the stairs but I wouldn't turn my head again. Turning away from the face of my death, I did what I had to do.

"Goodbye." I said with my last breath before my vision filled with blood.

I opened my eyes with a start, alert and ready. It took me a moment to understand my surroundings and take in all the other passengers who were staring at my sudden movements. I guess on a long-haul flight everyone was a little twitchy and the sight of me bolting upright gifted me with a few startled looks. It was fine, I was so used to those looks that it was second nature to me now. I was a master at feeling numb and I stared ahead as if no one else was around.

I scratched my arms out of sheer habit as the details of my recurring dream came back to me with a nauseating churn in my stomach. I tasted the familiar flavour of bile in my mouth. The dark aftertaste my dreams always provided. I looked down at my arms and I released a sigh when I saw the long sleeves of cotton that covered them. The dream wasn't how it had happened, but it was always the same way my mind played it back to me, no matter how wrong the details were.

"Did you have a nightmare, dearie?" I almost jumped as the first person in hours spoke to me. A plump, grey haired lady with a flower print top that looked like it had once been curtains smiled at me, as she waited for the only words I could say.

"Something like that."

DRAVEN

I

SOMETHING NEW

Old sights. Old smells. Old life.

Even if this was *New* England, for it didn't matter. Because as usual, the years all seemed to simply merge into one and the monotonous tasks were starting to once again weigh down on my soul. And finding myself now on a flight towards Afterlife was no different than it was last year or the year before that and so on.

"Dom, did you hear me?" I heard Vincent speaking and shook the cobwebs of melancholy from my mind.

"But of course," I said turning to face my brother knowing what I would find. That being, arms crossed and a perceptive smug look plastered on his face. Well, it was time to do what most brothers did in these situations, and that was to try and prove him wrong.

"You enquired to know why our sister decided to go on ahead of us." There, you smug bastard, I thought with a grin, especially when I saw his face drop. It was the same face he granted me whenever I bested him on the mats, something I was pleased to note happened often. Alright, so I wasn't in mind to mention how much it took to heal my vessel afterwards, as it had to be said, my brother may have been smug, but he was also one tough bastard right alongside it!

But as of late, I had found my mind elsewhere, so let's just say that I wasn't in a hurry to gift my brother with a victory any time soon.

"So, any idea as to why?" Vincent asked once he'd had his proof that I was listening. I shrugged my shoulders and replied,

"I don't know, why does Sophia do half the shit she does? As usual she is a law unto herself and does as she pleases."

"And most times I would agree with you, but this time...I don't know..." I watched as Vincent struggled to describe why he felt this time was different, which was when I started to think about her behaviour myself. It was true that the last few weeks she had been unusually quiet, but when you were as old as we were, then it was a common thing to find yourself out of sorts. By the Devil, but I could even sympathise with feeling that way myself on occasion.

Maybe it was time for a new project or business venture, as that usually kept him busy for a while.

"It's natural Vince, and it's not like we haven't been through it all before with her," I said as a way to try and ease my brother's worries. The funny thing was that Vincent no doubt had this same conversation to Sophia about me, for I was known for my dark moods far more than our sister was. But then I had the added weight of being overruling King of a hidden Supernatural Kingdom that lived among the entirety of the human population. A job that I didn't think possible to accomplish even half so well had it not been for the constant support and backing of my siblings. However, being what I was, then the task was primarily left up to me and for a good reason.

You see, Vincent was a king in his own right, ruling legions of his own angels. Just as my sister, who was a demon, ruled over her own realm. But I, well I was something else entirely.

I was the only angel/demon half breed in existence, which meant that with the power of both Heaven and Hell running through my veins, this meant there wasn't much I wasn't equipped to deal with. Of course, being stronger and more powerful than most certainly helped. But needless to say, that the three of us, well... we made a formidable and unbeatable force.

Now if I could just beat my own inner demon named boredom, then life would continue as it usually does, only with less of a bad temper for my siblings to have to endure. Gods, did I miss the old days! The days of wars to keep my mind busy and my hands even busier. But long ago had life lacked its lustre, and its purpose was becoming even further from the answer why.

But, of course, *I knew why.*

For shortly another year would be done with and just one more to add to the long list of ones lived through without her...without,

My Electus.

I tried not to think upon it too much, for the truth sometimes drove me to distraction enough that only a good fight would subdue such thoughts. But it was the nights that were the worst. Those endless, sleepless nights of asking myself when? When would she finally appear in my life as was prophesied? These were questions I would plague the Gods with but to no avail. For it was always the same answer, she will appear to me when the time is right. Which trust me, can get pretty fucking tiresome after two thousand years of waiting!

But seeing as it was the will of the Fates and essentially the fate of the chosen girl in question, then that answer was like an abyss my heart had long been suspended over. In other words, it was vast, and it was endless.

The only thing I did know for certain was that she had been born and by now would have reached the age of twenty-three. I knew this like I knew my own need to breathe. I had felt it that day as if something in my blood had fired up. After then I refused to take another to my bed. No doubt a foolish endeavour and would account for my mounting bad mood this last twenty-three years. Now do not mistake me, for I am no saint and far from one, meaning that even in a moment of weakness I had tried. I tried and failed. Because honestly, it had felt too much like a betrayal even before I set my sights on the girl. Which I assumed was all part of the Fates plan and why at times I hated them with a burning passion that branded a bitterness to my soul like it was somehow infected.

Now how I would feel about them when I am finally in her presence, I didn't know.

Unsurprisingly, I never spoke of this with my siblings or about my lack of women I took to my bed, for they would no doubt think me near to losing my mind. For what of the proof of her birth other than waking up one night after feeling as if my heart had been set aflame?

I even remember the dream as if it had afflicted me only yesterday. I was searching for something in the forest when I came across a mirror. I saw first my own reflection staring back at me, one very little changed since I was first gifted this body. But I heard something beyond it as if the mirror itself was a portal into the future. It was a woman's voice, and she was scared. I didn't think after that, I just heard it and ran, twisting my body side on ready to crash all my weight through to the other side of the glass.

However, all it did was stop me, making me bounce back as though it was made of Hell's black glass stone — a material used for many of the floors of my castle in my own ruling realm in Hell. Granted, it's not exactly what you would call a summer home, but it at least appeased my demon side to visit every now and again. Besides, Lucifer was only one being, and couldn't be expected to keep control over the entirety of Hell by himself. He is classed as a God yes, but even they could only do so much.

So, what had I done when faced with the near impenetrable force I was being denied entrance into...? I spent the remainder of my dream trying to prove that no will in Heaven, Hell or on Earth could keep me from her. In the end and after many attempts, I had taken a run at it one last time and finally created the damage needed. This happened when once close enough I had punched the centre with my fist and at the same time, released my demonic sword down my arm.

It finally penetrated the glass, but the power of it sent me flying backwards, skidding on a knee with my wings trying to create resistance against the force. A shock wave had come from the cracks I made and all that could be seen after that was a slim, feminine hand reach out and rest upon the glass for only a second before I had awoken.

I remember waking being so frustrated that I looked down to find the bedsheets torn and shredded between my demonic hands, with my talons still embedded within the material. In all of my years upon this Earth, I had never once remembered being so out of control.

Yes, I lost my temper, many a time in fact. But even then, I still remained in control of my demon side, keeping it locked down and for a good reason. I believe this was down to the angel side whose battle against the opposing force was a constant reminder to what could happen should I let such a power consume me and take control. Hell, if that ever happened, then I would be rendered a useless King and have to be judged myself. Naturally, this was not something I wanted to happen, which therefore was the reason for concern when my Chosen One was finally found.

This slight lapse in control was another reason added to many as to why I never spoke about this sudden change in my character with my siblings. And as if fate had also intervened at the time, my long-standing partner Aurora had also tried to make a mockery of me. Foolishly thinking to use jealousy as a driving force in fortifying our sham of a relationship. I believe I shocked everyone when my actions lacked the obvious blood loss and death they had all been expecting.

Aurora included. Which needless to say had been her merciless intent.

But no matter how beautiful and captivating I had once found the angel, I knew, like most did, that after a certain amount of time spent in her company, it soon became impossible to ignore the truth. That being that she was as black on the inside as she was light on the outside. Her soul was rotten to the core and held an ugliness that no amount of beauty could hide.

So instead of killing the poor fool she had tried to condemn to a near predictable death warrant, I had simply told him he was welcome to her. Something I deemed punishment enough in my eyes. After which, I then cast her out. An action that Sophia had naturally approved of and surprisingly, so had my brother. Meaning that up until then, I hadn't realised just how deeply their dislike for her had been rooted.

My only mistake had been a few years ago when she had appealed to the better and more angelic side of my nature in giving her another chance to prove herself at my council table. Oh, she had her uses among the seats, for she seemed to know a few valuable connections that came in handy from time to time. But what I hadn't known by doing so was the price of such kindness shown would backfire. For I was forced then endure a constant display and shameless attempt at securing my favour once more.

I had indeed put her in her place a few times now and the annoyance at this being deemed necessary, well let's just say that it left a sour taste in my mouth more than once. I doubted very much that it would be long before my temper snapped completely, and she would once again find herself being replaced at my table.

Sophia would, at the very least, be pleased.

But thinking of my sister did make me wonder of her strange behaviour of late. I knew of this deeper calling she felt the Fates had bestowed upon her when it came to my Chosen One. I had questioned it once when she would hound me like a Hellbeast yapping at my heels to try searching for her once more. Something I had done with no success, I might add. For even she knew as I did that it was a hopeless endeavour, as it was always prophesied that she would find me, not the other way around.

She would come to me.

A thought that I admit had tortured my mind and many a time toyed with the frayed old edges of my soul for I was forever growing tired of this eternal wait. And now, knowing that she was in the world somewhere… *finally…* was even harder than before. Because with each passing year I knew that it was simply another one for me to add to the list I would be forced to miss out on.

But of course, I wanted her to become of age, for I found it nothing but distasteful when a woman was taken too young, as was the case for more years than it had not. Something I was thankful not to allow in my kingdom when I was king, for a girl could still be just a girl even after she had discovered her first bleed.

It was too soon in my eyes, and thankfully my thoughts were mirrored throughout my kingdom. No, I didn't want some fearful little one and six in my bed… or should I say as times now expressed it as a sweet sixteen-year-old. No, I wanted a woman to warm my bed who had grown into her body with the curves a female should have. I didn't want to feel bone beneath my fingertips when I touched her, but soft flesh I knew would do nicely in cushioning against the hardness of my own body.

But alas, this was all just a dream for until I met her, then I would never know. My only clue had been a blonde-haired beauty displaying a golden fleece of my very own. Reason enough not to take one to my bed again until a weakness became too much in Aurora. The truth be known, I had simply wanted to feel something sooner than not, a clear mistake on my part.

"Dom?" Vincent called my name in question, and this time there was no getting away with feigning my interest in what he had been saying.

"We are landing soon," he informed me with an annoying and knowing chuckle. I nodded in acknowledgement as I was in no mood to divulge as to why I was acting in such a distracted way. No doubt he knew, for that was the thing with Vincent. He was the one who could read me like no other and just know how to calm my fiery nature. He knew far too much. In fact, sometimes he would simply look at me in a knowing manner that I often found infuriating. Simply because it felt like a weakness when another knew of my inner turmoil.

But then again, he was my brother and his love for me was the reason he worried. It was the reason he cared enough to help, and this would often come in the form of saying very little or nothing at all. For he knew nothing could ease the echoing ache I felt, as though a piece of me was missing. And sometimes, like now, that hole felt like a fucking chasm!

I watched as the world below became closer and it was when seeing this view that the theory God was just a kid with an ant farm could really take shape into truth. However, the Gods had very little say in humanity and the choices they made, for free will was, unbeknown to them, their greatest gift. If not also an incredibly destructive one.

I couldn't help but wonder though was she down there, in the world below me somewhere? It made me want to touch the window and see if it were warm, as the glass had been that night in my dream. But I was aware of Vincent watching me and let's just say that I loved my brother enough not think it necessary to cause him reason for alarm.

Damn it, but I wished I had just flown the plane as I had wanted to, but then it was as Vincent had said, what was the sense of having a pilot on the payroll only for him to be sat in the wrong chair as a passenger. Besides, Vincent and I had business to discuss, which unfortunately had been concluded an hour into the flight.

Our time in England had been a pointless one for no alliance had come from my meeting with the Hellbeasts' King, Jared Cerberus and other than finding some worthy entertainment for the night, it had been a useless endeavour. He was a stubborn bastard, I had to give him that. But alas, it looked to continue to be an endless hope that one day the rulers of our realms would reunite. Something I wouldn't be holding my breath in hope for, as it was something I had been trying to achieve for a very long time now and unfortunately with no alliance in sight, it was soon becoming a dying dream at best.

I watched as the plane came in to land and for some reason, I found myself more than eager to be off it. I don't know what had come over me, but I felt a sort of pull like some ancient instinct was kicking in and telling me to get off the plane. So, after barely even waiting for the wheels to stop turning, I had the door open and was dropping the steps to the ground from my private jet.

"Dom! What are you doing?" I heard Vincent calling behind me, but I didn't stop. I jumped down from the plane and found myself walking past the black Rolls Royce Phantom that was waiting for us. I then walked towards the main building of Portland's International Airport without even giving my mind time to think why. Suddenly I felt a hand restrain me back and I turned around to find Vincent asking what had gotten into me, but I barely even heard him.

I simply looked back at the main building and stared at it with such intensity I swear I could have rocked its foundations if I had wanted to. But instead, the only foundations that moved were my own when I experienced a feeling unlike any other rock me to my core. I couldn't explain it, but it was as though I could feel something coming.

Something life changing.

Something...

New.

Keira

2

New World

New sights. New smells. New life.

This was New England.

And this was my last-ditch attempt at making something of my life, something that would be better than my past. So, I hitched up my shoulder bag and bent my knees to pick up the two suitcases that held everything I wanted to bring with me into this new life venture. I felt brave and slightly empowered with the knowledge that I had actually done it. I had boarded that plane and let it bring me here to start over. Yes, this was going to be a good thing.

I looked up, nodded to myself and started to walk with confidence that lasted all of half a second. I made it two steps when one of the other herded passengers bumped into me from behind, knocking my bag from my shoulder and making me stumble a step.

"Good start, Keira." I muttered to myself. Of course, now instead of walking through to the arrivals gate at Portland's International airport looking ready to take on the world, I was dragging a bag along the floor and walking along being pushed and shoved like the rest of the cattle. But none of this mattered, not when I saw her waiting for me.

"Libs!" I shouted as I jumped up and down taking my bags with me and looking like an overweight bird struggling to take off.

"Kaz?" My sister said trying to look over the tops of heads and as soon as I saw an opening I went for it. I ran with my cases rocking behind me as though they couldn't keep up on their pathetic little wheels. 'Sod it' I thought dropping them not far from my sister and her husband who were both waiting for me. I ran into my sister's arms as she ran into mine. We embraced as though we hadn't seen each other for years, when in actual fact it had been about nine months.

"Kazzy!" She shouted in my ear making me smile at hearing my nickname once again. I looked over her shoulder at her husband Frank to see him wink at me before going to save my bags from the human stampede. He was a good man and one, luckily for me, who was built to handle the masses. I smiled as I saw everyone getting out of his way.

"Hey Libs, I guess you missed me then." I said laughing as I felt the air being squeezed from my lungs.

"Oh, I don't know, maybe a little." I laughed and nudged her on the arm after she finally let me breathe freely.

"Yeah right." I commented making her smile.

"Hey kiddo, you do know we don't have a shortage of rocks in this country, right?" He asked and then pretended someone with those heavy weight lifting arms was struggling to lift my measly cases.

"Ha, ha, whatever tough guy!" I said leaving my sister's side to hug my big bear of a brother in law. He hugged me like he meant it, which was something he always did and then lifted me up, causing me to do the whole girly thing and squeal in surprise. I had been lucky to get on very well with who my older sister had decided to marry but the only downside had been where he hailed from. I didn't mind him being from the US, for starters his accent was fun to have around but what had sucked was that Libby had moved away and that had been like saying goodbye to my best friend.

It had been hard at the time, I realised that, especially after certain things happened in my own life, things we don't speak of for obvious reasons. But we all knew it was what she wanted and for the most part, other than missing her family, she loved it here. And now I was about to discover why for myself.

"So how did Mum and Dad take the big send-off...did poor Mum do that sniffing thing?" She referred to our mother and her sweet attempt at trying to keep the tears at bay. This, however only ended in this endearing snuffling noise and I hated to say it, which reminded me and Libs like a pig sniffing out truffles...a very cute pig mind you.

"Oh yeah, there was truffle finding by the plenty" I said making Libby laugh as we had both discussed this habit before, ever since we were kids and Libby went off to camp with school. Anyone would have thought she had been called off to war with the way my mum tried not to cry.

We both laughed as we walked out of the airport and I continued to tell my sister all the news from back home. It was a strange feeling to know that pretty soon I would be pulling up to a new house and calling that my new home. But in truth I was more than ready for it as there were just some things you just couldn't get over, not unless you left the country.

The decision had been hard for my mum and dad as they had been torn between what was right for me and what was best for them. They had already lost one daughter to the States and the idea of losing another hadn't been very high up on their bucket list. I felt bad, but I knew sticking around was only making it worse. I was an adult after all and according to my passport twenty-one years old, so it wasn't as if I needed my parents' consent. In the end it was simply my own decision to make and I made it...truffle finding or not.

I wanted to do something with my life but like many at my age I was still at a loss as to what it was. I knew that I wanted to go back to college and start afresh, giving myself once again that reason to get up in the mornings. It had been so easy to lose myself into that dark place and now I was out of it, I never wanted a trip back there.

I found out from Libs that mum had already called her to inform them I got on the flight okay and when to expect me, which made me smile. I knew my parents would worry, it was natural for any parents but mine had even more reason to worry and I hated knowing that. I shook these dark thoughts from my mind before they had chance to develop further. 'You are not going there today' I told myself firmly.

"Man, its freezing!" Libby complained, and I suppressed a giggle. My sister hated the cold and if she'd had her way I would have been arriving at Los Angeles International airport if Frank hadn't been born and bred here. His family all hailed from these parts and this was where he wanted to start a family more than anything else in the world. It was sweet really and I knew my sister felt the same way, although it never stopped her from complaining about the cold.

"Still not acclimatised to the weather then?" I asked looking to Frank and seeing him roll his eyes behind my sister's back. This time I really had to suppress a laugh, or I would've got him in trouble. We found the car in the sea of metal and Frank popped open the boot, which I knew was referred to here as the trunk. He put in my bags just as Libby said,

"No and neither will you, just wait until you see it snow! We actually have to put snow chains on the wheels of our car." On hearing this Frank actually snorted a laugh after slamming the door and then bravely said,

"We?" Libby shot him a look and said,

"What? I'm a girl and I like heels...can you see me putting on snow chains when I am dressed for the office?" Frank smirked as he walked round to the driver's side of the car and said,

"Oh yeah, now I can...mmm." I burst out laughing at Libby's scowl that was only half way there due to her also trying not to laugh. It was nice to see how well suited they were to each other. They bickered like any married couple did but most of the time it was all in good fun, as there had been plenty of times they had been caught acting like teenagers.

We all got in the car and I smiled when I saw Libby playing with the controls in an attempt to make this car the warmest place on Earth. I saw Frank's secret smile as he checked out his wife's antics before pulling out of the space. I had always wondered what it must be like to find that kind of love. The type that brought on those secret smiles in sight of your loved one's quirks or the way their stories were always told in parts with the other filling in the gaps.

I always thought that the unique 'true love' couples could make every day mundane things, like cooking or cleaning look like a well synchronized dance. Or they knew what the other one was thinking with just a look or a single touch. And secretly I had longed to discover what it must be like but never having been in love myself, I was left only to wonder. But in the end, I was just happy my sister had found it and in doing so, set so many futures spiralling down different roads, which now included mine.

The rest of the drive to my new home was filled with Libby playing catch up on gossip on subjects I was at a loss to understand but I had to say, one car journey and I now knew by name all of the people that pissed her off at work. Libby worked as an interior designer for a company in Portland and she lived for it. Whereas Frank originally worked as bodyguard and now owned his own business recruiting other bodyguards for his security firm.

That's how they'd met, Libby and Frank. She was at a concert at the time and he was contracted to provide the security. She had been stood in the wrong place when a fight broke out and she had been knocked out in the process. She would have been trampled on if Frank hadn't been doing his rounds and seen the whole thing happen.

So, like a knight in a black t-shirt and jeans, he jumped from the stands and over the barrier to take my sister in his arms, shielding her from the angry mob that had started to join the fight. This quick action surely saved her from serious injury, as they needed three ambulances on the scene after the mob finally broke up. It was like a big halo hung around his floppy, honey coloured hair that no matter how many times it was pushed back always managed to make its way back in front of his kind, chocolate coloured eyes.

It was sweet the way she always told the story and when he first got introduced to the family you could almost see my father rubbing his hands with glee. As if a fine suitor for one of his daughters had just walked in and was soon to claim her hand in marriage. Ok, so it hadn't been that far off the mark as it was only six months later, and they were getting hitched...I think my father silently wept with joy that day.

As we pulled up the gravel driveway my mouth dropped open at the first sight of the house. I had of course seen pictures of the house via that beautiful thing we all called 'A way of life' better known as the internet. But now seeing it in person and I quickly realised my little laptop screen really didn't do it justice at all. I was amazed and just stood there wide-eyed and speechless. My mouth was still hanging open and a wide grin lit up Libby's beautiful face.

"So, I take it you like it?" It wasn't really a question as she already knew the answer.

"It's... it's so BIG!" I said without needing to exaggerate.

"Welcome home kiddo!" Frank said twisting in his seat to look at me before cutting the engine and exiting the car. Libby and I both did the same and I was shamefully left standing there all wide eyed and staring at the house whilst we let Frank do all the work. I was definitely overwhelmed.

"She likes it." Libby said as Frank retrieved all my bags in one hand, slammed the boot and grinned at his wife's statement.

"Of course, I like it, what's not to like...? But I bet you guys rattle around in a place that big or at least you must lose each other." I said looking up and up.

"Nah, she just needs a few rug rats running 'bout the place!" He said beaming at the idea of producing a family for his worthy home, one I had to smile at since he called it a 'she' like you would a car or a boat. I looked back to the house and saw Frank with key in hand already with my bags at the door. At this rate he would be inside with a cold beer in his hand, TV on and sat in his favourite chair before me and Libs had finished staring at the place.

As I said, the house was huge and very timeworn but in the best way possible giving it that ancient fairy tale touch. It had so much character I didn't know where to look first. The charming building was a large wooden structure with faded white paint that just added to the magic the place held.

Clusters of little nooks and windows of different shapes and sizes and slate coloured roof tiles came down at different points on the unconventional shaped house. The front of the house was framed with a large deck, which even had a swinging chair that looked as ancient as the building itself. Faded green shutters framed most windows, which were now nailed open after being retired during the installation of triple glazing. Still the effect was enchanting and the whole aura left no doubt, this was one well-loved home.

What astonished me more was not just the house itself. No, it was more the grounds it sat in. Positioned on the very edge of the White Mountain National Park, we were surrounded by deep forest and everywhere you looked were oceans of green. In fact, I think I was now looking at every shade of green on the spectrum.

The landscape was an endless tide of mountains overflowing with enormous trees that wound around the house like a barrier, encasing it in living, breathing safety. It was only when I followed them one by one did I notice a clearing to one side.

It drew me closer like a magnet as I walked forward to discover its treasure. Then there, in front of me, stood the most fantastic view I think I had ever seen in all my years on this beautiful planet. The vista exploded into a sea of even more mountains made from a lush green carpet of thousands of trees. Hell, it looked like millions!

The beauty before my eyes held me captive like a rabbit caught in headlights, taking my breath away. If I could cry, which I didn't do much these days as my tears had long run dry, I would have now. I wanted to show my pleasure in what I was seeing, but I was rendered speechless.

"As you know it was inherited from Frank's uncle." Libby's voice brought me back and I turned around to see that she had followed me to the clearing.

"How old is it?" I asked, hoping for a background story on the place.

It definitely looked like the type to have a few horrors in its past. It wouldn't have looked out of place in one of Stephen King's novels or even the family home in Hitchcock's Psycho.

"Not really sure, everyone in Frank's family we have asked can't really give us a date. But it's been in his family for generations." She made a strange face as she said this, which made me think there was more to the story.

"What is it?" I asked, as light heartedly as I could but from her face I knew this was it, any minute now she would spill the house's deepest, darkest secrets and then I would never sleep again. Not that I slept great anyway, but I didn't care. I still wanted to know, no matter how horrible it was.

"It's nothing really, just a bit creepy that's all." She leant around me to get a good view of where Frank was. When she was happy enough that he was out of sight, she continued,

"Well as I said before, Frank inherited this place from his Uncle..." She said whispering in my ear.

"Yeah, so what happened to him?" I asked whispering back.

"Well he...he committed suicide." She uttered this last part like a naughty word, waiting for my response with that usual sad look in her

eye. Worried I suppose that she might have said something that could 'set me off'.

"Where?" Was all I managed, praying it wasn't in what was to be my new room.

"Oh no, no....not in the house, don't worry." I think she understood my mortified look of dread.

"Oh well, at least that makes me feel better, I was about to think I was going to have to share my room."

"Share your room?" She looked confused about my answer as we made our way back to the house.

"Yeah, with a ghost or I'd have to move in with you and Frank, 'cause I think I'd be too terrified to sleep on my own." We both laughed at the thought.

"Nah, don't worry, if that ever happened I'd make Frank sleep in your room with his uncle. They would have something to talk about at least... being family and all." This just made us giggle some more but more from a way to shake off the eerie vibe the thought left us both with.

"So where did he do it then?" I asked getting back to the morbid story.

"Oh...well that doesn't matter." Was all she said and then quickened her pace back towards the house. This clearly wasn't the end of the story, so I knew I would have to get it out of her later, when Frank was out.

I followed after her, catching her up and said,

"Okay, show me this gorgeous house of yours!" Then I linked my arm with hers as we walked up to my new home.

I soon found myself sat on my new bed, in my new room, feeling so touched at all the effort my sister had gone to in making me feel at home. It was like leaving your childhood home a teenager and walking into this one as an adult. Obviously being my age, I didn't feel like a teenager anymore and hadn't for some time due to past experiences we won't get into. But my room back home was filled with all things from my childhood you never seem to be able to part with. It still had old posters of cheesy bands I liked and Trolls and beanie babies on the shelf gathering age old dust.

So, getting settled in this room took all of the four seconds it required getting to my new bed and sitting down. My new bedroom was at the very top of the house on the third floor, in the attic room which had been converted. There were other bedrooms in the house but this one definitely had the best view.

I was fortunate that the window was on the side of the house with the amazing clearing. So, this meant I had my very own personal view which was the serene vista of the national park. One that was lay out in front of me like a blanket of green ready to engulf the artist in me. This was why she picked it, she told me as we had climbed the second staircase. Frank had already carried my bags up and was now happily watching a game on the telly.

I surveyed my room and looked at all the effort my sister had gone to. It was amazing how well she knew me. There was a pine double bed with deep purple covers and a mountain of pillows to match. A bright purple lamp lay on the bedside table, which even had a copy of my favourite book on it waiting to be read.

It had been a while since I had picked up Jane Eyre, but I just loved the idea of dear plain Jane getting the rich and broody Mr Rochester, above the beautiful and wealthy Blanch. I was now looking forward to reading it again, only this time with a view like that to sit in front of.

I smiled at the pictures on the walls which represented our lives so far. There were ones by the sea whilst staying at my grandparents' house in Cornwall, done in sepia. And then family pictures printed in black and white, from holidays abroad to Christmases and Birthdays. It was nice knowing how treasured you were and it warmed my heart seeing the proof of just how much my sister wanted me here.

Unpacking my measly cases didn't take me long as there hadn't been much I had needed to bring over with me. My parents had been more than willing to send things over but deep down I knew there was nothing I wanted. This move was all about starting afresh and moving forward, which meant not dwelling on the past. Of course, this was easier said than done but I was here to give it my best shot. Besides when I had mentioned the magic words to my sister that we would need to go shopping it was almost worth coming with just hand luggage for her happiness alone.

After this I couldn't wait any longer to go exploring. So, I grabbed my jacket, kicked my feet back into my shoes and made my way downstairs.

"Hey, it didn't take you long, wanna cup of tea before you go exploring?" Libby said as she straightened up from the freezer compartment after retrieving tonight's gourmet meal.

"Nah, I'm good thanks, I won't be long, I'm sure to be jet-lagged soon."

"Okay, pizzas will be done in thirty minutes." With that she went back to preparing the pizza, which consisted of opening a packet and turning the oven on to full heat.

Pizza was about as much cooking as Libby did. If you couldn't just rip open a packet and bung it in a modern appliance, then it didn't make the grade with Libby. I was actually surprised Frank hadn't revolted or called mutiny by now the poor guy. Thankfully though cooking was one of the things I enjoyed doing, so was quite happy to do my bit and take over this side of things. Plus, I liked my stomach lining where it was and didn't fancy trying the food poisoning diet any time soon.

As soon as I opened the front door two things hit me. First, it was so cold that it literally took my breath away, turning it into a visible cloud of misty white and second was how fantastic everything smelled, helped by the lack of a polluting population.

I inhaled the heavenly scent of wet wood, damp grass and clear mountain air. I had spent so much of my childhood in the woods, that this smell brought back a flood of memories. Happy times camping with friends, nervous times, like when Johnny Carlson, my first boyfriend kissed me on that camping trip.

Then there were the sad times, like when I would argue with my parents (mostly about that boyfriend) and go running to the woods to be alone with my thoughts. But no matter what the emotion was, being there always made me feel better. Like an old friend giving me a big hug and telling me that everything would be just fine. It was as if somehow the elements of the Earth knew what I was feeling and worked to ease every crying breath.

I would just lose myself in the smells and sounds of the forest, sitting there for hours, knowing it was the one place on Earth I could truly be alone...somewhere not even my curse could find me. I tried to shake off these darker thoughts and focus back on the reasons I had come here.

I didn't want to be that whiny girl anymore. I didn't want to look up and find I had been sitting in the corner of a dark room holding myself and getting lost in what I had become...

I didn't want to feel *broken.*

I swallowed the hard lump that my body expelled at the bad memories and tried to inhale my new life. It seemed ironic that I was now living in a place that held 'New' in its title. Maybe it was a good omen and maybe that's why Libby had insisted to our parents that this move would be the best thing for me. After all she did know me better than anyone. A genuine smile curved my lips and it felt good it being there again. No, this time I was going to do it and nothing was going to get in the way of that.

I followed the stone path that led from the house and took note of the old wooden fence that ran on one side. It looked to be patched up so many times I almost felt sorry for Frank considering it looked more like a lost cause. It led into the woods and only finished when nature had started to win. Years of shifting earth and wild growth had broken up the stone flags until eventually it was swallowed up, creating its own trail.

I wandered further along the beaten path made now from man's constant footsteps, walking further away from the house towards the thick wilderness. The ground was making squelching sounds under my impractical shoes as the earth was muddy from the fine rain that had started whilst I had been unpacking. Another thing I loved was the rain. It just enhanced the feel of the place, the mossy floor sparkled as the sunlight touched it and the trees swayed in the wind that had now picked up.

Then the majestic forest suddenly took on a very different look as the clouds darkened angrily, hiding the sun. The fine rain turned to heavy raindrops that fell to the earth like little water bombs, drenching my hair flat and curling it around my face. I decided to turn back before I got too wet and in truth, the dark forest had somewhat lost its appeal. Also, I didn't want to get lost. After all, I lived here now and there would be plenty of time for exploring. Also seeing as I didn't know anyone in this town, I doubted my social calendar would be fully booked for quite some time.

With wandering thoughts clouding my senses, it took me a moment to realise why the skin on the back of my neck tingled. You know that feeling you get when you're sure somewhere close by eyes are drinking in the sight of you. Well it starts with the creeping sensation at the base of your skull and then quickly has you spinning round in unsure circles.

I scanned the earth's natural maze for any other sign of life and tried to listen out for any other sound than that of my heart pounding a frantic beat. The gentle tapping song of water hitting leaves was suddenly disrupted as a branch snapped close by. My head shot round without thought and then I saw it.

A hooded figure stood in the shadows…

Watching me.

Keira

3

VISITOR

My heart pounded an unnatural beat in my chest as my greatest fear flashed up in my mind.

"Not happening Keira, get a grip." I whispered to myself without taking my eyes off the figure before me. However, the person just tilted their head as if they could hear me from thirty feet away but other than that, they remained motionless. It was nothing short of creepy that was for sure.

"Uh...hey there...are you okay?" I asked thinking one of us had to say something first, as we couldn't just continue to stare at each other until the sun went down. Or God forbid, creepy over there decided to speak with their hatchet and write their reply in my flesh...Okay, new rule, no more horror movies now I lived in the middle of nowhere. Not in a place where hiding a body would be as easy as finding a swing in a playground.

"It's you...?" A female voice penetrated the still forest and I instantly relaxed at the discovery. Now I looked more closely you could make out the smaller frame wearing a woman's fitted jacket. It was black with a big wide hood that covered her face and flared out around her knees. Whoever she was, she even looked small from the distance between us and I myself was only five foot three.

"I'm sorry?" I asked in confusion just now letting what she had said filter through.

"It really is you…she said the time was now and here you are." The musical voice seemed to draw me in and I took a step closer.

"Do…do I know you?" I asked both trying to sound calm as if I might frighten her but also looking down, trying not to trip and break my neck on the uneven ground.

"Not yet Electus, but you will…and so shall *He.*" She said, and I shuddered at the silent promise in the way she said '*He*'. I shook my head and fiddled with the edge of my jacket sleeve.

"I think you have the wrong person lady." I said, and this inspired her to laugh gently…at what exactly I had no clue.

"Oh, I don't think so. You will learn who you are soon enough, don't you worry." I frowned before a humourless smile touched my lips.

"This is crazy, you don't even know me! Look, do you need to use the phone or something…" I looked back in the direction of the house and carried on speaking.

"…'cause if you're lost then my house is just…wait! Where'd you go?" I shouted as when I turned back the hooded woman was gone. I took a few steps closer to where she had been, my head whipping back and forth trying to find her. But she was nowhere to be seen.

"Did that really just happen?" I asked out loud. I walked over to the same spot she had been stood and looked around in all directions but there was nothing. It was strange and hard to explain but I felt drawn to her in some weird way. Almost as if she held the answers but what the Hell were the questions?

"You're not making sense." I said to myself, shaking my head and in doing so caught a small flash of light on the ground. Right at that second the sun was reflecting its rays through the tiniest of gaps in the thick tree canopy above and shining it down directly on a small white card. I bent down to pick it up and as soon as I touched it the magic that was lighting it up vanished. I looked up to see the sunbeam gone and the forest around me grew darker from where it must have hidden behind a cloud.

"Um, this must have fallen out of her pocket." I said still crouched down and now looking at the stark white business card in my hand. It was blank, and I turned it over to check the other side to find nothing but a black glossy side that also held no words. I was frowning down at it trying to make some sense of why it would be blank when I turned it back over. It was only on doing this that I saw it. Two words that were slightly raised and only when held in a certain way did it become clear enough to read…

'CLUB AFTERLIFE'

"Club After...Ahhhh!" I started to read it out when I screamed in fear at the same time falling backwards and landing hard on my backside. A massive black creature flew out from the forest floor coming straight at me. It snatched the card out of my hand, barely missing my fingers.

I still had my hands protecting the top of my head in case it came back when I finally braved a look. My head whipped from side to side, looking at all angles ready to protect myself once more.

"Jesus! What the Hell was that?!" I shouted with my hand going to my still pounding heart. Whatever it had been it was huge! I got up on shaky legs and brushed off the wet leaves and mud from my jeans and jacket once I was sure it was gone. Then my mind started to race. Was I seeing things again, was that it? Did this mean more pills for the crazy little Kazzy? God, I hoped not! I wanted to run back to the house and tell Libby and Frank about the girl but wasn't sure exactly what to tell them.

I closed my eyes and rubbed my forehead hoping this wasn't a sign of things to come. It was only my first day here!

"Great start Keira." I said scolding myself for seeing things. Well it was either that or admitting something weird was going on around here and I really didn't want to go down that route. Not when I hadn't even seen the town yet or had my first cup of tea.

But more than anything I hated the idea that there might have been a lost girl out there somewhere. And one with a few screws loose or still drunk from the night before, either way it wasn't a good thought. But then deep down I knew she was neither lost or crazy... or even drunk for that matter. For a start it wasn't as though I had walked far from the house. And let's face it, someone who is truly lost doesn't come across the first person they see and then sprout off a load of cryptic mumbo before doing a disappearing act.

But I couldn't chance it either so decided to try and reach out to her just in case. I mean she couldn't have gone that far.

"If you're still out there and lost, then keep walking north and you will reach my house!" I shouted feeling like an idiot talking to what appeared to be myself. So, with a shrug of my shoulders I turned around and left.

I could still see the end of the path through the trees but if I had walked any further it would have disappeared, replaced by a green wall of forest. I quickened my pace as the sky started to turn black and I wondered if there would be a storm tonight. I also worried that the girl could have been left lost out there to battle the raging elements. I shuddered at the thought.

When I finally got back in the house I kicked off my shoes by the door and went straight in search of Frank, who was watching a game.

"Uh...Frank?"

"Yeah honey? You enjoy your walk?" He asked not taking his eyes from the screen.

"Umm, yeah, it was great but...well can I ask you something?" I was still trying to figure out how to word this without sounding crazy.

"Shoot."

"When I was out there I thought I saw someone, do people often go walking out there?"

"Oh yeah, we get loads of hikers and kids knocking around out there. It's not that far from the house where there's a trail and further along is a clearing where they park their cars and stuff. If you saw someone then that's just the norm, although it looks like a storm is coming in." He said taking a brief look outside the sitting room window.

"So, if I saw someone, you don't think I should worry?"

"Nah, not unless they said they were lost. That trail is as clear as taking a walk in the park. So, don't worry your little head over it Kazzy. Now if you wanna worry over something serious, then I would worry about what your taste buds are about to endure." He said nodding his head back towards the kitchen. I laughed once and then said,

"I guess I'd better go check the kitchen isn't in flames, wanna beer whilst I'm in there?" I asked nodding down to his near empty bottle.

"That be a good call there Kazzy." He said smiling and I left him to his game to go assess the damage.

The smell of burnt pizza and oregano came from the kitchen as I walked in, only to see my sister wafting the smoke from the oven with a tea towel. This made me giggle and laughter soon followed as she started to blame the oven. One look at my face though was all it took for her to join in. It wasn't long before the sound of her grunting laugh had me in hysterics and my own unfortunate piggy laugh started making me snort until it almost hurt.

"At least I can assume the kitchen's not on fire...that or you're high on fumes!" Frank shouted from the sitting room.

"Well, I hope you like your pepperoni crispy and well... your crusts extra crunchy." Lib said ignoring Frank's comment and trying to slice into what looked like a charred concrete slab.

"You forgot black and cremated," I cracked and walked over to her to kiss her on the cheek.

"It will be just fine, I don't much like the crusts anyway." I reassured her only silently thanking the Lord that I didn't yet have any fillings in my teeth.

The pizza could have been made from drywall for all I cared, I was starving. She automatically poured me a glass of milk and handed me the plate. I headed back into the sitting room, with a beer under my armpit and noted that Frank hadn't moved from what I assumed was his regular seat. It was perfectly positioned in front of a huge flat screen TV with what looked like an American football game still in full swing. I was used to a different type of football, and this reminded me more of rugby only with a lot more padding.

"Cheers Kaz." Frank said not caring one bit his beer had been nestled under my armpit due to having no free hands.

Libby followed me into the room and was about to tell him to turn it over, when I shot her a look to say that it was fine. I didn't really mind what was on. Plus, he looked like a man possessed, shouting players' names I didn't know and calling them very different names instead.

I smirked when he first realised he had been caught by his wife and Libby didn't like swearing at all. His face now looked like a little boy who had been caught drawing on the walls with a marker or cutting his own hair with toenail clippers. I had to swallow my amusement and bite my smile.

So, there was one person in this world he did fear then. My small-framed sister stood waiting for the 'sorry', arms folded and pouting lips. Of course, she didn't have long to wait.

"Sorry babe, it's just this guy's a joker, let one right by and well..." He was cut off with just a look and a head tilt in my direction.

"Uh... sorry Kaz." The sheepish look on his face made me smile.

"It's okay. I've heard a lot worse." And that wasn't an overstatement, when I worked as a barmaid I'd had to learn to tune it out. Libby huffed and walked back into the kitchen to get her own gourmet meal as I looked down at my own, mentally cursing myself for not eating much on the plane.

I waited for my sister to come back into the room before asking the question that seemed to be bursting to get out of me. She was just sitting down when I spoke.

"So, have you guys heard of a Club Afterlife?" I said knowing even without the card as proof I would never forget the name. Both of their responses were equally telling. My sister dropped her fork with a clatter and Frank coughed.

"The more important question is how *you* heard of Club Afterlife?" My sister asked frowning at me like I was the one now swearing.

"Lighten up Libs." Frank said bravely, to which his efforts were only rewarded with a 'Humph' sound from Libby.

"Uh...I thought I heard some girls talking about it when walking in the woods, why...what's so bad about the place?" I asked after some quick thinking. I hated lying and one of the reasons was I sucked at it but what else could say, I found a card and then some freaky bird stole it...nope.

"Ha! What's right about the place more like, it would be a shorter list!" My sister said before taking an angry bite out of her pizza but then that probably wasn't a bad thing considering she would need the extra power an angry bite gave you just to get it down. Me, I just picked at a solid piece of pepperoni trying to think of a way to get the information I wanted.

"It's just a night club in town Libs, stop overreacting." Frank said rolling his eyes at my sister's dramatics.

"Oh yeah, you would say that, being that you're the one who supplies them with the security."

"Yeah and do you think I would do that if I thought there was anything suspicious going on there?" At this she just huffed then ignored him to say to me,

"He hasn't even met the boss. I mean who arranges security for their club and never meets their staff and then there are all the rumours..."

"Private people do that Libs, and as for the rumours, that's all they are...*rumours.*" Frank said interrupting her and emphasising the word. I almost asked about these 'rumours' but stopped myself in time, not wanting to rock the marriage boat.

"Well either way, you won't catch me going there." At this Frank burst out laughing making Libby frown. I smiled even though I was trying to figure out the joke and when Frank caught my look, he elaborated,

"It's one of those Goth places. Lots of heavy metal screaming and black makeup...not really your sister's scene." I smiled looking at my sister's pink fluffy slippers. She was as far from a Goth as you could get, and this wasn't just down to the footwear.

She had naturally curly, fiery red hair that was always perfectly styled. Instead of the normal fair skin she was tanned with a lightly freckled nose, this she got from our father. She had the most beautiful green eyes that looked more like jade stones or some deep lagoon you wanted to jump into on a hot day. They gave a lot of insight into her character and her feelings, which at the moment was utter distaste and that wasn't for the pizza.

"Sounds more up my street." I said knowing Libby would cut me a look...the place definitely had my attention now. Libby was about to comment when Frank beat her to it,

"Yeah you're into all that head banging stuff, aren't you?" I had to smile at this, as Libby rolled her eyes at her husband.

"I like my rock, yes, actually it would be pretty cool to get a bar job like I had before, if you know of anywhere that's hiring?" I asked thinking this was a great time to bring up the subject of a job.

"Don't you think it's a bit soon, you haven't even settled in yet and you know we're not expecting rent or anything?" At this I wanted to get up and hug my sister, but I also needed to reassure her that this was something I wanted to do. I hated being out of work but what I hated more was having free time to think too much into things and thinking about the past was a dangerous place for me to go. Plus, bar jobs were easy to get so it shouldn't be any different here.

"I know Libs but honestly I am ready to get back to work, it will be good for me. New start and all that." To this Libby nodded reluctantly before getting up to put her half-eaten pizza in the bin. I knew where she was coming from and she was just worried about me overdoing it but what she didn't realise was that it was more important for me to keep busy and my mind moving forward

"Actually, I have a friend who owes me a favour and if you want I can put a good word in to see if he's been looking for extra staff." Frank said leaning forward as soon as Libby had left the room.

"Yeah that would be great, is it like a bar in town or something?" I asked getting excited.

"Well put this way, you already said you'd like the music." Frank said with a wink and my heart started pounding. I wasn't sure why, considering I knew nothing of the place other than Libby didn't approve.

"Do you mean...?" I waited with baited breath to be sure I had it right, not even fully understanding why I wanted to work there so badly.

"Yeah, my friend Jerry manages the place, should be no problem, like I said, he owes me one."

"Wow, that would be great, thanks Frank."

"Thanks Frank what?" My sister asked, making her way through the arched doorway.

"Frank thinks he's knows a place," I said enthusiastically, knowing that Libby wouldn't see the good side to this.

"Then it's sorted, I'll have a word with Jerry tomorrow." Frank said looking pleased with himself on saying this last statement, as if he had won some epic battle. Libby on the other hand still looked sceptical but refrained from saying anything more on the subject. However, I doubted Frank had heard the last of it.

By the end of the game I was fighting a losing battle with my eyes to stay open. Libby had noticed how tired I was so had gone to my room and got the bed ready for me, which was sweet of her.

I made my way towards the bed like a zombie not really thinking about my feet and where they were going. It was as if they knew where to find the bed, so they didn't need me to think for them. This was good, as my head felt like my brain had been replaced with pink foam. I think I fell asleep before my head turned horizontal.

That night my dreams were strange and hard to decipher. I was back in the forest, but I was panicking because now I was the one lost. The weather was stormy and wild, producing a downpour that drenched my skin and the cold stung with invisible shards making my face numb. I kept slipping on the muddy ground where twigs and branches tore at my clothes from all angles. I was frightened as I heard the night's creatures come alive, but one sound cut through the storm and caused my blood to freeze.

It was the sound of a large bird calling out what sounded like a warning cry. I automatically ducked and cowered with my arms above my head as it was directly above my shaking body. I couldn't tell whether or not I was still crying, as my cheeks were both soaked from the storm and from fear. With quivering lips, I pleaded,

"I want to go home" in a whisper to myself but it was as if someone else heard my frightened plea. I looked up to see a bright glow light the angry sky and only when I blinked fresh tears back, could I make out the purple orb that started to pulsate and grow bigger.

It lit the forest life around where I knelt as it descended and all the black shadows of demons that had surrounded me backed away and began to retreat from the kill they had engaged. My fear doubled at the sight of hundreds of creatures all scuttling backwards like crabs in a desperate attempt to get away, leaving me with no chance of an escape. Some snapped jaws full of bladed teeth at me as though it was my fault they were being ordered to retreat.

By the time the last creature had disappeared from sight, I got up from my knees and studied the source of the light more closely. It now looked like a huge ball of gas that was effervescent. I could feel the power it emanated like a small sun, warming my face, creating little beads of sweat to replace my dried tears.

At first I was locked into place as my mind generated a mixture of possibilities, but in the end, sheer impulse took over and I started to move my feet. It seemed to feed from this, as with every step I took the more it grew. When I stopped moving closer it spoke to me.

"Come to me." The voice was purely hypnotic and hummed in my mind making me move my stumbling feet again.

"Yes, come to me...you belong to me." I felt my fear melt away with every syllable that flowed from it and into me. As if the energy was surrounding me in a heat source so comforting I could do little but obey. I took the last steps before reaching out to touch it. My fingertips were so close I could feel the tingle of my blood beneath the skin that covered them.

"Yes...be mine... Electus... The chosen girl... My Chosen One," it uttered before a man's hand emerged suddenly from the purple mist and encircled his strong fingers around my arm, encasing my limb in flesh

and bone. His effortless strength pulled me forward and off my feet into the fiery heat of darkness. The solid band of his arms captured me, securing me in an embrace, holding me locked to a concrete chest of muscle.

I wanted to scream out in fright as my vision came up empty in the black darkness, relying solely on the strong touch of a male to keep me safe. Why was I trusting this, I didn't know but for some reason I had never felt more safe.

I tried to move to see what would happen when the arms around me tightened possessively, pulling me even closer as the words of a very authoritative male spoke out his dominance,

"Mine!" He shouted as I felt my restraint slipping away into an endless abyss and my body collapsed into the arms of my dark possessor.

One word escaped my lips on a whisper…

"Yes."

Keira

4

Hooded Figure

I woke up, my eyes opening reluctantly to the sight of a red glow slowly coming into focus. The clock by my bedside told me it was six thirty in the morning and that I had slept for a good twelve hours. I decided it was best to get up as I doubted I would be able to sleep anymore no matter how tempting it was to stay in bed, if only to keep warm. I saw a blanket at the end of my bed and grabbed it to wrap around myself before braving the cold.

I looked around my new room and saw the perfect place to perch myself until the rest of the house woke. I grabbed the copy of Jane Eyre and I went to sit at the window seat of my quaint little attic room. As I walked over to the window I noticed the ice that had formed around the edges, like tiny white spiders trying to make their way to the centre.

Wrapping the blanket around myself I curled up to keep the warmth in like a cocoon and looked out at the eerie view in front of me. Rolling thick mist invaded the scenery looking as if it belonged in some horror film. I imagined werewolves or some crazed beast eating tourists. The headlines 'Campers Missing' came to mind.

Of course, this brought back flashes of what happened yesterday, and my thoughts not only went to the girl but also the creature that flew at me. I shuddered and pulled the blanket tighter before opening my book. I didn't want to think about it or other dark things that usually followed that line of thinking. I came here to get away from my past, not relive it on a daily basis.

I had read this book a million times before, but I just loved the story; the forbidden love of master and governess. The thought of nothing but this unstoppable force they held for each other, a love so strong that it could call out to one another between space and time. Okay so I admit, a crazy wife held up in the tower did get in the way a bit but show me a love story that didn't have its ups and downs. I always skipped to the part of the story where they met for the first time and missed out the depressing childhood bit.

But something wasn't quite right. I couldn't seem to focus on the words as I sat there flicking through the pages. It was as though something was playing on my mind and that's when the dream started to filter through. My eyes started to close as I replayed the dream, pulling it back from my deep subconscious.

*"Mine!"*The growl of a man's deep voice echoed in my head causing delicious chills to wrap around my body. This place felt safe and secure. His arms holding me as though they could protect me from the usual nightmares my mind had to face alone. But here...well let's just say...

Here, in his arms, I was untouchable.

"Good morning!" I woke suddenly to the sound of Libby's cheery voice entering my room. I pealed my face from the frozen glass and shamefully wiped away the cold drool from my cheek. I had to thank my lucky stars I wasn't stuck there, like that one kid we all knew growing up who was always caught licking ice from a frozen lamp post.

Libby was always happy in the morning. This was another trait we didn't share. I was not a morning person and I groaned as I unfolded myself from the window seat and the blanket I had been curled up in.

"Hey, what you doing over there? Surely the bed wasn't that bad?" She teased.

"Nah, the bed was great, but over here is a better view." I smiled then noticed what was in her hand.

"Oh God, you're an angel!" I said jumping up, forgetting about my tired limbs at the sight of a cup of tea. I eagerly took the cup from her hands and that first sip was like meeting an angel in Heaven. It felt good, warming me up from the inside as it slid down to my stomach.

"Mmmm nectar." This had been my only request before moving here. My mum was going to keep sending me a good supply of real English tea. I already knew from my sister's complaints that this was hard to come by as most Americans drank coffee, so this rule suited her just fine.

"So, what do you want to do today?" Libby said this with hope in her eyes. I think she had been starved of a good shopping partner for far too long.

"I'm easy, if you want to drag me around the shops, then that's cool with me." I said trying to sound as if I meant it. I didn't take as much pleasure in shopping any more, but it made my sister happy.

Her blissful face stared back at me and then glanced to my long sleeves. I instantly knew what she wanted to ask but she stopped herself at once, not wanting to upset me by bringing up the past.

Ever since the incident I hadn't shown any skin on my arms. I just couldn't bear the questions that would follow, and pity was not what I needed. So, I kept my scars concealed at all times, it was bad enough for my eyes to have to see them as a constant reminder. At least in this cold place I could get away with it with no questions asked. It was quite normal for everyone here to be wearing lots of layers to protect them from the bitter temperatures, so I told myself I would fit right in.

"It's fine, people won't notice." Libby said after reading my thoughts.

"Thanks." I said with a sad sort of smile that no doubt matched my pale complexion.

"Right, what's for breakfast?" I said with loads more enthusiasm than was needed.

"Umm...cereal. Sorry I really do need to go food shopping." I giggled thinking that my sister's idea of food shopping consisted of a quick nip down the frozen food section. At least if I went with her then I could get some actual ingredients.

"Cereal is fine, and I wouldn't say no to another cuppa." I said giving her a cheeky grin.

We had finally made it out of the house and on our way Evergreen Falls' mall before lunchtime. Libby took quite a bit longer to get ready than me. Of course, thanks to my new views on my appearance, I hadn't needed to apply make-up and my long hair was always pulled back and tied up in a secure clip. I used to dress and look quite different, making the same effort as Libby did. But now I just wanted to fade away into the crowd and not draw any attention to myself. Depressing I know but it worked well for me.

"So, do you know what you're looking for as there is this cool shop I know you're gonna love." I looked down at my ripped faded jeans and my scuffed up old skull converse knowing she wasn't talking about a Nike's megastore.

"Let me guess, its sells fashion gym wear?" I joked with a smirk.

"Ha! You in a gym, you're more likely to grow wings miss piggy snort." Libby sniggered then grunted a laugh which set me off.

"Oh yeah, you can talk, you sound like a..." The sight of a sleek black car coming the other way cut me off mid tease. With its unmistakeable grill and winged hood ornament you could tell instantly it was a Rolls Royce. The closer it got the more imposing and intimidating it became with its jet-black paintwork and tinted windows. Libby saw me looking in awe as the shiny beast cruised effortlessly past us and I watched it until out of sight.

"Since when are you into cars?" Libby asked dragging me back from what had kept me so captivated.

"I'm not." I said still looking behind me, almost sure it would turn back around and start following us...but where I had got that thought from I had no clue.

"Oh really? Then why is your jaw on the floor?" I didn't answer but just stuck my tongue out at her like back when we were kids. We were both silent a moment before Libby said,

"It looks like they're back in town then."

"Who's back in town?" I asked becoming even more intrigued with the soulful look on my sister's face.

"It doesn't matter, look we're here...let's park up and get shopping!" My sister said changing her mood now we'd arrived.

"Does it fit?!" My sister shouted through to my cubicle. I looked in the mirror at the long-sleeved top I had picked out and was currently trying on. It was one of those you could find in every colour but the only one I was interested in was black. I didn't really do bright colours which was why my wardrobe was made up of various shades of grey. I pulled down on the bottom after rolling it down my curvy top half and was happy at least it didn't show my belly button. That was one of the many down sides of having an ample bra size, shorter tops and a bad back later on in life...or so my mother tells me.

"Yeah!" I shouted back before whipping it over my head, making sure my hair didn't come loose. I liked having long hair but rarely wore it down. So it spent every day knotted up into a big thick twist, instead of how it used to look, long and thick golden blonde waves down my back. Libby used to say I looked like a surfer chick when I wore it down, even though I had never been surfing in my life.

I grabbed the stuff on the hangers I wanted in one hand and the ones I didn't in the other before turning around.

"Ahhh!" I shouted falling back on the chair as a hand coming through the curtain made me jump. It immediately transported me back into my dream last night and the man's hand that had grabbed me.

"What do you think?" My sister asked shoving through a chiffon dress that was exactly her style. My hand went to my heart in aid of slowing it down and I answered,

"Yeah, it's nice."

"Okay great, I am gonna try it on then. If you're finished wait for me by the shoes." I nodded to her hand as her face hadn't yet come into view and then realised I would have make my response audible.

"Okay, will do."

I grabbed my stuff that I had dropped on the floor and tried to get back to being organised before handing my unwanted items back to the assistant. The shoes were right outside the changing rooms along with the accessories, so I wandered over to check out if they had any fingerless gloves. I noticed the sunglasses and almost laughed when I saw they were on sale. Of course, they were as I thought it would be a while before anyone would be needing a pair, not when snow loomed just around the corner.

I was just picking up a pair that I knew my mum might like for their usual trip to Spain when something caught my eye in the mirror on the stand. It was a dark figure that moved across the shop and was looking at me. I turned around quickly but only in time to see them raise the hood of their jacket and leave the store. I took a few steps to follow but then my sister's voice startled me.

"Ooh, mum would like those." She said looking over my shoulder at the sunglasses I still held.

"Yeah, that's what I thought." I said distractedly, thinking to myself did I just see that?

We paid for our stuff and walked back into the main part of the Mall. It wasn't as small as it had looked from the outside, having all the usual shops from shoes, sportswear, formal wear and a funky looking alternative shop that Libby had mentioned in the car.

The shop named 'Rebel Rose' had all the usual stuff you would see in a shop like this, Goth, Rock, Punk and Emo. But the reason I liked these types of shops weren't for the clothes, although they were cool. No, it was for the fingerless gloves that Goths seemed to love so much.

I walked straight over to the accessories and looked at my options. Libby didn't look comfortable in a shop like this, but that was because she was a complete girlie girl. We had always been different that way. I liked the alternative look, never really following a fashion, just wearing what I liked whether it was 'in' or not. My favourite look had always been my pair of faded jeans and a fitted T-shirt. But now I was looking for a way to wear some of my short sleeve t-shirts without having to keep my jacket on.

I picked up a pair of black and grey striped long gloves that could be classed as sleeves. They didn't have holes for your fingers to go through but just a hole for your thumb, the rest of the material came down past the knuckles. This suited me just fine, the longer the better. I already had a few tops with sleeves like this. The thumb hole had always been a kind of comfort to me. Sort of like knowing that with my thumb securely in place, no one would ever be able to see my scars.

With this in mind I grabbed another couple of pairs, one in plain black and the other in dark grey and made my way to the counter.

The girl behind the counter was tiny and almost elf like. She wore all black, which made her bright pink hair stand out like a loud beacon, screaming for attention. The dark make-up around her eyes didn't make her look as fierce as she had intended. She still looked very friendly as she smiled at me. The girl took my items with spotty black covered nails and rang them through the till.

"You're new here, aren't you?" She asked in a bouncy, friendly voice which didn't match her 'I don't take any shit' appearance.

"Yeah, I just moved here, yesterday in fact." I said trying to sound casual.

"Wow and you're English!" She replied excitedly.

"Yeah, my sister lives here too." I indicated towards the door where Libby was stood waiting for me.

She looked at Libby and did a double take, not ever imagining us as sisters considering we looked quite different and not just in style. We were very different, like chalk and cheese. The only thing we had in common were our figures. We were both five three with small frames and slim builds, which we had inherited from our mother along with our curvy top half.

Libby looked more ready for the office in her dark brown pencil skirt with tights and boots that made her legs look great. The fitted red sweater that showed off her beautiful hourglass figure finished off the look, complimenting her red hair.

When she had come downstairs she had looked ready for a catalogue shoot not just a shopping trip at the local mall. I could see now why it had taken her an hour longer than me to get ready. I didn't wear makeup but thankfully I had lucked out on the skin department, only briefly going through the spotty phase in school. However, as punishment this then meant I was as pale as they came, and I always looked as if I had just woken from my crypt in the mornings.

"My name's Rachel Jane, but everyone calls me RJ." She held her hand out waiting for my response.

"I'm Keira...Umm Johnson, but everyone calls me Kaz." We smiled at each other as we shook hands. I hated telling people my full name, always holding my breath until it came out right.

"Are you at the college here?" I asked hopefully, as it would be nice to know at least one person before I started.

"Yeah, I'm going to be a freshman in a couple of weeks." Result I thought enthusiastically. Okay, I'd better keep this going, just keep talking, maybe she would give me her number.

"Great me too, just wish I knew the area better." I said hoping she would get my hint.

"Well, let me give you my number and we could meet up some time. Hey, have you heard of Club Afterlife yet?" My interest spiked on high alert when hearing the name.

"Yeah but I haven't seen it yet. I would love to check it out though." Hint, hint, I thought again.

"Cool, a group of us usually go, let me give you my number." She was already writing down her number on my receipt as she said this. She handed me my bag after ringing through the things on the till and taking my money.

"Give me a ring tomorrow and I'll let you know which night we're going there, that way I can introduce you to my friends."

"Okay great, talk to you tomorrow then." I said almost buzzing with excitement and that wasn't just from the prospect of gaining new friends.

"Cool, nice meeting you Kaz."

"Yeah, you too RJ." I made my way to the door and turned to wave only to find her already on her phone chatting away. I could have sworn I heard her mention my name.

"Well done you, Kazzy." My sister said putting her arm around my shoulder and pulling me side on.

"You got a date, I am so proud!" I rolled my eyes at my sister but couldn't help laughing at the same time.

"Oh my God, look at these shoes!" Libby shouted looking over my shoulder at the shop next to me. I looked but it wasn't shoes I saw. I squinted my eyes to see the dark figure stood watching me in the background which was being reflected off the store's window.

"I have to get them! And look 20% off everything in store...you coming?" Libby asked when she noticed I hadn't followed her inside.

"Uh...you go, I just want to check something out." She shrugged her shoulders and said,

"Okay, I'll meet you out front in ten," nodding to the front of the store. But my mind was elsewhere as I turned to find the dark figure was on the move. I decided to follow who I suspected was the girl from the woods as it was a similar jacket to what she was wearing. She had turned as soon as she saw me looking at her and her pace picked up, walking in the opposite direction. I, in turn, stepped up my pace as I didn't want to lose her but also didn't want to be seen running after someone in such a public place.

She took the escalators down to the lower level and I almost panicked as she went out of sight for a few seconds. I followed her, looking down momentarily as I chose my step but when I looked up she had already reached the bottom. I ducked, looking to see which direction she was headed until I was off the descending steps myself and found her easily in the crowd.

I excused myself through some people and quickened my pace. I didn't really understand what was compelling me to follow this girl, maybe it was the feeling I got that I was being followed myself and this was the question I needed answering.

I saw her disappear around a corner by a stand selling cookies and as soon as she went out of sight I jogged to catch up. I ignored the funny looks from shoppers and almost skidded around the corner in my haste to catch up.

"What the Hell?" I said out loud as I was met with nothing. It was a dead end and other than having some cash machines there was nothing. No shops, no toilets but more importantly no exits. She had vanished.

After standing there looking around in bewilderment for a few minutes I left feeling disheartened to go back to the shop where no doubt Libby was waiting for me.

"Where did you get to?" Libby said loaded with bags. I had to smile at the sight...Libby was a sucker for a sale.

"Found more than one pair then?" I asked trying to mask my confusion at not finding the girl. She lifted them up and said,

"They needed friends" making me laugh before helping her with her bags.

We had lunch and walked around nearly every shop the Mall had before deciding to call it a day. Finding the car was easy as the Mall wasn't that busy and most of the spaces were empty, which was surprising as when we found our car it wasn't parked alone.

"That's a bit weird." I said looking at the same sleek black Rolls Royce that had passed us earlier.

"Let's go." Libby said quickly stuffing her bags in the back seat and getting in the driver's side as though we were being chased by the Devil. I followed suit as she had already started the engine and as we backed out of the space I looked to see if I could make out anything through the tinted windows.

To my surprise there was someone in there already as the window started to descend and I gasped as the hooded girl came into view. But this wasn't the only thing that had me freaked. No, it was the sight of the figure sat next to her, still hidden in the shadows but his silhouette was clear. I say 'his' as there was no doubt it was a male but now I knew

I was losing the plot as I could have sworn his eyes had flashed purple as we drove past.

"Did you see that?!" I asked looking back at the car, but Libby had been too focused on getting out of there like a bat out of Hell.

The drive back gave me time to convince myself it had all been my imagination, one fuelled by a combination of jetlag and worrying about that girl in the woods. We got back after deciding to pick up takeout, much to Frank's delight and after eating some crispy noodles I was done for the day. I said goodnight and carried all my bags upstairs.

I had done well today. Okay, so everything I had bought was a shade rather than an actual colour but I'd picked up some warm clothes. I had bought a new pair of jeans, two sweaters and most importantly a warm black jacket. It was a long coat ending below the knees with a warm interlining. It had long sleeves that were more like gloves as they had a hole you could put your thumb through. It had a big hood that hung nicely when down and above all, it looked waterproof which was a must as Libby had told me how much it rained here.

It was fully dark outside my cosy window by the time I got out of the shower and dried my hair. I pulled on some warm sweat pants and an old t-shirt that I was using for pyjamas and a chunky woollen throw to put round my shoulders. I had put my long fingerless gloves on as soon as my arms were dry.

By the time I was ready for bed I had already heard Libby and Frank make their way up the stairs, calling it a night themselves. I decided to tiptoe downstairs to get a drink before I turned in and not remembering where the light switch was I braved doing so in the dark. I was just about to knock into the cupboard at the bottom of the stairs, when a sudden flash of lightning lit up every window in the massive hall, illuminating my way.

Of course, it also scared the life from my bones and I froze, too terrified to move, with my hands clamped around my mouth so as not to scream. Then it came five seconds after the light, the loudest bang and crack of thunder I had ever heard. I put this down to the location, as it must have echoed off the mountains because it seemed to go on for what seemed like minutes.

I remembered something vague from my childhood that for each second after the lightning strikes the waiting for thunder represents a mile. So therefore, the storm was five miles away. This was somewhat comforting.

It wasn't that I was scared of storms normally but being in an unfamiliar house in the middle of what seemed like nowhere didn't appeal to me. In fact, storms kind of fascinated me. The power of them was so immense. I used to like to think of them being created in anger by the almighty Zeus, forged by his own hand to be sent to the

Underworld ruled by his brother Hades. This was to be a warning of his impending wrath towards his treacherous brother living in the pits of Hell.

I nearly ran into the kitchen and turned on the light before the next angry blast of light could erupt. I grabbed a bottle of water from the fridge as I noticed that a heavy downpour of rain had now added to the night's stormy weather and left quickly, now changing a light foot for a heavy one. I took two steps at a time desperate to be in my bed for when the next one hit. Amazingly, I only stumbled once and considering the steep uneven steps to the attic that were consumed by darkness, I thought that I did pretty well not breaking something.

Once inside the comfort of my own room and seeing the warm glow of my bed lamp, I felt as if I could finally breathe. I got my cold body into bed just in time before the next eruption. The explosion of light and noise indicated to me that the storm was now right above us and Zeus was most definitely pissed off tonight! This was by far the worst storm I had heard in years. It seemed to last forever.

I didn't know whether it had finished or not by the time I finally fell asleep, but I awoke suddenly to the strangest sound. I lay wide eyed and breathing heavily as I waited for the sound again.

It reminded me of something trying to scratch their way out of my window. When I had been half way in between sleep and consciousness I tried to make sense of the noise, coming up with explanations in my mind as to what could be the cause of this irritating noise. My mind led me to a more familiar sound that our family cat used to make when she jumped up to my window ledge. Puddy, our big grey pet cat, used to scratch at the frame to get my attention hoping I would share my warm bed with her.

This thought quickly had me sat in an upright position, frozen and staring out into the darkness. The noise hadn't been something trying to get out but more importantly, something was trying to get in!

I sat waiting for the noise again hoping to God that it had only been part of my dreamy state and that I had imagined the whole thing. But then I heard it again and nearly jumped out of my skin. The clawing had become more erratic, sounding more frantic to enter my room and get to me.

My heart raced, it felt as if it would burst through my chest like the thing in the Alien movie. I still couldn't see what it was and knew that if I put my lamp on it wouldn't help. So, the only thing left for me to do was to get out of bed and walk over to my window to get a better look. The problem with this plan... I wasn't sure that I wanted a better look.

It was getting louder now, and I did think briefly about waking up Libby and Frank but then what if it had been nothing or was gone by the time I got back to the room. I would feel like one of those kids waking their parents up from a nightmare about monsters under my bed.

I decided that I had been through worse things and that I would brave it. It was just harder to get my legs to agree with my decision, as my body and mind refused to co-operate with each other.

Finally, I got to my feet and stood very still waiting for the noise to begin again, wondering if I would ever be able to get back to sleep not knowing what it was. I had to find out even though I was terrified.

I crept forward taking a deep breath with every step I took until the vision started to get clearer. The clawing was so violent that the glass sounded near to shattering at any second. Suddenly, I was beyond all fear and ran over to the window as fast as I could, tripping over the clothes I had left on the floor and falling into a heap on the window seat. This put me face to face with the creature trying to get inside.

Two huge black wings battered against the window in frustration as the thick set of claws on each foot looked deadly enough to rip through skin like a hot knife through ice cream. I sat staring at this enormous bird trying to destroy my window. I was fixated as I couldn't move.

It looked like a raven only more the size of a giant eagle. Its scruffy feathers all looked as if they had been pushed backwards. Not at all like the usual majestic birds I'd seen on TV. Oh no, this one looked bloody possessed! What had come over this creature to want to behave this way? It looked almost demonic with eyes bulging with a fierce hatred that glowed in the darkness. It was the look of a killer that had finally found its prey.

Just then a great scream rang through the dark sky.... no, not a scream but more like a roaring howl. I had never heard anything like it before. It sounded part animal, part man, part... *something else.*

The bird heard it too, pushing from the window frame and launching itself into the night and towards the direction the noise had seemed to come from.

My mind raced as I still sat at the window looking for any explanation as to what just happened. Had it even really happened or was I still asleep? Was this another dream and if so, where were my solid arms keeping me safe this time?

When I had been taking my medication I would often hallucinate, seeing strange things but even then, I was sort of aware that the reason at the time was due to the drugs in my system. This was not the same at all. Whatever had happened, one thing I knew for sure was that it had been real.

My mind wandered through any explanation I could think of, none of which made any sense. I finally crossed the room towards my bed when I stopped dead as something important hit me. The memory of the look on the creature when it too had heard the same blood curdling sound that ripped through the forest.

The same forest where something black had flown upwards scaring me that day. And that howl wasn't just some random sound the forest produced at this time of night.

No, this was something more, this was...

Its master calling.

DRAVEN

5

FINAL WHISPERS
IN THE AIR.

Finding Sophia that evening in my study lounged on one of the sofas was like finding a contented cat licking the cream off its paws. She was looking at her nails as if reminiscing of the last time they were used to kill something. It had to be said, that she was as beautiful as she was deadly.

Gods, but I would have felt sorry for her husband if he hadn't been considered too much of a blessing for Vincent and I. For he took the hellcat off our hands, figurately speaking. It didn't bode thinking back to a time when she was even worse than she was now and a brat we both adored, even when she was forcing us to loathe her at times.

But now, since Zagan came into her life and had far beyond exceeded all expectations, being that he had managed to tame the beast, well, at the very least, she no longer made our lives quite as difficult as she once had. The pale demon certainly loved her, for there was little doubt of that. But then again, he was also a brutal son of a bitch, so they undoubtedly suited each other, and both Vincent and I admittedly couldn't have chosen any better for her.

However, now Zagan was nowhere in sight, and I was left with the task of dealing with her. And after the night I'd had, then let's just say that my patience was likely to only stretch so far.

"Bad night?" she asked as if homing in on my thoughts, thoughts that many a millennia ago had been blocked from her. I rolled my eyes as I took my seat and snapped,

"What do you want, Sophia?" I knew it was bad when I saw the demonic smile seep through that porcelain skin of hers, turning her features to a baked sandy complexion for a second. Of course, she was beautiful to me no matter what side of herself was shown, the vessel or the mischievous demon that lay hidden beneath. The trials and tribulations of being a big she seemed to enjoy toying with.

"Is that any way to greet your wonderful sister?" she asked dramatically.

"I'm not sure, is it any way to greet your equally wonderful brother by reminding him of the cause for his foul mood?" I replied dryly making her laugh before saying,

"HA! I knew it, I knew you had been dreaming of her!" she said clapping to herself and making me groan aloud after rubbing a frustrated hand through my hair.

"Not this again," I muttered knowing that she would hear me.

"Yes, this again...seriously Dom, do you even want to find her or..." This was when I hit my limit, and this was known when I hammered my fist down on my desk in anger, splitting the heavy wood. However, she didn't even flinch, and this left me questioning if I had lost my touch.

"Enough of this!" I warned making her sigh before slapping her hands to her knees and getting up. Then, she walked over to my side of the desk with a grin I didn't understand, and then after patting my cheek she said,

"You will thank me one day, brother...one day, *very, very soon."* I shook my head at her, but before I could say a word she quickly made a demand of me,

"Now come on, you can take me shopping." I frowned and told her,

"You have a husband for that."

"Yes, but he is busy, and I cannot wait, besides Vince already told me you are on your way to the Forge." she said making me want to growl out my brother's name.

"Fine, but I have business to attend to first," I told her, and she simply kissed my cheek and said,

"But of course, you do." Then, with a knowing wink she left. Now, what by the Gods did she mean by that? I was still questioning this when I had dialled the number I needed and had started issuing orders.

"I am sorry, my Lord, but what exactly am I looking for?" Ranka, one of my most loyal subjects asked me, and I once again found myself rubbing a hand down my face, feeling as though I was losing a semblance of sanity just by asking this. But it couldn't be helped after the way I had felt when exiting the plane.

"I want you to check the passenger manifests for all incoming and outgoing flights at Portland International yesterday and get me a list of all passengers aged twenty-three and their details," I told her knowing that she was intelligent enough to know the reasons why without needing to be told.

Ranka had been with me since the beginning and was as I said, as loyal as they came. But she was also loyal to the cause and the Fates, so no matter what her own personal feelings may be for me, her faith in the will of the Gods came above all else.

So, we both played our parts and did this silently. Mine was to fake ignorance on her behalf, and hers was to do her job without the cloud of emotion getting in the way. And we had done this from the very beginning without question, which was why I wasn't surprised when she replied,

"It will be done, my Lord."

After this, I ended the call and released a heavy sigh asking myself what was I even doing? I knew the chances of finding what I was looking for just through a 'feeling' was unlikely. But then with an average of 180,000 girls being born a year and no more than 16% being naturally blonde, that still left me with 28,800 possibilities to search through.

Yes, I had done the maths, many times in fact, which was as far as my obsession would often take me. And like now, those odds seemed to be in the hundreds, which was worth a look considering how strong my reaction had been when stepping from that plane. And as much as I hated to admit to it, but Sophia had been right.

My dreams of her had started once again, and this time, there had been more than just a hand for me to see...

I opened my eyes the second I heard her soft cries battling against the sound of a storm overhead. The moment my eyes focused I knew it was a dream, for I was in what was known as a Void. It was a name given to a projected endless world that we sometimes used as a tool for newborns of our kind.

It was a safe environment for them to express their powers and test the limits of their minds without harming others around them or their new vessels. A kind of state of mind as you will, but for some, like myself, it can also be a manifestation of someone else's dream. Someone linked to your soul who is reaching out to you the only way their subconscious knows how. So, waking up within my own mind and finding myself in the Void only meant one thing,

My Chosen One was sharing her dream with me. Or from the sounds of it, more like a nightmare. This made sense as in her unconscious, but panicked state would cause her natural reaction to kick in. Meaning that the mere speck of supernatural ability in her would ignite and call out to what she considered was her safe haven...

Me.

This had never happened before, so I knew the importance of such a moment. Which was why I bolted upright a second after my eyes opened. Because that small and tiniest amount of power within her would only have accomplished such a task if she were near me. Which meant that finally, we were at the very least sleeping within the same state as each other...

Meaning she was close.

I got up from my bed still half-dressed from the night before, and that was when I saw it. The mirror was back, and the crack in the glass stone was still at its centre. But now instead of it being as black as night, it was clear as water and the picture it showed me was one that I had been asking the Gods to show me for thousands of years.

It was finally her.

I swear just the sight of her made me stagger towards the mirror as though I could barely get my own limbs to work in sync with each other. The sight rendered me incapable of anything more than one step at a time until I was at the glass. And once there, I could see a blonde beauty running scared through a wood caught in a downpour produced by the storm that raged directly above. Her skin was drenched and alabaster white as she shook in the cold. She was no doubt wearing what she had gone to bed dressed in, meaning she must have been too exhausted to change from jeans and a long sleeve T-shirt that was currently plastered to her shivering body.

I couldn't help but take in each factor, both of which added to my growing concern for her wellbeing and the obvious display of fear that was mounting. But to my demon side, well such a sight only ended up adding to my growing arousal. For the second I took in not only her startling beauty but also her delicious curves my demon growled its approval. Curves that pleased us greatly, knowing that indeed, she was all woman. But her face was still mainly in shadow as she ran half looking behind her at the mounting danger. I looked beyond her at what she saw and growled so low and threatening that the cracks on the glass started to branch out.

How dare they hunt what was mine to capture!

I watched as she started to slip on the muddy ground as twigs and branches tore at her clothes. Then I saw a familiar sight in the night sky, and I whistled too low for my Chosen One to hear. It was a call to my faithful pet who would have heard my command anywhere, even in my

Void. A place she was being pulled into, when in fact she was no doubt still tucked up in some large nest somewhere in the mountains.

But her mind was with me in this, which was why Ava swooped low and bellowed out to threaten all that would want to harm my girl, warning them to fall back for I was coming. However, the second Ava did this, the girl dropped to the floor and covered her head in fear. Doing so as if this hadn't been her first encounter with my pet and now making me wonder if Ava hadn't in fact gone and found my beauty first?

"I want to go home." The sweet and fearful first sounds of her voice drew me in like a moth to the eternal flame, and I slapped a hand to the glass. An action that unintentionally created purple energy to project outwards in a sphere of light. I watched as she slowly looked up at it, obviously only seeing the light and not the reason behind it.

I decided to use this to my advantage because if I was unable to go to her then maybe this way, I could get her to come to me. For it was possible that was the only way this would work. As after all, the Fates had stated as such, so it was time to test the theory and thus the reason why I decided to concentrate even more of my powers to my hand, forcing the light to grow and pulsate as if calling her towards it.

She looked behind herself to see that the creatures in the darkness had now started to retreat fully, knowing exactly what I was capable of, and now each fearing for their manifested lives. She sucked in a startled breath now she could see just how many beasts there had been lurking in the shadows and just waiting to make a meal out of her. It made me wonder where in her mind she had conjured up such Hellish creatures, for she couldn't possibly have known that they were in fact real?

But whether real or not in my world, I knew that no real threat other than her fear could have happened upon her. For if any had taken the chance to lunge at her, then she would have merely awoken far sooner than I would have liked. Which was why I intervened in taking control of her dream and those creatures in it. I couldn't chance this ending now, not when I was so close to touching her. For the second I did, then I knew the connection would be cemented between us and my chance at finding her would be greatly increased.

Eventually, she bravely rose from her knees and started to inch forward examining the light more closely. Her face was bathed in purple light, barely making it possible for me to see her features clearly and this made me frustrated enough that the purple light only intensified. This was when she stopped moving, and I felt my hand curl into a fist by my side in annoyance.

"Come to me," I told her, hoping that my voice would be heard. The second her large eyes widened further, a pair that looked as purple as my own did, thanks to the light, her feet started to move once more.

"Yes, come to me..." I started to tell her, now using now the power in my voice to beckon her closer and I was unable to help myself when I declared,

"...*You belong to me.*" I knew it was working the second I saw her mouth the soundless word, 'yes' in return, as if she was drugged. As if she was unable to fight my strength and control I held over her actions. It should have been wrong, but I didn't care. For I had to have her at all costs. I had to touch her, at least once to secure the connection before she was again lost to me. So, the second I saw her reach out, and hold her hand so close to my own beyond the light, one imprisoned cruelly behind the glass she couldn't see, I pushed once more. Only this time not only cracking her will but with it finally something else...

"Yes...be mine...Electus...the Chosen girl...*My Chosen One.*" The second the declaration was made my hand finally pushed through the glass as it didn't just shatter, it evaporated! Meaning that I could at last grab what was mine to take.

I took hold of her arm and quickly, before she could escape me, pulled her forward. She fell a step into my embrace, and the second I felt her trembling frame against my chest I wrapped my arms around her, binding her in my flesh and taking her as my prisoner. The purple light diminished from my hand and quickly started to plunge us both into darkness. I could feel her slight body fit perfectly into my own as I held her to me with absolutely no intentions of letting her go again. This was it, the moment I had been waiting for so long now, it had an eternity ago started to feel like an impossible dream.

But then she started to move as if testing the strength of my hold and forcing me to prove that I wasn't about to let her go. So, my arms tightened possessively, and I couldn't help the snarled demand slip through my lips,

"*Mine!*" However, the second I did, something happened that I couldn't have possibly foreseen. For the first had been like a prayer answered, one swiftly followed by the cruellest of endings, as first she whispered back,

"*Yes.*" Then the second that sweet acceptance was uttered from lips I still couldn't see, I felt my arms fall through her as she suddenly disappeared from my hold. She was gone, and somewhere in the world next to mine she had awoken.

I too awoke, but did so with what felt like my whole kingdom knowing the sheer force of my fury when I did. As I roared out into the night with enough force that it shattered the glass doors opposite my bed and caused some of the balcony to crumble into the gorge below.

Hence my foul mood the next day.

This had been made even worse when the reality hit me that I wasn't as connected with her as I had made myself believe would happen.

For I didn't wake knowing where she was in the world as I thought I would. I couldn't feel her presence, nor could I access her mind to find where she would be. No, instead all I had was a shadowed image in my mind of a girl I knew couldn't have been that far away.

So, needless to say, my patience for Sophia's antics had long run dry. And with the feeling of the girl's body still imprinted beneath my fingertips, then I was unsure I would even last the day without destroying something in my home.

My desk not included.

"Oh, you can just drop me off at the mall in town and pick me up later on your way back...*Dom?*" I heard my sister talking just after we passed a car coming in the opposite direction which for some reason took all of my attention. To the point where my head turned fully to watch as our paths crossed. I suddenly wanted to turn the car around and follow it, but my sister's voice had already given me the excuse to do just that. I watched until it went out of sight and then gave the driver his new orders and I did all of this before I even questioned why.

"You're not coming to Portland?" I asked once I was assured we were following the car and only feeling myself relax the moment I could once more see it barely ahead in the distance. Whoever was behind the wheel certainly was a little heavy on the accelerator, that was for sure.

"No, I thought it better to try something more local this time." she said nonchalantly, making me raise a brow at her in question.

"What?!" she snapped making me shake a head at her.

"I know not what you are up to, Sophia, but I can tell you now, that it is unlikely to end well," I warned making her chuckle.

"What makes you say that? For all you know I could just fancy a change for once." she said, this time making me laugh once in disbelief and in turn, she folded her arms in defence.

"Because I know you and have long been funding your expensive tastes, tastes I shall remind you don't tend to lean towards shops found in some small-town mall that is void of a single designer label." She shrugged and said,

"Everyone can change." At this, I couldn't help but smirk to myself and found myself ending the conversation by saying,

"We shall see."

Shortly after dropping Sophia off to cause some unknown mischief, I continued on towards the Forge, a nightclub exclusively for our kind. It was situated in a set of old warehouses I owned and was run and co-owned by my good and loyal friend Leivic. But right now, I could barely understand the urge I continued to feel which was to simply have the car turned around and make my way back to Evergreen Falls.

I had been annoyed when dropping Sophia off to find that I was too late in seeing for myself who had been in the car ahead of us.

"My lord?" the sound of my driver's voice shook me from my thoughts, and I looked up to see we were at the security gate.

"Change of plans, Fredrick, back to Evergreen," I told him without much cause other than a gut feeling.

"Very well, my Lord." was his reply before the privacy screen rose once more leaving me to contemplate my actions. I knew why I was acting out of character, and it was all down to that dream. By the Gods, but I swear I could still see the ghost of her image in the reflection of the glass I looked out of now.

I didn't know whether I wanted to hammer a fist through the glass or reach out and caress the invisible memory with the back of my fingers. Doing so just in case there was a possibility she could feel such a touch through the connection I allowed myself to hope for. I couldn't wait any longer, so I took my phone out of my pocket, and instead of calling Leivic to cancel our meeting, I instead found myself calling Ranka.

"Do you have any results?" I asked in a brisk tone that no doubt told her of my mood.

"I do, my Lord, but with so many passengers, I am trying to narrow it down to, well...to..."

"Natural blondes," I finished off for her as she knew well enough why I had suddenly rejected all fair-haired beauties in my Harem.

"Just send me what you have, Ranka," I told her knowing the list would no doubt be long, but now at least I was sure to recognise her... *wouldn't I?* Doubting myself wasn't common practice for me, so the unknown feeling was as distasteful as it was foreign.

"Yes, of course, my Lord."

"And Ranka, cancel my meeting with Leivic." I knew the moment I said this she would find it odd but thankfully she also knew not to comment. So, she acknowledged the order and I hung up to find I was to spend the hour back to Evergreen scrolling through the list of hundreds of female passport pictures Ranka had managed to acquire. They were all aged twenty-three as requested and were blonde, but by the time I made it back to the small-town shopping mall to pick up Sophia, not one single girl had been her.

However, I shouldn't have been surprised to find Sophia stood waiting next to the car we had been following. But what did surprise me was the hooded jacket she was now wearing. To say that it wasn't exactly my sister's usual type of attire was an understatement. We pulled up alongside the vehicle, and I waited before she was sat next to me with the door closed before turning to face her.

"What?" she asked, making me nod at her jacket that had a large black hood and one that still covered half of her face.

"Another change?" I asked in a knowing tone making her shrug her shoulders which wasn't good enough for me.

"Sophia, I don't know what it is you..." I started to speak, but then suddenly my vision started to waver as the brightest light erupted from outside the car. My hand shot out to hold myself steady even though I was sitting down, and I frowned through the blinding glare.

"Dom?" I heard my sister's voice reach me through the fog and I would have sworn that the sun itself had just fallen from the sky. I felt my demon growling at me just as much as my angel was trying to aid me in making sense of the intensity of it all.

"Drive on, Fredrick." I heard Sophia say in surprising calm as if she knew what this was. And it was soon discovered that she did considering the moment the car had pulled away and created some distance from the incident, the light began to fade.

"Better?" My sister asked of me, bending slightly as I was currently bent over with my head in my hands trying to rid myself of this feeling.

"What...what was that?" I asked still in my vulnerable position and glad that it had only been my sister in the car to witness it.

This was when I finally managed to open my eyes, and I did so just in time to see Sophia place a hand to the window and whisper her answer...

"A lesson learned."

Keira

6

New Friend &
Dark Stranger

The rest of the week went relatively quickly and well, more importantly without any more crazed bird incidents. However, it didn't keep me from wondering what the Hell had happened that night or with the hooded girl.

I had been for numerous walks and hiked as far as I could until I was sure I knew the area in hopes of seeing her again so that I might demand answers but there had been no sign of her. I soon moved on and tried to forget about it ever happening, which helped when I arranged to meet up with RJ for coffee at the Mall.

The week hadn't completely gone without some progress towards this new life I was trying to create. I had landed myself a job as a waitress at Club Afterlife, thanks to Frank's connections. Better still, this all happened without even needing an interview. All I had to do was show up for my first shift the following week. Libby didn't take this news well and acted as if working there was the equivalent to signing myself up to a death cult. I heard her and Frank arguing about it that night and I felt bad for him. But I was impressed to hear him standing up for himself and in doing so letting Libby know that this was not only what I wanted but also what I *needed.*

I really did need a job besides, from what I had heard from Frank, it was where most of the...and I quote "kids your age" hang out. Although trying to explain to someone in their thirties that being in your twenties no longer qualified as 'being a kid' was met with deaf ears.

At least there I would meet other people if the RJ thing didn't pan out. Luckily, I wouldn't have long to wait to find out as I was due to meet her in about twenty minutes.

Libby had been kind enough to offer to drop me off as she wasn't due back in work for another week. She had booked time off to help me settle in and show me around.

This included taking the time for us to sisterly bond on a hiking trip, which I quickly discovered to be a passion for her and Frank. She showed me the best spot to find on a clear day. Unfortunately, it had been cloudy and raining at the time, but it was still an amazing view. A brilliant place for a date, she told me with a wink, to which I groaned. It had been nice spending time together, almost like we were making up for lost time. In fact, the more time I spent here the more at home I felt and the more convinced I became that I had made the right decision...that was if I didn't die on the way to the Mall.

"Slow down, I'm not late Libs!"

"What? I'm doing the speed limit." She said, oblivious of the other angry drivers around her giving her the one finger salute.

"Yeah right, around the bends maybe. See that thing there, next to the accelerator? It's called the brake. Maybe you should think about using it once in a while." I only half joked.

"You just chill out about my driving and worry about meeting the Goth."

"What...I'm not worried!" I didn't even convince myself with this statement seeing as my voice went high pitched at the end.

"Okay, then why did it take you longer than me to get ready this morning? Plus, your room looked like a bomb went off and the clothes were the shrapnel." This was true, it was a complete disaster zone.

It wasn't that I was worried, but more apprehensive. It had been years since I had to do anything like this and it felt like high school all over again. The panic was more down to not knowing what questions were going to be asked. It felt like a test that I hadn't studied for...Hell, I didn't even know the subject. It was the 'where are you from?' and 'why did you move here?' questions that I was dreading. All seemed perfectly normal things to ask, but for me these were the times that my answers needed to be constructed from lies...And I was a really bad liar.

In the end I chucked on a pair of old jeans that had seen better days, a pair of trainers that had the same problem and of course a long-sleeved top that was grey with thin black stripes. My hair was wrapped up tightly into a twist which was held securely by a large metal clip. This had a butterfly on one side and a rather large point on the other.

I had bought this from a Christmas market the previous year thinking it would serve two purposes. One, with being made of metal it would be strong enough to hold up all my long thick hair and secondly, it would also make a useful weapon. And going off my track record the second was a comfort.

We pulled up in the parking lot right outside the main doors as it had started to pour down with rain.

"Well, good luck. I have some stuff to do but I'll be back here in about an hour...okay?"

"Yeah okay, no problem, I'll meet you here."

I got out of the car and ran towards the swinging doors and as I turned to wave, I just caught a glimpse of Libby making a speedy getaway. I would have to talk to Frank about her driving to see if he couldn't talk some sense into her. Thanks to her speeding she had dropped me off with ten minutes to spare. I walked over to the escalators and up to the food court. I remembered my way from last week's shopping trip and knew exactly which coffee house I was meeting RJ at, so I had time to find a seat before she got there, or so I thought.

I walked through the door to find a bright pink haired girl sat in the corner. She wore all black like the last time I had seen her, except for a very long multi-coloured scarf. It was wrapped around her neck a few times but still managed to make its way to her feet. Her hair was cut short and spiked into pink points at the back, a style that suited her look. She waved and stood up just in case the erratic waving hadn't caught my attention. I couldn't help smiling as I walked over to the booth she occupied.

"Hey Keira, how's things?"

"Yeah, good thanks, but you can call me Kaz, everyone else does." I said sitting down.

"Cool, so what have you been up to? Have you settled in yet?"

"Yeah, just about, I didn't really have that much stuff to unpack as most of it is still in England with my parents." I smiled at her look of horror.

"That sucks, are they going to send the rest of your stuff over?" If she had seen what most of it was then she wouldn't have thought this. Unlike most girls I didn't collect shoes or have handbags galore. Nor did I wear jewellery or really have anything of much value.

"Nah, but my mum said she would send anything I needed over to me. This was the main reason behind the shopping trip last week, I was in dire need of a warm jacket." She smiled at this last statement.

"Yeah, it gets pretty cold out here, just wait until winter and you'll be sleeping in that jacket!" We both laughed. She was so easy to talk to I didn't know what I had been worrying about.

A waitress came over to take our order but didn't look too happy at the task. She was quite old and haggard looking with white hair with some patches of grey. There were deep dark circles that lined her eyes along with the most wrinkled skin I think I had ever seen. The uniform didn't help her appearance as it was a pasty green shirt that looked to be the same colour they painted hospital walls. She looked ill and the colour brought out the green tinge in her skin.

"What do you want?" A rude harsh voice came from a pair of thin tight lips that looked like she was more used to sucking a lemon than chewing gum! RJ's bubbly voice answered first.

"Cappuccino, please." She turned to me but didn't meet my eyes.

"And you?" Was all she said, which sounded more like an order than a question.

"Hot chocolate, please." I always felt like a child ordering this, but I didn't like coffee and I doubted that they had English tea.

"Oh, and can I have a double chip muffin?" RJ's voice was the complete opposite to the waitress' whose name tag revealed her to be called Meg. She just gave a vague nod and walked away towards the counter to start the order.

"Wow, she was happy, must love her job." I said with a sarcastic tone.

"Yeah," RJ agreed and giggled,

"Don't mind her, she's never happy and she's been working here for years. I think she used to go to school with my mom but dropped out. She's been working as a waitress ever since."

I now understood why Meg wasn't the happiest person in Evergreen Falls.

"Ah, I see," was all I could think to say.

"So how come you moved to little old Evergreen, if you don't mind me asking?" And there it was. The dreaded question I knew was going to be asked and the one I didn't yet know how to answer. Oh, I knew the truth. I was running from my past and it had brought me here, but I couldn't come out with that for an answer. It always made me laugh the way people added 'if you don't mind' to the end of a question they really wanted to know. What was I going to say in reply, 'Hell yeah, I do mind!'

Just then the waitress brought us our drinks, which gave me a bit more time to think of an answer that seemed logical. She dumped them down and walked off.

RJ blew on her cappuccino and looked up at me with big eyes that were caked with thick black make-up.

"You were saying," she said as she studied my face for an answer.

"Umm... well I decided to move here because..." think Kaz, think!

"...because of Libby, my sister." I finished, mentally slapping myself upside the head combined with that inner voice, hand on hip, giving me attitude saying, 'smooth Kazzy, real smooth'.

"Your sister?"

"Uh...Yeah... she was kinda missing her family and stuff, so I decided to move here and start college in the new term." This was partly true as she did miss us in the beginning.

"Wow that was really good of you, you two must be real tight."

"We are, she's not just a sister she's a friend too."

"That's cool, I have a sister but she's younger than me and is going through her bratty teen years, driving my Mom crazy, along with us all for that matter!" We both laughed, and I couldn't help wondering if they were as different as Libby and I were.

"Yeah, I get on better with my brother Jack, he's two years older than me but we spend a lot of time together as we hang with the same crowd. He's into rock music like me... Hey, speaking of which, what type of music are you into, 'cause there's this great live band playing at this club called Afterlife. I think I mentioned it before in the store, but a bunch of us are going tomorrow night and it would be great if you could come." That word 'Afterlife' started to have a magical pull to it, one I didn't fully understand but I knew this was the perfect opportunity to learn more about it.

"Sounds great, I love live music and pretty much like most of the ones on your bag." I said nodding to her canvas bag that was covered in pin badges. She looked down herself and then smiled proudly at what I could imagine was her prize collection.

"Cool, so you're in?" She asked me referring back to the holy grail of subjects.

"Club Afterlife? Yeah, I know the place... I've actually kinda got a job there."

"SHUT UP! No way...*really?*" She had sat bolt upright, spilling frothy coffee over the edge of her cup as she looked ecstatic at this new discovery.

"Yeah, I start next week for my trial day, but I should be fine. I think so anyway, I mean I've worked in a bar before."

"Oh my God, oh my God! I can't believe it. You are so lucky. Everyone I know would kill for a job there... how the Hell did you manage that?" She said obviously getting more excited by the second.

"Well, my brother-in-law Frank knows the owner or something and well.... he just asked him, I think he must owe him a favour." At this her jaw dropped.

"Wait, hold on a sec...so let me get this straight. Does your brother-in-law know...*The Dravens?*" She whispered the name as though it was the town's biggest secret and my reaction felt like spiders dancing down my spine.

"Who?" As soon as the name was said, she had my full attention. It was weird, as if some bulb just flipped on in my head. Why did that name suddenly have an effect on me, as though I had heard it before in a memory or a dream I couldn't fully remember?

"The Dravens are a family who come here once a year. They are stinking rich, millionaires or even billionaires who knows. But they own the club and half the town for that matter and like I said, they come here for a couple of weeks every year to this tiny town. Nobody really knows why. They bring in loads of really crazy looking people, I mean *really* weird looking!"

"That's strange. I wonder what brings them here." I said out loud while this same question played on repeat in my mind.

"Like I said, no one really gets to the bottom of it, but we get a lot of these 'visitors' while they're here and they all stay at the club." She said this making "quotation marks" in the air with her hands for a more dramatic effect. It worked.

"What do you mean... they like, live there or something?" She could see my confusion and smiled.

"It will make more sense when you see the place, trust me. Which reminds me, are you up for it? Tomorrow night that is? The band's called the Acid Criminals. They do quite a heavy set, but it's worth it just for the dreamy drummer." She was getting carried away with herself and went on talking about the drummer for fifteen more minutes before we arranged a time to meet.

I really wanted to ask her more about the Dravens but chickened out, plus Libby was due to pick me up any minute. RJ's easy-going nature and friendliness had made the time fly by and I found myself looking forward to tomorrow night. I had a feeling that we were going to make an odd pair of good friends.

She walked down with me to the front entrance of the mall and waited with me until Libby's car was in sight. She continued to tell me about tomorrow night and who I was likely to meet there. The group included her older brother who apparently was dying to meet me. I couldn't understand why, but I figured she had said this to put me at ease about meeting everyone or maybe it was because in a town this small a new girl was probably a talking point. Especially one from England, well hopefully the novelty would soon wear off.

Libby waited while we said our goodbyes.

"Okay, see you tomorrow, oh, and don't forget your ID, they're really strict...wait what am I saying? You will be working there, durr, I forgot that!"

"See you then RJ," and with that I made my way to Libby's car and noticed she had the window cranked down despite the weather.

"What's on tomorrow night?" She asked, and I smiled as I got in the passenger side and waited for my interrogation.

"She's invited me to see this band tomorrow night."

"You must have made a good impression then, where's the band playing?"

"Club Afterlife." This was when her face dropped.

"What? I am going to be working there, I think it's a good idea if I go and check it out before my first shift." I said first trying for logic.

"Yeah look, about that." Here it was, I knew what was coming, the big sister 'Talk'.

"I was thinking maybe a quieter job would be more suitable to your situation. I mean you don't want to rush into things do you and you know if you're desperate for a job then I could see what I could do, maybe office junior?"

"Oh great, making coffee for thirty people and a whole load of photocopying." She looked hurt, so I quickly changed tactics.

"Look, I appreciate your concern, but I have done bar and waitress work for years and you know what I'm like around machines, they blow up if I just look at one wrong. I can't even get my mobile phone to work without calling Zimbabwe!" She laughed and with that the ache I got when I had hurt someone's feelings faded.

"Libby, I will be fine and anyway, what is it about this club you don't like?"

She made a face like she had just smelled some bad cheese and I knew this to be one of those 'things she shouldn't say' faces. So, I pressed harder.

"Come on Libs, what are you not telling me?" She hesitated.

"It's just…just you hear some really weird things about what goes on there."

"Like what?" I looked at her with a sceptic eye, which she refused to acknowledge.

"You hear some crazy stuff that goes on there and with the Dravens coming I'm not sure you should be there, that's all." Okay, hearing this name now was like waving a red rag to a bull.

"What do you know about the Dravens?" I asked, and she frowned before shooting me a questioning glare.

"More like, what do you know about the Dravens?" She snapped back. Well, she had me there. I mean I had only been here a week and I seemed to know about the town's favourite gossip.

"RJ told me that they're a rich family who come here once a year and nobody really knows why." I answered shrugging my shoulders like it was no big deal. She just stared ahead and for once concentrated on the road which was so unusual for Libs it was scary.

"Libs!" I shouted when I couldn't take the suspense any longer.

"Sorry but I...well I don't want to sound like some gossip queen, but I just don't like the stories I've heard about them. And no, I'm not just being dramatic like Frank thinks, but it just doesn't fit, the reason they come here. Why not some big city to do their business? Why this little country town?" She sounded a bit crazy herself as if she believed they were some secret murdering cartel.

"You think its drugs?" Although it didn't seem likely as that would be more fitting to a big city environment, not little Evergreen Falls, New Hampshire.

"No, I mean.... oh, I don't know. It just doesn't feel right, they bring all their own staff including bodyguards, which even Frank thinks is really strange. I mean why would they need them?" I had to agree with that one. This town didn't exactly scream bad ass, so what they would need protecting from I didn't know. But still, this was not really a valid reason behind thinking the worst of a couple of rich bigwigs coming to the area.

"They bring their own staff? I mean that's a little strange, but I guess they must entertain really important people and just want things to be right."

"Yeah, I guess," was all she said but didn't look convinced and this didn't seem like the only thing that bothered her about the Dravens. But knowing she didn't want to say anymore made me all the more determined not to give up.

"Come on, I can see there is more to this story." I insisted.

"It's just one story I heard and before you ask a million questions, I don't know much about the details!" She was getting touchy now as the truth unfolded.

"So, what was it?"

"A girl... she went missing." She said in a low voice and I couldn't help the shiver that went through my body when she said it. I could see I wasn't going to get more than that out of her, so I dropped the subject, not really knowing if I wanted to know more anyway. Not if I was going to be working there.

When we got back to the house there was an urgent message for Libby on the answer phone asking her to call the office.

"Are you okay if I pop into the office, this client is driving me crazy, he's always changing the design spec and..."

"I'll be fine Libs. Honestly, I could do with a wind down anyway. A good book and a cup of tea and I'll be set." I said interrupting her mid rant and finished this with a hug I knew she needed. She was out of the door and running to her car before I barely had time to shout...

"Not too fast Libby, take it easier with your right, I mean left foot!" She pulled a face laughing and just waved as she sped off down the driveway. I was still shaking my head as I closed the door.

To be honest, a bit of quiet time wasn't a bad thing and since I was feeling more positive these days, I wasn't as worried about where my mind would wander to.

I decided to go for a walk instead of the book and tea idea, so I grabbed my new coat and my keys. I followed the footpath Frank had mentioned was like a walk in the park and he was right that was until I went too far, and the undergrowth got thicker.

I was starting to love walking out here. It's the only time that I felt free, the only time when you can truly be yourself, with no one judging you. No one to have to act in front of, and most importantly I could let my emotions flow through my body with ease. To cry when I wanted and not feel guilty about whom it may be affecting.

But today's walk was different, not the overwhelming sadness and depression that used to sweep over me. Instead, it had been replaced by a wave of unanswered questions and a sea of curiosity. I kept finding myself thinking about the Dravens. Who were they? Why did they even come to this tiny town? And more importantly, when would I finally get a glimpse of them for myself?

I would have to restrain myself tomorrow night so as not to bombard RJ with loads of questions. I was hoping she would have been more forthcoming on the subject but once she had mentioned the drummer, he had become the main topic of conversation. The one thing she did say, which I found to be very disappointing, was that no-one hardly ever saw any of them. As soon as they arrived they spent all of their time upstairs in the VIP lounge and of course they had their own private party guest list, one that no-one who lived in the town was ever included on.

I didn't really understand why I was so fascinated. Why I was obsessing over them? But at heart I knew it wasn't 'them' I was dying to find out about.

No, it was *him.*

As soon as RJ had mentioned the name Dominic Draven, I had latched onto it like a good murder mystery book you couldn't put down. She only mentioned his name briefly, but it was enough to spark my imagination. Who was he and what did he look like?

By the time my brain had calmed itself down and started to get some real-life perspective, I had arrived at the spot I had been looking for, or so I thought.

I frowned as I saw a natural looking archway framed by the trees. I didn't remember this being here the other day and I was sure I had taken the exact same route with Libby. Maybe we came at it from a different angle. Yes, that must have been it. I convinced myself of this long enough to pass through the entwined branch arch but not before looking back over my shoulder one last time.

Once my doubts left me, they were quickly replaced by awe. The place was incredible. It didn't look like part of the forest. No, it was more like someone's secret garden I had stumbled into. Only instead of being surrounded by a stone wall to keep it hidden, the stone had been replaced by a wall of life. The forest enclosed the open space like a protective barrier with trees hundreds of years old all standing guard.

It was obvious standing here now that it wasn't the place Libby had brought me to, but it mustn't have been far away as it seemed to have the same view. This place looked like someone's property and I had just stumbled across their own private Garden of Eden. It was almost too astounding to be real.

Upon closer inspection the trees were different and more exotic looking. They had huge palms and vines growing on them with bright red flowers that looked very similar to hibiscus.

But this couldn't be right, it would be far too cold here for them and there were even more plants that would definitely not survive in this climate. How was this possible without a greenhouse or tropical climate? Yet here, in front of me, was the colourful proof. The blues, oranges and yellows of the Birds of Paradise and the bright pink bell shapes of Angel Wing Begonia. There was also sun bursting Dahlias and the beautiful purple and red Blue Dawns, which all lay around basking in the winter sun as evidence to this incredible place.

I walked into the middle, trying not to make a sound, only I wasn't sure why. It was so breathtakingly beautiful that it was like walking straight into a dream world.

There was not one murmur or movement for that matter, which I didn't understand. How could there be no wind in this big open space when there were clouds above me that were moving? There wasn't even the slightest breeze. I could feel my nerves kicking in and I started to tremble. I wanted to turn back, feeling something not right under my skin but I couldn't see where I had come in. Where was the archway?

In the stillness I heard a sound and knew I wasn't alone. My instincts kicked in and I pulled the metal clip from my hair, releasing long blonde waves down my back. My eyes darted from one space to another as I held onto cold metal. I spun round on one foot, my jacket flaring out along with my hair, only there was nothing but the beautiful cocoon of colour, radiant in the high sun.

Then suddenly, I heard another noise from behind me and as I spun back round I tripped on some uneven ground. I lost my footing and found myself falling to the forest floor. Letting out a yelp, I automatically put my hands out to break my fall losing my unconventional weapon in the process.

"Ah!" I shouted breaking the silence and feeling the wet moss across my skin causing my hands to slide. With my grip lost, I tried in vain to hold my body upwards. Instead, my hands flew out in front of me again coming into contact with something hard and smooth like leather. I swear I could now hear someone breathing, momentarily forgetting the noise I had heard before.

That was when I realised they were directly in front of me.

I lifted my head towards the objects my hands were touching but my hair had fallen forwards like a yellow blanket. I shook my head trying to part the sea of hair that was obstructing my view. I moved my hands quickly when I saw a pair of black men's leather boots I had been touching and I gasped in shock.

I tried to get up quickly but the earth under me had other ideas and I slid around as if on an ice rink. Then just as I was about to fall again, a large strong hand circled the top of my arm bringing back a wash of memories I couldn't explain. However, before I had time to think, another hand grabbed my waist, pulling me upright and preventing me from hitting the ground.

My eyes followed the figure from the ground upwards to find boots, jeans, a heavy belt buckle and a long black jacket that started at his knees. I worked my way up his muscular frame, feeling the heat generated from his body as he still held me tight.

He wore a dark t-shirt that showed the indents of a muscled washboard stomach and an incredibly wide solid chest with strong shoulders to match. Expecting to see a harsh hard face to match this warrior body, I reluctantly raised my head to look. I had to keep looking up at him as he was exceptionally tall, being well over six feet, making my eyes level with his hard chest. The face however wasn't harsh but extremely handsome. No, no, that wasn't merely enough, he wasn't just handsome...

He was breath-taking!

He was Mediterranean looking with very dark features and olive, sun-kissed skin. His jet-black hair was down to his shoulders but looked as if it had grown naturally into this style. He was very well groomed but still had a roughness about him with deep-set eyes that burned right through me. They were incredible, as if they were trying to see into my very soul, searching deep and finding what hidden secrets lay there. They were endless, dark pools of hard emotion framed by thick, long lashes. Not quite brown, more like onyx black, but they had a slight purplish edge to them, one I had never seen before.

He was truly startling to look at, so much so, that I couldn't stop staring at him. His hand finally released me and my body was left feeling cold, as if his touch had been sending a warm pulse coursing through my veins heating me up from the inside. My skin tingled as though it begged for his touch again. What was wrong with me? This guy could be anyone.

I took a cautious step back. He watched me in what seemed to be amazement, as if he was trying to distinguish if I were real or not. The heat rushed to my cheeks with being stared at and I tugged down at my sleeves nervously. I could swear after doing this I heard him groan but then he spoke, cutting off that thought.

"Are you alright?" His voice sounded like velvet with a cutting edge. Smooth and soft, but most of all a strong comforting essence encased every word. I was speechless and was just staring at him, finding it hard to turn away from his intense gaze.

What he saw in me I didn't know as his features were unreadable. His face was just so familiar to me, but I couldn't understand how I knew him. That was impossible, as I would have definitely remembered a man like this. I needed to make my lips work before he thought me a simple, staring mute.

"I'm...fi... fine...thank you." My voice didn't sound as cool and calm as I had hoped. His lips curved slightly as though amused by my obvious shyness and this made my heart skip a beat. My face blushed even more than normal, so much so it felt like my flesh was seconds away from melting away from my cheek bones. I had always disliked the fact that I blushed so easily, giving away my embarrassment for anyone to see, but at times like this I downright hated it!

"What is your name?" He seemed to be getting closer to me and for some reason I was backing away. I don't know why, but he really intimidated me. After all we were here all alone in the forest and I knew nothing about him. For some reason I felt both at ease, as if I knew he wasn't going to do me any harm, and scared, as though there was something not quite right about him. It was conflicting, so I didn't know whether or not to tell him my name. He looked shocked that I hadn't yet given him a response.

"It's alright little one, you can tell me," he said looking down at me, speaking in that soft voice, making me trust him even more but instead of giving him my name, I confessed my fears.

"I don't think I shouldn't be here." I said while looking down at my feet and trying to escape his dark penetrating gaze. It didn't help with the sheer size of the guy. I mean I was used to being around big guys with having Frank for a brother-in-law but this guy...well let's just say there are very few words needed to describe how I felt right about now and those would be 'Prey and Predator'. And it was easy to guess which part I would play in this little scenario.

"Oh really... then pray tell me, why are you?" I looked up, meeting a confident smile, which was the complete opposite to my own.

"I guess I got lost." He was shaking his head to tell me I was wrong.

"Oh, you're not lost, you're found at last and right where you need to be I think... Now for your name?" This sounded like an order, all velvet now removed, and I gulped down the hard, frightened lump in my throat before answering him.

"Keira...It's...Keira Johnson." His hand extended to mine offering it to me and reluctantly I did the same. But as he took my hand in his large grasp his grip tightened suddenly, and he pulled my body closer to his. This instantly took me back to my dream and I almost tripped into his body.

Warmth coursed through my blood once again making me lightheaded. He was looking down at me, but I refused to meet his lust filled eyes. Instead I focused on my surroundings trying in vain not to be affected by the intoxicating scent of raw Alpha male, leather and a spicy musk, all combined into one indestructible looking man.

"What's...what's happening?" I stuttered in a whisper, when I realised the lush Garden of Eden that surrounded us had started to fade away into a forest of demise. The exotic flowers began to wither and turn to ashes of grey. The trees blew in tornado winds that didn't reach us, uprooting them into splinters. The world began to spin with darkness and die as though in the presence of Death himself.

I choked back a scream and tried to pull away from this dark stranger's vice like grip. The movement caught his attention enough to pull me back and one arm snaked its way around my back putting an end to my plans of escape.

"Do not be afraid, for I will not hurt you." His face looked down and came closer towards mine. For a moment I thought he was going to kiss me as our lips were mere inches apart. I knew I would not have stopped him, even as the world around us had started to crumble away. Then he moved his free hand to my face, pushed my hair back from my neck to whisper something in my ear. Every touch sent a shooting desire down to my very core as I could feel his breath on my skin. At first it just lingered there before the words were released from his perfect lips.

His voice was light and soft as if trying to lure me into a trance as he spoke the words...

"Somnus, my Keira."

("Sleep" in Latin)

DRAVEN

7

FOUND AT LAST

$\mathcal{I}$ knew after that I should have been worried, for nothing as such had ever befallen me before. But I found myself forcing the car to a screeching halt by supernatural means the second I was able and near ripping the door from its hinges as I bolted from the car.

"Dom! Where are you…!" I heard my sister's worried cry fade the second I released my wings and took flight. I felt as if I had been locked in a cage for the first time in my existence and I was ashamed to say it, but panic had set in. I had never in all my years felt such a powerful force hit me and it had left me shaken and unsteady.

Thankfully though my wings were not affected and as I placed a veil of power around my flying form before a human eye could witness me, I flew up as high as I could. I swear I only managed to take my first steady breath the moment I breached the clouds.

I closed my eyes and remained as suspended, basking in the calm for as long as my wings could keep me there without feeling the strain. Then,

I let myself fall.

My wings folded, and I plummeted back to the earth drinking in the adrenaline and letting it flood my system as no doubt humans often did when jumping from a plane. But unlike them I allowed myself to get as close to the ground as possible before I released my wings and let the air against them take me back up. Doing so before swooping low and making my way to the ridge that overlooked my private cave. I just needed to think and try to figure out what was going on with me. Could it really be that after all this time she was finally here? That she had finally found me as the Fates had prophesied?

I had looked through all of the faces Ranka had sent me, but not one had stood out as being the girl from my dreams. I had wanted to roar in frustration and crush my useless phone in my hands just to put an end to my suffering. I swear, that by the time she actually stepped into my life, I would be a mere shell of myself or mentally insane. Which was enough of a sobering thought to get me to collect my thoughts and bury them. It was time to get back to the job at hand and the reason I was here...

To rule my world.

So, with this firmly in mind, I released my wings and flew back to Afterlife, swiftly landing at my balcony a short time later. It was also no wonder that by the time I was showered and ready to start the evening I was walking back into my club like a tightly coiled spring that no one wanted to see set loose.

Well, judging by her smirk, no one other than Sophia.

The night continued on as it always did, with my council each informing me of business that needed to be addressed, which at the very least kept me busy. In fact, it was only when I heard the slight call of Ava in the distance, did I rise from my chair and step out onto the balcony. One that was situated directly off the VIP area. It offered a clear view of the vista of mountains that surrounded most of the old abbey that was Afterlife. I'd had it moved here brick by brick and stone by stone all those years ago.

As for the town's folk, well they would never remember a time when it hadn't been here or a time from when it was being built. Only that from some point onwards, Afterlife became the talking point of their small town.

"What trouble are you causing now, old girl?" I questioned the dark, the moment I stepped outside and heard her call carrying across the trees. I was half tempted to tap into her mind and view her world, or at the very least see what it was that seemed to have caught her attention. But then I looked back through the glass doors to see my next appointment had arrived and it was one I wanted to be done with. So, I responded to my pet, by letting my demon cry out to her to come home and leave whatever prey she had no doubt been tormenting. But as I walked back inside, I also couldn't help but wonder...

Would that demonic bird of mine ever find another being she liked as much as she did me?

I walked back into the VIP area and made my way over to the head of my table before nodding to the next order of business now standing at the sight of my arrival. Then I said his name to indicate that he should sit and get on with this meeting before I let my foul mood dictate otherwise.

"Malphas."

The rest of the week came and went in its usual way, meaning that things had finally started to return back to normal. I'd had a meeting with my friend Leivic who was charged with many things, one of which was taking care of the Oracle, Pythia. Pythia was essentially a vessel for the Fates and a way for them to communicate with those of us living on Earth. Which meant that she had also been the first one to speak of my Chosen One, giving me a greater hope that my time for meeting my Queen was near. Well, that had been over two thousand years ago, so needless to say, the Oracle's words no longer brought me any comfort or hope.

But since that dream, then hope was something my mind wouldn't allow me to let go of. Which was why I insisted that Leivic have her brought out of hiding so that I could speak to her. However, even for a being as impatient as I felt right now, I knew this wouldn't happen overnight. Not when it was orchestrated so no one at any single moment knew of her whereabouts. Something that was just too dangerous to allow.

For if a being such as her were to get into the wrong hands, then it wasn't just my future in jeopardy but the very Fates themselves. It was everyone's future. The end of a prophecy that had been a whisper heard on the wind passed through every gateway found in the Janus Temple.

It would literally mean the end of time.

So, the Oracle remained hidden and frustratingly wouldn't be seen again until summoned from whichever far corners of the Earth in which she was hiding in plain sight. But arrive she would, and I, in turn, would be there the very moment to welcome her with a long line of questions. Questions all centred around one subject...

My Electus.

But until then I still had a job to do and speaking of which, where was Sophia?

"She mentioned something about creating something beautiful before watching it die, so my guess would be the woods again," Vincent answered after I had voiced this question aloud.

"I assume she is still aware that we have a kingdom to rule, along with many businesses to run?" I asked making him simply shrug his shoulders, looking in that moment as bored of life as I was these days. Yes, it was definitely time for a change and maybe one that should start sooner rather than later. Well, not before the Oracle had arrived, for I was going nowhere before first learning of any news that she might have in regards to my own fate.

"If I remember correctly, her very words had been, 'if our broody bastard of a brother wants me, tell him to come catch me before I decide to bring Hell to Earth just for something to do!' or something along those lines, as I could have just added the broody bastard bit myself." Vincent said, causing me to raise a brow at him. But then seeing how I had been this last week, then it was little surprise to me that I was pushing my siblings to take action. Sophia unsurprisingly being the first to challenge me. I raked a hand through my hair and swore in Cantonese before stating,

"Like I don't have enough to do."

"At the very least view it as it is no doubt intended to be," Vincent said making me frown.

"Which is?"

"An unwelcome distraction that may just prove one welcomed." He replied in Vincent's typical diplomatic style. I released a sigh and knew he was right. If this was what she intended, then indulging her was as harmful as it was simply to ignore. As peace never came from ignoring the likes of Sophia.

"Very well, but next time you can deal with her," I said getting up from my desk and making Vincent laugh, as he had no doubt heard me make the same threat a thousand times before. Vincent never 'dealt' with her but at the very least on occasion, he did try and rein her in. Appealing to what he believed was her more logical side. A side, I should mention, I myself believed lost long ago.

After this, I grabbed my long black jacket off the back of my seat before I walked onto the open balcony. It was one that was a part of my office and I released my wings, knowing it wouldn't be hard in finding her and this was the quickest way to do such. It was the sole reason for so many balconies such as this one that were situated around my home, offering easy access to the outside world. A way to stretch my wings or on days like today, when I needed to prevent Sophia from doing something foolish. Like allowing some poor unsuspecting mortal a glimpse into our world just for supernatural kicks!

I quickly located her with my mind and headed to the known clearing that quite a few walking trails led to. I just hoped that it was a slow hiking day or that Sophia at least had the foresight to cast a veil upon whatever it was that she was doing this time.

The moment I spotted all the extra colours a person wouldn't usually associate with the mountainous range of Evergreen, I knew I had found her creating 'one of her gardens'. Gods forbid she actually got her hands dirty and took up the hobby the more traditional way, for that may have even managed to keep her busy for a few years at least.

But no, there she was creating beauty with her mind that would only end up starting to fade to death the moment her influence left the once peaceful piece of Earth.

I let my wings fold, dropping from the sky as was my preferred landing.

"Ah, I did wonder when you would show and thankfully you will not be late." I frowned at her odd statement wondering if it were wise to enquire as I knew she wanted me to. I hated being coerced into what another wanted of me. Which was precisely why Aurora's actions had backfired on her. I was not a King to be led around by my coat tails and never would be, not even by whomever the Fates had deemed my equal.

But I had to confess this time I was intrigued enough to play along, at least for the moment.

"And what do you suppose I could possibly be late for? Unless you speak of the work you keep me from now in favour of this new madness that has afflicted you," I told her as she continued to produce exotic flowers one after another before she then moved on to an arched entrance. One made from entwined branches from the two trees standing guard to her little paradise.

She laughed in response before leaving her handy work now that she was obviously satisfied with her latest project. The clearing had been transformed into an explosion of colour thanks to the many plants you would have found naturally in warmer climates than this one. There wasn't necessarily an order or structure to her design, with walkways bordered by trimmed foliage. But more as if this had once been someone's special place now long forgotten.

A garden for the secret lovers.

Now, where that strange sentiment had come from, I did not know. But it seemed as though I wasn't the only one this overgrown paradise was affecting.

"Why, late for your first date of course," Sophia replied answering my question. I frowned down at her as she came to stand next to me clapping her hands as if freeing her skin from the dirt hard work would have gifted any other.

"Cut the shit, little sister and explain to me what it is we are doing here?" I said getting annoyed as I was seemingly pulled further into this charade.

"I believe the reason is about to step through that archway any minute now and trust me, Dom, it's not one you would ever want to miss...*Not when she has finally found you."* The second Sophia spoke of these last words I was lost to her cause. My whole body froze as if I had been tapped on the shoulder by the keeper of time himself. But even the God Janus had no control over my emotions. Not as they flooded my senses, making it hard to breathe, let alone having enough foresight or time to cast a veil around myself, as I felt a mortal presence approaching.

Just like Sophia had said.

I didn't need to look around to know that my sister had gone, leaving me to this monumental moment, being as it was one only ever destined for me to experience alone. To be honest, I couldn't have looked for her even if I had tried, for my will was no longer my own. No, it now belonged to the beating of one heart that I could feel getting stronger the closer it came to my vessel. My legs were rooted to the spot and my eyes unable to focus on anything other than the entrance I knew she would walk through.

And walk through it she did!

My Electus had finally found me.

A sight that nearly brought me to my knees for the first time in my existence!

By the Gods, she was beautiful! More than that, as there were no words yet spoken that were strong enough to describe such a being. The way she walked through the opening tentatively as if half expecting someone to shout at her. Something that in that moment I would have killed another for with little thought or regret.

It was just as if my whole being was being crushed by this overwhelming feeling of protectiveness. It was also one that was near crippling my restraint in order to keep my demon in check. The other side of myself that right now was one that begged and roared at me for one action to be taken. And that was for us to take her in our arms and steal her away from the rest of this world. One we deemed unworthy of being allowed to touch her, to look upon her...to bask in the near blinding glow of her pure soul.

Now I knew what it had been that day in the car. She had been there, and the Fates had chosen to blind me with the light of her soul, like a beacon I had unknowingly ignored. Well, now I could see it, and thankfully after time, it had simmered down enough for me to be able to see the human that had kept that heart and soul safe for me to claim.

And the sight was breathtaking.

She walked further inside and gasped the second she started to take in the beauty around her, one that dramatically paled in comparison to her own. She then turned around and took in the natural barrier to the outside world that my sister had created. The line of trees that in this moment were acting like sentinels keeping her locked within this green gilded cage she had unknowingly walked into. For there was no chance I would let her leave, not now that I had found her.

So, as I stood there, totally invisible to her, I started playing all the scenarios in my mind on what my first move would be. Of course, I could have just accessed her mind and took control, forcing her to come with me so as not to frighten her. Or I could simply put her to sleep and take her back to Afterlife with me, keeping her there until she came to understand her importance in my life.

Both of these were viable actions but if that were true then why did the idea of taking her free will leave a bitter taste in my mouth? I had been manipulating human minds for centuries in one way or another...so why was this any different if it was for the greater good and got me what I wanted?

Her actions suddenly stopped my thought process in its tracks as she stepped closer, the look of wonder still lighting up her face. I remained unseen, but I wondered if she would sense my presence at all, the closer she came? Well, I was about to find out as she reached the centre, so that she could look around and take it all in. And as she did, I, in turn, took in every inch of her.

She was wearing a worn pair of old jeans and running shoes that didn't exactly look practical for hiking, telling me she was an obvious novice at the preferred pastime around these parts. At the very least I could see she was wearing a warm, waterproof jacket, that had a large hood big enough, that if she had worn it up, then it would have concealed her face almost entirely. A thought that vexed me, for I would never allow her to hide from me.

She would hide nothing.

For all I needed was her name and within the hour I would know all about her life. Every single aspect of it and only then I would proceed with knowing what to do. But for now, I was reassured enough to know that she was going nowhere.

She turned back to face me and graced me with the porcelain features of her pale face. Her skin looked delicate enough to lick, and I could almost taste the cream, she looked to be bathed in. I itched to entwine our fingers and see if, as I expected, her fingers looked like milk against my honey tinted skin.

A pair of wide blue eyes looked up to the sky and frowned, casting shadows upon the apple of her cheeks thanks to long black lashes that were as real as they came. That's when I noticed that her eyes would change from dark blue to stormy grey with small flecks of green speckled around her pupils. Alluring eyes that were now starting to look worried.

She turned to look back at where the entrance had been, and for the first time in my life, I reacted in panic. I took away her only exit, knowing that it would only confuse her more and may even frighten her.

The thought didn't sit right with me but the thought of her leaving even less so.

She took a few steps away from me, and I couldn't help but reach out to her without thinking. Thankfully, she was out of reach from my grasp or that would have really scared her. Instead, a bird taking claim of a particular branch caused a stir within the forest and made her jump from the sound of wings taking flight. This caused a curious reaction within her for she reached up slowly and unclipped the metal clip from her twisted hair, releasing it down her back in a waterfall of golden waves that I could swear smelled like the sun.

If I had itched to reach out to her before, then now there was no hope of restraint as, with what I hoped was with the lightest touch, I managed to take a piece of it between my fingertips to bring to my lips before releasing her. She spun on one foot, holding the clip in her hand as if it had been a dagger, making me question in my mind,

'Now what makes you do such a thing, my beauty?' This was when my mind would have begun conjuring up the possibilities for such a defensive reaction, but before I could, she lost her footing and slipped on a moss-covered rock. Meaning she literally fell at my feet as if suddenly dropped from the Heavens as a gift from the Gods. Which in essence was exactly what she was for me.

My personal gift to keep for eternity.

In fact, I was so in awe of such a symbolic and significant moment that as I reached out to save her from falling the first time, unbelievably I had missed. Which in hindsight was probably not a bad thing considering having me suddenly appear from thin air like some magician was the very last thing I needed to explain right now. So instead, I allowed it to seem as though I had just stumbled across this poor lost girl in need of help.

Ha, that's it, you just try and play the hero here, I thought wryly, knowing exactly what I was. A half demon that right now was planning a hundred different ways of kidnapping her and keeping her locked away for our eyes only. Hell, if I were being honest with myself, then my demon wasn't the only one tempted by the idea!

But I knew that if she ever saw my true nature then that unconventional weapon of hers would no doubt slip from her grasp thanks to her fear, not just from her clumsy action. This certainly was a sobering thought and not one I had even allowed myself to consider before, when dreaming of this day and meeting my Electus. Even if it was always told that she would be human and indeed now looking down at her as she tried to regain her footing, she most certainly was.

Which then begged the question, how was a supernatural life for a mortal going to work?

In the end, this question evaporated the second she touched me, coming now in contact with my boots and discovering that she was no longer alone. She gasped and quickly scrambled to get up, trying in vain to shake her waist length hair out of her way. The scene would have been a comical one had it not been my Chosen One on the floor by my feet.

I was about to take matters into my own hands and lift her body from the ground when it looked as though she had finally found her feet. For once I was nervous about finally making that contact and touching her, unsure of what my reaction would be. Could I trust my demon to be gentle around her? Well, I was soon to find out as the second she looked to be on her way down again, I reached out without thinking and grabbed her arm.

A strange wave of memories assaulted me like a million pictures of a future together, yet not a single image I could pause long enough to make sense of. She would have heard my sharp intake of breath had it not been for her own which had been voiced louder.

I wanted to feel it again, so placed a hand at her waist wishing that the bulk of her jacket had not been in the way. However, it was a barrier that was both necessary and frustrating, for now was not the time for me to have her believe her saviour anything less than a gentleman. No matter how much I wanted to ravish her, starting with ripping open her clothes just so as I could make contact with her delicate skin. How soft would it be and what treasures would I find?

Humans were so fragile when it came to their vessels, females even more so. But what they didn't realise was that their bodies were a story of their existence. Each scar a conquest won and trophy of survival that should be viewed with proud eyes. Each freckle, mole, dimple or line developed because genetics were telling you a history of birth. A unique fingerprint covering their bodies and making them the person they should never be ashamed of being. Just like the way a mother's body was made to endure such a physical change that should be nothing short of celebrated, for it meant she was able to continue the Gods' vision in bringing a new life intended for the world. These weren't reasons to hide but reasons to be honoured.

And discovering the life my Chosen One had lived so far was as important to me as binding her soul with mine the first chance I got. It was as important to me as kissing those heart-shaped lips that she seemed to be trying to punish right now with her teeth. A habit that would surely unman me if she continued much longer. Just like the way her eyes worked their way up my frame and drank in the sight of me, just as I had unknowingly done with her earlier.

Meaning now, I couldn't help but ask myself what it was she saw in me as she continued to take in my face last of all. Now having no choice but to strain her neck due to our height difference. I was six foot four, so from the way her head only came to my chest I would have put her at no more than five foot three, give or take an inch. The perfect size for flinging over my shoulder I thought, trying not to smirk. An ideal portrait my demon enjoyed the thought of if his growl of agreement was anything to go by. An action he was now pushing at me to follow through with. And a notion I thankfully ignored, unless our first conversation was to be me politely asking her to stop screaming whilst I kidnapped her.

So instead, I kept silent allowing her to take in the sight of me, hoping that she was also branding my image to her mind as I had done with her. I could tell she was questioning my origins and no doubt decided on a Mediterranean ancestry. I suppose it was an easier fit than that of ancient Persian decent, with my jet-black hair, near black eyes and honey-toned skin, it was, after all, a typical assumption. One which would be even more confusing to her if she ever saw Vincent stood next to me, who was my polar opposite. The light to my dark most would say.

I continued to give her the time, but in the end was almost tempted to clear my throat just to sever the doe-eyed innocent look she was still giving me. One that only made me feel like the wolf in this picture and with his sights set on his next meal. This thought was a sobering one, enough that I released her before I could do something I would regret, like sink my fangs into that delicate neck of hers.

But the second I let go, I saw her take a step back away from me, making my demon want to growl back at her. So, just to ease its rousing, I sent a slight current of control through her, telling her to come closer. However, when she didn't, I couldn't help but look at her in such a way that I was allowing myself a moment of doubt, asking myself if she were real or not. I was tempted to add even greater power behind the command, but then that would have rid me of the sweet, confused expression she was now granting me. So instead, I decided to be the first to cut the silence, seeing as she was refusing to do so, as I had originally hoped.

"Are you alright?" I asked, now guarding my expression and choosing to give her very little as to what I may have been thinking.

"I'm...fi... fine...thank you." she said stuttering out her words at first as I was no doubt pushing against the boundaries of her nervousness. To which I couldn't help but allow a slight grin to creep through the calm façade I was portraying.

In fact, I wanted to hear more of her voice, so that I may discover her origins as she certainly didn't sound American. But then she started to blush, and I swear even the sight of that rose tint to her skin was enough to have me clenching my fists at my side. A physical reaction, just to stop me from reaching out and touching that now heated skin.

"What is your name?" I decided to ask, as was considered a reasonable request in such a situation. However, I had unknowingly been getting closer to her and in doing so, must have been frightening her, as she started backing away from me. This surprised me for I never imagined this would be my fated one's response.

Yes, it was clear that I obviously intimidated her, possibly due to my size, for I was far from slight of frame. But for her to now look actually concerned that I would harm her in some way, well that was utterly abhorrent to me. For I would have died for her right in that moment, without even knowing her name before harming a single cell her body produced. Which was precisely why I told her,

"It's alright, little one, you can tell me." I made sure to say this with a softer tone this time, no longer making it a demand to be obeyed but more like a request I hoped she granted. But once more she surprised me, and instead of giving me what I wanted, she instead confessed her fears.

"I don't think I should be here," She said looking down at her feet, and unable to withstand what she must have assumed was an unforgiving gaze. So, I decided to go with a different tactic and allowed my tone to take on a more playful one,

"Oh really... then pray tell me, why are you?" Finally, this made her look back up at me and in return finding what I hoped was an easy smile from my lips, in hopes of putting her at ease.

"I guess I got lost," she said, now gifting me with the strong hints of a Northern English accent. Chester maybe, or further north, like Manchester or Liverpool. Either one and it was only a faint hint. Which told me that she either hadn't lived there for a while or had influences from those in her family with a different accent she spent time with.

But this was a question for another time, as right now she had claimed to be lost, something I knew for a fact was quite the opposite. Which was why I couldn't help but shake my head, telling her she was wrong before divulging the truth,

"Oh, you're not lost, you're found at last and right where you need to be, I think... Now for your name?" This time when I asked, I let the undercurrent of authority lace my words, for I needed that name!

I knew it had worked even before she spoke as I watched in fascination when she swallowed hard, before then telling me what strangely seemed like only a half-truth,

"Keira...It's...Keira Johnson." I would have frowned in question, silently calling her bluff if I hadn't been aware of how nervous she was around me. How unsure she was and no doubt ready to run at any minute just to save herself the erratic pounding of her heart. One I could hear beating far quicker than it usually did.

So, I decided upon the very human custom of offering her my hand. Just the way she looked down at it as if assessing whether or not it was going to snap out at her, made me chuckle to myself. As if she were expecting it to clamp down on her like a predator's jaws would, well it was enough to have me once more hiding a smile.

But in the end, she reluctantly placed her hand in mine, gifting me with more than she realised. Which was when I hit my limit on allowing this space between us to continue, proving this when I tightened my grip, just as she had feared I would. Then, before she could squirm in my hold, I quickly tugged her to me, so that I could lock her body to mine.

I swear the second I felt her frame mould to my own once more, just as it had done in the dream, I was forced to close my eyes. This was to ensure that she couldn't see the purple flames I could feel seeping through to my human side, as was its natural reaction to do so.

It was only when I felt myself gain back control that I could once again look down at her, to see for myself that my touch was affecting her, just as much as it was me. It made me want to kiss her, to place my lips against hers and urge them open so that I could taste her. Something my lust filled gaze was no doubt screaming at her right now.

However, the elements of my sister's fantasy had other ideas as it was starting to wear off. Something little Keira here was witnessing for herself.

"What's...what's happening?" she whispered after fearfully looking around us for a moment, taking in the sight of such beauty now dying dramatically. In her eyes, it must have looked as though the world had been infected by the touch of death. A disease spreading amongst the Earth and a darkness now getting closer to us at its centre.

She moved a foot out of the way of the dying grass touching her and choked back a scream, before trying to tear herself away from my arms. Something I wasn't about to let happen! I let her know this the moment I pulled her back to me and banded an arm around her back so that she was going nowhere.

Then when I was assured that she could not escape me, I told her the truth,

"Do not be afraid, for I will not hurt you." Her eyes widened in response to this declaration, and the innocence I found there made me lower my face closer to hers. For I knew I had to bring an end to this meeting, no matter how much I loathed to do so. Because it wasn't her fear I needed, it was her trust. A trust I knew I would not gain by simply taking what I wanted or leaving her to experience this demise of the forest alone. So, with little choice left, I knew the best thing I could do for her was to make her fall asleep and believe this meeting to be a dream.

But I wasn't doing so without giving in to some small impulse. So, I raised a hand to her face and gently pushed the hair back from her cheek, marvelling at how soft her skin was. Then I lowered my head to her neck making sure to breathe her essence in deep. This time branding the scent of her to my soul. I then allowed my lips to gently brush against the tender spot under her ear before whispering my command, forcing her mind under my control and giving her what she needed,

But not what I wanted...

"Somnus, my Keira."

Keira

8

ALONE

I woke up on the couch with a blanket around me and I was alone. I felt strange, as if I'd had a dream I couldn't quite remember and when did I fall asleep anyway? I'm pretty sure I went out for a walk or did I dream that too? My head felt all fuzzy as though I had a hangover or something.

The house was empty, and it was dark but most of all, it was unnerving. I got up and went into the kitchen as my throat felt like a new place to store woodchips. On the way I grabbed the phone to see if Libby had left a message. Just as I turned on the lights I felt a cold chill run up my body. I turned to where it was coming from and noticed the front door was wide open.

My heart froze as a million thoughts went crashing through my head at once. The first being...was I actually alone? I ran into the kitchen and grabbed a knife from the counter and started to ring 911 but decided to hang up before I heard the first ring. What was I going to tell them? "I thought I went for a walk, found a Garden of Eden, and met the most amazing looking man I'd ever seen before, then waking up in a blanket with the front door open." Yeah, I don't think so. For starters other than the front door being open, it all sounded pretty nice to me.

Unless...no it couldn't be! I would have been warned.

I got that idea out of my head like shaking off cobwebs from my body and walked to the front door. There was no porch light on and it was quite wild outside. The trees were blowing angrily, and the swing chair's chains creaked. No wonder I was spooked. I closed the door and locked it. It could've just blown open. I tried to convince myself but knowing I would have to search the house didn't make me feel any better.

With all the lights on I checked the downstairs which, no surprise, was all clear. However, when I got to the last door I realised what was behind it. It swung open and I stared down into the darkness unable to step one foot down into the basement. My mind froze in fear and I slammed the door quickly as though fire from the pits of Hell was coming up at me.

"Shake it off Kaz, you had to unlock the door to open it, nobody is going to be down there." I said reassuring myself for not going down there and instead deciding to check the rest of the house.

I then checked the first floor, again turning on all the lights as I went. I swapped my knife for a baseball bat I grabbed from the cupboard under the stairs. I used that to open the doors as I braced myself for anything that might be there. Plus, I figured the bat had better swinging range.

The first floor was like the last, all clear, so by the time I got to the attic I was feeling pretty foolish. I opened my bedroom door and turned on the last light in the house. It all looked as I had left it that morning. Clothes were everywhere from getting ready to see RJ and not knowing what to wear.

I put the bat down and I started to pick stuff up, piling it up on my bed when I noticed something was wrong with the way I had left it. My copy of Jane Eyre, which I had left on my bedside table, was now gone. I was sure I had left it there. I was reading it last night and always put it there. This was strange, maybe Libby had taken it to read but then on reflection, I couldn't see it being a likely reason. Libby was more of a gossip girl and loved all the celebrity and fashion magazines. I don't think I had ever seen her read an actual book before.

I tried to look for it but gave up when I heard a car door shutting and knew that Libby or Frank must be back. I got up from looking under my bed and was just about to make my way downstairs when I noticed my window was open. How had I missed that? It wasn't even cold in here, why hadn't I noticed?

I walked up to it and the wind blew my hair around my face. But how did my hair get loose? It brought me back to my dream and I wondered where my metal clip was? I twisted it back up and knotted it, before trying to reach out to close the window.

"Hey, Kaz, sorry I've been so long, work was insane. Hey, are you alright? You look really pale...you feeling okay?" Libby said looking concerned.

"Yeah, I'm fine, I just woke up actually. I must have crashed out on the couch." She gave me one of those worried head tilts.

"Maybe you should get an early night, you still look beat and I wouldn't leave your window open you'll freeze up here. Talking about that, do you have enough blankets and stuff?" She asked and started fussing about the bed and folding up clothes, doing the whole mother-hen thing.

"Yeah, I must have forgotten to close it this morning. Say, did you borrow my book?" Her blank look said it all.

"What, Jane Eyre? Not unless there's a new one out that includes Orlando Bloom and George Clooney!" She gave me a cheeky smile and I tried to smile back but it was hard when my thoughts were all over the place.

"Sooo, are you thinking about taking up baseball or joining a club?" Libby said spying my weapon propped against the wall.

"Oh, that...well...umm..."

"No, it's cool, no need to explain...I think I will just take this downstairs with me." Libby said picking it up by the end like a dirty stick a muddy child had brought into the house.

"Cuppa?" She asked going out of sight not needing to wait for my obvious reply.

I slumped on the bed and in doing so knocked over the folded clothes tower Libby had made. I let out a sigh looking at it, but my mind was elsewhere. It was back in the forest and now searching my memory for another glimpse of *him.*

I could still remember the smell of the flowers and taste the damp air. And the feel of his touch that seemed to sear my skin couldn't be forgotten. Marking him there for all time...that...well that, I just could not get out of my head.

But what could I do about it? Nothing about what happened or didn't happen made any sense. Even if that place had been real, the part when it crumbled into dust should be enough to convince me otherwise. And there was my dark mystery man. Could my mind really conjure up such powerful perfection? I was so confused.

Had it been real?

I decided to have a shower to try and relax before bed. I let my bathrobe drop to the floor and stepped into the cubicle instantly feeling better as the hot water rained down over my body. I could feel my muscles slowly relax and the tension in my neck ease. I loved water, I loved everything about it, when it rained, the sound of a stream or a river, even the sound of droplets lashing against my window in a storm. But most of all, I loved the way it felt on my skin. As if it not only cleansed your body from everyday life but could also wash away any bad thoughts or memories, making you feel brand new.

Now, if it could only bring back old beautiful memories, then I would stay in here until I became 'Prune Woman' defender of the bathroom! I let my long hair fall down my back and held my face under the rushing water of the power shower, wishing it could be more like a waterfall in some exotic rainforest far away, somewhere hot and full of mystery. This immediately brought me back to my dream as I closed my eyes and let my mind wander in and out of blissful remembrance.

I had washed my hair and body with Libby's extensive supply of bathroom products, wondering if she wasn't a little bit consumer mad. There were six different types of shower gels and bottles of all shapes and sizes holding God only knows what. I used what I needed and came out of the shower smelling like a mixture of jasmine, honey and a touch of coconut. I would have to read the bottles more carefully next time otherwise I could come out of there smelling like a Piña Colada.

I hadn't realised how long I had been until the water had started to go colder and the signs of Prune Woman were starting to appear. I looked in the mirror at my face and frowned. I looked so pale even though I had just come out of a hot shower and the bathroom was still steamy. I wiped the mirror again with my arm and studied what the world saw when looking at me. My eyes were a boring greyish blue colour that looked more like the sky when there was a storm coming. They were big, but the only thing blessed about them was that they were framed with thick eyelashes that Libby would have given her right arm for.

I rolled my eyes at myself and gave up trying to find fault with everything. It seemed to be a theme with some women when faced with a gorgeous man that immediately you wanted to pick away the parts you didn't like about how you looked. I wish I could be more like one of those 'burn your bra' types as I thought that all woman were beautiful creatures if only we weren't our own worst enemy. But of course, I also believed beauty started within your soul as you could often find a beautiful woman made ugly through their actions.

I dried myself and changed into my sweat pants and a vest top with an old hooded zip up my dad had given me years ago. One he used to fit into until a beer belly had gotten to him. He knew it was one of my favourites. It had his old University football team logo on the front and it was lined with fleece inside. Most of all, it reminded me of home and kept me warm in more ways than one.

I scanned my room before getting into bed, mainly wanting to find my book. It was strange, my room looked as though someone else had been here. Had I taken it with me this morning? I would have to check my bag. I shook off the feeling and put it down to the stress.

I was like this when I first started taking the drugs the doctor had prescribed me. I didn't know whether I was coming or going. I would do something completely random and then wouldn't remember why or what I had done. It was one of the reasons I had stopped taking my medication. It made me numb and in my opinion, not a nice person to be around. The only thing I did still take occasionally was sleeping pills. Now they *did* work for me, but I still would be a bit hazy on the details before I slept as they made me a little incoherent should we say.

This made me wonder, could I have taken some after Libby had rushed out to work? It was possible. Was that it? My dream man was a drug induced fantasy? God, I hoped not! I couldn't think of anything crueller. Forget dangling a bloody carrot that was more like dangling a death by chocolate cake in front of a diabetic!

I decided it didn't matter. I'd done enough thinking about it. I got into bed and started reading some course material. It was about time as I was starting college in a week and they had sent me a reading list. I had an advantage though as I had already done the first year in England but as my plans had to change, I decided that it was best to start over from scratch. Towards the end I had missed a lot of work and found it impossible to catch up, not that I wanted to at that point. At least here, I might be ahead of the game.

I was looking forward to History the most. I loved History. I used to watch all the documentaries on the History Channel with my dad since I was a child, only now understanding them better.

My grandparents had a huge library in their house in Cornwall and it was full of historical books of all eras. I used to sit for hours on an old worn rug and look at all the pictures, imagining that one day I would go to all these old temples, tombs and monuments to see them for myself. I used to pretend I was an archaeologist and I would uncover all their mysteries and secrets.

But my favourite kind of history had to be mythological. I loved where the stories originated from. The fantasy behind them fascinated me. Ancient Greek, Egyptian, Aztec, I just couldn't get enough. I loved the drama of it all, the scandal of Gods, Kings and Pharaohs, it was my version of a gossip magazine. So naturally it was what I really wanted to study. The other classes I had just picked to fill the void. Art had been the only other passion of mine but not anymore. No, that had all changed for me now.

That incident had changed everything.

There was a light tapping at my door and I knew it to be a Libby type knock. She cautiously peeped around the door in case I had been asleep,

"Hey, how was your shower?"

"Great but I think I now smell like I work at a cocktail bar." She laughed as she plonked herself down on the end of my bed. This reminded me of so many moments in my childhood.

"You know me, I do love my bath stuff. So how are you finding it all? I'm sorry I had to leave you today."

"No, no, I was fine." My sister gave me a head tilted look and the disbelief was written all over her face. I mean I couldn't really blame her considering she had found me upstairs with a baseball bat.

"Come on Kazzy, you can talk to me you know." My heart melted. I didn't want her thinking I was losing the plot or this move hadn't been the right thing.

"I'm just trying to find my feet a bit...don't get me wrong I love it here and you were right, it's the best thing for me. I'm just worried about work and college and stuff, but you don't need to worry too." I smiled trying to reassure her, but I could see what was coming.

"Why don't you hold off for a bit with working. You could do with a rest and it's not the quietest of places." She pulled a face like she had just had her upper lip waxed. I couldn't help the laugh that escaped my lips and it felt good. Only once I started I couldn't stop. Libby saw the funny side and joined in. I could feel the tension lifting from my shoulders and gave Libby a big hug.

She flicked her red hair back off her face and looked more closely at me. She then reached out and pushed back a strand of my hair behind my ears.

"Wow, your hair is so long, I didn't realise, why don't you...?" She cut herself off knowing the answer. She understood I wasn't the same girl now.

"Never mind, but it's still a lovely colour," she said as she fiddled with the ends through her fingers.

"And you've still got dad's old hoodie, well I don't suppose it has fit him in a while." She grunted a laugh. She touched the sleeves and instinct kicked in, so I tugged down the material hiding my already hidden scars. This made her wince and she got up off the bed and made her way towards the door as if a memory had hit her and she didn't want me to see the emotion building up.

"Libs...I..." I started but she interrupted me.

"Get some rest honey." Then she left without looking at me. She was gone before I even finished a good night. I felt bad about this but understood that it wasn't only me that had been affected by what had happened.

I brushed my hair ready to plait it for bed and it squeaked as my hands split it into three parts. It was overly clean due to the amount of time I had spent in the shower. I hoped no one else was planning on having one as they would be in for a chilly shock.

I gave up on reading after only ten minutes. I just couldn't concentrate on college stuff with my mind now on other things. I had been so frustrated most of the evening that trying to forget about it seemed impossible. However, there was one aspect I desperately *didn't* want to forget.

Why couldn't men like that really exist in the world? Men just weren't that perfect, were they? Well ok, I hadn't really had an extensive knowledge of the other sex but from what I saw (or can remember) he was just staggeringly beautiful. More like a God than a human. Maybe I had read too many mythological stories.

I took my dad's sweater off and finally started to relax as I settled down my wired mind. I turned off my lamp and pulled the covers around my body like a cocoon. I could feel my heavy lids falling and knew it wouldn't be long until I found sleep.

Stirring from my sleep I woke frowning. Something was irritating me, and I turned my head looking to see how much time had passed. I had only been asleep an hour and I groaned in frustration. Then I heard it. The noise that must have woke me. I shot up fast...

It was back!

My head spun around the dark room looking for any movement in the shadows. The moon was out and there was a faint glow behind a cloud that would soon come into view. I held my breath not wanting to move. My body froze, and my hands were curled into balls, gripping so hard on the quilt that I was sure I would tear it.

I wanted to switch the light on but knew that it wouldn't help me see outside as I would only see my own pale reflection looking back at me. I waited for the moon as the tapping continued, only this time it wasn't as erratic. It made me too curious, so I bravely got up and walked over to the window seat. I strained my eyes in a desperate attempt to see the creature once more, but I was at a loss to understand why.

The moon was coming out now and it started to create more shadows in my room. Both relief and disappointment washed over me as there was nothing there. My eyes searched everywhere but still no bird and also no trace of anything that could have been making that noise. I was about to give up but decided to open the window. I didn't know why or what difference this would make but my hand still reached for the window latch. It was a bit tough but I didn't need to worry about waking anyone as nothing could be heard from up here in my attic room.

The paint flaked and the hinges squeaked as I pushed on its frame. The cold air hit me and went straight down my spine continuing all the way down my body. I held my arms around my ribs wishing I was back in my warm bed. Instead, I was stood here feeling like an idiot, freezing my butt off.

I poked my head out and looked down at the yard but there was nothing that had changed, still just a shed with some car parts dotted here and there. But no bird... nothing. What did I expect, my mystery dream man to be stood there with a handful of stones he had been throwing at the window?

I laughed at myself and pulled the window back to slam it shut. The noise startled me even though I was expecting it. What I wasn't expecting however, was the floorboards behind me to creak. I turned around too quickly and almost stumbled over the cushion from the window seat which had fallen to the floor.

"You have trouble staying on your feet, don't you?" That perfect voice. The one I had been trying so hard to remember. It was hypnotic. I didn't know what to do or to say. I just wished that I could see him as well as I had heard him.

The room was still black because the moon had disappeared again behind the safety of its clouds. I could just make out the tall, dark silhouette standing at the bottom of my bed, no more than four feet away from me. My heart rate must have tripled in seconds, yet I was still too scared to breathe. Speak Keira! I mentally yelled at myself.

"I umm...I mean... what are you doing here?" Was all I could think to say. What a moron I sounded! Wait...forget that, there's a strange man in my room and I was the one worrying about what I sounded like. Way to go Keira on getting your priorities right.

I couldn't see but I was sure he had a smirk on his face. I could hear it in his voice when he said,

"Yes, well apart from it being my right to see you, I also wanted to bring you something. You dropped this." He held out his hand to give me something, but I didn't move. And what did he mean by 'his right to see me'?

"There is no need to fear me. I would *never* hurt you." He emphasised the word 'never' as if it would cause him physical pain to go back on his words. His voice also did that hypnotic thing again and made my brain turn to mush. Even with all the mush, or maybe because of it, there was no way I could get my legs to work.

"Come here." That was until he *ordered* my legs to work.

I stepped forward cautiously and reached out as far as I could to take what it was he was holding. I was just about to get it when he moved so quickly. His movements were a blurry wave and I felt the hairs on the back of my neck stand up as I realised how close he now came to me. My hand had dropped to my side as I struggled to breathe again. He must have noticed my reaction because he whispered in the softest voice,

"Don't be afraid, little one."

I wish I could have found words to speak but I was numb and not all of it down to fear. Everything about him held me in some kind of spell; his smell, his body heat and most of all, the secret lure of that voice. I think I would have done anything he asked of me.

"I...I'm not afraid." I whispered in a cracked voice that sounded anything but convincing. He was so close, I could hear him smiling.

"Here," was all he said as he took my hand very slowly into his own. The heat that coursed through me almost blew me over. It was as if I had been struck by thousands of red hot pins of pleasure. My body literally ignited as I had never felt so alive. He turned my hand over ever so slowly as if not wanting to frighten me with any sudden movements, all the while his eyes never left me.

He held my hand in his with my palm raised upwards and with his other hand he placed something there. His weight shifted towards my body as he leaned down towards my ear once more as he had done in the woods. The words flowed from his lips in such perfection I couldn't breathe at the sound.

"I shouldn't be here yet, but I was curious about you, little one." This made me notice something else in his voice. He had an authoritative edge that made me shudder under his hands. Hands that dwarfed my own, making me feel every bit of the nickname he had given me. Hell, the hand that held my own could have crushed my skull with ease. I tried to swallow down a frightened lump as if I had a plum stuck there.

"About....*me?*" I asked, barely speaking the words. I was in shock. Why on earth would he be curious about me? He raised his hand up to my face and I froze. I could barely take a small breath. Meanwhile, the moon had come out, but he was still in the dark, unlike me. My pale face was now on show as he had his back to the window. The back of two of his fingers touched my cheek making me quiver at the warm path they left on my skin. I closed my eyes as the silent moments went by and his fingers continued to explore my heated face.

"Exquisite." His lips whispered against my forehead after he leaned in closer, cutting all space between us to nothing. My breath hitched at the word he used and this time instead of turning my insides to mush, he set them on fire. I was suddenly worried he could feel the points of my desire pressing into him thanks to my hardened nipples.

I looked up at him and I inhaled sharply when I saw for the first time his stunning features bathed in moonlight. I was right, he was Godly. And more incredible was that this Godly figure was smiling down at me. Of all the people in the world...he picked damaged little me to smile at.

"You will sleep, my girl and you will sleep well this night, understand?" It wasn't a question but a command, one I was almost positive I would not be obeying. I mean, who could sleep after meeting such a man in their room. No, sleeping would not be on the menu but fantasising...oh most definitely!

Then he broke the spell,

"Until next time, *my Keira,*" he whispered, and I loved the sound my name made on his lips. His whispered promise stayed in my mind like a drug working over my body. I could feel myself getting weaker until finally I couldn't fight off the urge to close my eyes.

My last thought, swimming happily through the current of bliss...

He called me *his.*

DRAVEN

9

No longer Alone

"*Sleep now, my Queen,*" I whispered once the girl was safely in my arms with her mind settled and lost to her sleep. Then I finally allowed myself to take a deep breath. For the whole time in her presence was like fighting a battle between right and wrong. A concept I knew well enough considering my sole purpose was to keep such a balance. But when my own mortality was put into question, I was at a loss on what my next actions should be. I knew what I wanted, but even I wasn't arrogant enough to believe that the two decisions morally walked hand in hand. For what I wanted and what was best for her I knew would only offer one of us the results we were looking for.

However, in the end, it was the memory of her slowly backing away from me that won over my selfish ways. For I didn't want her to fear me, just as much as I wasn't willing to control that fear by taking it forcefully from her mind. I didn't want to force my will upon her any more than simply making her sleep so as I could plan what my next decision may be. A decision that had been impossible to make when she had been awake and looking up at me with those eyes...eyes I found myself getting lost in and drowning myself amongst the doubts I had. I had never had to question my own decisions before, and now here I was, still at a loss on what to do next.

By the Gods, I knew what I wanted to do and that was to take her back to Afterlife and have her wake up in the only bed she ever belonged in…

"Mine." I startled myself the second my demon voiced this same sentiment aloud.

"Lucifer's blood, get a grip!" I scolded myself, giving my head a shake in hopes to rid my mind of these uncertainties and just make a fucking decision that didn't include kidnapping an innocent young girl who would no doubt wake up terrified. Okay, so the Fates hadn't exactly prepared me for this! In fact, looking back at it, I had conceitedly believed that when I met her, she would instantly know who I was to her and I would simply be able to claim her as my own.

Gods, but how wrong I had been.

No, the only option left to me was to find out where she lived and take her home, allowing her to wake on her own and believe this meeting had all been a dream. Then I would have time to think and plan my next course of action carefully. By the Gods, but could I actually be considering trying to date her as a human would? I would have torn a frustrated hand through my hair out of habit if I had been free to do so. Instead, I took another deep breath and tried to not let the scent of her invade my senses and influence my decisions as I knew could easily happen. Which meant I looked down at her sleeping face and asked her softly,

"Where do you live, beautiful?" I knew she heard me and the image she painted in her mind was of a house I knew, making me frown in question.

"Frank Miller?" I questioned making her murmur a single word,

"Brother." I frowned knowing that he didn't have a sister but a brother if memory served me right. It wasn't that I was in the habit of knowing immediate details of every resident who resided in Evergreen Falls, but the ones connected with my club I most certainly did. And Frank Miller provided the human security at my club, Afterlife.

Well, at the very least I now had a place to start, so that was something when beginning my search. Plus, I had a place to take her which was where I headed to next, releasing my wings and getting ready to blanket us from the world as we took to the sky. This was when I caught sight of something on the ground, so before leaving, I made sure it had been transferred to my pocket, for I wanted every part of her to remain with me.

After this I allowed my wings to do their job and the moment my feet left the ground, something surprised me. I felt her hands fist the material of my jacket as if some part of her knew what was happening now, and out of instinct, she gripped me tighter. As if clinging to me brought her comfort or security. I couldn't say that I hated the idea, quite the opposite in fact. Which meant I was half tempted to continue flying just to feel her holding onto me for a moment longer.

However, I quickly saw the roof of her house in the distance like an unwelcome sign that I should end this. So, I landed the second I could see a clear spot to set down, without any trees in the way. I then scanned the house for life with my mind, thankful when it came back empty, meaning I didn't have any other mortal minds to deal with. But when I looked at the house I quickly found myself trying to think back to why I had been here before, when it suddenly hit me, making me stop dead in my tracks.

"Ego Vereor." I hissed the name of the demon I had failed to deal with not that long ago, for she had escaped before being brought to punishment. She had caused the death of a mortal named George Miller, Frank's uncle, which explained the large house I once more found myself stood in front of. But I couldn't think of that now, no matter how much something was telling me too. No, first I needed to get my Electus settled. So, I retraced the steps I once made and walked up to her front door, opening it with my mind and allowing me entrance into her home.

Then I paused, asking myself what was next, as this was as far as I had found myself when making plans. Well, if I were continuing with the pretence that she simply fell asleep instead of taking a walk as she obviously intended, then laying her down on the sofa would make more sense. So, I placed her down as gently as possible, as if she had been made from the finest china, that even a whisper of the wind could have cracked.

Then I straightened up and looked down at her, knowing that for my plan to work I would need to rid her of her jacket. So, without wanting to wake her, I simply unravelled each fibre and allowed the memory of it to reappear hanging on the hooks by the front door.   Then I looked around for something to cover her with, as her temperature had dropped since I had taken her on that little flight. Making me realise just how fragile she was. I wasn't used to caring for mortals, and the idea actually scared me, something that was another first around her, for I was known not to fear anything.

I soon found what I was looking for and was about to cover her body, but something made me stop. I soon found myself staring down at her, asking myself once more if she was really here? She looked more like an angel than any other I had ever come across and yet somehow the things I wanted to do to her were far from heavenly.

Oh, they would feel like Heaven the moment I finally made her mine, but that was not what I meant. No, I meant the urge to tie her to my bed and spend days there with her unable to escape, continued to plague me as if this image was of my demon's design. I wanted to dominate her, to make her beg for me to allow her release, only for it to be denied over and over until I was satisfied her orgasm belonged to me and me alone. I wanted to make her cum with both the length of me breaching her hot opening, at the same time sinking my aching fangs into her flesh and feeding from her the way I quickly craved.

The thoughts of having her this way were so strong I felt my other form take hold before I even had chance to stop it. I felt my fangs lengthen and looked down to see the power of both Heaven and Hell engulf my hands in purple flames. By the Gods, but I had never had such a reaction before, not in the face of beauty or in the face of a battle. I had never once in all my years been unable to restrain that side of me until my will permitted it to surface.

And never before had I ever felt terrified of myself or what I could potentially do. For if this could happen simply by looking at her sleeping form, then what could happen should she do something more to tempt me? Gods, but I needed answers before I could potentially put her in danger this way. And it was no longer my own actions I had to fear but those of my enemies! For if they knew that I had found my Electus, then what other dangers could befall upon her?

No, I needed to plan. I needed to do my research and only make a move when I could first assure her safety, from both myself and any more of my own kind. That must be my first priority above all else. For I had waited for her for this long, so I simply refused to put her at risk or take the risk of losing her entirely, now that I had found her. Not just so as I could take her sooner and claim her the way I wanted. The way a King needed to. I would simply declare her under my protection and forbid all of my kind from going near her, which would have to be enough for the time being until I figured this out.

A reason why I now quickly covered her up, along with the tempting curves I could easily see now that she was without the concealment of her jacket. The roundness and swell of her breasts that begged to see if they fit within my large hands. The slight flare of her hips, giving me a natural place for my hands to hold her to me as I embedded myself within her body, connecting us the way I intended to for long hours to come.

"Fuck!" I hissed, the second my thoughts had taken me there once more and needed at that moment to leave the room. To just get away from her alluring scent for five fucking minutes so as I could think rationally! God's, but I was nearly begging for mercy just so that I could find a reprieve from this madness.

Was this what was known as falling in love? A notion that had once been so foreign to me that I had even pitied those who believed themselves to be under the very affliction. But now, well now it was those poor bastards that were having the last laugh, for karma was beginning to look like a swift kick in the gut. One I almost wished was in my seemingly constant erection, for I had been as hard as stone since holding her in my arms. A confession I utterly refused to be ashamed of, for she was mine to lust over.

But love?

Well, if love was the start of the madness of the mind, then I could actually believe in its existence. *Yet another first.*

In the end, I seemed to find myself at the very top of the house, drawn there no doubt because it was where her scent was the strongest.

It was her bedroom.

I took in the room, filing away even the most basic of details, knowing that it might help in discovering who she was. For I might have been resigned to the fact that staying away from her, for the time being, was the best course of action, but that didn't mean I wasn't going to continue to learn everything there was to know about her. Starting with the place she spent the most time in.

"Now, isn't that interesting." I mused the moment I saw the empty luggage and the fresh-looking tags I could see from here held one of the same flight numbers I had been scanning through on the passenger manifest. Yet this girl wasn't mentioned on any of the lists...had she lied about her name as I first suspected she had?

I didn't even need to question if she had been missed off by mistake as Ranka didn't make mistakes...*ever.*

Which meant there was more to discover about this Keira Johnson than there first appeared. Reason being why I got out my phone and rang her number.

"My Lord."

"Get me the flight information on a Keira Johnson, arriving the same date you have been looking into," I told her, knowing she would be confused but instead of asking questions, she simply said,

"It will be done, my Lord."

After this, I scanned the room for any more clues as to what it was she was hiding, *if anything?* I didn't know why I questioned her being here, but I knew in the way she gave me her name that something in her had been concealing a lie. But other than running a hand down her pillow as if being able to take her scent with me, I left her room.

Once more I found myself staring down at her sleeping form, now moved to curl up on her side, with a hand nestled under her head. So, without restraint, I lowered to a knee and ran the backs of my fingers gently down her cheek before tucking the short part of her hair behind her ear. Then I whispered my goodbye, doing so with a promise,

"I will see you soon, my little beauty."

Then I left, making it so that the door would unlock and open slightly the moment she woke, adding to the illusion of falling asleep with little thought of anything else, like locking her door. Of course, I wouldn't risk leaving it this way for the entirety of her sleep, knowing that it was quite possible for her to wake the moment my influence was taken from the house.

A task I loathed to do, but with little choice, I released my wings and increased the distance between us thanks to the sky. I had intended to reach my home at Afterlife, but instead, my feet touched the rock floor of my secret space. A cave that Ava had discovered long ago and one that I would often find myself coming to just to be alone and think. Ironically more often than not as these thoughts had nearly always led me to think about my Electus and who she may be. Well, now I had a vision of beauty to add to these thoughts and a voice still echoing in my mind as if every word she had said had been programmed on repeat.

She had been so nervous, yet brave enough to disobey me when making me wait for her name. She had backed away from me, but not once had she turned around and made a run for it. Not that she would have gotten far, for nothing would have been able to stop my natural reflexes kicking in and allowing my demon to make chase. Now, what I would have done once I caught her was another irrational decision I would have made, no doubt. Making me wonder if my decision now wasn't just as irrational? The choice made to keep away from her for her safety made me wonder if it was, in fact, the only reason?

I didn't exactly relish the idea of being out of control or out of my depth for that matter, two things I both seemed to be around her. No, I was right, I needed to take things slow, for both our sakes or I could end up doing something I regretted…like hurting her or making her a target for others to try. For there was one being on this Earth that I knew would be waiting for her arrival. Waiting for the moment my one weakness appeared, so that he could steal it away and no doubt use it to bargain with.

"Lucius." I found myself snarling out his name and dreading the day he discovered hers. He knew of Malphas' games and would be foolish in believing that he wasn't playing us both. Not when I knew his only alliance was to himself. We all had spies in this world and mine had long ago known of his association with Lucius. But we each played our part until someone called the bluff. Which up until now had been something I had been willing to continue…but that was until there was her.

A game I wanted her as far away from as possible.

The temptation to simply steal her away and lock her in some tower somewhere was nearly too tempting to ignore, and if at any point there was even the slightest possibility of this going wrong, then I needed to plan for such an event. Heaven only knew how such a thing would affect the type of relationship that was expected of me to have with her. As it was never in my mind to have my Chosen One utterly despise me for kidnapping her. Not exactly the perfect start to how I first envisioned this going. But Hell, at least I could no longer claim myself bored, for I hadn't felt this type of excitement for longer than I could remember. I couldn't even claim to have ever felt so many emotions new or old in a whole year, let alone only a few hours!

It was as if she had awakened something deep inside of me and at the moment, I couldn't think of what it was, but it was foreign that much I was certain.

I heard Ava arrive as soon as she landed by the entrance even though I had my back to her. She often chose to nest here, and usually, she left a mess of the place, scattering it with the remains her latest kill. The large cave that remained out of sight was nestled nicely in the rock face hundreds of feet up the mountain and mostly remained untouched, for I had little time to come here. Which was why I would simply manifest any furnishings I needed at the time to make my stay a more comfortable one. Like now, as I sat down in a cherry red leather Chesterfield armchair, with a wing back design so as I could lean the weight of my tense muscles against it. For now, I suddenly held more than the weight of my own world upon my shoulders but now hers as well.

"I assume you have already met her, my pet?" I said making Ava squawk back at me in return and come closer, perching herself on the arm of my chair.

"My Electus has finally made herself known to me, and yet my concern for her wellbeing has already overridden my need to take her...I must be losing my mind, old friend." I said feeling comfort in speaking this way with her. Oh, she understood, for she wasn't born of the Earth like any other golden eagle close to her large size. But her size and sleek shape was the only common sight they shared, for she was ink black, with feathers more like a crow or raven. Well, she proved a formidable force against her enemies, or should I say, *my enemies,* for she often fought by my side.

She was also my eyes in the sky, which was precisely what I wanted of her now...*her memories.*

"Come now, old girl, give me what I ask for," I told her knowing that she had already seen my Electus even before I did. But when she submitted herself to me, I discovered that she didn't have as much as I had hoped for. Like when she had followed Sophia into the woods and waited from above as she spied on Keira entering the forest directly behind her house. Then she swooped too low, scaring her into turning back, knowing that a storm was on the horizon.

The next time she saw her was the night Malphas had turned up at Afterlife, another being she didn't trust and with good reason. So, my pet had obviously taken it upon herself to play protector for the night but had gotten too close to Keira's window. This was when I had called her back from the balcony, now no longer wondering which creature I had saved from her torment.

The moment I severed the connection I stroked my hand down her back affectionately before praising her.

"Very good, my pet, you have done well, but no more scaring her...agreed?" I said, ordering this last part while taking hold of her beak playfully. She ruffled her feathers before shaking herself free of my hold, then she shuffled back a bit, getting ready for what she would deem her reward.

I rolled my eyes once as I knew what her motivation had been...*birds' feet.* Her favourite treat and one I had learned the hard way as there were most certainly downsides to sharing her mind. Either way, I produced what she considered a delicacy and threw it as far as my supernatural powers would take it. Meaning she would have to work hard at getting to it before it fell. She was off like a shot fired and once more I was left alone to my turbulent thoughts.

Thoughts that led me back to that house.

Back to a time I had forced myself to try and forget. Well, today I realised I had failed. As the moment I saw the image of the house in her mind, one of the Fates puzzle pieces had snapped into place, just as I imagined was their plan all along. One done to prevent little doubt in my mind as to who she was to me. Not that this had been needed, for it was as if a lightning bolt had struck me from above and one powered by Zeus' very hand.

But never the less, I couldn't help but think back to that day.

I had been too late to save the human, only learning of the Ego Vereor demon after the damage had already been done. However, Yvonne Dubeck, the 'Self fearing' demon, was now part of the 'Marked'. Meaning that now, it would not take long before she was found and dealt with in the same way all who interfered in a mortal life did. In this case, basically charged with sucking him dry and leaving a broken shell of a man behind. However, such actions against a human such as this weren't what made this case special, not when there had been thousands before her to do the exact same, forcing me to frequently play judge, jury and executor.

However, the house had been the difference.

I remembered it now, just like it was yesterday. Arriving at the now empty home with Vincent, Takeshi and Leivic at my side. Leivic had been the first to hear of the demon causing havoc in his sector, alerting me to the fact when I arrived that year. Leivic was not only a good friend of mine but was also what was known as an enforcer, a part of my council who instead of sitting at my table, had one of his own to command. He took care of this sector when I was unable to do so... as well, like the Devil, I too was only one man.

"Can you get a read on her?" I had asked Takeshi at the time, who was another of my most trusted council members and possessed a set of unique gifts of his own.

He was a rare breed of angel, known as one of the Holy Guardians. Or a Seeker as was another name for them. Their gifts came straight from Janus who was the God of beginnings, gates, transitions, time, duality, doorways, passages, and of course, endings. In fact, Takeshi was considered one of the most powerful of his kind, with only one other that I could think of that would come close. His name was Marcus, and he too sat at a council table, just one that wasn't considered any alliance to me...*yet.* For I still had hopes of one day forming such an alliance with the King of Hellbeasts.

But as a Seeker, this meant that Takeshi had a way of tapping into the past and seeing the truth behind what had happened in a place like this. A gift that certainly helped when casting judgement on those that were now being hunted. Oh, they could argue their case, but with the evidence of a Seeker against them, then the guilty had little left to defend.

However, what made this case different wasn't what Takeshi saw of Yvonne Dubeck, but it was what he saw of me! He had looked at me as if he were seeing me in two places at once and the second the future apparition clouded his vision, I too had felt it.

I had looked up at the house as I had done not long ago and felt the weight of an unconscious girl in my arms, only unlike today, when I looked down at my hands, at the time they had been empty.

"Do you see it, my Lord?" Takeshi had asked me, and I blindly nodded before running up the steps and through the front door.

"Dom, what are you doing?!" I had heard my brother shout from behind me, but I was lost to that same vision, the one my Seeker had just shared. I had run into the living space that had been long ago lost to despair. Dust covered every surface, and I could detect instantly that it had been a while since lived in. But I looked down at the sofa and wondered why I was surprised to find it empty. Shouldn't there have been someone sleeping there, I had asked myself. I heard my brother and Takeshi enter the home, but I ignored both. No instead I ran up the staircase and continued on until reaching an attic room that at one time had been used as a way to view the stars. An old dusty telescope and the single chair were all that really remained, other than the few piles of boxes labelled 'Christmas' that lined the walls.

But like the sofa, I had expected a bed with a purple quilt and the scent of a girl I couldn't rid from my senses of. In the end, I had left the house angry and confused, vowing never to think of this Gods forsaken place again.

That was until today.

Until I had finally realised what that vision had meant to me. How if I had just looked closer into it, then maybe I would have found her sooner. I knew that wasn't part of the Fates' plan for she was always meant to find me, but it seemed almost too cruel to bear. For what reason did they have to wait? Gods, but I had even agreed to have her brother's firm provide the security in my club for Hell's sake!

Why did I just ignore it that day, when all the signs were there?! It made no sense...I had made no sense!

The next thing I knew I let my anger get the better of me and found myself up out of the chair and with my fist embedded in the wall of the cave. I then tore it from the hole I had made and fixed the damage before the cracks could travel further. Then I shook the stone dust from my hand and walked over to the entrance bracing a hand against the side as I looked out to the view. My mind on only one thing...

The girl.

Then I took the metal clip from my pocket and looked down at it, already knowing what I was planning to do with it. I knew it was wrong. I knew it was risky. I knew how I should have stayed away from her like I vowed. But with my heart pounding in my chest, feeling as though it had only now really started to beat for the very first time in all my long existence.

Then I knew that I couldn't.

Because the truth was, that the sickness of obsession had already taken hold. It had already taken root in my soul, and even now I was feeling the weight of our separation lying heavily against my will power.

Which left only one dangerous question for me to ask myself...

"Maybe she could simply dream of me?"

DRAVEN

10

THE SEEDS OF
MY OBSESSION

By the time I realised what I was doing it was too late to stop, for my destination seemed to be the exact same place I told myself I wouldn't go back to. It was such a foreign concept to me, arguing with myself like this. I wished I could have said I was stronger, but in this, I was rendered under the pull of the Fates. Which was precisely why I found myself at her window like some stalker hoping for just one more look.

But surprisingly, she had still been asleep on the sofa at the time, which told me that she must still be trying to adjust to a different time zone. That or my influence on her had been more powerful than I first expected it to be. Either way, I found myself entering through her window instead of the front door as I had initially intended. But then I wondered if my presence would be something she would be able to detect if I was too close, and I didn't want her to wake just yet.

So, I checked the name on her luggage tag, which I should have done earlier. I don't know why the thought had only come to me later...well, that wasn't strictly true, as I wasn't exactly thinking rationally then! Or now for that matter, for here I was again, back to a place I vowed not to return to until I deemed it safe for her. But my own excuses and justifications had won the argument this time, telling myself this would only aid me in discovering her past quicker.

Which was why I now held the luggage tag in my hand, only to find out that she had been telling me the truth.

"Alright, Miss Keira Johnson let's see what it is you are hiding from me," I said aloud, now looking around the room with fresh eyes this time. I noticed a well-used shoulder bag lay discarded on the floor. So, I decided while I was already invading someone's personal space by stalking them and breaking into their home, then I might as well go all the way. I opened up the bag and ignored most of its contents, seeing as I was only looking for one thing... *her Passport.*

I found it and saw that, like her luggage tag, it stated that her name was indeed Keira Johnson and her date of birth would put her at twenty-one years old. I frowned down at the official document in my hand knowing that something just didn't fit. Mainly the fact that she should be two years older with a different birthday if my dream had been anything to go by.

I also couldn't help but note that the passport was very near brand new, which wasn't unusual as most people applied for a passport before travelling if theirs was out of date. Or they simply hadn't travelled before. But still, it stood out to me for reasons unknown.

I placed her passport back inside her bag, making sure it was in the same position as before, trying to rid myself of the doubts I now had. It wasn't that I didn't believe she was my Chosen One, for I would have known that even if I had been a blind man. No, it wasn't that but more a feeling of unease, as if there were more to this girl than anyone could have ever guessed.

A secret past maybe? Had that been what had brought her here? For I knew that it wasn't Frank she was related to but his wife, Olivia Miller. I ran a frustrated hand through my hair and noticed something new on her bedside table. I walked over to it, grinning to myself to find that she obviously liked the colour purple. As it was a definite theme to the room. Like the bright purple lamp that a book lay next to. A book I couldn't help but pick up.

"Jane Eyre." Ah, so she liked the classics, did she. I had read it some time ago when hearing it being talked about after it was first published back in the 1840s under a different name, Currer Bell. It had been an intriguing read at the time, painting this Mr Rochester as a man consumed by the misery of his own demons. Demons of a past that plagued him until a light had finally entered his life. One he had to lie to and conceal the truth from, just to make her fall in love with him.

I found it curious then that my Chosen One should favour such a story above all others seeing that this had been a book she had brought with her from England. Unless it had been a gift, one that also would suggest it to be a favourite of hers.

In fact, I continued to consider why, with the book still in my hands, when I heard my brother's call. I answered my phone quickly, unsure as to whether it would wake her or not.

"I am on my way," I told him before hanging up, knowing this was all he needed to know. Then I left, forcing myself to do so without seeing her again that day. For I already knew the true depths of the seeds of my obsession she had unknowingly planted. Seeds that had started to take root the second they were laid at my feet in the form of a beautiful golden-haired girl. One gifted to me by Heaven, in none other than a garden of Eden made by a demons hand. It would have been ironic had I not been half angel, half demon myself, and therefore simply making our first meeting even more poetic.

By the time I made it back to Afterlife the sun had set, and I found my brother on the rooftop waiting for me as I knew he would be. He was casually leaning against the stone wall that surrounded this particular section of the roof that was situated directly above my bedchamber.

He watched me approach and frowned at the book in my hands, before commenting,

"I hear that we have a well-stocked library right in our own home, you know, for the next time the urge takes you." I rolled my eyes and ignored his dry wit.

"I gather Sophia has told you." I deduced seeing as I received his call.

"Told me what? For I had assumed she had been with you seeing as that was the reason for your prompt and pissed off departure," Vincent replied, making me frown. But instead of answering him I grabbed my phone and dialled her number.

"Why hello there, dear brother, how was your first date...still going I hope," she answered making me growl, knowing that she had obviously been aware of my Chosen One's existence before I had.

"Where are you?!" I snapped, making her scoff once before informing me,

"I would rethink your being pissed at me, seeing as I had tried to tell you and besides, if I hadn't intervened today then just think how long it could have been for you two to have met, because unless she's into the goth scene, then a chance meeting at the club seemed unlikely," she informed me calmly making me want to growl. Mainly because she was right, the chances of us meeting at the club would have been unlikely. Not considering we usually remained out of sight up in the VIP, where I enforced a strict rule, that no humans were allowed in there. So, other than the one dramatic entrance we made, usually when first arriving and for the sole purpose of letting the town know we still existed. Like my sister had said, the chances of meeting would have been slim to none.

"Point made Sophia, now tell me where you are," I said hoping my tone was enough to get her to comply, as this was not the day to have my patience tested. Not when it had hit its limit the moment I had been forced to leave her for the second time that day.

"Well alright, I am currently breaking into the College's record office to find out what courses your dear little Chosen One has applied for," she said surprising me enough that I took a step back. For it hadn't even occurred to me that college could have been the reason for her now living here. I suppose it would make sense, for her sister lived here and was a logical choice if she wanted a change of scenery. But that didn't explain what Sophia was looking to do with that information. Information I myself would also be interested in knowing, but my mischievous sister didn't need to know that.

"Why?" was all I could manage to ask, as I looked up now to see that Vincent was looking as shocked to hear that my Chosen One had been found, for he could hear both sides of the conversation. He even mouthed the words, 'Is it true?'

I nodded, knowing that such news wouldn't just affect me but all three of us, as I wasn't the only one waiting for the prophecy to begin. Not considering it was said that my Electus was to be the catalyst into setting the wheels into motion. Wheels that included all the Kings of this world finding their own Chosen Ones. Which naturally also included my own brother.

But first thing first, and that was to ensure my own Chosen One's safety. My sister, however, wasn't thinking about this, she was simply playing matchmaker.

"Why do you think, so that I can join some of her classes, make friends and therefore keep an eye on her for you," she replied in an exasperated tone as if this little scheme of hers should have been obvious. But my reaction to it was to hold the bridge of my nose, mentally counting to ten and releasing a deep sigh so that I wouldn't lose my temper the way I wanted to at my little sister. For I knew that she was only doing what she thought was best for me and helping me...which right now, she most certainly wasn't. And Vincent knew this, which was why he took matters into his own hands and took my phone before my temper crushed it.

"May I suggest, little sister that you get your information and bring it back here with haste before Dom loses his sanity and decides to destroy that fucking college...yeah, thought so," he added before hanging up and handing me back the phone informing me,

"She'll be here in ten minutes."

A little time later I found myself standing out on my balcony with the same book in my hands staring down at it as if it held all the answers. When in reality, it held none. Mr Rochester had been just as selfish as I was by trying to convince Jane to live in sin the second she found out his dirty little secrets.

And what had happened...

She had run from him.

Which only begged the question, what would this Keira do when she found out all of mine? Found out that I wasn't human but in fact, far from it? Would she do as Jane had and risk her life by running from the safety of my home?

No, I couldn't risk such a thing, and thankfully my brother had agreed with my decision... *unlike Sophia*, who had been expecting to find Keira here at Afterlife, standing by my side the moment she arrived back. Thankfully however, our angelic brother had once again put his diplomatic talents to good use and at the very least got her to understand my reasons for caution. By the end of which, we were all in agreement that Keira's safety was to take first priority. Along with the decision in keeping her arrival to our world secret. Not until we could be sure that the moment she found out what we were, that she wouldn't make a run for it come the first opportunity. Something that would no doubt only end up getting herself kidnapped by the long list of potential enemies I had. Enemies that would no doubt also have a death wish, for that would be all they would receive if such an act were committed. Even the thought of it now nearly had me ripping the book to shreds, and it was only when the binding groaned, did I release my crushing hold on it.

However, Sophia hadn't been without her victories, for she had convinced me to let her join college under the pretence of making friends with Keira. Therefore, being able to not only ease her into what would become of her new life when the time came, but also to ensure that one of the most powerful demons was next to her as protection during the times that I could not.

I had also discovered how Sophia had known that she was to start college. Which was when I found what lengths she would go to, as she took over the mind of a waitress called Meg just so as to overhear a conversation Keira had with a new friend she had just met. She had overheard the talk of college and took it upon herself to gain the information she needed after that.

Information I myself had also had the chance to go over, telling me of her keen interest in history, seeing as most of her classes were on the subject, making me unable to suppress a grin. Well, that would certainly help, as it would give us at least one thing in common seeing how old I was and how much history I had witnessed firsthand.

Her other subjects were Spanish and no surprise, English Literature. Not considering the book I now held in my hands, for it was clear she liked to read. So, I wondered what she would then think of my library, making me start to contemplate getting more of the classics stocked there ready for her use.

"I am surprised you are still here." I heard my brother say from behind me, knowing before he entered the room that he had been on his way here. I didn't even look up from the front cover, simply ran my fingers over the name slightly embossed, seeing it now as the name I was only just getting used to saying...*Keira*.

"No good will come of me seeing her," I told him even hearing for myself the bitter tone it was laced with. This was when Vincent started laughing, making me now turn my hard gaze back on him over my shoulder.

"Oh no, letting the girl you want to make fall in love with you, dream of you most nights, oh yeah, that would be a mistake indeed," he said making me frown.

"You jest?" I asked making him laugh even harder this time.

"Yes Brother, I jest...Hell' Dom, even the Gods jest right now, for if you think it is expected of you to stay away from her after all this time, then you will surely wake on the morn and find yourself a bloody saint!" I groaned, making him chuckle as I raked a hand through my hair.

"Then you think I should go to her?" I asked needing to be sure and to be honest, just looking for the excuse to allow someone else to take the decision from me, for it was currently killing me!

"That depends, do you want me to buy you a monk's habit? Yes! I think you should go to her," he said making me grin.

"Well, I would hate to disappoint my only brother," I replied making him smirk. Then he slapped me on the back and said,

"Better not chance it then, for I am a fickle being." I laughed, and it felt good to finally relieve myself some of the tension. After this, he left calling behind him,

"I will tell the council you have more pressing matters this evening and who knows, maybe such news will finally relieve Sophia and I from a night of Aurora's presence." At this I scoffed, knowing that the time to rid myself of her was a situation I was going to have to face before situating my Electus by my side.

"Then I wish you luck with that prayer," I shouted back as I saw him grant me his middle finger over his shoulder, as a way of goodbye. I grinned in reply to the action before looking down at the book, now flicking it to the page I had memorised. It was the part of the story when Jane had return back to Thornfield Hall and described how she felt that coming back to him was like coming home. It was also a part that I wanted Keira to read and find the significance of it when she was to remember meeting me in something other than what she was led to believe was only in her dreams.

And speaking of dreams...

It was time to invade hers.

DRAVEN

II
THE POWER OF A NAME

 entered her room with ease, once more deciding her window was to offer more direct access. Thankfully, it was a large dormer window that opened wide enough to accommodate my size. So, using the front door wasn't needed and would only be considered wasted time, for this way put me at the bottom of her bed in seconds.

Just the sight of her and I felt my lungs expanding as I took in a deep breath. Seeing her now and I could feel the tension of the day leave me just by knowing that I was back in the same room as her. Was that how it was to be from now on? That I would only get a moment of relief when I was in her presence, for if that was the case, then I didn't hold out for much hope of relaxing for a while.

These thoughts left me the moment I saw her begin to stir in her sleep and I looked behind me to see the wind had picked up outside and was causing a nearby branch to tap against the glass. I was about to snap it with a thought when I decided against it, curious now to see if she would wake and hoping that she would. So instead of preventing the sound, I made sure it continued, only louder this time. Then I stood back in the shadows, keeping my presence unknown for now.

I watched as she moaned, before begrudgingly turning her head to look at the clock, checking the time. I didn't know how long she had been asleep but seeing as she had slept already, then I doubted she had been in bed for long. Her groan of frustration told me I was right, as she seemed annoyed. Something I found equally fascinating, for I wondered how she would look when angry?

In fact, I quickly found myself wondering many things about her. Like what she sounded like when she laughed? What colour her eyes turned to when she cried? What habits she would have, for I only knew about the biting of her lip when nervous. A distracting mannerism indeed, that had me only craving to take the action up upon myself and rid her teeth the burden, therefore tasting her lips for my own gratification.

Which had me asking myself if I would soon see the tempting sight once more when I finally let my presence be known to her? For I had little doubt that she would be nervous again when finding me in her room and now dominating her personal space.

These questions vanished the second I saw her bolt upright in what looked like fear, making me feel a moment of guilt. Which be assured, was a very foreign emotion for a King like me to experience. But as I watched as her head frantically looked around the room, it was precisely what I started to feel. Especially when she held her breath as if waiting for something to happen. Even her hands were curled up into fists, gripping on to her quilt in the same way she had unknowingly been gripping onto my jacket earlier.

She reached out for the light, only stopped herself before she turned it on, telling me she had just realised that if she did that, then she would lose all hope of seeing what was beyond her own reflection. But no matter the fear she obviously felt, she was brave enough to throw the covers aside and slip from the bed to go and investigate.

She seemed to relax once the moon came peeking out from behind the clouds, creating more light in her room and showing her that there was nothing there as she had feared. Making me wonder if she had believed it to be Ava knocking at her window once more. It had most certainly scared her the first time, so it stood to reason that it would do so again.

She even smiled to herself as if she felt silly finding nothing there and the sight caused me to suck in a breath. For how was it possible that she was even more breathtaking than when I first saw her?

Was it thanks to her skin that was illuminated, now being bathed in the moonlight? Or the way her hair hung down to one side like a thick chain of gold, braided to her waist? I decided it was all of these things that started with that secret smile of hers, one I wished to have seen in the light of day.

She seemed to be unsure of what to do next but whatever thoughts were playing on her mind, opening the window won above all else. It seemed a bit tough for her to budge and watching as she struggled with it, didn't sit well with me. Never before had I been so compelled to help another, to the point my hands curled to fists at my sides, just to stop myself from reaching out to her. In the end, I was simply left with no other option than to give it a swift kick of power to get it to open the moment she applied more pressure.

I then watched as she shivered from the cold, before hugging herself, as if to fight off the chill. That was when I noticed the sleeves on her arms weren't attached to the thin vest she wore to bed. I frowned, wondering why someone would go to bed wearing long, fingerless gloves up past their elbows? Especially when there were other ways to ward off the draught an old, big house like this one could create. Why not just wear more than a vest?

I felt myself still lingering on this question, only leaving it for another time when I heard her chuckle. My head shot up suddenly, wondering if she could see me, for what she would have found funny looking out the window I couldn't guess. But instead of finding my answer to the enigma that was this girl, she slammed the window shut and spun quickly as if scaring herself.

However, her erratic actions ended up causing her to almost stumble over a cushion that had landed on the floor. It was also at this point that I could remain hidden no longer, for the impulse to tease her was too much to bear without voicing the words.

"You have trouble staying on your feet, don't you?" The moment she heard me was the moment she could now see how close I was to her, for I stood at the bottom of her bed only feet away from her. I half expected her to cry out for help, or at the very least scream...*something I wouldn't have allowed for long.*

But she surprised me for other than a sharp intake of breath she remained silent. I then waited for her to respond to seeing me here in some other way. As after all, she had just discovered a stranger in her bedroom like some thief in the night, ready to steal her life away...little did she know that it was her I wanted to flee with, not her meagre possessions.

"I umm...I mean... what are you doing here?" She finally responded, and I would have laughed had it not insulted her. So, I contented myself with a smirk instead, for she certainly didn't have her priorities in order if finding me here wasn't enough to cause alarm.

But wait, had she remembered me from this afternoon? No, surely not, that would have been impossible, for I had made sure to take away the memory of our first meeting. Unless fragments had remained? Well, if that were true, then it would mean that she would have one of the strongest minds I had ever come across on a mortal. Half of me hoped not, seeing as it would make coming here difficult, especially if I wanted to continue making her believe it was all a dream.

And I didn't think myself strong enough to stop seeing her, which was why when I finally answered her question, I did so with a possessive tone I couldn't control.

"Yes, well apart from it being my right to see you, I also wanted to bring you something. You dropped this." I told her now holding out her hair clip in my hand for her to take, hoping for her to step closer. However, when she didn't trust me, I couldn't help but feel it in my chest. A kind of pain and hurt I couldn't explain, for I had never been afflicted with the emotion before.

But then I had to ask myself why would she trust me? I had given her no reason to trust a man she had only just met and one that had essentially just crept into her room. If I was being honest, then neither of our reactions to each other were what you would have called conventional. As becoming a night stalker definitely wasn't in any plan I would have made when thinking of first meeting my Electus.

"There is no need to fear me. I would *never* hurt you," I said, hoping she would hear the way I emphasised the word 'never' as if it would cause me physical pain to do such a thing. What was it about this girl that had me acting so out of character?

I wanted her to trust me, more than she trusted any other soul on Earth. But I wanted her to do so of her own free will. Oh sure, I could have just forced that trust upon her mind, but then it would no longer be considered a gift, or a treasure earned.

However, when my words of reassurance were obviously not enough, as she still hadn't taken a step towards me, I decided to let a hint of authority coat my next command. Even if still refusing to inflict my will over her decisions.

"Come here." Finally, that worked, and again I barely held back a grin when I saw the way she stepped forward so cautiously. Even the way she reached out as far as she could, so as still trying to keep the distance between us had me near grinning. For I wasn't about to allow that to continue for long.

So, the very moment that her fingertips barely whispered over the metal clip, I made my move, no doubt making her question how I had moved so fast. Once more she sucked back a startled breath the second I eliminated the space between us. However, the sound of her erratic little heart beating wildly in her chest might have been from fear, and again, this wasn't something I would allow. So, making sure that my tone was a gentle one, I told her,

"Don't be afraid, little one." Her reply ended up surprising me.

"I...I'm not afraid," she whispered back in a small voice that spoke of anything but the meaning of her words. Unless...could there be another reason behind her reactions towards me? Was she speaking the truth and it wasn't fear that was making her heart pound? Could it be what I hoped? I couldn't help the knowing grin from appearing, deciding to put my theory to the test.

"Here," I said now reaching down to slowly take her hand in mine, marvelling at the heat I felt emanating from our contact. In fact, it nearly rocked me back on my heels for the connection was so strong, my breath was stolen from me, making this yet another profound moment.

I turned her hand over, keeping eye contact so that I could tell the moment that her look of awe turned to one of fear, happy in the knowledge that it hadn't yet happened. I placed the clip in her palm and knew in that moment that the internal struggle within me was like fighting a battle of three sides with my humanity at the centre of it all. My demon simply wanted to collar her neck with my bare hands before forcing her to submit to the plundering of her mouth. To feel her pulse beating beneath the skin on our fingertips as it increased with her arousal.

But then my angel was screaming caution for this wasn't a single night of passion we craved but a hundred lifetimes of it. We didn't want to feed from her fear but feed from her sexual release. Oh, what a meal that would be...I swear the very thought of it would have had me drooling, had I been a lesser being!

And these turbulent thoughts only ended with me confessing my reasons for being here now.

"I shouldn't be here yet, but I was curious about you, little one," I said in a hard tone as if she had just purposely torn the truth from me. When in fact, she was as innocent as they came in this picture. Because there was only one villain here and it wasn't just the demon part of me.

"About....*me?*" The sound of her shock made me want to growl. As if she could barely believe how something like that was possible. Seriously, had this girl looked in the mirror lately? Sure, so she wasn't what the world would class as a conventional beauty, one you would find plastered all over glossy pages with their natural features hidden under layers of product. And I understood, thanks to having a sister, that there was nothing wrong to what she liked to call, adding a frame to the masterpiece when referring to a woman wearing makeup.

But I also wanted to feel skin beneath my hands when I was finally able to touch the face of the woman, I had been waiting for all this time...not makeup. Which was why I couldn't resist bringing my hand up to her face now and running the backs of my fingers across her tender cheek, one bathed in the moonlight.

My gentle actions caused her to close her eyes as if she was also trying to burn the memory to the forefront of her mind, so that it was never far from her thoughts. Thoughts that unfortunately I knew I would have no choice but to take away from her, as now was not the time for her to know me yet.

No, this time *was for me only.*

So, with that in mind, I placed my lips to her forehead and whispered exactly what type of beauty she had gifted me.

"Exquisite."

Then as if both of my supernatural sides knew what their master was planning next, they took action by pulling her closer to us, as they feared my next decision was already made.

For it was time to let her go... *for the night at least.*

But then I wanted to growl in triumph as I felt her body shiver in my arms, and I knew it was from the lust we both felt enveloping our senses. For her nipples hardened within the centre swell of her ample breasts, allowing me to feel them through our clothes, only wishing now that it was against my naked skin.

Then she looked up at me with those big wide, innocent eyes of hers and I swear I was a man rendered incapable of speech. I very nearly had to clear my throat just to push past the emotions she was causing to swell up within the stone confines of my heart. I even felt myself smile at the thought of what this little one had the power to do to me.

So, trying to take back some of the control I issued her with a parting order before I would take over her mind. And this time, I would make sure that I didn't miss any piece of me left there.

I hated the idea of eradicating myself from her memory, but I just couldn't chance it right now. No, there would be time for her to know me and soon, I was sure of it. So, I told her,

"You will sleep, my girl and you will sleep well this night, understand?" I expected her to nod, but instead, her shy gaze found her feet, something I wouldn't allow for long. So, I hooked a finger under her chin and lifted her face to look at me as I offered her my promise as a way of goodbye...

"Until next time, *my Keira,"* I whispered, already weaving the spell of control on her mind. One that started to work the moment her eyes fluttered closed. So, I lifted her slight frame into my arms, loving the feel of her there and wishing I had more time just to simply keep holding her. But instead, I carried her back to the bed and laid her down as I had done earlier that day when placing her on the sofa. I then granted myself the tempting and torturous few minutes to simply stare down at her, wondering what it would feel like to have her naked in my arms and unable to hide anything from me. I wanted to be skin to skin. To feel the swell of her breasts against me when she inhaled deeply, the second my fingers explored her most sensitive parts. To span my hands around her waist, to prevent her from moving too far from my grasp. By the Gods, but I wondered if in fact, I would allow her from my bed at all when I finally allowed myself to claim her!

I was quickly losing myself and my focus as I encouraged these little fantasies to play out by not yet covering up her delectable body with the covers like I had intended on doing.

But then something happened. Something so unexpected, that when a single name left her lips, it shocked me to my core!

It was the moment she whispered a single name in her sleep…

"Draven."

Keira

12

GETTING READY

When I woke the window still held the last few shreds of night. I rubbed my eyes and wondered what it was that I had been dreaming about. I sat upright and stretched out my arms yawning when I heard the thud of something hitting the wooden floor. I leaned over and picked up my copy of Jane Eyre. I must have fallen asleep reading it last night. How strange, I couldn't remember anything.

I looked at the clock and saw it was 6:30 am. I rubbed my eyes and pulled back the warm covers. I got up and regretted it immediately as the cold air hit me. I quickly rushed into the bathroom wishing I owned slippers as I dragged my frozen feet across the hard-wooden floor. I decided to get back into bed when I had finished as it was much warmer there. The house was still quiet, and I was in no rush to start the day in this weather.

I grabbed my book and noticed something attached to one of the pages. I shook my head at the unbelievable sight as I removed my metal hair clip. How it got there I didn't know, but I had a vague memory that I had lost it. I opened the book and my first thought was it had been placed there for a reason. The point was positioned as though to draw my attention to a part in the book I knew well.

It read...

"An impulse held me fast,-a force turned me round. I said,-or something in me said for me, and in spite of me:- "Thank you, Mr. Rochester, for your great kindness. I am strangely glad to get back again to you; and wherever you are, is my home--my only home."

I held the book open on the page staring at it for a long time, trying to comprehend why it should be marked on this page. My mind didn't feel like my own. It felt as though I had dreamed the last couple of days. I tried to recall what I had done yesterday but my mind came up empty. The last thing I remembered was meeting RJ at the mall and talking to Libby on the way home. But it finished there. What on Earth?

My train of thought was interrupted by the noises my stomach was making. I realised I was starving. Did I even eat anything yesterday? Jesus, I couldn't remember that either! How strange but more than anything else it was utterly frustrating.

I grabbed some thick socks from one of the drawers and put them on my feet as quickly as I could before they turned to blocks of ice again. I tried to be as quiet as I could when I crossed the landing and went down the stairs. The steps creaked under the weight of my body making them sound as though they were moaning at me for waking them too.

Once in the kitchen, I flicked on the light switch and headed for the huge double door fridge. My eyes hadn't quite adjusted to the light as it was still dark outside and as always, raining. I grabbed the carton of milk and put it on the table, got a bowl, spoon and hunted for some cereal. I found one called Captain Crunch and thought I would give it a try. I clicked the kettle on and put a teabag in a mug, thus completing my breakfast.

Libby walked in the kitchen dressed in a fluffy robe with slippers to match. She looked like a pink marshmallow but hell, at least it looked warm.

"Nice." I said waving my hand up and down motioning to her ensemble. She gave me a smarmy smile before saying,

"Frank bought these for me last Christmas and trust me, you'll be wanting some in winter."

"Why, does it come in black?" I replied with a cocky smile of my own.

"So, how did you sleep?" She asked as she sat opposite me with her own bowl and spoon in hand.

"On my side mainly." I giggled.

"Ha, ha, very funny, you know what they say about sarcasm don't you?"

"Highest form of wit, oh and I don't recall the rest." I said as I put my bowl and spoon in the sink after finishing my breakfast in record time.

"Yes, and the lowest form of intelligence! Also, we do have a dishwasher." She said nodding to one of the cupboard doors it was no doubt hidden behind.

It felt so normal to be talking like this with my sister. The way we were before my shit hit the fan.

"What?" She asked, looking at me as if she wanted in on the joke. She was so beautiful, even now when her hair was loose and suffering a funky case of bed head, it just gave her a more natural beauty, unkempt and wild. Like some Amazonian princess.

"Nothing really, just reminiscing. You in work today?" I asked trying to change the subject.

"Umm...well no but..." she paused, and I clocked the guilty look right away.

"It's ok, you gotta work. I'll be fine Libs. Plus, I've got my big night clubbing to plan for." I winked.

"Ah yes, the Acid... umm... something or others. Yeah, good luck with that." She said now being the sarcastic one.

"Acid Criminals actually and they sound rather cultured." I said this last part in a posh English accent, and Libby couldn't keep a straight face. We both laughed.

"Well, like I said, good luck with that! Hey, but didn't you say RJ has a brother?" Her cheesy wink said it all.

"Yes, but you know that won't mean much to me. I don't date, remember?" I said firm enough to get it through.

"Okay, okay, I was just saying. You know they go crazy here for the English accent right." She winked again at me which had me quickly rolling my eyes.

"Umm.... well in that case I'm just gonna have to practice my American accent then." I couldn't keep the smirk from my face. I got up to take the second mug of tea that Libby had poured me back upstairs when I heard Libby ask about my book. I stopped in the hallway and backed up a few steps.

"What did you say?"

"Did you find your book?" She asked, her mouth still full of cereal.

"Umm, when did I lose it?" I was confused, did she take it and was she the one that attached my hair clip to it?

She looked even more confused.

"Yeah yesterday, you were asking me if I had seen it remember." She looked slightly worried at my non-responsive face. I honestly didn't remember even speaking to Libby after she had dropped me off after the mall. My mind was a blank and Libby was shifting slightly in her seat and had put her spoon down waiting for me to answer her. Her face was about to quickly shift to worried, so I decided to lie.

"Oh yeah that, sorry. I found it under the bed, must have forgotten. I've slept since then Libs." I smiled trying to play the dumb blonde act, only my acting skills weren't my finest attribute.

She answered me with a nod and picked up her spoon again, which indicated that she was at least satisfied with my response.

Once upstairs in my room, I examined the book again and read the entire page over and over, trying to make sense of the significance.

It was the part in the book where Jane had returned from her aunt's house after she had died, and Jane was returning to Mr Rochester. She felt like she was home or more like wherever he was, was her home. The thought lingered there in my mind like a lost memory trying to find its way back through the fog. I gave up making sense of it all and put it down to coincidence.

I got into my baggy jeans and double layered top, which had long grey sleeves and a plum coloured outer t-shirt. I also put on a thick knitted cardigan that was far too big for me. I decided to do some housework and take the burden off Libby. I started in the bathroom, which was really my own personal en-suite. It was the only other room on the top floor so naturally I was the only one who used it.

It only had a shower, sink and a toilet in it but it was big enough to house a bath. It was decorated in a whitewashed style that reminded me of a beach hut. There was a corner cupboard that housed extra towels and lots of empty shelves waiting for me to fill them with everyday things.

I cleaned the beautiful arched, wooden mirror that hung over the sink and around the little shelf at the bottom which had a candle on it.

Libby walked in just as I had finished the sink. She was dressed in a black suit that looked fantastic on her. It was tight fitting and had a thick belt under the chest. A bright white shirt showed underneath at the collar and cuffs. She wore heels that looked far too high to be comfortable, the type that I would most definitely fall down in.

"You look nice." She smiled and tried to twist a stray curl back into her bun.

"Thanks. And you're sure that you'll be..."

"It's ok, you don't have to worry. I told you I will be fine." I would have hugged her but my rubber gloved hands that smelled of bleach wouldn't have mixed well with the power suit.

"I'm just going to do some housework and maybe try and get some reading done ready for next week."

"Ok, well I'm off now. Frank's already gone so you've got the whole house to yourself. What time are you meeting up with the 'Goth Gang'?" This was no doubt her new nickname for my hopefully soon to be friends.

"Umm, I'm not actually sure on that one, RJ said she'd ring but I will ring you on your mobile to let you know the details."

"Don't you mean 'cell' phone?" She said in her best American accent, which was about as good as mine, and that was pretty weak.

"Oh yeah, don't want the locals getting all rallied up 'cause there's a stranger in town." God, my red-neck accent sounded more German. I laughed at myself.

"Nope, but I think the town will be more pre-occupied with the other newcomers, the scarier ones." She said this bit in a dire tone and she wasn't laughing. Why did she dislike them so much? Had she even seen them? 'Cause from the sound of things, not many people had.

Libby looked at her watch and soon rushed off saying she would be late if she didn't leave now. I shouted my goodbye and combined it with telling her to watch her speed but was met with sound of the front door slamming.

I went back to cleaning shaking my head. I couldn't wait to start work and college as I was getting seriously bored. But thinking about tonight I was both excited and nervous. I didn't really know what to expect but at least from what RJ had said I had high hopes for the band being good, or at least the drummer being hot.

I spent the rest of the day trying to find things to do as unfortunately my list of jobs didn't take as long as I thought they would have. RJ had called to confirm I was still 'up for it'. I think she was excited about being the one to introduce me into the 'Goth Rock' society. To be fair though, any would do at this point. I just needed to get out and would have joined the chess club if I had to.

It made me miss my little Ford Fiesta. What I wouldn't do now just to be able to get in a car and drive around and explore the place. After ringing Libby on her "cell" and informing her of the plan, I finished getting dinner ready.

I had made a casserole so all they would need to do was heat it up. I'm sure even Libby could handle that without burning it. Or maybe I should put in into bowls ready to just shove in the microwave. That way she wouldn't have to light anything. I chuckled to myself as I remembered the pizza on my first night here. It was time to get ready for the big night, so a shower was first on the agenda. I had done the girlie thing and asked what RJ was going to wear, not wanting to stand out. Not that I ever really wore anything to stand out, but still, I had to check.

I had been quite relieved to find out that the place wasn't the dress code type. I was just going to stick to my old faithful blue jeans that weren't as baggy as my usual ones and a long sleeved black top with a v neck. This one at least had black embroidery across the neck giving it a bit more of a layered look. It had a bit of a gypsy vibe to it giving it a retro feel. I thought it would pass for the alternative look that I was aiming for.

It clung quite tight to my skin, which showed off a little too much of my figure than I liked, so I added a hooded top which was also black with red piping around the edges. It had a huge hood that would give me lots of protection from the weather should we have to queue to get into this place. It also had long sleeves that went right down past my knuckles.

I dried my hair, which had taken me the longest part to get ready, as it always did. It was just so long and thick, it looked more like a shaggy rug hanging down to my waist. My hair had always been a head turner. I used to enjoy the compliments I received, but now I just wanted to hide it away, with tonight being no exception.

I tied it into a knot and secured it up at the back with my strong metal clip and I had this down to a fine art. The shorter bits at the front fell down framing my face, with one side thicker than the other. I examined myself in the long mirror in my room and I was satisfied that I didn't stand out yet hopefully didn't look too much like the newbie I was.

Libby was already downstairs finishing her dinner off and was mopping up the juice with the baguette I had asked her to get when I called. She looked as if she had enjoyed it.

"A bit of a change from fast food?" I said as I joined her at the table. She would have replied with some sarcastic response, I could see it in her eyes, but she was too engrossed in her food to bother.

I loved watching people enjoy my food. I had always enjoyed cooking, ever since my dad had shown me how to make potato cakes with left over mashed potatoes from Sunday dinner.

"Yum...mmmmy, that was delicious, thanks. Frank is going to love that when he comes in. Hey, can't I say that I made it and win some brownie points?" I smiled gratefully at her.

"Since when do you need brownie points? Frank adores you." I removed her plate before she started to try and eat the pattern on the bowl.

"Umm, is there..." I changed direction from the sink to the stove before I had chance to get the bowl wet. I dug the big spoon in the mixture and poured her another bowlful.

"Only if there's enough." But this last statement was said while she was digging into the hot mixture of meat, gravy and vegetables.

"It's fine, I made enough for leftovers. I know how much Frank eats and anyway, you didn't answer my question."

"About?" She said with her mouthful.

"Brownie points." I said reminding her.

"Yeah, well he may adore me but not my feet and I could kill for a foot rub. Those shoes were crippling me by the end of the day and well, you see he's got these really big, strong hands that..."

"Okay, okay, I get it! Please, spare me the details." I said making a gagging motion but getting it all wrong as I laughed.

"You look nice by the way, didn't want to wear your hair down? No, I don't blame you, not in this weather." She said answering her own question.

"You not eating before you go?" She added.

"I had some earlier." I said lying as it was easier than saying I couldn't eat because of my nerves.

Libby nodded her head toward the clock on the wall and I followed it dreading what it might show.

But it only confirmed my time had run out...

Afterlife here I come.

DRAVEN

B

PAST MYSTERIES

After she had unknowingly shocked the breath from me, I laid her gently on the bed, positioning her long braid beside her with care and marvelling at how soft it felt. I could tell she had not long since showered before going to sleep for it was still slightly damp at the folds and her natural scent now held the hint of something more. Jasmine, coconut and the slightest touch of something sweet, like honey. I then wondered at her choice, filing it away in my memory vault for when she would find herself living in my home, calling it her own.

A day I hoped wasn't long in coming.

I ran the backs of my fingers across her gloved arms, frowning down at them, knowing that it was odd. She didn't have any medical reason to wear them, or at least not one I could detect. But then I couldn't be one hundred per cent sure of that until I had looked at her medical history as I intended on doing. For I would leave no stone unturned, not where my Chosen One was concerned. Which included finding out just how it was that she had heard of me.

So, with that in mind, I committed the most invasive act one of my kind could do to another, and that was delve into her mind, looking for all thoughts of me. An act that should have been easy, only the second I breached her subconscious, I quickly realised just what an impossible task I was up against.

Her mind was unlike any other I had ever encountered before and was a damn fortress! In the end, the best I could hope for was casting memories of me to the far corners of her mind, rather than taking them completely. Which meant it was highly likely that only the sight of me could trigger all that I had worked hard at trying to conceal.

I just couldn't understand it! How was it possible for her to have built up such walls of defence when she was but a mortal? This wasn't something you were born with but something you spent a lifetime creating. Gods, but it was as if she wasn't just trying to keep out one soul that might have deeply wounded her, but instead an entire world! Even my brother wouldn't have been able to breach such a barrier, and I hated to admit it, but he was more powerful than I at the task.

But then, as startling as this revelation was, at the very least it offered me some comfort in knowing that even the most powerful being capable of controlling any mind would no doubt struggle with Keira's. And there was none more powerful at it than my enemy, Lucius. The Vampire King and once a being who I had considered a friend who ruled by my side instead of against me.

"What is it you are protecting behind those walls of yours, sweetheart?" I asked softly knowing that she wouldn't answer me. Her powerful mind wouldn't allow her to be vulnerable and give up her secrets like that. Well, it was confirmed, for I had no other option than to find out the hard way.

So, with this in mind, I left the clip she had once more dropped the second her mind fell into a slumber and this time decided to leave a piece of my own thoughts behind with her. I found the right page in the book I had brought back with me and secured the clip so that it pointed down at the passage. The one I found most relevant at this moment in time. For I wanted her to feel as Jane had when finding her soulmate waiting for her...

"Soon, my Electus...*soon you will find your eternal home.*"

Before long I found myself back at Afterlife and yearning for her even more than I had before leaving here in the first place! I wanted to growl in frustration, for it hadn't helped as I thought it would. At the very least I could tell myself that it was a necessary evil, as the sooner I left her, the sooner I could start my research.

I had already spoken to Ranka only to find out what her luggage tags and passport had confirmed. But I had instructed Ranka to delve as deep as she could, finding me everything on the girl, which was why I was surprised when I received a phone call only an hour later.

"I am not taking this as good news," I told her as a way of answering the phone.

"I am afraid not, My Lord," she replied, making me want to crush my phone before I could hear what I knew was coming. Because my instincts about the girl had been right...she was hiding something, and something big.

"Tell me."

"There is no history of a Keira Johnson older than a year, eighteen months maximum. Anything before that isn't real."

"You mean it was staged?" I asked, my tone saying it all.

"Exactly, my Lord."

"Your thoughts?" I bit out, angry at what I feared the answer to be.

"At first glance, I would say maybe a witness protection program." This too would have been my own guess, for it was the most logical explanation. But it also meant that it complicated things immensely. Oh, I would still discover exactly who this girl was, but it just meant exercising that age-old practice called patience...something I had very little of when it came to my Electus.

"And what of her family?" I asked, not holding out much hope on this side of things either.

"I am afraid I am still digging on that front, as all we have so far is her sister, who changed her name when she was married. All details before that seem to be lost or purposely misplaced." Ranka said making me once more want to embed my fist into something, preferably the reason my Chosen One felt all this deception necessary.

"I see...has there been any medical history in the eighteen months?" I added after thinking back to her gloves. I waited the minute it took Ranka to find the right files, and I could have sworn my patience failed me at half that.

But even so, I waited because I knew that Ranka was as efficient as they came and she no doubt had a lot of information gathered already. It was just unfortunate that most of it was a lie. Years of a life generated and make to look real, so it went by unnoticed to those who may have been looking for it. So, the only important question now was... *why?*

Why her? What had she seen or been involved with? Had she been coerced into being a witness for the prosecution in a murder case? Or was it personal and someone was after her? In the end, Ranka's answer brought me out of my murderous thoughts and back to my last question.

"Yes, from the looks of things she was prescribed Temazepam."

"Sleeping pills." I ground out knowing now that my last words to Keira this evening, had obviously held a deeper meaning for her than I intended.

"On more than one occasion, yes."

"Then she would also have to be seeing a therapist, find out who and get me those session notes by any means necessary," I ordered making Ranka end the call with the usual,

"It will be done, my Lord."

I threw the phone to my desk after this and leaned back in my chair, finally taking note of my brother who was also curious about what I had discovered.

"That didn't sound reassuring," he commented dryly.

"Far from it," I growled before running both hands through my hair and holding my fists embedded there, very near ripping every strand from my head, just to give me something else to focus on, something other than the frustrating puzzle that was Keira Johnson.

"So, she's a ghost."

"More like a Gods be damned Phantom! I swear sometimes I look at her and spend half of my time convincing myself she is real and the other half questioning my own sanity, for she is too perfect." I confessed.

"Besides her past," Vincent reminded me, making me frown.

"Yes, besides her past." I was forced to agree, as it was definitely looking more complicated than I had originally assumed it would be.

"Maybe it isn't as bad as we think, who knows, it may just be a disgruntled ex-boyfriend who can't take the hint." Vincent offered innocently enough but ended up making me hammer a `fist down on the desk, as was quickly becoming a habit because of this girl.

"Or maybe not." Vincent quickly corrected knowing that thinking of another touching her was not the wisest picture to portray right now. Especially one that was unwilling to leave her alone and forced her to run. No, if such a being lived, then he wouldn't be for long, mortal rules or not! For there was always the exception to the rule, and right now, I was it.

"Look, I get that this is difficult for you, and I know your reasons for taking this slow, something I happen to agree with, but now after finding out...well, nothing about the girl, wouldn't it be better to reconsider keeping her at arm's length...you could, you know, try things the conventional way and simply ask her..." Vincent said making me slash a hand through the air and tell him,

"No!"

"But why not, I just don't see..."

"Because I don't trust my demon around her, alright!" I snapped finally admitting the truth and feeling weak for the first time in...well, in an eternal life so far. This was when he finally started to get it, and I knew this when his crystal blue eyes flashed white, and his skin looked touched by the Heavens, as his angelic side shone through. Not that this response wasn't surprising, as it wasn't often after all this time, we found ourselves astonished by anything anymore.

"It is pushing at you?" he asked in a gentle tone, one said out of concern.

"Only every time I am around her and the times that I am not," I said bitterly before admitting,

"When I am without her, my demon pushes for me to go to her and when I am with her... well, then he pushes for me to simply take her, and I do not speak in the most gentlest of ways here, brother."

"Would doing so be such a bad thing, for surely as your Chosen One then she must naturally feel drawn to you?" Vincent argued making me argue back,

"And what about when I go too far? Like today, when it very nearly made me wrap my hands around her throat just so that she couldn't escape our first kiss? It wants to dominate her in a way that would no doubt only end up terrifying her. And well, without knowing her past, then I could end up doing more damage than I could ever imagine." I told him, making him now understand exactly what I meant. As for someone even more dominant than I in the bedchamber, then he knew the damage such a lover could inflict with the wrong partner.

"Alright, so I will admit, collaring her with the palm of your hand might not be the most subtle first kiss you may want to aim for here, but honestly, I believe this feeling will calm."

"It's been one Gods be damned day, Vince!" I argued, slumping back in my chair as if being kicked in the chest by the Devil laughing at me.

"Exactly, like you said, it's been one day."

"So?"

"So, cut yourself some slack! Gods, Dom, so yes your demon is fighting you on this, but don't forget he, along with your angel have been waiting just as long!"

"And your point?"

"You just need to give it some time, and you will see, things will settle. But listen to me Dom, as I doubt that will happen unless you continue to see her and at the very least when she doesn't know about it. Because the answer is as simple or as hard as you wish to make it. The longer you go on fighting your true self, then the harder it will simply continue to push." I knew he had a good point, for there was only one way to get my demon used to being around the girl, and that was contact...a contact I couldn't fully trust.

"I think this is what is referred to as a catch 22...So, you're suggesting what?" I asked, not really seeing a way around this myself.

"Find a middle ground. Keep her in your sights, reach out to her at night like you just did and make her forget until you are ready and assured your demon is under your control. Then simply take her when you are ready." I listened to Vincent's wisdom and was thankful for it, as it brought me comfort to know that another soul in the world understood. Now, if I could just continue to access her mind to do so, then that plan should work perfectly.

Yeah, because everything else about this was going to plan just perfectly, I thought wryly.

The Fates certainly had a lot to answer for, that I was sure of!

'An impulse held me fast, a force turned me round. I said, or something in me said for me, and in spite of me:- "Thank you, Mr. Rochester, for your great kindness. I am strangely glad to get back again to you; and wherever you are, is my home--my only home.'

The moment I heard these words being softly spoken by a woman's voice, I bolted upright. I looked at the large grandfather clock I had in the corner of the living space on the far side of my bedchamber and saw that it was 6:35am. Had I dreamt what I had wanted to hear or had she awoken and found the book as I intended? Was I already that connected with her as I hoped?

"I swear the Gods are laughing at me right now," I groaned to myself at the same time falling back to the bed and flinging an arm over my eyes. Something done in hopes of blocking out the fucking hundreds of questions that had plagued me about her when first trying to grant myself the reprieve sleep would hopefully ensure. Well, it had worked for...I looked up again at the clock...for three fucking hours!

Well, at the very least I had awoken in my bed, even if I was still half dressed from where I had frustratingly dragged my shirt over my head, before collapsing on top of the covers.

I couldn't understand why I had been so tired, not considering a being like me could go weeks without sleep before my vessel started to show signs of weakness. It was the same as eating and drinking, only needing to fuel our bodies when they informed us of such.

You see, our vessels may still, in essence, be human, but our supernatural sides were what continued to repair broken or damaged cells, creating new ones in the process so that the ageing process slowed down dramatically. For me, strangely though, I had only ever had one vessel, which I believed was down to having the power of both Heaven and Hell entwined within my soul.

However, Vincent and Sophia had taken possession of a few bodies in their time, and I was just thankful that once they did this, that it didn't take long before their preferred features returned. For I had to confess, it would have felt strange looking upon a different face but the one belonging to my brother or sister. So, a few days of rest was all it usually took for their old selves to return and I had to admit, it was a feeling I had never experienced, so knew nothing beyond the days I spent waiting.

But just because our vessels worked this way, that didn't mean many of us didn't eat regularly or find a drink in our hands once darkness fell. We simply did these things because we enjoyed them, not because we needed them. I myself, was partial to a fine cognac or a 65-year-old scotch I happened to keep in my reserve. Oh yes, living 'topside' as Earths plane was known to most demons in Hell, certainly had its advantages. And now I could add a young blonde beauty to the very top of that list…that was if I ever managed to get her into my bed and locked in my arms long enough to claim her as my queen.

I looked down at the strained denim that was currently resembling a small tent thankful at the very least that my kind couldn't suffer afflictions such as blue balls. Or I would have found a fist around my cock more times than not, these last twenty-three years of celibacy!

Which only added yet another question to the long list gathering about her and it wasn't about my large morning erection I was now choosing to ignore. No, it was about her age. For if her identity was a fake, then it was very likely that her date of birth was, which meant…

Suddenly I had my phone in my hand and was dialling Ranka's number once more. As always, she answered on the second ring.

"My Lor…"

"The date of birth I told you to look for when going through the passenger manifests, use that to see if you can locate any birth records from hospitals based around Liverpool, England. Maybe even Manchester or surrounding areas. Cross-reference all parents and get me a list of all the ones that gave birth that day who now have at least two girls…I am unsure as to whether there could be other siblings." I told her, annoyed that I didn't have more to go on…well, that was until Sophia strolled into my bedchamber unannounced as usual. But this time I couldn't be too vexed as she did at least bring with her some useful information.

"She only has one sister."

"And you know this how?" I asked unable to hold back the sharp accusing in my tone.

"I listen." Was her only short and vague reply.

"Very well… Ranka you know what to do." After this I hung up the call just as Sophia was obviously making herself comfortable, telling me she had something else to say. But one look told me what it was, so I got in there first.

"Vincent spoke to you."

"He might have and besides, so what if he did, I believe as the one who found her, I do have some rights in these plans you keep making without me." She had a point, just one that in this moment I didn't want to confess to.

"The girl is solely my concern."

"And what of her past, for unless you are willing to find out these little facts yourself, then I believe what you need is a spy, and I happen to know a very friendly, and I do say so myself, a well-dressed one." I rolled my eyes as she motioned down to herself, making her chuckle as it was clear that unlike me, she had yet to find the need for sleep. As even at this time of the morning she was still wearing an expensive, midnight blue evening gown.

"When do you begin your classes?" I asked knowing there was no point in arguing and besides, I hated to admit it, but she was right. At least one of us had to get close to the girl and she was the most likely candidate. And it wasn't as if she hadn't proved that in this case, there was power in knowledge. Of course, I had just assumed when first meeting her that I would be able to access her mind and find out all this information for myself. But then again, that age-old saying in my world came back to remind me that 'assumption was the mother from where all mistakes were born.'

"Next week, but that is not what I came here to discuss with you." No, it never was that easy, I thought sardonically.

"I am all ears, Sophia," I said mockingly again making her laugh.

"Yes, well I was thinking more 'All eyes'... as in, on you...you know, as you make your grand entrance tonight down in the club...oh, don't give me that look, Dom, as you know, it's all part of the façade. Besides, it's what half the town actually comes here for." She argued making me groan in frustration.

"Don't you think I have more pressing matters to deal with, like the arrival of my Electus, something I have only been waiting for since the beginning of my time." I reminded her but to no avail.

"Yes, but technically you have only been waiting for over two thousand years, for the Fates stated at the start, that a gift such as she, would prove the wait of a thousand lifetimes...so..."

"So, if you think that has made it any easier, then you are mistaken, for the last I checked, two thousand years was not a small measure of time," I snapped back, wishing now I was having this conversation in front of a punching bag I could destroy before just replacing it with another.

"Look, I get it, you're going to be broody, pissed off, bad-tempered Dom for a while, but that still doesn't negate the fact that we have a business to run and that includes getting people through those doors as always. Which means doing as you do every year by making a grand entrance, hence becoming the talk of the town and bringing greater meaning to yet another boring year for them all," she said making me actually groan at the thought. Then I opened my mouth ready to argue this matter further when she held up a hand and continued,

"Then you can go back to playing detective and secret guardian all you want. But tonight, it's time to rough it up with the common mortal folk for all of five minutes... and besides, you will be soon dating a mortal yourself, so Hell, just call it research!"

This was when she made her exit, and I found myself wondering if it was yet possible for a Supernatural King to get a headache through stress...

Well, there was a first for everything.

Keira

14

AFTERLIFE

Not one thing was what I had expected.

We had driven further out of town than I would have thought necessary and when Libby had reminded me that it was on the outskirts of town, she hadn't been exaggerating. It was more like in the middle of nowhere!

We drove along the main road for what seemed like forever and then turned down a small one lane road which was covered either side by thick forest. It almost looked like a dark green tunnel, which didn't help my nerves. The angry tunnel, more like the mouth of Hell, opened up into a big clearing that looked like a car park. Libby drove round to the front, but I couldn't get out.

I was stunned.

The place was enormous and astonishing. I hadn't expected it to look anything like the picture of beauty that was before me. Libby noticed my surprise and just nodded saying,

"I know, nice isn't it?" Nice! Nice wasn't a word I would have used. Out of this world, stunningly beautiful, truly amazing, breath-taking, anything than just plain old nice! Surely her being an interior designer would have evoked a better response from those red glossy lips of hers.

"It's more than nice Libs, it's incredible!" I said gobsmacked.

It looked so out of place and yet it didn't somehow, as though it had always been there. It looked hundreds of years old but surely it couldn't be. It wasn't like any club I had in mind or any that I had ever seen for that matter.

In England, a lot of nightclubs just looked like pubs or normal buildings. One I used to go to was an old cinema, but this was like a bloody manor house.

I couldn't see the entire house (house, what an understatement!). It looked as if it went further back but was surrounded by thick forest so only the front was exposed. It was made from thick stone blocks that were once, I suspected, a lighter shade than they were now. This was due to weathering I guessed and it reminded me of Bath, a city in England, which was famous for its old Roman baths and sandstone buildings.

One side was covered in a thick blanket of rich green ivy that curled its way around the windows, looking as though it was trying to overtake the building, but only reaching so far. This certainly gave it a creepy vibe. The entrance was as grand as the rest of the building with its impressive stone archway jutting out. Big thick black gates stood open on either side that looked strong enough keep out an army when closed.

They had been secured back to allow access into the club where people were now entering. However, there were no lines outside with rope barriers as I had expected. In fact, the only thing that made it resemble a club was the two huge monster security guards who stood on either side of the gates. I looked at Libby.

"Frank's?"

"Yeah, that's Cameron and Jo, they're nice guys. I met them at last year's Christmas party." She laughed as if remembering something and as it turned out I didn't have long to wait for her to fill me in.

"Jo got so drunk doing too many vodka shots with Frank that in the end his mum had to come and get him." She gave a smug laugh.

"Well, have a good night, just give me a ring and I will get Frank to come and pick you up... it's fine." She said before I had chance to say I would get a taxi.

"He's working late anyway and said he wanted to pick you up."

"Okay." I said not believing her for a second and knowing this was more likely down to Libby worrying about me.

"You'll be fine, go get 'em kiddo." She said trying to sound positive.

I got out of the car reluctantly and turned to shout bye.

"Have fun and relax, you look as though you are going to pass out!" She said through a small gap in the passenger side window. I was being ridiculous; the place wasn't that creepy. I watched as Libby's Ford disappeared into the fog before I turned and made my way towards the imposing entrance.

My eyes took in every raw edge, every stone block and every arched window. I noticed how the forest to the right side looked thicker and wilder in some way. When I narrowed my eyes, I thought I saw a massive balcony on the right side of the building. I wanted to take a better look but when I started off in that direction I caught the quick glimpse of a large figure standing there. I chickened out and turned my attention back to the main entrance.

I walked slowly, barely hearing the gravel crunching under my old purple Doc Martins, due to the loud pounding of my heart. I caught sight of the two men standing there by the entrance waiting for me to come closer. They eyed each other as if amused with the look of dread on my face. They could no doubt tell I was a newbie.

"Evening." Was all the shorter one said. He had a kind face which didn't match his coarse, hard voice. Both were wearing thick black jackets that made them look even bigger. The smaller one didn't look as fit as the taller one did but he stood looking at me now as though he was about to speak. I looked at the taller one as he was looking at me impatiently for something. Had he asked me a question?

"I said ID!" He snapped impatiently. Oops, come on Keira don't piss off the big men.

"Yeah, sure." I replied, swallowing hard as I reached in my pocket and grabbed my new licence. They eyed it carefully and then all of a sudden, their features transformed. Well, at least now they were smiling at me instead of scowling.

"You're Frank's sister-in-law?" The taller one asked me enthusiastically (the one with the intolerance for vodka shots).

"Uh, yeah." I said warily not knowing if Frank would want them to know that.

"Ah Hell, him and Libby have been waiting for you to come for months! It's damn good to finally meet you, I'm Jo and this is Cameron." He held out a big bear like hand for me to shake and I was touched that Frank had mentioned me. His hand swallowed mine up as I placed it in his and he shook it gently as though eyeing my little breakable body.

I nodded hello to the other guy while Jo still had hold of my hand. He was turning it around and I looked at him curiously to see what he was doing. He stamped it and I examined the red word 'legal' across my skin.

"We allow a lot of age groups in here, but they need ID to drink and you fit the bill." He said with a big infectious grin on his face.

"Do you want me to come in with you and make sure you get to your table?" Jo asked, and I almost visibly cringed at the idea. I mustn't have done too good a job at hiding this as he laughed.

"I take that as a no." He said in good humour.

"You're just not cool to be seen with, buddy." Cameron laughed hitting his friend on the back. I chuckled nervously hoping I hadn't offended him when a more pressing matter came to mind.

"Wait...did you say table?"

"Yeah, one was reserved for you and your friends. They're already in there. Go on in, honey." Cameron winked at me, just as a couple of young dark dressed youths were coming up behind me. They turned to them and said "ID" in a less friendly manner than I had received.

I smiled to myself and thought bless Frank for doing this. It was a nice perk being related to my big brother-in-law and I didn't feel as nervous as I had before. I would have to remember to thank him later and also for giving me a lift home.

After walking past the imposing gated entrance, I found myself staring at a massive set of wooden doors that looked as if they once belonged to a castle. The deep oak was encrusted with black iron studs and both doors were left open for guests. I couldn't help but touch them as I walked over the threshold.

They were warm, which I found odd. I studied them for a few seconds before I entered. There appeared to be a symbol carved deep into the middle of each door. I think it was some kind of family crest, but it was hard to make it out, as some people behind me were trying to get past. I walked through them getting the strangest feeling, one that made the hairs on the back of my neck stand to attention. But it wasn't through fear.

No, if anything it felt like...

I was coming home.

"Hey Kaz, you made it!" RJ said sounding shocked. Had she really thought that I would have stood her up. Maybe she could sense my reservations on the phone.

"Yeah, of course, wouldn't have missed it." I said trying to sound enthusiastic, which wasn't hard, as now that I was here I was really looking forward to the night. It was as though something had made its way inside my body giving me the most amazing rush of confidence. As if something wanted me here and knew that to get me through those doors I needed some help. Well whatever it was, it had worked.

"Follow me, you need a drink!" She said with a huge smile on her face, which didn't match the Gothic vamp look she was going for. She was in a tiny black mini skirt with chains hanging from it everywhere. I wondered how it didn't fall down with all the extra weight. She teamed this with a black top with rips slashed across the chest revealing bright pink netting underneath. It matched her hair, which was as pink as ever but was pinned into twists at the front and when she turned, she had a chaos of spikes at the back. To complete the outfit, she had on a long black jacket that went to the floor. It looked military style with lots of big round metal buttons going down in a v shape either side.

We made our way through the crowd towards what I assumed was the bar. It was sweet the way she kept turning around every now and again to check I was still following. I could understand why she did this as it looked as if the whole town was here and the place was so big it could have easily have been done with room to spare. I had to keep my eye on RJ's bright pink points so as not to get lost in the mass of bodies. This was proving difficult as I couldn't help but stare everywhere.

I had never seen anything like it. Inside didn't really match the outside, a bit like old battling new. On the outside it looked like a stately home from the sixteen hundreds but on the inside, well that's where it started to look more like a club. One with a definite twist. The massive open space could have been built around some ruined church. The shell remained, with its really high ceilings and massive stone arches everywhere. The whole ceiling was a series of them that all mingled together, interlocking and then going off in different directions like the type you see in a grand cathedral.

The room was separated into different levels with seating around the outside in booths. The interior was lush and rich looking with crimson reds and deep purples. There were great wrought iron chandeliers that hung down from where the bigger arches met in the ceiling. All were lit with candle bulbs which flickered for effect. The same style lamps were along the walls in a random fashion. The walls were of the same stone as the outside, but they weren't weathered, so still had their natural softer colour. This gave the room a warming glow as the light reflected from the pale stone.

I was amazed by my surroundings, as if I had been transported back in time to a medieval age. Only I don't think there would have been quite so many scary looking people here back then. Words like witch hunt, devil worshipper and burned at the stake came to mind. There were so many people dressed in black it almost looked like a cult gathering. Some of them stared at me as I made my way past, trying my best to keep up with RJ. We were nearly at the bar as the crowd began to get thicker. She stopped in front and turned to face me with a huge grin across her black lips.

"You ok?" She said with a little bit of concern in her eyes.

"Yeah I'm fine. I just didn't expect it to be so busy." She laughed as though I had missed something... something very important.

"Well it's not normally this busy until the Draven's come here and the Acid Criminals aren't that popular, so it's great for your first night that they're here early." She said and clapped her hands together like a child.

"What, the Acid Criminals?" I was confused, still not understanding the reason behind the mass of people who looked more like they were attending a Gothic comic convention than a nightclub.

"No, no...not the band...." I was about to ask when she suddenly shouted the reason with pure unrestrained excitement,

"The Draven's!"

After receiving this bombshell, we finally got served after about twenty minutes of trying to push our way to the front. Well RJ pushed, and I followed. Now, once again, I was following RJ back to where her friends were waiting for us. My mind was now elsewhere and instead of being nervous about meeting new people I was consumed by seeing *them*. I looked around and I knew I wasn't the only one as people seemed to be buzzing with excitement.

RJ grabbed my hand as it was obvious she knew where we were going.

"Come on! The table's just over near the stairs and will have the best sweeeet ass view ever!" RJ said dragging out the sweet part and giving me a satisfied smile.

They were situated near to the mezzanine level and one of the immense staircases that led up to it. There was another one that mirrored it on the opposite side. Both of which created a perfect frame for the centre stage. It was a raised platform high enough for everyone lower than it to have a clear view of the band playing.

The layout of the place was perfect for the purpose it served. It was the classiest night club I had ever seen, one that you would have expected to find in a big cosmopolitan city, not a remote little town in the middle of the wilderness.

"What's up there?" I asked as we passed the staircase on the left that had two enormous men guarding it as if it held the crown jewels up there. I thought that Jo and Cameron were big, but these guys put them to shame. The story of David and Goliath popped into my head.

"Ah, now that's a good question my dear Kazzy, as that up there is the one and only VIP area." She said dramatically as she eyed the giants.

"That's where the Draven's spend all their time, it goes further back than you can see." She elaborated motioning her hand backwards.

"Not that I have ever been up there myself," she continued with a slightly bitter tone.

"But my dad has his own building company and one of his guys went there last year to do a job, which is strange 'cause they usually get their own people in to do stuff like that. I guess they got desperate or something... Anyway, I got my dad to describe it in every little detail to me and then of course passed that important information on like any good town gossip." She smiled proudly. I laughed back, not being in the least bit surprised and also making a mental note never to tell her anything that I didn't want ending up on the town's bulletin board.

By this time we had managed to make it through the alternative looking crowd to the booth that housed all of RJ's 'Goth Gang'...that wasn't actually that Goth at all.

There were three of them in total. Two guys and one more girl all sat round a massive half oval seat covered in red velvet. There was a table in the middle already filling with empty glasses and bottles waiting to be collected. As soon as they saw us they budged round to make room for two more bodies. RJ took one side and I sat opposite her.

"That was a nightmare, I think next time I would rather die of thirst!" RJ complained as she sat down putting her bottle of Bud on the table, ready to make the introductions.

"Everyone, this is Keira!" She announced to the gang and I suddenly felt like I was being introduced to one of those 'self-help' groups.

"Uh... Kaz is fine." I said trying not to sound shy. Of course, it didn't help when I had all eight eyes studying me. I sat down and rested my bottle on the table as my hand had started to go numb with holding it so long.

"Hi Kaz, I'm Lanie." I smiled in reply to a pretty girl with short bobbed hair. She had a kind face and small oval glasses that sat upon a tiny delicate nose. She got up to shake my hand and I leaned forward to reciprocate.

One by one they all introduced themselves and I started to relax once I wasn't the main topic of conversation any more. I was relieved to be chatting about starting college. They all lived locally apart from one, Charles, or Chaz as he liked to be called, who had also just moved here.

Chaz was cute looking with a baby face that looked like it still hadn't fully matured. He paid a lot of attention to RJ, but she didn't seem to notice. Every now and again he would stare at her and smile to himself, one he thought was hidden. The other guy was Andrew or Drew as he also preferred. He confessed himself to be a bit of a geek. He was studying computer engineering and loved to play World of Warcraft. He started to go into detail about the game or 'community' but he could have been speaking Japanese for all I knew.

"Leave it out Drew cap!" RJ said throwing a piece of the beer label she had been playing with. She was a good shot as it landed on his head and rolled down only to rest on his glasses. Everyone laughed including Drew.

I learned that he and RJ had grown up together as neighbours and had been best friends for an age. The nickname Drew Cap continued throughout the night. Drew was tall and very thin with a face to match, but he had the most amazing deep brown eyes with hints of toffee in them. They were big, very expressive and they seemed to like what they saw in Lanie as they kept glancing towards her general direction.

They all made me feel very welcome and I felt at ease telling them about myself (well to a point) but they all had a laugh with the different things that I said and started with all the "say this…say that" malarkey.

Libby was right, my English accent had gone down well with them all. I didn't think it would be long before they had me doing impressions of the Royal family! But I took it all in good fun and was having so much of a good time that I didn't realise when RJ's brother turned up. It was very embarrassing to find that he was behind me the whole time I had been slightly snorting like a pig with laughter. I didn't realise until RJ looked up.

"Hey, there you are, I thought you were going to miss the band starting but they're not on for another ten." My face went bright red with embarrassment as I could feel his eyes on the back of my head. I turned around sheepishly to see a very handsome face smiling down at me.

"Well hello there giggles, I'm Jack. You must be our English rose, Keira." He said in a very confident smooth textured voice. I blushed again like a nun in a nudist colony. I hated receiving compliments. I never knew how to react, not wanting to be rude but most of all not wanting to be the centre of anyone's attention.

"Jack, don't be a freak, you're embarrassing her!" RJ said coming to my rescue… well sort of.

"I apologise for my brother, he was dropped on his head a lot as a child." I lowered my head to hide my grin.

"Don't you mean hit on the head and by you!" Drew said now joining in the debate.

Jack leaned down to my face and with a cheeky grin that would make any heart melt and said,

"Sorry about these two, there's no stopping them when they get going. Let's start over, I'm Jack and I don't have any problems with my head." He smiled at the end of this speech, replacing the cheekiness with a charming wink.

There was something so likeable about him it was hard to keep from smiling to myself. He looked a bit like a rough catwalk model. One you would see in an advert for a Gillette shaving product, as he had the stubble and messy hair for it.

His hair was brown but with streaks of gold cast lightly through it. It flopped around in every direction as he moved, his streaks getting caught in the warm glow of the club's lighting. His eyes were a warm hazel that matched his hair and they were framed with long lashes. But none of these were his best features, oh no, it was his very heart-warming smile; the kind of smile, that when it appeared would light up his face, transforming it entirely.

He sat down next to me as we all budged up once more. Drew and Chaz seemed happy about the close proximity that Jack had created. But now we all looked more like couples, there being three girls and three guys. This thought made me nervous. The last thing I needed when moving here was any complications and guys always bring complications. Especially when they looked like Jack.

"So, we have you to thank for the table?" Jack asked, and I smiled thinking about Frank.

"My Brother-in-Law supplies the security here." I said clarifying when RJ jumped in,

"Yeah and the lucky cow also got a job here too!" I grinned when she winked at me no doubt assuring me she was joking with the 'Cow' comment. I looked back to Jack to see him looking slightly concerned but then he hid it almost immediately as RJ cut him a look. It was strange.

"So how do you like our cold little town?" Jack asked with a crooked grin, as his arm rested slightly on the back of the velvet seat behind me.

"Umm, to be honest I haven't really seen much of it, but what I have seen I like. My sister and I went hiking the other day, which I loved." This made his eyes react as though I had said something to spark his interest.

"Oh, you like to hike? I do too, well growing up here, there's not much more to do. Until this place opened that is." I wondered how long this place had been open. RJ had said the Draven's came here every year.

"I know all the best spots if you would ever like an expert guide," he continued nudging me at this last part.

"Best spots of what?" RJ said with an abrupt manner.

But before she could get her answer the crowd started to shift and people that were sitting were starting to rise to try and get a better view of something. I found myself thinking that considering the band wasn't that well known they sure were getting a lot of attention. I thought out loud and said,

"So, I'm guessing the next band's here." I directed more at RJ as she was now stood like the rest of them. Jack and I were the only ones still sitting.

"You guessed wrong," she said through a wide black lipped grin, now nearly standing on the seat to get a better view. I noticed Lanie was doing the same only with her height she didn't have the same problem as RJ.

"This is going to be awesome!" And with that her hands went to her face in what looked like pure joy!

"Is she like this at Christmas?" I asked Jack who wasn't looking as thrilled as he rolled his eyes at his sister's behaviour.

"Sadly no, nothing gets her this excited. I really don't understand what it is about them." He said in a bored tone, shaking his head slightly.

"Them?" Was I missing something? And that's when my mind kicked into gear and realised what all the fuss was about. RJ's excited squeal just confirmed things for me.

"The Draven's!" She went so high pitched I could just imagine all dogs within a ten miles radius howling in pain.

"Ah," was all I could mutter as I was trying to sink further down in my seat and angle myself away from where everyone was straining their necks to see. Jack seemed to notice my movement.

"Well, it's nice to see not everyone here has Draven fever." He said smiling down at me but receiving RJ's middle finger in retaliation.

"Nice and very lady like sis," he said laced with sarcasm. Then the whispers started, which indicated they were here. I don't think that anyone had even noticed that the next band was already on the stage and ready to start their first song.

Heads turned towards the front entrance where I had not long since walked through. Then it was strange, like something from a Godfather movie when the Don walked in. Everyone who had been staring was now trying not to look directly at them. From what I could make out they were now passing through the crowd and it looked a lot easier than when we did it. People were now parting as if Moses was leading the way.

The music had started right on cue, as though trying to divert some of the attention. If anything, it just enhanced their entrance making it more dramatic. I tried not to look but found myself glancing up every now and again, wishing the commotion would soon be over. I don't know why but I was embarrassed for them. I would have hated to have all those eyes watching me…so I didn't look as it would help having one less pair of eyes watching them.

But there was also another set of feelings that were coursing through my body and mind. Ones I couldn't understand. I felt nervous again and my arms began to itch, as though the well concealed scars beneath my sleeves were burning.

I sat on my hands trying not to fidget too much. My heart raced uncontrollably, and I was thankful the music had started, as I was sure you could hear my body's erratic behaviour. I tried to concentrate on my breathing, slowing my inhaling down the way the doctor had shown me to control my panic attacks.

What was wrong with me? Why was I acting so crazy? So, it was just some rich family that had a bit of mystery to them, they probably just wanted to be left alone. I started to relax my thoughts. Yes, this was good, keep this up Keira, I commanded myself. But then something RJ had said to me earlier struck me.

The stairs!

The bloody stairs that led them up to the VIP area. The very stairs that we were all sat right next to. That's why RJ had been so happy about our positioning. She had known that they would have to walk right by us to get there. Okay I wasn't so calm now. Then, as if to make matters worse, Jack was having his own rebellious feelings towards them and got up swiftly, declaring,

"I think I've had enough of the theatrics, I'm getting a drink." and left, leaving me fully exposed in view of anyone who walked by. With the crowd parting in front of us, we would now have a clear view of the Draven's, almost like being in front of the stage at a concert. RJ gasped in delight and Lanie sighed with contentment.

I, on the other hand, had stopped breathing.

Because there, in front of me was...

Dominic Draven.

Keira

15

The Dravens

I was like a small, helpless woodland animal caught in the sight of wild prey. I knew it was dangerous but still I had to look. I tried to tear my eyes away from the most perfect being I had ever seen. And Holy shit! This man was incredible. He was just too perfect, like a Greek god sent to torture me for my sins. I think if Air Force One had crashed through the building I still wouldn't have noticed and would have died still staring.

I was aware that I was staring and hoped that no one else noticed. Not that I thought this was an issue, not with Dominic Draven around as I could now understand what all the fuss was about. He had a sort of magnetic pull to him, something unnatural, almost haunting but utterly mesmerising at the same time.

He was ahead of all the rest, so I knew he was the one in charge. A little further back there were two men that caught my eye, one of which was gargantuan. The crowd didn't stare at him and it was no wonder as his face was just as intimidating as his size. He had deep coloured skin like leather that had seen too much sun over the years and it was full of what looked like potholes. Maybe from a severe case of smallpox I wondered. Of course, being the size of a seven-foot wrestler, I doubted many people questioned his looks.

The man on his other side was tall and athletic looking, with very white blonde, straight hair that you could just see under his large black hood which concealed most of his face. I could have sworn that I noticed what looked like tattoos down one cheek. Then he came closer and it soon became hard to miss the startling difference between the whitest skin of an albino and the ink that featured down one side. I don't know why but he reminded me of the white knight on a chess board being taken over by the opposing dark side.

Behind these two, who looked like guards, were two other men, one dressed in a Japanese robe and had kind Asian features. His raven black hair was slicked back and he had a distinct sharp point to his chin. High cheek bones matched oriental features that spoke of a nobility lacing his blood line. He stood next to another man who was all light next to his dark.

He was angelic looking and in stark contrast to the others but had eyes that suggested otherwise. They were like black ice with a cruel harsh glint to them. His skin was almost luminescent, even in this low lighting it glowed as if he had just spent the day basking in the sun's rays. His hair was cut short creating a halo of tight golden curls, reminding me of a handsome antique doll. His face however was set in firm lines, screaming out in both arrogance and pride.

But all these were insignificant factors, shadows in the background, behind the God that stood in front of them. They moved according to the way their master moved, scanning the crowd for anything unexpected.

He was slowly approaching now and looked straight on as if oblivious to everyone. All the girls (and some guys) had the same look imprinted on their eager faces. They all wanted to be seen by those seductive eyes of his, to be noticed.... Well everyone except me.

I looked down at the table now trying to resist the urge to look again, but I knew he was getting closer as I could feel my heart rate going through the roof. It was RJ that made me fail my objective.

"Oh my God, he's looking this way!" She whispered through half closed lips. Then I did the unthinkable. I looked up meeting a pair of intense eyes that amazingly, were also staring back at me.

Arctic. Black. Consuming.

He had paused in front of our table and the bodyguards behind him looked just as confused as the rest of the spectators did. We had both frozen and were using precious time to drink each other in. It was as if we were now the only two people in the room.

The feelings he invoked attacked my system, flooding me with too many new sensations to deal with. Like lightning had struck and now all

I felt was electricity coursing through my body. If I thought my heart rate was going crazy before, now I thought I was going to go into cardiac arrest! He wouldn't move his intense stare from my face and I blushed every shade of red in the spectrum. However, something inside of me would not yield. I sat up a little straighter as a mere slice of bravery gave me the strength to match his gaze. I thought I saw a small glimpse of a smile, but it was gone as quickly as it came.

I could almost hear RJ hyperventilating. He looked the pinnacle of dominance, standing there with all the club's eyes behind him watching his every move. Like waiting for a mythological warrior to issue his first command to his armies. Although with his massive body dressed in a black designer suit, he looked more like a modern version of a warrior. Maybe 'Commander of the Night' would be more fitting.

There was just something so unnerving about him...no not only unnerving but almost unearthly. The whole club seemed to be at a standstill, my heart included. It was as if he was searching for something in my eyes but then he frowned, breaking the spell and obviously coming up empty. Then his expression turned harsh and his frown deepened, pulling his eyebrows tighter together. This released his hold on me and I finally lowered my face and turned my back to him to hide my shame.

I could still feel his presence as though he had somehow buried his essence under my skin. I couldn't help but scratch at my scars that started to burn under layers of clothing. I don't know how I knew but I could feel his eyes taking in my movements. Then something snapped. A link shattered. I noticed RJ's eyes following him and then they turned to me indicating that they were no longer in sight. I could finally breathe.

"Oh My God, what the fuck! What just happened? Did everyone else just see the Prince of Darkness himself just stop to look at our table...do you two know each other?" RJ asked me, now on a mission. She eyed me curiously and then looked back at Lanie for back up.

"Yeah, what was that? Did he know you? Did you recognize him?" Lanie said now joining in the Spanish Inquisition.

"No!" I said a bit too abruptly, as if it had hit a nerve. But then my mind went into overload when she had asked 'Did I recognise him?' That was the nerve that had hit bullseye...and holy mother did it hit me hard!

I did recognize him.

That's the reason I had the reaction when I saw him. He was the man from my dreams. The dreams that were now starting to flood back to me like a crashing wave. Yes, they were all so clear now, so clear in fact that it was hard to think of them as just dreams. They had seemed so real but why did I forget about them. And more importantly why was a man, who I had never seen before tonight, the exact same man that I had been so vividly dreaming about the last couple of days? None of it made any sense!

The girls didn't look convinced and neither did the guys for that matter.

"Well, the way he was staring at you, maybe he knows you." RJ shot Drew a look for saying this and he shrugged his shoulders replying 'what?' to her dirty look.

"What did I miss?" Jack said as he came back holding a tray full of drinks.

"You will never guess what happened." Chaz said in a high-pitched voice trying to mimic one of the girls.

"Oh, please tell me this was finally the year that he tripped and fell on his rich, pompous ass!" He said raising his hand and dramatically slapping his forehead with the back of it. I moved closer round to give him room as he resumed his place back next to me.

"Sorry dude, guess again."

"Oh, I don't know, some girl flashed him to get his attention and even then, I doubt he would have looked, he's probably gay you know." He said with a wicked smile. I just stayed quiet, still embarrassed from the memory. My thoughts were doing a pretty good interpretation of Formula 1.

"No flashing needed, he took a fancy to Kaz though, couldn't stop staring at her." Ok, I was going purple now. I had to get away from everyone staring at me and it wasn't just my table, it was the entire club!

"I ...I gotta go to the bathroom!" Was all I could manage to get out. I felt like I was going to be sick. I know it was a silly reaction to have but I couldn't help it. I just needed to get out of there. I pushed my way through the Gothic Draven fans over to the bathrooms. I knew the direction as Jack had pointed to them in reply to my rude exit. I saw the neon sign glowing like a beacon as it was near the bar on the same side of the wall as the entrance.

Once inside, I could feel myself calming down like the air in here was clearer. There was no one in there apart from the reflection of myself staring back at me horror-struck. I looked terrible! No worse than terrible, I looked ill. I was so pale and my eyes looked almost black. I felt so ashamed, no wonder he was staring at me. He probably thought of me as riff-raff, wondering what a plain, fragile little thing was doing in his club!

I ran into the cubicle not being able to stop what was coming next as I threw up the one bottle of Corona that I had consumed. Thankfully, I only heard the door open after I had finished. It sounded like two girls and no guessing needed as to who they were chatting about.

"And oh my god did you see his body, he gets finer every year. What I wouldn't do to have a night alone with that man!"

"Tell me about it, now there's a man that I bet has good equipment, if you know what I mean!" A girl's giggle followed.

"Yeah and I bet he knows how to use it!"

"Yeah baby!" They both giggled again stupidly like superficial teenagers. I found myself angry at them being so vulgar towards him. I was just about to leave when I heard more.

"Yeah, but did you see that girl he was staring at... urgh." The silly cow then made a gagging noise. I was furious even though I was in the same frame of mind just a moment ago but still, it wasn't the nicest thing to hear.

"I know right! She wasn't at all pretty, nice skin I suppose but way too pale."

"It was just make-up, I bet my life on it." Well, I sure hoped that this girl didn't get into any unforeseen accidents on the way home on account of my skin type, I thought to myself angrily.

"Well, I bet he was only staring because he couldn't believe she got in his club and if we would have been sitting there we probably would be in the VIP area now!" Oh god, it was getting worse. Now they were clearly deranged!

"We are going to have to come earlier next time and try for those seats."

"Yeah, then he won't have to be put through that sight again!" They giggled again only this time making high-pitched squeals. My blood boiled as I walked out of the cubicle, head held high. I knew that they were young from the sound of their undeveloped conversation but they were practically kids. They were applying lip gloss when they saw me and their faces dropped.

I washed my hands that were slightly shaking in anger and dried them. Once I had finished I made my way to the door but just before I left, I turned to say my piece.

"Oh, and by the way, he might not be into pale and plain but I'm pretty sure he's definitely not into kids, so why don't you two run off home before you miss Hannah Montana!" I walked out with the biggest smile on my face, leaving them with their mouths still hanging open. As I walked back still grinning, I looked up to stifle a laugh and noticed a pair of eyes that were watching me in amusement themselves.

I could see the VIP area clearly from back here and it looked full of people, which was strange, as not one person had gone up the stairs after them. Maybe there was another entrance to it for the 'special guests'. These little factors were irrelevant compared to the statue of a man staring back at me now, just as he had before. He wasn't as clear up there in the low light, but I could have sworn I had seen the flash of white brought out by a smile. He was so damn enigmatic. I stopped smiling and put my head down determined not to look again as I hurried back to my seat.

The rest of the night went quickly and without any more incidents. Jack insisted on staying with me while I waited for Frank. The others were going on to Drew's house but as I was getting picked up I didn't want Frank having to wait up for me any longer, so I declined the offer.

"Are you sure? I could drive you home? I've only had one beer." Jack said with a hopeful look in his eye.

"I'll behave," he added with a mischievous wink.

"Thanks, but Frank's probably on his way now... rain check?" I said hoping he wouldn't take it the wrong way. I mean, maybe before at a different time, I would have really gone for someone like Jack. He was really warm and sweet to be around, with a happy-go-lucky nature that was infectious. You couldn't help but smile around him.

But I didn't want him to get the wrong idea. How could I get it across that I didn't date? Maybe I could hint to RJ about the whole 'not dating' rule. But what was I saying, I was being conceited enough to believe he wanted to be more than just friends. He was just a nice guy, plain and simple.

"Okay, okay I give in, but how would you like to meet up and I will show the big bright lights of our small town?" I raised one eyebrow and said,

"Bright lights?"

"Oh yeah, there's one really bright street lamp on 5th, no really, you should see it, Vegas has nothing on us baby!" I laughed, and he smiled down at me sweetly, his hair flopping over his eyes. He was really tall, I hadn't really noticed in the club. He had long legs and a wide chest that went out in a v shape from his waist. He wore jeans that were ripped at the knee and a t-shirt with an Iron Maiden picture on it, underneath a combat style jacket.

"I will have to get your number off RJ, so next time we can arrange for me to pick you up and take you home again, that way you don't have to wait here in the cold." He paused and touched a single finger to my chilled cheek.

"We don't want that pretty skin of yours to get any paler." I blushed as always and smiled not knowing how to respond.

"Or I could just keep embarrassing you, that seems to put some colour in those cheeks," he said laughing and then nudged me, trying to get me to smile again.

"I can wait on my own if you're cold, I feel bad you waiting with me like this," I said trying not to offend him.

"Plus, they're going to be waiting for you at Drew's." I added trying to sound light hearted.

"Are you kidding? I don't mind waiting with you, besides RJ and Drew are probably just brawling around on the floor, which I've seen a hundred and one times before and trust me when I say it gets old. Nah,

I would much prefer being here with you." I blushed again, hoping he didn't notice.

"Brawling?" I said trying to imagine the two of them, 'The Goth and the Geek' going at each other.

"Yeah, and I would put my money on RJ any day, she fights dirty, at least that's the way I taught her." He gave me a wink as the penny finally dropped. He'd been teasing me.

"You shouldn't tease gullible people, it's against the nice guy law." I teased back.

"Oh, but where's the fun in that?" Then he rubbed his hands together and blew into them. I couldn't help but feel guilty but then he stopped suddenly.

"Wait...you think I am a nice guy?" He asked beaming at me. The only reply he got from me was a laugh. He joined in and went back to rubbing his hands.

"Are you sure you don't want to go. I'll be fine, the club's not even closed yet and the doormen are only over there." I said pointing over my shoulder.

"I think I'll survive, plus if I get frost bite you can nurse me back to health. I would be expecting first class health care though, sponge baths, back rubs, dangled grapes...you know, all the extras included." He was in front of me now and he poked me gently in the ribs. I, of course, being very ticklish, giggled and to my embarrassment snorted a little as well. I stepped back as a wicked grin spread across his face and he held out his finger threatening to do it again.

"What an adorable sound you just made," he said mocking me but trying very hard not to laugh. Just then Frank's car came into view and Jack nodded as if to ask, 'if that was him'.

"Yeah that's Frank. Thank you for waiting with me Jack, it's been ...amusing," I said smirking back at him. I went to turn but before I could go he said,

"Oh, come here," and then wrapped his big arms around me in a bear hug. He whispered down into my ear,

"It was very nice meeting you Keira," and then let go and walked away, waving over his shoulder. I composed myself and got in the car a bit red-faced. Frank turned to me and said,

"Boy, you sure do make friends quick, kid." The fact that he called me kid made me smile.

"So how was it?" He said as he pulled away nodding briefly towards the doormen. I looked back at first the doormen to see them waving but then something else caught my eye. A lone figure on the balcony to the side of the club stood there motionless and watching. I had to wonder...was it him?

"It was good, everyone was really nice." I said realising Frank was still waiting for my answer. I noticed his lips curve into a mocking smile.

"Yeah, I noticed that, he seemed *real* friendly," he teased aiming a thumb over his shoulder back at where Jack and I had stood.

"It's not like that." I said getting defensive.

"Sure, sure, I'll say no more but I'm warning you, your sister might grill you when you get home."

"What, she stayed up?" This was bad. She would want every minor detail about the whole evening and unless I could convince Frank not to mention 'the Jack thing', I was screwed! She would push it and push it until I repeated every word he'd ever said to me and then never let me forget it.

"Umm... Fr..an..k" I said in my sweetest voice dragging out his name.

"Y-y-e-e-s-s" he said doing the same.

"Could we kind of not mention the whole Jack thing to Libby?" He raised his eyes and a cunning smile crept across his lips.

"Oh, its Jack is it?" Damn! I tried the puppy dog eyed thing and then...score! I knew it would work. His features turned to putty in defeat.

"Okay, okay, I promise, not a word." This was why I loved Frank.

"Thanks, only I would never hear the end of it." He was on the main road now and I knew there wasn't much further to go.

"No, neither would I. She's still having a go at me for getting you that job. Speaking of which, did you see Jerry?" I smiled thinking back to it. Frank had rung him to let him know I was going to be there and must have given him a description of me because at the end of the night Jerry the Manager had come over to introduce himself.

He also asked if I could start earlier due to the Dravens' unexpected arrival. The place had been packed tonight and there didn't seem to be enough bar staff. I told him that wasn't a problem and he looked thrilled. Added to that, he also looked tired and worn down. I wasn't surprised with the night he must have had.

"Yeah, he did, thanks for that. He asked if I could do a small shift, starting tomorrow."

"That's great but..." he shifted slightly in his seat, looking uncomfortable.

"But?"

"But Libby is going to shit kittens! I try and tell her that she worries too much about you, but she can't be reasoned with," he said looking sympathetic to my cause.

"I know but I can handle it. Her heart's in the right place." I didn't like where the conversation was leading so I quickly changed it.

"Oh, and by the way, whilst it's in my head thanks for sorting out that booth for us tonight, it was manic busy."

"What you talkin' about, kid?"

"You know, the table you had reserved for us." Frank gave me a vacant look and then shook his head.

"Sorry honey, that's nice but it wasn't me." I frowned thinking back to who could have reserved us a table but more importantly, why would they?

"It must have been your friend, Jerry."

"I doubt it as he's a great guy but as tight as they come and those seats are normally bought for the night."

"Really?" I asked now even more confused. He nodded, and we didn't speak of it again. However, my mind went into overload trying to figure it out and of course my thoughts led me back to the sight of that lone figure stood on the balcony.

How long had they been watching?

And more importantly...

Was it him?

DRAVEN

16

UNEXPECTED GUESTS

"Well, it's that time again, gents," Vincent commented with a smirk to the others that sat in the limo, saving the wink for me and making me roll my eyes.

For unfortunately, on this occasion, my sister had been right. It was time to make the grand entrance I always did. For the simple fact remained, that to keep the club as busy as it was, at least one sighting a year was needed.

Mortals were fascinated by the unknown and 'The Dravens' were at the very top of that list, especially in a town like this. It was in fact what kept the place busy all year round as no one really knew when we would turn up. But only that when we did, at least one sighting was needed to keep that gossip wheel turning and tonight was no exception.

It was very near capacity, which meant that the neighbouring towns must have also got wind of us being here. But of course, that was no doubt Sophia's plan, for she often liked to spread the rumours herself, using an unsuspecting mortals lips of course.

The truth was that more often than not, we had arrived before this grand entrance and like today, usually started with my sister nagging me to do so. In fact, the one year I utterly refused only ended with giving her the evidence she needed to prove herself right. As the clubs accounts were down significantly the year after. But it wasn't profit that was important here, for all three of us had more money than we could possibly spend in over a hundred lifetimes. Hell's blood, but we gave more money to charities than most billionaires made in a lifetime!

No, it was the effect it had on the town that mattered, and I had to confess, it was a town I felt responsible for. The club brought in tourists who chose to come hiking here above all the other hundreds of possibilities the United States had to offer, simply because they also got to say they spent a night at the infamous gothic club, Afterlife. And as much as some locals hated to admit it, our club was the reason their little corner supply shop hadn't gone out of business, no matter how heinous the acts they believed were committed here.

And because of all of these reasons, it was why I found myself pulling up outside my own club with my council with me. All minus Sophia, who strangely, never included herself in these dramatic entrances. I didn't usually have all of my council with me, but it just so happened that we had come from a meeting in Portland. There was word throughout my enforcers that there was a potential traitor working for me. But with very little information to go on, it was unsure whether or not they were situated at Afterlife. And with so many people under my command, finding a spy was like finding a needle in a Hell stack, as Sophia liked to say.

Either way, this news hadn't exactly put me in the best of moods, for the timing couldn't have been worse. I, at the very least, had it on good authority from my sister that Keira's day had been uneventful, in a preferred, safe way. If I remember correctly, my sister had made a distasteful sound before telling me on the phone,

"Are you sure her real name isn't Cinderella, for she has been cleaning and cooking all day!" I would have laughed at how horrified she sounded at the prospect, that was if the image she created hadn't taken hold of my mind in a different way.

Which meant I had spent the rest of the meeting thinking of her in a different time. Wondering what I would have done if I had met her back in the 1800s for example and finding her as my new servant girl. What would I have done if walking into my office I found her on her hands and knees, doing her chores and oblivious to the lord of the manor who now stood behind her? One now admiring not her handy work but the fine shape of her behind, one that I wanted to take hold of and fit within the frame of my own body as I claimed her.

By the Gods, but the fantasy alone made me feel like the horny adolescent I had never had the chance to be! But even after I had calmed my lustful mind for her, I couldn't help but think about how our first meeting would have gone if in a different time. I had been a Lord or a King in so many of them, which made me realise now just how untouchable I had made myself. Now I was just a rich businessman, dealing with more mortals than I ever had before, but even now, I knew the truth of my actions.

But back then I wondered how she would have entered my life unless being that of high society herself. Even now I think to how foolish I had been, as I was about to be seen at my club for the one and only time a year. Meaning her chances at finding me, had it not been for Sophia's intervention, would have been closer to zero. And whose fault was that other than my own.

Meaning that our meeting each other could have ended up being years later. And to think of all the time, I would have wasted by making myself so closed off to all but who was considered the elite of society. Oh yes, I had been a fool indeed. But one thing had come from this realisation, and that was I most certainly owed a lot to my sister.

So, with this in mind, I exited the car along with my council and entered Afterlife, doing so just as the band's first song started to play for the night. And as it did every year, every head stopped and turned to the sight of us, parting the already packed floor to make way for our arrival. A hush of silence swept through the large open space. One that looked more like a cathedral converted into a place of sin, for the blood reds and deep purple soft furnishings that were the only hints of colour running throughout the club. It was a subtle gothic feel, granted more by the high arched stone ceiling, the twisted wrought chandeliers and the pale stone block walls. Walls that reflected the high beams coming from the stage lighting over the dance area creating the 'club' vibe.

It had to be said, I was proud of this place and concentrating on its interior now was easier to do, than allow myself to be overwhelmed by all the voices trying to scream their way into my mind. You had to just let them all flow over you and not start pinpointing one voice, as before you knew it, the whole room would be screaming at you.

I confess that I usually didn't find such a task hard, but this time it was different. As if I was off my game and the reason was an obvious one. As spending, most of my thought process consumed by a blue-eyed blonde goddess would certainly do it. A girl known for the time being, as Keira. I had to say, I liked the name, but its meaning surprised me, for it actually meant 'Little dark one'.

"Oh boy, it will be interesting to see how this goes." I heard Vincent's voice behind me speaking to Takeshi who he was stood next to. I glanced a look back only to see him nod ahead of him to a booth next to one of the double staircases that lead up to the VIP area. Of course, the second I did this, I felt as though I had once more been struck down by one of the Gods, for the sight impacted me the same as it had done only yesterday.

For there was my 'Little dark one' who was all the light of Heaven, despite the name. And incredulously, she must have been the only one in the whole club currently not looking at me but instead down at the table. Something I found fucking ironic!

"Oh my God, he's looking this way!" I heard her friend whisper the moment I had finally reached their table, finding myself unable to move away from it. It was as though she had a cord tied around my heart and had suddenly yanked at it. Well, if that was the case, then I must have had my own hold on her, for I couldn't help but force my will upon her, commanding her mind,

'Look at me.'

At this unspoken command, she did, telling me of the ease of controlling her mind when she felt vulnerable or even emotional, which I quickly noted for the future. But none of that mattered now, not the second our eyes finally met. And I knew I would have no choice but to allow her to remember.

I could vaguely hear the confusion of my council, all but Vincent and Takeshi who knew exactly who she was to me. But everything else in the room seemed to evaporate around us, leaving just the two souls meant to be together alone in a room full of people.

I just couldn't take my eyes from her, no matter how much her blush deepened because of it. But then she surprised me, as even through her obvious shyness, she wouldn't yield to my intense gaze but instead challenged it. It was only a subtle change in her demeanour, but by sitting up a little straighter made it difficult to fight the grin I wanted to grant her in return.

I could hear the usual erratic pounding of her heart that I seemed to ignite within her whenever she was around me. And the second I saw her nervously pull down on her sleeves I frowned seeing once again the hint of gloves there even under her long sleeves. But why? I saw her scratch at them as if she didn't even know she was doing it and I didn't like how intense she was when doing it.

"Brother, I think the locals are getting restless." I heard Vincent speaking in my mind, something that rarely happened unless I was open to allowing it. But he was right. I had to move as I couldn't just continue staring at the girl all night without speaking and now was hardly the time to introduce myself. And besides, what was she doing here? Ah, but

of course, it started to make sense as one name was growled by my angel this time...

Sophia.

She had known. But of course, she had! Damn her, but she had played me yet again! I felt my expression turn to one of annoyance before I could stop it and instead of excusing myself in an attempt to rectify this strange meeting, I simply ended up making the girl wonder as to what my problem was.

I stormed up the steps, noticing the way she lowered her head as if looking deflated by my abrupt departure, causing my mood to turn from black to that of a raging storm in seconds. I walked right up to my table and found Sophia there sat obviously enjoying the show immensely.

"In my office...*now!*" I ordered, making her not even try to hold back the grin. Even her husband shook his head at her as it was obvious his wife had been up to no good again if she had been the cause of such a foul mood. I stormed to the back of the VIP and through the grand double doors that were the entrance into our home. A building that went much further back against the mountainside than any mortal could have imagined. It was a home certainly big enough to get lost in and was considered a castle in its own right. But right now, I couldn't have given a shit how grand it was or how large, as long as it took me less than five seconds to get to my office, so that I could verbally tear into my dear little, interfering sister!

"You wished to see me?"

"Don't you dare play innocent with me Sophia, not when you planned this!"

"Yes, yes, so what if I planned it, but if I hadn't, then I knew you most certainly wouldn't!" she argued back as Vincent quietly closed the door behind us both.

"Damn it, Sophia! How do you expect me to do what needs to be done when she is here in my fucking club!" At this, she rolled her eyes and told me incredulously,

"Oh, stop being so dramatic Dom, so the girl is here, so what."

"So what...*so what!?* Did you not just see what happened down there!" I pointed out to her along with pointing to the door.

"I saw you make an arrogant ass out of yourself if that's what you mean?" At this, I saw red, and the Gods be damned relishing in it when she saw me take a swing out of one of the stone pillars in my office.

"And whose fault was that!" I roared at her which was when she got in my face, squared up to me and roared back,

"Yours, you idiot!" Vincent took a deep breath as if he had been dealing with the two of us going toe to toe for far too many years to remember, so put a hand to my chest and said,

"Dom, try and calm yourself."

"And you, can you for once not purposely antagonise our brother, one who is clearly dealing with something beyond either of our comprehension."

"Speak for yourself, I found my husband!" she snarled back making Vincent frown down at her before informing her sharply,

"Yes, and we all remember how that went, you found something you wanted, and as usual you simply took it! Lucky for you at the time that it was something that wanted to be taken. However, this is not that time nor is the situation the same. I know you are only trying to help, but you must understand that blindsiding him is not going to achieve getting him any closer to the girl, but only end up pushing her away."

"Yes, well pushing her away is precisely what will happen if he reacts like that again to seeing her," she snapped making me growl.

"I think it is safe to say that Dom is out of his comfort zone here...wouldn't you agree?" Vincent said motioning for me to jump in, however right now, all I could muster was folding my arms and glaring at her.

It had to be said that over the many endless years the three of us had been together on this Earth, that fighting with one another was a common occurrence, as was natural for anyone after spending so much time together. And even though my sister often acted out this way in doing what she wanted, with what seemed like little consequences, I knew that deep down, now was not one of those times.

Which was why I released a deep sigh and walked up to her. Then I wrapped an arm around her shoulder before pulling her into me for an embrace, taking her off guard. I then kissed her forehead and told her,

"I know you are only trying to help, little sister, and trust in my words now when I say that I will be in your debt for eternity, for the gift you helped bring to my feet but from now on..." I paused releasing a deep sigh before telling her,

"...All I ask is you show a little restraint." She too allowed all the steam to expel from her argument as she hugged me back before looking up at me with those big beautiful chocolate brown eyes and said,

"I shall try..." I let out a premature breath and was about to leave my office to go and see if the girl had left or not when Sophia quickly added,

"...But I make no promises." I sighed again as I left, hearing her defending herself to our brother claiming innocently,

"What, you think that will be the last time I will reserve a booth for her?!"

It was my first real smile of the day.

Thankfully, *the second came shortly after it.*

I walked back into the VIP and ignored my table of council members who I knew were awaiting my arrival. But business would have to wait, for there was only one face I wanted to see in that moment and I was hoping that during my argument with Sophia, its beauty hadn't left my club.

Seeing her downstairs with her friends had been an experience I hadn't prepared myself for, as I was getting used to only seeing her alone. And admittedly, when I finally had her all to myself, I found it hard to imagine myself sharing such pleasure gained by being in her presence. I was a selfish being, I knew this, and when it came to my Chosen One, well I didn't expect to be any other way. But even so, the jealousy that had struck me had been one that shocked me to my core, for I had never felt the emotion before in my entire existence!

To see those other humans sat with her, able to converse with her openly was something I was yet unable to do myself and the thought had infuriated me beyond words. In fact, the only hope I latched onto was that this feeling would ease in time, once she was by my side and going nowhere. Only then I could come to terms with sharing her with the world. For I knew she was not an exotic pet of mine to put in a gilded cage to simply admire.

She had a life and would continue to live it whether I was meant to be her sole purpose or not. She also had a family, one I doubt would approve of me stealing her away for years on end. Or hiding her away in a tower somewhere until I was assured of her safety...maybe Scotland might be a good option.

I soon found my musings cut short the second I approached the edge of the balconied mezzanine part of the VIP. One that was open to the club underneath and provided a perfect view over the whole floor. Also, because of the way the lighting was engineered, it was purposely done so that very little from down there was seen up here unless of course you were stood at the edge, as I was now. And what was I trying to achieve by such...?

I wanted her to see me.

It didn't take me long to locate her, even if her mind was difficult to find amongst the sea of others that were all screaming out at me. But a quick scan of the room told me there was only one place left and moments later I was rewarded by the sight of her coming from the restrooms. A sight that this time, took my breath away for another reason, for strangely, she seemed to be laughing to herself. Just the sight of her radiant smile had me imitating the emotion, for it was the pure joy on her face that also put the same on mine.

Then, as if feeling it for herself, she looked up and found me standing here looking down at her. It was a single moment shared that I hoped was enough to erase the hard look I had given her down by the booth she had been sitting in. A booth my sister had secretly arranged for her and now, looking back on it, I was glad of it. As it meant that I was finally sharing a small slice of my life with her. Even if she didn't know it yet. But in doing so, it made me yearn to know what she thought about Afterlife? What she would think of my home, one that soon, was possibly to become her own?

I continued to stare at her, as was my right to do so. But my gaze must have become too much for her, for she shook her head a little and broke the connection, quickly finding her feet and hurrying back to her seat. The action made my fingers itch to take hold of her chin and force her gaze back to mine. It seemed I was quickly discovering the problem I had with her hiding herself from me.

After this, I turned now she was no longer gifting me with her attention when something made me stop. I wanted to know what it had been that had made her laugh, for she obviously had found something funny in the restrooms. It turned out that I didn't have long to wait, as I took over another's mind who was stood close by the restrooms. A moment later I saw two young girls exit who looked barely legal to be out this time of night, let alone drink. Then I heard them speaking, and it all became clear what Keira had found so funny.

"How dare she! Saying that we looked like kids and he wouldn't be interested in us!"

"I know, what a bitch! Just who does she think she is anyway, so he was staring at her, so what!"

"Yeah, exactly! Like she was anything special and saying that we should run off home before we missed Hannah Montana! Uh, god I mean how old is that show!" I had heard enough and left the human I had been using, so that I didn't have to listen to their whining any longer. But I did so grinning as it was obvious now that Keira had caught them speaking about her in the restrooms. Something she must not have taken kindly to or the assumption made that my attention was of a different kind than intended. For she must have known why the sight of her had struck me unable to move away from her?

Didn't she?

Which now begged the question...had the memories that I had hidden from her been brought back to the surface of her mind due to seeing me? It was quite possible, for I wasn't sure just how deep I had managed to bury them. Well, one thing was certain, as after tonight, keeping her at arm's length might be harder than I first anticipated. Especially if she planned on becoming a regular visitor at the club.

I turned to my guard who was positioned by the top of the staircase and nodded down to the two girls that I would bet' at least one of his lifetimes both carried fake ID's.

"Check their ID's and remove them if false. Then inform the doormen to be more vigilant next time." I ordered making him bow before leaving to fulfil my command. Then I took out my phone and found myself giving in to the impulse as I took my seat at the top of my table, typing one name into Google…

Hannah Montana.

The night proceeded but it was far from usual. My mind wasn't on business as it should have been and only a select few on my table knew the reasons why. Takeshi, my Seeker, knew of my Chosen One due to his gifts and Zagan who was my lieutenant also knew, thanks to being Sophia's husband. No doubt quickly learning of her antics from Vincent. Little good that information had done I thought with a frown as she was currently toasting the champagne glass to his own as if congratulating herself on her few days' achievements.

"What did you expect, you did praise her for her interference, which you do realise rendered all your other words after that obsolete," Vincent told me, leaning to my side and making me raise a brow at him in question…one I hoped was swiftly answered with, 'I am joking'. Unfortunately, he simply whispered what Sophia now thought I had given her,

"Greenlight."

And as if to prove his point I watched as Jerry, our floor manager who ran the club below approached Keira as she was putting her jacket on. I decided once more to take a closer look, so I took over the mind of one of the band members, who was now packing away equipment.

"Hey, Keira isn't it?" Jerry said, approaching her and holding out his hand for her to shake, making me grit the human's teeth until it was likely to cause the vessel toothache.

"I'm Jerry, your brother in law Frank told me you were coming in tonight." I watched as recognition registered on her face, making her for the moment scrunch up her nose and in turn making me stifle a grin, for the expression was one I found adorable.

"Oh yes, sorry, it's been one of those night, I guess," she replied with a shrug of her shoulders, telling me that she was still affected by our earlier encounter.

"Yes, well sometimes this place can do that to you, especially first-timers…it's definitely got a certain aura to the club. Anyway, I spoke with one of the owners, and they agreed with me that if you're free, how about starting tomorrow night, as we could certainly do with the extra staff, now the Dravens are back in town." On hearing this I knew there was no way to prevent the damage I was doing to the poor mortal I was using, as I felt the crunch in my mouth as I gritted my teeth once more.

I wanted to hiss out my objections but then again, right now who was I but some nosy looking bystander.

Well, one thing I was certain of, and that was Jerry certainly hadn't spoken to me about hiring someone new, for I think I would have remembered! Which only led to one culprit...*damn you, Sophia!*

"Yeah, that would be great! I'm not exactly busy," she added as if this was an afterthought and was said in a melancholy tone. Now making me realise that she might be struggling a little in this new life she had obviously embarked on.

"Ah yeah, well that will soon change no doubt, as soon as college starts back up, you won't be short of shifts, take my word for it. Right well, I better get back to the cashing out, but I will have someone here ready to show you the ropes tomorrow night, and I am sure we will get you settled in no time at all." Jerry said reassuring her and making her nod her head in appreciation.

After this I thought my torment would have been over but how wrong I was. I had just been about to leave the vessel to his unfortunate toothache when I noticed a boy approach Keira. They conversed as if they knew each other, making me realise he must have been one of the boys at her table but absent when I first walked in. I watched as he said something that made her laugh and suddenly, I felt like committing murder.

"Hey dude, Jesus, lighten up on the equipment yeah, not unless you wanna be without sound at our next gig!" Another voice brought me out of my murderous haze long enough to realise I was currently winding one of the cables between my hands as if ready to make a noose. I suddenly left the vessel, reclaiming my own and I did so hearing two things, one was the whining of the boy I just left,

"I swear dude, one of my fillings just crumbled out of my fucking tooth!" and the next was the order I just gritted out, knowing at least my own teeth were up to the task of withstanding my own rage.

"Sophia, a word!"

"Oh, Gods' blood, what did I do this time!?" I ignored the question as I stood from my chair and this time, made my way onto the balcony, for I didn't want to miss as Keira was leaving. It was situated to the side of the building but still offered enough view of most of the large open space in front that was used for parking cars. It also had a good view of the long driveway that swept in from the main road. But right now, as I stood side on, I could see people emerging, knowing that she would soon follow the crowd.

"Tell me you didn't arrange for the girl I am trying to keep at a distance to get a fucking job here!" I growled unable to hold back my temper, for it seemed this was a day to have my limits pushed, mainly over and over again by my own sister.

I heard her sigh behind me, but I refused to look at her.

"Okay, so I know how it looks."

"You mean that you are purposely trying to defy every damn order I make!"

"Believe it or not brother, I am thinking of the girl's safety," she told me this time making me whip around to face her, almost expecting her to be mocking me. However, her face told me she wasn't. She was, in fact, telling me the truth.

"Explain." I gritted out the only word I could in that moment.

"Think about it, okay, so you want to distance yourself for the time being, giving you time to discover who she is and what enemies she might face."

"I am aware of these facts, Sophia, so get to the ones I am not."

"Well, then consider this, after she starts college next week there will only be three places she will be spending the most of her time. Her home, a place I know you are having watched by your bitchy pet Ava, her college where she will have me to watch over her and now here, where she will be spending most of her free time, where you yourself can watch over her from afar." I released a deep sigh after hearing all of this, now seeing for myself her logic. I was almost inclined to smirk at the idea that some worry would be taken from my shoulders...that was until Sophia added something more,

"Free time, that I should have mentioned she won't have much of, you know, to do other things...*like date."* Then she nodded down at the front of the club, and I could see her now stood there alone with the boy who had approached her. Even from up here I could see him flirting with her and making contact any chance he got. Yes, suddenly I could see Sophia's point, very well, in fact, as now I was in half a mind to order Jerry to ask her to start her first shift now. But the damn club was closing and right now it was obvious she was waiting for a ride home.

A car that couldn't come soon enough.

Because this time when I felt the jealousy raging through me, it caused my hands to crush the top of the stone balustrades I had been leaning against.

Hands that now craved a human neck to snap!

Keira

17
FIRST NIGHT

"*Why can't I control you?*"

I woke up suddenly with his voice still echoing in my mind. But then I heard the phone ringing and knew it wasn't just the sound of his voice that had dragged me from sleep. I left it to ring as there was no way I was making it downstairs in time. It wasn't long before RJ's excited voice could be heard leaving a message.

I looked at the clock thinking it was way too early for phone calls but to my utter shock I had slept in. I never slept in this late so was surprised to see it was almost lunch time, which meant I only had hours until my first shift.

I got up, rushed through a shower and called RJ back after listening to her message with a towel still wrapped round my head.

"Yeah, he wouldn't shut up about you last night at Drew's. I think my big bro has a bit of a crush!" RJ said after telling me I was a big hit with everyone.

"Oh, I think he was just being nice." I tried in vain, but this didn't sway her efforts.

"Trust me, there is being nice and then *there's being nice!*" Thankfully she soon forgot about this subject however her next wasn't any easier to hear.

"Hey, speaking of being nice, what was up last night with tall, dark and dreamy staring at your ass?"

"I was sat down, RJ, there was no ass looking." I said going red just thinking about it.

"Yeah, yeah, you know what I mean. He couldn't take his eyes off you!" I bit my lip just thinking back to it and even more so to the dream I'd just woken up from.

"RJ, he was frowning at me. If anything, I thought he was going to have me kicked out of his club!" At this she started laughing.

"What?" I asked frowning now myself.

"Oh, come on, did you not see him first playing all Mr Lusty, he only frowned when he realised you weren't dropping to your knees and begging him to take you...which by the way, officially makes you the coolest person I know." I laughed and cringed at the same time.

RJ ended the conversation by making me swear to tell her everything about my first shift at Afterlife. We also arranged to meet up for our first day of college as Jack had offered to show us around as he was in his third year already. I had to admit knowing I wasn't starting college on my own was comforting. And now with having a new job things had really started to fall into place more quickly than I ever imagined.

I was feeling so good that I decided to call my mum and let her know how things were going. The conversation didn't last long as she had a spinning class to get to, but she was obviously thrilled to hear I was doing so well with the move. We promised a time to speak for longer, only next time on Skype so Libby could also be there.

Pretty soon I found myself getting ready for my first shift and this was where the nerves kicked in. The thought of going back there made my palms sweaty again. I didn't know why.... well okay, that wasn't entirely true as I was pretty sure I would be more at ease if the Dravens weren't there.

What was it about that man that had my body in knots? And the word intimidating didn't even begin to cover it. Of course, now there were the dreams to explain. I mean, how can one man I had never laid eyes on before, end up being so real? I had tossed and turned over these very questions all last night.

It was a strange mixture of nerves and excitement as the clock ran down. Every time I thought about last night I tried to put it down to nothing, but that one look just kept creeping its way back into my mind like a little bug munching away at my brain.

By the time Libby got home and walked in through the front door she was greeted by the sight of me sat at the foot of the stairs facing her. I had my jacket on and bag next to me all ready to go, which she obviously hadn't been expecting.

"Oookay…" Libby said dragging out the word like she was worried as she slowed her motions down from hanging up her jacket.

"I was kinda wondering…" Libby cut me off when she took back her jacket knowing what I was asking.

"Let's go then." She said turning back around and out of the front door. I got up and only then realised I had been sat there way too long as my butt felt numb. I grabbed my bag and followed Libby to find she was in the car with the engine running.

"Okay, so where to?" Libby asked as I sat down but before I could answer her she got the wrong idea.

"You look nice, you have a date don't you! It's with that Jack guy isn't it?"

"No, it's not but wait…how did you know about Jack?" I asked already having my suspicions.

"Do you really think I don't know when my own husband is keeping something from me, besides he does this thing with his lips that looks like he's sucking a lemon. Oh, that and he's ticklish, so he was easy to break." She said smirking at me and now I knew what all the raucous laughter was last night.

"Well he obviously wasn't that easily broken." I said cringing at what was coming next.

"What do you mean?" She asked looking sideways at me.

"My date isn't a date at all. I'm actually starting work tonight…and technically this isn't being dressed up…I just thought I would make a bit of an effort, being my first shift and all…" I said rambling in hopes of skipping the lecture. She closed her eyes briefly as if trying to find the right words when I beat her to it.

"I know you don't think I should work there but honestly it's fine. In fact, I'm really looking forward to getting back into work and besides, I can't have you and Frank driving me around forever. I need a car and with that comes the need for money." Libby let go of a big sigh at this and instead of the argument I was expecting she shocked me by saying,

"Okay. I get it. I might not like it, but I understand you wanting your independence and after what happened, well it makes sense." I felt my muscles tighten when she brought up the past, but it was gone as quickly as it came. Libby wasn't going there, which meant I didn't need to go there either.

"Thanks Lib's. You know I love you, right?"

"Yeah, yeah, I love you too, which is why I had Frank promise me that his guys will be watching out for you and if you get any trouble, then ass will be kicked."

"Alright, kinda scaring me now Libs." I said laughing but she still made me promise before I got out of the car to let Cameron and Jo know if I had any problems.

It was a clear night but still cold and crisp. I pulled my long jacket collar closer up to my face keeping my neck warm. At least it would be warm inside. I was about twenty minutes too early, but I was sure that wouldn't matter. I knew tonight would be mainly showing me around, but that part excited me. It was just such an amazing place. I could imagine some Lord or Lady owning the town and this was where they resided.

But that thought sobered me pretty quickly considering which 'Lord' did in fact live here...well for the time being at least. And from the sound of things, that *Lord* did own most of this town. A man I was going to be working for. Now this thought got my pulse racing. I got a hold of myself and made my feet move forward.

The same doormen greeted me as I approached the door which made my nerves calm slightly. The place was empty at this time and looked three times as big as it had done last night. You could now see much more detail that had previously been lost in the mass of bodies concealing it.

The bar area was made from a glass front with metal entwined through it. The metal was made to look like a thorny vine that was piercing the glass and at each point it did, it was surrounded in a blood red tint. It looked like a piece of art.

The rest of the bar followed on with the theme, housing big glass shelves with vine metal supports, holding a variety of different bottles of liquor upon them. Some of which I recognised and some that looked imported from God only knows where.

"Hey, you're early, that's good!" Jerry was coming towards me not looking quite as flustered as last time. He was tall and very thin, and he reminded me a bit of Nosferatu, as he was bald and had the palest skin I had ever seen, even paler than mine. He held a constant fear in his eyes and he moved nervously from side to side. He didn't strike me as a club Manager, and I couldn't see the kindness in his eyes that I had last night.

"I hope that's ok," I whispered, not knowing what else to say. He nodded as though distracted by something. His eyes seemed locked and he stared behind me with a frightening gaze. I was just about to turn and look but he blinked twice and turned back to me abruptly.

"Okay then, let's get you started." I turned to follow him but not before looking in the direction he had been fixated on. He had been staring at the VIP level but whatever he had been staring at was now gone and you could only make out faint shadows that didn't seem to be moving.

"Now there's only one thing to warn you about, we only have one rule...but it's very important you understand." He was speaking in hushed tones but then he stopped and looked around as though he was about to tell me a deadly secret. He leaned in close and I could smell a sour tinge to his breath, which made me gag slightly.

"Nobody goes upstairs...EVER!" He said, shouting this last part louder than the rest. I couldn't help taking a startled step backwards. This place didn't seem real, like this guy was an actor and I was on some weird 'caught on camera' show. The ones where they trick some poor unsuspecting fool that it's all real and they get a big kick out of their scared witless reactions.

"Ooo...kay" I said drawing out the word.

"Yes... I mean no, *no-one* goes up there unless instructed. They have their own staff and the VIP area never closes whilst the Draven family and guests are here...I mean there, up there!" It was like deciphering a conflicted code talking to this man!

"No problem, got it." I said a little too over enthusiastically. Thankfully this seemed to throw a spanner in his babbling.

"This is Mike and over there is Hannah. Mike will be showing you the ropes but don't worry we will just have you collecting glasses tonight until you get...uhh...*a feel for the place.*" It was odd the way he said this last part, as if there was something amiss. He scratched his head with a violent rub that made me jump slightly. I was sure I saw him twitch before he did this. Then abruptly, he turned and almost hovered away.

He was odd to say the least. I would have to ask Frank about him later when he picked me up, that was if I was brave enough to find out.

"Hi, sorry what did he say your name was?" A voice talking to me brought me back to Earth.

"I don't think he did, but its Keira or Kaz for short."

"Don't worry about him, he's a bit of a weirdo, but you will get used to it. Of course, it's worse now the Dravens are here, he won't relax until they're gone again." He stood with his arms folded looking very defensive, which made me think that he'd had a few problems with the manager, ones he'd like to share.

"His brother Jerry is the more relaxed one." Ah! That explained a lot. It wasn't even the right guy.

"Twins?" Although it was obvious, I said it anyway.

"Yeah, that was Gary, but they are nothing alike, that one's a bit... how can I say...a bit special." Oh, Okay that explained it I thought, feeling a bit guilty.

Mike stayed with me all night and he turned out to be a fun guy. He reminded me of Frank's younger brother Justin.

Justin was around my age and I had met him once at their wedding. He was a lot like Frank, easy going and sweet natured but his looks were the opposite. They were both very handsome but in different ways. Frank was more like a cute cuddly bear, big and burly. Justin was a baby-faced beauty, but boy did he know it. I would be the first to admit that when I first saw him I had a bit of a crush, and if he hadn't brought a girlfriend with him to Libby's very English church wedding, then I'd have hoped for more.

The bar started to get busier as the time got on. I didn't even realise that a band had started to play until it was finally time for me to collect some empties. Mike begrudgingly left my side to go and help serve at the bar. I weaved in and out of all sorts of people, who looked like they were trying to belong to something greater in life. Wasn't that what we were all doing in some way, trying to belong to something better than ourselves? Trying to evolve our thoughts and expand our minds to different exciting new possibilities. Wasn't that what escapism was all about?

Sometimes reality just doesn't seem enough. In my mind I held so much faith in fantasy. It was safer for me that way, because in my fantasies the things that happened to me in my real life, those were the dreams... No, not dreams but nightmares. It was as if they hadn't happened and that's how I coped. I decided that the hurt could be numbed, that I could lose myself in a perfect state of ignorance. After all, 'Ignorance is bliss'. However, this didn't make the cloud disappear completely, but it helped me get from one day to the next without bringing anyone else down with me. It was my curse, no one else's.

So, as I walked or more like ducked, squeezed and pushed my way through all these troubled looking souls, I found it was a bit comforting to, well... 'fit in'.

The night went very quickly, and I hadn't realised that my two-hour trial night had turned into my six-hour trial. Now I was outside taking out the trash and it was fully dark. Luckily, I had rung Frank and arranged for him to pick me up later. I smiled when I heard Libby in the background asking, 'is she alright, does she need me to go and pick her up now?'

Mike had shown me where the bins were and the number to get back through the security doors that had a four-digit code. He told me to just remember a square, 1452. His fingers touched the keys in the order that made that square and I nodded saying "got it" not wanting to give blondes a bad name. But now I stood here alone behind a closed door, not getting that fuzzy lift that the club's music and atmosphere gave off. No, now I was looking behind me at the looming forest, that looked too close for comfort and wishing I had taken Mike's offer to do the bins.

Now I was alone. Of course, the fact that this side of the building was completely surrounded by an eerie black wall of forest didn't help with my jellified backbone. I automatically started to look around but when my eyes scanned the side wall they found a black abyss that didn't seem to end. How big was this freakin' place?

I shook off the feeling that someone was watching me, getting that tingling feeling at the base of my skull again. I started to walk to the place Mike had shown me where the bins were hidden. Great.... hidden! But of course, they were I thought, rolling my eyes to no one.

I struggled down the steps with my heavy load and nearly slipped as the temperature had dropped significantly, covering the Earth's surface with an icy blanket. My gloved hand caught the metal supports and I steadied myself letting out a nervous giggle. I picked up the sacks I had dropped and walked slowly around the corner to where I had been directed. My feet crunched the icy gravel making my heart quicken. It was so stupid to be scared.

"Man up Keira, its only bin duty." I said reassuring myself.

I could see the 'dumpsters' as Mike had called them. I wondered if I shouldn't go back and ask for his help, they were so big I didn't know if I could even lift the lid. I paused and turned back to the door where a faint glow of the security light could be seen around the corner of the imposing stone wall. It cast shadows across the ground making my mind wild with images that weren't there. The light caught the icy gravel making it look like glass or mirrors, sparkling in millions of directions.

I tried to focus on the job at hand. The quicker I got this done the sooner I could be inside safe and warm. I pushed the lid and it opened only to come crashing back down again missing my fingers by mere centimetres.

Okay, it was going to play hard ball... then bring it on, stupid pain in my ass plastic top! I bent my knees down, planning to launch myself upwards, hopefully giving it enough momentum to keep going until it was back on itself. Okay, here goes. I took a deep breath, flung my body upwards and pushed the lid's lip as hard as my little frame could manage. But it wasn't enough.

My hands were gripped on the inside where the lid had been and was now crashing back down angrily. I didn't have time to move, just had time to wait for the pain to hit.

But the pain didn't come. Instead, the wind did. A gust that was so strong and powerful, it pushed the lid back with an almighty thunderous crash. The plastic bounced back and forth until it cracked under the strain. It made me jump backwards landing on my backside with a thud of my own. That was going to bruise, but Hell, it was better than eight broken fingers. I got up and wiped down my jeans and rubbed my sore bottom. I picked up the stupid black sacks and threw them with shaky hands into the dark pit.

"What was that!?" My voice shook in response to the noise that had just cut through the dark silence. Okay definitely time to leave. But hey, why was it so dark? Shit! I hadn't noticed before but where did the light go? There was no longer any glistening floor or shapeless shadows. Oh God, the security light had gone out!

There had been a noise, I was sure of it. The sounds of trees rustling, then a branch snapping had me frozen in pure dread. It must just be an animal. But what if it wasn't? Okay, breathe. Just breathe.

I stared into the surrounding trees but there was nothing to see. Just tall black shapes that entwined themselves closer to me, like a wooden cage I couldn't escape from. I could feel my chest getting tighter as it was getting harder to breathe. I tried to tell myself not to panic and to get back to the door, but my feet were rooted to the spot. Fear had me trapped in time and I felt my scars almost burn their way through the material that concealed them. My blood froze, and my eyes filled with tears.

Memories came rotating back at me over and over, hitting me hard like a bloody sledgehammer to the chest. Repressed memories assaulted me and flooded my brain. It had been a night like this, cold and hauntingly beautiful. Only then I had never been afraid, I had seen its beauty and not the living nightmares it could bring; the evil lurking in wait amongst its flawless settings.

I had stood waiting unaware of the danger that night held in store for me. And after expecting something sweet to come along in reality the only thing waiting for me was horrifyingly evil and sour. Then I heard a noise I would never forget but wished more than anything in the world that I would... *That I could.* Had it been a warning? It was the last noise I ever heard before Hell had truly found me.

Before I changed.... *before he had changed me.*

A single tear escaped my eye and ran down my cheek towards my quivering lips. But something happened before it got there, it stopped...no it didn't just stop... *it froze.* I could now move. It pulled my focus out of its mental confinement and I raised my hand to my cheek. There my fingers peeled away a single frozen tear drop.

My eyes then started to focus on a familiar sight. For there in front of me was an image getting closer, flying through the trees so gracefully as if there wasn't any forest in its path. It glided through the black evening air, tilting its wings as if to catch the cool breeze.

The bird from my dream was back.

But more importantly...

Where was its master?

DRAVEN

18

NEW EMPLOYEE, OLD FEARS.

I took flight the moment I saw her get into her brother-in-law's car, knowing if I had stayed then I would have committed the biggest sin my kind could commit...*a mortal death.* I had caught only half of their conversation, but it had been clear he intended to see my Chosen One as something more than a friend. A thought that at the very least I was happy to see that she seemed disinterested in... if not a little too nice about it, for my tastes. As I would have preferred a more forceful 'No, get lost dick head' type of response, followed by a swift kick to his tiny genitals that would have been the 'icing on my cake' as they say.

"Fuck! What is becoming of me?!" I scorned myself the moment I landed at a particular clearing that was a usual spot for hikers to take advantage of the panoramic views. It also looked over towards my cave in the distance and was another place I sometimes came to when I needed to clear my head of whatever problem I was facing at the time. And as King, then there were always problems to face, but by the Gods, there had been nothing like this! I swear it felt as if I were being constantly ripped apart by an Aeolus eye before being put back together again.

Aeolus was the God of wind and Perses, the God of destruction. Both of which were commissioned to create this incredible and constant energy. A vortex that combined the two deadly elements and merged them so that the worst of Hell's prisoners would be encased inside such a force for eternity.

It had actually been a gift for Hades from his brother Zeus to use as punishment. And it was one Hell of a punishment at that, and one I still had yet to see with my own two eyes. A punishment definitely reserved for a person's mortal enemy. But then I thought about enemies, and I was sure that no matter how much I hated the human boy for taking an interest in Keira, then really...*could I blame him?*

Hate him for it, yes, without a doubt, but blame him? No, I most certainly could not. And I was left wondering when the time came, who would a girl like her choose? She didn't strike me as the type who would be impressed with money or an expensive suit. A thought that made me look down at myself now and see just that.

But then she was my Electus and sent to me personally by the Fates themselves, so surely that was to mean something to her when the time came, and I could finally make my move?

Alright, so if I were honest, then this would have been so much easier if I could have just controlled her like I could any other mortal. That way she would soon forget about this sandy-haired boy with his easy and charming grin, one I wanted to permanently eradicate from adding to his boyish charms with a slice of my sword.

Maybe I could at the very least plant the idea of him having herpes in her mind?

"Oh, fuck it!" I said aloud before taking to the skies once more and quickly finding myself outside her house. I stood by the tree line, watching her through the window as she laughed with her sister in the kitchen. She looked to be making a sandwich and stopped every now and again to add some dramatic action to her story, swinging the buttered knife in her hand as if it weren't even there. Then she turned back to her chore and once done, lifted the whole thing to her mouth and took a large bite, still trying to tell her story, despite now also trying to consume her meal.

And throughout the whole thing, I only managed to ask myself why I found this little scene such an endearing one? Why wasn't I put off by such behaviour? I had once believed that all females should be graceful and ladylike creatures. But now watching this little act, I couldn't help but wonder what I had been missing out on all this time.

There were so many sides to her I just didn't know yet, but I found myself eager to learn them all. Like what had her sister just said to her that made her throw her head back and laugh like that? As if it had just burst from her, making her slap a hand down on the counter and nearly spill her glass of milk. And another thing, what human past the age of elementary school still drank milk?

Gods, but she even wiped her mouth on the back of her hand before taking another man-sized bite from her sandwich. But yet here I was, utterly fascinated and yearning for the day I got to witness all of these things for myself first hand.

Soon this happy little scene was interrupted when Frank walked in and swung his wife around before whispering something in her ear that made her giggle. Keira rolled her eyes as if suddenly feeling like the third wheel in this picture but the smile in her gaze was easily seen, even from where I was stood. She was obviously happy for her sister, that much was clear. As there was not a single shred of jealousy to be seen and the selfless joy in her eyes made me only want to kiss her for it.

Her sister left the kitchen shortly after this, making sure to grab a beer for her husband, something that made Keira laugh to herself this time as she now faced the window. She was shaking her head as if a memory of what made her smile still lingered. Then she continued to finish her meagre meal, now looking out to the tree line ahead as if getting lost in her thoughts.

I knew she wouldn't be able to see me, but for a few small seconds, it was almost as if she were looking right at me. Then she looked down and released a deep sigh, before turning away from the window and switching off the light as she left the room now bringing an end to my sweet moments of discovery.

I don't know how long I waited, trapped in my own thoughts, by the time all the lights went out in the house, but I made sure that it was long enough after this before I went to her window. I wasn't intending on waking her up this evening, for I didn't have it in me to take another memory away from her. However, I needed to know if it were at least possible for me to gain enough control over her mind, in case her feelings for this boy increased. I knew it was wrong, but as a man on the edge of his restraint, and one already stepping far past the boundaries of what was right and wrong, I felt as though I had little choice.

She was mine.

It was that simple.

She just didn't know it yet.

The moment I saw her, it was as if every hard, tense element in me softened...all but one, and it just so happened to be the one I was ignoring until I could get her in my bed. But this time, I referred more to my angel and my demon. Both of which were wound up tight enough that I could foresee a day on the mats in my training room before too long.

She was lying on her side, one hand under the pillow and another fisted in the quilt with a foot poking out to the side of the bed. Even the sight of one thick sock almost hanging off made me smile to myself.

Why was it only now I was starting to notice the little things? Sure, I been all around the world and been captured by the natural beauty it had to offer. As when owning some of the most exclusive property money could buy, then a view was something that came hand in hand with such a luxury. And as someone whose favourite pastime included spreading my wings and taking to the skies, then trust me, a beautiful view was something I most certainly appreciated.

But observing human life and finding the beauty in that...well, that was something I was starting to feel ashamed to say I never did. I was simply arrogant enough to believe they should be thankful that what I did do was to be considered enough. For keeping the balance between our worlds had never been an easy feat. But anything beyond that was, quite honestly, not something I had even thought about. They had always been lesser beings in a sense, as having very little to no power meant little respect in my world.

But then here was this innocent beauty who had enough power to bring a King to his knees. So then, who was I to claim such a being was lesser than myself...for she unknowingly held all the power. A profound realisation brought forth by the simple sight of a sock falling from a dainty little foot.

"I am losing my mind," I stated on the other side of the glass with a shake of my head. Then I gave in to my impulses and let myself inside, approaching her bed and only wishing that I could snatch her from the night.

Once again, I saw that she had plaited her hair and it was currently coiled around her pillow as if at some point she had thrown it over her shoulder in annoyance. But just seeing it lay there, having dreamt of such a golden fleece, well, all I wanted was to fall asleep next to her with it wrapped around my fist. Oh, the comfort I would feel in knowing every movement she made would alert my lonely soul to her presence.

Which was why I reached out for it now and tucked it further back, so that it wouldn't get in her way again. I didn't know why she struggled to sleep, or if she still did for that matter. As from the looks of her now I would be content in thinking not.

But if she did, then once with me, I would make it my mission that she found the nights peaceful ones, and my preferred choice of drug would be to simply exhaust her body beforehand. Also, to flood her mind with oxytocin, which was the body's natural pain killer. Now once accompanied by the release of endorphins from as many orgasms as I deemed her body could take, then I foresaw little trouble in sleeping for my Chosen beauty.

Looking down now and I had to agree with the remedy also working for myself, as I was hard as steel and certainly due for a peaceful night's sleep. Which forced me to face why I was here this time, and unfortunately it wasn't to test either of those remedies of restful sleep.

So, I did what I had come here to do and committing myself to yet another line crossed as I accessed her mind, something that was far easier to do than when she was alert and awake. Then I crept into her thoughts without making my presence there known. Once more I came across the fortress of her mind, something she had built up with incredible strength and not something I was ever willing to try and tear down. However, all I wanted was to pluck away any deeper feelings for the boy she met tonight and cast them as far as they would go.

And I knew no matter how innocent an act I tried to make it or justify such a thing, it didn't make it any less intrusive than it was. But with my sanity on the line, then I feared I had no choice. However, in the end, it had been a pointless endeavour, as she was giving me nothing. Not one single thought of him. Not even when I pushed that little bit harder. For all that happened was a wave of strength that ended up shutting me out completely.

I almost staggered back, not from the force of it but from shock. I knew now that if she woke with her mind engaged in such a defensive way, that I would even have a hard time getting her to sleep again. In fact, I didn't know how long I could push my luck with that and just how many secret nights like this one I had left with her.

Which was why I brushed back the shorter parts of her hair so as I could see all of her face. Then I leant down and whispered against her skin,

"Why can't I control you?"

And then I was gone.

The next day I was thankful that business had kept me busy, but it hadn't been enough to rid me of thinking of her. I often asked myself if this obsession would ease once she was claimed, but somehow I wasn't holding on to much hope. Of course, it hadn't helped my tense mood when hearing that very little progress had been made in trying to find her real identity. I hadn't blamed Ranka for this, for I knew she was doing everything in her power to get me the information I wanted. However, that didn't mean she was clueless to my displeasure.

Frustration wasn't something I was used to dealing with, as usually if a problem arose, then there was always some solution found. And in business, it was no different. As normally, if you threw enough money at a problem, it would eventually stick like glue and find itself solved the very next day. And mostly by people who would want to line their own pockets and wouldn't have minded taking a vacation to the fourth level of Hell named Greed…

Now Lust was the one they really needed to watch out for!

"You're looking at your watch again," Sophia commented without looking up from whatever gossip-filled glossy magazine she currently had her head in. Why she was even in my office, I had no clue. I just knew that by the time I had showered and was in a fresh new tailored suit, one by some designer you wouldn't be able to pronounce unless you spoke Italian, she was lounging on my teal coloured sofa in my office. A gaudy looking piece of furniture if you asked me, but one Sophia had insisted on, and at the time, I hadn't felt inclined to argue.

"Why are you here again?" I asked as I fixed my onyx cufflink.

"I was just wondering if there was anything, in particular, you wanted me to find out when I start classes next week."

"I think you know your history, Sophia," I commented dryly. She granted me an impervious look in return and said,

"I was, of course, referring to your golden-haired Electus."

"Her real name would be nice," I said looking through the paperwork on my desk and contemplating just setting it all alight with the click of my fingers, just to save me some time.

"Then I take it you have had no luck from the Mohawk?" Sophia said making her distaste for my loyal chief officer known. However, I ignored her derogatory comment and gave her, her answer.

"No, not as of yet."

"Then maybe I should just go meet with her now and introduce myself," Sophia said smoothing down the tight red skirt part of her outfit. She reminded me of some old movie star, with the classic dress sense and the way not a hair was ever out of place. My sister had always loved the finer things in life, which was why it always looked so out of place seeing her in battle still dressed the same way, only covered in another's blood with a smile on her face.

Of course, the complaining would always commence after all our enemies were long gone, dead and dispatched. Even if she always seemed to have fun during the violent act. But then sex and violence often went hand in hand for a demon, so having her clothes ripped off shortly after by her husband was usually problem solved for the pair. Sophia, when ridding herself of bloodstained clothes and her husband ridding himself…well, ridding himself of her whining and shutting her up on the matter I can imagine.

But Sophia was a strange creature, in the sense that she always had an unusual phobia…*germs.* Something in the early days Vincent and I teased her about mercilessly seeing as it was unusual for a demon to even have a phobia, let alone to be something so irrational. For it wasn't as though we could even contract a disease, let alone die from one!

But now, thanks to this being the era of personal hygiene and Sophia having more products to choose from than she knew what to do with, then there was no longer any need for her to bathe ten times a day for fear that she missed someone sneezing on her. As I said, a strange concept really considering it was impossible for her to get sick and something Vincent and I often wondered hadn't slipped through from her first vessel?

See there were many types and breeds of demons and angels, but essentially only two ways to become one on Earth. The first was a soul was granted a vessel through the Gods' favour or through punishment when you became one of the fallen. Named as such for an angel or one of the ascended, for the demons that were banished.

However, being here through punishment usually meant losing your wings and sometimes being stripped of your power. But then the other way was to have a recent death appealed, and request for the soul to be transformed into an angel or a demon. For the 'keeper' or 'King' in my case, believed their souls to offer a greater purpose to serve on Earth's plane, than the place where they had initially been intended for.

Once a request was accepted, this was when it was preferred their mortal bodies be healed and reused for the soul they were originally born into. The power then of a demon or angel were merged with what was once a human soul. One as such was head of my security, Ragnar, who had once been King of Denmark and Sweden.

But getting back to the present time and with it stopping Sophia from interfering any sooner than she had to.

"No, I think we just allow the girl to settle into her first shift without being faced by who she would only consider as one of her bosses. Which may be something else to consider when first introducing yourself, as I believe befriending her first before announcing who you are in her work life, would be wise." I watched as Sophia digested this idea and I swear the Gods were playing a trick on me when she actually agreed. In fact, I wondered if this were akin to winning a battle against the mighty Devil's beast Abaddon!

"I think you're right, that might be wise." I swallowed carefully, making sure not to let my tongue go down with it, and nodded, which I believed was called, 'playing it cool' by human standards.

Minutes later Vincent entered and as a way of hello frowned at me in question.

"What is it, Vince?"

"Oh, nothing really, I just wondered what it was you were still doing in your office when the girl you have waited for your whole life arrived twenty minutes ago?" I bolted up out of my seat and looked at my watch.

"She was early?" I asked making Vincent grin.

"She was indeed and obviously very keen." I could hear the teasing tone, but it was one I ignored as I grabbed my suit jacket from the back of my chair and left my office. The club wasn't yet in its usual full swing as they would say, which I suppose was a good thing for her first shift. I could see her clearly from up here as she was being shown where everything was behind the bar. This was by an employee named Mike who was currently opening up the glass washer and showing her how best to load the empties.

I had to say that seeing her now working in my club, I was torn. Half of me wanted to agree with Sophia that having her working here now gave me the perfect excuse to watch her from afar and ensure her safety.

But the other half of me hated to see her having to work at all, wanting nothing more than to go down there, tell her that she was fired from that job and that instead she could be my secretary or some other job that wouldn't have had her on her feet all night and put her in even closer proximity to me.

I decided to quickly bury these thoughts before my imagination ran too far ahead of me. But what was I saying, for I was already envisioning her in a skirt for ease of access, so as I could take her on my desk, after first pushing her back with a hand to her neck and ripping away any silky bit of material that concealed her from me. Then I would dip my head to the centre of her milky white thighs and promptly begin my feast, taking my time as I made a meal out of her and tasting her nectar right from the source.

A definite treat this king was more than ready for.

The rest of the night I found myself content and even started to relax a little as I watched my obsession down below as she weaved her way in and out of the crowd. She spent most of the evening collecting empties, and it was only when nearing the end that Mike called her over to show her where to dispose of the rubbish. I was at least comforted to know that he was carrying those heavy sacks for her as they exited outside. But then I quickly became concerned again when he came back inside alone. He had been called back to the bar for the last orders rush, meaning Keira was still outside…*alone.*

Something I didn't like, not one bit. Which was why I found myself standing from my table abruptly and making my way to the balcony. Once outside and looking below I knew that was where the large bins were kept slightly off to one side and tucked further back. Directly below where I stood was the side exit door that had a four digit control panel that I feared Mike had forgotten to mention.

So, I threw up a veil and let myself drop to her level, making sure to do so quietly, so as not to startle her by the sound. I did so just in time to see her look around, now scanning the black forest that lay directly ahead. She was still stood at the top of the steps as if needing to first make sure it was clear of any danger before venturing down. I frowned knowing that something was off, but I couldn't put my finger on it.

Then, with these thoughts still roaming for answers in my mind, she grabbed her load and started to make her way down the few steps. The problem with this was the overwhelming urge to help her as I was forced to watch as she struggled. Even very nearly slipping on the now slippery steps, thanks to the slight frost that had started to take hold of the night. But before I could reveal myself, she saved her body from hitting the steps as her gloved hand grabbed hold of one of the railings.

Gloves again? I was about to question it further in my mind when a sound took all my attention. She had actually let out a nervous giggle before picking up the bags and continuing down until her feet were soon crunching on the frost-kissed gravel. Then she took a deep breath and scolded herself.

"Man up, Keira, it's only bin duty." I found it odd that she had referred to herself as Keira if this weren't her real name. Especially as she currently believed herself to be alone. Unless it was her name and it was the surname that was the fake? I would have released a frustrated sigh, had I not feared her mind able to hear it. There were just too many questions still left unanswered, and I didn't like it one bit. Just as I didn't like watching her struggle with those bags.

She continued to drag them over to where the large industrial sized bins were when I saw her swallow hard at the obvious problem she now faced. As she took one look at the height of them dwarfing her own and then back at the doors as if debating with herself on whether or not to go and ask for help.

I swear I almost growled in frustration the moment she made the wrong decision, and it was times like this that her strong mind very nearly infuriated me, for I couldn't control it!

No, instead I was forced to watch as she tried in vain to push the lid open, only to see it come crashing down, barely missing her fingers. I was suddenly torn because I felt helpless, knowing that if I just used my mind to open the lid, that would no doubt scare her as my sudden appearance might. But then what if a gust of wind were to do the job for me?

"Alright you stupid lid, time to play hardball!" she told it after bending her legs, readying herself to propel her body up and gaining the height needed. Something I knew wouldn't work, no matter how much she looked adorable when speaking to it and telling it who was boss.

But never-the-less, I was forced to watch as she followed through with her plan as she jumped up as much as her legs would allow. Now only pushing the lid up slightly higher this time. And unsurprisingly, it wasn't enough, and she knew this the moment it started to come crashing down, giving her little time to move. Her eyes widened in panic before wincing, as she waited for impact. Which would have included the pain that would follow from having eight broken fingers.

But of course, I would never allow something like this to happen, so instead, I sent a burst of energy towards the lid, forcing it back with a crack and letting her believe it was a strong wind that had saved her. However, it didn't entirely go to plan, for I forgot that I was dealing with someone who obviously had a clumsy streak and therefore fell backwards. She landed on her backside, moaning in pain as she did.

After a stunned moment or two, she got back to her feet and rubbed a hand along her sore bottom before picking up the bags and muttering in annoyance as she swung them around one by one, up into the bin. But then the echoing sound of each bag crashing against the metal caused a skittish animal in the distance to run further into the forest, cracking branches as it went.

"What was that!?" she suddenly shouted in panic, and it cut through me like a blade. It was the first real time I had seen such fear in her eyes, and the sight was one that became immortalised forever on my soul. It was the first time in my life that I could class a sight witnessed as one that haunted me and one I vowed to do everything in my power to prevent from ever happening again.

But before I did that, first I needed to understand where that deeply rooted fear was coming from.

She started to look around in desperation which was when I noticed the security light had timed out. However, I could still see her thanks to my superior eyesight, which also meant that I could now see much more.

More than she even knew that she was giving me.

A piece of her terrifying past.

Keira

19

WHISPERED LIPS

One look at the bird coming at me again and I ran back towards the door, which wasn't easy in the dark. I fumbled my way along with my hands sliding off the wet stone wall. Of course, the Heavens had decided to open and with the rain beating down hard it made everything slick.

But thankfully the moon had come out from behind the trees and was leading the way. I didn't know whether or not the creature was still out there. I had not waited long enough to find out as now I didn't have the safety of glass from my window to protect me.

I could feel something watching, but it didn't make me feel as scared as I had been before. It made me feel warm and safe. I couldn't explain it but whatever it was, it was comforting. However, it still didn't change my need to get back inside.

"If only I had more light." I hadn't realised that I said the words out loud instead of just thinking them until, to my great surprise, the security light flicked twice before illuminating fully. It lit up my pathway to the door, which wasn't as far as I had thought it had been. But wait, oh damn! I had forgotten the bloody password! Oh God, what was it?

I almost fell on the steps in my haste to get to the keypad. I fumbled with the keys pressing them too fast to even register. Oh, come on, think. Think damn it! A square that was it! 3256. No, that wasn't it, 1254 again no.

"Oh, come on, please work!" I said in a panic, whipping my head back and forth in case anything was behind me. The feeling that I was still being watched still hadn't left me. Then something different started to happen. A calming wave overtook my body, travelling its way down from my neck to my hand like some soothing touch I couldn't see. Then the feeling of a larger hand taking my own and gently forcing it to move invaded. Almost like a lover coming up behind me and taking matters into their own hands.

My mouth dropped open but there were no words. I just gasped taking in more cold air. The hairs on the back of my neck stood on end as if a much bigger body was getting even closer to my trembling frame. My head even tilted to one side as I felt the hidden breath there before it travelled down my body as though I was waiting for the kiss that never came. My finger moved gracefully over the digits in perfect order as though they weren't attached to the rest of me.

1...4...5...2. and the door clicked. My hand gripped the cold metal handle pulling it down. When the door opened easily letting the warm air and light seep through the gap, I finally took a much-needed breath. My hand was quickly released, and I was once again capable of moving of my own accord. I spun round quickly trying to capture a glimpse of I don't know what. My eyes came up empty, just as my mind did. I could not explain any of it. Only that whatever it had been, had been truly...

Magical.

The rest of my shift came and went in a bit of a blur. Mike had given Gary a glowing review of my first night, so I now officially had the job if I wanted it. I knew in a town like this getting this job was like winning the lottery considering how many people would kill to work here. So, I accepted gratefully and was now stood outside waiting for Frank with a smile on my face.

Jo and Cameron were kindly giving me their congratulations on getting the job before I even told them. I took note of their ear pieces and gathered news travelled fast around here. Speaking of which Jo put his hand to his ear and after listening for a few seconds they both hurried inside. I knew something must have been kicking off back in the club for them to have rushed inside like that as you rarely saw them leave the entrance.

I started walking slightly away from the club, so it was easier for Frank to pull in and pick me up. I looked back to Afterlife and my eyes wandered over to the side of the building where the bins were situated. I rubbed my hands thinking of the warm sensation that overtook my body earlier. My hand hadn't been my own and the feeling hadn't completely left me. No, it had stayed with me in a more delicate form, but it sure felt good. It made all the fear go away and was replaced by a warming bliss so intense it had me struggling to keep my secret smile hidden.

"Hey Blondie!" A guy shouted over to me and in my reminiscing state I hadn't noticed the two guys now approaching me.

"Do you need a lift somewhere?" The other guy asked, and both were carrying beer bottles.

"Uh...no thanks, I'm waiting for someone." I said taking a few steps back the closer they got.

"Aww honey, don't be like that. Why wait when we are right here." The guy sniggered to his friend nudging him on the shoulder.

"Yeah, why don't you come with us? We know a little place where we can all get to know each other a little better." I rolled my eyes at the jerks that obviously had issues with a girl saying no, so I decided to make it clearer for them.

"Look, I don't mean to be rude, but I am not interested, so just move along." They both laughed holding up their hands and mocking me,

"Whoa, you know bud, I think she's trying to blow us off."

"Yeah and after we have been so nice to her." The other butthead said. I turned back to face Beavis when he walked up closer to me and said,

"I think you just like being a cock tease and playing hard to get, so stop being a little bitch and play nice." Then he grabbed my forearm and I freaked. I hated being touched on my scars, so I yanked my arm free and stepped in to face him.

"Listen tosser, I said no! And you ever touch me again it will be the last thing you ever do, as my boyfriend is on his way and will kick your dodgy, gormless ugly ass face!" I said wishing that swearing came more natural to me. I had to admit when their faces dropped, and they started backing away I felt good.

"Okay, okay, we're sorry! We didn't mean anything by it...we don't want any trouble now."

"Yeah, yeah...no...no trouble, we're just leaving." They both stuttered out in their haste to leave.

"Yeah! You'd better run!" I said rolling my shoulders and puffing out my chest. I turned around still watching them over my shoulder when I walked straight into what felt like a wall. I bounced backwards only to be caught before I fell on my bum. Unyielding arms secured me not only upright but also pulled me a step closer to his body. I had that dreaded feeling of who I would find when I finally looked.

I blew some of the loose hair that had fallen in front of my face as I raised my eyes to his, only to find the one man I had been obsessing over. Like in the club we had a silent moment pass between us, one that was shattered with the sounds of the two guys freaking out in the distance. His head shot over mine, which wasn't hard given our height difference. His frown put mine to shame and was scary enough in its own right.

"See they don't come back." He ordered to one of the men with him in a voice I had not yet heard, and I shuddered at the authority in it. The massive guy I had seen him entering the club with last night looked like a battle-scarred Viking. He was possibly the biggest guy I had ever seen and one that would have me quaking in my boots if he merely said 'boo' to me. He grunted in response before following orders and leaving the two of us alone.

Meanwhile I was still trying to think of something to say when he beat me to it.

"It is not wise standing alone in the dark." He told me, and it almost sounded like a threat. I went to take a step back and the arm he still held around me tightened possessively before letting me go. The feeling it created being so close to him was intoxicating and the spell was only broken once we had some space between us.

"Uhh...Okay, well thanks. I guess I needed to add a few inches to my threats eh." I said raising up on my tiptoes and looking him up and down knowing I would need bloody stilts to match his height. However, I knew this was the wrong thing to say when his frown deepened.

"This is not a joke. If you have a boyfriend, then I suggest informing him of the dangers that can occur when leaving a beautiful girl waiting alone at night." My breathing hitched when he called me beautiful and I exhaled in a puff, not knowing what to say. It came out as a wheezing noise and one perfectly shaped eyebrow arched at the sight of my strange behaviour. What, had he never seen a girl flustered before? Being as handsome as he was I very much doubted it.

"Uhh... I would say that to him...but there is no him...boyfriend, I mean...just me." He didn't say anything to this but looked over my head once more and I followed his gaze to see headlights illuminating the trees. Just then Frank's car came into view.

"Your ride?" I nodded too scared of what else to say as everything that I'd said so far had made me sound simple.

"Don't let this happen again, *Keira.*" He whispered in my ear and my body froze with the feel of his lips so close to my skin. I still had my eyes to Frank's car coming closer but all I wanted to do was close them and sink back into the strong body behind me.

"I promise I won't..." I said turning back round to face him to find he was gone.

"What the...?" I muttered in sight of his disappearing act and I looked everywhere to see if I could spot him.

"You ready, Kid?" Frank asked through the window and I nodded my head even though I was in no way ready to leave yet…and after what just happened, I didn't think I ever would be.

It didn't take a genius to know my mind was elsewhere and Frank gave up after his third attempt at a conversation. At least with the smile on my face he knew from the power of elimination that my shift had gone well.

The same thing happened once we were back at home when Libby tried to ask me how it went. I saw Frank shaking his head at her as if to say, 'don't ask'. I walked over to where she was curled up in the armchair, kissed her on the forehead and said,

"I am beat, gonna sleep, it was a good night, loved working there, night, night."

"Uh…night." She said shocked when I just turned around and left for my room after kissing Frank on the cheek and thanking him for the lift home. I walked away to the sound of Libby asking,

"Is she pissed?"

I was definitely drunk but not from alcohol. I ran up the stairs taking two at a time. Once inside my room I stripped off my work clothes and draped them over a chair by my desk. I then pulled out some clean baggy clothes I used for pyjamas. I let my hair down, running my fingers close to my scalp. I couldn't help moaning out loud at how good it felt after a day of weight twisted at the back of my head. I brushed it, plaited it and then finished getting ready for bed.

While brushing my teeth, I thought about how my shift had gone and how much I had enjoyed getting back in the swing of working again. But this was a fleeting thought quickly replaced by what happened after work. For starters he knew my name! And what had he been doing out there in the first place. Did he usually take midnight strolls in case there were damsels in distress? This thought didn't make me happy and the jealously was irrational.

I decided to think back to nicer thoughts, like how it had felt to have his arms wrapped securely around me, almost as if he hadn't wanted to let me go. This was a nice thought to be having when about to get into bed being as it was one of the main places I wanted a certain someone to join me. After all I was only human! But not only that, I was also woman enough to know that when a man like him is around then that affects you in places you normally have to touch to be affected. Well, that meant something in my book. So, with this in mind, my hand wandered down under the covers and did the next best thing a girl could do when having a devastatingly handsome man on the brain.

For the act to play out to its fullest, I transported myself back to that first night in the club. I was now sat there in that booth wearing a black, barely there dress of silk. I was also alone and this time when the doors opened only one man walked in. My breath caught as my pleasure increased at just the sight my mind created. He was utter perfection and that perfection was once again walking right up to my table.

I bit my bottom lip, both in the realms of fantasy and bland reality. He homed in on me and stormed through the mass of people with only one thing on his mind...*me.* This time, the world didn't part for the powerful looking man getting to me. No, in my mind I wanted him to work for it and as his long legs ate up the space, he most certainly worked it good. Damn good in fact, thanks to the way his muscular frame looked in a black suit.

Once he got to me he looked almost wild and the intense gaze told me one thing was on his mind. Before I even got a word out, that look of restrained lust snapped and he hauled me up against him. I think my knees would have given out if one of his arms hadn't banded itself around my torso.

The other hand travelled excruciatingly slowly up my side, brushing my breast as he went, extracting a moan from my parted lips. His hand continued its exquisite journey upwards until the whole of his hand was stretched along the column of my neck. I had closed my eyes, hiding myself from the intensity of his soul-searching eyes. This was allowed to happen for less than a second before I heard the possessive growl coming from deep within him.

"Look at me!" He commanded. At the same time his hand fisted in my loose hair, forcing my head back to look up at him. I gasped when I saw the purple fire burning in his eyes. Eyes that looked as though they wanted to devour me whole. I was caught in some mental web he intended to keep me sealed in and at this point I never wanted to escape. Even when his head lowered fully, welding my personal space to join his own.

"You *never* hide from me." His intimidating order was enhanced by the growl on the word 'never' and I shuddered in his arms.

"Say it!" He added and when I hesitated, his grip tightened in my hair but holding back from developing it into too much pain.

"I..." I tried to get my brain to work harder and somewhere along the line this fantasy was slipping out of my control. But how?

"Say it. Now!" His voice broke not only argument but also any hesitation. So, I gave him not just what he wanted but what we both wanted...

A small forever.

"I will never hide from you." I whispered, and I heard the breath leave him quickly. Then, before I knew what was happening to this runaway fantasy I clearly no longer controlled, my head was forced into

another angle. Where now his perfect lips descended and just before the connection was made, he whispered above me,

"Good girl" in the softest voice I didn't know could come from such obvious strength. His arms pulled me tighter at the same time my world exploded. He took control of my lips in a way that caused a need in my toes to curl. On a gasp, he took his opportunity to drive the connection home and home is how I felt when Dominic Draven was kissing me. It was completely soul consuming and I felt myself break into pieces as I came apart under my own touch. The orgasm tore from me with such force I could only hope I hadn't screamed the name I felt leave my lips.

"Draven!" And with that one name coming from deep inside my core, I felt that at that moment all was right in my world.

"Keira." That was until I heard my own name being spoken aloud, breaking through the euphoric fog. My eyes snapped open and I shot up, seeing my room in darkness but more importantly, without a moving shadow.

"It couldn't be." I whispered but even as my mind was grasping back reality, my hand raised. My fingers touched the tender lips that felt slightly swollen from receiving a commanding kiss like no other. But that wasn't the only thing I felt there, or the most important. No, in the end it wasn't just the kiss itself that was the only thing to stay rooted deep inside me, it was the word spoken afterwards. A name whispered.

My name whispered...

Over my kissed lips.

DRAVEN

20

SECRET GRIN

In that moment, I realised I have never known the true meaning of restraint before. I had thought just being around the girl and not being able to touch her was bad enough. Not being able to claim her the way my intense lust was pushing at me to do. But I soon understood in that moment, it all meant nothing to what I was experiencing now. For the need to help her, to take her in my arms and comfort her was beyond all the pleasures of the body. A realisation that once more rocked not only my soul but also that of my angel and my demon, for they too cared for nothing more in that moment.

Which was why watching now was near excruciating. The way she was quickly allowing herself to give way to blind panic and I watched her internal struggle, as it was getting harder and harder for her to breathe. Well, the whole thing was like finding myself in a personal Hell. Yet I knew I could do nothing, for if I were to make myself known now, then I would only end up frightening her more.

Or so I told myself.

For it was a battle I continued to fight when I saw her tears and realised what I was witnessing wasn't a new fear born from the present, but it was a personal fear created from the past. This was when I could stand it no longer, thanks to the moment I saw that single tear fall towards her quivering lips.

I was going to make myself known in hopes that I could soothe her enough into trusting that I meant her no harm. But first, that falling tear had to stop. I don't know what compelled me to do so, but I made it freeze against her skin, so that it wouldn't be allowed to fall without me first being there to catch it.

Swiftly after this, I watched as she raised her hand to her face so she could peel the cold droplet from her skin, one I was happy to see melted and was quickly absorbed back into her palm. Her tears were mine to comfort and mine to control, I thought with an angry vow to myself. One I knew deep down I couldn't possibly have the power to enforce, but at the very least it brought me comfort when feeling as useless as I did right now.

So, just as I was about to step forward from the shadows of my veil, I noticed that she started to get herself back together. However, this was to be short-lived, for the next fearful event was only around the corner and had quickly started to take hold on her senses once more. And this time the fault was mine, for Ava had felt my inner turmoil through our connection and was currently making herself known as she started to fly through the trees.

I quickly sent her away with a single silent command, but it was too late, Keira had already seen her. Which was why after one look, she quickly made a run for it. At the same time, the forces of nature decided to rain down on us, making her short journey a slippery and dangerous one. So, I followed her, remaining closer than before in case she was to fall and then I would have no choice but to reveal myself, something I still didn't want to do unless absolutely necessary.

However, I knew I wasn't without my influences, so I sent a wave of reassurance to her, finding that like this her mind was much easier to explore. Making me realise that the key to unlocking her mind was fear, grief, upset and panic, none of which I wanted to exploit just to get my answers.

So instead of accessing her mind fully and finding what I wanted, I focused only on reversing her fear and bringing her back to calm. She looked around a little and then spoke to herself,

"If only I had more light." Well, her wish became a command I was only too happy to grant her and was one I only had to think of before the security light illuminated the space around us. Her eyes widened beautifully in surprise before she located the door again and continued to run towards it, only pausing the moment she realised it was locked. She then turned her attention to the keypad in a comical way, as if only now remembering that it was the last thing left that was still keeping her out of what she deemed was her safety.

She released a deep sigh and proved my suspicions correct when she started randomly pressing numbers in hopes of finding one combination of four digits that worked.

"Oh, come on, please work!" she said, continually checking behind her to make sure no one was creeping up on her. Gods, she was beautiful, even in her panic. The deep midnight blue colour her eyes had changed to was a startling contrast to the paleness of her milky skin. I even found myself mesmerised by her hair, that was now wet thanks to the rain, turning her golden blonde to darker shades of honey caramel that stuck to her skin. I even found myself reaching out to touch her face, only to fist my hand before pulling back in frustration.

I wanted to touch her. To reach out and take her in my arms without first needing to think of the repercussions such an act would cause. And I knew one day soon I would be free to do this, but this knowledge while waiting for it didn't make times like this any easier.

So, in the end, I decided to take control and ease her panic by taking advantage of it, doing the one thing I didn't want to do. I took hold of her mind now it was at its most vulnerable and masked the sight of myself. But not the feeling of what I was doing now. I started by running my fingertips gently down her neck, flooding her senses with a soothing sense of calm.

Then I allowed my touch to travel along her shoulder and down her arm until I found her shaky hand before taking it in my own. I started to slowly raise it back up to the keypad, noticing now how her mouth had opened slightly, and her head had tilted as if inviting my touch back elsewhere. But she had no clue as to what she was doing by tempting such a dangerous being as I. For I couldn't help it as my fangs lengthen at the sight of such exquisite skin being offered to me. I had never felt such an impulse to taste the essence of someone's lifeblood before, but knowing hers was but a hairsbreadth away, was like offering water to dying man!

And one taste would then replace that water for a drug offered to an addict, for I had no doubt that was exactly what would have become of me. A sobering thought indeed. So instead of giving into the highly tempting and highly erotic impulse, I simply extended her index finger and slowly moved it over the right sequence of numbers, soon making the door click. Then with another hand holding hers, I too raised it up so that she could now take the handle and pull it down, allowing her access back inside my club. Then the second I released my hold on her, I also released my wings and shot upwards back to the balcony for I could no longer conceal myself from her.

It was as if I had used every ounce of self-restraint against going too far and taking what I wanted, meaning the power needed to hide myself had failed me. Something that had never happened to me before!

It was a good job I had made this quick decision, for I heard her spin on a heel quickly as if trying to see what force it was that had possessed her body in such a way.

I found myself only able to breathe once more the second I heard the door slam shut, knowing now that she was safely inside and safe from an unknowing growing temptation.

Safe from my demon.

Moments later and after I had taken the time needed to calm my own pounding heart, I found myself storming back into the VIP and then straight into my office. I ignored all on my council table, who no doubt had wondered at my strange behaviour and unsurprisingly, was joined shortly after by Sophia and Vincent. The moment he closed the door I started barking orders.

"I need that fucking name!" I bellowed with enough of a temper to crack the walls. I was like a man consumed by rage knowing that something had happened to the girl. And from the looks of her fear tonight when looking at those woods, I would be close to guessing it was abduction!

Of course, this thought was enough to render me of unsound mind, one that at that moment was incapable of thinking rationally. But I couldn't help it! Just the thought of something like that possibly happening to her, well it was enough for me to tear fucking England apart if the offender was still unfortunate to be alive! For I could vow if this was the case, then it most definitely wouldn't be a soul left untouched for long, not before I allowed my demon to get his hands on him!

"Try to calm, Dom and tell us what happened," Vincent asked making me growl, but at least that was all I did, for his presence did manage to calm me somewhat.

"I just witnessed my girl utterly terrified that her past was coming back to haunt her. A past I know not one fucking thing about because I don't yet have her Gods be damned name!" I told them both, making them grant each other a look.

"I want to be informed the moment it is time for her to leave," I ordered making Sophia wisely nod once before telling me,

"I will tell Zagan to watch out for her." I nodded in what was the only thanks I could offer in that moment due to my unrelenting temper. Yet no matter how threatening and dangerous I must have looked to Sophia I was simply a big brother in need of comfort. Which was why she glided over to me and hugged me, before cupping a small hand to my cheek. Then she said,

"Have no fear brother, for we will soon know her and once we do, we will then kill all who have ever caused her harm." Then she rose up on heeled tiptoes so as to kiss my cheek before leaving the room and her sweet sentiments of murder behind her.

"She is right you know, I know it is frustrating, but we will know who she is soon enough," Vincent said once Sophia had left the room. I ran a hand through my hair, gripping the handful gathered at the base of my neck a moment longer.

"I fear I do not have the patience needed for this, Vince," I confessed making him smile sympathetically.

"When does anyone when matters of the heart are concerned, for we were not born into this world to then learn these types of emotions from our parents as mortals do. We have but only been gifted time into which to discover them as and when single moments occur. And well, as for love, it has never been an emotion that goes further beyond how we feel for each other. And as you can no doubt now surmise for yourself, that common knowledge would suggest that it is as far from the types of sentiments towards siblings as you could get." Vincent said and as usual making perfect sense. Which was why I deflated in my chair instead of destroying it as I had first wanted to when walking in here.

"Perhaps it is also the reason why Sophia is trying to speed up the process, being the only one of us who truly understands the concept and what it supposedly means to be in love," he added no doubt to trying to plant the diplomatic reasoning behind the next time Sophia planned to take matters into her own hands. Something I knew as well as he did would happen again.

But I understood his meaning, for she only wanted me to be as happy as she was when finding her soul mate. I remembered what she had been like before Zagan came along. Meaning I could very much believe in the power of love and what it had the ability to do when changing someone for the better.

"I know Vincent, I just wish that her demon wasn't laughing its ass off at me as it decides these things," I commented wryly, making my brother throw back his head and laugh.

"Yes, well I doubt there will ever be a chance of that, not when you're clearly her favourite brother to tease." I made a scoffed grunt which only ended up making him chuckle before he said,

"I will leave you to your thoughts."

Thoughts I wasn't sure I wanted to be left alone with, as for once my solitude didn't bring me as much comfort as it once had. But I needed to make a phone call, and I could only hope that it would bring a sweeter ending to my day.

"Tell me you have news," I said instead of any wasteful formalities when speaking with my chief officer.

"I may have a lead but needed to first inform you that it is one I will have to follow up personally," Ranka told me, and instead of asking what it could be, I simply said,

"Take one of the jets and leave as soon as you can."

"Thank you, My Lord."

"Keep me informed," was my only reply to this.

"But of course... and My Lord..."

"Yes, Ranka?" I said releasing a sigh that couldn't be helped as I rested my head in my hand, now propped up upon the desk.

"I believe it won't be long now," she told me just before I thanked her and hung up the call, hoping that she was right. For I feared that my patience was on death row with little time left.

Not long after this Zagan informed me that the girl had finished for the night after accepting the job. Jerry had informed that she had done well, which was no surprise there. For having witnessed her work ethic all night and discovering that it was one focused on hard work and keeping busy.

But in all honesty, she could have broken every glass in the club for all I cared, for she would have found herself with the job regardless.

I stood, buttoning up my suit jacket as I left my office, needing to see that she left here safely until I allowed myself the luxury of driving her home myself. I watched just as she left through the front doors but frowned as I saw a commotion happening with the last few customers of the night.

Now I care little for a fight, however, what I did care for was that Keira was now stood outside alone as the doormen had quickly rushed inside to provide their aid. I had a bad feeling in my gut, and I wondered if what had happened earlier was still lingering on my mind. I didn't want her to feel scared while waiting alone, so decided I was within my rights to leave my own club and just happen upon her standing there...right?

"Ragnar, you're with me," I ordered after motioning for my head of security to come over to me before we did something we rarely ever did and that was walk down the main staircase. Just the sight of us was enough to break up the fight, but I didn't want the sight of them being thrown from my club to interfere with this 'chance meeting' we were to have. So, one nod to my own security that stood guard at the bottom of each staircase was enough to get them to take charge.

Meanwhile, I ignored all the bewildered looks of shock sent my way and focused on just getting outside. And by the time I did, I once again wanted to commit murder for the second time that day!

I had just walked out the door to see a man grab her by the arm, which I very soon intended to break but before I could act, she did so herself by wrenching her arm free and actually squaring up to the large man.

"Listen tosser, I said no! And you ever touch me again it will be the last thing you ever do, as my boyfriend is on his way and will kick your dodgy, gormless ugly ass face!" she shouted with her hands on her hips and looking close to kicking him where it would hurt the most.

I swear my mouth would have dropped open should I not be faced with these two cretins that were itching to die. It wasn't just from the strange choice of her words that had me shocked, as it was obvious that swearing and insulting people wasn't her forte.

But it was more from the total difference from how I had seen her earlier when too scared to move. As back then she had been terrified by the mere hint of danger, yet now it was here staring her in the face, and she looked ready to fight to the death because of it!

But the conundrum that was my Chosen One would have to wait until I had dispatched these two wasted vessels. So, I took a threatening step closer to Keira's back, with Ragnar doing the same and allowed my eyes to show the hint of the demon beneath. A sight that would have looked as though the pits of Hell were being projected from their depths.

I also looked to Ragnar and nodded, allowing him the unusual pleasure of scaring the shit out of a mortal. Something that he was able to achieve in the seconds it would have taken someone to click their fingers.

He was known as one of the Devourers, granted down to him the power from his Norse Gods, and would have only been described as what a mortal would claim to be a real-life monster. But for the moment, they would no doubt simply try and grasp the meaning for their moment of madness. As now they would see a face without skin and fleshless bone covered in small holes. Holes made from when Ragnar received his punishment from his enemies and was literally bitten to death in a pit of snakes. A poison that seeped deeper into his flesh and carried over into his new life as one of my demons.

For even demons had scars.

They would also see the hint of demonic lips patched together with hammered metal plates reaching up to his jawline. No nose to speak of, just two elongated holes where it had once been, and a pair of eyes lost to the endless looking shadows surrounding where they should have been. Only now two simple white dots staring down at two men who have just had their nightmares confirmed as real.

But two seconds was all that was needed for their eyes to widen in panic before quickly backing away.

"Okay, okay, we're sorry! We didn't mean anything by it...we don't want any trouble now," they mumbled, quickly regretting not only praying on a girl alone but no doubt their entire lives full of misdemeanours after witnessing what they just had...*Hell on Earth.*

"Yeah, yeah...no...no trouble, we're just leaving," the other agreed as they turned around and ran with more speed than they no doubt ever had before. I had been about to go after them when Keira's 'tough' voice brought me back to the reason I was here.

"Yeah! You'd better run!" she said rolling her shoulders and puffing out her chest as if proud of herself for single-handedly fending for herself and scaring off two of life's losers. Then she turned still watching them over her shoulder and therefore not looking where she was going. Meaning that my clumsy new waitress walked straight into me instead of making the dramatic badass exit she had obviously been planning on.

The moment she did, I felt her body bounce away from me, and she would have fallen had I not caught her. Then, as if my reactions were as natural as breathing, I instantly tightened my hold and pulled her a step closer to me. This meant that when she finally braved a look up at who had caught her, she did so by straining her neck back. I swear the cuteness of her next actions nearly had me lifting her fully into my arms and taking her back inside with me. As she now tried to blow the hair from her face because I currently had her arms locked to her sides from my hold on her.

Then, as I looked down at her and in turn, her up at me, suddenly everything else around us evaporated to someone else's memory, for I only had eyes for her. And I was happy to say it seemed as though she only had eyes for me.

By the Gods in Heaven, but it was almost as if I was connecting directly with her soul, for her eyes started to show me everything. All her emotion, all her feelings, her insecurities, it all played out there in those dark blue depths. It was like looking into the ocean and asking yourself of the world that was hidden beneath.

A world I simply wanted to immerse myself in and never leave.

But leave was exactly what I had to do for our moment was soon broken by the sound of my mistake. Two mortals that were now facing a reality of what they had just seen, a vision that hadn't just belonged to one but to both of them. It was time to eradicate their memories, but before that, there was no reason my old friend couldn't be granted some fun.

"See that they don't come back...*and make sure the one who touched her falls and breaks his hand,*" I ordered, adding this last part in Ragnar's mind so that Keira wouldn't hear of the violence, I wanted to be inflicted.

I was still frowning over Keira's smaller stature wishing that I could have been the one to act out my wishes but then I tensed my hands and what I found in them was more important right now than vengeance.

I watched as Ragnar walked away, making sure we were alone before I told her my thoughts, as I was still angry at the fact she was waiting out here alone, so that something like this could happen. So, before she could speak as she looked close to doing, I beat her to it.

"It is not wise standing alone in the dark." She didn't like this, but I liked her reaction to it even less for she tried to take a step back. My own reaction in return was one that couldn't be helped as my hold on her automatically tightened. For I was unwilling to let go on her terms but doing so only my own a moment later. She looked down and hugged an arm around her middle as if the memory of my touch still lingered, before finally speaking.

"Uhh...Okay, well thanks." This part she mumbled slightly before obviously deciding on another way of breaking what I imagined her to believe was an awkwardness between us. So, surprisingly for someone so shy, she tried for humour, telling me something new about her.

"I guess I needed to add a few inches to my threats eh?" she said getting to her tiptoes before rocking back a few times and now also looking me up and down as if to indicate the differences in our height.

I would have laughed and in fact, very nearly did. However, I couldn't help but remember her earlier threat to the men when speaking of a boyfriend. Which in turn made me hold back the growl that threatened and now seeing her humour as deflection of what could have been a serious and dangerous situation.

Of course, it also didn't help that now I was only seeing the boy I had discovered was named Jack as this 'boyfriend' she had been waiting for. Which was precisely why I ended up snapping at her,

"This is not a joke. If you have a boyfriend, then I suggest informing him of the dangers that can occur when leaving a beautiful girl waiting alone at night." Hearing the way her breath hitched instantly made me feel guilty for being so short with her. But then she made a strange sound as if she was struggling to breathe, making me raise an eyebrow in question down at her. This was when she granted me a verbal gift and a lot more than I had ever hoped for.

"Uhh... I would say that to him...but there is no him...boyfriend, I mean...just me," she informed me with a small smile and a slight shrug of her shoulders. I then wished in that moment I had the time to think of what to say to her in return.

Like how I wanted to tell her that I was glad to hear it and hoped it stayed that way until I was ready, being no longer a danger to her. How I just needed the time to subdue my demon and make him understand what having her in our life meant. How I needed to go slow.

How my demon and I needed to be gentle and above all, how we didn't want to frighten her. But I didn't get a chance to say anything other than two words, as I saw headlights pulling up through the tunnel of trees.

"Your ride?" She turned to see for herself and nodded, but before she could look back at me, I stepped closer to her and whispered my command in her ear, letting my lips linger against her skin for a moment longer.

"Don't let this happen again, Keira." Her body froze as she sucked in a deep breath but before she could answer I was gone with the start of her promise made still lingering in the air. I then watched as she got in the car and still turning as if looking for me. A reaction that made me grin to myself from the shadows that concealed me.

It was only when her brother-in-law's car went out of sight that I finally came out of the darkness, meeting my chief of security as he joined me where I stood.

"I trust you were successful?" Ragnar nodded once and informed me,

"Both men soiled themselves and one with broken bones called out for his mother."

This time when I grinned...

It was all demon.

DRAVEN

21

FINDING THE SWEET

Giving in to my impulses by going to her room at night was starting to become the sole focus of my days and the hours leading up to when I knew she would be asleep. And I knew that by doing so I was also neglecting my duties as King. But the way I looked upon it, was that I had dedicated and devoted my whole existence to my kingdom and keeping the balance for the Gods. Well now, it was my turn.

And my time was now my own.

Which was why I soon found myself outside her window, only this time what I saw was the last thing I had ever been expecting! For there she was, all relaxed in bed and with our brief exchange obviously still playing on her mind. Or at least this was what I hoped for as I watched her hand wander down under the covers.

My girl was obviously sexually frustrated.

Once there I saw her inhale sharply the second her fingers made contact with her intimate self and the constant rubbing of that tight bundle of nerves made her body quiver as her fantasy took hold. I knew that I couldn't allow such an act to continue without being a part of it. So, I tried once more to take hold of her mind, finding that there was a new emotion to add to the list of ones that made it easier to gain access.

And one I was more than happy to exploit this time, for any sexual gratification was to be gifted by me and no other, which included herself.

Meaning that if I couldn't touch her myself, then whichever fantasy she had planned, I decided to make it one of my own, unknowingly giving her a taste of what it would be like with me. But I confess, that at first I was curious. Which is why I decided to see how the start of her sexual story played out, after first slipping into her room. Doing so only when I was confident I had a complete hold on her mind.

I found myself sitting down on the bed next to her and twisting to the side so that I could watch her as she moaned slightly in this dream-like state I had put her in. But then I closed my eyes and opened the door to her fantasy image. And to my surprise found myself doing so at my own club. I looked down at myself to see that I was wearing the same suit I had been wearing the night I had entered the club with my entourage behind me. But this time there was to be no council at my back or a sea of people parting at just the sight of me.

I wondered at this and smirked to myself as it was obvious what she wanted to see...*she wanted me to work for it.* The little vixen was playing with the Devil, that much was clear, and I don't know who was enjoying it more, her or me.

In the end, I gave her what she wanted, knowing now where I would find her. Well, she had better be alone in that booth for if I saw that boy there with her, then this little fantasy of hers would start with blood being shed. And I very much doubted that was what she had envisioned!

But then the second I saw her all other deadly, jealous thoughts fled me, as I swear the sight she had created was one right out of my own dreams, not hers. By the Gods! I even nearly stumbled back a step when trying to push past one of the customers and finding their strength with the upper hand. For I was stuck incapable of moving a full minute at just the sight of her.

She was currently sat at the booth and thankfully alone. But this time she no longer hid that delectable little body under layers of cotton and denim. No, now it was a barely-there whisper of black silk that clung to her pale skin, one that now made it look as though she had been dipped in ink.

Her hair was loose and flowing down around her in stunning golden waves. It looked thick and luscious as it now shimmered under the club's travelling lights. Smokey makeup made her eyes more exotic and sinful, along with lips painted red... lips I wanted to see gasping for air as I stripped her bare and kissed a trail down to her core, one she currently kept busy with her fingers.

This time I shed myself of the shock that kept me powerless to move in favour of getting to her quicker. Now I simply pushed past the faceless crowd that were quickly becoming shadows in this dream. Just the bodies needed to recreate that night and start rewriting something new...*something sweeter.*

I saw the way she watched me and bit her lip at the sight of me cutting through the mass of people, making my intent clear. I swear by the time I finally got to her, I must have looked like a wild man teetering on the edge of madness! Which was why this time there would be no more caution. She wanted to see the real me, well then, I would give her that...*I would give her this piece of me.* And I did this by grabbing her hand and hauling her hard against my chest before locking her there by wrapping an arm around her upper body.

I looked down at her as she gasped and no matter how her makeup suggested otherwise, along with her seductive dress, she couldn't mask the innocence in those eyes now staring back up at me. Those questioning eyes that asked me a million questions yet were too afraid to word even one. Eyes that told me so much, yet at the same time told me nothing...eyes I never wanted to leave me.

And ones that widened the moment I started to test her. I let my hand travel slowly up her side, taking care to brush purposely against the side of her breast, smiling the moment her lips parted, and a moan of pleasure slipped through. But I didn't stop there, for I continued until giving my demon what he needed, this time collaring her throat.

It was a possessive action, as much as it was one of claiming. It was a way for us to feel the life we own beating beneath our hand. It brought us comfort, and for the first time since meeting our Electus, my demon relaxed, fighting me for control no longer.

But I myself was quickly getting lost in her beauty, and my gaze must have been one she found too much to bear, for she closed her eyes, shutting the intensity of it all from sight. Something I wouldn't allow for long. For now, was to be her first lesson in what it meant to be with a man such as I. So, I released a slither of my demon, growling before issuing my first demand upon her,

"Look at me!" I ordered, at the same time burying a fist in her hair so as I could control her movements and get her to look back at me. I know my actions didn't hurt, for that wasn't ever my intention. Not unless it was to be a bite pain delivered with the sweetest of pleasures and one I hoped to get her addicted too soon...*one day very soon.*

It worked, as her eyes widened, no doubt taking in the purple flame I could feel burning in my own eyes. And I knew in this single moment, that like this, having her in my arms and about to make her mine, that I would never be able to fully hide from her what I truly was. Not all the control combined from Heaven and Hell could have prevented such a thing. Telling me now that when the day finally came to claim her, then to do so she would first have to have seen my true self, my true nature. First, I would have to be assured that she wouldn't run from it. For it was that or simply tying her to my bed until I could prove to her that I meant her no harm but only endless hours of pleasure.

Which was why I issued her with her first warning by lowering my head, commanding her space and telling her,

"You *never* hide from me." I found myself growling the single word of 'never' and making her shudder in my arms. However, I knew this was not from fear, for I could smell the musk of her arousal flooding my senses and near making me wild enough to taste it. But first I needed to hear her compliance...*my demon needed it!*

"Say it!" I demanded more forcefully when she hesitated. It was given to her as a slight warning, allowing her to see that it wasn't wise to keep a demon on the edge waiting, even if she wasn't fully aware of such yet. I strengthened my grip, once again being mindful not to cause pain but just enough to get her attention.

"I..." she mumbled softly, and I felt my restraint was on a knife-edge.

"Say it. Now!" I commanded sternly, knowing this was what we both needed. I had to have her submit to me, and she had to understand that by doing so I was in fact, giving her the power over me. It was the only way our relationship would ever work. For if she gave herself to me the way I needed, the way I craved...if she let me rule over her, then I would, in fact, be her slave.

I waited for her mind to play out the depth of what it was I was really asking for, making me wonder if she had any idea the magnitude of the words she would next say. The weight they would hold...the promise in which they would immortalise and brand on my soul.

Which is when she unknowingly gave me her own forever,

"I will never hide from you." She whispered, and my reaction was an audible breath leaving me before my actions could speak far louder than any promise I made in return. I took her face in my hands and tipped it to one side so as I could then grant her our first kiss. But before I ruled her lips, I first felt compelled to gift her with the praise she deserved, for she had pleased me more than she could ever have known.

"Good girl," I told her before then crushing my lips to hers letting go of her face so that I could lock her in my arms. She gasped, and I took my opportunity in slipping my tongue inside and in doing so, getting my first taste. Now asking myself if it would be the same when I was finally able to do this in the realms of reality. For it felt incredible, and unlike anything, I had ever experienced before. It felt as though she was connected to my soul and sparking to life something deeper within me, speaking to every nerve ending this vessel of mine possessed.

However, I wasn't the only one affected, for soon I could feel herself building up as the orgasm was about to tear through her own senses, and it was all just from the image of a kiss shared in her mind. One that was yet to be real enough to remember against our skin, which was when I decided that no, this wasn't enough. I wanted her to remember the feel of my lips to hers, not as a fantasy but as something she could actually feel.

A lasting memory only one of us would understand.

So, I opened my eyes and twisted my body before placing a hand down by her side. Then I leant down just before she was on the verge of erupting for me and placed my lips gently against hers, finally making a moment of it my reality.

The second my lips made contact, she screamed out my name against me as her body convulsed when her release tore through her.

"Draven!" and I could no longer help but whisper back over lips I wanted to own and claim every day for the rest of my eternal life.

"Keira." The second I said her name I knew that I was breaking the spell I had cast and doing so the very moment I said it. But I no longer cared, for I couldn't let that moment go by without giving her a piece of myself...a piece of my own vulnerability.

And then I was gone.

Now letting the darkness slip in place of my body. She sat up suddenly as if in hopes of catching me still there. I then watched from the window opposite, veiling myself, as she touched her lips, now tender from both the dream and the imprint I had left there.

"It couldn't be," she whispered to herself, making me smile and with one parting last look at her, now combined with the feel of her own lips imprinted on mine.

And with the lasting taste of her in my memory, I was finally granted the conclusion to the day that I had hoped for...

I found my sweet ending.

22

Friends & Drunks

The rest of the week came and went without any more incidents. I had worked three more nights at the club and was getting the hang of it. I was now at the stage where I could serve behind the bar. Mike had become my little protector for the week. Bailing me out when I got the complicated fancy card machine wrong, sticking up for me when customers were rude and most importantly taking out the trash. This I was most grateful for.

I tried to ask about the Dravens, as my curiosity got too much for me one night, but everyone was always so vague. No-one would reveal any useful information about them. It was always the same story, as though rehearsed.

There were two brothers and a sister. The head of the family was the older brother Dominic Draven. I wasn't sure if I had seen the other brother. When they first arrived there were only men, so I knew I hadn't yet seen the sister. Dominic, I had seen twice in the flesh and the rest in my dreams, but that had been enough to start my obsession.

My thoughts always seemed to be about him. I didn't really understand why. It was as if he had a power over me that just wouldn't fade. There were the obvious reasons, of course. Like he was the most remarkable human being I had ever seen. He was stunning like a transcendental Godlike creature making him completely heavenly. But on the darker side, he looked intensely strong, almost invincible, as if he could have been a Spartan or Trojan in a past life...even dressed in Armani.

I found my eyes wandering up towards the first floor more times than I could count but then my head would look away quickly before I got there. My cheeks would flush just thinking about him and when I had been waiting for Frank. Thinking about the way he'd looked at me that night, with those consuming eyes piercing through me, ablaze with fiery passion, devout and excruciating.

I had to convince myself on a daily basis it was nothing, just to function. My daydreams about him were getting ridiculous and were ever constant. Being at work was the worst and also the best. That was when I felt it most, like a magnetic pull drawing me towards him. But it was my embarrassment that kept me rained in and stopped me from looking.

I was the only one with this restraint however, as everyone else in the club seemed to stare in his direction. Of course, you couldn't really see him, just shadows of people up there. But no one ever went up or down the staircase. And considering there were always people up there I had to wonder where they all went, did they stay there? Like some luxury 5-star hotel? Well if that was the case, then Hell, where did I check in!

In fact, the only time I had ever seen anyone walk those steps was with Draven himself a week ago. It was all very strange especially when not one person seemed to know anything about them, yet they had been coming here for years and owned half of the town. It was as if the whole of Evergreen was part of some weird conspiracy with the Dravens at the head of it all. And needless to say, I was the little outsider in this X files episode.

Getting back to reality I grabbed some clothes before I was late for 'Fresher's day' at my new college. With something black and grey in my hand I put it over my head not really knowing what it was, but it had sleeves, which was all that mattered.

It was joined by a pair of faded jeans, which had seen better days. They were a bit too long for me, so they were badly ripped around the bottom. Every now and again I would have to pull a bit off as they got caught around my trainers or 'sneakers' as they were called here, which was funny 'cause you never really got much chance for sneaking in everyday life.

"You ready because I think RJ is here?" Libby shouted from at the bottom of the stairs. I had found her in the kitchen at an ungodly hour trying to make me a full English breakfast. Of course, it looked like it had been cooked with Plutonium. I had eaten as much as I could with my teeth screaming in pain as I crunched my way through what could have been lava rock. Pity we didn't have a dog, having said that, I don't think even a dog could have digested this and animal rescue would have been on our case.

"Yeah, I'll be there in a minute." I grabbed my bag, putting the strap around my head and my jacket on top. I didn't need gloves today as the sleeves I wore had a thumb hole. I ran down the stairs and slipped on the step, landing on my already bruised bottom.

"Ouch!" I complained.

"You okay?" Libby shouted up and I grumbled out my reply,

"Yes." It didn't venture a guess that it was going to be one of those days.

It took what seemed like an age to get away from Libby doing the whole mothering thing.

"I have done this before Libs, it will be fine. I'm not going off to war." I gave a little salute and made for the door. Poor RJ had been waiting for so long she had cut the engine.

"Sorry about that, my sister can be a little...neurotic at times." I gave her an apologetic smile, but she didn't seem fazed, just as happy as always. Extremely happy, in fact she couldn't keep still.

"So, come on tell me everything, and don't leave a thing out, even if it seems insignificant I still want to know." She clapped her hands and started the engine. She had a comical little car that sounded angry as she pulled forward. It looked like an old VW but the badge had fallen off the front, so I couldn't tell.

The conversation about the nightclub had continued all the way to the college and she hadn't been joking about the small details. So, by the time we got there RJ had been filled in on all the details...well, all except one. I never mentioned about Draven in the carpark. No, that one I wanted to keep for myself. It was as if it was sacred to me.

"We will never get a space nearer to the campus, plus Jack said he would meet us here." She gave me a wink which I ignored. 'Here' was a car park surrounded by trees that were turning different shades of reds and oranges. It was a little further away from the main campus, which was fine with me as it had finally stopped raining.

In fact, the sun had come out from behind its clouds transforming the once dreary day into a utopia of sun bursting colour. It made me want to pick up a paint brush for the first time in a long while. I shuddered at the thought.

I grabbed my bag from the back seat as RJ did the same. I slammed the door too hard and little flecks of rust started to snow from the door. Oops!

"Sorry about that," I said with a sheepish grin.

"Oh, its fine, I get a shiny new one when I graduate, but to be honest I don't think it will last till then, so you go ahead and bang it all you want!" We both started laughing and didn't notice when Jack had come up behind us.

"What's so funny? What did I miss?" He instinctively came towards me, grabbing my canvas bag off my shoulder and giving me a wink. RJ didn't miss it and put her finger in her mouth, accompanying it with a gagging noise.

"What about my bag?" RJ demanded as she flicked Jack on the ear. He winced and dodged her punch on the arm that followed.

"You're fine with your own bag. You have a strong sturdy back, like a camel." He patted her on the back, which sounded more like a slap. They were a typical brother and sister. Full of banter and fooling around but deep down at heart you could tell they adored each other.

We all walked towards the campus, which looked more like a town of its own. There were huge red brick buildings all situated in their own little woodland, matching the colour of the trees that surrounded them.

RJ and Jack were obviously used to the place, as they didn't look half as impressed as I did. I didn't say a word all the way to the main building. I just stared wide-eyed at my beautiful surroundings, thrilled I would be seeing them daily. It was like something from a movie. It looked far too posh to be a college, well ok maybe Oxford or Cambridge I could understand but here? No wonder my parents hadn't wanted to disclose the amount they must have coughed up. A small fortune!

I had tried to contribute, having saved up a small amount during the summer and I also had my inheritance. My Grandfather had left us all a substantial amount of money when he passed away. I was too young to understand at the time, as he passed away when I was only two years old. My amount was still gathering dust in the form of interest in a savings account and I still hadn't touched it, even though it was legally mine once I'd turned eighteen.

My father's father had been a kind man who had a number of businesses in Liverpool. He had only one son, my father, who he brought up on his own after his wife had died during childbirth. His father adored him, telling him daily how he reminded him of his mother. They were very close but due to hard times my Grandfather spent most of his time working and building up his small empire. He therefore enlisted the help of his sister Olivia, whom my sister was so proudly named after.

She was a widow and childless and as a result, a very lonely and depressed woman. After a series of failed suicide attempts she finally found happiness being a surrogate mother to my dad. She also adored him and spent the rest of her days tending to his every need. They were inseparable, like two peas in a pod as my dad had described. So, when she had died it had been like losing a mother all over again, only this time one that he knew.

My Grandfather, however, had sold his businesses for a small fortune, knowing that my dad wasn't really interested in running them. He then retired and moved abroad living out the rest of his days in the sunshine. My father hadn't realised how much money he had saved over the years until the reading of the Will. Of course, it had all gone to my dad as there was no other family left. My mother had told me that he'd nearly had a heart attack when he found out the amount.

He split it three ways, putting mine and Libby's into a savings account. My parents bought a bigger house with their share, where they still lived today. And the house my Grandfather had in Spain they kept as a holiday home.

Libby had already used some of her money emigrating here and remodelling the house Frank had inherited. Our parents had paid for their wedding, being only too eager to get her hitched and "on her way" as my dad had joked. He also told Frank there were no refunds available, in other words 'Best of luck and no bringing her back!' We had all laughed at this part of my father's speech at the wedding.

"Earth to Kaz, is anyone reading me?" What, oh RJ was staring at me with a confused look in her eyes. I had been daydreaming again.

"Sorry, I was in my own little world, this place is amazing." She shrugged as if she was used to eating breakfast at the Taj Mahal.

We walked up the mass of steps towards the main building which was swarming with students. There were tables everywhere topped with banners all advertising different clubs and sororities. People buzzed around like clones in matching t-shirts and sweaters. There were so many people shouting, all the voices seemed to merge into one. The odd "Try out" and "Wildcats" could be separated from the rest.

Not surprisingly no-one flagged us down, as one look at RJ sporting her usual Gothic attire and they quickly looked away. I grinned to myself realizing what a perfect match we were. She dressed this way to be noticed and to stand out. I did the complete opposite, shying away from any form of attention. What was funny, however, was that we both did each other a favour. I didn't draw any attention away from her and she was scary enough that she didn't bring any attention my way. Granted, it was more in my favour than hers, but I was still happy about it.

Now Jack, however, was a different story. He stood out from the crowd and for all the right reasons. With every step his long legs took he was admired... or envied. Girls winked and giggled in silly girl fashion and guys nodded in respect, some even used coded hand gestures which were all foreign to me.

He was extremely popular, but he had been here for two years. He also seemed perfectly at ease showing us around despite the funny looks RJ was getting. I suppose he was used to it with RJ being a heavy Goth, but it didn't stop him introducing us to his friends when they stopped him. He even put his arm around my shoulders in a playful manner when introducing me to a group of them. I received plenty of evil looks from the girls but wicked smiles from the boys.

I couldn't quite understand it. It was as if he was proud, but I was at a loss to know why. I must have looked even plainer and boring compared to the living billboard model that stood next to me. My cheeks would flame every time he introduced me while RJ just nodded looking bored. She played ice queen very well... I, on the other hand, was not so down with the cool, calm and collected act.

The rest of the day was filled with tours of the campus, a lot of which I didn't need to go on as I wasn't living there and little lectures of groups we might join. Also subjects we were taking and charity events etc.... but by the end of the day I felt mentally exhausted.

Jack decided we needed a drink after such a hectic day, so we all went to a local bar near the campus. We met up with Drew and Lanie and it soon became apparent things had progressed between them as they were more than a little friendly with each other.

We all walked the short distance to the bar and 'Willy's One Eyed Joe' was no Club Afterlife that was for sure, in other words, it was a complete dive. We all walked through the decrepit doors to find the inside very much like the outside...dilapidated. It was in desperate need of a makeover...Hell the place needed re-building!

The walls looked as though they were melting, with a mixture of paint and paper that was trying desperately to get to the floor. There was a strong smell of disinfectant in the air and I looked down to see the tiles had also seen better days. With patches of broken and new that didn't match the originals, in fact nothing matched in the whole place. Chairs and tables were all odd and scruffy, making me wonder if they had ever been new.

We sat at one of the big booths in the corner and it creaked in pain as we all sat down. I noticed I was the only one who didn't look completely at ease. The rest looked very relaxed and used to this place, seeming oblivious to the state that surrounded them.

"Joe... hey Joe!" Jack shouted towards the bar, which had also seen better days. A big fat man with a jolly looking face turned in surprise. There were only two other people in the whole place and they were sat at the bar. Must be regulars I thought. I could spot them a mile away.

"Oh, hey guys." The guy looked more like a Father Christmas look alike than a jolly owner of this place. He came over and met Jack halfway.

"Hey Joe...uh, how's business?" I almost choked. Was that a joke? But Jolly Joe just smiled and replied shaking his hand.

"Not too bad, could be better though. The bikers rally is passing through next week, which always brings business in." Jack nodded his head looking as if he didn't quite know what else to say.

"Say how's your ma?" The conversation turned a different course about family and other stuff I didn't quite catch.

"Yo Joe, could we get a round in, I'm spitting feathers here!" I had to hand it to RJ, she sure had a way with words. Joe waved in acknowledgement and walked back behind the bar. Jack resumed his place next to me and got cosy. We all started chatting about college stuff when I couldn't help noticing one of the guys staring at us all from the bar. Actually no, he wasn't staring at us all he was just staring at Jack. I frowned finding this odd and when Jack noticed he too followed my gaze. He found the guy scowling at him, so Jack just shrugged his shoulders and put his back to the guy.

"Didn't I tell you that this place had it all... *even crazy drunks."* He winked at me putting his arm around my shoulders and giving me a squeeze. I laughed but it didn't sound right as the guy's intense stare was creeping me out. He looked like he wanted to rip Jack's arm off and beat the crap out of him with it.

"Yeah I know but seriously that guy is acting like you scratched his car or something." Jack smiled down at me and then raised his hand to push back a stray bit of hair behind my ear and I tried not to flinch so as not to offend him.

"Don't worry your pretty little head over it, that guy doesn't know me."

"BARTENDER! Another drink!" The drunk shouted startling us all as he pounded his fist on the bar.

"Ahh!" Jack shouted standing up as his drink tipped all over him, soaking his pants.

"Way to go Bro, real smooth now you look like you've wet yourself!" RJ said giggling to herself and Jack sent a fake angry scowl her way and then gave her the bird saying,

"Bite me!" Jack said over his shoulder as he walked to the rest room. I felt bad for him as I didn't even see him move so had no clue how it even happened. But I guess my attention, like us all, had been on the aggressive behaviour coming from the drunk.

"Alright Billy, keep your hair on, geez...what's with you today man?" Joe said coming to refill the guy's pint and the one called Billy, just shook his head as though just waking up from a dream.

"What?! What'd I do?" He asked as though the last ten minutes hadn't happened. Looking at him now he looked completely different. I would even go as far to say he was dopey looking with no aggression whatsoever.

RJ got from her side of the booth and came to sit closer to me, taking Jack's seat.

"He's got it bad for you Kazzy girl." She said nudging me talking about her brother. I bit my lip as I didn't want to be having this conversation. It was strange, like I needed to be cautious for some reason. I looked towards the bar once more and saw Billy still shaking his head as if he didn't know what had happened. But it was no longer Billy that took my interest, no now it was the other guy who seemed fixated on me and RJ. It was almost as if he could hear what we were saying. He saw me looking and met my gaze head on then something flashed in his eyes; a purple glimmer that must have been a trick of light.

"So?" RJ said nudging me and breaking the connection.

"So?"

"Yeah so, as in, sooo are you interested?" This was a tough question to answer so when the mobile phone I borrowed from Libby started singing Abba, I sent up a prayer of thankyous. I answered it before it could ring off getting Jerry on the other end asking me if I could work tonight.

"Yeah, no problem I just have to see if I can get a lift in with my sister or…"

"No, no, that won't be a problem. I have already sent a car for you. It's on its way and will be out front soon." I frowned as he hung up, so I didn't have time to question anything.

For starters, how did he know I was going to say yes?
But the biggest question of all…

How did he know where I was?

DRAVEN

23

BROKEN GLASS

"Don't you find it odd?" Sophia asked stepping closer to where I was stood, currently watching Keira's third night working below.

"What?" I asked wishing I could get back to my private thoughts.

"The way she refers to you as Draven." I had wondered at this myself, but then I told Sophia the same thing I had deduced from it.

"She doesn't know me as anything else...I am not yet Dominic to her, and I suppose referring to me as 'Mr' Draven in her own thoughts isn't personal enough."

"Does it bother you?" she asked, and I finally turned around now that Keira had gone out of sight into the back room, no doubt to gather more stock.

"Yes and no." Sophia laughed once and said,

"Vague as ever." Making me raise a brow at her before giving in and telling her,

"It bothers me that she doesn't yet know me well enough to speak my chosen name, but then I find myself satisfied, for she is the only one to refer to me by just Draven. A name that now feels strangely like hers, as if the name belongs solely to her to speak it as she wishes," I told her making her smirk as though she knew something I didn't. But like myself, she refused to divulge further. Instead, she simply nodded, murmured an ambiguous,

"I see," then moved away to join the others at our table, now leaving me alone once more to my thoughts. I saw Keira coming from the back room carrying a crate of bottles and frowned. I hated seeing her working just as much as I enjoyed it. A reason why I had ordered that from now on the one named Mike was to take out the rubbish and if not him, then Jerry, for I would not have a repeat of what had happened on her first night working here. But then, as I watched her carrying her heavy load, I wondered if I could get away with taking that duty from her also.

Which sparked the beginning of my dilemma, for like I said, I hated seeing her working just as much as I enjoyed this hidden time she was unknowingly gifting me. For just having this job had now enabled me to watch her for the last three nights without being forced to do so when she was sleeping. Which also meant that in that time I had also learnt a great deal about her personality.

Of course, I was still frustratingly in the dark about her past, but this was something Ranka assured me wouldn't be for much longer.

But what I did manage to discover was that Keira was a kind, thoughtful and warm person that people seemed to gravitate towards. She was always polite and greeted people as if they had been friends for years, even when they were simply asking her for a drink to purchase.

She was also a hard worker, for when there was no one to serve she wouldn't just stand around chatting and waiting for the bar to fill up. She would make herself busy, and she would do this by going out to the floor with an empty basket and collect empties. Or she would grab a cloth and wipe down the sides or like she was doing now, restocking up the bottles and potentially saving a job for the end of the night.

But the side of her that surprised me the most was discovering how funny she was. She was quick-witted one moment and silly the next. She didn't mind laughing at herself and did so freely when seeing what I already suspected was a clumsy side. It even made me wonder how many self-inflicted bruises she had concealed under her casual attire. Quite a few I could imagine seeing as tonight alone I had seen her walk into the corner of a table, hitting her hip hard enough to see her rubbing it and mouthing the word 'oww' as she walked away. Then there was when she caught a finger in the glass cleaner, shutting it on herself accidentally.

The night before she had bumped her head on the lip of the bar top when rising too quickly from retrieving the change that had slipped out of her hand, before making it back to the customer. I swear I was either clenching my fist in frustration from not being able to help her myself or shaking my head in exasperation at her antics. She was a liability to herself that I was sure of.

But my favourite part about the nights were the times she would give in to her impulse and look up to the VIP as if hoping to see a glimpse of my world. Was she looking for me when she did this? It was in these moments that I wished I could have given in to my own impulse. To wait until the end of her shift before approaching her and asking if she would like to join me for a drink. Then I would take her hand in mine, smirking when seeing that nervous little lip bite of hers. One she often did when looking up here, and then I would welcome her into my life.

But each night I simply let her go, watching from the balcony until she was safely in a car and heading back to a place I didn't want her to call home. For this was her home, *her Afterlife*. She just didn't know it yet, but she would. When the time was right.

Which unfortunately wasn't tonight, so I prepared myself the same as I did every night that I was forced to watch her leave. However, this time was slightly different, for the moment the bar went quiet she didn't pick up a cloth this time. Nor did she leave the bar to pick up empties. No, she decided to engage in conversation with Mike and my curiosity got the better of me.

I could have heard their conversation from up here, but with the music and other people still lingering on until last order was called, I decided it was easier to take hold of one of the vessels that was drinking at the bar with friends.

"So, I know you probably get this a lot, but I was just kind of wondering, you know…" Keira said before nodding up to the VIP and looking slightly red-faced as if embarrassed to be asking. But then I guess I wasn't the only one whose curiosity was getting the better of them. It was comforting to know.

"Oh, well, to be honest, there isn't much to tell, at least not for a mere mortal like me," Mike replied making me suddenly break the glass in the hand of the vessel I was currently using. This made his friends respond by laughing, and I played my part the best I could. But then I turned and accepted a cloth given to me by Keira who was smiling at me sweetly.

"Did that drink have a bite to it?" she asked with a smirk, and for a moment I couldn't respond, struck dumb and glad that when it happened, I was in someone else's form. In the end, I simply nodded making her smile again before she started to pick up the pieces of broken glass.

"Here, allow me…I don't want you cutting yourself." I said taking the piece from her hand with care and hearing it being said in a voice that wasn't my own.

"Thanks, but I've got…"

"I insist." I interrupted quickly, nodding to Mike and asking,

"Bin." He smirked as if he knew what I was doing, and half expected me to follow up this conversation by asking her out. But instead of commenting he simply handed me a small bin they usually used for broken glass. I then made swift work of picking up the mess I had made, healing the small slices I had inflicted on the vessel before it was given a chance to bleed.

I heard the jeers behind me from his friends now calling him Casanova, but I purposely ignored them.

"Do you need a replacement?" she asked me once I was done and handing her the bin back. I shook my head thinking it was probably safer not to have something breakable in my hand when she was near, as she had a habit of igniting that type of reaction from me.

"Okie dokie." she said comically, making me question what those two words together meant. I then tried not to make it too obvious as she rejoined Mike before I had interrupted their conversation abruptly.

"But like I said, there isn't much people really know about them," Mike continued.

"But how is that possible? I mean they come here every year, don't they?" Keira asked making me realise that my little blonde waitress had learned a few things of her own.

"They do, and they also spend a shit load of money on this town, which is why it pisses me off when you hear anyone bitchin' about them...you know, the older folks who don't want to admit how much they did for our once dying town," Mike told her making me suddenly feel like giving the boy an increase in his wages. For he was correct in saying that one of the reasons we had chosen this town was not only for its direct connection to one of the biggest portals into Heaven and Hell but also because it was, in fact, a dying town.

There was no business able to keep their doors open thanks to the lack of passing trade. The mining that had once lead to the town being built in the first place had long since become obsolete. Which meant there were no jobs, so the next generation had no choice but to relocate to Portland. Therefore, leaving this small town with nothing left to offer the world...until there was us.

We had the college built, which brought the young back to the area and the club brought back tourists. Which in turn meant any hikers that came started to take notice of the surrounding beauty and thus giving the town yet another avenue to exploit, one never before taken advantage of.

Suddenly life seemed to bloom as jobs were created, helped by the modest little shopping mall that opened and just so happened to have a silent investor who signed the bill. Meaning that we owned even more of this town than the town knew about. But year by year buildings were restored or rebuilt, and our thanks for such charity…? Distain from those that should have known better, for the elders were the ones that should have remembered their once dying town's history. A distrust fueled even more from the young, outrageous gossip that happily, only ended up filling my club every night.

Now that was what I called a balance.

"But then it doesn't help when they are only ever seen the once and never allow any of us 'townsfolk' up there," he added nodding to the VIP.

"You mean you have never been up there before?" she asked, clearly shocked.

"Nope, what Gary told you that night was right, no one is allowed up there, which includes us lot down here. One girl who used to work here simply walked up a few steps at the end of one of her shifts and got fired on the spot and escorted to her car." Keira looked totally stunned at hearing this and swallowed hard while glancing at the staircase as if seeing it play out for herself.

Don't worry sweetheart, that wouldn't happen to you, I thought, wishing I could have said the actual words, for now, she actually looked scared.

"But hey, I am not knocking it, as it's a good job and the best pay around. We get paid holidays, sick days and all the benefits, like health care. So, you know what, if they don't want me going up there and I get to keep this job, then that's fine with me," he said, no doubt giving her a friendly heads up. One that she didn't need, for I had no intention of letting her go, no matter what it was deemed she had done wrong while working this job.

But this obviously gave her enough to think about, and because of it, I now hated how dejected she looked. After this, their conversation ended and with it my need to stay in this vessel any longer. Besides, his friends were starting to make it more obvious that I was not participating in their conversation. So, I left, returning back to my own slice of the world, one that she would now deem totally untouchable.

So, it wasn't surprising then when the time came for her to leave, it was the first time she never glanced back up this way, and I felt it like a stone-cold kick to my chest. And, as if trying to keep hold of the sweet she had given me, it was the reason I took out my phone and yet again found myself asking Google…

'What does Okie Dokie mean?'

So here I was, with this obsession spiraling out of control, for I was to spend my time playing a new game, one I would have named 'stalker dominos'. A game primary played when she attended her first day at college and what I knew would be all days after. But by doing so meant that I could follow my Chosen One around by jumping from one vessel to another, thus keeping a close watch on her. And in doing so, I quickly gathered that this day was more of an 'introduction' for she didn't actually attend any lessons.

This would have been fine if it hadn't meant I was forced to watch the cretin named Jack act as though he had some sort of claim to what was mine. At one point, I had even pushed passed him, using my shoulder and wishing I had chosen a bigger vessel before doing so, as then it might have taken him off his feet!

At the very least in all of this, I had been granted a small mercy, as Keira had been nothing but polite...meaning that had been all she had been to the boy. She showed no interest other than that of friendship, even if the boy obviously needed a swift kick in the head to see it for himself.

But I could tell. There wasn't nearly half as much lip biting or blushes like she would grant me. There also wasn't an elevated heart rate whenever he would purposely make contact with her, something I was close to strangling him for by the end of the day.

But then I watched as a group of them all met up and made their way to a bar nearby. A place I growled at, knowing first-hand the reputation it had and the degenerates that were known to go there. Besides, the place looked one bad storm away from crumbling to the ground, and the name said it all, 'Willy's One-Eyed Joe'. I doubted an innocent like Keira realised that the owner had named the place after his own cock!

But no matter how amusing the locals found him, I didn't want my girl anywhere near this shithole he owned or anywhere near the asshole who had brought her here for that matter!

So, I left my vessel, no doubt dazed and also wondering what he was doing outside this biker's cesspool before scurrying off to whatever life's daily chore I had stolen him from. Then finding myself sitting in my office back at Afterlife once more, I quickly made a call.

"Mr Draven sir, what can I do for you?"

"I want the new girl in tonight," I told him cutting straight to the point, so that I could get back there.

"Oh...okay, well I could call and see if she can do it, but then if not I know Mike is always looking for more shifts, so I..."

"No. I want Keira. Call her now and inform her that we are sending a car to pick her up," I ordered and in a tone that left no argument, not that Jerry would even try.

"Of course. Yes, I will call her now, sir. I admit she is a very good employee," he added no doubt trying to discover the reasons for my insistence, but I didn't have time for that.

"She is indeed. Now ring her, Jerry." Then I hung up before quickly locating which vessel I wanted to take control of, for I could sense a number of humans in the bar. Not that there were many to choose from, which wasn't surprising considering the business was no more than a year or two from closing.

I located a vessel sat at the bar, one of only two to choose from but by the time I got there, I could see this Jack now sat next to Keira and getting far closer than I would have liked. I watched as they conversed about the day and all the while I was gritting my teeth and cursing Jerry for no doubt taking his time in finding her details so as to call her.

Strangely, I noticed it was Keira who spotted my intense gaze upon the two of them, doing so way before all the others. Was it possible that she could sense when I was near, even if it was a feeling she couldn't yet put her finger on? I had noticed her look at me a few times in my chosen vessels for the day, but then she had shaken away the feeling as if putting it down to paranoia.

Soon the boy wanted to know what had caught her attention and quickly found my deadly gaze directed his way. But instead of being concerned as he should have been, especially with me staring at him as if I wanted him dead, he simply shrugged his shoulders and said,

"Didn't I tell you that this place had it all... even crazy drunks." Then he winked at Keira and sealed his fate when he put an arm around her, giving her a squeeze. An arm I wanted to rip off and beat him unconscious with.

Damn it Jerry, fucking ring her!

"Yeah I know, but seriously that guy is acting like you scratched his car or something." I heard her say, now getting concerned for him and making me just want to rip off the other arm also and finish the job! Hell, fuck finishing the job with something as useless as his arms, I wanted to skewer him on the end of my blades the second he touched her face when brushing back a piece of her hair.

"Don't worry your pretty little head over it, that guy doesn't know me," he told her, and that was when I hit my limit. I pounded a fist on the bar, playing every bit the drunk and at the same time making sure the assholes drink knocked all over him, making it look as though he'd pissed his pants, something he would be sure to do if he ever encountered me alone!

"BARTENDER! Another drink!" I demanded just before I heard him cry out in shock making me grin down at my almost empty pint glass.

"Ahh!"

"Way to go, Bro, real smooth now you look like you've wet yourself!" The one with pink hair told him, making her a welcomed friend for Keira in my view.

"Bite me!" was his reply before disappearing into the restrooms which I was hoping was riddled with some disease that rotted the skin.

"Alright Billy, keep your hair on, geez...what's with you today man?" The barman said, which was my cue to move on to the next drunk who was also sat at the bar.

"What?! What'd I do?" The vessel I had just left said, obviously utterly oblivious to the last ten minutes I had possessed him, as they always were.

I then watched, being more subtle this time as the pink haired one named RJ positioned herself next to Keira and suddenly I was rethinking about my approval of their friendship, especially when she said,

"He's got it bad for you, Kazzy girl." She then nudged her and nodded to the bathroom where her brother was hopefully contracting some fungus on his genitals.

Then Keira did the strangest thing, she automatically looked to the bar, and our eyes locked briefly. It was only a moment, but it was enough for me to recognise an unconscious magnetic pull she had towards me. A thought that made my other side break through a moment, before I was able to control the impulse, no doubt showing in my eyes.

"So?" RJ said regaining the attention and breaking our connection.

"So?" she repeated in question, and it was obvious even from here that she was trying to avoid answering, giving me hope of what that answer may have been. But then the moment RJ pressed further, Jerry decided to unknowingly torture me some more and chose that moment to call.

"Yeah so, as in, sooo are you interested?" This was an answer I too would have liked to have heard but the sound of some old disco music coming from her bag had no doubt been the welcomed saviour Keira had been hoping, as now she seemed totally relieved.

I watched as she answered her phone and listened to Jerry's request that she work tonight.

"Yeah, no problem, I just have to see if I can get a lift in with my sister or..." She was quickly cut off, no doubt being informed that I had ordered a car to be sent for her. The cute little wrinkling of her nose confirmed this as confusion soon replaced her relief.

And for me, only two things now played on my mind. The first was wondering what her answer would have been to her friend?

And the second...

Jerry was getting fucking organised!

Keira

24

PROTECTING BEAUTY

Introduction to Historical Thinking was my next class. I grabbed my map out of my bag and found a quiet corner to read it. All my classes had names of buildings and room numbers next to them to make it easier. But easier, it was not. The place was as large as a town. It would take me half an hour to walk from one class to the next. Luckily, I had a few free periods between classes so I made it on time but there was nothing free about them.

Starting college had been hectic, but to be honest I had loved every minute of it. History, Spanish and English Literature had been whirling around my head for days, leaving no room for anything else. The only time that didn't belong to my own mind was in my dreams.

My dreams still held that one face, as though scorched inside my mind for all time. It was as if something else controlled me, planting images and fantasies that seemed so real I would wake to find myself asking if he was still there. I would also find myself going to bed early in the hope of dreaming of him and then when I did, I would wake in a blissful state of euphoria.

Although, this didn't make it very easy when at work, I would fixate on the staircase using every ounce of self-control I had to not going running up there and making a fool of myself. I hadn't seen him since that first night I had worked, but in my dreams he had not faded. If anything, his image was getting clearer with him dominating my nights.

The dreams varied slightly, but the one concept remained. He would always come to me in my bedroom. I would wake (in my dream) to find him there at a distance watching me. I was never scared but I was always wary. After all there was a strange man, whom I hardly knew anything about, sat at my window seat or standing by my desk staring at me.

He was always so perfect. Like a living statue you would have found at the Trevi Fountain in Rome. I would find myself staring back trying to make out every detail, but the moonlight was never enough. I would start to sit up to get a better look at him which was when he would make his move. He just seemed to be beside me in a blink of eye and I was always left wondering how he had got to me so quickly.

I would freeze, locked in his penetrating gaze. He would smile down at me, causing my heart and lungs to work erratically. I held my breath waiting for the next part I knew was coming. He would raise his hand and touch my cheek with the backs of his fingers. The way he touched me was always so soft as if he was handling something so breakable and delicate.

But I didn't understand how as when I could finally focus on his hands they looked too strong to be so gentle. He'd trace the line of my blushed cheek all the way to my chin, lifting it slightly when he got there leaving a warm trail on my skin. He'd tilt my head closer to his face and I could feel his breath. It was cool like the fresh air when it snows and the scent was like nothing I had ever encountered before. It was hypnotic, and I'd feel my head spin with every breath I would take.

His face would be very close, yet I still couldn't move, not that I would have wanted to. He would trace his finger across my lips and I would feel every touch with tiny little electric pulses, as though my lips were having an emotional attack, mirroring my own mind. I just hoped he didn't notice how they quivered at the very sight of him. That confident smile again. He knew what he did to me and he enjoyed it.

I would try to speak but his velvet voice would intervene saying only "Ssshh, be still," which would blow more mind-numbing venom my way, infecting my brain's functions making me do nothing but obey.

I knew that soon the dream would be ending but hoping that this was one of those nights it would last a little bit longer. Every so often he would stay, if only seconds more but it would always end the same way. It was when I was starting to focus that this would normally happen. The time when I would try desperately to grasp onto whatever was feeding this delusional fantasy, driving it to its most pleasurable peak.

And that peak would most certainly be worth waiting for, although cruel in its own right as it also signified the end. One look in the reflection of his dark depths became evidence enough that we both knew what was happening. My eyes became pleading for him to stay and let the dream continue on, taking us to the next level of intimacy but his look never mirrored my own that way. No, it was like something inside him was holding back, whereas I was trying to hold on.

His hand would find its way to the back of my neck and it would send ripples of desire down my spine. My body would arch upwards slightly in response. His big strong hand would hold all the back of my head and entwine his fingers through my hair. I was glad I was unable to speak as every fibre in my body wanted to let out a moan. He would then lean his face to mine as though we were one and his lips would gently touch mine, but he did not kiss me. He just held them there slightly making contact. Then he would whisper...

"Sleep my Electus, sleep for me."

And once more I would obey.

Then that would be the end. I would wake suddenly to find it was morning and I was most definitely alone. That still wouldn't detract from the contentment I felt. It was as if I had taken happy pills and most of the time it would last all day.

"Hey, heads up!" Pink hair flashed in my peripheral vision, along with something hurtling its way towards my head. I turned in time to catch a soda that I wouldn't be able to open for a while.

"Hey, good reflexes. So, you got a free period?"

"Yeah, but I'm probably going to spend that looking for my next class." She smiled.

"What, no chauffeur driven car to take you to class *my Lady?*" RJ joked but I blushed all the same. That night had been strange to say the least as I had never had a job where you received transport to work before, especially in a car that was worth more than some houses.

"Uh no." I answered RJ smiling.

"So, come on, what was that all about? I mean it's not exactly the norm." I had to agree with her there.

"I asked Jerry about it when I got there but he just gave me some management spiel about how any girl working there who doesn't have their own transport now gets it provided so they get home safe." RJ whistled before saying,

"Wow, are they going for workplace of the year or something? I mean, how many girls even work there?" I frowned as I thought about this before answering her,

"Well I have no clue up in the VIP as you don't meet any of the staff..." RJ gave me a weird look but I carried on,

"…but downstairs, it's just me and Hannah…oh and some other girl I haven't met yet who collects glasses on busy nights."

"So, they must be pretty happy with the new rule then." I thought on this for a second.

"No not really as they both have cars." RJ smirked and nudged my arm playfully.

"So just you then Miss Special Treatment" This made me blush even more. Thankfully though she dropped the conversation making her point and went back to helping me find my next class.

"Well lucky for you I know my way around this joint…where we off to?"

"Wakewood Hall and I would sell my soul right now for a clue as to where it is." She laughed,

"Aww, come on now Kazzy, wouldn't you want to save your soul selling for the right buyer? I know who mine would be… mmm, oh yes." Ok, well she had me there and I was pretty sure we were both thinking of the same person. If only she knew just how deep my little fantasies about Dominic Draven really went.

"Come on, I'll walk you there and on the way tell you about the most amazing bit of gossip I have ever heard, better than the time Mrs Waterman tried to stab her husband over their last ding-dong."

We walked towards the building I needed, and RJ didn't take one breath the whole time, I was sure of it. The girl was a machine! She told me of when poor Mr Waterman nearly lost his life due to half a bottle of wine and some badly prescribed meds. From that day on there had always been a more than ample amount of Ding Dongs in the Waterman household. Oh, and just to clarify, a Ding Dong is a chocolate cake product not a door bell like I first thought!

"Ok, now for the real juicy stuff, did you hear who is going to be enrolling here?" She was red faced and bouncing as though she couldn't contain her excitement any longer, but this still didn't stop her from prolonging it.

"Enrolling…? I thought it was too late to enrol." She grinned, enjoying the fact I was out of the gossip loop.

"Well I don't think that would ever stop this person, seeing as her family puts a Hell of a lot of dough into this place each year." She pointed to the building in front of us that looked old and imposing. It was a huge brick building that could have been a school on its own.

"Welcome to the newest edition, Wakewood hall." I couldn't help but smile, knowing that I had most of my history lessons in this gorgeous place.

"This was the latest gift, last year it was a new sports complex." She waved her hand as though this had been a donated bench for the gardens. So that's how the college had been so grand for such a remote place, it must have a multi-millionaire for a benefactor and I didn't need to guess as to who that was.

"That's one Hell of a gift!" I replied still in shock, but she hadn't finished telling me the gossip of the year. So, I pressed for it

"You were telling me..."

"Oh yeah, and anyway that's why she can get in any time. I doubt she would even have to pass a single class! They wouldn't dare fail her, that's for sure." Ok, now I was lost, was she ever going to tell me who this bloody girl was!

"And...she's?" She rolled her eyes clearly loving every minute of my blondness.

"Well isn't it obvious, its Dominic Draven's sister!" Okay now she had said it, then yeah it had been obvious. But Draven's sister studying here, did that mean they were staying? RJ was talking to me now doing her usual overload of information about the girl's name, subjects and full timetable, she was like some confessed stalker, but I wasn't taking any of it in.

I just kept on seeing his perfect face in the dim moonlight, feeling the essence of him as more of a myth than human. Now it was just such a normal thing for him to have a sister who was enrolling here. My imagination had run wild and I was going to have to get it under control. It was getting ridiculous! What did I expect? He was after all just some normal rich guy that happened to be the most handsome man that I had ever seen. I just needed to get a grip!

But deep down I knew what I had been feeling and there was some truth behind it. There was just something different about him, something...*unnatural.*

"You're so lucky, but hey, you're going to be late." So instead of asking her why I was so lucky as I had missed most of the conversation, I said goodbye and went to try and find my next class.

I got there with only minutes to spare but the class was nearly full. There were a few seats left but they were dotted around like holes in an old sweater. I found one in the middle in a cluster of empty spaces.

The room filled even more with only the space left next to me and the obvious lack of a tutor. There was a hum of whispers and a continuous nervous tapping of a foot from the girl behind me. Any other day it would have driven me over the edge of my already fragile sanity but today my mind was too busy being filled with thoughts of Draven.

Then silence descended as a man walked towards the desk at the front. He slammed his bag down, followed by a pounding from his books. He did *not* look happy. You could feel the room instantly tense as everyone seemed to straighten up at the same time, causing a wave of creaking chairs.

He cleared his throat and began.

"This is not a class for easy credit so if you don't want to work hard then I suggest you take up the creative arts for those easy A's and stop wasting my time." He paused and looked about the room. One guy got up but kept his head down, hiding his shame.

"Ah, we have a taker, try woodwork I hear it's a slam-dunk." The class let out a series of nervous noises. The lad left taking with him the tension in the tutor, which seemed to please him as if the initiation process was over and he could now continue.

"I am Mr. Reed, Head of History. I will be taking many of your classes and believe me when I say I do not accept excuses for any reason as I don't care for them. So, unless you are on your death bed in excruciating pain and expelling every liquid from your body, I do not accept absence, just as I don't accept tardiness." This was directed towards the door as a face had appeared in the little porthole. She knocked and we all held our breath, instantly feeling a mutual sorrow for what was about to occur. We could feel the humiliation ready to erupt as the handle pulled downwards, letting the unsuspecting girl into a pit of misery.

She walked in with such grace I think even Reed was taken aback. The classroom actually gasped. She was just so stunningly beautiful, you could almost hear all the breaking of hearts from the boys and the envious mental screams from the girls. She glided through the door in a way that would put any ballerina to shame.

Reed composed himself ready for the kill and stared at the girl who just smiled sweetly in return.

"I do not accept anyone late to my class, but as it is the first day, then I will make an exception. However, if this were to happen again then you will be removed from my lessons and failed on any paper which is due, do you understand?"

"Of course, and please accept my most sincere apologies." Her voice sang out reminding me of one very similar. She was small and elf like, with beautiful black hair that resembled silk as it hung down in curls to her shoulders and bounced as she moved. Her skin was almost translucent with a rosy tint to her cheeks. She looked like a china doll, as though her face had been painted in some way. It was an ancient looking beauty, one you would find on the Sistine Chapel ceiling or the works of Bouguereau.

She looked around for a space and you could see guys standing ready to give up their seats for this lovely creature. I put up my gloved hand and the tutor nodded in my direction. You could hear the groans of disappointment. She walked up the steps and people rose out of their seats to let her through to the middle, I moved the bag that I had put on the other seat and moved one of my books off the now occupied table.

"My name is Sophia and..."

"Excuse me Miss 'I want to disrupt the class' I have had about enough of you today." I don't know what came over me but I felt compelled to stand up for this poor innocent girl. After all, I was the cause of her now being punished. So, I did the unthinkable. I broke my one rule and drew attention to myself.

I stood up only to get a better view of the students gasping at my madness, some even held their breaths.

"Uh..." I had to clear my throat as the words would not form.

"It was not her fault, I asked her a question and she was answering me." I managed to say, not as forceful as I had hoped but at least it made sense.

"And pray tell, what exactly was that most essential question, as now you have all the class' full attention, we're all just dying to know what is more important than my lecture?" His words burned as I started to realize his full meaning. Every head in the room had now turned to look at me and I was in my own personal Hell. I could feel my palms start to sweat and I rubbed them together as I tried to continue.

"I just asked her if she had a book or if not, would she like to share mine." I said trying to sound confident.

"What a Good Samaritan you are, and your name would be?" Oh shit, how long was he going to keep this going? I could imagine it from now on. I was going to be a target for every question, the butt of every joke and the bullseye for every sarcastic comment that would escape those small chewed lips.

"Keira," I stammered as I sat back down, trying to indicate the end of my humiliation.

"Well Keira, I assume I can continue and would hope you are going to show the same dedication in my class as you have done with your unprepared friend there."

I just nodded in response and tried to ignore the stares I received from every eye in the room.

"Well, now that that little drama is over, open your books to page 68, for those of you that have them that is." His tone was cutting, and I knew that my chances of this blowing over and being forgotten were not going to happen any time soon.

"During this lesson you will see that reading and analysing text is central to understanding and knowing history. In this class you will understand the importance of facts. You will live and breathe the intensive study of books and documents from varying historical fields and periods." He continued like this for the rest of the hour, loving the sound of his own voice. Well at least someone in the room did.

The girl next to me and I didn't say another word to each other throughout the class. She did, however, keep smiling at me as if I was some kind of saviour. She wrote the words "thank you" in her notebook in the most amazing ornate handwriting I had ever seen. She pushed it my way for me to read, never taking her eyes off the Himmler lookalike down at the front. It was the large forehead and the shifty eyes peering from behind small round glasses that gave him the appearance of the Head of the Gestapo. Hitler would have been proud to see his lieutenant's reincarnation dictating history.

I scribbled in my not so neat handwriting *'no problem'.* My handwriting looked as though it had been written by a toddler compared to her flowing calligraphy. The lecture continued and made History sound excruciatingly boring. Something I love so much could easily be destroyed by this man's voice alone.

He continued on just like all the first lectures I'd had. The introduction to History was a little wasted on me as I had been studying it all my life. So, as his boring voice droned on, I let my mind drift to other thoughts. Like the fact I was working at the club tonight and the possibility of seeing Draven again created a buzz of anticipation within me.

The class finally drew to an end and I realized that I had missed most of it due to my daydreaming. I would have to pay more attention in future or I would definitely be caught out in the firing line. I was already an easy target in Reed's mind.

I got up grabbing my books and as I was putting them in my bag I noticed a pair of doll like eyes examining me. I met them with a curious look of my own.

"You have lovely hair, why do you wear it back?" Her question had caught me off guard and I started to stammer my answer out.

"Uhh well...it...it gets in the way. But thanks." I couldn't believe that this enchanting looking creature was complementing me when her hair looked like it had been styled ready for a photo shoot for Vogue.

We both walked down following the mass of numbed students trying to escape before another word leaked from Reed's mouth, when something caught my eye. Reed was talking with a student and they were both looking our way, but it was Reed's expression that held my interest. He looked as though he was in shock. It was as if something the boy had told him was about us but wait, it wasn't *us* it was *her.* He was staring at Sophia but now he looked troubled.

She didn't seem to catch the same horror in Reed's eyes that I had or if she did, she didn't hold much consequence to it. I shuddered as we walked out of sight and I realised she was still smiling at me. I felt as though she was studying me more than just being friendly. Was there something more behind her smile or was there just something in my teeth? Either way I felt my tongue run over them just to be sure.

"Thanks again for bailing me out back there, he's a real piece of work, right?" She said as she followed me and people were staring at us in a curious manner.

"Yeah, he's a bit scary but I think we handled it ok, though I bet next time we will get bombarded with questions." I said making her laugh at this and she held out her hand ready to receive mine.

"It was nice to meet you, Keira." I placed my hand in hers and the warmth I found from her soft skin was comforting. She seemed to read my thoughts and smiled once more before she left, saying over her shoulder,

"See you soon." My hand tingled slightly then went very cold along with the rest of my body...*Strange.*

"Who was that?" RJ's asked as we both watched the back of my new friend disappear out of sight.

"No one...how was class?"

RJ went on about her day and I happily listened, not really wanting to tell her about my little run in with Dictator Reed. And I didn't really know why I didn't tell her about Sophia. I guess I just felt a weird connection with her at the end of class. I couldn't explain it, but I'm pretty sure she felt something as well and in a strange way it felt like kinship. Maybe that's why I had felt so compelled to defend her to Reed. In the same way when RJ asked me about her, I wanted to keep her friendship to myself in some selfish way and protect her from RJ's personal prying.

We were nearly home when RJ's word by word account of her day had finished and my mind hadn't retained any of it, luckily though she hadn't noticed.

"So, what you up to tonight, 'cause a couple of us are going to Afterlife, there's this great group playing and....." I stopped her mid-sentence before I forgot what she'd asked, and we were nearly at my house.

"I can't, but I will see you there anyway as I'm working. Maybe I can join you if I get off early."

"Oh my God, you are so lucky you work there, I would have to keep sneaking a peek upstairs." She giggled at the vision. If only it was that easy, I thought bitterly.

"Yeah right, have you seen the security they have, those guys give new meaning to steroid abuse... breakfast, lunch and dinner." I said this last part getting out of the car turning to add,

"See you later."

"Yeah laters, you lucky Biatch!" RJ was still laughing as she turned her little car around and I watched her go out of sight. Only laughter wasn't on my mind. No, there was only one thing to occupy my thoughts and it included 'lady luck' putting me in the same room with a certain someone...

One Dominic Draven.

Keira

25
VIP

J had grabbed my usual black top and jeans, only this time swapping long sleeves for a vest top as it got quite hot in the club especially with lots of enthusiastic Goths swarming the bar. But that was the bonus working at a place like this, the gloves didn't stand out.

I wore my hair in its usual knot, tied up by its clip. There was nothing to suggest that this wouldn't be just like any other night at the club, but I had a strange feeling that was gnawing at my stomach. Maybe it was just after the weird effect meeting Sophia had on me or maybe I was just hoping something might happen. Either way I just couldn't shake off the feeling.

"Oh Kazzy!" Frank shouted up to me as he must have been ready to go. I had told Jerry on the phone that I didn't need a lift for my shift tonight as Frank had already offered. In truth I had been relieved when Frank had offered this. I didn't want to sound ungrateful, but it was getting a bit embarrassing now as I was the only one being chauffeured around in a flash new car. The last thing I needed was for people to think I was getting special treatment and if anything, RJ said was to go by then rumours spread like wild fire in this town.

I grabbed my bag and rushed down the stairs not wanting to keep him waiting. However, on the last few steps I faltered to a stop as I was met with Frank holding the front door open. He had a big grin on his face as I took in the sight yet again of a big shiny black car waiting for me.

"Did you win employee of the month or something, 'cause I gotta tell ya, that's a nice perk?" He said with a wink and I closed my eyes and sighed before descending the last three steps.

"I thought you were a barmaid, not a stock broker?" Frank asked laughing at his own joke.

"Ha, ha, not a word of this to Libby." To which he burst out into raucous laughter...my response was an unimpressed look which only fuelled his amusement.

Great...just great.

The club was quiet when I first walked in and the band had only just arrived. I recognised the drummer to be the same guy RJ had given her number to on my first night here. No wonder she was coming again tonight. What was their name again...Acid um...Acid Criminals. Actually, they weren't half bad.

Mike and Hannah were both working tonight and another girl I hadn't seen before, but I knew her to be Cassie Jones. Hannah hadn't kept it a secret of her dislike towards the girl.

"You watch, she will be all over Mike like a fly on shit. Not calling Mike shit of course, but you know what I'm getting at. She will hang around him all night like a lost kitten digging her claws in ready for the attack! That girl is poison." Of course, she hadn't been the first to warn me about her. RJ, the 'town crier', had filled me in with knowing everyone in Evergreen. Of course, she had told me every sordid little detail. Was there anyone in this town she didn't know? Well, I immediately thought of one and couldn't help looking up.

RJ had used some choice words when describing Cassie, which had surprised me seeing as they were both Goths. But there was no comparison, RJ informed me. Cassie wasn't a real Goth. She was now just the flavour of the month being Emo.

She was one of those who changed with whatever was "in" at the time. Apparently, the number of alternative looking people increased this time of year due to the new arrivals, most hoping to get noticed and make their way into the VIP. Cassie was no exception and she wanted it bad. Her father knew some important people in high places and had wrangled her the job here. But she was still only seventeen and couldn't serve behind the bar, so she collected bottles and glasses as I had done on my first night.

RJ had said the difference between herself and Cassie was that unlike most, RJ was a Goth with style and didn't dress that way just to have an excuse to look like a slut like Cassie. At this point, Lanie had also jumped on the bandwagon, adding her own story that included an older married man who also happened to be one of her teachers. This was a lethal cocktail destined for trouble. Luckily no one seemed to find out about the sordid little affair but the whole town still knew about it, which I found a little confusing. I really didn't understand how that worked, but Lanie carried on telling me more about the little hellcat.

I stood talking to Hannah at the other end of the bar, watching as Cassie did everything but fling herself into Mike's arms. She flicked her hair and bent across him trying to show him more than just her cleavage. He clearly wasn't interested, trying everything apart from smacking the hormonal girl to one side. Poor Mike shifted awkwardly trying to avoid her advances, when he saw me. He winked and walked over leaving her mid-sentence, which had her almost shaking with anger. She saw me and looked like a bulldog chewing wasps.

"Hey Kaz, how's college? You had the dreaded Reed yet?" Mike had kindly forewarned me about Reed, but to be honest, I thought he was exaggerating with his description of him. Of course, now I knew that if anything, he hadn't said enough.

"Yeah, it's going ok and wow, you weren't kiddin', he really does put the Grimm Reaper to shame, doesn't he?" He let out a hearty laugh that reminded me a bit like a pirate. Hannah had left us to talk about college with a smug smile on her face as she was enjoying the evil glares I was receiving from Cassie. She finally strutted her way over to us on impractical looking heels with her face like thunder.

"Who's your friend Mikey?" He cringed at the sound of his name. He mouthed the word "sorry" before turning to face her.

"This is Keira, Keira this is Cassie." He clearly wasn't enjoying the introductions.

"Hey," was all her two brain cells could muster and I just nodded in response. She was clearly happy with herself that plain old me wasn't any competition. She turned her back to me rudely and carried on.

"So, Mikey, do you think you could sneak me up there tonight?" She asked as she flicked her bleached hair for the millionth time and popped her gum. I couldn't help the laugh that escaped my lips and she shot round giving me daggers.

"Yes... is something funny?" She had her hands on her hips like the spoilt teenager she was, and it made it harder for me to keep a straight face.

"Nope," was all I said before turning to help Hannah with the cleaning. I felt sorry for the girl. I mean, the very idea of her trying to sneak upstairs and not getting caught by the massive security guards was almost too funny...she was clearly delusional.

The night got busy and I wasn't surprised that both Jerry and Gary were managing the club tonight. Luckily Gary was manning his station from somewhere else and Jerry was behind the bar with us. Although the bar was manic, we kept on top of it and it reminded me of old times. Jerry kept coming up to me and telling me what a good job I was doing and how impressed he was that I had picked it up so quickly. I reminded him that I had worked in a bar for years and that's why I could juggle serving customers and remembering large orders. After that he just kept coming out with comments like 'Keep it up kid' and 'She's a trooper this one' which was sweet and endearing.

The large orders were mainly from the groups that occupied the many booths surrounding the club. Jack had come up to the bar with such an order. He had wanted to get someone else to serve him so as not to bombard me with remembering eight drinks, but I had impressed him with my multi-tasking skills. I wasn't surprised that the barracuda Cassie had helped him take the drinks to his table. Jack would be her next target, but I could understand why. Excluding the VIP area, he was the most attractive person in the room and it didn't go unnoticed.

The bar area quietened down for a brief moment and I made my move to the ladies, but when I returned I found Jerry stood waiting for me with a crate in his hands looking impatient. I took a look in the crate to find bottles of green liquid with old foreign labels on them. He didn't look his usual calm self.

That was when my night started to get very weird...

"I need you to do me a favour. You need to take these up to the other bar."

"Uhh... other bar?" I looked blankly at him, feeling like an idiot.

"You know, up there." He motioned with his head to the balcony and my mind went into panic mode. Was this a joke or a test? The one rule I was told, Hell, the whole town knew the one rule of Afterlife, and now after less than two weeks of working here he was asking me to break it. Was this man insane?

"Why me?" I said this last part out loud and then repeated it when he stared blankly back at me.

"Why me, why not someone else? Maybe someone who's been here longer, I know Cassie would want to..." What was I saying? Was I really going to give up my one chance to finally go up there, especially to the Emo Barbie herself? I was torn as the Mr Hyde in me was screaming YES! YES! But the reserved Dr Jekyll was terrified at what a bad cocktail of events this could turn out to be.

"That's why it has to be you, you're the only one who doesn't go on about it..." No, I just fantasise about Draven everywhere I go and dream about him almost kissing me in my bedroom every night. Oh no, that wasn't worse, I thought sarcastically.

"I need someone that won't do anything stupid and will be quick, in and out without... umm...well without getting noticed." He said this last part as if it had offended me, but it had been the truth. I was the only one who didn't stand out. I played my last card in the hopes he would fold.

"What about you or Gary? I could watch the bar and..." He cut me off, no doubt already anticipating that was what I was going to say.

"I can't leave the bar unsupervised and Gary starts to go into meltdown whenever you mention the VIP, so that's a no go." He said thrusting the crate into my hands and left, taking my silence for a yes. I stood motionless for a moment contemplating what to do. I looked down slowly and was surprised when I saw nine green faces looking back at me. The old bottle labels were all the same, no name, but all held a beautiful green winged fairy lying naked sipping a green cocktail.

At first, I had wanted to call Jerry back and tell him no, but I chickened out. I also thought about just dropping the box and making a run for it but that wasn't a practical solution either. I liked this job and didn't want to lose it. I started towards the staircase wondering how I was actually going to make my feet move up each step. I was nearly there when Gary came out from nowhere, scaring the life out of me.

"Not those stairs, there is a door around the other side of the stage, that's what they use." He said this as though they were some alien life force that didn't belong here.

"O...kay." I said dragging out the letters as if I wasn't freaked out enough. He looked as nervous as I was. What the Hell did he have to be nervous about? I was the one who was being thrown to the bloody rich wolves.

I walked in the direction he had nodded to when his hand reached out and grabbed my arm. His grip tightened as his face went whiter.

"Be as quick as you can for your own sake!" Oh great, that was a confidence builder!

I carried on towards the stage and I could see the door he had been talking about. No wonder I had never seen it before, as it was well hidden. I was just about to put my crate down to open the door when two huge guys came out from nowhere making me jump. My nerves doubled. I kept my direct gaze from theirs and tried to think of what I could say. I half hoped they wouldn't let me up. But of course, they just opened the door for me without saying a word. I walked through, jumping again as the door slammed behind me sealing my fate.

There was no going back from this 'oh shit' moment.

Once inside, I took a moment to try and calm myself as I was pretty close to hyperventilating. It was like something you would have found in a castle. The staircase was huge! So big you could have pushed a grand piano up it and still had room either side. It was all made out of the same stone as the rest of the building, only instead of blocks it looked as though carved from one big piece. It was incredible.

I put the crate down and straightened my arms and fingers. There were red marks and deep impressions across each finger. They then made cracking noises as I moved them in and out of a fist. My thin puny arms weren't up for the task as they ached and I had only made my way across the club. There was a door the same as the one I had walked through opposite to where I stood. I was tempted to try it, but the fear of being caught was greater than my curiosity.

My feet moved up the ancient looking steps as if they had a mind of their own. The walls were bare but for the wrought iron candle holders, only this time they didn't hold flickering light bulbs for effect. The light from the flames didn't seem as if it would be enough, but there was an ample amount of light to take in my surroundings. There was also a matching banister with twisted iron making its way up the staircase alongside me. There were two doors at the top of a small landing mirroring the downstairs. I knew which door it would be but as before, I still had the same urge to try the other one.

I could still hear the rhythmic hum of the Acid Criminals getting louder as my heartbeat was matching the bass. I stopped behind the carved wooden door and wondered 'what next'? Should I knock or just walk in? I decided to just walk in. After all, would anyone hear my knock? I held my breath, put down the crate and turned the ornate handle. Here goes, I thought with my bottom lip firmly between my teeth.

I walked into what seemed like the dressing room for some Gothic production and everyone's eyes were on me. I pretended not to notice, happy that the lighting was an ambient glow which hid my bright red face nicely. I could see the bar clearly on the other side of the room and a path through the chairs and tables full of the strangest looking people I had ever seen in my life.

I looked around, taking in as much as I could as I struggled my way to the bar. The room was breath-taking. It was like something from a different era. Maybe more like something you would have found in a stately home hundreds of years ago. But there were also new, modern aspects to the place. The mix of old and new worked well together. There were the same twisted wrought iron fixtures that ran throughout the entire club, but they were lit by candles instead of electricity. I doubted that this was to do with the electricity bill and more to do with the authentic setting.

The furniture was a mix of antique carved chairs and modern metal tables with lush fabrics that covered them in luxury. There were dark red rugs that were scattered on the floor over black slate tiles. The walls held nothing but light fixtures and twisted iron artwork. These were beautiful pieces, all entwined metal flowing in and out of each other. Some held metal roses attached to vines. Others were in the shape of the moon and the sun but were being attacked with metal claws. It was by far the strangest room I had ever seen.

But stranger still wasn't the room itself. No, it was the groups of people occupying it. I tried to keep my head down but that proved difficult. Like taking a child to Disneyland and asking them not to look at the parade. I was so engrossed, I momentarily forgot what it was I was doing here. I stepped around the pathway that led to the bar on the other side, trying not to meet all the eyes that were staring at me.

Some were kind looking, others harsh and nasty like those made more intimidating by the blood red contact lenses they wore. Their clothing was something else entirely. Some wore normal everyday outfits, but others were dressed very differently. One group all wore what looked like eighteenth century costumes that seemed as though they had just stepped out of a classic period drama.

Another group looked as though they could have been extras from a Vampire movie, with long black coats and long black hair to match. Eyes like red pools of hate and lips curved into sadistic grins. I shivered as I walked past.

I would say my mind was playing tricks on me with my imagination to match. But there was so much fuel in here for my over active brain, that I couldn't tell what was real and what was in my head. I could have sworn that at one table I passed, they all snarled at me. And this particular group all had halos of tight curls of white hair and gleaming silver fingernails that looked like sharp metal spikes. No wonder I gasped.

I was coming to the middle now, walking in front nearest to the balcony. I could see quite clearly all the people below which seemed so normal in comparison. They were all dancing and busy socialising, completely unaware of the horrors that resided in the VIP. It was weird to think that where we couldn't see anything they were all looking down on us and could see everything. I could now understand why no-one else was allowed up here. People would be terrified and rumours would spiral out of control.

It had me wondering what type of business this was. What could warrant all these different kinds of people to meet like this? It was like something from a horror film convention and they were all dressed up as their favourite characters. I had expected business suits and fancy looking models hanging over them as paid pleasure but not this.

I tried to concentrate on the job at hand and shake off the creepy vibe that licked at my skin. I was directly in the middle where the balcony widened into a semi-circle and jutted out from the rest. I turned, half expecting the reason why this part was bigger and knowing that this was the best view showing the entire floor below. I was surprised as nowhere was hidden. But I wasn't surprised by what I found.

I tried so hard not to look but it was as if I was going against the Gods of nature by not turning my head. My eyes burned as I was fighting a losing battle. I knew he was there, I could feel him. It felt bizarre, like the sensation I got when I dreamed of him. I would seem to be awake, but also not. I couldn't really explain any of it, not into words that would make sense anyway.

I turned to see a large oval table that mirrored the shape of the balcony. It was on a raised dais so anyone on the table could look down at the unsuspecting fools who thought this place held rich suits. This was clearly to show the importance of the people who sat around it, as if this was even necessary as it was evident enough without all the theatrics.

The table was the biggest one in the room with everyone sat on a high backed wrought iron chair. However, there were no chairs at the front of the table to obstruct the view from the head of the group. The head of the table being of course, where Dominic Draven himself sat.

He was the most breath-taking person in this marvellous room. He seemed higher than everyone else and the chair he sat upon looked more like a throne. It was twice the size and looked even more amazing with him sat upon it. The back which twisted up from the legs was ornately carved from wood, like the spindles you would have found on a staircase. They met at the top in an arch, which was intertwined with iron. The middle had the same crest carved into it that I had noticed on the entrance door. There was a centre section covered in purple velvet for his back and I guessed this was also the same on the seat. The arm rests were made from what looked like stone or maybe marble. But these small factors of where he sat were unimportant compared to the living masterpiece that was sat upon it.

He didn't seem to notice me, so my eyes didn't move from his perfect face. I was so enthralled that I didn't even take in the other people around the table. He was the only one my eyes could see. I followed his body up from the waist, as I had done that first time in the forest clearing in my dream, but I had remembered every detail correctly.

He wore a black pin-stripe suit with waistcoat with a black shirt and tie. My eyes followed the material as it widened for his powerful looking shoulders until I paused at the neck. My heart fluttered, and my stomach ached in knots, knowing I had reached my favourite part... *his face.* But I chickened out. I couldn't bear to look into his eyes, scared to see what I might find there.

After all,

I was breaking all the rules.

Quickly pulling myself back to reality I walked with my head down towards the bar. It wasn't far from the central table, so I didn't have much further to go. The bar was a match to the one downstairs, only on a slightly smaller scale. It was the only thing in the room that reminded me that I was still in the same club and not some European castle. There was one man behind the bar and now I was suddenly nervous for a new reason. Confrontation.

I walked up to it placing the crate down on the bar's counter, when the man turned towards me. Having had my entire mind concentrated on everything in the room it had made me forget the aching pain in my arms and hands. They were now burning. I straightened them out again as I had done before but now the imprints the crate had made wouldn't go away.

"Are you alright?" A silky accented voice had asked me something and I looked up to see a man smiling sweetly at me. He looked from Moroccan decent with a soft dark tint to his skin, deep dark eyes and long black hair past his shoulders. His eyes were kind which was comforting compared to the wave of scrutinising looks I had received crossing the room.

"Sorry?" I said feeling stupid, as the first person to talk to me up here must think me a simpleton.

"I was just asking if you were alright my dear, you must have carried that a long way and no offence, but you don't look built for hard labour." He chuckled to himself at this last part.

"Yeah, I'm fine thanks. I was told you needed this crate and so they sent me...well Jerry sent me...I mean not sent me... asked me." I needed to stop talking. I was babbling on like a lost child. He couldn't keep the smile from his face as he must have known my reason for being nervous.

"Okay, well thank you very much, we did need it quite badly as we were down to our last bottle and we are extremely short staffed ...due to umm...well let's just say compromising circumstances." I didn't really understand this last part and couldn't imagine anyone using the term 'compromising circumstances' as a way of saying someone either quit or got sacked!

"I'm Karmun and you are?" He held his hand out for me to shake and I leaned over to offer mine in return when someone shouted my name.

"Keira, is that you?!" The same familiar voice that I'd heard today in history was now speaking my name behind me. I moved my hand from hovering towards Karmun and turned to face her. Only a combination of surprise and fear that the girl had followed me up here not knowing the rules had my body rebelling against my orders. I lost my footing and fell sideways into someone. It wasn't Sophia as I had hoped as she was opposite me now grinning. The person I fell into was still holding me upright and I was about to turn to face them with a chorus of apologies, when Sophia giggled and spoke the name with which I was only too familiar.

"Nice catch! Keira, I would like to introduce you to Dominic Draven." I lifted my head and saw his perfect face staring down at my scarlet cheeks and I hung my head in shame. I straightened myself up and instinctively stepped away from him. I was still warm and branded from his touch on my skin.

His eyes followed mine and I managed to say a quiet 'Sorry' that anyone would barely hear. He looked me up and down with hard unimpressed eyes and my knees weren't up to the task of keeping me up straight. I tried to regain some control to prevent any further embarrassment.

I couldn't understand how Sophia knew him and then it hit me. Maybe she was his girlfriend. She certainly fit the bill. She was beyond beauty and perfection. She was the very meaning of desire and the reason artists and writers had a muse. I suddenly felt a sickening feeling in my stomach. I would never, in a million life times, be good enough. Not for a man like this.

But then she said something that answered my unspoken thoughts and it all made sense.

"Brother, this is Keira, the girl I was telling you about."

Keira

26
Offer I Can't Refuse

Brother! She'd called him brother, of course it all made sense now. Even down to why RJ was calling me lucky before class. She had known that I had the same class as Sophia. I would have to start paying more attention to people and less time daydreaming.

Now I knew, I could see the resemblance in them both. They had a way about them that drew you in and held you captivated as though under some secret spell. I could imagine that her effect had worked on guys as well as her brothers had worked on me. It was obsession plain and simple.

I stood silent as she was recreating the events of this afternoon, but her brother looked more than unimpressed, he just looked bored and most of all, rude. He stared at me as though I was an intruder, just some outsider that needed to be removed. Maybe the shit on his shoe would be the right analogy.

His eyes were the only thing different from the way he was in my dreams, but they had just the same, if not more of an impact. He didn't even look away when my eyes met his. He just kept on with the malevolent glare as though his sister's words had meant nothing.

"I didn't realise you worked here, what a small world." Sophia smiled. At this she received a harsh look from her brother, as though someone had clicked their fingers to get his attention away from me. One she ignored and carried on.

"Actually, we don't usually have people from around here working up in the VIP. You can understand we don't like the gossip that a small town generates but seeing that you haven't been here long then maybe you could help us out."

"What?!" This was the first word from Draven's lips and for once it wasn't worth waiting for.

"That is not a good idea, Sophia." He paused to look down at me, which wasn't hard given his immense height and then continued,

"She does *not* belong here." It was like being punched in my chest with a battering ram. I squeezed my fingers into fists until they hurt just to stop the pain in my head and my heart. I couldn't believe how different he was from my dreams. There he remained soft and kind, but here was a different matter entirely... he was unnecessarily cruel.

"I don't agree. We need staff up here and I think she deserves a chance, or do you no longer trust my judgement?" She was fearless as she now stood facing him, looking up into his deep black eyes. He didn't look at me again but only ended the discussion by adding his own dark judgement on the idea.

"Sophia, you know my thoughts on the matter, so let it be on your head when this goes wrong. Do not forget our ways, sister." He said with a terrifying glint in his eyes and a deadly flex in his strong jaw line before leaving Sophia and I alone. I watched as he walked away, not taking my eyes off his impressive figure. I knew Sophia was watching me, but I couldn't help it. I still couldn't believe that he was just speaking about me as though I wasn't there.

I wanted to hate him! I mean, what was the worst that could happen? I would break a glass or get an order wrong. It wasn't astrophysics! I was just serving drinks. And yes, it was a little bit different, mainly down to the weirdo people that I would be serving. But come on, who did he think I was... a bloody axe wielding psychopath? Did he think I was going to serve them drinks with a severed hand?

"Don't mind him, he's...well he's always cranky around new people. But he will get used to you." If this was supposed to comfort me it didn't!

"Maybe it's not a good idea and I don't mind working down there." She didn't look convinced.

"No really." I added.

"Well you get better money up here and I want you to, it's the least I can do, and we're friends right?" It wasn't so much a question, more of a statement. She had known, as I did, that we would be instant friends.

I decided to deal with this tomorrow as the mental whiplash where Draven's words had attacked at my soul, still seared deep. I would just explain tomorrow after class how I appreciated the sentiment but would have to refuse.

"Okay, when would you like me to start?" She gave me a smug grin and said,

"Tomorrow night would be great. I'd better go but I'll see you in class." She gave my arm an affectionate squeeze and left in the same direction as her brother had. I needed a minute to take everything in, but a voice interrupted my thoughts.

"Well, it looks like I will be seeing a lot more of you now you're going to be working with us up here." Karmun smiled and winked at me before continuing on with his duties. Well, at least two people seemed happy about having me up here. I was so confused I couldn't think straight. I knew I had to move but my brain was too busy trying to process all the information. I was just standing there like the fool I felt. I wanted to run from the room, anything to get away from the essence of him still lingering in the air around me.

A waitress pushed into me hard enough for it not to be an accident and I turned in time to see a blonde bombshell beauty scowl at me. This was enough to bring me to my senses and I looked for a way out that wasn't past his table, but I couldn't see one. So, I decided to ask Karmun. I leaned over the bar and watched as he was pouring a green liquid into what looked like a fountain, like the ones you would find at a cocktail party.

However, this one was different. It had a tube in the middle, which was where the liquid was being poured. It was moving around the glass container like a twister tornado and as a result the liquid had a reaction. It was changing colours from greens to blues to black and then back again. I was fixated. Then a button was released and the liquid would start to flow out of four taps into goblets below, stopping automatically when filled. These he placed on a tray for the blonde to take away. The whole process was fascinating, so when he noticed me and came over I was taken aback.

"Are you alright?" He said looking at me with concern in his expression.

"Oh sorry, but I was intrigued by what you were doing. I've never seen anything like that." I commented nodding to the liquid still swirling round in the glass cylinder.

"It's absinthe and it's a favourite around here, but you will soon get used to it tomorrow night as it's what most of them drink." He nodded towards the tables of people as he said this. He must have mixed something with it when I wasn't looking, as there was no way anyone could drink a cup full of that stuff straight! I had heard about it and knew it had been illegal for a long time due to its strange effects and its ridiculously high proof.

"I was wondering if there's a more discrete way of getting out of here?" I cringed as I said it, feeling weak and pathetic for asking, but he smiled taking the feeling away and replied,

"Sure, I understand, it's over there near the entrance to the outside balcony. There's a staircase before the double doors, you won't miss it. Just look for the big gangster looking guys."

"Thanks, and I guess I will be seeing you tomorrow then." I shook his hand as I didn't get chance to before and he looked touched that I had remembered.

"Sure thing and don't be worried you will be fine, I will look out for you." He gave me another trademark wink and left again to carry on with his cocktail making. I felt a bit guilty, knowing I would be turning down the job tomorrow and yet knowing this, I had still repaid his kindness to me with lies.

I headed in the direction he had shown me, happy in the knowledge that I wouldn't have to walk past those judging eyes of Draven's again. I rounded a pillar and the stairs came into view as they were slightly hidden from the rest of the room, out of the way which was perfect for me. I noticed as I got closer not only the usual Hercules standing guard but the frosted glass double doors that must have led outside to the balcony Karmun spoke of. I had a sudden urge to open them and take a peek but realised I had spent way too much time up here already and Gary and Jerry must be having kitten human hybrids by now! I wondered what they would say when I told them of Sophia's request.

As I walked downstairs, I could see Jerry pacing up and down the bar like a hungry cougar. But that wasn't the only thing I noticed as I was now walking down the stairs where everyone could see me. All eyes stared in amazement and the embarrassment level reached new highs. I could see RJ nearly jumping out of her seat to get to me. I tried to play it cool and not notice but that was proving impossible, as now there weren't just stares to contend with they had now been joined with whispers.

I could hear the 'Who is that girl?' and 'Why's she so special?' But this time I just raised my head up and hid my shame, because all these facts were insignificant in comparison to the feelings that were heating up inside me. I didn't know what hurt the most, the fact that he had been so mean and disgusted towards me, or the fact I'd finally realised what an utter bastard he could be.

After all, what did I expect? It wasn't like he was the man from my dreams. No, he was just the empty shell. The image to put with the kindness and warmth he had shown me in my dreams. I knew it was too good to be true and I couldn't have it both ways. No one that gorgeous was ever going to have a personality to match.

These thoughts brought me all the way to the bar without even thinking about it. Thank God for autopilot that's all I could say. Jerry spotted me then came stomping over to me with a hard, red face. I had guessed that this wasn't going to be easy but man, did he look pissed!

"What the Hell took you so long?!" He pulled me to one side and not in a friendly manner.

"I sent you up there because I knew you were the only one who didn't want to go, so I knew you would be quick, so what...? You thought that you'd have a good look around, take a tour, 'cause it's my ass on the line!"

Oh yeah, he was definitely pissed. I couldn't deal with this now, not after the cold backhanded slap of pain that Draven's words had inflicted. I was about to turn, not say a word but just leave and never look back. Then I heard his phone ring and frustrated he fumbled for it in his jeans pocket.

His eyes looked down at the screen and then froze in what looked like fear.

"What did you do?" He questioned me, and I frowned, shaking my head to indicate I had done nothing. He didn't look convinced as he cautiously put the phone to his ear as though it might explode.

"Uh...yes, can I help you?" His voice was shaky and his eyes were everywhere.

"Oh, I see...no, no, of course that won't be a problem. No, I'll take care of that personally. Yes, I understand, and it won't happen again...please allow me to apol..." It was clear he was cut off and I felt bad for him. He turned to face me but smiled instead of the evil glare I was expecting.

"So, you have been promoted upstairs. Well done, you must have made quite an impression for me to have received that call." I didn't know what to say so I didn't respond.

"Well, you start tomorrow night and don't worry, you won't have any problems from anyone. I've been instructed to take care of any gossip." He said this with controlled bitterness.

"Look I'm sorry, I didn't know. See, I met Sophia in my History class and..." He tilted his head before interrupting me.

"Sophia?" He stared blankly at me and I continued,

"Yeah, Sophia... Mr Draven's sister. Didn't you just speak to her on the phone?"

"No, but I guess that makes sense now...anyway, you start at eight and wear all black." He started to walk off but my curiosity wouldn't let him leave without giving me the information I needed to know.

"Then who was that on the phone?" My pulse quickened waiting for the answer that I hoped for. I didn't think he was even going to answer me at first as he didn't stop, but then he just looked over his shoulder and said the name I wanted so badly to hear.

"It was my boss, Mr Dominic Draven."

My shift had finished soon after the call and now I had to explain things to RJ. This wasn't going to be easy. All I wanted to do was go home and try and make sense of what had happened. I couldn't get my head around it. Why would a man who obviously didn't want me anywhere near him be ringing Jerry to make sure I didn't get any trouble from anyone? The only explanation I could fathom was that his sister had put him up to it.

I felt angry at myself for even thinking...no not just thinking but hoping that it could be just an inch of what I only wished for. Of course, he didn't care. I mean why would he? I was nothing to him, a thorn amongst the roses that surrounded him.

"OH MY GOD! Tell me everything!" RJ nearly bounced into my arms as I walked over to their table. It was situated on one of the lower levels not like the booth we'd had reserved for us before.

Everyone was there except for Jack, but they all watched me as if I had just met the president. I just wanted to scream by this point and run all the way home. Why did things have to get complicated so quickly? I felt like a bloody magnetic force that attracted trouble. I just wanted to be normal, but I guess you had to know what normal was to begin with. I had never been 'just normal', I knew that much.

Ever since that day at the fairground my life had changed. Hell, who knows, maybe even before then. She had seen it, something in me that had scared her. She had looked into my eyes and feared for what she had seen there. So, she had changed me.

RJ thankfully interrupted my thoughts as the real-life nightmares of my past started to invade my conscious state. Not here, not now. It wasn't the place for my demons.

"Sooo... come on, don't hold out on me, what was it like?" She looked like a child who had just found the golden ticket to Willy Wonka's. I sat down and they all waited for me to speak. I was now wishing that I hadn't agreed to meet up with them after work.

"It really wasn't that big a deal, just some weird looking people who drink a lot of absinthe. But honestly, that was it." I tried to sound casual but I didn't even convince myself, so I had no hope.

"Aww come on, you have to give me something! All these years everyone has been waiting to go up there and they pick you. No offence." Everyone kept saying that to me but I was so far past caring, I couldn't even see the insulting line that people kept crossing. I mean I agreed with them, which was even more pathetic. Did I have even an ounce of self-confidence left in me or had the monsters destroyed me completely?

"Look I hate to burst the fantasy bubble but it was nothing, no cult, no blood sucking, not even a voodoo doll. Nada!" I think this was the most animated they had all seen me get, so I guess it got the right message across. Basically, I wasn't in the mood.

"Not even Dominic Draven?" She asked in a deflated voice with her grin gone from her Gothic black lips. It pained me to hear anyone speak his full name as if I had the right to be the only one. Who was I kidding? I thought about the question and answered it with a half-truth.

"No, Draven wasn't there." It was true. The Draven that I had constructed in my dreams didn't even exist. I had just used the thought of him and combined it with his good looks and my need for a kind, comforting stranger. Someone who knew nothing of my past and wouldn't judge me but love me in some small way for who I was and not who I had become.

I decided it best not to mention the job offer I had received, seeing that I would only be turning it down anyway. So, there was no point in prolonging the painful, scrutinising looks I was receiving from everyone in the room. And that was just from taking some bottles up there for Pete's sake. What would they do if they knew I had turned to the dark side and joined the VIPs? Grab their pitchforks and hoes... I think I'll pass.

I looked around the table and all faces dropped with disappointment, all except one. Chaz looked amused and concerned at the same time. I didn't want to stare like he was doing back at me, but his eyes were fascinating. They flashed a different colour ever so slightly, but I was sure it was in my mind, so I tried to blank it out. This was harder than I would have liked as he was now grinning at me and it was only when Lanie started to talk to him that he seemed to snap out of it. It was as if he had momentarily been taken over by pod people.

"Hey there pretty lady, how you doing?" I hadn't even noticed that Jack had turned up after the Spanish Inquisition. He said this putting on a half Texas accent and half Joey from Friends. It was the first time I had smiled all night. Then it burst, spoiled by RJ's reconstruction of the evening's events.

"Oh my God Jack, you'll never guess!" She didn't wait to hear one, or to take a breath.

"Our little Kazzy here only got singled out and sent upstairs to the V...I...P." She mouthed the letters, dragging each one out for more effect. Jack didn't look shocked and like a gentleman he didn't make as big a deal out of it as RJ had or still was for that matter.

"So how was the Master of the Universe and his disciples, just thrilling I bet?" RJ scowled at her brother's sarcastic remark.

"Shut up Jack, what do you know?" He laughed in response.

"Oh, come on sis, it's all bullshit, smoke and mirrors. Anything gets this place rallied up and everyone loves a good rumour," he said trying to sound more light hearted, as he could see RJ's explosive side coming through.

"Well, that's the thing... it's not always just rumours though is it Jack?" She stared at him with a knowing looking, as though this would jog some memory of his.

"Leave it out Rachel!" It was the first time I had heard anyone say her full name. At Jack's outburst, she backed down as though he had shouted at her for the first time in his life. Which had me wondering, what had I missed? It must have been something bad. For two reasons, the first being if the town's biggest gossip hadn't told me about it and secondly, it would have to be something pretty big to get her to back down so quickly.

I felt even more awkward now and I needed some air, so I decided to make my excuses and go outside.

"Hey guys, sorry I'm going to bail. RJ I'll see you tomorrow, ok?" I got up and started to put my jacket on, when Jack grabbed one side and helped me with the other arm. I froze as he was so close to my scars but thankfully it was over quickly, and he didn't realise my hesitation.

But then I noticed Chaz had resumed his glaring at me, only this time his stare was no longer one of amusement and had been replaced by one of abhorrence, but this wasn't only directed at me. No-one else seemed to notice and just before I lowered my eyes, I saw the deepest colour of purple flash in them before once again Lanie spoke to him, breaking the spell.

"I think I'll join you outside for some air, it's a little crowded in here tonight." Jack said clearly still angry with RJ and it was strange to see his face in this new light. His soft features turned hard and made him look more like a man, taking away his boyish charm. However, it had been replaced by something else. He now looked insanely sexy instead of cute.

We both walked outside, and I couldn't help but look back at the balcony one last time before I left through the huge carved oak doors. There my eyes played tricks on me as I could swear I saw a dark figure staring back, but I looked away quickly, knowing I was only seeing the things that my mind wanted to.

I let the cool air sweep over my body and cleanse my exposed skin. It felt good to be outside. Even the smell of that place did strange things to me. I couldn't think in there as it played with my emotions. But out here I could think clearly and more importantly, rationally.

"You ok?" I had almost forgotten Jack was with me and felt embarrassed when he noticed me with my eyes closed.

"Yeah... sorry. I just really needed some air and to get away from all the stares." I don't know why I chose to add that bit, but I felt like Jack was becoming a good friend and one that wouldn't judge me.

"I know what you mean. I just hate it when they come here and the whole town hypes up all this crap about them. I just wish they wouldn't ever bother coming back." He sounded different, like something about the Dravens hurt him personally, but I couldn't think for the life of me what it could be seeing as the Dravens didn't have anything to do with the locals.

My phone suddenly started singing 'Gimme, Gimme, Gimme' by ABBA and I fished around in my pocket frantically before it started to get louder. I would have to remember to change the ring tone once I got home.

"Nice, hey if you wanted to boogie, then all you need to do is ask." He laughed, giving him back that warm glow I was used to. I smirked back before answering the phone.

"Hello, oh Frank... is everything alright?"

"Hi honey but bad news I'm sorry but I'm going to be late, things got a bit crazy here but I'll ring Libs and ask her to come and pick you up." At that very moment as if on cue the usual black car rolled up.

"Well, it looks like that won't be a problem anymore." I said conveying across my frustration in my tone.

"The car's there again, isn't it?" He laughed when I groaned in response.

"Man, he must have it bad."

"What do you mean?" I asked thinking this was a strange comment.

"Never mind Kid, I won't ring Libs. Catch you later." I said goodbye and flipped the phone shut. Jack was still smiling at me with a huge grin on his face.

"It was my sister's phone and what can I say, she loves ABBA." We both laughed, and it felt good in spite of the car. I had already told Jerry that I no longer needed the special treatment, but someone clearly wasn't listening.

"Come on, I'll drive you home if you want. Warning you now though, it's nowhere near as fancy." He was walking towards the car park before I could object. I looked back to the black car to see the chauffeur looking back at me, so I did the only thing I could think to do. I gave him the thumbs up and then pointed to where Jack was walking to his blue pickup truck.

I could just see the look of disapproval from the chauffeur who never said a word to me, but I didn't care. They needed to get the hint, so with that in mind I ran after Jack.

"Hey wait up!" He turned to me and smiled, putting his arm around my shoulders.

"I told you it wasn't as fancy."

"Looks great to me." I said taking in the slightly battered pickup. Just at that moment the sounds of an engine revving and wheels spinning made us both look back as we caught the car driving out of sight. We both looked at each other confused and Jack shrugged his shoulders.

"He must have really wanted to drive you home."

"Bored I guess." I said as I got in the truck.

Once inside, Jack cranked up the heater and switched stations from the death metal to something softer. Then he turned to me and said,

"Sorry sweetness, no ABBA." I couldn't keep the smile from my face when I replied,

"Ha, Ha, I told you it was my sister's phone." He leaned over and nudged my arm saying,

"Yeah, sure it was." He was such a tease. But this was one kind of attention I wasn't minding as much. I really wanted to ask him what RJ had meant, but I didn't want to spoil his good mood as I had witnessed the change in him earlier. It must be something of a delicate nature. Maybe I would subtly ask RJ tomorrow on our way to college.

We were just chatting about friends and college stuff when he asked me outright about something of a delicate nature himself.

"So, how come I always see you wearing gloves?" I don't think he expected my reaction, so he couldn't have been thinking the obvious. I sunk down into my seat and looked out of the window before thinking of what to say, when I noticed something moving with us...no, not moving but more like following. It was quick whatever it was and very dark with a bluish tinge when the moonlight hit it. Like a fast-moving black cloud.

"What's that?" I said pointing to my passenger side window. Jack looked but by the time he turned his head it had gone. Great, now he just thinks I'm seeing things. Well, it wouldn't be the first time and no hope of it being the last.

"I don't see anything. I suppose the effect of the VIP is playing tricks on your mind." That smile again, if Helen of Troy had the face that could launch a thousand ships then Jack's smile held the male equivalent.

"So, what did happen up there? You didn't seem yourself when you came down and you were up there a long time?"

"How do you know...I mean, you only just arrived when I..." He shook his head hiding a smile while he was pulling into the dirt road leading to my house.

"I got there earlier but was sat at the bar with some other friends. I asked if you were working and Mike told me where you were, so I waited."

"So that's why you weren't shocked when RJ told you, you already knew." He nodded as though embarrassed about something, but I couldn't tell what. He had pulled in front of the house and cut the engine. The lights were on and I saw a curtain move. It must have been Libby.

"The ABBA fan?" He asked chuckling to himself.

"Yep, she's also taken on the role of my mother, warden and caretaker seeing as my real one is in England. She's sweet though but a little paranoid. She doesn't like me working at the club and also doesn't trust the Dravens." I said this last part to try and prompt something out of him.

"She's a smart girl." He said with a distant look, as though the thought of a bad memory had re-entered his mind. I decided to call it a night, feeling bad for him. I didn't like seeing him all serious, it was just like a puzzle piece that fit but was the wrong shade.

"Well, thanks for the ride." I opened my door and noticed Jack also getting out. He walked round to meet me and said,

"Please allow me to walk a lady to the door." He put on a southern accent and tilted an imaginary hat taking my hand adding "Ma'am" for effect. He made me chuckle and the dreaded snort showed itself. He laughed as he walked me up the porch steps to the front door. He still had hold of my hand and I was going red with embarrassment. He then stopped in front of me and leant down to my ear, which shamefully reminded me of someone else. I felt guilty for even thinking it but I couldn't help the way I felt about Draven.

Jack whispered in my ear.

"Did I mention it's the cutest thing, that little snort of yours." I held my breath knowing what was coming next. Maybe if I had never had this weird obsession thing with Draven going on, then this would have been what I wanted. But that fact remained, I did still feel the same and I didn't want to hurt Jack's feelings in the process.

He was turning his head towards my lips and his arms were moving their way around my upper body. I hadn't yet decided what to do. If I stopped it, it would hurt his feelings but if I didn't, then I was leading him on.

My mind was reeling off excuse after excuse in the seconds it took for his lips to close the distance but then something happened. He paused suddenly and his arms that were around me went rigid. I lifted my head but saw his eyes were elsewhere. His arms dropped, and he moved to stand with his back to me facing something I couldn't yet see.

"What the Hell is that thing!?" I looked around his shoulders and saw a familiar sight.

My stalker bird was back...

And it looked enraged.

DRAVEN

27

TAMING THE SHIT STORM.

"*Sleep my Electus, sleep for me.*" This was the way in which I would say goodbye every night that I went to her. Then waking her from her dream at the time and letting her believe in a new one. I quickly found myself getting addicted to those little moans of hers, or the quivering of her lips as if in anticipation of the kiss I never granted her.

Some would have considered the act cruel, for I knew in those moments that she wanted me, as much as I craved to have her. But I didn't want our first real kiss to be one lost to the realms of a dream and with only me to remember it. I wanted it to be a moment neither of us would ever forget, no matter how many lifetimes we lived through.

So, I would silence her, telling her to be still and do as I softly commanded of her. I can't express, in these moments, how much she pleased me when submitting so sweetly. Moments that were over in only minutes but ones that lasted days, for the effect on me was like a drug, one I never wanted out of my system.

So, every night I went back for more, wishing that just for a moment it was enough of a hit to my senses to last longer. But I had to confess, it was getting harder not easier. I wanted her so badly, I swear it was like a fever had taken over my soul.

I admit that I had wanted to monitor her first meeting with my sister, which had already occurred earlier that day, but she had made me promise to allow her to do so alone. I had, of course, argued this decision, only to end up agreeing that I needed to trust in Sophia's capabilities to make friends with her. Something, in her words, that was 'without being judged by stalker boy over there'.

This was, of course, said to Vincent, who once again found himself playing referee in the middle of one of our disputes. In fact, I didn't know who would be more exhausted by the time I finally made the girl mine, me or Vincent.

But in the end, Sophia had won, and I had begrudgingly let her take charge of this 'chance meeting' she had planned. Well, now it was the evening, and Keira was due in work any minute. I had continued to arrange for a car to bring her to work and take her home again. For I felt no reason not to do so, as it offered me peace of mind that in these times she was safe. As to what her thoughts were on this matter, and to which I knew others no doubt deemed as 'Special treatment' I didn't know. But I vowed I would be the one to drive her home this evening, unbeknown to her.

However, little did I know at the time that this night was to be different in more ways than I ever could have predicted. And it started when I walked back into the VIP after taking a call, to see Sophia on the phone herself, only it was the one situated by the bar. Something I naturally questioned as it was not a usual sight.

It was a busy night, for the entirety of the club, thanks to what the college deemed as 'student night', along with the new arrivals for the VIP. It was the time of year that all heads of their states and sectors had the chance to come to me and present me with any problems they were facing. These issues were anything from human matters, financial business or the increase of demonic or angelic population. But more serious matters mainly included any sightings of those classed as the 'Marked' which was a list of our 'most wanted'.

The arrival of which also brought with it the workload that would follow, for these meetings were often long and tedious. Of course, there were often the trials too, in which this year there were to be four in total.

Afterlife wasn't just special for obvious reasons, the first being that it was what I classed as my main home. But also, because it was one of only a few homes that included the tools in which doing my job was made easier. Like the prison in the lowest levels, that housed some of the world's most dangerous supernatural criminals all still awaiting their sentence. Or the crypt that surrounded our tree of life, the one that connected both Heaven and Hell together and became a place of worship for my kind. For living eternally wasn't for everyone and some wished for those lifelong vessels to be put to rest when their souls moved on.

There were other things in these levels also, like my personal vault and the Temple where numerous events took place, including where sentences of crimes were to be passed down. Something that also meant that Afterlife acted as a kind of hub for the leaders of their kinds and heads appointed by myself, to come to when situations deemed it necessary.

However, unless it was classed as an emergency, where they would have to travel to wherever I was in the world at the time, then these problems could often wait until we came here once a year. This then giving me the opportunity to solve most issues raised before our time here was through.

Needless to say, we had a few places like this one throughout the world, making it easier for my subjects to gain access to what was needed. Afterlife just so happened to be one I also liked to call home more often than not.

I walked up to the bar just as Sophia was ending her call.

"Problem?"

"Just that we have run out of absinthe again and the last of our reserves got misplaced and put downstairs."

"Then have someone fetch it," I said frowning at the simple solution.

"Which is exactly what I was doing and hence the phone call," she replied in a sweet but sarcastic tone. I frowned making her grin before saying,

"Shall we?" She then held out an arm to indicate that we get on with the next meeting. I nodded and followed her there unable to help myself to a quick glance at what my girl was doing down below. It had been busy, so she had spent most of the time behind the bar. Something I was thankful for, as it was positioned directly opposite the VIP area.

Therefore, what I considered a most convenient place to watch her, especially when I would find my thoughts always leading to my new little waitress. A few times I had wanted to find a vessel next in line to order drinks just so as I could hear her speaking to me.

But then the next head of state would sit down opposite me, and work would begin all over again. In fact, it was only after the latest one had left, thankfully with nothing more to say than all in his sector was good. Well, other than the potential of a rogue in the area, after that I couldn't help but release a frustrated sigh.

"Why not just give in to your impulses and do as you have wanted to do all night," Sophia whispered leaning into me. I nodded knowing it was useless, for I could fight it no longer. So, in response she shook her head before the next person could take the seat of the last, telling them silently to wait, for their King was not ready for them.

Then when all was clear to do so, I picked a vessel close to the bar thinking I would find her quicker this way. However, the moment I took possession of the girl's eyes, I noticed Keira was nowhere to be seen. I frowned wondering had she possibly gone to the restroom? So, I went in search of her there. One look at the line and I swapped vessels with one just walking in, only to find that Keira wasn't in there either.

So, after one last look around the club, quickly jumping from vessel to vessel, I was very close to panic by the time I came back into my own body, now, at the ready to bark out my orders. But the second I did, I swear I very nearly swallowed my own tongue. For there now in front of me was Keira leaning over the bar and extending her hand to my barman, up here in the VIP! I was up and out of my chair in seconds and just in time to find Sophia next to her, saying her name in feigned surprise. That was when I knew exactly what this was...

A fucking set up...*A...fucking...gain!*

I was over there in a blink of an eye, knowing such a move was risky with a human now up here, but it couldn't be helped. Lucky that I had in the end, for she turned too quickly, and her clumsy manner soon took over, as her foot caught on the lower part of the bar. She fell sideways and into my arms leaving me thankful for taking the risk so that I was here to catch her.

"Nice catch!" Sophia commented happily before explaining to her who I was,

"Keira, I would like to introduce you to Dominic Draven." This was said with a hint of smugness, making me frown hard enough, I swear if I blinked my face could have cracked! I then watched as she lifted her head slowly, giving it enough time for her once pale skin to heat like the burning sun had touched it. The second she saw me she quickly dropped her gaze, and stepped away from me, making me want to growl in anger. I didn't want that response from her but the complete opposite!

"Sorry," she mumbled quietly making me near enraged. Had she remembered nothing of me in her dreams? For now, she acted as if any moment I was to lash out at her, physically hurting her and the thought had me furious.

"Brother, this is Keira, the girl I was telling you about," Sophia said finally cutting through what she no doubt hoped was not just tension but also the rage she could feel emanating off me in waves. Hell's blood, the entirety of the VIP could no doubt feel it coming from their King, as I could hear the whispered whimpers of fear.

"She graciously saved me today from getting into trouble with our new history tutor, who, well let's just say is certainly a piece of work." Sophia carried on this way, no doubt to try and put the girl at ease, something I found unable to do myself right at this moment. No, for all I could think of was a room full of the most powerful of my kind, now all watching this scene play out and no doubt asking themselves why I hadn't yet had her removed from the VIP. A place that was well known for not allowing humans into, under any circumstances.

This was my own strict rule.

So, despite them being loyal subjects to me, I was not unaware of the potential dangers from this leaking out. Which meant my next response would only end in setting me further back with the girl than I ever intended to happen.

For, in reality, I wanted to take her aside and engage in what would be considered a 'normal' conversation with her. But given how the audience I knew was at my back, there was only one course of action for me to take. And it just so happened to be the very last one I wanted to carry out...*I had to be mean to the girl.*

So, I gave her a look that spoke volumes to how I was pretending to feel, looking her up and down in an almost disgust. I also sidestepped when doing this so that those around the room could also see my reactions to her. I even openly glared at her, giving her nothing but my feigned indifference to her. And her reaction to this... she looked, well she looked,

Utterly devastated.

Although I will admit, that she at least tried to hide it somewhat well, but not enough to fool me. For after what I had observed in her personality and her natural reactions to people and situations, I knew exactly when she was putting on a brave face.

"I didn't realise you worked here, what a small world," Sophia said, finally drawing away my attention and unfortunate aim in trying to intimidate the girl, something right at that moment, I fucking hated myself for!

But I snapped my gaze back to my sister and the lies I heard spewing from her mouth with ease. I granted her a deathly glare she of course ignored and when I heard the reasons why I thought one of us had finally gone insane!

"Actually, we don't usually have people from around here working up in the VIP. You can understand we don't like the gossip that a small town generates but seeing that you haven't been here long then maybe you could help us out."

"What?!" The outburst was something I was unable to keep in before I took a disbelieving breath as I screamed at her to back down in my mind.

"That is not a good idea, Sophia," I said first before adding what I knew would be the last effort at showing my people my feelings on the matter. So, hoping they would buy into the show and Keira wouldn't I looked down at her. Then as if to seal my fate in words alone I said,

"She does not belong here." Lies! It was all fucking lies and all because I didn't want my secret getting out that I had found my Chosen One! I swear if I had felt like an asshole before in my lifetimes, then it was nothing compared to this moment! I could even see the second the pain had been inflicted for she actually flinched as if I had struck her down.

By the Gods, but even her hands had curled into fists, and I didn't know if she wanted to hit me or was just trying to prevent herself from crying. Well, I would have taken the first a hundred times over than a single moment of witnessing her tears! Even if the Gods knew that right then I deserved it and far worse.

Even Sophia looked shocked, giving me a look as if to ask me what the Hell I thought I was doing, making me grant her exactly the same look back.

"I don't agree. We need staff up here, and I think she deserves a chance, or do you no longer trust my judgement?" she challenged, and I swear I felt a vein pop at the side of my temple. It was such a deadly look I could feel myself giving her that I could no longer look at Keira again, for fear that I would actually frighten her. And after being so cruel, then I doubted she needed any more reasons added to the list to hate me!

"Sophia, you know my thoughts on the matter, so let it be on your head when this goes wrong. Do not forget our ways, sister." I told her almost now imploring for her to hear the inner meaning of those words. For it was her safety on the line here, and she had already unknowingly sabotaged me in gaining her heart!

I then left, storming through the tables of people and into my office, ready to let loose the wrath of the devil!

"Fuck...FUCK!" I roared hammering both fists down on my desk and near splitting the thing clean in two! I felt as if I had blown every chance of ever making her mine, just because I had a fucking act to play in front of my people!

But what else could I have done? For there was already knowledge of a traitor among us, and now Sophia thought to what, parade the fucking fact that I had found my Chosen One to the world so that they could kidnap her the first chance they got and right from under my fucking nose!

By the demonic Gods, what in Hell's soulless pool of fire, did Sophia think she was doing!? Well, she had just thrown the poor girl to the fucking wolves that's what! And now how was I to explain why there was a human working in the VIP? Gods, but I was their King for fuck sake, I wasn't supposed to have to explain anything to anyone! Yet if I did not, then such a thing would spread like soul weed throughout my kingdom, leading straight to a million other conclusions, ones which would undoubtedly include weakness...*as in mine!*

No, I would have no choice but if I allowed such, then to announce her as my Chosen One and put her in even greater risk than before I'd had the chance to protect her fully. Something achieved only when having her fully situated by my side and living in my home. And not something I could exactly accomplish yet until I had actually had a full-length conversation with the girl, let alone fucking bed her!

Gods be fucking damned! What a cluster fuck this was!

I don't know how long I was venting out my rage when I could stand it no more. I needed to see what damage I had inflicted, for she was the only one who mattered. So, I took hold of a vessel nearest the bar and saw her walking down one of the main staircases. This was no doubt so that she would be saved having to walk past my table in case I had been there.

This thought was just another lash of pain. I felt that I had inflicted upon us both. But then I saw her look up and her eyes widened as she noticed Jerry who was pacing the floor behind the bar and looked close to having an aneurysm.

I also noticed how she looked as though she was trying to ignore the obvious stares she was receiving from the rest of the club. Not surprising either, as they rarely saw anyone walking down the main staircase that framed either side of the stage area.

Then I saw Jerry march his red face over to her the moment he spotted her, making me want to growl at how angry he looked at her. I knew that this was my fault. After all, I had made it clear enough in the past that under no circumstances was there to be any member of staff allowed up into the VIP. Which meant that right now, he was only taking that job seriously. But that still didn't mean I cared for the way he spoke to her. After all, *I was responsible for it all.*

"What the Hell took you so long?!" he said yanking her to one side, and this time the glass that broke in my hands was one I cared little for cleaning up. I ignored the reactions around me and got up, moving my vessel closer to the two of them.

"I sent you up there because I knew you were the only one who didn't want to go, so I knew you would be quick, so what...? You thought that you'd have a good look around, take a tour, 'cause it's my ass on the line!" Jerry snapped, and I knew that only part of what he said was true. As what he didn't know was that when Sophia had called down earlier, claiming to be out of absinthe, she had planted the idea to send Keira in his mind...a fact I was absolutely sure of.

But I could take no more of this. So, I decided that it was time for some damage control. I fully returned to my vessel quickly and rang Jerry's number, knowing that he would answer it promptly.

"Uh...yes, can I help you?" Jerry asked, clearly unsure and no doubt fearing for his job, for he was certainly well paid. Something I was now reconsidering thanks to the way he had treated Keira. And because of this, I let my anger be known, for no one was to speak to her that way. And no one who wanted to continue to live would touch her like that ever again, not unless they wanted me to rip their fucking head off!

"I have sent Keira down there to inform you that she has been promoted to working up here in the VIP, which I gather won't be an issue for you," I said letting my authority known in my tone alone.

"Oh, I see...no, no, of course, that won't be a problem," he replied stumbling for his words as he was put in his place.

"Good. See that she starts at eight tomorrow night and wears all black. I also want you to take care of gossip, for there is no reason for Keira to suffer the bitter reaction of others because we have singled her out this way." I added knowing of the bitterness she would no doubt have to endure from others for accomplishing something no other staff member ever had.

"No, I'll take care of that personally," he replied now changing his tune which lead me on to my last and final warning.

"And I see from up here that you didn't even give her chance to speak before listening to her reasons as to why she was up here so long. So next time I suggest letting them speak and not putting your fucking hands on an employee unless you wish for this establishment to find a law suit on its hands? *Do I make myself clear?*" I said hoping to make my point, one in fact, I wished to have worded quite differently, adding my own personal death threat. Something along the lines of 'if you lay your hands on what is mine again, then I will break every bone in that offending appendage, making your pain a lasting memory every time you try to even sign your fucking name!'.

Yeah, something like that.

However, I refrained and reworded it as professionally as possible, impressing even myself at my restraint.

"Yes, I understand, and it won't happen again..."

"Be sure that it doesn't!" I said ending the call before letting him finish his grovelling.

"Please allow me to apol..."

"NO!" I shouted slamming my phone down on a table I had only just fixed with my mind.

"So, I take it this means she got the job then?" Vincent commented after entering my office, no doubt hearing the whole conversation before walking through the door. My growl was all the response he got before he spoke again.

"Okay, so granted, that was a bit of a fuck up."

"Understatement of the fucking millennia there Vince...seriously, what the blazing Hell was she thinking?" I asked after running a hand through my hair and banging my elbow down on the desk just for the jolt of pain I needed. I would have punched something but in all seriousness, I was making far too many holes around my home, and half of them forgetting to fix.

"Honestly?" he replied, and I waved a hand out like I could barely care anymore, I was just that fucking tired of Sophia's shit.

"I think this time she was thinking about Keira."

"What, about the one thousand different ways in getting her killed?!" I shouted now lifting my head up and looking at him.

"She's a fucking mortal, Vince, so we both know what that means!" I reminded him making him back down a moment because he knew what I meant. But I continued regardless.

"So, until I can make her mine and start merging my immortal essence with hers, she will be too vulnerable, even with the ability to heal her. And for that to happen, I need time Vince, Gods but I need fucking years! Time, I swear Sophia is trying to strip from me!" I watched as Vincent took all this in and you could see that he was trying to look at this from both sides.

"Or time she is trying to grant you quicker. Look I know it's hard for you to see right now but your caution could also end up being your downfall. Yes, I agree, tonight's actions were rash and impulsive, but just think about it, you wish to one day soon immerse the girl into our world...*yes?*"I didn't reply, but my look said it all, meaning he continued anyway.

"Then you are never going to achieve that by keeping her from it. At least this way you can ease her in and let her see for herself that there is nothing to fear from us, even when she finds out the truth of what we are. For instead of dropping something like that on her when she does not yet know us, then that is when fear will play a part." I fucking hated that he had a point!

"But think brother, if she has spent time up here, surrounded by our people and never once come to harm, then surely hearing such news will go hand in hand with trust. For she will know we speak with such knowledge and certainty when we say we mean her no harm?" I listened to everything my brother had to say, and I had to confess it once again made sense. Familiarity might very well be the key to gaining her trust before telling her of our world and might mean less chance of her running from it? I didn't know all the answers, but it was something I was willing to find out.

But now for the main problem in all of this,

"And what of the dangers of allowing such?"

"It's simple." At this I frowned, disbelieving such words.

"Lie."

"Lie?" I asked shocked.

"Or tell our people only half-truths, whichever you prefer," he stated as if this were easy.

"And within these lies you wish me to tell, what grounds do you suppose I make them?"

"I don't know, get as creative as you want. Tell them the Fates have claimed her as being a descendant of the Gods, and she is under your protection." I made a face telling him no one would believe such a thing and I told him why.

"But she is human."

"Ah, but is she fully? Consider it, no one can access her mind or her thoughts. Meaning that no one can feed on her emotions…something unheard of in a human mind. So, will it be so hard to convince others that she is special and in need of protection?" Vincent argued and making a good enough point that it had me now thinking this could possibly work.

I had told Vincent all about her 'locked' mind, one he had found hard to believe at first, but then no doubt found out the truth for himself the next night she worked. For he only said one thing to me before I bid my council a good night that eve.

'You are right Brother'.

"And what is then to be done about concealing our kind from her the times she is working here?" I asked, believing this an even bigger spanner in the works as they would say.

"Easy, explain how it is the Gods' wishes that her true identity is not known to her until the Fates deem it right. So, a pretense of humanity is needed to be upheld around her. And due to this, it stands without reason that the yearly meetings should be postponed until you believe it safe enough for your new charge to be exposed to such dealings."

"There will be those that won't believe it," I argued making him shrug his shoulders.

"There will always be rumours Dom, as you will never be able to control that, but at least this way you can be assured of her safety, as no one would dare harm her from up here. And hopefully, who knows, potentially speed up the process in claiming her, for like I said, trust is going to play your biggest enemy in that, if you don't want her to run from you."

Again, he was right. Which meant that by the time we left my office we now had a firm plan in place for this new shit storm Sophia had purposely let loose in my lap.

My only hope now was that it was to be a case of a problem solved and by that I meant…

A pissed off human girl I could tame.

DRAVEN

28

ENRAGED AND CAPTIVATED

By the time I had finished speaking with Vincent, I found that Keira had finished her shift and was currently sat at a booth with her friends chatting and looking uncomfortable. No doubt this was because she was being bombarded with questions by her pink haired friend.

I decided that my curiosity was too much for me, so I located one of the quiet ones sat at her table and took over their vessel as was quickly becoming a regular occurrence for me these days. In fact, I had lost count of the number of mortal bodies whose minds I had claimed since first meeting her. But I just knew that it had been more than I had in the last decade combined!

The moment I took possession, I was at least calmed by the knowledge that a certain boy I wanted to watch Ava maul to death wasn't at the table.

"Aww come on, you have to give me something! All these years everyone has been waiting to go up there, and they pick you. No offence."

The pink haired one known as RJ was in the middle of saying and I wanted to growl in Keira's defence.

But one look at my Chosen One now and I had to say, she looked close to snapping herself, making me realise just how much my words had affected her. The guilt I felt made me nearly crush the bottle in my hands, another thing that was starting to look like habit when I'd taken hold of a vessel around her.

"Look, I hate to burst the fantasy bubble, but it was nothing, no cult, no bloodsucking, not even a voodoo doll. Nada!" she said throwing up her hands and proving that Sophia had been right, she wasn't the 'gossiping' kind of girl. I then watched as this RJ seemed to deflate back in her seat as if utterly disappointed before then asking in a gentler tone this time,

"Not even Dominic Draven?" Now this question had me automatically sitting up straighter, thankfully a reaction no one else took much notice of. I was of course, deeply intrigued to hear what her reply would be and I almost dreaded it as much as I craved it. However, in the end, it was one answer I didn't relish hearing,

"No, Draven wasn't there," she said in a disheartened voice, as if she meant every word, making me realise that the way this was said held a much deeper meaning. It was only in this moment that I realised just how deeply she must have already felt for me, for why else would my words have affected her so badly?

This thought gave me something to focus on and more importantly, it gave me some much-needed hope right now. But then, when I looked at her dejected expression, I found that even though I was happy in the knowledge, she felt this strongly for me, I was also concerned with how far I had pushed her? Which was why I felt my eyes change, flashing with my other side before I had a chance to stop it the second she looked at me.

This hadn't been the first time, and I had to ask myself, why did it continue to do so? It was almost as if she were unknowingly trying to draw that side of me out and I found I had barely any will to stop it.

And she noticed, for her eyes widened the moment she saw it, and I couldn't help but smile back in return, trying to secretly convey to her who I truly was. I know it was foolish, but on some level I wanted her to know that I was watching her. That I cared enough about her to do so. But then this only lasted mere seconds as another girl on the table spoke to me, forcing my attention away from Keira as I had no choice but to leave this body.

My own had been in its blank state still stood by the edge of the balcony. It was almost like being asleep with your eyes open, blinking and mirroring the eyes of your vessel. But the link between the two was never fully severed as the moment your body felt anything from another's presence to that of a single touch, your mind was alerted to the fact.

"Is that going to be a problem?"

"That depends," I responded on a growl, as I watched the boy, Jack who had merely been sitting at the bar with some other friends of his, was now making his way towards Keira.

"On what?" Sophia asked, now feeling it safe to come and speak with me after no doubt being asked to give me time by Vincent. Wise advice after the damage she had caused in the last hour.

"On what you can discover tomorrow when speaking with the girl," I told her, now tearing my eyes from the sight of the two of them talking. Half of me wanted to retake hold of the vessel I had been using, but I knew it was safer to wait until his conversation was finished with the one I now knew was named Lanie.

I homed in on the others, who also seemed to be deep in conversation and as a rule, we tended to stay away from these, as engaging in conversation as a person you had no idea about was often...how shall I say...*awkward.*

"Vincent told me of your plan," Sophia said, this time edging on the side of caution. Um, wouldn't you know, perhaps she was learning, after all, I thought scathingly.

"A plan you forced me into." I snapped.

"Yeah, well it's done now, and for the record, I knew you would think of something," I growled at this, and the second she chuckled I quickly reclaimed my early statement, for she had learned nothing. Then, as she started to walk away, I issued her a last warning,

"Sophia."

"Yes, brother?"

"Interfere again without my knowledge and I will have you banished from the girl and from Afterlife until this claiming is done...do you understand?" The second I heard her suck in a shocked breath I knew that she got it. She now understood the full severity of what she had done. For I had never threatened anything like this before.

I looked back at her as I waited for her compliance and noticed how it all started to sink in. Something I hoped actually stuck this time. I really did, for all our sakes, including Keira's.

In the end, she didn't answer, she simply nodded and left, leaving me yet again that day to feel guilty. As I hated using the threat but in all honesty, I was at my wit's end, and I had no clue how to handle it any longer. All I knew was that I could no longer allow her to make my decisions for me, as the girl was my sole responsibility, something she was making increasingly difficult each day. Not considering I was constantly questioning what she would do next?

Half of me had expected an argument from her but then again, I think with one look at the problems she had caused, and no doubt thanks to our brother's intervention in explaining those to her, then she knew that this time, she had gone too far. Besides, we may have been equals in family, but I outranked her in station, for I was her King.

The hierarchy was a strange one, I grant you, as I was not the only King on Earth's plane. There were many considered Kings in their own right as they each ruled the race of their people. And this usually meant that they were chosen to rule from being the first of their kind or being the most powerful. Either way, the two usually went hand in hand, and in my world, power was everything.

In fact, the only exception to the rule was a being named Adam, or better known as his true name, Abaddon. He was without a doubt the most powerful being alive and the only one with enough force to destroy entire worlds. He had been, in the crudest explanation, the Devils experiment gone wrong. For it was like bringing up a child monster and then asking them to play nicely.

However, the only one he ever decided to play nice for was one of the most unlikely of characters I had ever met in the entirety of my existence. Her name was Pipper Winnifred Ambrogetti and if I thought of Sophia as a handful, when compared to her, Sophia would have been classed as a saint!

Pipper, or Pip as she preferred was a shadow Imp and a relatively powerful one at that. However, she was also known to be easily influenced and manipulated, due to having a slightly child-like demeanour and personality to match. Meaning that she more often than not made bad decisions.

Unfortunately for her these bad decisions orchestrated by another ended up causing one of the highest death tolls in England and other parts of Europe at the time of her crime. This was due to unknowingly introducing another round of the bubonic plague that resulted in her being sentenced to the deepest levels of Hell. I know this, as I was the one to cast such a sentence having no choice in the verdict, no matter how endearing the creature was to be found.

However, in an unusual twist of events, she somehow found herself the plaything of this uncontrollable beast Abaddon. Ironically, she was only ever cast his way as a fun snack to amuse her jailors as she met her end. Needless to say, this didn't happen but instead the beast found in her his soul mate.

But because of this he then destroyed a large piece of Hell the second they tried to take her away from him, done in an attempt at using Pipper to control him. However, such a beast was uncontrollable, and his destruction would not cease until she was returned. Something Lucifer decided pretty quickly once he realised that his kingdom was getting smaller by the second.

After this, unsurprisingly he didn't trust for Abaddon to remain in Hell, so granted Pipper leave, to try and find him a vessel, if such a thing were possible. The only way they achieved such a feat was using the power of all the kings together to put him to sleep, meaning for the one and only time in history, Hell was a vulnerable place. And hence my own time in having to leave this world to then go and rule it in Lucifer's place...*not exactly a time I relished, I assure you.*

However, it ended up granting me even more power, one of the largest armies in Hell and a castle erected in my honour and gifted to me to reside in during my time there.

My father had been proud indeed.

Thankfully though, it hadn't taken Pipper too long before she found the right man for the job and his name was Adam. The rest was history and thankfully one that doesn't include the destruction of Earth the second she managed to merge the two souls...a slight worry at the time.

Now they are married and he makes it common knowledge he is happily ruled by his wife who makes it her mission in life to sexually torment him at every opportunity. And he adores every minute of it, according to Sophia. For the two were thick as thieves for a very long time. Now, of course, Pip and her husband work and dedicate their loyalty to Adam's sire, Lucius. Someone who I had charged at the time to aid Pip in this near impossible endeavour. But that was another story and one far more bitter than I cared to admit.

I shook these thoughts of the past from my mind before getting entirely lost in them and refocusing on my future below, who was currently getting up from her seat. I decided I wanted to hear more, so I took hold of the vessel I had favoured before, just in time to see Keira putting on her jacket. I frowned the second I saw this leech named Jack grab the other sleeve, helping her into it. I was just about to focus all my hatred on the boy when I noticed something no one else did. Keira had frozen at the mere brush of contact with her arms before wincing to herself the second it was over, only then taking in a deep breath of relief.

I couldn't help but look at her, questioning now the new levels there were to discover what she could be keeping from me. This time I don't know what she saw in the vessel's eyes, but she could tell something was clearly amiss. Well, that made two of us, for she definitely wasn't what she seemed.

"I think I'll join you outside for some air, it's a little crowded in here tonight." The boy Jack stated now glaring at his sister RJ, making me wonder what I had missed when speaking with Sophia? I could hear the girl next to me trying once more to involve me in conversation, so I released the body and let her have at him and deal with his sudden confusion.

Then from back in my own vessel, I watched with gritted teeth, and an unyielding hold on the railings, as Keira and the vermin walked through the doors. I was somewhat comforted when I at least saw her take a moment to look back at me, directing her gaze up at the VIP and no doubt seeing the dark silhouette of my brooding figure watching her. One that now moved towards the balcony the moment she was out of sight, for I wouldn't allow it for long, not with the threat near hanging off her arm like a fucking primate!

I pulled my phone from my pocket the moment the doors disappeared into the slices cut into the stone walls either side.

"Bring the car around for the girl." I said before hanging up, having no patience for 'My Lord' bullshit right now! I knew that this order would be carried out immediately, which was all I cared for right now. I ended up missing the beginning of their conversation but watched as she started to fumble in her bag for her phone.

"Nice, hey if you wanted to boogie, then all you need to do is ask." The boy commented, annoyingly now trying to make her laugh as that awful music blasted from her phone. It was easy to hear them from up here with no interference usually found in the club.

She smirked back at him before answering, and I was at least satisfied that she hadn't laughed like he had intended for her to.

"Hello, oh Frank... is everything alright?" Keira answered first showing her concern and not thinking of herself or her situation first like so many would have. She was a selfless soul.

I couldn't hear Frank's reply from this far away, but it was easy to surmise, and besides, it didn't matter for I could hear the car coming from around the corner of the building now. A part of Afterlife where we had a hidden row of doors so that my many cars could get out with ease, for I kept a large part of my collection here.

The moment she saw it, I could see her face drop, and a blush deepened her pale skin. It was a moment I would have laughed at, as I knew that she had told Jerry that it was unnecessary and no longer needed. Something he had conveyed to me a few days ago and I had purposely ignored.

And well, looking at her face now, as I said, my first impulse was to laugh. Had I not been more concerned with taking control of my driver and ordering him to release his mind to me for a short while. This was so I could be the one to drive her home as I had always intended on doing that night.

I could have forced the issue as his King, had my driver not accepted, but it was common courtesy to ask another of my kind, no matter what your station was. Of course, he relented it willingly as I knew he would, for most under my employ would have done anything I asked.

"Well, it looks like that won't be a problem anymore." I heard Keira's reply and fought a grin after first creating an opening at the driver's side window. She sounded exasperated, and it was becoming clear that maybe Sophia had been right, that being singled out this way was something she found confusing and embarrassing.

From this distance, I now heard Frank's response on the other end of the phone.

"The car's there again, isn't it?" he asked with humour lacing his tone. Keira's only response was a groan, now confirming her true feelings on being driven home. Damn it, but I could sense an 'I told you so' on the horizon from one very smug sister.

"Man, he must have it bad," Frank said making me tense...was it possible that there was at least one human around her who had taken my actions for what they were and guessed at my true feelings for the girl? Well, it would seem so, and I had to say, this Frank just earned my respect for it.

"What do you mean?" she asked as if utterly shocked at the possibility and in total denial...foolish girl, she knew so little.

"Never mind Kid, I won't ring Libs. Catch you later," Franks said deciding to let her continue to be naive, as it was obviously easier to deal with than it was the truth behind my actions.

"It was my sister's phone and what can I say, she loves ABBA," she told the boy once she hung up making me sneer their way. I wondered how long she would make me wait, or should I say the driver, as I knew from speaking with him that she was always polite, always buckled up her seatbelt, always thanked him but more importantly, was always prompt at getting inside.

Something she wasn't right now.

"Come on, I'll drive you home if you want. Warning you now though, it's nowhere near as fancy." The cretin stated ignoring the car and now walking towards his own that must have been parked. Surely she wouldn't choose his offer... *would she?*

She looked to her unfortunate choice of friend and then back at me sat waiting for her. Then, unbelievably, she gave me the thumbs up and then pointed to a piece of shit pickup truck that looked ten years past scrap heap age! The fucking thumbs up! I couldn't believe it, she had actually chosen that fucking death trap over my Mercedes-Benz S600 Maybach! Granted it wasn't the Phantom, but still, it was a fucking nice car!

I watched as she ran to catch up with *her friend*, one who was quickly developing a death wish, making me wonder if it was time to get in contact with a death dealer and see if he hadn't somehow been one soul missed off their books.

After this, my anger wouldn't allow me to concentrate on whatever trivial words they exchanged, I just took my rage out on one of my two hundred thousand dollar cars. But from the sounds of the way I nearly blew the engine's pistons, it looked as if I was soon to be one down in a fleet of many, for it only just made it as I wheel spun it out of sight.

I couldn't watch the result of my mistakes being played out anymore. It was time to take action and do something I loathed to do. It was time to take over the mind of the boy and force him to act in such a way that Keira would never forget. It was time to play the asshole!

So, I concentrated on reaching out to his vessel and was about to take hold when suddenly I was cut off! I frowned and tried again, only this time, with more force than I ever had to use before with any other mortal being. Keira not included, for I had never tried to claim her vessel, nor would I ever, even if I could!

But this was different. It was as if I was just about to make a connection, allowing my mind to get to that place in theirs and then suddenly a door would slam shut on my efforts! I didn't understand it, why would such a thing happen? I knew it wasn't my own abilities, for I had jumped from vessel to vessel more than I ever had before in such a small space of time. Making me momentarily wonder if this was the reason?

But even that ceased to make sense, for there were times in battle I had been forced to use the same tactic hundreds of years ago and didn't find myself affected then. No, there must have been some other reason, one I intended to find out. But that would have to wait, for right now, I had more pressing matters, and they all centred on a shitty blue pickup truck containing an asshole driving it, and a naïve beauty that belonged to me sat alongside him.

So, even as I said that I would no longer watch as the results of my mistakes played out, I was quickly exchanging one body for another. Only this time, one with wings and a sharp enough beak for stripping flesh from bones.

I found Ava out on the hunt, one I forced her to give up in order to loan me her eyes, for I wanted them on my girl. I knew this was the safest way, for if I had gone to her house myself and saw what I thought I was going to see next, then no will in the world would have stopped me from making a rash decision. Something at this delicate time, I couldn't afford to do.

So, I quickly located their car, ignoring the pining of my pet asking me to go back for her kill. No, instead I calmed her as we flew with our minds entwined and told her that it was a meal given up for my Chosen One. She soon understood and forgot about her next kill, swooping low and getting too close to the window on Keira's side. I eased her to stay back but not before the panicked blue eyes of my girl caught sight of us.

I decided to get to the house before them, hoping to perch ourselves out of sight so as we could watch unseen until the time came to reveal ourselves. Should, of course, the unfortunate reason arise, something I was fucking praying to the Gods of Hell wouldn't!

"Well, thanks for the ride," I heard her say as she opened the truck's door, noticing the slight slip of her feet before getting to the ground. She looked unphased by it, as if it were such a common occurrence that, unless she actually hurt herself, most of the time it just went by unnoticed.

Unfortunately, the creep got out of the piece of junk also and started to make his way round to her side. Then as if this was some piss poor show of Oklahoma, he took her hand and said in a southern accent,

"Please allow me to walk a lady to the door." Then tilted an imaginary hat. I swear if I had been in my own body, I could have nearly swallowed my own tongue, before forcing him to choke on his!

But more absurd yet, was that Keira actually chuckled and I would have been furious at her as well, had I not then in that moment witnessed a new sound coming from her...*She snorted.*

I swear Ava's beak dropped because my own was doing the same back at Afterlife! What by the Gods had this woman done to me! I found myself mesmerised and at her fucking mercy just simply because I heard the adorable animal sound coming from her! One that should have been nothing short of ridiculous. However, this was not the case, for it had me fascinated.

It was...well, cute of all things!

For obvious reasons this wasn't a word, I found myself often using, as I couldn't even remember ever finding anything cute, let alone the sound of a small farm animal!

But then my blood ran cold in both bodies, for the boy leaned in close and whispered words that should have been mine,

"Did I mention it's the cutest thing, that little snort of yours?" Soon my hatred turned to utter loathing, and before I knew what I was doing, I roared up at the skies, from the balcony at Afterlife, cracking the fucking foundations and rocking the trees back on their roots, just from the force of my rage!

For now, he was leaning in to claim that first kiss that also should have been mine! There was no way I could stand for it and let such a thing happen, not in Hell's chance was he getting that piece of her!

So, the moment his arms went around her, I stretched out my wings, allowing Ava's true nature to be known, for Keira's back was to us and the dead boy standing, *well his wasn't.*

He opened his eyes a single moment before reaching her lips, and that was all it took for fear to take hold. He saw us for who we really were and even if, for only a split second, it was enough.

"What the Hell is that thing!?" he shouted, just as we charged, no longer as the demonic bird from Hell but as just as an unhinged part of the wildlife.

Unhinged and out for blood.

Keira

29

Dreaming of my Draven

As soon as I had laid eyes on the bird it took flight, pushing from the porch banister where it was perched. Jack had been freaked.

"What the Hell was that thing doing? Not like any crazy ass bird I have ever seen! Shit me, was that an eagle?!" I didn't even know if he was talking to me or himself, but he hurried a short,

"Goodnight," and went back to his car still muttering.

It was the one time I was thrilled the bird had reappeared and it also confirmed that it wasn't just my imagination. It had been real all this time.

Libby was trying to act casual when I got in, sat on the couch watching TV. Well, if she wanted to put on a convincing show then she shouldn't have put the TV channel to Football highlights. She hated most sports. I pulled her up on the bluff.

"Who's winning?" I said trying to hide my smile.

"What, oh uh... Liverpool." I very much doubted that, seeing as she was watching an American football game.

"Umm, strange that as I didn't know Liverpool were playing the Broncos this week... that should be an interesting game." I laughed as I watched her realise her mistake.

"Okay, so I wasn't watching the stupid TV."

"No, really? I would never have guessed, but you were watching something." I was making my way to the kitchen when she followed me.

"There's some pasta still left in the fridge." I opened it up to reveal a car crash of a meal left in a bowl. I couldn't understand how you could burn pasta. I would have to think of something quick to cook tomorrow before work.

"It's ok, I just fancy some toast." I put two slices of bread in the toaster and filled up the kettle.

"You want one?" She nodded in response and I grabbed two mugs out of the cupboard.

"So, he seemed nice, was that Jack?" I knew it wouldn't take long so I sat down and joined her.

"Yes, that was Jack and we're just friends." I knew she just wanted me to be happy, like she was with Frank. In her way she thought that if I could just meet someone nice then everything would work out. Well, what she didn't know was that I *had* met someone, but tonight just confirmed he was *far* from nice.

"Oh... do your friends always kiss you?" I knew it! She'd been spying on me.

"Libby! What were you..." She cut me off.

"Toast." She pointed towards the smoke coming from the bread inside and I reacted with waving a tea towel about trying to get rid of the smoke. I removed the charred bread and changed the setting down from five to two. No wonder it had burnt.

"See, I'm not the only one who burns things," she said in a smug tone.

"Well, maybe if it wasn't on the highest setting then I would get toast instead of charcoal and anyway, don't change the subject. Why were you spying on me?" I put the black squares in the bin and decided to give up on the toast idea and just settle for the tea. I poured the boiling water into the two mugs and let the teabags brew.

"I wasn't spying, jeez you're so dramatic. I was just checking to see who it was and I saw him about to kiss you, so I stopped. But man, he's cute and tall. Didn't think you went for blondes though? I always thought it was tall dark and handsome you liked?" I passed her tea and sat down giving her one of those looks.

"Libby, it's not like that, he's a friend."

"Does *he* know that?" Okay, so she had me there, but I really didn't want to talk about it, so I changed the subject.

"Anyway, how's that new client going?" I knew this would work. She loved to talk about her job and when she got going it was as if she had entered a different world.

Libby chatted until Frank walked in and then I made my excuses and went upstairs to my room. It was finally nice to be alone. I got ready for bed hoping that I would dream of him. Not the asshole version I had met tonight but *my Draven.*

"NO!" I shouted at myself. It was getting out of hand and I needed to stop it all! I knew what Draven was and he was out of my reach. It was pointless to dream of something that wasn't real. I went back into the bathroom and filled a glass and grabbed my sleeping pills off the shelf. This was one night that I needed to myself.

Back in the club the band played but it was surprisingly empty for this time of night. Jerry came over to me with a tray in his hand, looking flushed and his brother followed behind. It was the first time I had seen them both together, but it was only Jerry that spoke.

"You're needed upstairs again but you need to be quick." He handed me the tray, but I shook my head at him.

"No, I turned down the job. I'm not working up there and you can't make me." I finally said it and it felt good, unfortunately it was short lived.

"No, but Draven can. So, hurry up!" Now this did scare me. I didn't want Draven to speak to me again, so I gave in. I took the tray and headed for the back staircase when Gary spoke in that disturbing voice of his.

"Be careful not to bleed." What the Hell! Why did he say that? I' turned to demand what he meant but neither of them were there. What was with that dude? Did they teach 'creepy' at his school or was he just born weird. I mean, I know that Mike had called him 'Special' but come on.

I went to the doors that led to the staircase I had used last time, but something was different. There wasn't the usual muscle standing guard, so I shrugged my shoulders and I pushed the doors open. It was strange without the hum of people busy enjoying themselves down in the club. It made it more eerie.

The door at the top was open, unlike last time and I walked through after a moment of hesitation. Once I was inside, the door slammed shut sealing me in along with my fate. I dropped the tray and tried opening it but it seemed stuck or worse... *locked.* I turned to the room, which was the same as I left it the night before. There were the same groups all sat at exactly the same tables and I walked the same steps I had done the night before. Thinking of the one friendly face I could find, I walked towards the bar in hopes of seeing Karmun.

I was getting close to the centre table and my hands started to shake. I really wished there was a different way to the bar but it had been cleverly positioned. I took a deep breath letting my lungs fill with air so that I didn't have to breathe while I walked past. I wasn't sure why I did this, but I was almost convinced that the very scent of him had me feeling strange. I wouldn't look. I wasn't going to look. I promised myself not to look.

I looked.

Of course, I did. I was weak. However, he didn't look back. I tried to move my eyes but they wouldn't listen to my silent pleas. He wasn't wearing a full suit tonight. He wore a tight fitted t-shirt instead of a shirt and tie but had kept on the jacket. My God, he looked sexy. I started to mentally undress him and stopped before it got too much to handle.

I found myself thinking what his skin looked like in the glow of candlelight. More than ever I wanted to touch it. Would it be soft or hard under the strength of his muscles? He leaned over to the Goddess next to him and listened to what his sister was whispering to him. Then my cover was blown as his head snapped up too quick for me to react. I almost ran the rest of the way to the bar.

I bumped into people on the way but what I saw in them wasn't the same as last night. My curse! It had come back to haunt me, and I screamed. But no one looked at me, even when they pushed around me. I dropped the tray and bottles smashed around me in slow motion...but wait, hadn't I already dropped the tray? This thought was soon lost in sight of their faces...they were monstrous! I was terrified, and I wanted to run. NO, no, no, this couldn't be happening. Not now...not again!

I began to run but it felt as though my legs were made of metal. I could hear the crunching of glass beneath my feet and the heavy thunder of my own heartbeat. I was looking for the way out of this Hell but as I passed each table, the horrors kept showing themselves in wave after wave of demons.

There was one whose skin looked as though it was melting from the bone but it just smiled as though what I was seeing was normal. I gagged at the dripping skin and lipless grin. I ran past another table of men who didn't have faces but teeth. That was all, just teeth that locked together like prehistoric sabre-toothed tigers. Their lips started from their foreheads and went down to their chins with just deadly teeth, but their faces kept twisting and contorting into their normal faces, the ones I had seen last night.

I couldn't get a grip. I turned around looking to hide from them only to see more monsters. The table I thought looked like Vampires were actually a table full of broken skulls that bled through the cracks. They turned to look at me and pointed to me with broken fingers that kept fading into the air like they were made from the ash of cremated corpses.

I grabbed my head and sank to my knees wanting to curl up into a tight ball saying, 'There's no place like home,' over and over.

I could see from the corner of my eye a figure coming over to me before I made my secure ball. Everything was blurring, like when I was a child. I couldn't make out what was real and what was my madness. The figure was getting closer and every instinct told me to run but I was paralysed with fear. I hung my head and let my hair cover my face and the tears started to erupt from eyes that couldn't take any more.

"Please make it go away." I whispered like a frightened child.

"I will little one. Don't worry you're safe now." When a voice answered me, I realised that I had begged for this out loud. I recognised the voice, but I no longer cared.

"You can open your eyes now, don't be scared little one." A hand touched the top of my head before it flowed down to my chin and lifted it slightly. I opened my eyes as he had instructed and saw that I was back in my familiar bedroom.

Oh, thank you God!

I was in my bed and it had all been a dream. I saw the room just the way I had left it and I started to relax my tense muscles from the ball I was still in, but then I froze mid-stretch. If this was a dream then why was there a figure stood over me now? I shot up out of bed before I could think and dragged the covers with me, nearly tripping over them.

"Whoa, easy there... you're alright, I won't hurt you." He walked towards me with his hands up as though I was holding a gun. He looked as he did in the dream, only he wasn't wearing a jacket, just a t-shirt and black trousers. I instantly looked down to make sure I had gloves on which he noticed. Thankfully I did.

"I didn't touch you." He said in a soft tone taking my fears about exposing my scars the wrong way.

"I know you didn't but...but what are you doing here?" I tried to keep my voice steady, but it was proving difficult with my heart going so fast it felt like a jet engine firing up.

"I should go." That wasn't the answer I was hoping for and said the first thing that came to mind,

"Please don't!"

"You want me to stay?" He seemed surprised and I wondered if he'd looked in the mirror lately?

"I don't understand. Was...was I dreaming...*am I still dreaming?"* I added in a whisper.

"No and yes, it was a nightmare but now, well that's a different matter." He had slowly been making his way towards me and I shivered with the breeze that flowed through my open window. Was that how he had entered my room? And what was with the cryptic messages?

"What about now?" I asked as he bent down, not taking his eyes from mine for a second. I could see him smile in the dark when I asked this. I knew what was coming. This was the time that he would leave. It was the same smile I would always get when I didn't want it to end. But what was I saying, there was no way this was a dream, it felt too real. *Far too real.*

He held something in his hand as he came so close to me now that I had to arch my neck back to see his face. He looked down at me.

"Are you cold?" He raised his free hand to my face and touched my skin with the back of his hand, running it down my neck. This had to be real! I closed my eyes as my nerves became tense, hoping his next move was the one I had waited what felt like an eternity for.

He answered his own question.

"Yes, you are." Then with one swift motion my covers were around me like a cloak. He pulled me closer gripping the quilt like a collar on a jacket. I could feel him breathing as he got closer still to my face. I, on the other hand, had stopped breathing altogether, afraid that he would leave me as always. I needed to speak. I needed answers even if they were just in my dreams. There were things I simply needed to know.

"Thank you. But please... I need to know." There was just enough light from the moon for me to see one of his eyebrows rise. I carried on before I lost track of what I was saying.

"Is this real, are you real or am I still asleep?" He gave me what seemed like a sad smile and answered me,

"Yes, you are, but you won't have another nightmare. Not tonight." His voice sounded harder and somewhat possessive.

"But why, I mean...you..." I didn't know how to word it and he picked up on it.

"Why do you keep dreaming of me, you mean?" I nodded, half knowing why. I was sick. I was obsessed, and my dreams were only one of the symptoms of my sickness.

"I don't know why, but I will tell you one thing..." His hands moved up from the makeshift collar until his fingertips caressed the cool skin along the column of my neck. I couldn't help the deep quiver coming straight from my spine. Then he made it worse and added to the spell he had over me by speaking the words I longed to hear.

"I like it." He lowered his head, so he could see my eyes when he said this, and I could feel my skin burn under the hand that still held my neck. He smiled again as though feeling the evidence for himself.

"But why?" I finally asked. The reaction I got made me shiver as his fingers on my neck tensed and held me there, tightening his grip. His thumbs applied pressure under my chin, forcing me to look up. My breathing hitched when I saw the intensity directed down at me. I tried to move back when I saw the flash of purple create a ring of fire around his black eyes. However, this move wasn't permitted as not only wouldn't his hands release me, but he slowly shook his head.

"You asked me why." He reminded me, but I couldn't concentrate. Not when one of his hands moved so that he could caress my bottom lip with the pad of his thumb. I only managed to nod and even this was made more difficult as his fingers had now started to explore my t-shirt's low neckline.

"Please." I pleaded for anything more. His hand fisted in the material and for a moment he looked close to tearing it from my body in response to that one barely uttered word.

"The reasons why will be known in time, but for now..." He said quickly letting go of my clothes and I made a small sound of protest before it could be stopped. Although there was no need for it as he framed my face with both his hands and pulled me closer so that his lips could whisper the rest over my skin.

"...never doubt yourself Keira, you are so beautiful." I couldn't help but allow my eyes to close as his words washed over me. He thought I was beautiful?

"I..." A noise faintly heard in the distance interrupted me and caught his attention. He looked at the window as though something was calling.

"Time's up my little one." But before he could do his usual disappearing act I stepped away from his hold. He looked shocked as though this wasn't what he was expecting. Well, if this was my dream then I was in control, wasn't I? Although it sure never felt like it.

It pained me to be far from his body, but I needed something different to happen. I wasn't ready to let go of this yet. I moved to the corner of my room putting distance between us, which he didn't seem to like at all. I could even make out the hard lines of his displeasure from the other side of the room.

"Why do you have to go if it's my dream?" I bravely stated the obvious but was still retreating, backing into a corner. I looked down for a split second to make sure I wasn't going to do my usual tripping over act.

"That's a good question, but unfortunately one I cannot answer." The breath of his words hit me across my lips, as he was once again so close to my face. I couldn't understand it. How had he reached me so quickly?

Before I could react, his hands gripped my hips roughly and tugged me into his body. He grinned as though he found my startled breath amusing and then slowly leant down to my ear. I held onto his biceps just for something to anchor myself to in the flood of sensations he was causing to my body. Then it came. The whispered words that would end one of the nicest dreams I had ever experienced. And as always, his last words lingered in my mind, making it impossible to ignore such a commanding voice.

"Sweet dreams my Keira, for this time I promise..." He paused, which mirrored my breathing and then I felt him inhale deeply the scent at my neck before he vowed against my beating pulse,

"....to protect those dreams."

DRAVEN

30

PROTECTING HER DREAMS

Swiftly after I finally had something to enjoy as I saw the boy nearly soil himself seeing as he couldn't get away quickly enough. The second I heard the truck door slam shut I released Ava of her duty, now to go back to whatever prey she was stalking, as I went back to mine. I was back in my body in half a second, and I was then back at her house in under five minutes flat.

I landed with a thud, hiding myself the moment I did, and I watched as the kitchen light came on and Keira entered the room smirking. Her sister followed behind and I decided this time I wasn't going to miss the conversation. So, after throwing up a quick veil around myself, I got close enough to hear what was being said not far from the kitchen window.

"There's some pasta still left in the fridge," her sister informed her, and she opened up the fridge. Then she looked down only to quickly shut the door again. Then as she turned away from it, she pulled a face like she was going to throw up, only doing so after assuring herself that her sister couldn't see.

"It's ok, I just fancy some toast," she claimed pulling two pieces from the bread bag and popping them into the toaster. Then she filled up the kettle and asked if her sister wanted a drink. So far, it seemed quite normal, and I wasn't holding out for much insight as to what nearly just happened, that was until,

"So, he seemed nice, was that Jack?" her sister asked, now going down in my expectations for viewing him as such. But then I held my breath, waiting for the reply I was hoping for,

"Yes, that was Jack, and we're just friends," Keira said as she joined her sister at the small kitchen table. Alright, so it wasn't the exact words of, 'Who that little prick, no he's just some asshole I was using for a ride home in hopes of pissing off my boss, who was a cruel asshole tonight, but despite all that, someone I am actually in love with'...that I had been hoping to hear but granted, it was better than nothing!

But then her sister made a good point when she asked,

"Oh... do your friends always kiss you?" Now her response to this was what I most wanted to hear.

"Libby! What were you..." She was soon cut off by the smoke coming from the toaster and Libby informing her of such.

"Toast." After this, I watched in fascination once more as she took a piece of cloth from the counter and started waving it around before removing the two charred pieces of now black bread before dumping them on the counter. Then I noticed her frowning down at the dials on the machine before changing them.

"See, I'm not the only one who burns things," her sister argued making Keira laugh once, shake her head and tell her,

"Well, maybe if it wasn't on the highest setting then I would get toast instead of charcoal and anyway, don't change the subject. Why were you spying on me?" she asked as she now deposited the inedible pieces in the bin and simply settled on making her tea.

I had expected her to replace the bread for two new slices to toast, but she didn't. I frowned at this. Had she not been hungry? Was she eating enough? And was she getting the right types of food inside of her?

Gods, but what was wrong with me! I needed to get a grip if I was concerned about the girl's eating habits. Even ones that did seem to be rather sparse and out of sync. But then I tried to remind myself that she had been taking care of herself for a lot longer than I had known her, so who was I to decide on what she preferred? As long as it never affected her health, then it was one aspect of her life I need not meddle in.

"I wasn't spying, jeez you're so dramatic. I was just checking to see who it was and I saw him about to kiss you, so I stopped. But man, he's cute and tall. Didn't think you went for blondes though? I always thought it was tall, dark and handsome you liked?" Now hearing this certainly peaked my interest, for if that was her type then could that have been why she seemed so nervous around me?

Was it her attraction to me physically that made her bite her lip or stutter her words? Which meant, that around the boy, could it be as she said it was, did she only view him as a friend?

Thankfully her next words confirmed this and gave me the peace of mind I had needed.

"Libby, it's not like that, he's a friend."

"Does he know that?" her sister asked, and I had to agree for if this was her feelings on the matter then prolonging the boys deluded hope would only make matters worse. And selfishly, what I actually meant by this was to prolong my annoyance in keeping him around.

After this, their conversation turned to more mundane things, something I could tell was purposely engineered by my Electus. I decided that I needed to give us both some space for the evening, knowing that I now had more questions raised. And for once, they weren't about the girl.

No, they were about the asshole and why I couldn't access his mind? For I found it odd that I had come across two mortal beings like this for the first time in my existence and both within weeks.

So, I took to the sky once more and found myself striding into my office after landing on the balcony. Then, I pulled my phone from my jacket before removing it completely, throwing it to the back of a chair. Then I rolled up my sleeves and got to work for the night, starting with trying to find out why I couldn't control a human parasite named Jack.

I don't know when or how but I opened my eyes and found myself stood on the ground floor of my club with the band playing but strangely, most of the place empty. But even more surprising was to discover who I was stood directly behind now...

"Keira." Her name slipped passed my lips on a whisper but one that should have been close enough for her to hear. However, she didn't turn but instead she just watched as Jerry rushed over with a tray in his hand and his brother following closely behind.

"You're needed upstairs again, but you need to be quick," Jerry said abruptly, handing her the tray and in turn, Keira started shaking her head at him.

"No, I turned down the job. I'm not working up there, and you can't make me." She said forcefully, and the pain in those words made my chest ache, for I had caused this.

And I knew exactly what this was...

She was dreaming.

"No, but Draven said. So, hurry up!" Jerry said snapping at her this time and I found it curious that even in her dreams she referred to me as Draven. I shook my head in frustration. As after what Jerry had just said, I knew now which part I was to play in this dream of hers...*I was the villain.* And could I really blame her after the way I had acted? No, I could not.

But then something else happened, and it was something I hadn't been prepared for. Just as Keira gave in and headed to the back staircase so that she could access the VIP, Gary stopped her and whispered over to her,

"Be careful not to bleed." That was when I knew what this truly was. It wasn't a dream like I thought...

It was a fucking nightmare!

In that second, I woke up, bolting upright from my bed. I quickly dragged some clothes on that were closest to hand and found myself outside on my balcony in less than thirty seconds. Then, without any other thought, I took off into the night, getting to Keira's window in just under five minutes.

I entered into her room and could see for myself she was still trapped in her nightmare for she was tossing and turning, mumbling in her sleep. I got closer to her, moving slowly for if she woke suddenly, I didn't want to frighten her further. That was when I heard what she was saying, over and over.

"There's no place like home, there's no place like home" Hearing that softly spoken plea broke my heart. Making me realise that I had no choice but to first access her dream and try and fix whatever it was she was seeing that was terrifying her. It was time to cancel out her 'villain like' image of me and replace it with another... *The hero.*

It didn't take me long to access her mind, as her fear was very near being screamed at me. Unsurprisingly, I found her up in the VIP area of the club on the floor curled up, holding herself and with her face hidden by the curtain of her hair. Again, the sight broke my heart, for she seemed totally frozen by fear. I looked around to see that whatever images she had seen, they had all blurred and vanished the moment I stepped into her mind as if they themselves had been afraid of my presence. Now it was just my hope that she wouldn't be the same.

I knew the moment she felt my presence for she whispered a desperate plea,

"Please make it go away." I knelt down in her dream to her level, still being cautious about touching her too soon. I didn't want her to wake screaming in fright, but to do so calm and trusting, reasons why I made my tone as gentle as I could, telling her,

"I will little one. Don't worry, you're safe now." She recognised my voice. I could tell this the moment she first tensed her body. But just before I could move away to give her some space, she instantly relaxed again, giving me the green light to move forward. So, this time I left her mind and came back to reality, where she was still asleep in her bed. Something I knew I would have to put an end to if she were to get a peaceful night. For if I left now, she would only find herself back there once more.

So, I decided to take the chance, in hopes that I would be able to control her mind enough to be commanded into sleep once more. As I was no fool and knew that the more I pushed, the more her mind fought me, making coming here harder and harder to control.

But right now I didn't care. No, all that mattered was saving her from herself and putting a stop to her fears.

So, I told her,

"You can open your eyes now, don't be scared, little one." Then I gently laid a hand on top of her head before caressing her cheek with the backs of my fingers, still taking the time to marvel at how soft her skin was. Then I curled my fingers under her chin and lifted with only enough pressure to get her to open her eyes and look up at me.

She blinked a few times, in an effort to make sense of her surroundings and bat away the last few cobwebs of her dream that tried to cling to her mind. I knew she had done this when I saw her body relax, lowering her legs and loosening her arms from the protective position she had put herself in. But then it was as if my presence was an afterthought, and it had just kicked in, as she paused the stretching of her limbs.

Then, after a single moment of gazing slowly up the length of my body, she reached my face, which was when she froze. But, before I could say anything, she bolted from the bed, taking the covers with her and coming close to tripping over them. However, she managed to stay on her feet this time, and I started to walk towards her with my hands up in a gesture that meant her no harm.

"Whoa, easy there... you're alright, I won't hurt you," I told her, and I frowned when she looked down at herself as if to check to see if I had touched her or not. I wanted to be angry at this but in reality, what right did I have to be? She didn't yet know me on a personal level. But only as her boss and someone on many occasions who had been abrupt or rude to her. So, what else was she to think when finding me in her room? Which is why I forced myself to un-grit my teeth and told her as gently as I could,

"I didn't touch you." She looked shocked a moment and then looked back down at her arms as if something just dawned on her before telling me quickly,

"I know you didn't but...but what are you doing here?" This was when I realised that she hadn't been concerned with me touching her at all. She had just been worried if her arms were concealed or not, which they were, *just like always.*

Which meant only one thing. She wore them for only one purpose...to hide what was beneath them. This was when my heart really started to ache, for there was only one explanation for someone to do such a thing...*shame.*

'Oh sweetheart, what did you do to yourself?' I asked in my mind, hoping it wasn't what I suspected it was, for I couldn't imagine what she must have been going through to feel as if that were the only way.

I looked at her now and replayed back her question, knowing now that it was possible that due to previous issues she may still have, that me being here right now might only be making matters worse.

So, I told her,

"I should go." But then her quick panicked reply surprised me. Especially when she stepped forward, reaching out to me as if she wanted to grab hold. Then she pleaded,

"Please don't!"

"You want me to stay?" I asked, confessing my shock in my tone. But she didn't answer me. No, instead she wanted her mind put at ease, something that would have been difficult seeing as I didn't want to lie to her.

"I don't understand. Was...was I dreaming...*am I still dreaming?*"

"Yes and no, it was a nightmare, but now, well that's a different matter," I confessed, even though I knew this wouldn't have been enough for her. But then she looked to the window I had left open in my haste, now grabbing her attention as the cold blew through and made her shiver because of it.

"What about now?" she asked ignoring the cold, whereas I would not. So, I bent down, doing so slowly, so as not to startle her and making sure to keep eye contact. I also couldn't help but grin, for she seemed more concerned with the chance of me leaving than me actually being here. Did that mean my rash and abrupt actions tonight didn't inflict as much damage as I thought? Well, it was time to test that theory.

So, I stepped closer to her until she had to arch her neck back to still keep contact with my face. I looked down at her beautiful soft skin, one bathed in moonlight and made even paler from the chill. Then as I raised my hand to touch her, asking her at the same time so that she would know my intentions,

"Are you cold?" Then I ran the back of my hand down her cheek and neck, making her close her eyes as a shudder rippled through her body. I knew then how much power I held over her. The power to affect her body and mind the way I always hoped I would. But instead of making the next step as I wanted to and from the looks of things, like *she wanted me to,* I answered my own question.

"Yes, you are." I then took charge of her care by casting out one end of her fallen covers behind her, so that it landed on her shoulders. Then I caught that end, gripping it tight so as I could pull both sides together around her shivering frame. But instead of letting go as I should have, I only ended up gripping the makeshift collar tighter, pulling her closer to me and looking down at her with only one thing on my mind...*tasting those awaiting lips.*

But then she spoke, and I could barely believe that she thanked me, as if all memories of earlier tonight had simply evaporated.

"Thank you. But please... I need to know," she asked adding to her thanks and making a single eyebrow of mine rise as I looked down at her.

"Is this real, are you real or am I still asleep?" she asked, making me realise just how frustrating this all must have been for her. Yet my half smile was more to do with the idea of her dreaming of me and trying not to focus on how little I could give her, as I knew now that anything I told her would have to start with a lie. For what other option did I have? She couldn't be allowed to know that these times were real yet, not until I was ready. *Until she was ready.* As I knew that with a single truthful word spoken, that would only end up opening up the flood gates on questions, she would ask. Questions that right now, I just couldn't deem it safe enough to answer.

Questions like, how did I keep getting up here? How did I keep making her fall asleep? How did I keep accessing her dreams and why was I always watching her? Well, unless I wanted to come out with the answer, 'I am a rock climbing, hypnotist stalker who has claimed you as my next victim', then I saw little options left. As the truth would have had her really screaming in fear!

So, in answer to her question, I told her as a vow,

"Yes, you are, but you won't have another nightmare. Not tonight."

"But why, I mean...you..." She paused stumbling for her words, but I knew what she meant.

"Why do you keep dreaming of me, you mean?" I asked knowing the moment that I did, she was embarrassed. Almost as if ashamed, as if what she was doing was wrong. But I wanted to eradicate this from her mind and let her know that it was in fact, the opposite. That she had every right to dream of me, for I belonged to her and no one else.

But in the end, there was only one way to get her to feel at ease without delving too deeply into the real reasons why. So, I decided to give her a piece of my feelings.

"I don't know why, but I will tell you one thing..." I paused long enough so that my fingertips could trace lines up the column of her neck and I leaned closer so as to emphasise my next few words as the truth they were,

"...I like it." Then I grinned the second I saw her eyes widen in surprise, for she really had no clue of the strength of power she held over me. Only acting as if I was the one holding it all and using it against her.

"But why?" she asked making me wonder if she had looked in the mirror lately and witnessed the way her soul lit up everything about her from something as simple as a smile? Was the girl blind to all that was her?! I was a King of Kings, ruled an entire world, and yet one strange piglet sound had me struck dumb. One wrinkle of her nose had me grinning, one doe-eyed look up at me could bring me to my knees. And the sight of a single tear in her eyes made my heart feel as though it was fucking torn open! And yet in that one question, she had not a single clue!

Not one.

Which was why my fingers tensed on their own, tightening my grip on her neck but taking care not to frighten or hurt her. But I wanted her to understand, to see herself the way I saw her. So, I forced her to look up at me with my thumbs pressing against her chin and her breath caught in her throat the second she saw the intensity in my gaze. One she tried to step away from. Of course, this wasn't something I could allow, and I could feel my demon respond to such a challenge as it no doubt flashed its warning in my eyes.

She didn't struggle, knowing that she was going nowhere still locked in my hold, but I shook my head in warning again, for I didn't want her to push my demon too far.

"You asked me why," I said reminding her and myself that I was yet to answer her question. But I had to confess I was quickly getting lost in the sight of her. Just looking down at her innocent beauty, one that was currently at my mercy. Which was why I couldn't help but tease her and torture myself at the same time. I ran the pad of my thumb across her soft, pink lips, wishing it to be a journey made with my tongue, so as I could taste those breathy sounds, she made for myself.

Then, at the sight of her heaving chest, no doubt from trying to maintain a steady rhythm to her breathing, I couldn't help but push her just that little bit further. And myself for that matter as I traced my fingers along her low neckline that offered me a delicious sight of what I would soon be in store for. I felt her nipples harden even through the makeshift cloak I had put around her, and I was half tempted to let it fall, just so that I could see them peeking out for me. But then these thoughts fled me the second she uttered just one word. A word that if she had been naked beneath me now would have ended up being my undoing.

"Please." The sound of such coming from breathy lips made my fingers halt their soft exploration and the next thing I knew I had a fist full of material in my hand, ready to tear the fucking clothes from her quivering body. She sucked in a quick, sudden breath which was enough to sober me into realising what I was close to doing.

"The reasons why will be known in time, but for now..." I told her pausing as I let go my forceful hold on her before taking a more gentle approach. First enjoying the small sound of protest she made when she thought I was letting her go entirely. My heart lifted knowing that this more dominant side of me didn't scare her but only managed to increase her sexual need for me. For I could sense it coming from her in lustful waves, making it harder for me to keep a firm hold on my restraint. Especially when all I wanted to do was give her first-hand knowledge of what I could do to her with my hands. Hands that she made clear, she didn't want to leave her.

But I knew if I crossed that line, then there would have been no coming back from it and she was too important to risk losing. So, I forced myself to take hold of her face instead, so that I could pull her close and whisper the mere kiss of a promise over her skin,

"...never doubt yourself, Keira, you are so beautiful."

"I..." She started to speak when the sound of Ava calling out in the distance, told me that I was needed elsewhere. It was as unfortunate timing as it was not, as I didn't know how long my restraint, or willpower would last around her.

"Time's up, my little one," I told her expecting her compliance but as usual, she surprised me. As one second she was in my grasp, and the next, she was not. She had slipped free of my hold and continued to move away from me, making my demon want to growl. However, a frown was all I would allow as she started to position herself in the corner of her room.

At first, I questioned why, hoping it wasn't done out of sudden fear, but then she spoke, and I couldn't help but feel elevated to know the motives behind her sudden actions.

"Why do you have to go if it's my dream?" She missed the knowing grin I displayed that was all demon this time, as she looked down briefly to check that she wasn't going to trip on something. And knowing her, then it was a good call or, so I was quickly learning.

It also allowed me to use the speed I needed to get to her without her seeing how fast I moved.

"That's a good question, but unfortunately one I cannot answer," I told her the second her head snapped back up, and she found me only a hairsbreadth away from her. She sucked in a quick breath of disbelief, and I had to admit, that I was starting to become addicted to the little sounds she made whenever I was close. I also relished in her question, liking that she was needy for me to stay. Especially after I had feared I had ruined my chances with the girl. Well then this, this was quite a revelation.

But before she could fully react, I decided it was time to show her who was in charge of this 'dream' I had forced her to believe in. So, I suddenly grabbed her hips and yanked her tight against my body. Then I smiled once again to myself when hearing her increased heart rate and knowing she was nearly panting being this close to me. I then leant down, getting as close to her ear as I could while lifting her slightly to make the connection easier.

She quickly felt the slight elevation and gripped onto my muscles hoping to steady herself. But other than the thrill I now felt at having her touch me, then really, there had been no need, for I would never have let her fall. Gods, but I didn't even want to let her go, knowing just how right her body felt in my hands. It was like the strangest addiction. Just to feel her skin beneath my fingertips was a connection unlike any other. The heat, the spark of that single touch, it was as if powered from some Heavenly source, not even I was aware existed. So no, I didn't want to ever let her go but instead found myself near desperate to drown myself in the sensations. To bury myself in her sweet little body and stay there for hours making it mine.

However, for now, I would have no choice but to let her go. So, I let the angelic lure to my voice take hold of her senses and infect her mind with just the right amount of influence so as not to alert her mind to the intrusion.

"Sweet dreams, my Keira, for this time I promise..." I paused, taking a last bittersweet moment before I had to say goodbye, to breathe her in deep, burying my face in her neck and finishing my sentence against her quivering skin and erratic pulse,

"....to protect those dreams."

31

CHILDHOOD

As soon as those words had been uttered, my mind instantly found sleep then just as quickly awoke, as though they had been echoing round and round in my mind until finally bubbling up to the surface. It was still dark outside my window, but it was closed as though it had never been touched. My heart sank instead of the usual rush of pleasure I would normally feel. I tried to piece together the nightmare, which had then erupted into the second-best fantasy yet; the first being the one that included a kiss.

It had seemed so real I could barely believe it was just constructed from stunning visual memories and sweet fictional ideas. Mainly ideas of what I longed to do to Mr Arrogant himself. In fact, the only reason I still believed they were all just dreams, was because any other explanation was impossible. The man despised me that much was clear. To him I was an intruder who didn't belong, not only in his world, but most definitely not in his club. So, what did my mind do to rectify this? I conjured up a sweet centre to go with his delicious hard candy casing, instead of the bitter aftertaste spending time with Draven really produced.

I got up, wrapping a knitted throw around my shoulders, as I was about to do something I hadn't done for a very long time. I walked over to my white washed wooden desk and took out the supplies I needed from one of the drawers. Libby had put a load of art stuff in one drawer in the hopes that one day I would start up my passion again. As it turned out she had been right. I held the pencil in my hand as though I had been Harry Potter finding the right wand.

Libby and I had both shown a passion for art since a young age. But Libby then went on to develop a taste for interior design, begging our parents to let her decorate their lounge at the age of sixteen. Ever since then, she had known what her calling in life had been, and she was a master at it. I, on the other hand, had developed mine in a very different way.

You see, I had a secret. The deepest and darkest of secrets. I was different from the rest. I had always known that one day it would catch up with me. Like a personal realm of demons I just couldn't hide from and no matter how much I closed my eyes, they were there...they were always there.

Waiting in the shadows of what was left of my mental control. Waiting until the day I finally broke and gave in for the very last time. The scariest thing was it really didn't feel like that far away. It started when I was younger, one year when we all went on vacation down to Cornwall to spend the summer with my mother's parents.

My grandparents lived by the sea, which would attract various types of tourists. The summers would be buzzing with people from all walks of life and was a breeding ground for all types of entertainment. Everyone would wait with excitement for the famous travelling circus and fairground to come to town.

Only this particular year would end up being a life changer I would never forget.

My sister and I went skipping through the crowds with giggles and smiles, taking in all the wonders our eyes could see. Fire eaters, acrobats, men that would eat swords, stilt walkers and clowns with sad faces, squirted each other with water filled flowers. The rides with happy screams of excitement and the smells of sugar treats and hot dogs filled the field, transforming it into a child's blissful playground.

It had been my first time at a fair, well one that I could remember anyway. I was nearly seven so I couldn't go on every ride like Libby, but I didn't care, I was just so happy to be there, that I could barely contain my excitement. Libby and my dad had just come off a roller-coaster called the 'Inferno Twister' when I started to ask about the candy stand over near the 'House of Fun'. My mother had waited with me and bribed me with the chance of candy-floss if I waited like a good girl. Given my love for all things sweet, this wasn't a hard task to comply with. But as soon as they came in sight, it was all my mind could think of.

"Libby, take your sister to get some teeth rotting sweets before she gnaws my hand off." My sister laughed and took my hand in search of the red and white stand.

"What's gnaws mean?" I had asked innocently enough, when the crowd started to get thicker due to the end of a show in the big top. My sister's hand squeezed mine in vain just before I broke away. I couldn't see for bodies all moving in different directions. I was pushed along with a family who weren't speaking English and I couldn't hear the sound of my sister's voice calling my name over a language that I didn't understand.

Finally, after following them, I was left standing in a quieter part of the fairground where there were no rides or stalls. I was on the outskirts of the park. I stood with a wet face from tears of panic when a woman with a kind voice approached me. She was dressed strange, with a number of red and purple scarves around her head like a turban. I remembered seeing people dressed like this in some of the books in my grandparents' library and I recognised her to be a gypsy.

She wore a white shirt with big sleeves and a red dress on top that tied under the bust with ribbons crossing over. Her arms were covered in bangles and gold bracelets with what looked like coins hanging from them.

She wore multiple sets of matching hooped earrings. But her hands were covered in so many rings that you could hardly see the skin on her fingers. One caught my eye as it was shaped like a silver dragon's head and its mouth opened up as though it had swallowed her entire finger. The teeth on the end looked sharp as the spikes interlocked and clamped together.

"Are you lost, young lady?" I remember thinking it was nice to be called young lady instead of my usual "Little squirt" Libby called me.

"Yes, I can't find my sister, she was taking me for some sweets." She smiled showing a full set of yellow teeth, like ones you would find on an elderly person after a life time of heavy smoking. Her tanned skin was awash with lines of age and I noticed a small red star close to her right eye, nearly lost in the wrinkled folds.

She looked at me strangely, staring deep into my eyes. Even as a child, I had known that something wasn't right about this woman and remembering the golden rule of childhood, I took a step back saying,

"I should go and find my parents and I shouldn't be talking to you, you're a stranger." I turned to leave but somehow she stood facing me once more.

"How did you do that?" Her red lips curled up on one side revealing a yellow fang and she bent down to the level of my young face.

"Magic!" She said and with a movement of her hand she produced a pretty pink flower. She gave it to me and then straightened up revealing a less creepy smile.

"My name is Nesteemia, but my friends call me Ness. I'm a palm reader."

"What's a palm reader?" I was at my questioning phase wanting to know absolutely everything there was to know about anything.

"I can tell you your future my dear, by touching your hand."

"How? I hold my sister's hand all the time and I don't see anything." She bit her lip trying to hide a smile that would no doubt turn into a laugh.

"You have to know the magic to be able to see." I nodded my head understanding, thinking she could be a witch. I held out my hand with a firm mind and said,

"Show me please." This would turn out to be the biggest mistake of my life because when she took my hand in hers what I saw next truly terrified me... and the gypsy.

She closed her eyes as she ran her heavy metal covered fingers across the palm of my cold small hand and she started to chant words I didn't understand. I got scared and tried to pull away but she held on tighter, stopping me from removing my now quivering hand. She opened her lids, but her eyes were somewhere else. Rolling back into their sockets so all you could see were the cloudy whites of them. She started to shake her head and her eyes, that had turned blood red in colour, were now flickering back and to as though trying to read the lines in a book a million words a second.

I looked around searching for anyone who might be able to help me, but I hadn't realised she had pulled me further from the fair. We were now completely out of sight. I tried to speak and scream but when I opened my mouth no sound came from it. It was as if she had put some sort of spell on me, forcing my silence. I was helpless, wishing I had never even wanted candy-floss in the first place.

She started to slow down her breathing and her eye movement was less erratic. She looked at me but now she was the one who looked scared. Fear caught up with her body making it vibrate as mine once did, as though what she had seen in my future had been so disturbing she couldn't contain the terror. I stopped struggling now as a new fear had gripped me.

What had she seen?

"What is it? Tell me... what did you see?" I asked in a panicked voice. She just stared at me not speaking a word but she wouldn't let go of my hand.

"TELL ME!" I managed to scream bringing her out of her comatose state.

"It's all true, but it can't be...you can't be real...what trickery is this?" I didn't understand her babbling, so I struggled once more to break free of her fierce grasp.

"Let me go!" I said over and over but she wasn't listening to me. She just kept saying the same words over and over.

"It has come, it has come." Finally, I could see someone coming this way and tried to make another run for it. She caught sight of them before I managed to draw attention to us both and she clamped her other hand around my mouth, pulling me back behind a work shed, out of sight.

"I will make you see ready for your master, young mistress." I didn't understand, and I shook my head under her grasp.

"Be still," she ordered as she grabbed my arm and held it out with my palm facing upwards. I was losing the strength to struggle anymore and was giving up. The tears streamed down my face and on to the hand of my captor. She held the dragon finger out pointing it at my palm.

She said something that sounded like a command, only it was in a different language.

"укусить!"("Bite" In Russian) Then my eyes saw something impossible. The dragon's head moved, opening its mouth wide releasing its teeth into a biting position. I mouthed the words *'Don't!'* and *'No!'* But the sound was muffled by her hand. The dragon bit down hard on my palm making small puncture marks with its teeth. I cried out in pain wanting this nightmare to be over, wondering if I was ever going to see my family again. She whispered in my ear yet more words I couldn't understand.

"Θα τελειώσουν σύντομα ένας γενναίος" ("It will soon be over, be brave" In Greek)

She pulled her hand away from my lips and I was in too much pain to say anything apart from cry. Then she repeated the same words once more to the dragon ring and placed it to her own palm letting it once again taste blood. At least this time it was hers. Unlike me she smiled at the pain as though welcoming it and pressed it tightly to my own bleeding hand.

"It has been a pleasure, Electus. Until next time."

These were the last words I heard until my mother's voice woke me up. I opened my eyes to the room my sister and I shared in my grandparent's guest house. I first thought it was all a dream as I looked down at my hand for a cut in my skin but it wasn't there. I later found out that my parents, along with a number of fairground staff, had found me curled up asleep near the tool shed. There was no sign of a gypsy woman and nor had there been one working the fair that year. I tried to tell my parents but without proof they put it all down to a traumatic nightmare.

I, too, had been convinced until the day I saw her again.

It was on my seventh birthday, we had all gone out to an American themed diner where they served burger and chips (Or fries as it was on the menu), which was a favourite of mine. Afterwards we all walked along the shore to get some ice cream, spotting one made with traditional Cornish clotted cream. I pointed it out as though the colourful ice cream van was a beacon drawing me in.

I walked right up to the open window already knowing the flavour I wanted, when I noticed something familiar. The man who served me had the same deadly red tint in his eyes as the gypsy in my dream. I tried to shake it off, but the red kept getting deeper and deeper until it soon looked as though his eyes would overflow with blood. I stepped back before giving him my order, when my father's voice came up behind me making me jump.

"Whoa, hey kiddo, what flavour are you getting?" I didn't answer as my dad walked past me giving the man three orders for himself, my sister and my mum.

"Honey, what you having...? Come on, make your mind up." My dad was getting impatient as he could see a line forming behind me. I still couldn't speak. Why couldn't he see what I was seeing? He turned to give me a look that translated to 'if I don't pick soon I wouldn't be getting one' so I mouthed a silent 'chocolate' and he frowned at my strange behaviour. He passed me mine with his hands full and walked towards my family who had sat down on a nearby bench. I was about to follow when the man from the van shouted,

"Hey Guv, you forgot your change" in a thick Essex accent.

"Oh Honey, could you grab that for me?" I froze knowing I would have to explain myself if I refused. Maybe I was just seeing things. That had to be it. No one else in the line looked freaked. People moved out of my way to let me pass as I reached up my hand to receive the money, but the man grabbed my hand forcefully and my eyes met the gypsy woman's face, the one that had haunted my dreams for weeks.

Her eyes were bleeding and the blood dripped down her face. There it gathered into thicker drops until finally onto people's ice creams that lay in the holders. Customers still took them and licked away as though they were consuming the blood of a witch like demonic strawberry sauce. And nobody seemed to notice this mad looking woman as she was pulling me closer to the window. They were just going around me as though I was merely a traffic cone in the road.

"Now you will see...7....7....7 and I will see you again at 7...7...7" she kept repeating the number over and over as she let go of my hand. I fell back, and an elderly couple helped me off the floor, picking up the change that the crazy gypsy had dropped around me. I looked back and the ice cream man's face smiled, saying,

"Are you alright, love?"

I couldn't understand what had just happened and my parents just thought my tears were from when I had fallen and lost my ice cream. But from that day on I would see things that made people's nightmares seem like happy cartoons. My nightmares started to come to life when I wasn't even asleep. I would be on a bus or in a car and one minute I would see just a normal person and then I would see them change into something utterly terrifying.

Sometimes I would see them with scales where skin should be, or their hair would move as though they were floating underwater. Then there were the very scary ones, the ones that had black empty holes where their eyes should be. Sometimes these holes would glow red and the cracks in their skin would light up in reaction. It would move under the cracks as though thousands of tiny little creatures were trying to claw and scratch their way out from under what looked like a dry a riverbed.

Others would flicker back and forth like the top of their heads kept screaming. As if the other side of them was trying to escape. These would let out a screeching sound so high pitched that I would have to put my hands over my ears and they would always ache afterwards, leaving me with a ringing in my fragile mind.

I now lived in fear of when I would next see one, soon becoming withdrawn and nervous. I tried to tell my parents about my fears but they put it down to everything and anything. They would tell me off, sending me to my room, and then my mum would get so upset about what she was hearing. I would cry to Libby, pleading with her to believe me but as the months went on she did less and less. I had no answers to any of her questions, so why would she?

"Why can no one else see them?" She would often ask but I just hung my head feeling helpless in a secret world no one else could see. Occasionally, I would see a kind looking one but even these were disturbing. They would glow with eyes bright, but their veins would move as though you could see the blood flowing through their bodies. But it was normally a bluish light that would follow through into their backs to what looked like wings. These too would sometimes differ in shape and size and also type of material.

I remember one woman looked as though hers were made from clear plastic bags stretched out onto long thin twig like fingers that curled at the ends. But the images would flash in and out so quickly that sometimes they would change. It got to a point where I didn't know what was real any more.

One day at school it was getting too much for me when a new teacher had asked why I was crying and why wouldn't I go outside to play with the others? When I had replied 'Cause there's a boy in my class that's a monster,' she had rung my parents to come into the school. The meeting had lasted the rest of the day with different teachers and staff being involved. No one spoke to me but my father came out and barely looked at me. My mother just placed her hand on my back and said,

"Come on, we're going home."

Nobody said a word in the car.

Later that night I had heard my Mum and Dad having an argument and I had tiptoed to the landing to hear. I found my sister there already with her face full of sorrow. Marks down her cheeks revealed she had been crying. The voices downstairs grew louder and I could make out that my mother too was crying.

"But she's not sick and I won't send her to that place!" My mother said between sobs.

"You know I don't want to send her there either, but what else can we do?" Tears filled my eyes at all the trouble I had caused. I wished I could erase it all. I wished I could go back to the happy kid I once was and then none of this would be happening. My sister turned to me and wiped away my tears.

"I don't understand why this is happening to you but I know you're not faking it. However, mum and dad will send you away if you don't do something." She looked at me with pleading eyes and her face blurred through my watery vision.

"Send me where?" I tried to control my sobs so as not to alert my parents that we were listening.

"The school thinks you should be sent to a special hospital, so you can be monitored by doctors and therapists." She lowered her head in shame to be the one to tell me this.

"They think I'm crazy, don't they?" She nodded, and a single tear rolled down her pink cheek.

"What am I going to do? I don't want to go, I'm scared Libby." She held me close to her, hugging me tight, not wanting me to be taken away. She leaned into my ear and said one word.

"Lie." My head popped up and looked at her. She was serious.

"What?"

"Lie. Tell them it was all a lie to get attention, tell them a girl at school put you up to it, tell them it's scary films you have been sneaking downstairs to watch, I don't know, but tell them anything so they won't send you away!" She was almost as desperate as I was but she'd clearly had time to think about this.

I nodded saying,

"Okay, I will but Libby, what do I do about keeping the monsters away?" She looked worried at my response and sadly said,

"I don't know but let's deal with this problem first."

It felt so comforting to hear my sister's semi-belief, so it gave me the confidence I needed to do what I did next. After telling my parents one of the excuses Libby had come up with, everything went back to normal pretty quickly. Apart from my seeing things I could not explain, my life went back to the usual young girl's life I had originally had.

Only now I had to fake a lot of things. Why, for example, I would jump at nothing and looked shocked at some random person walking passed. But my parents were more than happy to believe that I was fine. If only for just one day they saw the same things I did. I would sometimes dream that this would happen but then felt guilty about it instantly. I would never wish this curse on anyone. Even at such a young age I still knew the consequences such a life altering event had on one human mind.

However, it all changed again six months later when Libby came running into my room with an idea. She had recently seen a documentary of a man who travelled around the world talking about different cultures. My dad was watching it as he did every week when my sister took notice of one part in particular. It was when he tried to take a picture of the Aborigines, they held up their hands in protest. The guide then explained why this was.

Spiritualists would claim that the human image on the mirrored surface was akin to looking into one's soul. The spiritualists also believed that it would open their souls and let demons in. Aborigines believed that taking one's picture, took part of one's soul. It somehow kept it locked away.

Locked...that was the key.

This was how her idea was born. She thought that if taking a picture of someone let demons in then maybe taking the picture of a demon would somehow contain them. But it didn't quite make sense and I could hardly go around taking every one's picture just in case. So, she came up with another way. She told me to try and draw them whenever I saw one. Maybe this would act as a sort of prison for them to be locked out of my mind. It was something I had never thought of, so I did as she asked and started sketching them every time I saw one.

I found that every time I did this it would lock the image from my head and I wouldn't see it any more. The effects didn't stop there. Because after years of seeing these living nightmares they grew less and less, until one day I realised I hadn't seen one in over a month.

However, they didn't go completely. They were now only coming to me when I was asleep. I would play back part of the day and somewhere there would be one changing into something horrible but as long as it remained in my dream, I could cope with it. I would then get up and draw what I had seen and keep it in a hidden folder, locking it out of my head forever.

The next time I saw the same person, they would be just like everyone else and I wouldn't dream of them again. By the time I hit my teens the dreams had also stopped, only coming back to me a few times a year. I owed it all to Libby and she would never know the full extent of what she had done for me. She had saved me from my curse.

Now, of course, I was back to my own unusual therapy, drawing the visions that had come to me in last night's horror. Of course, the difference now was that I had a knight in not so shiny trousers and t-shirt, but man what a knight he was! It was worth being so scared in the mists of Hell to see the Heaven there waiting to pull me out. It was just a pity that he too was just a fragmented version of the truth.

Draven at the club and Draven my knight were miles apart. It was just a shame that the only one of those who was real actually disliked me. I sat back staring at the pictures of faces made up of teeth and shuddered at the thought. But this time I didn't have a book I could add it to. This time I would have to start a new one, for new nightmares.

And I had a feeling this was only the beginning of my recurring past...

My Curse was back.

Keira

32
FALLING FOR
DRAVEN...LITERALLY

I went downstairs just before the morning light filled the kitchen. No one was up yet, and I was thankful for it. I still felt strange from the night's events and Libby would no doubt pick up on it. Hopefully, I could get away with not seeing her until later today before I started work.

The thought of work gave way to new worries. It would be even harder now, knowing that everyone would soon find out I was about to turn down a once in a lifetime opportunity. For them maybe but for me, more like a recipe for disaster.

I sat and wondered as I played around with my breakfast, one I couldn't eat. I let my mind go over every detail of the dream. Had he awakened me from a nightmare in a dream? How was that even possible? I searched my room before coming down here for any evidence of the possibility that it could have been real. But I was living in hopes for an impossible reality. What had me so fixated? He had completely seduced my mind but more importantly...

Was there anyway of going back?

But did I want to even if I could? I knew the answer. There was no turning back now. He had ruined all chances for me feeling like this about anyone else. Jack had made it perfectly clear about his feelings last night, but I had shied away from his attentions, yet before I would have relished it. I would have really gone for someone like Jack. He was funny, handsome, charming and above all a perfect gentleman. But Jack wasn't the problem...*I was.*

And I knew what my problem was, I was attracted to the one guy who didn't care and never would...or was that true? His actions contradicted his behaviour at every turn, even from the very first time he saw me in the club he went from hot to cold in seconds. Then there were the jerks outside the club when he came nobly to my aid. Not to mention the chauffeur driven car and the phone call to Jerry. To say I was confused was an understatement.

I carried on fighting with my own thoughts like this until I got out of the shower and I had to finally concentrate on something else, like getting ready. I realised I was running late when I heard RJ's little car beep it's pathetic horn. It sounded more like Road Runner. I ran downstairs with half wet hair trying to put it up into its usual twist but it wasn't co-operating. The sides hung down wet and wavy. I got in the car after a quick goodbye to Libby and Frank and must have looked as if I'd been dragged backwards through a car wash.

"Hey, you ok? Just woken up by any chance?" She laughed and started the engine into semi life. She rubbed the dash saying,

"Come on old girl, you're warm now." I laughed, and the car spluttered into motion.

"Believe it or not I woke up at 4:30 this morning." She shot me a look in disbelief.

"Tell me you weren't getting ready this whole time?" She eyed me up and down, already knowing that I obviously hadn't.

I sat fiddling with my seat belt waiting for her to start back up the interrogation.

"So...good night?" She smiled, half biting her lip to contain herself. But now with that look on her face I wasn't sure what she meant. Was it about the VIP or Jack?

"It was ok. Look I'm sorry I got all weird last night but you know I just hated all the attention, that's all." She nodded, still smiling like I was missing the joke.

"But you must have liked the attention from someone... *right?"* Ah ha, so she was talking about Jack. I was now wondering what he had said as I would have to be careful.

"I don't know what you mean." Ok, she wasn't stupid and she shot me a look to prove it. God, it was like having CSI Grisham on the case. I'm surprised she didn't have a lie detector strapped to my ass.

"Oh, come on, we all know Jack likes you and he drove you home and..."

"And...and what?" I decided the best way to play this out was good old faithful 'playing dumb'.

"And what happened next?" Well at least this was confirmation that Jack hadn't said anything, which meant that I could get away with also not saying anything.

"Ok... so what did Jack say?" Another smirk, she had taken my asking the wrong way.

"He didn't say anything, that's my point, which is how I know something happened. He's only secretive when something's going on." Now I was starting to feel really bad. I was going to have to make it clear to Jack as I didn't want to hurt his feelings.

"Nothing happened. Jeez, you're like a pit bull with a lamb chop!" She laughed and seemed pleased with the analogy. I carried on talking in a more serious tone.

"Honestly, nothing happened, he's a good friend, we chatted and he was the perfect gentleman but that's it." I said making her sigh in defeat.

"That's a shame. I really think he likes you and it's been so long since his last girlfriend." Her cheerful tone dropped but I couldn't understand why. I mean, it's unusual for a sister to really care who her brother dates, unless she was a friend.

"Why, what happened?" Now it was *me* being nosy. RJ must be rubbing off on me.

"I shouldn't have mentioned it, forget I said anything." What! This coming from RJ, gossip queen extraordinaire, now how could I let it go?

"Can I just ask, does it have anything to do with the Dravens?" She whipped her head round to stare at me in amazement but come on it really wasn't that hard to put two and two together.

"Who told you!?" She looked upset as she raised her voice and gripped the steering wheel as though she was going around a circuit.

"Was it Lanie? That little..."

"No! No, sorry but I just guessed and after what you said at the club last night about some stories not being just gossip and something that Jack said, I just kinda put it all together." She relaxed her muscles a little and slowed her speed, not that the little car went much faster, if anything it just made more noise.

"I shouldn't have said that last night, I hope he's forgiven me." It was horrible seeing RJ sad, it looked wrong in the same way when Jack looked angry last night. It didn't suit either of them.

"I'm sorry I said anything, let's just forget about it." I said trying to be a good friend, even though I really wanted to know.

"Okay I would tell you, but this really is the one thing that isn't my place. But I'm sure he will tell you soon, he does really like you... you know that, right?" I did and I wished I could do something about it but I couldn't. I wasn't that girl any more. So, I said the only thing I could think of, without giving away too much information.

"I like Jack, I really do, but I just don't date anymore...call it a bad experience." She rolled her lips back into her mouth and nodded getting the idea.

"Boy, somebody must have done a real number on you." I just nodded holding back the tears.

She really had no idea.

The rest of the day flew by without any more talk from RJ about last night. We spent lunch outside as the sun was out for a change and most of the students were taking advantage of the freak weather. There was still a chill but nothing a hooded sweater couldn't handle. The rest of the gang met us as RJ had sent a mass text inviting everyone. There was the usual lot and four others I didn't know. They seemed like Jack's friends, as they kept nudging him as soon as they saw me. Jack came over to sit by me and asked sweetly if I was cold. I said I was fine and we continued to talk about our day's classes.

I wished, at this moment, I felt that tingle that you get when you're sat next to someone you fancy. I mean, what was wrong with me? He was gorgeous and today was no exception as he wore a faded Led Zeppelin t-shirt with a leather jacket and a hooded zip up underneath that looked warm. Oh, and his usual faded jeans with rips at the knees. His hair was untamed and floppy, but it could have been styled by Toni and Guy, as he looked once more as if he had just come from a photo shoot for Men's Health magazine. His big shoulders leaned in towards mine as he sat with his body turned into me. He wanted to be close that much was clear.

"Wow, now why won't Mum and Dad buy me one of those?" RJ's eyes nearly bulged out as she stared at a huge brand new, shiny black Range Rover that had just pulled up less than twenty feet away.

"Because Mum and Dad don't have ten grand to spend on anything let alone over hundred grand for a car." Jack turned his head back round in disgust as if knowing who was in it.

"Is that a Range Rover Project Kahn?" One of Jack's friends said, as though he wanted to go up there and start licking the bodywork. Another answered his question with amazement himself.

"I thought they were only available in Europe, man that's a sweet ride." Every student was now staring at it as they went by. Some even took pictures with their mobile phones. Jack had leant into me as if to try and draw my attention away from who it was.

"So, I was kind of wondering if maybe you'd like to catch a movie one night?" Oh no, was he asking me out on a date? I was starting to think of how to form the words when RJ saved me.

"Oh my God, Kaz there's a stunning looking girl waving to you." I turned my head round and saw Sophia's perfect figure standing there in a designer dress, waving one manicured hand at me. I got up and went bright red as everyone, but Jack was staring at me with their mouths wide open.

"I'd better go and see what she wants." I walked over to her and the big black beast of a car that was still burbling behind her. I heard RJ say as I walked off,

"Is that who I think it is?" And then a murmur of whispers continued about the mystery girl.

"Hi Keira, I thought we could walk to history together." She embraced me as if she hadn't seen me in years. The scent of her perfume nearly knocked me out. She smelled like a luxury flower garden and I imagined the Hanging Gardens of Babylon to have the same effect. She was about to link my arm but then stopped.

"Silly me, forgot my bag. Do me a favour and just grab it from the back seat, would you? I need to tell the driver when to pick me up." I shrugged and said,

"Sure." Then, as if I had just been programmed to do so, I opened the car door. It was slightly high for my 5ft 3 inches to get into without heaving myself in using the side step. So, I opened the door, looked down to get my footing and pushed myself up. This turned out to be a colossal mistake as I overdid it and fell forward into the back seat. I would have been fine if it didn't turn out that the back seat wasn't empty as I would have hoped...or prayed. No, because instead of face planting into a leather seat, I did so into a man's lap.

"Oh God, please no." I whispered into a suit pant leg.

"Keira?" And with that one name said, I knew no amount of wishing would make the man I'd fallen into turn into someone I wasn't obsessed with.

"Unfortunately." I muttered, too low for him to hear. I held my eyes tightly closed for a second, knowing I not only had to apologise, but also had to move off his lap considering I was pretty certain I had outstayed my welcome...that and my shameful encounter with a certain part of his anatomy.

"I...I...am...am so, so sorry, Mr...Draven." His last name came out strangled as though it physically hurt me, knowing this was the first time I was saying his name to his face. Or more like his crotch...oh shit, God, damn, bugger, shit, shitty, shit, shit! I cursed in my mind holding in the much needed F word.

"Keira it's..." He started as his hands curled around my arms to help pull me up. The strength in this move practically dragged me the rest of the way in the car and now I found myself facing him, with the shorter parts of my hair covering most of my scorched cheeks. Then my heart must have stopped beating for a whole minute as disbelief struck. Draven raised his hand and with one gentle sweep, he pushed the hair from my face and tucked it back to rest behind my ear.

"Keira." He whispered my name and my reaction couldn't be helped.

"I'm dreaming." My first thought flew out of my mouth, not just skipping the 'saying stupid shit' filter but blowing the damn thing to smithereens!

"Am I interrupting something?" Sophia asked her voice so full of mischief that I started to wonder if she hadn't orchestrated this little 'accident'. Upon hearing her voice, mine and Draven's reactions were the same and sudden. We both separated, only Draven's hand lingered where my cheek had once been for a few seconds before it made a fist and then dropped to his side. I bit my lip and braved a look up at the man's face, which made me ache with wanting. His dark eyes cut to me and I saw a flicker of gentleness before they morphed into harsh black ice. Now all I saw there was cruel indifference.

His fisted hand uncurled then tensed again before he leant down to pull out a Gucci bag to match the dress and shoes and everything else about Sophia's outfit. This prompted me to move back as though I had been stung by that same hand. Draven's eyes never left me and I didn't think it possible, but his look went from furious to glacial.

"I...I am so sorry, Sir." I said again as I got all the way out of the car and before I could see his reaction to my mumbled apology, I fled from sight. I was leaning with my back up against the car trying to find my breath, when I heard Sophia speak,

"Thank you, Dom, see you later." She said sweetly and then started laughing at the growl she received in return. I wanted to run. Instead I just turned around to face the other direction and held my head down. She came back to where I stood and linked my arm.

"Come on then, let's get the dreaded Reed over and done with." I plastered on a smile and waved goodbye to my friends who were starting to disperse themselves. They stared in amazement but only Jack looked hurt. Sophia noticed as he was now glaring at her full of hatred in his eyes.

"Who's that, your boyfriend?" I choked back a nervous laugh and she looked at me with a strange expression.

"No, why would you think that?" She smiled and looked back in front as we walked towards the entrance of our building.

"Well, it was actually my brother who noticed you... umm...seemed cosy sat there, deep in conversation. I guess he just assumed." I couldn't speak. I just did that strange little grunting noise I had done earlier. Like trying to swallow a big pill that was stuck half way down. Why on Earth would he even mention me, let alone notice me?

"Nah, that's just Jack my friend RJ's brother... I...uh...I don't date." I said as it felt like this was the theme of the day. I felt like a quiz show contestant where the presenter introduces you in a dramatic loud voice saying your name and something about your personal life only mine would read:

'I'd like to introduce our next contestant Keira Johnson. Keira enjoys obsessing about her boss, who barely knows she's alive. She's come over from England due to being cast out, likes drawing the monsters she sees in her head and most importantly enjoys explaining on a daily basis how she never dates... COME ON DOWN!'

I could have added a lot more, but I did want to make it through the day without feeling like a complete loser. After all, it was bad enough that I had Reed for my next lesson, not to mention the news I had yet to tell Sophia about me turning the job down. With her cute little doll like face it was going to be like telling an entire Kindergarten there was no Santa.

We both found our seats, which so happened to be the same as last time. I got the same old stares as we took our places but with one look from Sophia they stopped, along with the whispering. Everyone knew who she was now and from the look of things they were all just as intimidated as I was. I decided to wait until the end of class to mention the job. It would at least give me another hour to think of what to say. It was amazing to think that last night I had thought this would be easy, now I wasn't so sure.

"So tonight, are you okay to start at seven instead of eight?" Worst luck in the world and trust this to be a day when Reed was late. She noticed me looking towards the door searching in vain.

"Reed's having car trouble, he will be late." She snickered like a naughty child, but I didn't know why.

"How do you know that?" I asked as she smiled a wicked grin but it was still cute on her.

"I overheard one of the other tutors... so tonight?" Well here goes, I was going to have to get it over and done with at any rate.

"Well about that, I was thinking that maybe it wasn't such a good idea." I tried not to look at her, but she turned fully facing me with her arms folded. I looked into her eyes and she looked confused and hurt. I felt like the child catcher out of Chitty Chitty Bang Bang!

"Why, I don't understand... is it me?" What! How had she come up with that reason?

"No, no, of course not, it's just I think that it would be easier if I just stayed downstairs, your brother looked really hacked off about the idea of it and well..." she smiled and cut me off mid-sentence.

"Don't worry about him, he's already warmed to the idea. Our family is very private and he doesn't trust new people. But it's no reason not to take the job, he just needs to get used to you being around." She relaxed as though this had convinced me.

It hadn't.

"Still, I think that it would be best..." Again, she jumped in.

"It will be fine. Look, we really are desperate for some new staff and you haven't been tainted by all the lies and gossip of this small town, plus it's a lot more money."

"It is?" I didn't want to sound shallow, but I really did need a car soon and if I could do it without dipping into my life savings that would be a plus.

"Oh yes, it over thirty bucks an hour." Wow now that was a lot more than I was expecting. I wondered why it was so much. Did you have to donate blood at the end of each shift or something?

"Okay, that is something to think about." I said, and she smiled at her near triumph.

"You saving up for anything?" What, was she reading my mind now?

"Yeah, I really need my own car. I can't keep relying on my sister and her husband or chauffeur driven cars for that matter." I gave her a look but it was one she ignored.

"And on friends?"

"Yeah sometimes, I mean me and RJ ride together here most days, but it would be nice to be able to drive as well, so it isn't always her that does it." I was kind of getting the feeling that she was digging for information, but I couldn't for the life of me figure out why?

"And from work, will Jack be driving you home from now on?" For a minute I was considering if she could be a spy for Libby. What was it with all the questions?

"Uh..."

"We were told you passed on being driven home last night." Sophia smiled as my face must have blushed.

"I don't want to sound ungrateful, as I think it's great you provide that...it's just, well it's kind of...see the thing is..."

"It's okay, I did tell Dom it could be embarrassing singling you out like that."

"What do you mean?" I asked feeling my chest getting tight.

"Sometimes he just rattles off his orders and doesn't really think about the little things." At this my mind was in turmoil. I didn't know what to make of it but now one thing was confirmed. Draven had given the order for my safety.

Just then Reed came racing in all red faced and panting. He had what looked like oil down his shirt in little spots and his trousers had marks at the knees as if he had been changing a tyre. I smiled to myself as I thought of a little thing I like to call...

Karma.

DRAVEN

33

FALLEN, CAUGHT, LAP

After that night I had to confess my concerns about the boy being a threat to my claim on her were definitely lessening. Not only having heard so from her own lips, when claiming they were just friends. But also doing so to her sister, who was no doubt a person she would have confided in if there were deeper feelings to confess.

But then again, I had yet to hear her make any such claim on her true feelings for me. So, maybe I was wrong in this assumption. Maybe she was just a very private person and speaking on such matters of her heart didn't come easily to her at all.

Either way, I was satisfied and found some relief in how she acted around me when we were alone. The rapid pounding of her heart, the breathy responses, like the sharpness of breath whenever I touched her. Even her unwillingness and arguments made last night when hearing how I would soon leave, for it was clear she didn't want me to go. It all pointed towards the girl feeling our connection and thankfully because of it, I had not yet ruined my chances to claim her heart due to the mistakes I had already made.

So, for the moment, I was at least satisfied in one area of this complicated situation, that this 'Jack' was nothing more than a pest that would only buzz around her for so long before giving up. For she was making it clearer by the day that she was not interested. Now if she would just let him know that, then I could consider it at least one problem to tick off the list, as unfortunately, there were many.

Also not doing this sooner rather than later would have been preferable I thought on a growl as we pulled up close to where Sophia's next class would be. For there, sitting on the large blanket of grass, one now filled with groups of students all taking advantage of the warmer day, was Keira next to none other than the fly.

"Is that going to be a problem?" Sophia asked in response to my growl, no doubt more than willing to take care of the 'problem' for me. But no one else knew what I had discovered about the boy last night and therefore didn't know that the 'problem' couldn't actually be fixed. Which was why I decided to use Sophia as the spy she always intended to be.

"Ask her if he is her boyfriend," I said cringing at the term I just used but knowing it was standard terminology in this time period. It just sounded so juvenile, and not a term I ever wanted to be heard when being referred to in Keira's life. Now soulmate, life partner, fiancée or husband, were ones I was very much looking forward to.

"Consider it done," she said opening the door and getting out which was when I had an afterthought.

"And Sophia..."

"Yes?"

"Tell her I was the one asking." Sophia's smirk was her only reply before I watched as she started waving Keira over to us, now the expensive and luxury 4x4 had gotten everyone's attention. A vehicle that was so high off the ground that I doubted Keira would have been able to get inside unaided, giving me a thought. For if I ever had the chance to drive her home, then maybe this should be my first choice? That way I would get the excuse to lift her inside it myself. Placing my hands at her hips as I had done last night and exciting those sweet little sharp breaths from her. By the Gods, how difficult it had been in letting her go! But business had come between what I wanted and what duty had claimed of me.

I watched as Keira blushed when making her way over to my sister, granting her a little wave in acknowledgement. Then she looked to the car still parked, before lowering her face and tucking some fallen hair behind her ear. Did she know I was in here? Was that what deepened that blush? I decided to keep watching, intrigued by her responses and wondering if her mind was on last night as mine was. Had she spent the day questioning the time as a dream, as only half of me hoped?

"Hi Keira, I thought we could walk to history together." I heard my sister say to her, knowing my time seeing her through my own eyes was nearing its end as Sophia linked arms with her. I was just about to order my driver to continue back to Afterlife when Sophia decided to intervene once more, and I was just thankful that it was done in a way I finally approved of.

"Silly me, forgot my bag. Do me a favour and just grab it from the back seat, would you? I need to tell the driver when to pick me up." Of course, I knew this was a lie, for our driver knew her schedule better than even she did.

No, it was a ruse just to ensure a 'perchance meeting' between us. And suddenly I was thankful for the invention of tinted windows as I knew she couldn't see me sitting back here waiting for the sight of her shock and how much I would relish the expression. Would she wrinkle her nose again?

However, as per usual with this girl, it was me that ended up being surprised, for her actions were as such I couldn't predict, despite her clumsiness, something I had already noted.

"Sure," she replied as she opened the door without looking ahead but instead down at her feet, no doubt trying to figure how she was going to get inside to retrieve the purse in the first place. I watched as she heaved herself up and in doing so, overstepped it, as she literally fell into the car, losing her footing and letting her hand slip on the leather when she tried to save herself.

The result...*she landed face first right into my lap.*

This time, it was I that sucked in a startled breath, one that wanted to quickly turn into laughter when I heard her praying into my leg,

"Oh God, please no."

"Keira?" I said her name alerting her to the fact that her whispered prayer had gone unheard, as it was now my extremely hard package, she had her face resting against. But then again, what could she expect, for I was usually hard the second she merely said the word 'hello'. So having her face there and now playing out a live feature of at least half of my sexual fantasies of her...well, let's just say there was little point now in trying to hide the fact of what she did to me.

"Unfortunately." She muttered her answer no doubt hoping I wouldn't hear, and I had to put a fist to my mouth to prevent my chuckle.

"I...I...am...am so, so sorry, *Mr...Draven,"* she quickly started to say as she tried to scramble up, unknowingly placing her hands in places that were not making this any easier on my straining manhood. But it was the unsure way she had said my name that meant the humour of the situation fled me. She had sounded so unsure when saying it that my heart ached once more. So, I took control of the clearly embarrassing situation for her and plucked her up from my lap, pulling her fully into the car. I continued to do this until she was now seated next to me.

"Keira it's..." I started to say when her beauty once more captivated me enough that I couldn't finish that sentence. But instead, I raised a hand to her face and in one gentle motion swept the hair from her face, tucking it softly behind her ear.

"Keira." I then whispered her name, trying right in that moment to convey so many things.

"I'm dreaming," she muttered as if not meaning to but unable to help herself, for she looked as though she wished she could have taken it back and was close to covering her mouth with her hands. It was so utterly adorable that I wished to have also covered her lips, only doing so not with my hands. I had never wanted to kiss someone so much in my life before that it became almost painful to hold back.

"Am I interrupting something?" Sophia then asked, no doubt thinking that Keira needed saving from any more embarrassment, something that instantly put me in a foul mood. The reason for this was that the moment she heard Sophia, she moved away from me so quickly. It was almost as if she felt we were doing something wrong and forbidden. Even my hand, that moments ago had been cradling her cheek, still lingered in the air as if suspended by stolen time.

A hand that soon made a fist before I let it fall to my side in annoyance at being interrupted. In fact, all I wanted to do now was yank her back to my side, slam the door with my mind, lock it and order my driver to speed away!

I watched then as she braved a look my way, biting her lip and making me close to acting out on the temptation. I felt my gaze soften when looking at those beseeching eyes that held a million questions yet not quite brave enough to ask a single one. Then I heard Sophia clear her throat and my gaze hardened before it had managed to turn fully away from Keira's startled look. I only ended up hoping she hadn't believed it directed at her but at the troublemaker by the door.

I reached down and pulled out her bag, handing it to her and conveying my feelings clear enough that she rolled her eyes at me before Keira could notice. But my eyes were now back on the girl and seeing the way she shied away from me only managed to piss me off even further.

Why was it that in her room alone she displayed her feelings without guilt or shame but now, in front of my sister, she acted as though being with me was nothing but a sinful act? Well, she would soon know the full meaning of sinful, for I would spend long endless hours teaching her the true meaning of the word! And with her naked and tied to my bed, unable to escape me or my hands that craved to touch her!

"I...I am so sorry, Sir," she mumbled as she got out of the car, very near running from sight and making me want to hammer a fist into the side of the car! I swear to the lowest levels of Hell ,and to the highest reaches of Heaven that I didn't understand why it felt as though every time I took a step forward with this girl, I was being dragged back six more!?

I knew my time with her had affected her, for I could feel her presence still leaning against the car and hear her trying to regain her breath.

"Thank you, Dom, see you later," Sophia said before closing the door on my growl and laughing because of it! I swear, by the end of all of this, it wouldn't be the girl that would be the death of me but my own fucking sister!

I pressed the button to the intercom and barked a two worded order,

"*Afterlife, now!*" Then I pressed the button again to switch it off, only I ended up doing so that hard that my finger went through the casing, creating a hole in the panel. I looked at it for longer than I needed to, feeling the twitch in my jawline as I fought my temper from exploding...that's when it became clear.

It was going to be one of those fucking days!

My only hope now though, was that it wasn't going to be one of those fucking nights.

I had to say that I hadn't been wrong, for the day dragged on, as waiting for Keira to arrive at my club for her first shift up here in the VIP felt like waiting for a damn solar eclipse! I was actually nervous! Me, a fucking God in my own right! Nervous because a mortal girl a foot smaller than me was entering my world. And I just prayed to every other God out there that she liked it enough to want to stay forever!

Fucking nervous, I thought as I shook my head and downed back my next drink, just wishing it would relax my nerves the way I had hoped the ten before it would. I don't know how many times I had looked at my timepiece, but it was verging on ridiculous and every time I did Sophia's chuckle beside me was making me one step closer to murderous.

I swear my moods were so changeable that even I couldn't keep up! I had been ready to tear into Sophia (not literally), but the second she entered my office and told me a list of all the things I wanted to hear, the memory of her interrupting us in the car fled my mind along with my stewing anger.

Keira had told Sophia how she and Jack were just friends and had been quite adamant at that. So pretty much confirming what she had told her sister also. Keira, although admittedly after some persuasion, accepted the job, even if she first turned it down because she believed I didn't want her there. Which she couldn't be blamed for considering I had pretty much given birth to that assumption for her last night. The last piece of good news was that she had also asked her to come in an hour early, meaning my Hell in waiting would be reduced for she was due in the VIP in ten minutes.

However, this wasn't all she told me, for this was Sophia we were talking about. So, I knew there was always a bad side. Meaning all I needed to do was raise a single brow and say,

"Out with it, Sophia."

"Well, a slight hiccup."

"Which is?"

"After she told me that she and the honey-haired blood sack weren't an item, she also informed me the reasons for that was that she doesn't date...at all," Sophia said making me frown for a second before replying confidently,

"That won't be a problem, Sophia." Now she was the one to frown before folding her arms and saying,

"No?"

"I don't intend to date her, Sophia, I intend to claim her as my queen and marry the girl," I stated, making her laugh once without humour and say,

"Whoa, that's a little heavy there, Dom, may I suggest at least taking her out to dinner first and getting the girl some flowers." Hearing this I granted her a brief, wry look up from the paperwork I was going through as I was yet again at my desk.

"I don't date, Sophia," I stated, making her chuckle.

"Oh, jeez let me think, who do you remind me of again?" she said sarcastically.

"Good, then we will have something in common, now if you have nothing more to add..." I said, pausing and hoping she would get the hint. Something I knew she hadn't when she blurted out,

"She wants a car." I frowned a second before repeating,

"She wants a car?"

"Yes, that's what she is mainly working for, so she can save up and buy a car." I thought on this a moment and realised it made sense, for it was clear she didn't like relying on anyone or considering herself as a burden. That much was clear about her personality.

I picked up my phone and dialled the number.

"What are you doing?" Sophia asked, but I ignored her and continued my call.

"Yes, My Lord?"

"Fredrick, what cars do we have in the garage with the highest safety rating, as whichever one it is, I wanted it delivered to Miss Johnson's house before seven pm." I asked before the phone was suddenly plucked out of my hand by Sophia.

"Cancel that order, Fredrick" Then she hung up making me growl.

"Why did you do that?!" I shouted.

"That wasn't exactly what I meant here, brother." she said rolling her eyes as if now conversing with a child.

"You said she needed a car."

"No, I said she was saving up for a car. Big, big difference here," she said holding out her arms to indicate just how big she thought it was. However, I disagreed.

"I fail to see the point you are making here."

"Clearly," she groaned making me growl her name in warning. *"Sophia."*

"Okay, so here it goes. You have a girl who hates being the centre of attention and blushes as easily as the winds changes. You also have heard her express on a few occasions now how she doesn't want to be treated any differently or singled out by being the only one chauffer driven to work and back. But she is working hard at trying to earn money to buy herself a car, so as to be more independent and not be a burden to anyone...so your answer to this is to give her a two-hundred-thousand dollar car!"

"Again, and your point is?" I asked calmly.

"AHHHH I give up!" was her dramatic response, combined with throwing her hands up in the air.

"Alright, so I will concede that the timing to do so might not be the best..."

"You think?!" she interrupted mockingly, meaning I granted her a pointed look before continuing,

"...So, because of such, I will wait. But I warn you, all it will take is one more occasion involving a piece of shit blue truck and an even bigger piece of shit human, and one of my cars will be on her drive whether she agrees to it or not!" At this Sophia released a big sigh before shrugging her shoulders in acceptance. But then just before she left my office, she issued me a warning before doing so.

"Well, in that case, Dom if that happens, then if I were you, I would look up two more things on google."

"And they are?" I inquired with a prompting and unconcerned shake of my hand.

"A local florist and the meaning of the word... *grovel."*

And with that she left, leaving me with the question,

I wonder what Keira's favourite flowers are?

For obvious reasons, soon after this, I found myself needing a drink and after a cold shower, (something I had taken up since trying to tame a certain part of my anatomy around her) I re-dressed in a suit and was at my table with a drink in my hand an hour before her arrival. That was now fifty-five minutes ago and ten, no, now eleven drinks past. And at number eleven was when she finally arrived and unfortunately it was not a pleasant start for her. She looked up at the VIP first and then back at the bar as if unsure where to go first. Then she saw Jerry and decided to inform him of her arrival first.

"What are you doing down here, you should be up there already! At least you remembered to wear black," he snapped at her, and I growled, making Sophia put a hand to my arm the second he practically pushed the girl towards the VIP.

"I will handle it," she said pulling out her own phone and dialling his number. I didn't end up hearing whatever threat she made as she walked away from the table and my thoughts were elsewhere. At the very least Jerry now looked like a dog with his tail in between his legs, so that sight was somewhat comforting.

But then she finally reached the VIP and once again brought meaning to my day. She was wearing all black as Jerry had pointed out, and it made her skin look even more transcendental than usual. Now with the darkness managing to bring out more of the paleness. It also made her eyes a shade darker, and I wondered if she was getting enough sleep because of my little visits?

Her hair, as usual, was twisted up and held there with a sturdy clip which was there purely for practical reasons, not as an embellishment. And in my opinion, she didn't need any as I knew that she would have been at her most perfect when naked, without makeup and with her hair down and preferably lay stretched out on my bed waiting for me.

Thoughts like this seemed to consume me, for when seeing her I could think of nothing else but what it would finally be like to have her to myself. To be able to walk straight up to her now, throw her over my shoulder and walk back into my home, sealing the doors behind us, so as there was no escape for her. To not have her fight me but to just submit, well these were thoughts that played heavily in my dreams.

What would she have done right then had I stood from this table, grabbed her hand, and yanked her to me, as I had last night? To then take her face with my hands before kissing her as my only hello. What of the future for us if I allowed this to happen?

If I was to rewrite the past and pave this new start by claiming her now?

Would she run or stay?

Keira

34

First Night Take Two

When the class finished, RJ was standing waiting ready to walk me to my next class. It was so sweet the way she did this but whenever I thanked her she just waved it off as no trouble and said that she had a free period. When the truth was she was worried that I would still get lost.

Sophia was still behind me, so I decided to introduce them.

"Sophia, this is my friend RJ, RJ this is Sophia Dra..." RJ jumped right in there before I even had chance to finish.

"It's nice to finally meet you. Kaz has said nothing about you to any of us. I think she was trying to keep you to herself." I frowned at her, but Sophia looked more than pleased on hearing this.

"It's nice to meet you too, but I must confess I have the upper hand as Keira has told me all about you. I do love your hair." RJ was just about ready to sell her soul to this girl just for the compliment alone. RJ was a sucker for flattery but to have someone as super humanly stunning as Sophia, this must have been classed as an honour.

"Thank you so much, the colour's called 'passion for pink'." Sophia nodded and continued to say,

"Yes, I was admiring it before. I have seen you in the club a few times." At this, I couldn't help the snort that escaped. This was a huge understatement as RJ practically lived at Afterlife. But I couldn't help notice in Sophia's responses, the cautious replies and how she was always careful on how she worded things, wanting to create an illusion she was just like the rest of us. The way she had said "In the club" instead of "My club". After all it was a family business.

They continued to make small talk and RJ beamed over everything she said. I was the third wheel of course, but I didn't mind. I just wasn't looking forward to the ride home knowing it would be nonstop Sophia this and Sophia that. But she was smart. Even after RJ's bombardment she never really revealed anything about herself. She just kept the conversation casual and kept enquiring about RJ, deflecting each question back on itself.

Of course, RJ didn't notice.

On arriving home, I waved goodbye to RJ and smiled to myself as it looked like she was still talking about Sophia. No one was home yet so I decided to cook Spaghetti Bolognaise as it was quick and Libby and Frank could just heat it up in the microwave. I was like a robot on autopilot not really thinking about what I was doing. My mind was on tonight and on all the things Sophia had said.

Why hadn't I just said 'no' to working in the VIP? Or maybe subconsciously I wanted to work up there, just to be closer to him. I was most definitely a glutton for punishment that was for sure. I wasn't concentrating and burnt my hand on the stove. It woke me out of my zombie state and I ran over to the sink to put some cold water on it, but it was too late it was already starting to blister. Great that's all I needed... more scars!

I heard keys in the door and realised the time was getting on. I dried off my hand and examined the big red blotch on the side of my palm near my little finger. Thankfully Frank walked in instead of Libby.

"Oh, hey Frank, how you doing?"

"Hey, yeah I'm good, better now I've come home to this... mmm." He said smelling the air and went straight over to the pot to lift the lid.

"All she needs to do is cook the pasta okay and try not to let her burn it this time." I patted him on the back as I walked past making my way upstairs.

"Are you kidding me, that woman could burn ice cream!" He laughed at his own joke sounding like Doctor Hibbert from The Simpsons. I was running up the stairs when I remembered I was starting earlier and would have to get a lift, so I went back downstairs into the kitchen, where I found Frank burning his mouth with a spoon in his hand.

"Ah ha, caught ya!" He dropped the spoon and held up his hands.

"Okay, you got me, I'm busted. What time you working tonight?" He was such a great guy, like a real brother. And that wasn't just because he would do anything for me. My sister was one lucky girl.

"They asked me to come in early, at seven if that's okay...oh and before you ask, no chauffeur driven car tonight." He laughed and joked,

"Why, who did you upset?" I smiled and made a lips sealed gesture across with my finger. It was time to go and get ready, so I jumped in the shower and let my worries continue under the warmth of the water that rained down on me.

I got to work in a fluster with only five minutes to spare. I wasn't sure what to do so I went up to Jerry who was behind the bar with Mike. As soon as Mike saw me he walked off to the other end without even so much as a head nod. What was his problem? Had it started already, was I forever going to be the outsider and shunned? Jerry came around from behind the bar and pulled me off to one side.

"What are you doing down here, you should be up there already! At least you remembered to wear black." He was not happy, but he kept his voice steady although a little strained.

"Well, I didn't know if I should look in with you first or just go straight up there." He nodded as if this was normal, but he just kept looking around anxiously as though not wanting to be seen...this didn't help with my nerves.

"Okay, well you just go up the staircase that you went up last night and they will be expecting you...but go, go, you don't want to be late!" At this he turned me round almost pushing me out of sight. Then he walked off with his phone vibrating and once again he looked as though he didn't want to answer it.

I shook off the feeling of dread or at least tried to as I took the same steps that I had done last night. I kept telling myself that it was just one night and if it was that bad then I would leave. Yeah, I would just turn around and walk out. I could do that.

This little pep talk I was giving myself wasn't helping much but it was the only thing making my legs move in the right direction. The club was quieter at this time, which made it easier. Not as many staring, gossipy faces as last night. The band members setting up watched me as I went by, near the door closest to the stage. One guy winked at me but then his friend came and whispered something in his ear and he quickly looked away. I wondered what it had been.

The same huge guys stood watch, but they didn't even look down at me this time, they just automatically opened the doors to let me in. I decided once inside to run up the stairs otherwise I might not go through with it and the last thing I wanted was to draw any attention to myself by being late.

This time there was no music and no comforting hum of people from down below. It felt more like I was entering a portal to a different dimension instead of just working the VIP in some swanky club. Maybe if there weren't as many weird looking people that were drinking up here or at least some normal looking ones then it wouldn't feel quite so daunting. It made me wonder even more about the type of businesses that the Dravens were into that would warrant such a strange array of people.

I walked through the doors at the top after taking more than a few deep breaths. Like before, everyone turned and stared but only for a split second, as if someone had flicked a switch that made them all turn back round at the same time.

I walked to the bar as I had done last night still not knowing what to expect. My heart rate went up yet again when I knew I would have to pass the top table. I bit my lip as I always did when being unable to control my nerves and gripped the strap of my bag tighter over my shoulder. I put my head down and promised myself mentally I wouldn't look.

I... Would... Not... Look.

This I repeated over and over in my head until I had passed, completing the ultimate goal of self-discipline.

I finally took a much-needed breath when I got to the other side and was safely at the bar. I held my eyes closed and raised my head slightly as I inhaled.

"Well, look who's back. Hey honey, you ready to start your shift?" My eyes opened to find the kindest face looking back at me. There was nothing I needed more than a friendly face right now as my confidence was at an all-time low.

"I'm ready. Put me to work." He motioned for me to come behind the bar and I followed to where he pointed for me to get through. Behind the bar was just like any other bar apart from it being immaculate. You could have done surgery behind there it was so clean. There was a place for everything and most of the glasses were so fancy I was scared to touch anything.

There were masses of green bottles all lined up on their own designated shelves. No two bottles the same. All were different in shape, size, label and even material, some being glass others being made out of metal, pot and even wood. Along with the many different bottles there were unusual glasses to match. Even goblets, tankards and sake cups lined the shelves below. Most of these were made out of different materials, ranging from stone to copper, silver and gold. Some were plain, and others looked as though they belonged in the Tower of London with the rest of the crown jewels.

Karmun saw me looking and said,

"Ah yes, we have a lot of different liquors that you won't have seen before, we import specialised drinks for each of our customer's needs." *Needs?* That was a strange way to put it, but he was foreign so maybe he meant something else.

"You can put your stuff back here in this little room." He nodded down to a few steps from behind the bar into a small office style room.

"I'll give you a minute," he said smiling.

I looked about the room taking in my surroundings for a moment, amazed for the first time to notice the lack of things, rather than the splendour I was used to seeing in this place. There was a desk with no paperwork or computer. There were shelves with no folders, just old looking books. Also, there were no personal belongings from any of the other staff members, so I wondered what this room was even used for and why was I the only one that seemed to be using it?

I put my bag down and took off my jacket, hanging it on the back of the only chair in here. There was thankfully however, a gilded mirror that looked far too much like an antique to be in this tiny back room. I studied my face quickly realising that instead of my usual deathly white skin my cheeks were flushed, giving me a warm glow. I placed the cold backs of my hands on them to cool them off and curled a stray strand of hair that had escaped from my twist. I took another nervous breath, knowing it wouldn't be my last one tonight. So, with my head held high, I walked back out to take my shift by the horns!

For the first night Karmun thought it best if I just took it easy and collected empties as I did downstairs on my first shift.

"It will also give you chance to get a feel for the place, but you must understand, up here we do things differently." I was not surprised. Nothing about this place was normal so why should the work be.

"I am the only one who gets the drinks ready and the girls take them to their assigned tables, but they never change tables, you understand? That's our one main rule, okay?" It was the first time I had seen him serious, so I took the rule as set in stone.

"No problem." I said assuring him I understood. But I wondered if I was only collecting empties then who would be serving my tables?

"You're going to be doing the tables nearest to the bar. There are ten tables in your section and these are over here." He pointed to the ones surrounding the bar area. The tables went from one side of the bar to the other, ending up near the staircase I used when leaving last night. They were all along the same wall and thankfully none of them went near the top table.

"We have six girls in total, including you and they too all have their own sectors. See the small Asian girl with the pigtails? She does the same sector as you but on the other side leading from the main staircase you see there to the staircase at the back where you came in. Her name's Akako." He pointed to the staircase where I had first seen Dominic Draven and his bodyguards walk up, to the other end of the wall where I had just come from.

The girl I spotted was like a china doll, she wore what looked like a black school girl dress but then I remembered there was a name for people who dressed like her...what was it called...? Gothic Lolita, yeah that was it. She looked adorable until she turned around showing scary yellow contacts that were haunting to look at. She saw me and bowed her head in respect.

"Then there's the middle, which is split into three sectors. The parts that are not raised both have six tables that sit Mr Draven's more important members."

"Members?" I asked wondering what type of club this was exactly?

"Clients." He corrected and then pointed around the large raised area that only had the one table on it. This one, of course, I knew well.

"You can see the girl with long green hair, that's Zarqa. She covers the left side and the other girl with the short black hair, that's Rue and she covers the right." He continued, and I wondered how I was ever going to remember so many strange names in one night. He pointed towards each girl in turn and I couldn't have picked a group of girls so different in all my life.

The one that worked on the left with the green hair was very beautiful with green eyes to match. She wore a black corset with green ribbon tied up each side. The black trousers she wore looked like leather and the heels she had on made me wonder how she made it through the night without limping.

The other girl looked more boyish but the bust she had under her tight black T shirt proved just the opposite. She looked like a punk skater with long shorts and army boots that reminded me of the 'Avril Lavigne' look, only she had short spiky black hair that was shaved on one side. I could now only see the back of her so didn't get a look at her face, but I did however notice the blonde bombshell who was dressed like a high-end prostitute buzzing around the top table.

Karmun noticed me looking and continued on with his introduction to the VIP area.

"Ah, that's Layla and the other girl with black and red hair is Lauren but everyone calls her Loz, they both work the top table." I looked up at him sensing there was more he wanted to say.

"What? They have two girls for just the one table?" I said in disbelief, not understanding why on Earth they would need two waitresses for what... no more than seven people!

"Yes, and you are never to approach this table, if you have anything to ask then come to me first, okay?" He said this in a firm yet steady tone. It was most definitely a warning, but it just made me even more curious as to who this man Dominic Draven really was. And unfortunately, in this case the internet had proved useless. Apart from a few local sites mentioning their thanks for donations, the Dravens were off the social grid. There wasn't even a damn picture, something I had developed Tourette's syndrome over for a good hour cursing my screen.

"So, there you have it, it's as simple as that. Just stick to your tables and you will be fine." He walked back to the bar and as I followed I noticed that RJ was right, it was a lot bigger than it seemed from downstairs. Looking to the back of the room there stood a pair of double doors that I hadn't notice the night before.

They were huge and carved the same as the grand oak doors at the front entrance. At each side of them were magnificent stone pillars that framed the entrance and joined the ornate stone arch above. Unusually though, there wasn't anyone guarding these doors. There was, however, just something about them that looked threatening and imposing. Almost as if they took on a life of their own, something demonic that sent shivers down my spine.

"What's in there?" Normally I wouldn't have even asked but it was like staring at Pandora's Box. There was something inside me that needed to know more.

"You should stay clear of those doors." And that was all that he said on the matter. It was as if I was being tugged from either side, good versus bad. The good girl side of me wanted to take this advice and stay away but the other side, the side I suspected the monsters fed from, was daring me to run towards the doors. I wanted to tear them open and run to whatever they were concealing. I could even hear the voices... *do it...do it.* I wrestled with the demons inside me and walked away...

For now.

Keira

35

BEAUTIFUL PAIN

It didn't take me long to get into the job at hand, as a monkey could have done it just as well. The tables contained the same colourful characters as the rest of the place but luckily for me my tables seemed to seat the nicer groups. The people that sat at all of my ten tables were nice to me and smiled as I took away their empties. Some even passed over the glasses that were hard to reach.

One table had people friendlier than the rest and even asked my name and introduced themselves as the family of Shinigami. Of course, I didn't know what this meant, but they seemed pleasant. They all shared the same striking eyes of the lightest blue colour, almost as if they were transparent, but they held a depth and sincerity to them, I couldn't help but feel at ease as they stared back at me.

The band started to play, but for the first time since working here I heard a woman's voice over the microphone. It was a more mellow sound than what usually came from the speakers, but it still held a rocky edge to it. She sang about an infatuation with a dark eyed stranger and how within 24 hours the love would turn bitterly into death. The message being that he would inevitability become the death of her.

For reasons out of my body's control, I looked at the table that I had been avoiding all night. What I found there was both alluring and terrifying.

As always, whenever I saw him not in my dreams, he was wearing a suit, this time black with a dark red shirt and black tie. For some reason this added to his dominating features. His face looked even more cruel and unimpressed than usual. Maybe it was my added presence that did it. I couldn't seem to take my gaze from his eyes that were exhibited as cold and black like the darkest of winter nights. He sat in his chair with a masterful grace, his strong shoulders set back against the stone that mirrored his muscles. He looked deadly and indestructible.

He made me shudder.

Karmun kept a close eye on me the whole night but this wasn't in an intimidating way but more like a friend who wanted to look out for me. He shouted me over as I had just finished clearing the last of the tables with empties on it.

"What's up?" I said, just as one of the other waitresses came over to the bar. It was the one with short hair, what was her name again …Rue, that was it. She turned to me and extended her hand, but I couldn't keep the shock from my face when I saw her eyes. They were the freakiest eyes I had ever seen. They were all white apart from the tiniest of black pupils left in the middle. There were scars and what looked like burn marks around her eyes, creeping their way down the cheeks.

She was blind.

"Nice to meet you, I'm Rue and you're Keira, right?" She said in a cocky voice as I took her hand and shook it, noticing a strange tattoo of an eye in a tribal style on the palm of her hand. I looked at the other hand to find another identical one in the same place. She looked directly into my eyes, which I found amazing considering she couldn't see them.

"Hi, nice to meet you too." She smiled and let go of my hand, turning towards the bar with no problems. She didn't even need a cane. She was quick and nimble and grabbed her tray of drinks from Karmun, turning one last time to my face and said,

"Welcome to the House of Crazy, I hope you stay." And that was it, she was gone. I knew blind people's senses were heightened but she was truly gifted, to look at her you would never have guessed she couldn't see as well as the rest of us.

"So, how's it going?" Karmun asked me, as though it was my first day at a new school. I suppressed a little laugh and told him the truth.

"It's been fine."

"Okay well, why don't you take a break and get some air." He handed me a bottle of water from under the counter and nodded for me to take it.

"I'm really okay, I don't need a break. After all I've not been here for more than an hour." His lips curved up into a knowing smile and said,

"Keira it's nearly ten." What? It felt like I hadn't long since started. This place was like a time warp. I grabbed the water and went to duck under the hatch behind the bar when he stopped me with a hand and said,

"Why not go get some air, the balcony will be quiet."

"Okay" I said confused as he had a strange look in his eyes when he said this, just like when someone is told to say something out of character. Or maybe I was just being paranoid. Either way, I walked over to the staircase I had used last night and knew the doors to the balcony were next to them.

I was about to push them open, assuming they were just like any other doors, but oh no, not in this place. As soon as my hand came into contact with the cool glass they disappeared into the wall out of sight. I walked through the opening into the dead of night and shivered as the air hit me like a cold shower after swimming in a heated pool. I closed my eyes from habit, something I always did when first walking out into a winter night. Although technically it was Autumn or "Fall" as they called it here. But to me, whenever the weather got cold and the rain or snow showed, it was winter's way of saying a premature hello.

I heard the doors closing behind me with a gentle hum and the noise from the VIP was abruptly cut off. The balcony was huge, a room of its own. It was framed with marble pillars and in between was a wall of stone balustrades. The top part was wide enough to sit on if you were brave enough, which I wasn't. There was no seating of any kind and the floor was spotless, even though there were massive ferns in Chinese pots either side of the doors, not to mention the surrounding woods. Yet not a stray leaf or needle from the ferns was to be seen.

Vines worked their way around the pillars, hugging them tightly yet there was no evidence of where they came from, so I guessed they had made their way up the side of the house, mixed with the ivy.

The view in front of me was a blanket of deep surrounding blackness. There was no moon out and if it hadn't been for the lamps on the walls I wouldn't have been able to see my hand in front of my face. The lights cast an eerie glow that reflected off the marble floor making me feel uneasy. It was not an ideal place for someone with an overactive imagination that was for sure.

I unscrewed the top of my bottle and took a couple of long swigs not realising just how thirsty I was until I had felt the cool liquid slide down my throat. So, it took me by surprise when I heard my name being spoken from behind me.

"Keira, so here's where you've been hiding." I turned around to see Sophia for the first time tonight. I don't know why, but whenever I did get the guts to look over to the top table, all my eyes managed to find was his face.

"Hi Sophia, how's your night?" She smiled and looked over her shoulder as though she heard something there. She smirked and turned back to answer me.

"It's productive and as it just so happens it's about to get even more interesting but enough about my night, how's your first shift going? Are you going to come back for more?" I thought for a moment and answered truthfully.

"It's been a piece of cake. I'm a bit surprised as you were right, nothing to worry about." I screwed the cap back on my water bottle and pulled down on my top feeling like a shabby homeless person compared to the beauty before me. Her hair hung in perfect spiral curls and the purple dress she wore fitted like it was tailored to her goddess like figure.

"Good, that's great! Well why don't you join me for a drink after work to celebrate your first shift?" I looked down at my scruffy black flat shoes and knew the answer I would give her wouldn't be one she'd want to hear.

"I don't think that's a good idea, Sophia."

When I heard the response I was about to give not coming from my own lips, but from those of the man I was both terrified of and obsessed with, I kept my head down even more. My last breath caught in my throat and it actually felt as though my blood had stopped flowing through my veins. It was just like before when all I wanted was to be invisible, a fly on the wall, never to be seen until it was time for him to leave. I just wanted to look at him from a distance... that was enough but stood here I was too vulnerable.

"And why not? She did well and I think she deserves a drink!" I liked Sophia but right now, I just wished she would back down from being my new spokeswoman. I had to add something before I ended up being the reason for these two to battle it out.

"I...I appreciate the invitation, but your brother's right, I will have to pass, but thanks." I did it. I did the unthinkable. Okay, so I did it with my head down, but it was the first time I had spoken in front of him without needing to say the word 'Sorry'. Hell, I was just lucky it made sense and was in English, although I had stuttered a bit.

I looked only at Sophia and she pulled a face as though I had just stolen her favourite doll, ripped its head off and then threw it to a Rottweiler to play with. So, because of this, I felt like I needed to add something more.

"How about another time, okay?" She smiled a little and I could feel Draven's eyes on me, but I still couldn't look. I was just wishing this could be over so that I could get back to my job.

"Alright, but soon and I won't take no for an answer." She seemed happy with this last little demand, but I found it more adorable than serious.

"Sophia, you're needed." He said this with such authority, however Sophia just shrugged her shoulders and nodded, but before leaving she hugged me and said,

"See you tomorrow." At this I was sure I heard her brother's disapproval in the form of a low growl. I hugged her back but went bright red at the embrace. Normally I would have been fine but under the scrutinising eyes of her brother, the blood in my cheeks gave away my feelings only too clearly.

She left us alone and I found myself playing nervously with the bottle in my hands. After a moment of silence and him clearly not moving, I went to go around him when suddenly he grabbed my arm stopping me.

I felt the heat as the first touch rushed through the thin material of my top and through the gloves underneath them. It penetrated my skin and pierced my heart as though he had been made from a pure sexual current. I was taken aback to say the least and didn't know how to respond, but the shock made my hand drop the bottle. Before I even had chance to bend down to retrieve it, he had it in his other hand passing it to me.

"Here you go." He said with a hint of softness in his voice as a prompt to take it. This was what made me look up into his eyes for the first time and I regretted it instantly. His eyes were filled with so many emotions it was hard to pinpoint just one. They were so intense I felt as though I could look into them for hours, getting lost in their beauty, they were truly mesmerizing. He looked back into mine and spoke again without releasing my arm. Instead, he ran his hand down its length until he got to my fisted hand. He lifted it closer to his face as though about to examine it in detail.

"I...what are...?"

"Ssshh." He interrupted me with a gentle tone and started to uncurl my fingers with his much larger ones. Once my hand was flat, he turned it over by my wrist making me flinch. His eyes shot to mine in question as his grip tightened over the scars, he thankfully couldn't see. After a moment of searching for the answer in silence he finally let it be and turned his attention back to my hand. Then he ran a single finger over the burn he found there, and I closed my eyes at the beautiful pain it caused.

"How did you hurt your hand?" His question made my eyes snap open. I shook my head at him with a little motion, hoping this would be enough, but then he frowned.

"Keira, I asked you a question." This caused me to swallow hard before needing to clear my throat to voice my answer.

"I cook." I blurted out and then quickly realised how dumb that just sounded. So, I added to the dumb with a little more dumb, 'cause evidently if your name was Keira, you could never have enough dumb!

"I mean I did it... earlier that was...eh, Spag Bol for my sister and Frank, he's my brother-in-law, you see I like him to have a good meal and my sister isn't the best cook and..."

"I know who Frank is." He stated, and I just thanked the Gods his voice had shut me up.

"You do?" I couldn't stop myself from asking.

"I do." He answered simply, and I felt like slapping myself upside the head saying a loud 'Durr'! But of course he knew who Frank was. Frank was the guy who provided security for downstairs.

"Of course you do." I said quietly, although in my head I was screaming 'IDIOT!' to myself.

"Next time you will be more careful, yes?" The way he asked didn't sound anything like asking but more like demanding. I could only nod in response and when I did he dropped my hand. This broke the connection as though cutting the wire that powered my heart for a short time. I lowered my eyes to hide my shame.

"Sophia tells me you expressed your feelings to her on being driven home." On this 'oh shit' moment I looked straight up at him.

"Well I...I...did say something, yeah but I'm...I mean, I did say I was really grateful and I am...really grateful that is but..." He held up one hand for me to stop speaking and put me out of my misery.

"I understand. However, your safety is a concern as a member of my staff. Therefore, I will forgo the *embarrassing* chauffeured car..."

"Thank you, I really..." He cut me off abruptly as I made the cardinal sin of not letting him finish his sentence.

"But in return I expect to be notified if Frank or your Sister is unable to provide you with transportation."

"Okay, that shouldn't be a..."

"I am not finished." My eyes widened as I bit my lip. I felt like a kid being told off.

"If this happens then I *myself* will drive you home, is this clear?" In this moment I just hoped my mouth hadn't dropped open. Was he serious?! I could barely get my wits in order before he started speaking again.

"Karmun tells me you did well tonight." I nodded not knowing what to say in response. I still couldn't look into his eyes, again feeling that if I did I would never be able to escape them.

He moved a step closer to me and I could feel the heat from his body. I closed my eyes not being able to prevent my shy habit, but I don't think he noticed my weakness. He leaned down slightly as he had done so many times before in my dreams.

He was more than a full head taller than me, but he closed the distance between our bodies to mere inches. I could smell his skin and wanted to inhale more deeply to take in every scent. But I didn't. No, instead I froze, locked into my position like a scared animal.

"Come back tomorrow then, if that is the case." And that was it. The delicious torture was over with those words still lingering in the air as he left me standing alone, nearly hyperventilating.

One thought was all that was needed...

My heart was in big trouble.

I was still thinking about my encounter with Draven when I was at home getting ready for bed. I had been in a zombie like state for the last hour of my shift and the ride home with Frank.

I was still in shock that we had actually spoken to one another. Okay, it wasn't actually a really long conversation, but it was better than him just insulting me while I stood there not saying a word. But more than anything I was in a numb state of shock that he demanded to know when I was without a ride so that he could drive me home! Himself...personally. He and I, in a car together ...alone! How had this happened? One thing was for sure, my need for a car just reached desperate levels.

I could still feel goosebumps appear on my skin whenever I allowed myself to think about how close he had been, so what would a drive alone with him make me feel? I had thought that the real thing would have been more realistic than in my dreams but as it turned out my dreams had been spot on. The smell was the same, the heat and connection I felt whenever he touched me. It had all felt just as real as it did tonight. I couldn't understand how that could be, but whatever it was, I wasn't complaining.

I decided to try and unwind as I picked up Jane Eyre and started to read where I had left off, but I kept imagining Draven as Mr Rochester. The similarities were starting to mount up. He too had been harsh calling Jane a witch the first time they met. But she soon warmed to him after a time, chipping away his rock exterior to find a soft centre that loved her, even though she was plain, penniless and above all...
Broken.

I would love to believe that my own story could hold such possibilities like that outcome, but in an age obsessed by beauty, money and greed I doubted even for a second that Draven would ever think of me the way Rochester did about Jane. But it was harmless to fantasise...wasn't it?

I put down the book after only three pages, frustrated that everything had to come back to Draven. I turned off the light and said a silent prayer for sleep to come without visions of the monsters that had now decided it was the right time to come back into my life. As if my life wasn't complicated enough!

I drifted in and out of sleep but woke up when the tossing and turning was too frustrating to even try to sleep. I got up and went into the bathroom thinking that my sleeping pills might help, even though they hadn't last night but who knew, tonight could be the night for change.

I was about to swallow the two pills in my hand when I heard something. I turned to face where the noise was coming from and stood deadly still, trying not to breathe. I waited but there was nothing, so I put it down to my imagination.

I swallowed the pills and walked back into my room. I heard the rain start to lash against my window panes and put the noise down to that. I went over to the window seat and sat down, listening to the rain until the pills started to make me drowsy. I looked out at the angry night sky and jumped when lightening erupted, illuminating the clouds and silhouettes of the trees. I put my hand to my chest and laughed nervously at my jumpiness.

I counted the seconds until the thunder and knew it was close when I only got to six. Even though I knew it was coming I still jumped again when it cracked the silent sky, filling it with a boom. I shook my head and laughed again at myself at how jittery I was. Then the lightening hit again only this time it didn't just light up the sky.

I looked down into the garden and for a split second I could see a figure under my window looking up at me. I didn't take my eyes away from it but now without the lightening it was too dark to make out who it was.

I strained my eyes and waited for the next flash of light to reveal the mystery. The storm was getting closer as now I only got to three seconds until the thunder erupted. I could see the figure moving slowly and it looked as though it was motioning me to come down to join him. I could just about make out that it was a man, being far too tall and bulky to be a woman. He moved his arm up and his hand was waving at me.

I waited and waited for some more light. If only the moon had been out, I could have seen him clearer. Whoever he was he wore a long jacket to the ground and a hat. The hat was like one you would have seen from those old corny detective shows called a trilby. I could only see his mouth and chin as the hat concealed half his face, but my mind was processing where that hat looked familiar.

I was sure I remembered someone wearing one like that but where? I didn't have to wait much longer to find out as the sky lit up in three different places giving me more than enough light as the storm was now directly above the house. What my eyes saw there was scarier than any nightmare or any monster I had ever seen.

For there, under my window, beckoning me to join him...

Was my past.

DRAVEN

36

BURNING TOUCH

In the end, I simply watched transfixed as she was forced to get to the bar area by walking past my table, and I waited for the single look of acknowledgement. One where I had planned to make it known I appreciated her presence with a nod of approval in return. However, I never got the chance, for she didn't even raise her head my way, not once!

In fact, the only evidence to suggest she was aware of me at all was the deep blush that bloomed across her cheeks and ever so slightly down her neck. Because of this, I decided to see if I could access her thoughts at all. But all I heard was a repeated chant,

'Don't look, don't look, don't look,' said like a mantra in her mind.

Of course, I couldn't help but grin.

I spent the rest of her shift listening first to Karmun explain how things worked, and what section she would have. He had been Afterlife's VIP barman almost as long as the place first opened as a club. Meaning he was a valued and trusted member of staff who I knew would make things easy for her. I had decided that after making my announcement to my people about her importance to postpone business until further notice. To which, unsurprisingly there were no complaints, and only a few matters deemed urgent enough that they were dealt with before the parties returned back to their designated sectors.

Leaving me with my usual entourage of loyal servants who all had their own jobs within Afterlife and the businesses I ran. The VIP was a place to relax and one where my people could feed without harm to anyone. Especially as no one would dare to go too far in my presence with any mortal down below. And the Gothic nightclub offered a wide range of people, with an even wider range of emotions to feed from. Meaning it was a win, win, as no one hardly ever suffered any ill effects from such things. As feeding from humans gathered in large numbers barely affected the individuals. However, constantly feeding on a single human over a long period of time was likely to end one of three ways, suicide, murder or madness.

Hence the reasons it was utterly forbidden. But even my own kind had addictions, and these were usually the drug of one particular favourite mortal of theirs that they couldn't seem to stop feeding from. Now if they stopped before matters went too far, then it was possible that they could be rehabilitated, just as any mortal addict would be given a chance to do. However, death was usually the punishment if no such restraint was shown and it ended in a mortal's end.

So, with my word meaning law and keeping this choice firmly in their minds, all of my people had been warned to keep their other sides on lockdown while the mortal was among us.

I also, personally, had the seating rearranged so that her sector was with the gentler souls, who would put her at ease and would surround her with the more positive energy they preferred to feed on. Of course, this had been another strict rule of mine, for no one was permitted to even try and feed from her. Explaining that she was off limits in every way possible!

Of course, they didn't need to know that it would have been impossible to feed from her. But I knew that divulging as much would only raise more questions, and gossip didn't just start and finish down below with the townsfolk. So, everyone had their orders and so far, the night was going smoothly and to plan, making me at least start to relax.

I had told Karmun that I only wanted her collecting glasses again this first night and it was clear she took the one task very seriously. As, if it didn't have any liquid in it, then it didn't stay there for long.

However, the one thing of the night that hadn't gone to plan and was starting to grate on my wary nerves was the fact she had barely even glanced my way. Not even the once meeting my eyes, and I would know for I watched her most of the evening. In fact, I could only imagine that my people must have thought that I was taking this 'charge from the Gods' very seriously indeed. For I doubted they had ever seen anyone take my interest like this ever before.

"Explain to me again, why is she here?!" Aurora hissed making Sophia do the same in reply,

"I suggest you remember your place and don't question your King again!" I let this slide, for I had no patience for some petty bitch arguing at my table. Besides, Sophia had handled it well enough, and I wasn't about to undermine her own authority. Also, the spoilt look on Aurora's face right now only told me that she would soon storm off, granting the rest of us a peaceful evening for once. In fact, her only friend at the table seemed to be Celina, who admittedly never rocked the boat with anyone.

In the end, I cared little for it as Keira's shift was nearing its completion, and I wanted the opportunity to speak to her alone before she left. Even if I couldn't be as I wanted to with her yet, I still wanted to ensure a meeting between us. One, so as she felt welcome here and after last night, then by me most of all. The Gods all knew that she deserved far more!

So, I nodded to Karmun to indicate it was time for her to take a break and then looked towards the balcony, knowing he would understand my orders perfectly well. Which was why he motioned her over, handed her a bottle of water and suggested she get some air.

Then once she had gone through the automatic doors, Sophia stood up beating me to it.

"What are you doing Sophia?" I asked placing a hand on her arm. She smirked down at me, leaned in a little closer and whispered,

"I think it would look odd if I didn't say hello to my friend all night...don't you?" Then she patted my arm in a patronising way and winked at me before walking away in the direction I myself had been hoping to take. A growl rumbled from me as I downed my drink, making Vincent chuckle next to me.

"Well, I think it's safe to say, that life certainly isn't boring any more," he said, now drinking back his own brandy, only doing so while keeping an amused eye on me. I took a deep breath, downed another drink and thought with a growl,

No, it most certainly wasn't.

"Wow, two minutes, brother, I am impressed," my brother commented now looking smug after I had risen from my seat.

"Bite me," was the only comment I made back, which was so uncharacteristic of me, it made him nearly choke on his drink as he tried to swallow through the shocked outburst of laughter. It was I that then walked away smirking.

I made it to the balcony doors more quickly than I should have if I were also portraying myself as human, but thankfully she was outside, and I didn't give a fuck, as I was King and it was, do as I say, not as I do!

So, as I ate up the space between us, I had only a second to wonder, what her reaction would be to me this night?

I walked through the balcony in the middle of yet another scheme my sister was plotting as I heard what was a ridiculous offer made, no matter how much I wanted it for myself.

"...Well, why don't you join me for a drink after work to celebrate your first shift?" Keira instantly looked down at her shoes and was about to speak, which from the looks of it, there was no doubt she was ready to decline. But this was when I got there first,

"I don't think that's a good idea, Sophia," I said trying not to sound as stern as I feared I did. However, I heard Keira's breath catch as it did so many times before when first alerted to my presence and it was starting to make me paranoid and question... *was this a good thing?*

"And why not? She did well, and I think she deserves a drink!" Sophia argued as I knew she would, but remarkably this time it was Keira who intervened before I could.

"I...I appreciate the invitation, but your brother's right, I will have to pass, but thanks." Once she had finished, I had the sudden urge to simply take her face in my hands once more, tilt her head up and kiss her. Thus, giving her a whole new reason for those addictive little, surprise intakes of breath of hers.

But then I also wanted to kiss her until both our worlds simply evaporated around us. Until it all turned to dust and we were the only two people left in the entire world, for then at long last I would get her to myself, sharing her with no one!

However, one look at her trying to hide her gaze from my currently intense one and I would have to say that she was utterly, fucking clueless to it all! *Gods, if only she knew.*

She looked to Sophia, concentrating so hard, it was as if she were fighting some magnetic pull I was trying to force upon her, for she still hadn't looked at me. But one look at Sophia's obvious disappointment at having her plan foiled and Keira felt guilted enough into saying more.

"How about another time, okay?" she said in a sweet tone, one that would have been impossible to argue with, even for Sophia. Which made me begin to wonder, had I actually found a being on Earth who could handle my sister better than anyone else? Well, it seemed as though she was the only one she listened to, for she backed down soon enough and even did so with a smile.

"Alright, but soon and I won't take no for an answer," Sophia replied with no malice in sight, just simply acceptance delivered in a warm manner. In fact, it was my first indication that Sophia really was developing a real friendship and love for this girl. One that obviously went far beyond being a spy, but more so in looking out for her best interests. It couldn't be denied that it was a bond I would relish in seeing flourish, as long as it didn't ever interfere with my own relationship with her. Or take her time away from me, for that was also something I wouldn't allow. But once again my mind was getting ahead of itself and pictures of our future together clouding the present and the reason I was standing here now. So, I decided to speed things up in order to get my alone time with her before she was gone yet again from my world.

"Sophia, you're needed," I said knowing that she wasn't, just as well did she. But instead of the challenge I half expected she simply shrugged her shoulder and hugged Keira goodbye as if they were already life-long friends. Again, I would be lying if I said the sight didn't touch my heart.

"See you tomorrow." Of course, that warm memory was annihilated the moment she said this, as jealousy overtook the emotion. As Sophia would be seeing her and could in effect, at any time she wished, being that she was classed now as a 'good friend'. I, on the other hand, felt a fucking miles apart, and not one Gods be damned step closer to her, other than being classed as her boss. A title I did not fucking relish in, that was for damn certain! So, because of this, I couldn't help the slight growl of disapproval that escaped before I could rein it in.

Finally, my sister left and for the one time that day it felt as though I could finally breathe! I noticed the way she still kept her gaze from mine and instead of speaking, played nervously with her bottle of water. I was curious as to what she would do, so I allowed her the time of silence. Now wondering how long she would allow, what she would no doubt deem as awkwardness, to last. I grinned when it was less than a minute.

She must have assumed I desired to be out here alone, and that wasn't happening with her stood there, so she moved, trying to make her way around me when I stopped her. I grabbed her arm with enough of a grip to prevent her from leaving but making sure so as not to cause harm or to alarm her of such intentions.

However, the shock of such an action caused her to drop her bottle, and before her eyes could track the motion, I caught it before it hit the floor, doing so with my free hand. Our connection when touching each other was so strong you could almost taste it, as though the air had been statically charged.

"Here you go," I said gently, passing her the bottle and for the first time, the kindness in my tone she took for a sign to finally look up at me. At last, this was what I had been waiting for all night. The moment to be alone with her and let her see a softer side to what she deemed the 'real me'.

I found myself, as usual, getting lost in her wide-eyed gaze, looking at me now as if she half expected me to take a bite out of her...little did she know the truth behind that statement, for to bite her, I most certainly wanted to do. As for creating harm, then that couldn't have been further away from the truth of what I wanted to do to her. Making her scream in pleasure, being very close to the top of that spectrum.

But then these thoughts fled me as I remembered something from earlier. It had been while watching her collect glasses from the closest table to my own. A red mark that was now on her hand which hadn't been there before, and I now wanted to know what it was.

So, I ran my hand down the length of her arm, taking note of the gloves she always wore underneath her long sleeves. I continued down until I felt her tightly curled hand held in a tight fist. Not one as if ready to hit me but done more as if to prevent herself from reaching out and by holding herself back from touching me. It was a curious action but one I ignored for the moment as I took her hand and lifted it up for my inspection.

I could hear her heart beating wildly throughout it all, no doubt asking herself if she were silently dreaming as she had done today when questioning my actions in the car.

"I...what are...?" She stuttered as if struggling with what to ask first.

"Ssshh," I ordered her softly, knowing that my actions were about to speak louder than her words ever could. Then I went about uncurling her little fist by force, only satisfied when her hand was flat and cradled in my much larger one. All of which she didn't fight me on until I managed to turn her hand over and skimmed the inside of her wrist making her flinch. My gaze shot to hers, raising a brow in silent question, daring her to tell me why...to tell me what she was hiding.

But she never said and instead gave me a pleading look in return, making me momentarily tighten my hold on her. I tried to be satisfied just knowing that I would find out soon enough, but I had to confess it was difficult in that moment to let it go. But her pleading eyes were what granted me the strength of will to do so, and the relief in her expression when I did was a bitterness I could almost taste.

I decided to ignore my inner resentment, arguing with myself that I had given her little reason to trust me yet and time was the only solution. So, I focused back on the reason I wanted to examine her hand in the first place, soon discovering that she had clearly burnt herself. I frowned, wishing I could simply heal it. Especially when running a single finger over the open blister, one she had obviously spent the night catching against things, for it now looked raw and sore, enough for the slightest touch to cause pain and make her close her eyes.

"How did you hurt your hand?" I asked making her look back up at me and in response to simply start shaking her head as if it was nothing. Well, it wasn't nothing to me, which was why I reminded her firmly,

"Keira, I asked you a question." I nearly grinned when she swallowed hard and blurted out,

"I cook." I would have let her see my smile this time if she hadn't quickly started to elaborate on this brief statement, meaning she did so trying to look everywhere else but at my face... no doubt thanks to her blush.

"I mean I did it... earlier that was...eh, Spag Bol for my sister and Frank, he's my brother-in-law, you see I like him to have a good meal, and my sister isn't the best cook and..."

"I know who Frank is," I informed her just to save her the embarrassment I knew she would feel after her nervous talking, something I had quite enjoyed listening to, as I think it was the most she had ever said to me in one sentence.

"You do?" she asked surprised, again making me want to grin as I saw the moment it dawned on her why I should know him.

"I do."

"Of course, you do," she muttered quietly, looking as if she now wanted to slap herself and the sight was an adorable one. But I didn't want her feeling this way, for she clearly had no idea how fascinating she was to me. So, I got the conversation back on track and did so by showing that I cared, even if it came out as more of a demand.

"Next time you will be more careful, yes?" I said knowing this would no doubt be a hard promise to make for someone so clumsy. However, instead of conceding this as I was hoping she would, she simply nodded as if not knowing any other way to respond to me.

So, seeing now that I was only making her nervous again, I let go of her hand, making her lower her gaze from my own. A habit of hers that I didn't like and would have mentioned it to her, had it been the right time to do so. But instead, I decided to bring up another matter which I wished to discuss with her, eager to hear her own thoughts on the matter with me, and not with Sophia.

"Sophia tells me you expressed your feelings to her on being driven home." Now, this got her attention, for she looked back up at me as if she were a child about to be reprimanded by an adult.

"Well I...I...did say something, yeah but I'm...I mean, I did say I was really grateful, and I am...really grateful that is but..." Once again, as much as half of me enjoyed hearing her nervous ramblings, I knew the right thing to do was to put her at ease. Hence why I held up a hand to stop her and once again, the relief was easy to see.

"I understand. However, your safety is a concern as a member of my staff. Therefore, I will forgo the embarrassing chauffeured car..."

"Thank you, I really..." I decided to interrupt her for I had not finished, and she would soon know the full extent of my concern for her.

"But in return, I expect to be notified if Frank or your sister is unable to provide you with transportation..." She quickly interrupted me, and obviously eager to please.

"Okay, that shouldn't be a..."

"I am not finished," I told her making her bite her lip, an action I enjoyed immensely, and that delightful wrinkle of her nose I wasn't even sure she was aware of doing.

By the Gods, she was cute.

"If this happens, then I myself will drive you home, is this clear?" Her look of shock was priceless and again a reaction I relished. I let go the fact she didn't answer me but instead continued on with what I had already planned on saying.

"Karmun tells me you did well tonight," I told her, again prompting those sweet little expressions and blushes from her. But I was unsatisfied when she wouldn't look at me, so I decided to take her limits a step further. I stepped closer to her, far too close to be deemed necessary and she even closed her eyes as if trying to physically absorb the memory of me. This was the reaction I had been hoping for and for that matter, been pushing for, as I needed proof my harsh behaviour last night hadn't impaired the future of our union.

But this wasn't without its difficulties, for being this close to her, with her scent breeching my senses and softness of her skin just begging for my touch, it tested the very core of my willpower.

I wanted her with a fever I had never known but instead was forced to continue playing this little charade until a time my full feelings were to be known.

"Come back tomorrow then, if that is the case," I said before I was gone, leaving her to what I knew were confusing and turbulent thoughts.

Thoughts I could only hope that one day...

Mirrored my own heart.

Keira

37

A Trip Down Horror Lane

I screamed and screamed until my lungs needed more air. I was gripping something as it felt like I was being smothered. I must be in a bag... That was it! He had found me...it was happening again... No, no, no! I had to get free. Someone must hear me...they had to hear me! I screamed again and again. I could taste the material over my face and I could smell the sweat from my body as I twisted and turned.

I was scratching and clawing at it in hopes of escape. Not again, not again! The screams just kept coming. I was using all of the air left in my lungs and then the material lifted from my face as I heard a familiar voice saying my name.

"Kaz, Kazzy it's okay, it's okay, it's just me...calm down, you're okay now, it was just a dream." My sister was smoothing her hand across my forehead, looking as pale as I must have been. She helped me sit up as my mind started to fight its way back to reality. My breathing slowed, and the tears started to flow from my sore eyes.

"I'm sor...sor...sorry." I mumbled through hiccupping sobs. She smiled and took my head into her arms, letting me cry freely into her shoulder.

"Is she alright?" Frank stood near the door with a baseball bat in hand looking like he was ready for action. She waved an arm behind her back at him in response and he nodded once before leaving me in Libby's arms, like a small frightened child.

"Feeling better?" She said after ten minutes of hysterics.

"I'm sorry for that, it was just... I haven't had a dream like that for a while. I guess it really hit me." I took the tissue out of her hand and wiped my eyes and runny nose, feeling a little embarrassed.

"It's fine honey, but the way you were screaming I think Frank was ready to bust the door down, and it wasn't even locked. I think sometimes he thinks he's Jack Bauer from 24!" We both laughed and I instantly felt better.

"Poor Frank, he looked worried." I said feeling guilty.

"Well, at least you know you have a big brother in the house to protect you." That was more comforting than she'd ever realise.

"Was it about him?" She asked carefully, not wanting to upset me any further. I just nodded, feeling my eyes fill again. Her face looked both angry and sad at the same time.

"Try and get some rest, do you want to take some pills?"

"It's okay I already...oh no wait, that must have been in my dream. In that case yeah, I better had." She got up and went into my bathroom but then came back out again with the bottle in her hand but no water. I was about to protest that I could never swallow pills without some form of liquid, but she handed me an empty prescription bottle.

"But how...? That's strange, there were loads in there yesterday." I couldn't understand how the bottle was empty. I had only taken some the night before and the bottle was over half full.

Libby glanced at me with a weird look, obviously not knowing what to believe but clearly she was worried, so I told her about the part when I had taken some pills in my dream.

"Maybe I was sleep walking and tipped them away. I really don't remember." Her face softened and she got me some she had been given when she pulled her back out about six months ago.

"These will knock you out so take two now and I will wake you in the morning, but you know this means you're going to have to speak to another therapist to get any more pills, don't you?" I nodded, not liking where this was going. The last thing I needed now was to 'talk about my feelings' again. It was beginning to look like my old life was trying to catch up with my new one... *again.*

The next time I woke it was morning and Libby was waking me up with a cup of tea.

"How are you feeling this morning?" I looked at her through blurry eyes and saw that she was all ready for work, which could only mean one thing ...I was most definitely late! RJ would be here any minute. I jumped out of bed and raced towards the bathroom but Libby stepped in my way.

"What's the rush?"

"I'm going to be late, how come you didn't wake me sooner?" I said with a croaky voice from last night's 'Sob-a-thon.'

"Because I thought you would want to sleep in, as it's a Saturday." Oh, I must have been more confused last night than I thought. I assumed when Sophia had said 'See you tomorrow', she had meant in class but she had really meant at work.

"Oh yeah, so it is, but you're dressed for the office?" I stopped rushing to get ready and went to sit back down on the bed to drink my tea. Meanwhile, Libby was picking up some clothes and putting a pair of my shoes back in the wardrobe.

"I'm sorry, I know we were supposed to spend the day together, but this client is breathing down my neck to get this job done and if I do a good enough job on this one, then I might have six other show homes, so it's a big deal." She smiled with enthusiasm but also looked guilty as well.

"It's fine Libs. I have loads of studying to do and plus, I'm thinking while the storm's passed I will take advantage of the dry weather and go for a walk." I needed to go and clear my head after last night and I couldn't think of a better cure.

"Okay, but tonight I will make up for it. We will order some pizzas, pop some corn and watch a girlie movie." I laughed at her take on an American accent. I loved the idea of spending some quality time with my sister, so when I told her that I couldn't because I was working she looked wounded.

"I'm sorry, but hey I'm off tomorrow, let's do something then, okay?" She nodded and added,

"Okay, but I still think it's all too much, all this work for college and the club... you're going to collapse." She was a little bit right. If I didn't get some decent sleep soon I was going to drop.

"It's only until I have enough to get a car and then I will cut some of my shifts, besides, I can't expect you and Frank to keep chauffeuring me around, back and to." I held up my hand to stop her from continuing with her protests. I also mentally added on the part where now I had Dominic Draven to contend with and the threats of him driving me home.

"I know you don't mind doing it but I do, it's not right that you have to keep picking me up at such late hours and plus, I don't want to push my luck with RJ." She admitted defeat and gave up.

"Okay, I get it. Plus, I know you must want your independence back." I smiled at her knowing she only said all this because she worried and because she loved me.

"I will see you later...and Kaz..." She paused on her way out of the room as she held on to my door frame.

"Yeah?"

"Try and relax today, you know... take it easy, okay?" I replied with a 'Scouts honour' and saluted.

I spent some of the day catching up on college work and 'trying to relax' as Libby had instructed but I found it hard to concentrate. My mind would wander over to darker thoughts that solely consisted of the dream. It was irrational to think this way, but I couldn't help feeling crushed under the weight of disappointment. It wasn't just that last night he had managed to worm his way back into my life, no it was more the lack of someone coming to *rescue* me from it.

In my last nightmare, Draven had come to save me from the monsters, which made the nightmare less petrifying. But in the one last night, that was the one where I had needed him to save me the most and he hadn't shown. As a result, I couldn't keep my mind off my past no matter how much I tried. It was so bad at one point, I was half considering the bottle of vodka that Libby had down in the liquor cabinet.

But that was a bad place to go and I knew it, but sometimes just the thought of going that low to numb the pain was all I needed to knock me back out of it again. I decided this was the right time to go for a walk and try and find the place that Libby and I had hiked to. It was a nice clear day at least, despite the cold but once I started walking I would soon heat up.

I grabbed my jacket, which had a big hood, just in case it decided to pour it down. I put my mp3 player in my pocket, turned it on, placed the headphones in my ears and grabbed the keys. I knew the direction I was heading for, so I set out, losing myself in the music and the scenery around me. I half wondered if I would see that girl in the woods again and realised I hadn't thought much about her since those first few days when I arrived. At least I hadn't seen her again, which made me wonder if she had followed me that day or if it had all been in my head?

I mentally shrugged my shoulders and followed the rough pathway that led deeper into the forest. I continued until I got to the part that forked but for the life of me I couldn't remember which way we had taken. For some reason though, I had the biggest urge to go left, as though something was pulling me that way. There was that little voice inside that said it wouldn't be a good idea but I didn't listen to it. No instead I listened to the rebellious voice that told me not to be so cautious.

After about twenty minutes along my chosen path the forest floor started to get a bit more hard work, as if this had once been a regular walking spot but that had been a while back. It looked as if the earth hadn't been disturbed in quite some time. There were a lot of branches to duck under and pull back to allow me to pass and at one point there was a fallen tree that made me change course due to its size. It looked freshly up-rooted and the air was filled with the scent of freshly dug earth. Maybe it had been from the storm last night.

Another twenty minutes or so of walking in this direction was all it took to make me regret my decision, fearing now that I would never remember my way back. I stopped and pulled my headphones from my ears to find that I could hear the sound of running water and realised there must be a stream nearby. As soon as I heard it, all I could think about was how thirsty I was. I followed the sound a little off the track I was on and it wasn't long until I found it. The little scene was so pretty I wished I had a camera with me.

The ground around it was softly covered in moss and it curved its way around each little rock and stone like a blanket. The forest echoed the sound of the water rushing along and I bent down closer to take a drink. I rolled up one of my long fingerless gloves, freeing my hand to cup the crystal clear water.

I made a noise when my skin came in contact with the freezing liquid, as it was a shock but at least a refreshing one. I got up once I'd had enough and followed the stream upwards for a while before coming to an opening. The light pierced through the trees as they separated, creating a clearing like the one that I had seen in my first dream about Draven.

I stepped into the light screwing up my eyes, as they had grown accustomed to the shade the forest provided. I walked forward and soon realised that I was at an opening by the cliffs. There were trees that surrounded a log cabin, which was on the very edge of a sheer drop and the National Park opened up in front of me, reaching for miles. It reminded me of the view outside my bedroom window with wave after wave of lush green forest.

I couldn't help but smile at the beauty and started wondering what the people who must have lived in the cabin were like. Not only must they have liked to live life on the edge 'literally' but they must have loved the forest and its beauty. It was one of the best views of scenery I had ever seen.

The log cabin looked long abandoned with windows smashed and cracked wooden panels as though it had once been kicked in. The door was nearly hanging off its hinges and had also seen better days. I walked closer, feeling that I should be shouting to see if there was anyone else around. I don't know why, it was obviously a long time since it had been lived in, but I just felt that maybe I wasn't as alone as I should have been.

I put that thought to the back of my mind and put my foot on the wooden steps leading up to the front door. The wood creaked under the weight of my foot and I looked around making sure I wasn't being watched. Seeing nothing but the wall of forest looking back at me I walked onto the porch and looked through one of the windows by the door. One of the panels was missing so I crouched down and peered inside, telling myself that this was as far as I was going to take it.

It looked as abandoned on the inside as it did on the outside. There were a few bits of handmade furniture but most of the stuff looked broken up and piled up near the doorways and windows. That's when I noticed the rest of the windows that faced out towards the cliff had been boarded up in what looked like a hurry.

The front door had the most furniture next to it but it had been pushed backwards. Like something had burst through the front door spreading it along the floor in its path. I couldn't understand why anyone would do this, what were they trying to keep out?

I got a weird feeling in the pit of my stomach as I felt like it was time to leave. A gut feeling had me believing something really bad had happened here. I started walking backwards off the porch not wanting to take my eyes off the door. Almost as if I did, someone might come bursting from behind it at any moment. This of course wasn't the brightest of moves as I caught my foot and fell backwards off the steps.

My body hit the floor sideways and I hit my head on one of the rocks that lined a path towards the front door. I closed my eyes as a shooting pain exploded around my skull. I tried to get up but failed a few times as the ringing in my head made it hard to focus. I finally got up to my knees and felt for any damage.

My hand went to the cause of the pain and found a sticky liquid. Great! Now I was bleeding. I looked at my hand covered in deep crimson and tried to remain calm. I wasn't going to die from a little cut and I had overcome my fear of blood years ago, with little choice on the matter.

I made it to my feet, wiping the blood off my hand on the ground as I rose. I could now feel it trickling its way down my cheek. I took off one of my gloves, wiped my face and held it to the rest of my cut, hoping it didn't need stitches. That's all I needed for my shift tonight, a big gash on my head and a blue bulge to match it. I just prayed it didn't look as bad as it felt. I started to walk back in the direction I had come from and I was hoping that nobody was home when I got back. Libby would freak out as it was, but if I could at least wash the blood out of my hair, that would be a bonus.

Then I remembered the stream and that I could use that to clean myself up a bit just in case she was there. But where was it? Had I gone wrong somewhere because it was near the cabin wasn't it? I turned in every direction but I couldn't make out anything familiar. How far had I walked away from the path I came along? My head was starting to feel really fuzzy and my vision clouded with the pain. I quickly stuck out my arm, holding myself steady on a tree until I regained my balance.

It was then that I heard it. I couldn't understand where it came from but I followed it anyway, knowing that it must lead to people. Someone was singing faintly in the distance or was it music being played. I couldn't tell the difference as it didn't sound like anything I had ever heard before. It was a beautiful hum that changed into words I couldn't understand. Maybe I would come across some hikers that had a map...and obviously a stereo.

I twisted around branches and foliage following the sound that echoed through the trees. Whenever I would go slightly off in the other direction it would momentarily get louder in the direction I should be going.

I was in a daze and couldn't feel the throbbing in my head any more, all I could feel, taste and think was the noise that I followed. For all I knew it was leading me deeper into the forest and I would be lost forever, but for some reason I wasn't worried. It was as if I was on some sort of mind control drug. I was completely hypnotised, and I was mellow and calm as I picked up pace to find this astonishing sound.

I wasn't sure how long I walked but it didn't feel like more than mere minutes. It was just getting louder but I still couldn't see anything that would make that noise. I was now on a path and my feet didn't have to work as hard to move along. I broke out into a run as it felt like I was getting closer and closer.

I could hear more words now but still it was a language that I had never heard. I was nearly losing my breath as my chest ached with the strain. I wasn't the fittest of people at the best of times and I hardly ever ran but there was just something spellbinding about the sound that filled my ears and took over my brain. I was nearly there now, I could feel it. I could see an opening in the trees, as the light got brighter with every step.

Then the sound was gone.

The entrancing song had stopped as though the power had been cut, just as I walked out of the trees into the front of the house I knew well. I couldn't understand any of what had just happened. I looked around for signs of life, maybe a passing car or music that Libby had been playing but that still wouldn't have explained it. I followed music that led me home. I was sure of it.

I went into the house and walked upstairs, dumping my jacket on the bed and kicking my shoes off. I don't know when, but I'd lost the glove I used to soak up the blood. I removed my remaining glove and pulled my ruined top off, ready to get in the shower. I knew nobody was in, so I walked to the bathroom and grabbed a fresh towel from the cupboard on the way. Once in the bathroom, I examined the damage in the mirror.

Thankfully, it wasn't as bad as I had dreaded. It looked worse because of the dried blood on my face and hair. The cut wasn't deep enough to need stitches and I knew I could get away without needing to see a doctor. There was an angry bruise around it that I could hide with my hair and with a skin coloured plaster, I thought I could get away with it without anyone noticing.

Libby was back when I got out of the bathroom and I didn't have time to hide the evidence of my fall.

"Oh my God, what happened to you?" She ran over to me and fussed around my head, tightening her fists and sucking air through her teeth, the way people did when they could imagine the pain.

"It's fine Libs, honestly, it's not as bad as it looks." This was a bit of a lie. Actually, it was a big ass lie because as soon as the music had stopped, the pounding pain began again.

"Tilt your head and let me see, you might need stitches." I tilted my head in her hands and said,

"It's okay, I looked in the mirror and it's not that deep, I will be fine with just a plaster." She grabbed my hand and started to pull me down to the kitchen, where she kept the first aid box.

"Sit under the light." I did as instructed and she pulled a box down the size you could have fit a Christmas turkey in! What did she keep in that thing? Spare body parts!

"So, are you going to tell me how this happened?"

"It was no big deal. I just tripped and hit my head on a rock." She was cutting up little strips of tape into tiny lines and was passing them to me to hold.

"This might sting a bit." She sprayed some antiseptic on the open wound and I cursed like a pirate.

"Nice...very lady like." she teased.

"Sorry, next time it feels like my skin's melting off I will calmly say "Oh fiddlesticks, terribly sorry my dear but that did sting a wee bit." She laughed at my posh accent and carried on by pulling my skin together before sticking it in place with the little strips she'd cut, acting like make shift stitches. She covered that with a bigger plaster and said,

"There, that's better."

"Thanks mum." I gave her a kiss on the cheek and left to go back upstairs.

"So, do you want me to call work for you?" I turned and looked at her in disbelief.

"Why on Earth would I want you to do that?" I laughed at the thought.

"Because you hit your head and could have concussion or something." I shook my head and smirked at the idea.

"I didn't break my neck Libs, I only bumped my head. I think I'll be fine for work." She shrugged her shoulders and said,

"Okay, only making sure."

Once I was ready, I studied myself in the mirror and tried to position my hair so it covered the plaster completely, only every time I moved my head, my hair would move with it. I gave up and decided just to keep my head down and hopefully, no one would notice.

Just before I was ready for leaving the phone rang with RJ on the other end. She wanted to ask me if I was working tonight and if I needed a lift home as Jack was the designated driver for this evening. I accepted the offer as I knew Frank couldn't pick me up tonight anyway as he was working late and I didn't like the idea of Libby driving in the dark or worse still, getting a lift home with Draven.

"Tell Jack thanks." I said as the conversation was coming to an end and I needed to leave so as not to be late for work.

"It's okay you can tell him yourself later, as I'm sure he would much rather hear it from you anyway." She finished the sentence with a naughty giggle and hung up. I put on my jacket and took my bag from Libby as she held it out to me.

"You ready?" I thought about the question for a minute and wondered was I ever ready to be in the same room as Draven?

The answer was always the same...

Never.

DRAVEN

38

SCREAMS IN THE NIGHT

The moment I heard her screaming in the night, my blood ran cold. I wasn't asleep this time and was up from my desk in a heartbeat, knocking my chair back in my haste. I had heard it through our connection as if she was terrified and unknowingly calling out for her protector. I even heard Ava calling out to me seconds later, informing me that something was seriously wrong.

I cannot explain the panic that I felt, only that I had never experienced anything like it! It was like a surge of emotions making me near mindless with worry, questioning every possibility! Had she been kidnapped, had she been attacked, had she woken early in need of a drink and fallen down the stairs, breaking bones, thanks to her clumsiness?

By the time I got there, I must have had a hundred different scenarios in mind, and not one of them was as simple and harmless as a nightmare. Which was precisely what it turned out to be. I couldn't believe the depth of relief I felt when I couldn't smell her blood on the air or see flashing lights belonging to emergency services outside her door.

However, what I did find very nearly broke my heart, for she was sobbing in her sister's arms.

"I'm sor...sor...sorry." I had never heard her so upset, and I swear it felt like I couldn't breathe through it. I clenched my fists on her window frame with enough force I could feel the splinters of wood cracking beneath my palms. Ones I quickly had to fix before the glass planes cracked with it. They couldn't see me out here, as I veiled my appearance using the darkness, something that was always easier at night. And one of the reasons for using vessels in the day, as it took far less energy to do so, than what I was doing now.

"Is she alright?" Suddenly the appearance of Frank at her door with a baseball bat held firmly in his grip brought my thoughts back to what had happened. I was at least satisfied that she had a protector in the house and a big one at that, as he wasn't far from my own larger physique. But this wouldn't have mattered unless up against another human, as one of my own kind would have dealt with him swiftly. This was a sobering thought indeed.

I watched as his wife quickly waved an arm behind her, telling him without words that she had this covered as Keira continued to cry on her shoulder. Something I was forced to endure for the next ten minutes or so, which felt like a fucking lifetime! All I wanted to do was storm in there and whisk her away to my secret place. Declaring she was mine to protect and she was mine to comfort, and a fucking baseball bat wasn't going to stop me!

But the frustrating fact remained that I couldn't do any of this, as right now it wouldn't have helped her but only made matters worse...*for both of us.*

"Feeling better?" her sister asked after she seemed to have calmed.

"I'm sorry for that, it was just... I haven't had a dream like that for a while. I guess it really hit me." Keira replied making me growl low enough they wouldn't have heard, but I frowned hard enough if felt the ability to crack my face! Now all I wished to know was what dreams she was referring to and did this have something to do with her past?

Her sister continued to comfort her while I was still asking myself what she could have dreamed of that made her so terrified? Which was when I received my first clue when her sister asked cautiously,

"Was it about him?" I swear the moment she nodded in return, my whole body went ridged! As this could only mean one thing and it was the only time in my life that I wanted to be wrong.

Someone had harmed her.

After that, there was no way I could stay there and not make myself known, so for fear of discovery I left. But I did so feeling guilty, as after her sister offered to fetch her some of her sleeping pills I knew what she would find. For I had taken them away from her and now, along with her only means for a peaceful night's sleep.

At the time my motives for such had been in fear they would do her more harm than good, as I didn't know at the time just how heavily she would rely on them. I didn't want anything like that coursing through her veins and possibly doing damage. I didn't want her becoming dependent on any type of drug, not unless that drug was me.

But now, I realised my mistake, for she obviously only kept them on reserve for times like now. So, I decided for the moment to give her enough space, while I too took the time to process this. Then I would check back on her and see for myself if I couldn't help her sleep.

I had noticed them after the first time she'd had a nightmare and made my rash decision then, tipping them down the sink and leaving the empty bottle behind. But not before I had checked to see where she had acquired them and from which doctor that had prescribed the medication. A lead that Ranka had been currently working on these last few days.

Which was why I was intent on calling her now as there had been something else I hadn't wanted to share with anyone, but after tonight, then I felt as though I had little choice. So, I flew to the mountain clearing that overlooked the national part and pulled out my phone.

"My Lord."

"Did you find the psychiatrist?" I found myself snapping, telling her instantly of my dark mood, one I feared would only pass once this search was all over.

"Yes my Lord, but unfortunately upon searching his office, it became apparent that he is not the organised type and only notes on his current clients are kept there," I growled making her quickly add,

"I did, however, learn that he has moved several times in the last year and that he keeps his older case files in his home." I frowned.

"Then why have they not yet been retrieved?!" I barked with irritation.

"He is leaving for a conference tomorrow, and therefore I thought it prudent to wait so that I have more time to search through his hard copy files along with his computer where I might find more evidence. I am hoping for a timeline of events that I can work back from, my Lord," she said, and this made sense for even though she could just make him unconscious, it meant less concentration on the task at hand for the duration. This way she would have unlimited time to do a more thorough job.

"Good idea," I stated as I knew she was doing a good job and felt it needed to be said. But she knew there was something else bothering me.

"My Lord, you require something more?"

"I feel there has been a development in discovering her past so I want you to extend the search, one that should be enough to tie only one person to the results," I said taking a deep breath and holding the bridge of my nose with my thumb and forefinger.

"Alright, do you wish to send me the…"

"I want no trace of this, Ranka, this is to be done off the radar with no trail," I told her knowing that even if she found this request a strange one, she wouldn't have said it. So, it was unsurprising she simply responded with,

"Understood." I released a deep sigh, knowing I was about to confess what were my biggest fears and in doing so what there could be for me to discover. But I needed to say it. I needed to…*admit it.*

"I want you to add to your search all girls that may have been either attacked or abducted and cross-reference these with the girls who have been admitted into hospital with self-inflicted injuries," I said pushing it past my lips like it was poison. I didn't want to believe it, but all evidence was suggesting this was the most likely case.

"Self-inflicted injuries?" Ranka enquired knowing she would need something more specific. So, I closed my eyes and said with gritted teeth,

"Slit wrists." This created an audible silence on the other end, and I knew why.

"But, my Lord, if that is true then…"

"I know what it means, Ranka," I said interrupting her, unable to hear another say it. As there was only one place attempted suicides find themselves and I didn't even want to think about that.

"I will add it to my search, for with this new information, I don't think it will be long. A day or two." I nodded which was a habit, even for me despite knowing that no one could see the action.

"And Ranka."

"Yes, my Lord."

"No one else is to know, do I make myself clear?" I said knowing this would go without saying, but even so, it was deemed too important not to.

"Taken to death and beyond, my Lord," she replied as was her way.

"Then I will leave you to your work," I replied making her bid me farewell before I hung up.

Then I found myself needing to actually sit down for I feared my legs wouldn't carry me any longer. I would have liked to have said the reason was my failing strength, but it would have been a lie. No, it was because all I could see were my own nightmares playing out in front of me on repeat. Every terrified look I had witnessed on her face all because I hadn't been there in time to save her from an unknown enemy.

I hadn't been there in time to save her from herself.

In the end, I didn't know how long I remained there, sat on the cold damp ground staring out into the dead of night. I didn't know what would end up being worse, not knowing the details or discovering them, for there was no coming back from something like that. Once I saw for myself what she had possibly gone through, then I knew I was crossing a line. A line I myself would have drawn in the sand in the first place.

But I knew deep down why I was digging so hard. Because how could I honestly predict the damage I could unknowingly inflict if I didn't know what she had been through. Her fear was something I could deal with, I could comfort or manage in the future. *Her fear of me however*...no, I could never have that! Meaning that I had no choice, for when the time came then that line was getting crossed, no matter how hard it could prove to be.

Moments later I flew back to her window to find her thankfully fast asleep and looking peaceful, making my heart ache for her. I just wanted to scoop her up in my arms and take her with me, cradling her to my chest and keeping her safe forever...

Even safe from her dreams.

The next evening it was unfortunate that I had been in my office when Keira was due to arrive as Ranka had informed me that she had found all the information of Keira's therapy sessions and was forwarding it to me via our private server. Meaning that I had been hoping to read it before she had arrived. But then Vincent walked into my office with a frown upon his face, telling me I was about to hear something that I didn't want to.

"The girl?" I said making him nod his head.

"She's just arrived."

"And?" I prompted knowing there was more to this.

"And I take it she was not followed today?" he asked making me suddenly stand from my chair and demand,

"Why, what happened?!"

"Calm yourself, she is alright, but I fear she may appear a little less than the perfection you're used to seeing," I growled at this and gritted out,

"Get to the fucking point, Vincent!"

"I was just speaking to Karmun, who was concerned she may not be fit for work, for it seems your clumsy little waitress lost a fight with the floor today, as she fell and hit her head," he told me with a half-smile, as he had learned for himself how clumsy she was after seeing how many times she had bumped herself or tripped when working below.

But hearing that she was hurt didn't calm me, even if relief was something I felt from learning now that this was all that had happened.

"Is she alright? Has she been seen by a doctor?" I asked quickly making him lift his hands up in surrender.

"I'm just the messenger here and not a very informed one at that. He said she looks pale, paler than usual and has a cut and big bruise on her forehead. But there are no stitches which he can see, so it's unlikely she went to have it looked at." He replied making me growl once more. Foolish girl! She could have a concussion or even an underlining head trauma which might cause greater problems and risk to her health!

"I need to see her!" I said rounding my desk and heading to the door when Vincent stopped me.

"Whoa, there Dom, just stop a second."

"No, she is injured," I stated the obvious.

"Yes, I know, but she isn't exactly bleeding to death out there calling for a priest or reciting her last will and testament," he said making me frown.

"Not funny."

"Alright look, she has simply had a bump to the head, something I foresee you having to deal with often in your future and long lifetime together, seeing for myself how clumsy she is. But what do you intend to do now, demand to see her head and then tell her you want to play doctors and patients?" The thought, I confess, was a tempting one. But I shook the sexual thoughts of having her lay spread out on a bed for me to examine and back to the problem at hand. Which at the minute was my brother and his damn logic!

"You do realise what underlining issues can become of a head injury?!" I argued making him fold his arms across his chest and remind me,

"You're not the only one with a doctorate Dom." I rolled my eyes making him carry on trying to break through my thought process.

"Look I get your frustrations, but you can't force her to go to the hospital, no more than you can force her to go home."

"The Hell I can't! She cannot be allowed to work!" I said, at the ready to drive her home myself!

"Well, you can try, but I would have thought you would have wanted her here, seeing as I am sure you know what signs to look out for better than her sister would...*having a doctorate and all.*"Vincent added this last part in a sarcastic tone to himself, but I ignored the jibe for he had a point. At least if she were here for the next few hours, I could monitor her myself and be assured if she needed medical attention or not.

"Fine, you made your point, Vince," I told him making him shrug his shoulders in a way where he didn't doubt for a second that he ever would. I then walked to the door but paused before going through it, looking back over my shoulder at him to ask,

"Is it bad?" This obvious display of concern for her wiped the smug look off his face.

"I don't know, for I haven't yet seen her for myself but when I asked Karmun the same thing, he merely winced and said, that it looked painful." I winced myself when hearing this before I was out the door with a growl.

Because right now her past could wait,
Keira and her pain could not.

The next hour was excruciating to watch as I was just getting angrier by the second! I just wanted to storm over there, pick her up and take her to lie down in my bed. A place where I could then examine her and for once my sexual urges had nothing to do with that image. I could see that she was obviously in pain and I had made a move to get up a few times to aid her only to be reminded by Vincent for me to give it time.

Time that hit its fucking limit the second she walked into the back room for a moment. I motioned for Rue, one of my other waitresses and our resident witch over to the table.

"Clear Keira's section Rue, she is done for the night." She nodded, no doubt knowing why after seeing for herself the damage to her forehead and commenting on it once when they were by the bar together. I had yet to see it up close myself, but even from a distance, the bruise was developing angrily.

"Of course, My Lord," Rue replied, before hurrying off to do as instructed before Keira had finished in the back room, no doubt having a much-needed sit-down. I had given it long enough and was motioning for Karmun to check on her when she emerged looking paler still.

"You need to go home, you don't look well," Karmun told her as I instructed him to after sending this message in his mind, but one look back at my table and something in her decided to disagree.

"I feel better now, I've just taken some pain killers, and they should start kicking in soon," she told him, making me growl again.

"Dom," Vincent said my name in warning which was only when I noticed my demon had reacted by gorging thick lines into the wood at my armrest, as my nails had turned into his thick black talons. Ones strong enough to have slashed their way through metal sheeting. I closed my eyes a moment and took the time to tame him, pushing him back and forbidding him to do anything rash. Like storming over to her, throwing her over our shoulder, spanking her fine behind in warning and taking her back to our chamber so as we could heal her. Then, of course, we would make her ours. Of course, I didn't disagree with this fantasy my demon had quickly planted in our mind, it was just unfortunate that I had to tell him no.

But then I thought back to her decision and had to ask myself, why had she disagreed? Had it been down to the harsh look I was giving her? Had displaying my mood so openly backfired...it looked like it, for I would have thought she would have seen my disapproval of her being here when injured and backed down.

I had been wrong.

"Wow, stubborn much," Sophia commented, as she too knew of Keira's injury, one discovered the second she saw it for herself. I for one had been sitting here, chastising myself for not having her watched more carefully during the day. As I had come to understand when listening to her conversation this morning with her sister, that she was to spend the day at home, and therefore I had little to worry about. Clearly, I had underestimated the dangers of even a 'home environment' could present for my Keira.

Well unsurprisingly after this point it only took her another ten minutes later to realise her mistake. I watched as she stumbled her way to the bar, saving herself from falling and told Karmun that she was going to get some air. She grabbed her bag from the back room and unsteadily made her way to the doors, nearly falling through them in her haste to get outside. This told me one thing...she was going to be sick.

Karmun nodded to me to tell me something I already knew.

"Okay, so intervening now would be a good plan," Vincent said sheepishly.

"You think!" I snapped back as I shot from my seat and stormed over to the balcony doors only hoping I wasn't going to find her passed out on the floor. Damn my brother and his shit logic!

I walked through, smelling the vomit, and quickly detecting that her choice for expelling such was one of the large terracotta pots situated either side of the doors, offering the only decoration on the balcony. But I couldn't care less as my only concern was for the little beauty stood against the wall, currently using it to keep upright.

The beads of sweat were glistening on her pale skin, and with a shaky bottle of water in her hand, I wondered how long it was before she passed out completely? But then the second she heard the doors open she instantly dropped the bottle back in her bag and hid something behind her back, making me frown.

Especially when she looked up briefly, saw me and then quickly lowered her head again. So, I decided to play dumb and pretend I didn't know of her injury, as I wanted to see if she would lie or if she would trust me with the truth...

Her first test.

Keira

39

A Drive Never to be Forgotten

By the time I had arrived at work my headache went from a light throbbing to someone going at it with a jackhammer. I was regretting not taking Libby's advice. I tried to ignore it, but it was persistent, so I took a couple of the painkillers that I kept in my bag before I started work.

Once upstairs I pulled the short bits of my hair forward to try and hide the huge bruise and lump that had now fully developed. It was amazing that in one short car ride it had changed so much. It was now different shades of blue and purple and also had crept its way down one cheek along with a little scratch. There was no getting around it, my face looked a mess and no amount of hair across my forehead was going to conceal it.

I walked in front of the tables with my head down, letting my hair flop limply around my face. I didn't look up until I bumped into the bar.

"Hey sweetheart, how are...Wow that's a real shiner. Now that looks painful. What did you do, lose a fight with a bus?" I smiled timidly at Karmun, not wanting to draw any attention to myself.

"I fell," was all I said before going around to the other side and into the little room in the back. Looking in the mirror I lifted my hair again to re-evaluate the damage but, Eek... It didn't look pretty. The lump had grown and was making the plaster lift on the side that was near my hairline. I tried to pat it down, but it had lost its stickiness and wasn't co-operating. I rolled my eyes to the ceiling and inhaled a deep breath before walking out to start my shift.

This was great, only my second night at this job and I already looked like I'd been in the ring with Rocky Balboa! I was just about to walk through the door into the bar when I heard my name, only it wasn't being called, it was being spoken. I couldn't see who it was without showing myself, so I waited. I didn't recognise the voice as the band had started but I was sure it was male. I waited but didn't hear anything else, so I walked out. There was no one there apart from Karmun.

"Are you sure you're okay to work?" I wanted to tell him no but knew that wouldn't look good so instead I lied.

"Yeah, I'm fine, it looks worse than it is." He didn't look convinced but gave me a tray of drinks anyway and pointed to the table. After about an hour of waiting tables my head was starting to spin slightly, so I went into the back and took a couple more tablets as they didn't seem to be touching it. I knew this wasn't safe, but I just wanted the pounding to stop drumming against my skull. The music wasn't helping being that it was a very heavy rock band called 'My Pretty Little Nightmares.' Well, they didn't disappoint being as they were, at this very moment, my nightmare. The drum and bass mirrored the pain I felt, and I sat down for a minute holding my head in my hands. I needed to get a grip.

I could do this! I was only doing a short four hour shift tonight anyway so only three more hours to go and I could go home to bed. But then I was forgetting that Jack was taking me home tonight and Frank was working late. Well, I would just have to call Libby and ask her to come and get me, because I didn't know how I was going to last another three hours let alone the rest of the night downstairs socializing.

When I went back out I noticed most of my tables had been cleared for me and Karmun's worried face was waiting for me.

"You need to go home, you don't look well." I was about to agree when I noticed Draven's cold hard eyes staring at me, making me change my mind. I didn't want to give him the satisfaction of being right. He didn't want me working up here in the first place and after only one night, being sent home would prove him right. Nope, I don't think so. I would rather slog it out.

"I feel better now, I've just taken some pain killers and they should start kicking in soon." He shook his head a bit but I knew he was caving. He handed me the tray again and added,

"Okay, but if you feel dizzy or sick then you are going home and no buts." I nodded and took the tray trying to hold it as steady as I could.

The customers started to look at me strangely and I wondered how many times I had bumped into their tables. I was losing my perspective on my surroundings as my vision kept going blurry. It had only been another hour but I was fading fast. Maybe Libby was right, maybe I had suffered concussion.

I got back to the bar and nearly fell but managed to hold myself up without dropping. I was feeling sick and needed some air badly. I grabbed my bag and told Karmun I was going to get some air on the balcony. He just nodded but I wasn't sure it was to me. I had never felt this dizzy before and kept shaking my head to make it go away, but it was having the opposite effect and making me want to vomit.

Once outside, I couldn't help what was coming and ran over to the huge plant pot that was closest to the door and threw up in it. Luckily, I hadn't eaten much throughout the day, so what came up was mainly liquid and bile. My throat burned and I took the bottle of water out of my bag and took a large gulp, only it felt like liquid fire as it went down.

The cold air on my skin was welcoming as the heat from my body was causing little beads of sweat to form around my temple. I wiped them away with the back of my sleeve and dug into my bag for some more tablets, knowing now it would be all right as I must have thrown up the last lot. I was just about to get two out of the bottle when the door opened suddenly, letting out a burst of warm air and music. So, I put the hand that was holding them behind my back and hid them from sight.

I was about to say I would be back in a minute, thinking it was just Karmun who had come out to check on me, but I was wrong. It wasn't Karmun and no amount of wishing would make it so.

Draven walked through the glass doors and looked around finding me leaning up against the wall using it for support. I lowered my head quickly so he couldn't see my face and felt the heat rush to my cheeks, making my head spin even more. Why me?

Of all the times for him to need some air, I would have to be out here, after just vomiting in his plant pot moments before and looking like I had been hit by a car! I looked truly awful and even though I knew it wasn't the best of times to be worried about what I looked like, in front of Draven it was just hard not to.

"Keira, what are you doing out here?" God, why did I have to love how my name sounded on his lips? I couldn't believe that my obsession didn't falter even when I was feeling as bad as this. My sickness for Draven obviously ran deep to the core.

"Sorry... I...I was just getting some air but... I'm umm...I'm done now." I turned to walk back in still keeping my tablets out of sight, when his large solid arm came out in front of me. I quickly stopped in my path and was rooted to the spot. His hand stretched out resting on the stone wall. His arm had become a barrier of solid muscle preventing me from leaving. I noticed he wasn't wearing his usual suit but a black t-shirt that clung tight to the curves of his defined chest and rippled stomach. A long black jacket that went to his knees added to a 'bad ass' exterior.

"What do you have in your hand?" His voice was hard and stern, making my lips quiver in response. Then his tall body leaned in towards mine slightly as it had done last night, and I got the same sensation of energy coming off his skin. My head started to spin more and I held the wall for added support. Now with my back fully flat against the stone my heavy breathing became the issue.

"It's...It's nothing." I curled my fingers around the bottle tighter, but my palms were sweating and they were starting to slip. I tried to put them in my pocket, when his other hand snaked around my back. I couldn't help the gasp at the feel of his touch as he gripped my wrist in a vice-like hold, pulling it back round to the front of me. My pulse went through the roof and I looked up at him for the first time meeting his terrifying black eyes.

He took my hand in his and peeled my fingers from around the orange bottle and looked down with disappointment in his eyes. I, on the other hand, was trying to string two words together but couldn't due to the tingling heat that travelled its way around my body from his touch.

"I do not allow drugs in my club." I shuddered at the sound of his authoritative voice, which filled the night air. I wanted to defend myself. I didn't want him thinking I was some kind of junky! So somehow, amazingly my lips formed the words.

"It's not drugs, I mean...well yeah, it's drugs but just normal pain killers. See, I hit my head today and just have a bit of a headache." This in fact was a huge understatement. It actually felt as though my head was going to crack open allowing my brain to come oozing out in something that resembled a strawberry smoothie. I could also feel that I was fading fast, and my head looked down so that he couldn't see, also I was going slightly cross-eyed trying to stay focused and that was never a good look.

"Let me see." He ordered as he lifted his hand to my head. I thought I was going to die with shame. I was saying over and over in my head, *Please don't, oh please don't*. And for a split second he actually stopped as if he had heard my secret plea. But then his hand touched my chin, lifting it up so he could see my face better.

God knows what colour my cheeks went but they felt on fire, so it couldn't have been good. I couldn't look at his eyes, so they found a spot on his shoulder to stare at. But his hand didn't stop there as it moved up to where the lump was as he now pushed my hair back. I bit my lip so hard that my teeth almost pierced the skin. His fingers touched the cut very gently and when I thought that it couldn't get even worse, I realised that the plaster must have come off at some point.

He sighed as though upset with something and said in a softer tone,

"This doesn't look good. You shouldn't be here, you probably have concussion." Oh great, now him too. Well, wait until Libby heard this one, something Draven and she agreed on. Only then I remembered I was yet to tell Libby I was working in the VIP but knowing what her reaction might be I decided this was one story that was better left untold.

I didn't want to back down now I'd come this far, so I decided to be brave and tell him no.

"I'm going to be fine, I only have another hour or so and I will be okay until then." I moved to walk back inside, but because I'd been stood in the same spot for a while I hadn't noticed that the only reason I was still upright was thanks to the wall. My feet gave way and I would have stumbled if it wasn't for Draven who had caught me by the waist. His strong arm was circled round my stomach and his other hand was gripping my side sending sparks of pleasure up my skin.

"I don't think that's going to happen," he said with a hint of smugness to it. Was he making fun of me?

My top had risen slightly, and his skin was now in full contact with mine. The heat off his fingertips left marks of intense stimulation on my back and this was made worse when his grip tightened against me. I closed my eyes as the rest of my legs finally gave way and I was soon fully in his arms. He lifted me effortlessly, pulling my body closer to his.

I was so embarrassed, I started to object. Shaking my head slowly and saying,

"No, it's okay... I can walk, really," in a pathetically weak voice, as my head was now spinning.

"Easy there, I've got you now and I'm going to get you home." His face was full of concern as he stared into my eyes. It was the first time I had seen this softer side to him and it gave him a different, yet sexy look. But then I knew I must have been dreaming as surely he wouldn't take the time himself to care for me, an important man like Draven. I must have fallen asleep in that little room. That was it! I just prayed that Karmun found me and no one else.

It felt so real though, and would there be this much pain if it wasn't? I was vaguely aware that we were no longer alone. I could hear Draven giving orders to someone and I was pretty sure it wasn't me as I was still nestled safely in his arms. Arms that felt solid, as though they had been fortified with steel and I wondered if this was how Louis Lane felt when she was in the arms of Superman. By now anyone else would have just put me down due to the strain.

I could just make out bits of what was being said and I heard the words *'Car'* and *'My Lord'*, but I must have imagined this last part unless there was something more to Draven than I knew.

When I heard the door shut I knew we were alone again and waited for his next move. He leaned his head down and pulled me up closer to his face as he whispered,

"Close your eyes." I did what he asked, as if the warm scent of his breath hypnotised me. He turned my face inwards so it was against his solid shoulder and he moved his jacket so that it covered my head, shielding me from what was about to happen. I couldn't prevent the shudder that crept its way up from my spine at the feel of his large hand gripping the back of my neck.

"Now don't look or this will make you feel worse." I didn't understand what he meant, but I nodded under the material that smelled like warm leather. Then all of a sudden we were moving but I had no clue as to where. I mean, we were still outside, I was almost certain of it. I couldn't hear the music and the noise of people inside.

Also, there was still a chill in the air even though I could only just feel it, as I was next to Draven's soothing warm skin. In these arms I felt as though nothing in the world could ever harm me. I almost fell asleep with the calming effect of being moulded to his body in this protective cocoon. It was only the blazing pain in my head that kept this moment from being the most blissful experience of my life.

I couldn't explain how we were moving, as it didn't feel as though Draven's body had any movement at all. It felt as though maybe we could have been gliding but it was probably down to the fact that I didn't know what was real or what was fantasy any more. Then whatever it was came to an end as I jolted slightly in his arms, as though he had just jumped and this was the landing.

He was walking now and I couldn't contain the urge to look any more, so I turned my head slowly so as not to draw his attention. However, he must have felt my movement under his jacket because he pulled me in tighter still. I could feel his heart beating against me and my own heart quickened because of it. This just felt so intimate that it was hard not to get carried away.

By the sound of his footsteps it appeared as if he was walking on a stone floor and the chill was taken out of the air. I knew we must have been inside somewhere, as now it felt as though we were moving down a staircase. My body jolted slightly with each step and I couldn't help my hand grabbing on to the material of his T shirt as though to steady myself. I was also sure that I felt him look down at me when I did this, but I couldn't see his face as my head was still buried into his shoulder.

When we unfortunately stopped, I held my breath waiting for him to put me down. His arms must be killing him by now as I was sure no man could carry a body for this long without any pain. But surprisingly he didn't put me down. No, instead I heard the creaking of a door's hinges and he carried on, letting it slam behind us. I jumped at the noise and he squeezed me tighter as though telling me through his actions that I was safe.

We carried on for a while longer and as if hearing my thoughts, he finally spoke

"Not much further now." His voice was strong and steady and amazingly wasn't even strained slightly from the weight of me. I mean, I knew he looked fit but I had no idea he was super human! The guy was a machine.

We went through another door into a room and I knew this was the end of our journey as his arms and grip loosened around my body, allowing me to turn my head and peek through.

We seemed to be in what looked like a car dealership. There were so many new cars I couldn't name them all as there must have been at least twenty. It looked more like a museum considering some of them were on their own display mounts. Some were covered in sheets and there was one that looked extremely old. But the strangest one of all looked like it was in its own glass room. I knew then that I was most likely dreaming, as I was sure I could see it shake as though trying to get out. What the Hell was going on in my head?

We weren't alone and Draven was walking up to a man who wore a flat hat and a long grey coat.

"Will it be the Enzo or the Phantom my Lord?" I had no idea what he was saying but I think he was asking Draven which car he should take me home in and then there was that *Lord* thing again. I just couldn't get my head around it. I was getting ready for his hands to let me go and even though the pain was now creeping its way across the back of my head, I was still encountering more pleasure in Draven's arms than I had ever known. Pleasure I wasn't ready to let go of yet.

"No, I will take her back in the Aston," he said in his usual commanding tone. The man nodded, adding,

"Very good Sir" and went off to open the door to a very low silver sports car. It looked more like a panther than a car, with its sleek curves and angry grill. I was almost scared to be put into it.

"It looks as though I get to drive you home sooner than *you* thought." Draven said with a soft tone and a smirk I could see clearly.

"Oh...umm...it's okay, you don't have to...I know you're busy and...with stuff...I have my phone in my pocket, Libby can be called...she has a phone..." I said all this knowing my brain wasn't making much sense and at the same time I wanted to smack myself for sounding so stupid...although my head hurt enough already.

"No." How he said that one word was as though it was final and made me bite my lip so I wouldn't argue against it.

With my body still curled in Draven's arms he walked up to the Aston and lowered me into the seat. He was so careful, as though I was made from fine china and he was scared of breaking me. As he put me down his hands slid from under my legs and his face nearly touched mine, he was so close. I couldn't breathe and again closed my eyes, being scared that I might find his gaze fixated on me.

"Are you alright?" Once more his voice was soft and steady as he said the words so close to my own lips. I kept my eyes closed and could only nod in response as I still didn't believe this was happening to me.

"Good girl." I thought I heard him whisper, but then the door closed making me jump. Had he really said that? I opened my eyes and tried to focus them to the light.

Inside the car was like nothing I had seen before. The seat that I sat in was curved up around my body and it reminded me of a racing car. I think they called them bucket seats. In between the driver's side there was a curved middle console with controls I didn't recognise. For all I knew he could have been James Bond and this was where you fired the rockets and ejector seats.

The rest of the car was black leather and cream interior, with a chrome finish. The steering wheel looked more fitting for a master's hand like a sword to a warrior. It wanted to be driven, as if beckoning or daring you to touch it, to see if you could control its power. The silver wings that were embedded in the middle just added to the feel of the machine, as though created by the Gods themselves.

This car was definitely made for a man like Draven.

I didn't know much about cars, but I would bet my life on it that this car cost a small fortune. I jumped when the driver's side opened and Draven's long muscular legs stepped in. The car was facing a stone wall and it didn't look as if there was going to be enough room to pull forward to turn around but thinking about it I couldn't see a garage door of any kind so I wasn't sure how we were going to get out. Draven must have noticed me looking around and read my thoughts.

"Put your seat belt on," he said while looking at me and he soon had me biting my lip again. Then the lights went out plunging us into darkness. I couldn't help the uncertain noise that escaped and his voice remained calm and said,

"Don't be afraid. Trust me." I don't know why but I did trust him. If there was one person I didn't trust, then that was myself.

I lifted my hand to my head and held it there trying to stop the aching. We were still in the dark and thankfully he couldn't see the discomfort in my eyes.

"Try to relax and the pain will ease." His deep voice cut through the silence as he killed any ideas I had that he couldn't see me in the dark. I looked over to him and for one tiny second, I could see a purplish tint where his eyes would be and then it disappeared as the engine burst into life.

The beast came alive around us, sounding like a hundred thousand warriors charging into battle. Then the stone wall in front of us reappeared in the blaze of the headlights, only now seeming closer than it had before. He revved the engine as though taunting the beast and all of a sudden, I became disorientated by the thunderous roar and the immense force that pinned me back in my seat. Then in fear, my mind focused on the wall, I closed my eyes and gripped the seat ready for impact!

But it never came, instead we seemed to be getting faster and I never could imagine death to be so painless. I wondered if Draven had been my angel to deliver me to Heaven or my demon to drag me to Hell. But as I started to compose myself I realised I was still breathing and in one piece.

"You can open your eyes now." Draven said with no emotion in his voice. I did as I was told and opened them to find we were on a road, but we were going so fast that I couldn't make out where, as everything was a blur outside my window.

I couldn't help but ask

"Where did the wall go?" A quiet laugh came from his lips and a smile that I hadn't seen before. It was hard to tell in the dark with only the faint glow of the dash to show the expression on his face, but his eyes changed from their usual cold black to the hint of purple that I had seen before.

"That wall was the door and it opened just like any other, which you would have seen if you hadn't had your eyes closed." The blood rushed to my face and I was glad that the light in the car wouldn't pick it up. I truly was going crazy and now Draven knew it too.

"Let me ask you, do you really believe I would have driven us both through a stone wall?" He laughed again at the thought and I was getting hotter. He was making fun of me and rightly so, but I had to defend myself in some way.

"Well, how was I supposed to know you had your very own bat cave? And considering it didn't look like a bloody door and I've had a knock to the head, maybe you could cut me some slack?" Oh my god! What did I just say? Where did that come from? And more importantly how was I ever going to take it back? I looked out of the window and once again was nearly pulling all the skin off my bottom lip. I was now wishing more than ever that this was a dream. What must he be thinking? The man had just carried me God knows how far and was driving me home in this awesome machine and that's what I decided to say! What an idiot... IDIOT!

"Bat cave?" I shot him a look and thought I could just see the hint of his lips twitching as though trying to contain a smile. My only answer was a groan that couldn't be helped. He must have seen my head drop shamefully, so his next words were gentle and sincere.

"You're right. I'm sorry, you weren't to know. I hope I didn't scare you too much." I was also sure he sounded a little bit guilty as he asked me about being frightened. I was scared to open my mouth again in case something equally stupid came rushing out like verbal diarrhoea. I coughed clearing my throat before saying,

"It's okay, I guess my mind just plays tricks on me sometimes." He turned his head towards me, taking his eyes off the road. I wasn't sure this was a good idea as it felt like we were going over a hundred miles an hour. He looked as if he wanted to ask something but stopped himself. I was burning to know what it was, so I turned and asked,

"What?" I didn't know where all this new-found confidence was coming from. Then I started to worry about the bang to my head and wondered if that was the reason.

"You don't think like other people, do you?" His face was serious, and I realised that he wasn't making fun of me anymore. He actually thought I was crazy. This was like a flaming arrow to the heart. I was so sensitive about my mental health it was like my Achilles heel. When I didn't respond he looked at my face for the reason why. I must have looked like a spoilt child because I just folded my arms and looked out of the window. I mean, what did he want me to say, 'Yes Mr Draven, I am a freak!'

"Trust me Keira, that's not a bad thing." He said this, and his hand moved as though he wanted to touch me but instead he let it drop to rest on the gear stick. I was about to answer him, but the car filled with the sound of ABBA and my heart almost stopped. The words "Gimme Gimme Gimme" sang over and over and when I didn't move he said,

"I'm pretty sure that's yours." And laughed again, only this time he couldn't wipe the smirk from his face.

I fumbled with the phone in my trouser pocket and said a weak,

"It's my sister's phone." But I doubted he believed me. I looked at the number and I knew it was RJ. Shit! I had forgotten them completely and answered the phone wishing this night would just end and my humiliation with it.

"Hey RJ, look I'm sorry...Oh... hey Jack, I thought it was, oh no I had to go home, I wasn't feeling too good." Draven all of a sudden went very rigid and his hands tensed on the wheel. I didn't understand why the sudden change, but I carried on with the conversation, wanting to get off the phone as quickly as possible.

"Yeah, I'm sorry I was going to call, no its okay I'm nearly home." Jack didn't sound pleased and Draven didn't look happy.

"No, I'm fine, I just hit my head, No, no, in the woods not at work. Look, I will talk to you later, okay? Honestly, I'm fine it's just a scratch." Draven shot me a look as if to say *liar*

"Okay yeah, well I'll talk to you tomorrow then, sorry what? Who am I driving home with...uh..." Shit, shit, shit, I didn't know what to say? I didn't think that Draven would want anyone to know about this, so I said,

"Frank, yeah... okay then... see ya." I let out a sigh and put my head back against the seat. My head felt like it was splitting in two. I could feel a pair of eyes staring at me, but I didn't want to look. The atmosphere had changed since the phone call and I wished I hadn't answered it and had called from the house instead. I felt as though I should say something, although I couldn't think of anything but,

"Sorry about that, I forgot that I was getting a lift home with some friends." My voice went back to its usual embarrassed tone. I knew the confidence thing wouldn't last.

"Frank?" I had to think for a second, then it hit me maybe he wanted to know why I had said it was Frank driving me home instead of him, but why would he care.

"I didn't...uh...didn't think you would want anyone knowing...you know." I nodded to the dash to indicate the car and his sharp gaze locked on to mine.

"You think I would have an issue with anyone knowing I was driving you home?"

"I...well, what I mean is, you and your family...you know that I don't say things, I can be discreet, and I know you like your privacy and rightly so, I just figured..." I just figured I really needed to stop babbling! Thankfully though, he visibly relaxed and then even smiled.

"Keira, its fine and I know you don't talk about me or my family." Hearing him saying this gave me a warm feeling that was deep enough to penetrate my bones. After all, this didn't sound like the words of a man who hated me. I wanted to say something more, but we were pulling into the gravel drive and I knew I would soon be getting out, saying my goodbye. I told myself that I wouldn't linger, I would just say thanks and get out.

He stopped the car and cut the engine. Then it hit me, the very last thing that I wanted to do was...

Get out of his car.

DRAVEN

40

DRIVING BEAUTY

"Keira, what are you doing out here?" I asked her as gently as my dark mood would allow. The next words out of her mouth only meant it was a test she quickly failed,

"Sorry... I...I was just getting some air but... I'm umm...I'm done now." She turned ready to try and walk back inside, which was when I made my move. Oh no, you aren't going anywhere, my fragile little lamb I thought, the second my hand slapped to the wall in front of her, blocking her path...*and her escape.*

I then watched silently as she looked along my arm, before following it down my body, to find I was no longer wearing my usual suit this night. I had planned on changing before I had heard that she was injured. So, she found me now wearing a casual black t-shirt, dark jeans and the same leather jacket I had been wearing the day we first met. Half of me wondered what she was thinking right now when taking in my muscular form. The other half voiced what I wanted to know,

"What do you have in your hand?" I let my tone be that of her boss demanding an answer, hoping she would take it seriously enough to answer truthfully. I even added to the intimidation by leaning closer towards her, overtaking her space. But her mind was obviously spinning, for she shifted so as more of the wall was holding up her weight and therefore hiding her hand from me completely. Then she told me in a weak tone,

"It's...It's nothing." I looked down as she started to fumble with her pocket, obviously trying to conceal the small pill bottle I could see there in between her trembling fingers. Fingers I decided to take the burden from, as I curled an arm around her back, feeling for myself her overheated skin.

Then I found her wrist and forcefully pulled it to the front of her. This was the point she finally looked up at me, as I started to peel her fingers away from what she seemed ashamed off. The label stated they were simple paracetamols and a mild pain relief, which then begged the question as to why she seemed so embarrassed about having them. Unless they were something more, hiding inside this unsuspecting bottle?

Which was why I pushed her further for answers.

"I do not allow drugs in my club," I told her, knowing that she would end up defending herself and thus giving me the true reasons why she was out here, which was what I really wanted from her.

"It's not drugs, I mean...well yeah, it's drugs but just normal pain killers. See, I hit my head today and just have a bit of a headache." Ha! A bit of a headache, yeah sure you do sweetheart! For starters, she could barely focus. I almost shook my head in my disbelief. But then at the very least, she admitted to her fall, so I guess it was a small victory for me, as we were getting closer to the truth.

"Let me see," I demanded softly, as I lifted my hand giving her no choice to deny me. But then the gentle plea of hers was heard being whispered in my mind, as in her panic she had unknowingly reached out to me. Even though I was the one currently causing this anxiety.

'Please don't, oh please don't' Her haunting plea continued to echo in my mind, even forcing me to stop for a moment before deciding to continue. She needed to learn that she could trust me and most of all, to keep her promises made to me...

She would never hide from me.

So, I took hold of her chin and lifted it so that she was forced to look up at me, hiding those worried eyes no longer. But after a mere glance, it was as if she could stand it no longer, for they focused on my shoulder, telling me she was nearing her limit here.

So, I continued to do as I had wanted to since she arrived and that was to examine her injury. Once I could see it properly, I found the large lump after pushing back the hair she had used to try and conceal it. I then looked down to see her expression was one of apprehension, for she had her eyes closed tightly and was biting her lip so hard, it would have been classed as self-torture. So, I decided not to take any more time than was necessary, and after examining the deep cut I found there, I knew now that she indeed needed medical attention.

I released a sigh and told her my thoughts,

"This doesn't look good. You shouldn't be here, you probably have a concussion." I was then about to explain what was to happen next when she beat me to it, having her own ideas on the matter.

"I'm going to be fine, I only have another hour or so, and I will be okay until then." A fact she tried to prove when moving, and something I knew she would fail at. For that wall behind her had been holding up her weight now this entire time, something her body had become reliant on. Which was why I was more than ready to catch her as I did the second she tried to move away from it on unsteady legs.

Of course, having the excuse to wrap an arm around her once more was something I welcomed, despite the circumstances.

"I don't think that's going to happen," I told her in a tone that could be classed as both arrogant and cocky, considering I had just been proven right. Then she shifted slightly, but it was enough for her shirt to rise up, now allowing me access to her soft skin, meaning that smugness was soon swept away and replaced by a wave of lust.

I couldn't help my reaction to her as I tightened my grip for fear of losing the feel of her body beneath my fingertips. And I wasn't the only one this intense contact was affecting, for her legs swiftly gave way completely. Something I relished in for I easily swept her up in my arms, holding her meagre weight tight against my frame. I could tell this action embarrassed her as she started to object, but there was very little fight behind those words.

"No, it's okay... I can walk, really,"

"Easy there, I've got you now, and I'm going to get you home," I told her, gently soothing her fears and letting her know that she was in my care now. She seemed to blank out for a few moments, no doubt as she tried to control the spinning sensation her mind was fooling her with. In that time one of my men stepped into sight, having no doubt been summoned by Vincent who would have known what was happening now.

I decided to give him his orders in a way she wouldn't understand,

"Tag pigerne ting og få dem klar til at vente i garagen. Informer min chauffør, vi vil snart være der." I said speaking Danish and telling him to take the bag she had dropped when collapsing in my arms, one that had a jacket spilling out of it and inform my driver that I was coming.

"He will have a car waiting My Lord." I nodded letting my subject go and hoping that Keira was in too much of a haze to question why I was now being referred to as 'My Lord'. I waited for him to leave and decided what I would do next. I had intended to simply walk her back into the club and down the back passageways to the underground garage.

But now I had her like this, then there was no way I was putting her down, and I knew that walking back inside would have caused too much of a stir among my people. And if I were being honest with myself, I didn't want to share this moment with anyone.

Which meant there was only the one option left and it was a risky one. So, I lifted her slightly so as I could whisper down to her, hoping this time she proved her trust in me.

"Close your eyes." I waited for her to comply before I reached up a hand from her back and turned her face against my shoulder. Then I used my mind to cover her with my jacket so as she was hidden and cocooned against my chest. Not that she would have known as I could feel the confusion coming from her mind in waves. She was questioning if this was a dream or not and in aid to try and calm her, I imprinted the feel of my hand on the back of her neck, even though both my hands were around her body.

Then I warned her,

"Now don't look or this will make you feel worse," I said making my decision to drop to a hidden entrance slightly below this one. From first glance, it just looked like a decorative feature added to the side of the building. A small single person sized balcony that was all twisted wrought iron curled round in a semicircle. But there was no door or opening to speak of unless of course, you knew how to access one.

There were very few people who knew of this secret entrance into Afterlife and for good reason, for it didn't just grant you access into the club but somewhere much more forbidden. It was essentially a long tunnel that at different points had other tunnels running from it like tree branches. However, at the end of the tunnel and after first travelling a long way down, it would bring you out by my treasury, one situated just outside the crypt. Beyond that was the prison and Temple. But there were many secret passageways hidden throughout the entirety of my home, ones that only the three of us knew about. And a few that were for my personal use only.

And now here I was, already sharing one of our secrets with a girl who didn't even know who I was in this hidden world of hers. I shook my head to myself, wondering what had happened to my once good senses. Then I looked down at the sweet girl in my arms, and I knew precisely where it had gone...

Lost to my heart.

So, with this deep and profound sentiment still lingering in my mind, I took a leap of faith and hoped that one day soon it would pay off, for it felt in this moment as if she held all the power. The power to grant my heart the reason for beating or the power...

To destroy it completely.

So, I did the only thing left in my control and in that single moment,

I trusted her and I jumped!

I felt her holding on to me and whimper a little in the confines of my jacket as we landed on the metal floor. But like I had asked of her, she didn't look. Then with my own gaze looking directly at the stone wall, I uttered the words that would open it, making sure to do so, so as she wouldn't hear me.

"Persae Calorem" I spoke the Latin for 'Persian Heat' and waited for the doorway to appear before walking through the small space, one only made big enough for one person to walk through single file. Thankfully it was still wide enough for me to continue holding her this way, without her legs touching the sides of the wall.

It wasn't long before I was ducking through an arched opening as it was one of the first branches off the main central tunnel that would lead directly back to the club. The whole place was a honeycomb of tunnels, hallways and corridors that connected the large building from all four sides. As one thing no one would have guessed from first glance was the way the building was constructed.

It was similar to a castle in design, for the centre section was cut out, but instead of holding a courtyard like most castles would, this one held the Temple's domed, golden roof barely even level with the lowest floors of Afterlife.

But whatever the size of the building above then the lower levels were at least twice that and thanks to its constant veil, wasn't visible unless you were granted access into the 'home' part of Afterlife. So low flying planes or helicopters weren't a concern, for all they would see was a large panelled roof section, one framed by a series of connecting rooftop gardens, walkways and staggered tower tops made from interlocking large stone blocks.

It was a fortress.

Feeling Keira beginning to stir in my arms brought me back to my situation, and I tucked her closer to the cradle of my body, knowing that her curiosity would only hold out for so long. It wasn't much farther now as we would soon be back inside the main building and the chill in the air would be gone. I rounded the corner and saw the staircase that would take me directly to the underground parking that housed my large collection of cars.

It was one of many, only with a distinct difference. As it was common knowledge that I collected Ferraris and had done since the first one built holding the badge back in 1947. It was called the 125 S in a maroon red colour, as it was pre the famous Ferrari red and powered by a 1.5l V12 engine. An extremely rare car seeing as there were thought to be only two produced. I remembered seeing its debut on May 11th 1947.

A date I remember due to the new passion it fueled being that it was at the Piacenza racing circuit that I first saw it being raced. After this, I quickly had one commissioned to be built and helped fund the company's rocky start. Their unfortunate bad luck included everything from factories being bombed and their first car seeing little competition, both of which were thanks to the war.

Of course, there were other cars in my collection, for I also had a taste for classic English built cars, like Aston Martin, Rolls Royce, Bentley, Jaguars and if I needed to go off-road, Land Rovers. However, in 1963 Ferrari's rival was introduced as Lamborghinis were born, meaning this was a natural brand of car to be chosen by my own rival...*Lucius.*

Something no doubt done just to piss me off as it was widely known for this to be the Vampire King's car of choice. Just as another twist of the blade we both believed had been delivered by each of us back in the 1940s. This had been when things turned sour between my once right-hand man and myself. But that bitter time was not to be thought of now, even if he had tainted my collection somewhat by letting it be known of his own obsession with the rival car brand. However, I had received my revenge of sorts when bidding for a car I knew he was interested in, having one of his lackeys there at the time bidding on it.

It was named the Sesto Elemento and was a concept car to explore just how far Lamborghini could push its carbon fibre structure. Hence the name Sesto Elemento, which meant the 'sixth element' in Italian... the sixth element being of course Carbon. And Lucius had wanted it...*badly.* Which was why it was the one and only Lamborghini in my collection.

I looked down the moment I started to take the staircase as the jolting of her frame must have made her grab onto me, as I felt my T-shirt tighten against my shoulders and chest, from where she now had part of it bunched in her fisted hand. I don't know why but the small gesture felt as though she were offering herself that step closer to me. Like it was a small whisper of time, I knew I would always remember, for it was to me as significant as the first time I ever saw the rising sun.

It felt as if...

As if I was her anchor.

The moment we reached the bottom I opened the door, wondering if she even asked herself how I did so without my hands leaving her body? Well if she did, then she didn't say anything but just continued to hold on to me for the rest of the duration. But then she jumped at the sound of the banging of the door behind us, and I gladly gave in to the impulse to squeeze her tighter, telling her she was safe with me.

"Not much further now," I informed her, knowing that she must have been wondering this. Which unsurprisingly was what finally led her to peek out just as I went through the last door entering the large open space. One filled with a lot of expensive cars...my pride and joy.

Well, that was until there was her.

Now the whole thing could burn for all I cared, as long as keeping her with me throughout eternity was the reason for those flames. The second I felt her straining to see, I relaxed my hold on her so that she could see for herself where we were and in doing so, sharing a little piece of me with her. But then as I watched her taking in the room, of course, it wasn't surprising which one she focused on.

The little Bastard!

Ha, if only she knew what that car really was, then she would understand its reason for being fully encased within that glass surround. One that was sealed with casting symbols Rue had created. Locked away so as it could never harm another living soul again as trying to destroy it had failed many times before its final resting place.

Unfortunately, this car became the embodiment of what happened when you willingly sold your soul to the Devil for fame and fortune. For a time frame on such a bargain is never written in the contract so to speak, and at aged only twenty-four, James Dean died just at the beginning of his promising career. However, through his early death, his wish was granted for he wanted to be one of the most famous people on Earth, for not only his acting but also his racing.

But that was the thing when selling your soul to the Devil, for he will grant you your wish. But in doing so for Dean, that meant he was to die young, barely tipping the top of his game after winning a few awards for his acting. And then, well, dying by driving his own car before even getting to the intended race days later. A story that would be immortalised long after his death. Hence becoming one of the most famous names known for both his acting and then shortly after, racing to his death.

But the moment he died, it became apparent that this was one soul who didn't want to leave this Earth when he should. Which meant that this car was only ever meant for one owner and every single piece of it after that 'Devils' crash' caused injury or death to the individuals who came into close contact with it.

Because, the story didn't end with James Dean, it only really began. For it soon came to my attention that the 'Little Bastard', which was aptly named for the Porsche 550 Spyder, then went on to claim the lives of at least three more mortals and injured more than a dozen just through its sold parts alone.

I had ordered it to be rid of once the problem reached me. However, it had other ideas, for whilst being stored in the garage that my men burnt down, a fire that was supposed to claim the last pieces of its cursed chassis, had only ended up surviving the blaze untouched.

In the end, I realised the power of James Dean's immortality infused within the car upon his death and was too powerful to destroy. Hence why it suddenly went missing without a trace when being transported back to its owner in Los Angles back in 1960.

The moment it came into my possession it became clear that throughout the years the car was repairing itself now being surrounded by supernatural means. So, what had once started out as a wreck in a glass cage now became what Keira was looking at today. Looking as pristine as the day James Dean first took a ride with death and lost more than his life but his mortal soul as well.

Needless to say, I turned with Keira still in my arms, no longer wanting her to look upon it, for she should never be tainted by such evil. So, I walked up to my driver and after a brief look around the room, saw that the Aston Martin One-77 was the closest to one of the retractable doors. These had been made to look like the stone walls surrounding the rest of the underground garage.

My driver gave me two options he thought I might like and I chose neither, for I didn't want to wait as Keira looked to be in more pain than before. Which wouldn't have been surprising considering she might have thrown up her last pills before having time to fully take effect, the reason why I had found her trying to take a few more. Something, in the end, I had foolishly prevented her from doing.

"Very good Sir," my driver said, nodding respectfully before opening the door for me on the sleek, two-seater that was another one of my favourites. They had only made seventy-seven of them, hence the name and at the time it had been over a million well invested, for she was a fast little beast, just how I liked my cars. She could reach 220 miles per hour and hit 0-60 mph in 3.5 seconds and doing those speeds simply felt as if I was flying on land!

And now I was finally getting one of my wishes granted, for if I couldn't yet fly with her in my arms, without her being unconscious like she had been on the first day I met her, then this was the next best thing. Now if only I could have gotten away with locking the doors and driving to the ends of the Earth with her, I thought wryly.

But instead of entering into any more thoughts of fantasy I leaned in close and told her,

"It looks as though I get to drive you home sooner than you thought."

DRAVEN

41

BOY BE GUILTY, GIRL BE FOOLISH

"*It looks as though I get to drive you home sooner than you thought,*" I said with a grin, for I knew she would remember what I had warned her of last night. A promise to drive her home should a problem arise in getting a ride from anyone other than Frank or her sister. An order I know she was surprised on hearing at the time and one she seemed even more shocked at now, seeing it come to fruition so soon.

"Oh...umm...it's okay, you don't have to...I know you're busy and...with stuff...I have my phone in my pocket, Libby can be called...she has a phone..." she said, mumbling some of it and rushing the rest as if needing to say it and all the while doing so with a rising blush to her cheeks.

"No." was the only answer she received to this and it was said stern enough that it gave her nothing to argue against. I knew this the second she bit her lip again as if holding her next words back. I then lowered her down into the passenger seat with care, making sure to get as close to her as I could. I even smirked to myself the second she closed her eyes and took a deep breath as if to try and calm her racing heart. But then I feared it might have been done from pain, so asked her,

"Are you alright?" When her only response was to nod, I knew then it was from being so close to me, no doubt aiding in making her head spin. It wasn't arrogance that made me deduce this. For yes, even though I would admit to owning what some would class as the failing personality trait, it was said because she had the same effect on me. But yet throughout all of this strange ordeal, she had done as I had asked, passing my tests in trusting me and now she was sat in my car waiting for me to take her home with only a slight moment of protest. Which was why I whispered down at her,

"Good girl" before closing the car door. I then waited for my usual driver to hand me her bag and jacket, things she had obviously forgotten about. I slipped them into the trunk, before taking off my jacket and handing it to my driver to take away with him. Then I opened the driver's side door and found her looking around the inside of the luxury car with wide eyes. I suddenly found myself wondering if she liked this car and pondered if so, then how possible it would be to locate another for sale. But then Sophia's past argument soon put a stop to these thoughts.

She watched me as I folded myself inside before then looking around the car, obviously curious as to how we were going to manoeuvre ourselves out of the space, seeing as what lay ahead of us didn't look like a door. And I, in turn, was curious to see what her reactions would be, so decided to say little on the matter.

"Put your seat belt on," I said, instead giving her this instruction and in turn meant the moment she complied she was soon biting her lip once more. A habit that was becoming increasingly distracting. But then Fredrick, my driver must have turned the lights out as he left, for it plunged the large space into darkness, one that must have been unsettling for her. Well if the sharp intake of breath was anything to go by.

"Don't be afraid. *Trust me.*" I said once more trying to gain that trust and one I was about to test yet again. Only she lifted a hand to her head as the pain was obviously increasing and I tried to inject a wave of influence into her mind to try and ease it. However, giving that she had a defensive mind, one made even more so thanks to the new intense circumstances, it made this nearly impossible, which was why I suggested,

"Try to relax, and the pain will ease." She looked to me then, and no doubt asked herself how I could see her and her actions too well in the dark. For it became clear that she didn't like showing people what she considered a weakness. Another endearing quality of hers and one, she would soon learn, she couldn't get away with when belonging to me.

I turned on the headlights, and revved the engine, listening to its roar before the purr, and driving forward the moment the appearance of the stone wall was gone, dropping down into the gap in the floor below it as it was designed to do.

There was actually five separate doors, all with the same systems along the side of the building, and each had been engineered with the sole purpose...to keep people out. Hence why they were made to look like part of the building, for it could be said I was a little paranoid about leaving my precious car collection alone for months on end. But then again, I also housed billions in bank vaults all around the world, so it was only the same.

Or at least this is what I told myself when having the near million dollar security system installed. Vincent had simply laughed at me, something he stopped pretty quickly when he realised I had also included his extensive bike collection among the vehicles protected. Oh yes, then he had changed his tune pretty quickly. Sophia, however, had just shrugged her shoulders and said,

"What, like I would give a shit if anything was stolen, as I know you would just buy me a new one." Then she had walked away from her brothers with a smirk. Also leaving her husband shaking his head as if he didn't know whether to laugh or to fling her over his shoulder and run off into the night with her. I knew which I would have preferred for only one would have granted us peace for a few days at least.

But, in regards to my triple layered bomb proof doors, Keira now looked slightly terrified. Which was when I realised that she had closed her eyes and braced for impact. Doing so because she believed me to be mad enough to drive us both into a wall.

"You can open your eyes now," I told her slightly annoyed that she could think such a thing but trying not to let it show in my tone. She was after all, unwell at this current moment, so there was no need to cause her any more discomfort. But then she surprised me by admitting it and asking,

"Where did the wall go?" I couldn't help my response, but I laughed, all shreds of my annoyance long gone in sight of her innocence.

"That wall was the door, and it opened just like any other, which you would have seen if you hadn't had your eyes closed," I informed her with my amusement still lingering, and it was enough, I soon realised, to cause her to blush. But it wasn't enough for me to get the hint for I couldn't help but then go on to ask,

"Let me ask you, do you really believe I would have driven us both through a stone wall?" Her response to this however was the very last one I would have guessed coming from her.

She was pissed off, that much was clear. However, it only ended up adding to how I found most of her attributes...*it was adorable.* Like an angry kitten swiping out pointlessly at a tiger.

"Well, how was I supposed to know you had your very own bat cave? And considering it didn't look like a bloody door and I've had a knock to the head, maybe you could cut me some slack?" the moment she had finished I found myself utterly stunned. Not something that happened often to an Elder Kind like myself, a reference used to beings older than a few thousands years.

But yet here I was, sat next to my Chosen One, a girl who up until now has been nothing but shy and submissive towards me, and she has just chastised and reprimanded me like a child for basically teasing her. And what did I want to do now because of it? I wanted to pull this fucking car over, haul her out of it, bend her back over its frame and kiss her senseless for being the first person other than my own family for not taking any shit from me!

I wanted to growl her name, adding 'my little vixen' at the end before getting rid of that painful pounding in her head the natural way. By igniting the body's natural pain relief with a good old fashioned mind altering orgasm! I wanted to flood her body with endorphins and praise her for being my good girl and taking all of me into her hot little body. By the Gods, how I wanted this woman!

But my extreme lust was also being overbalanced the second I saw her reflection in her side window, now looking worried and as if chastising herself for speaking so honestly. But she didn't understand the gift she just gave me, for that was what I wanted from her. I didn't want just another loyal subject to serve me and do as I commanded. I wanted an equal to stand by my side, and up until this moment, I had never realised just how important this was to me.

So, with that small slice of guilt now eating at me and trying once more to process this fairly new emotion, I decided to pick out one of the points of her comment,

"Bat cave?" I questioned, allowing a grin to play at the corners of my mouth. She groaned in embarrassment, but it was enough to cut through the tension mounting in the car, one I had started. So, I told her in a sincere tone,

"You're right. I'm sorry, you weren't to know. I hope I didn't scare you too much."

"It's okay, I guess my mind just plays tricks on me sometimes," she confessed, and I thought about that. Was she saying that she was more open to the possibilities of accepting the unknown? Usually, people simply feared what they didn't know. But there were those among mortals who were quite open to believing in the Supernatural and instead of running from it, they did everything in their power to prove it was real.

Could it be possible Keira already believed in my kind? I wished in that moment there had been an unsuspecting way for me to word such a question.

"What?" she said as if knowing there was something I wasn't saying, making me realise she was extremely intuitive.

"You don't think like other people, do you?" I finally said, realising the second I saw her reaction that I had worded it wrong. Especially when she folded her arms and refused to look at me. And for what I knew could have no doubt been for the remainder of the drive, had I not acted upon resolving my mistake quickly.

"Trust me, Keira, that's not a bad thing," I told her wanting nothing more in that moment to reach out and touch her. To prove my words with actions of comfort, something I rarely ever felt compelled to do until meeting her.

In fact, I would have said more but that Gods' awful disco music started blaring from her pocket, making me suppress a shudder in memory from that horrifying era that was the 70's. But right now, I couldn't resist the playful tease as she froze in shame.

"I'm pretty sure that's yours," I said to which her blushing face brought me no end of enjoyment, making me smirk when she offered,

"It's my sister's phone." But laughing at her in harmful jest ended up granting me a swift kick from Karma if such a thing could be believed. For when I found out who it was on the phone, I felt as though I had been hit by it! Meaning that I had to try very hard not to give in to my demon's natural urge to growl, while also not envisioning the neck of a certain mortal and twisting the steering wheel into a figure of eight!

"Hey RJ, look I'm sorry..."

"Hey Kaz, it's me." I heard his interrupted reply making Keira now look my way as if trying to gauge my reaction to this, making me curious. Did she know of my jealous nature, one admittedly only brought on by her?

"Oh... hey Jack, I thought it was..."

"It's okay, just my phone died on me, so I used RJ's to see if you were still joining us?" I heard him say on the other end making me wish that wasn't the only thing that died on him tonight, for an elephant or a blue whale would have been more preferable. Both could crush bones well enough, but at this point, I would even be satisfied with a box jellyfish!

"Oh no, I had to go home, I wasn't feeling too good," she replied, and I waited for the point when he would no doubt ask who it was that was driving her home. I didn't have to wait long.

"Oh shit, so do you still need a lift because I would be happy to drive you?" Ha, too late asshole, I thought now having no choice but to hide my smug grin, one that yet again Karma soon stole from me.

"Yeah, I'm sorry I was going to call... no, it's okay, I'm nearly home."

"Oh alright...well, I hope you're okay? Is it serious?" he asked making me wish I could have just grabbed the phone from her hand and thrown it out of the fucking window after telling him, 'She's fine with me, now fuck off!'

Unfortunately, Keira kindly replied for me.

"No, I'm fine, I just hit my head."

"Where, at work?!" He shouted in annoyance, making me want to point out that shouting at someone who just admitted to hitting their head wasn't the smartest of moves!

"No, no, in the woods not at work. Look, I will talk to you later, okay? Honestly, I'm fine; it's just a scratch." I couldn't help but snap my gaze to hers, silently calling her on her lie, one that admittedly I didn't mind so much, seeing as it was directed at the cretin, not myself.

"Alright, well if you're sure." Yes, she is fucking sure dickhead, now get off the fucking phone before I start making imprints of my fingerprints on the steering wheel!

"Okay yeah, well I'll talk to you tomorrow then..." She added, and even I could tell she was trying to get off the phone quickly, only prince fucking charming wasn't getting the fucking hint!

"Sorry what? Who am I driving home with...uh..." Now, this was when I found myself holding out for my own name to be said, wishing to have seen his expression myself as punishment. However, it never came, but instead, the lie did and thus completing my lesson of karma for the day, I thought with a grit of my teeth.

"Frank, yeah... okay then... see ya." She finally hung up the phone, and in turn, I finally released my punishing hold on my car, seeing for myself it hadn't made it unscathed as there were slight indents in the leather on the wheel. Something I would fix once she wasn't around.

I had just been about to ask her why she had lied when I noticed she had let out a sigh and now rested with her head back against the seat. She looked exhausted.

"Sorry about that, I forgot that I was getting a lift home with some friends," she divulged as if feeling as though I deserved an explanation. But in that moment, I cared little for her friends but more as to why she had lied to them about me.

"Frank?" I only needed to say his name for her to understand what it was I asked of her.

"I didn't...uh...didn't think you would want anyone knowing...you know." My gaze once again shot to her, for I was astounded.

"You think I would have an issue with anyone knowing I was driving you home?" I questioned, letting my tone speak of my surprise and trying to control my anger at the thought. Because honestly, if this were true, then what did she think of me? Did she believe there would never be a chance for us? Did she believe me so far from her reach, when it, in fact, it felt as though she was even further from mine!

"I...well, what I mean is, you and your family...you know that I don't say things, I can be discreet, and I know you like your privacy and rightly so, I just figured..." Upon hearing her reply, I was thankfully able to relax a little, putting it down to reasons of gossip and her loyalty towards me and my family. I even granted her a small smile in return before telling her in a gentle tone,

"Keira, it's fine and I know you don't talk about me or my family."

Thankfully after this, I was pulling the car onto her gravel drive, as to be honest, I didn't think it would survive me and my turbulent reactions much longer!

So, I cut the engine and looked to find my next shock of the day.

Keira obviously didn't want to get out of the car.

Which meant only one thing...

She didn't want to leave me.

Keira

42

DRAVEN AND DOCTORS

Draven got out of the car and walked around to my door. He did all this before I had time to react, so I grabbed for the handle but couldn't find one. He opened my door and looked as though he was about to carry me out.

"I'm fine to walk now, thanks." He backed away slightly but leant with one hand on the car over my head.

"Alright, prove it." He said being cocky, as if he knew I would fall. Of course, he was right. As soon as I tried to stand I nearly fell back into the seat. He grabbed my hand and pulled me up, then in one swift movement had me safely back in his arms once again.

"I told you I was fine." I muttered in a pathetic attempt to save face. I felt his lips get close to my ear and he muttered right back,

"And I told you to prove it." Okay, so he had me there.

"I'm really okay though, just a bit wobbly, but I'm good now." His hold tightened in a way of answering me without speaking and if I was being honest, I had no real desire to leave his arms. It was now I realised for the first time he didn't have his jacket on anymore. He must have taken it off before getting in the car, but I was too shocked to notice much back then. We both should have been freezing in the cool night air, as I too was without a jacket but being snuggled up close next to him there was no way that would happen. He seemed to radiate heat and I sucked it in like it was warming my soul.

I could feel the definition of forearm muscles and large sexy hands that held my body in an iron hold. My heart did another one of its trademark flutters as I wished for this gesture to be for another reason, one of a more erotic nature. He walked up the steps and the door was opened by my poor sister who was already in her pyjamas with bunnies and carrots patterned over them.

Ah, it looked as if it could have been worse after all. I could be in his arms right now wearing them. The look on her face was one that I would never forget. Her jaw actually dropped open. I doubted that she had ever seen Draven before, so the sight of me in the arms of the most astonishingly handsome stranger was enough to make any woman's jaw drop. Hell, mine did and that was just in my dreams.

Draven smiled at her and I decided to speak, as Libby hadn't yet.

"I'm fine, it's just my head was...well you were right." She shook her head slightly and moved out of the way letting Draven come in with me still in his arms. Then he spoke and I thought Libby was going to pass out.

"She fainted at work and has been a bit unstable on her feet, so I brought her home... to get some rest." He said this last part as a hint to get some sort of clue as to where he might put me down but she still didn't say a word. However, we did get a semi-response as she pointed to the stairs.

"It's okay, just put me on the couch." I was already embarrassed enough as it was, but picturing him in my bedroom made me blush, along with wanting to attack him and tie him to my bed where he could never escape. The thought of him lying on my bed was enough to make my mind burst with pleasure and I didn't know if I could hide my secret fantasy about him without moaning and giving myself away. As it was, I was going to have no choice in the matter as he ignored what I had said and went for the stairs, carrying me up them as though I weighed nothing at all. My sister followed behind like some bunny loving robot.

He reached the first landing but kept going as if he knew where my room was. He leant down to my face and said softly,

"Is your sister Libby alright? She hasn't spoken a word."

"Yeah, and it's a first." I said under my breath so only he could hear. He tried to hide a smile. I was in shock... did he just find me funny?

When we got inside my room, he looked around for a moment before finding what he was looking for... *my bed.* I knew this was the end, so I inhaled deeply taking in his scent for the last time, wishing more than anything in the world that I could keep this intoxicating smell with me forever. This was the moment I was both dreading and dreaming about. There was just something about a man who carried you to bed, that made my blood boil. But this man, well there was no other who I could imagine ever topping this, even if I wasn't going to remain in his arms for much longer.

He placed me down tenderly and said,

"Here you go." And that was enough to make me close my eyes and bite my lip, yet again. But he hadn't moved. Did he want to say something more?

"You'd better watch that lip of yours or before long you won't have anything left of it..." He leant down closer and I received the next shock of the night, when he continued,

"...and that would be a shame indeed." One side of his mouth curved up into a mischievous grin and my heart was in need of fanning itself. Was he...? Did he...? *Flirt with me?*

"Would it?" I asked under my breath, so he wouldn't hear.

"Definitely," he said over his shoulder as he had turned to face Libby, who had now joined us. How had he heard me? I was pretty sure I had only mouthed the words more than actually saying them. And had he really meant that?!

Poor Libby must have regained some life back when walking up the stairs, as she was now smiling at him.

"Thank you so much for bringing her home, but my God Kazzy what are you trying to do, scare me to death?" Oh great, she was back. And she just had to call me Kazzy, like I was five all over again. Draven smiled at this and went to stand next to her.

"It was no trouble, but I would get her to a doctor tomorrow as she might need an X-ray." He said as though they were a parent and teacher talking about me as if I was a bloody child.

"No! I mean... no, that won't be necessary, like I said I will be fine, no doctors...I wo..." I nearly shouted this, but the pain cut me off and my eyes watered. Draven frowned and Libby noticed.

"She doesn't like doctors, ever since... well..."

"LIBBY!" I shouted, warning her not to add anything else to that sentence or my life would have ended there and then. Now Draven's full attention was on my face. I could almost see the cogs turning in his head. He looked as though he was burning to know why I had just reacted this way. Luckily, the conversation was interrupted by Frank running up the stairs shouting about the Aston Martin parked in the drive.

"Libs, have you seen that car? Man, whose is..." He was cut short once he entered my bedroom and saw the answer to his question standing there with his wife.

"Oh shi... I mean Mr Draven, Sir." At this Libby froze in horror, as she'd finally twigged who he was. But Draven turned to Frank and held his hand out to him and calmly said,

"Please, call me Dominic." Frank shook his hand as though he was meeting a celebrity. Libby also shook his hand but once more she couldn't speak. I couldn't help thinking that this was a blessing.

Frank looked over to me in the bed and said,

"Hey kiddo, what's up with you? You alright?" Great, now it was Kiddo, what was next, a bottle before bedtime and nursery rhymes?

"It's no big deal, I fell and now everyone's fussing." I couldn't look at Draven anymore. It was hard enough believing any of this was still happening. Nope, there was definitely no more worries about this being a dream! Frank stepped closer to see for himself what all the fuss was about and then made a face like he tasted something sour in his mouth.

"Damn kid, that don't look good, where did you fall? In the ring with Bruce Lee?" Great, the one person I thought I could count on and now he had turned to the dark side. And just when I thought it couldn't get any worse, Libby found her voice again.

"No, she did it in the woods and then she went to work with concussion, collapsed and Mr Draven here was good enough to bring her back...*himself.*" She added the last part as though it was some secret code she was trying to get across that Draven *did* in fact drive me back here and why the Hell would he do that!?

"Well, I will leave you all and Keira, I don't expect to see you working back in the VIP until you get the all clear from a doctor ...understood?" Draven said with his authoritative tone firmly back into place. Great, well this night really couldn't get any worse if it tried. Oh no, I was mistaken, because what came next was far worse than anything that had happened this night, because Draven's next words would haunt me for the rest of my life.

"Oh, and if I were you I would give her a bucket just in case, she was a bit sick earlier." Oh dear god! He had known all along that I had vomited in his plant pot! Life just couldn't get any worse.

"Oh my, okay I will do that...and thank you very much for taking care of her but wait... did you say the VIP?" Libby unfortunately hadn't missed that bit and now I was going to pay for it.

"Yes, this was Keira's second night working the VIP area. Did she not mention it?" Draven's eyes looked questioningly at me but I looked away from his gaze.

"No, it must have slipped her mind." Libby said, keeping her voice steady and smiling.

"Goodnight Keira and get some rest." Draven said this as if he knew I didn't sleep well. I could only nod in return and his gaze flickered down to my bitten lip, before he turned to my sister. He said his goodbye and left my room with Frank walking him out. I could hear Frank saying,

"Umm, could I just ask what model is the Aston...?" Then his voice trailed off downstairs.

I wanted to die of shame! It was so bad that tears started to well up in my eyes and thankfully, Libby put it down to the pain. She came over and sat on my bed to feel my temperature.

"Oh Kaz, it will be alright, I'll get you some pain killers." And then I remembered, Draven had taken mine away and he still had them. But then I noticed Libby opening up a bottle of pills that was on my bedside table. It was the same bottle he had taken, but how? He must have put them there when he put me down and I had just missed it.

Libby went into the bathroom and came back with a glass of water in one hand and an empty bin in the other. I raised my eyebrows and she said,

"Just in case."

She handed me the water and I finished it in one, along with the two pills. Strange, they looked different somehow, but I looked at the bottle and it was the same one as before. So I shrugged it off putting it down to my spinning head and immense headache. After all, this was one of the weirdest nights of my life, so why should it start suddenly making sense?

"Try and get some rest but wake me if you need anything or if you start feeling worse." She kissed me gently on the forehead and I told her I would be fine as she left the room, leaving me with the confusing images of tonight's events.

No, I would never sleep, that much I was sure about. I lay there and wondered how on Earth I was ever going to face Draven again. What must he be thinking of me? The most ironic part was that if I had just left when Karmun asked me to, then I could have avoided all of this humiliation. Then my mind drifted to the nicer parts of tonight. The part where I was in his arms for so long and the way he held me close, as though needing to protect me in some way. Wasn't that worth all the humiliation in the world?

He now knew things about me. Like where I lived, who I lived with and even where I slept. But wait, I was missing something here. When had I told him any of that? I hadn't told him any directions to my house but, yet he knew exactly where it was. I didn't tell him my sister's name yet on the stairs he mentioned it. And most of all, how did he know which room was mine? How would he have known that I slept on the top floor in the attic? This wasn't making any sense. There was something different about him.

He wasn't like everybody else and by everybody else I meant... *human.*

I laughed off my ridiculous thoughts. What was I thinking? Not human? I needed help. Maybe this bang to my head had affected me more than I thought. I'd probably told him these things but didn't remember because I was in pain. Or the best explanation was he'd looked at my records. I mean, I don't remember filling out a form but I did get the job thanks to Frank, so maybe he filled something in for me.

I still had all my clothes on, so I kicked off my shoes and wormed my way out of my trousers. I was about to take off my top when I stopped myself. I lifted it up to my nose and inhaled, allowing my senses to be overwhelmed with the delicious smell of his body. I pulled the top over my head, only leaving my underwear and a vest on, but I held the top in my hands and then positioned it close to my head so that I would fall asleep with nothing but that scent to consume my mind.

I woke up the next day to find that I had slept through the whole night having only one dream and it had been perfect. I only had vague images and flashes of Draven being back in my room. But while he was there I would feel the soothing touch of his hand at my temple brushing the hair from my bruise. I would feel his lips graze softly over the damage and then his kiss would linger as if it wanted to travel to other areas of my skin.

I felt his fisted hand bracing either side of my body, taking his weight on the bed and I would hear gentle words being murmured sweetly into my hair. In my dream, I didn't know what he was saying as it was in another language, but just by the way he spoke told me enough to know the deeper meaning. He felt protective.

After this I was even more surprised that I had managed to fall back asleep, but when I had it was down to Draven's words telling me to do so.

I looked at my bedside table and noticed a mug of cold tea, as it must have been sat there a while. I looked at the clock. Oh wow, it was nearly one in the afternoon. I hadn't slept this much since being in the hospital. It took me all of two minutes to realise that what had happened last night was in fact not a dream. And a mixture of pleasure and pain rang deep in my mind.

There was a little tap at my door and then it opened without waiting for a reply.

"Hey honey, how are you feeling today?" My sister's kind face poked through the doorway and when she realised I was now awake she walked right in.

"I'm still a little sore but I will live to humiliate myself for another day I'm sure." I said in reply and she smiled and looked a little confused.

"What is it?" I said wondering what else could have gone wrong last night.

"Well, I think you will need to get dressed, as the Doctor's here." What! No way, never going to happen... what was she thinking?

"Aww Libs, why did you go and call a doctor? I said I was fine and..." She cut me off, holding her hands up in defence.

"I didn't call a doctor."

"What! Then who did?" She smiled, clearly amused with the answer.

"He said that Mr Draven sent him." Oh no, was she serious? This wasn't some cruel trick instead it was just a cruel reality. What the Hell was Draven doing by ringing a Doctor?

She left the room giving me some privacy to get changed, telling me she would give me ten minutes. But my mind wouldn't concentrate, as it was still fuzzy and lightheaded and not just with the huge lump protruding from my forehead. I got up and wobbled like one of those inflatable clowns you hit for fun. My brain wasn't up to the simple task of walking to the bathroom. Once I finally got there I washed and brushed my teeth, but my throat still burned from last night's vomiting and the thought once more made me shake my head in shame.

Once I'd finished in the bathroom, I grabbed a pair of black sweat pants from my drawer and put on a fresh pair of grey sleeved gloves and a maroon coloured top with a faded football logo of my dad's old university team. I brushed through my hair quickly pulling it into a ponytail and then went to sit back on my bed waiting for a doctor I didn't want.

"May I come in?" A voice at the door asked and begrudgingly I agreed.

The man who walked in was at least in his fifties and had a familiarity about him that I couldn't put my finger on. His kind eyes were very dark blue and deep set. He had a square jaw and a caring smile that lit up his face making him look like a sweet guy. This made me relax slightly but I was still cautious. I hadn't had a lot of good experiences with doctors and as a rule generally stayed away as much as I could help it.

"Keira, I presume. It's nice to meet you my dear, I'm Doctor Spencer." He held out his hand for me to shake and smiled showing an impressive amount of very white teeth.

"Hi, it's nice to meet you too." Okay, so I lied, but what was I going to say, 'I'm dreading it so please get it over with'.

"Mr Draven tells me you took a nasty fall in the woods and was feeling some ill effects of it last night." This wasn't really a question, so when I didn't answer he came over to the bed to look for himself. He carried a black leather bag, one you might expect from a doctor, and placed it next to the bed as he sat opposite me.

"Do you mind?" He nodded to my head and I shrugged my shoulders in return. He then lifted my hair out of my eyes, very much the same way Draven had done, and the memory made me shiver.

"I'm sorry my hands must be cold. If you could tilt your head back for me, I will take a closer look." I did as instructed as he poked around the lump and cut that was in the middle of it. Then he took out a small torch, stethoscope and then the thing I was dreading the most...something to measure my blood pressure.

"That looks nasty. You should really have gone to the hospital and got some stitches." He tutted and shook his head as though I was a disobedient child. So, I said the only thing in my defence, which so happened to be the truth.

"I know, but I kinda have a thing with hospitals." I said as his eyes fell on mine with a weird look of empathy.

"Bad experience I take it?" He replied as he shone the flash light in my eyes to measure my responses.

"Something like that," I said before he wanted me to follow his finger. It was strange, his eyes looked at me in a heated way and I felt something strange around him, the same as I felt around Draven. It made me wonder if they were somehow related. I could imagine Draven looking like this when he got older. He was handsome for an older guy, like Harrison Ford or Robert Redford.

He asked me about my symptoms last night and how I was feeling now.

"I feel a lot better today after a good night's sleep." I said, knowing he would be the one I would have to convince to let me go back to work. He raised an eyebrow and asked,

"Do you usually have trouble sleeping?" Ha, what an understatement!

"Yeah sometimes...well I mean lately." I wished he wouldn't pry. That was the worst thing about doctors, they had a way of picking up on everything. And they were usually right on the money.

"Do you take any medication for it?" Shit! I knew if I went down this route, I could easily predict where it would end.

"No." I don't know why, but he looked at me as if he knew it was a lie because he repeated my answer, which was usually a pretty clear indication when someone doesn't believe what you're saying.

"Yes, well let's take your blood pressure." Great, the bit I was dreading. This was the point they all thought I was a nut job!

"If you could just roll up your sleeves for me." He was getting the strap ready to put on my arm and I paused not knowing what to do. He nodded to my sleeves when I didn't react, so I gave in and did as I was told and rolled them up over my elbow. He looked down at the gloves and frowned.

"Are you cold?"

"I suffer from bad circulation, cold feet as well. Do you mind if I keep them on?" He didn't seem convinced and said,

"It won't be for long." And he was about to roll them back when I whipped my arm from under his hands.

"Look, I'm sorry Doc, but I have this thing with people touching my arms. Let's just put it down to an accident and leave it at that... okay?" He nodded and looked sad, getting my full meaning on the subject. After all he was a doctor and I gathered he had seen this type of behaviour before.

"Alright, let's measure it on your neck, should we?" His jaw tightened when he looked at my arms and then softened when he touched my neck.

"I appreciate it and I assume that all this will remain confidential?" I nodded to my arms and he knew what I meant. I was at least happy to see we were on the same page.

"You mean Mr Draven?" He smiled, and I didn't understand the meaning behind it. I nodded, not wanting to say his name in front of him.

"Mr Draven is only concerned and wants to know when you will be fit to go back to work, anything else will go no further than this room." He said making me relax my tensed arms and sigh in relief.

"Thank you." I said with strained emotion. I don't know why but I trusted this man and I couldn't for the life of me understand why. He handed me some pills to take that would help with the swelling and pain. He also re-covered the cut, taking Libby's make-shift stitches off and re-applying medical ones. He then left the cut uncovered letting the air get to it. I also noticed him studying me and I could see his eyes lingering on my father's old sweater for a moment before my voice pulled back his attention.

"So, this means you will tell Mr Draven I'm fit for work?" I asked in the hope that his answer would be the one I wanted to hear.

"Yes, after three days of rest and depending if you're fine in that time and have had no more dizzy spells, then yes I will." That was not what I wanted to hear.

"Aww come on Doc. Look, I feel fine, great even and I don't want to lose my job or anything." I was hoping guilt would work but with the smug look on his face he wasn't buying it.

"I very much doubt that would happen and if I find out that you haven't taken my orders on board, then I will ring up Mr Draven and tell him you're not fit for a week." Oh great, a Doctor with a PhD in manipulation as well as medical.

"Okay, okay, three days off work." I shook my head at the thought of not seeing Draven till then and the pain once again came back to my head.

"Not just work, college too." I pulled a face as if to say Hell no, but he continued with 'Doctor's orders' and gave me a note to be handed in to the academic office at college.

"I can't. Look you have never met my History teacher! You have to be dying to get away with not turning up for one of his classes." He laughed as though I was joking.

"I will speak to Mr Draven. I know his sister is in the same class, so I'm sure she could have a word with him for you." Oh God, that was the last thing I wanted. I had caused too many problems for Draven as it was.

"No...! I mean, no thanks, that won't be necessary, I think I have caused more than enough aggravation for Mr Draven without involving him in any more of my problems." He looked hurt at this and again I was baffled by it.

"That's not how Mr Draven thinks. I have known him a long time and he has always taken care of his staff."

"Oh, I have no doubt, but he was very kind to me last night and considering it was only my second shift, I think he has done enough for me to last my life time. I wouldn't like to push my luck." I said with the memory of me in his arms hitting me again like a battering ram.

"Never enough." My head whipped round to his, on hearing the words that were barely spoken.

"Sorry, did you say something?" I asked wondering if I had mistaken what he had said.

"I said, fair enough. Well, in that case, I will be off to report back to the man in question." He got up and held his hand out again to shake mine goodbye. I placed my hand in his and the heat coming from his skin shocked me.

"Goodbye Keira, it was a pleasure meeting you and until next time." He said and then let go of my hand, leaving me feeling confused. Why would he say until next time? What a strange thing for a Doctor to say, because let's face it, when was going to see the doctor ever a good thing?

As soon as he was out of sight, I fell back on the bed and covered my face with my hands saying out loud,

"What must he think of me?"

"What must who think of you?" Libby's voice sprang from behind my door as though she had been waiting for the doctor to leave. I was not in the mood to talk to Libby about any of this, so I said,

"Sorry Libs, but my head is still killing me, so I'm just going to take some more pain killers and try and sleep it off... can we talk later?" She nodded and closed the door, leaving me alone to fight with my thoughts.

I grabbed the pills that the doctor had left and pulled the covers over my head as little tears started to fill my eyes.

Tears that screamed...

Heart-breaking trouble.

DRAVEN

43

BROTHERLY ADVICE

I got out of the car and walked around to her side proving that she wasn't getting rid of me so quickly. And besides, a gentleman walked a lady to her door, or in my case, a demonic gentleman carried one. I watched as she looked around for what I was guessing was the handle, when I beat her to it. Then I leaned in ready to pick her up when she bit her lip only to let it go again just as quickly, before informing me,

"I'm fine to walk now, thanks." I doubted that, but I thought it best for her to learn this for herself. So, I raised an unconvinced eyebrow and rested a hand over the door before telling her,

"Alright, prove it." She now didn't look as confident as when she first made the claim, but she tried it anyway, nearly falling back onto the seat when her legs weren't ready for her. But instead of letting this happen, I grabbed her quickly, pulling her up and out of the car fully before taking out her legs with one arm and catching her back with the other. Then I turned and started walking us both towards her front door but nearly chuckling when she muttered a defiant,

"I told you I was fine."

"And I told you to prove it," I replied lifting her slightly and speaking directly into her ear. The shudder she tried to hide made me grin before pulling back.

"I'm really okay though, just a bit wobbly, but I'm good now," she said trying once more, and in response to her weak argument, my only answer was to hold her tighter, letting her know without words that she was going nowhere. So, I continued to her front door, suddenly wishing it was a mile away, just so as I could continue to hold her for a little longer. However, her sister soon opened the door, looking ready for her bed but definitely not ready for the sight of me carrying a close family member into her home.

Keira even comically looked to her and then to me and back to her sister again as if silently asking me why her own sister hadn't yet spoken. Well, I had no answers for her but was just thankful when she decided to intervene.

"I'm fine, it's just my head was...well you were right," she said confirming that I hadn't been the only one who thought working tonight had been a mistake on her part. Her sister soon responded after this but not yet with words, for all she did was move out of my way. I decided to take control of the situation and inform her,

"She fainted at work and has been a bit unstable on her feet, so I brought her home... *to get some rest.*" I said before just walking towards the stairs like I owned the place or had the right to be there. Thankfully, in the end, she got the hint and pointed at them, but Keira obviously had other ideas and quickly interjected,

"It's okay, just put me on the couch." Of course, I ignored this and started up the staircase, needing no direction on which room was hers. If she thought this was strange, then she didn't say. However, I wanted to know her thoughts and seeing as the sister was yet to speak, I thought it best to start there. Besides, it gave me another opportunity to get close to her again, as I whispered down at her,

"Is your sister Libby alright? She hasn't spoken a word." Her witty response made me want to chuckle, even if it had been said under her breath,

"Yeah, and it's a first." I granted her a smile, and in return, I got those beautiful wide, questioning eyes. Was she surprised that I found her funny? It looked to be that way, which made me wonder. Was I always so stern around her that she believed me void of any sense of humour? Well, it was time to show her that not only could I find her funny, but I could also flirt with her, something I decided to do the moment I set her down on her bed, doing so carefully.

"Here you go," I said, leaning in close as I knew that if I lingered long enough that she would...ah yes, there it was, that poor punished lip of hers. This then gave me a chance to tell her,

"You'd better watch that lip of yours, or before long you won't have anything left of it..." I paused so that I could lean closer still, delivering to her what I hoped she would realise was my first sexual tease,

"...and that would be a shame indeed." She sucked in a surprised breath, barely audible this time for I would have missed it had I not been so close. My own reaction to this, however, she didn't miss, for a playful grin tipped up one side of my lips, growing in size the second I saw her reaction...*good,* for I cannot keep being the only one surprised by the other.

"Would it?" she asked herself under her breath, even after I had moved away giving her space, meaning that I shouldn't have been able to hear it. But it was too good an opportunity to miss, so I looked back over my shoulder at her and replied,

"Definitely," Then just as her mouth dropped open in shock, I looked back at the door smirking one second and looking serious the next by the time her sister followed us into the room. Only doing so after obviously stopping to grab a dressing gown and try and hide her obvious love for furry woodland creatures and vegetables that were printed all over her night clothes. Clearly yet another strange fashion I would never understand for an adult. Yet not one as bizarre as 70's 'Bellbottoms', I thought being haunted by that era again for the second time tonight.

Finally, her sister had come to her senses enough to speak by the time she was walking through the door.

"Thank you so much for bringing her home, but my God Kazzy what are you trying to do, scare me to death?!" she said aiming this at Keira, who amusingly looked close to snapping.

"It was no trouble, but I would get her to a doctor tomorrow as she might need an X-ray," I said, making a point of her going to get medical help so that I could be assured there was no underlining problem.

"No! I mean... no, that won't be necessary, like I said I will be fine, no doctors...I wo..." Keira started this by shouting out her panicked thoughts on being forced to go to the hospital, something she obviously was very opposed to doing. And now telling me the reasons must have something to do with what she had concealed beneath those gloves she always wore. I would have pressed further on the matter if her sentence hadn't trailed off thanks to a fresh new wave of pain.

"She doesn't like doctors, ever since... well..."

"LIBBY!" Keira shouted out her sister's name in warning, preventing her from explaining further. I had been tempted to discover what it had been, while it had been in her sister's mind and so easy for me to find. But then I heard her husband arriving through the front door and knew where he was headed after showing his appreciation for my car.

"Libs, have you seen that car? Man, whose is..." Frank stopped dead the second he saw me, having already briefly met me once before. I wished I had known at the time what he would mean to my Chosen One, for I would have spent more than a minute with the man. I also would have said more to the man than a basic acknowledgement when being introduced to me once by Jerry.

"Oh, shi... I mean Mr Draven, Sir." Yes, definitely should have spent more time being cordial to the man, I thought inwardly wincing.

"Please, call me Dominic," I said now shaking his hand and giving him the time I should have back then. Frank had a friendly face and an easy smile, but his grip was fooling no one, for he was not a man to get on the wrong side of if you were but a mortal. I liked this about him and instantly started to respect him more than I would have when first meeting him.

He soon turned his attention to Keira and as natural as any biological big brother would, he showed his concern.

"Hey kiddo, what's up with you? You alright?"

"It's no big deal, I fell and now everyone's fussing," she replied, and at this, I fought a grin again, as it was becoming clear she really wasn't one for enjoying the 'limelight' as it was known. Frank took a closer look and hissed through his teeth before saying,

"Damn kid, that don't look good, where did you fall? In the ring with Bruce Lee?" I also had to agree with him, as in the time since the balcony the bruise had deepened in colour.

"No, she did it in the woods and then she went to work with a concussion, collapsed and Mr Draven here was good enough to bring her back...*himself.*" Her sister informed him, giving him a look that was about as subtle as Ragnar shopping for ladies underwear.

"Well, I will leave you all and Keira, I don't expect to see you working back in the VIP until you get the all clear from a doctor ...understood?" I said making my intentions known and giving her fair warning for what she would find at her door tomorrow morning. Then after a brief shy look from Keira, I turned, ready to leave but paused next to Libby, to inform her,

"Oh, and if I were you, I would give her a bucket just in case, she was a bit sick earlier." I knew this would embarrass her, but I wanted her sister to know to keep a closer eye on her throughout the night. I glanced back just in time to see her roll her eyes up at the ceiling as if silently asking the Gods why her.

Again, she made me want to smile.

I also realised that I wasn't the only one watching as Frank had seen my reaction and was clearly making his own assumptions in his mind. Ones I had no doubt wouldn't be long in coming when being voiced to myself in private by the man.

"Oh my, okay I will do that...and thank you very much for taking care of her but wait... did you say the VIP?" The sound of his wife speaking to me now made me redirect my attention, for was it possible that Keira had been keeping secrets from her sister too?

"Yes, this was Keira's second night working the VIP area. Did she not mention it?" I asked granting Keira a questioning look, one she looked away from, no doubt with a mixture of guilt and shame. Now, why hadn't she said anything I wondered?

"No, it must have slipped her mind," her sister said trying to keep the strain from that sentence when really it was accusing in its own right, making me realise my little beauty had some answering to do once I left. Something I decided was time for me to do, for I had outstayed my welcome.

"Goodnight Keira and get some rest," I told her trying to convey how I wished her sweet dreams and no more nightmares. But then before I could help it, I also homed in on her bitten lip, reminding her of my little tease earlier. No surprises, Frank walked me out of the room.

"Umm, could I just ask what model is the Aston...?" he said, and I knew this was said as a ruse so that was what the two sisters thought the conversation was about. But I knew better, for Keira's Brother-in-law, clearly had something on his mind. I answered him of course as he walked me to the door and followed me out.

"Look, Mr Draven..."

"Dominic, please," I said nodding for him to do so and something I rarely permitted those I didn't know well to do. But Frank had already earned my respect just for being someone who cared for my Chosen One's wellbeing and therefore he deserved my time in listening to what he had to say.

"You ever shorten that?" he asked curiously, making me grin before saying,

"Sure, Dom is fine."

"Alright then Dom, first I wanna say that I know what you do for this town and I respect that. I do, despite all the bullshit rumours you hear going around, I know whatever it is you do in that club of yours, it's your business. But that being said, I ain't stupid, I have my men working in there who say that your shit is run as smooth as fucking silk." I retained my calm when hearing this and tried not to smirk, for if only he knew what actually went on in my club. But Frank continued, and for the moment, I let him.

"No drugs, no underage drinking, no putting up with shit, they fight, they sell, or they cause trouble, and their ass is outta there with a firm warning not just to the club but in regards to the whole town," Frank said, telling me nothing that I didn't already know. But no matter however much I appreciated the sentiment, I still wanted him to get to his point, for it's like they say, I had shit to do!

"I also know that because of you guys, the crime rate is near none fucking existent, and you pay to keep it that way. Or so my buddies at the station tell me, as they are well paid, well informed and the station is well funded, which isn't down to charity fairs and little old Mrs Fundy's bake sales like she would have you believe." I laughed at this, knowing of the old crone and her disapproving campaigns to have us shut down. Apparently, we offended God! Something Sophia found a great deal of amusement in whenever we happened to drive past one of her homemade posters stapled to a lamp post.

"So, you see, I may not listen to the bullshit people spread, including that of Mrs Fundy and her church groupies, but that don't mean I don't listen. Best piece of advice I ever got was from my Pop when he told me an easy smile and calm nature was the best disguise anyone could ever wear for having people underestimate you. Something that was never a bad thing, for it could be used as your greatest weapon in life, especially if you were willing to shut up and listen."

"I get that." I agreed with a nod.

"Yeah, I bet a guy like you does," he commented without malice. But still, I folded my arms across my chest and leaned back against my car door, before saying,

"What's your point, Frank?"

"My point is that I took that advice and spent the rest of my life listening. So much so that it helped me find the woman of my dreams amongst an ocean of screams." Now, this had me intrigued for it seemed Frank was not only in the asking mood but in the storytelling one as well. Meaning that I may be in for a chance to get some information about Keira, something I was severely lacking in at this current moment.

"...I heard hers calling out the loudest for help. Changed my life that day of that fucking concert. I saw her flaming red hair like a beacon in the crowd and knew a girl needed my help, and there I found my woman. But the story didn't end there," he said looking back up at the house as if expecting to see her in the window staring down at him. But then I realised he didn't just mean to see her, which is when I answered for him,

"You mean her family." He looked back around at me and smiled as if we were both on the same level of understanding.

"The first day I met her, Christ but you should have seen her! Brass balls I swear." He chuckled to himself which was when I realised he wasn't talking about his woman anymore, he was talking about mine. Suddenly I found myself hanging on his every mortal word.

"I mean, I'm a big guy and yet she just opened the door to me, welcomed me in and looked me up and down with this big grin on her face. Then she told me,

'Yeah, I totally see it, now let me give you some tips big bro... chocolates, total way to her heart but no caramels, hates those... favourite flower is the lily... loves men being a gentleman, so opening the doors, letting her go first, that type of thing... hates men with their top buttons done up on their shirts, so undo that now... favourite part on a guy is his forearms so I would roll up those sleeves too... calling her beautiful as a nickname has always been a secret dream of hers... definitely got the green light to make the first move at the end of the night... Oh and last of all, no swearing, that's a huge turn off and will prevent that green light. Now follow all these things and your good to go and will find yourself hitched in no time!'...then she pushed me towards the bottom of the stairs where Libs was walking down em and whispered, *'Now go get her handsome!'...*"I couldn't help but grin when hearing this brazen account of her, wondering now, where did it go? I had seen a hint of it in the car when driving her here after she believed I was mad enough to drive us both into a wall. But that had been the only time.

"...And after that moment, I knew two things, one was that she was right, I was going to marry that beautiful girl walking down those steps and the second, was that I would love Keira like the sister I never had." Frank said finishing his touching story and one that also ended up giving me greater insight to Keira's warm and loving personality. I would have even thanked him for it, but I knew he wasn't finished.

"Now those two girls in there mean the world to me..." I held up a hand and said,

"I know where this is going, Frank." But he surprised me as he shook his head and said,

"No, you don't, as you couldn't possibly know. No one does. You see that girl in there isn't the same Keira I met that day and as much as it fucking pains me to say it, I don't know whether she will ever make it back. But that's not my story to tell, it's hers and one, no offence to you Dom, but I am not sure would ever happen, for she doesn't even talk to Libs about that shit." Now at this, I was frowning, and he couldn't have known in that moment what it was he was giving me. So, I took the opportunity to press deeper.

"What shit Frank?" He could see how serious I was and just how much I cared, which was no doubt what he was trying to gauge in the first place. But then he told me, and it made my blood turn to ice before being near engulfed in the flames of anger,

"Christ, Dom, shit you wouldn't believe! The type of shit no one, not even your worst enemy you would wish on. But it happened, and it happened to one of the nicest people this world has in it. It happened to someone I consider a sister and that knowledge eats me up inside as I know it does Libs. Now, why am I telling you this…?" I released a sigh that should have been a roar of rage.

"I won't hurt her Frank," I told him, knowing this was what he wanted to hear.

"Oh, I know that, for I vowed long ago that anyone who ever tried again would find the bottom of that ravine over there as their final resting place. But then, even I know there is more than one way to hurt somebody Dom, and I suspect that you know that as well," he said, making his final point. Which was when I needed to admit to someone other than the tight-knit of my own family just what my intentions were.

"I…well I…" For once in my life I struggled to put something into words making him chuckle once before helping me out,

"I know you like her Dom, any fool could see that." I raised a brow at him making him laugh again,

"A guy like you doesn't have one of his waitresses chauffeur driven around this damn town, and he certainly doesn't stand outside watching her back when two low life scum bags from out of town come hassling…yeah, I saw your guy dealing with them that night," he said surprising me. But then if he knew how I felt about her, then why this conversation now?

"I can see you're asking yourself why, and this is the thing, I may know you like her and for someone who never shows any interest in any of the girls in this town, then I know it means something when it happens…" Well, at least I had that going for me I thought dryly before he continued,

"However, what I say now needs to be said for my own piece of mind. After all, you don't know me, and I know even less about you I can imagine. But I know Kaz, and that gives me the right to say this, something I am guessing you're not gonna like much, but here it is…" No, he was right in that, I wasn't going to like this.

"She is not a fun time girl. She is not an itch to be scratched, and she is not a conquest to be won. She also isn't just for the duration of your brief stay here as a way to pass the time. She is a lifer…a keeper and the type you settle down with, marry the first second you can and thank your lucky fucking days you get to be with a woman like that. I know, as I was the lucky bastard that got her sister who is the same."

"I know she is none of those things Frank!" I snapped trying not to growl at the implications and getting more frustrated by the second.

"Good, then that means you're not an asshole and also means you're either staying in town for good or leaving her alone, because breaking her heart isn't an option here!" he stated making his point at last but instead of letting me then make my own he continued, and in the end, I was the one that gained from it.

"She has been through more than any of us could ever truly know, but my guess is the only way to describe it is going to Hell and back and barely surviving it! What she needs now is a life of good and pure. And if you're telling me right now that your it, then hey, I will back the fuck off and bid you goodnight my friend. But if you can offer her any less than that, then this ain't gonna end well. For in there, those Williams sisters mean the fucking world to me, and now they are under my roof, which means I will be the one protecting them," he said and unknowingly giving me the very last piece of the puzzle I had been waiting for.

Her real name!

Williams.

He continued on, but I was hardly listening,

"And if that includes making bad decisions by taking a chance on a rich businessman that's only around once a year..." Finally, I put up a hand to stop him and gave him not only what he wanted to hear but also what I needed to say. After all, for what he had just given me, he had no idea just how much he deserved it.

"You have nothing to worry about, for I can assure you, I won't ever be leaving this place unless she is with me, that I can fucking guarantee you," I said in such a way that wasn't only my own vow for him to take seriously, but also as a way of ending this conversation. I turned around indicating as such and was just opening the car door when he said,

"Oh shit...you're actually in love with her?" I paused with my hand gripping tighter onto the frame, nearly crushing it for the weight those words held upon my soul. I thought about those words. Those simple fucking words that were actually anything but simple!

Words that had never held any substance before. They had only ever been a myth, a fucking fantasy created in the minds of those only ever eager for more. Words that had been used and abused time and time again until they simply unravelled into meaningless letters lost in a sea of mortal lies. For I myself had never uttered that four-letter word to anyone in my eternal lifetime and up until now, I had never thought I ever would. But then here was a man asking me if I loved someone, he considered a sister.

A girl that was my Chosen One, yes, but that never meant that I *had to love her.* It didn't ever force that emotion on me or force me to feel something akin to what one could only imagine that word even meant. But now, even just thinking of her, seeing her face in my mind, her eyes looking up at me, her smile, the bite of her lip, it was all there like a blinding light I was unable to shield myself from.

It was a truth.

It was an absolute.

It was the end and the beginning.

And it had quickly become my everything.

Which was why it was unsurprising to me when I looked back at him over my shoulder and said,

"Of course, I am in love with her."

DRAVEN

44
TORTURED TRUTH

Franks' eyes lit up as if this had been all he had needed to hear.

"As you can understand, I would appreciate this conversation staying between us, one that I am sure you would prefer to be kept left unspoken also," I said before leaving, knowing that he too would realise what he had admitted here tonight. He nodded and then walked back up the steps just as Libby had opened the door, no doubt wondering what was taking her husband so long.

"Oh, you're…"

"Sorry honey, we were getting carried away talking." He told her with a grin, and then he turned back to me and said,

"It really is a nice car you got there, Dom," I smirked back at him and nodded in thanks, which was for much more than the compliment to my car. Then he put an arm around his wife, and I smiled to myself when I heard him say to her,

"Come on, beautiful, let's get back in the warm." Then they closed their door as I got inside my car and started the engine. Knowing now that any time I heard him call his wife that, then I would only ever think of Keira and how she obviously liked to play matchmaker.

But no matter how much a sweeter thought this was, right now, it was the last thing on my mind. Because not only had Frank let slip her real last name, he had also confirmed my biggest fears...

Keira's past was a lot worse than I could ever have imagined.

I pulled out of Keira's drive and was on the main road before I made the call, the sound of Ranka's answer coming through the car speakers.

"My Lord, did you not get the documents I sent?" She asked obviously associating this with my reason for calling.

"Yes, I did, but that is not why I called," I told her as I had yet to read the file she had found in the psychiatrist's home. It was still no doubt sitting in my private server waiting to be opened on my laptop. But the moment I heard of Keira's injury, then everything else had been deemed unimportant.

"My Lord?"

"I discovered her name Ranka," I said knowing that once I had said it, then there was no going back from learning the entirety of her secrets. There would be no walking away from the truth.

"Then we are nearing the end My Lord, for that is the last piece of the puzzle." I nodded, more to myself seeing as there was no one else to witness it. Then I looked out into the shadowed walls of the forest either side of the road, ones blurring in sight of the speed I was travelling. I didn't know what I expected to find there, but it suddenly made me stop the car with a screech of tires.

"My Lord?"

"I will call you back," I said then hung up and didn't really know why but threw my phone onto the passenger side seat and shouted,

"FUCK!" Then I hit my palm down against the centre console, making the display screen crack. Then I grabbed my head with both hands, gripping handfuls of my hair and asking myself what it was I was fucking doing?!

Why did this feel so wrong?!

This had been the break I had been waiting for...*hadn't it?* All I had needed was that name, and I would have her entire life unfolded in front of me as I had wanted from the very first day, I had met her. And now, all I could see was this new life she was trying to create for herself as one I was trying to unravel again. A past life so horrific, she couldn't even bring herself to speak to her own family about it, no doubt wanting to save them the pain. And now here I was digging it all up and at some point, knowing that it would all be discovered by her what I had done.

And there it was again...That useless emotion I was beginning to loathe.

Guilt.

Because the reality was, she hadn't trusted me with this information, and I wasn't fooling myself, for I knew we were far from that point. So, the question remained, was I really willing to allow time to grant me the chance of her telling me, or was I going to take it from her?

Was I going to make the call?

I looked down at my hands resting on the steering wheel and never before had they looked so empty...so unlike my own. But then I knew now what was missing...*what had always been missing*. Because now I knew what it felt like to have her in my arms. Now I knew what it was like to hold her close and the immeasurable amount of pleasure I felt from that one simple act alone. And just like the four-letter word, I had learned in one night the true meaning of, for it wasn't something you said or an act you did because it was expected of you. It was a *need* you felt pulling at your soul, one that worked in conjunction with the tugging at your heart. The same feeling now that was screaming at me to do the right thing. It was telling me to wait. To wait for what I hoped she would one day give me willingly.

But then my demon reminded us of the possible threat to her, one that could still be out there unpunished and suddenly her screaming in the night was all I could hear. No more laughter, no more secret moans or surprised little gasps. No more smiles, blushes or lip bites were all I could see.

No, it was her tears making her eyes look like glass fragile enough to break. It was her frame shaking in fear and pale skin that became that of a ghost. It was an image of her screaming my name in desperation as she was lost in a dark cabin unable to escape her own nightmares.

By the Gods! The image was powerful enough in my mind that when I lifted my head from my hands, I now found them shaking! I didn't know what had come over me, but it made me grit my teeth, fist my hands and frown down at my knuckles turning white. Then I snatched my phone from the seat next to me, rang the number and said only one thing before hanging up and speeding off into a night I knew had only just begun.

My own personal nightmare, only this time it was one I had asked for...

"Keira Williams."

Two hours later and I found myself sitting at my desk shaking my head as I pushed the printed file away in annoyance. Like Ranka had said, she had sent me all that she found on Keira's sessions with this doctor, and unsurprisingly there had only been two. And it seemed to me that she told him very little and the reasons were just so she could get her prescribed sleeping pills.

But that didn't mean it didn't hold any clues. Like when he asked her if there had been any suicide attempts made and her answer had been a very firm and resounding 'no'. Now, she could have been lying, but then I had also played the audio files Ranka had found, where she was asked the same question. Just hearing her voice in these sessions brought me comfort, even if her voice sounded strained and upset. As if she was trying to hold something back and was on the edge of something catastrophic.

Frank had been right, Keira had changed. But he had been wrong about one thing, and that was if she was ever coming back to the girl he used to know. For hearing this, then he could guess that she was still fighting for it. Fighting her way out of those memories that no doubt still held her captive. I could hear it for myself, that fight in her even then. The way she challenged the doctor as if predicting his thoughts and knowing where he was taking his next line of questions.

At one point he asked her what she was hoping to accomplish from these sessions and she laughed without humour, making the sound feel almost foreign. As if not coming from her at all. Then she told him dryly,

'A good night's sleep perhaps.'

'Then help me understand the cause of why you're not getting one.' had been his reply and once again she laughs, and it was so far from the sound I was used to that it made me tense.

'I know the reason, just because you don't doesn't mean it will change why or stop it. Only pills will do that,' she informed him frankly.

'Then why come here for my help at all?' he asked making me frown, for even I knew what her reply would be.

'Because I can't just walk into a pharmacy and buy them over the counter like I hoped,' she answered honestly making me smirk.

'And if I gave them to you without knowing the reasons why, what is stopping you from taking them all in one night at a time when you feel it all gets too much?' He asked making me grip onto the side of my desk so hard my fingers bit into the wood in an unyielding grip. But it was her reply that really struck me, for you could hear her chair scrape along the floor as she got closer before telling him,

'Alright Doc, I will tell you why, because a person doesn't fight through the Hell they have had forced on them, only to survive, get home and then take their own life because they can't cope with no longer being out of that Hell." She paused for a minute and strangely asked,

'Can I ask you a personal question?'

'Sure,' he agreed, obviously as curious as I was to see where this was going.

'Do you like Stephen King novels?' she asked making me frown.

'Yeah, as a matter of fact, I do,' he answered sounding surprised. But then what she said next made it all become clear.

'So do I, and my favourite is the Novella, Rita Hayworth and Shawshank Redemption, from the book Different Seasons,' she said in a strange voice as if thinking back to it often during hard times, something the psychiatrist would have picked up on if he'd had been any good at his job!

'I know of it, yes.' He said although even I could detect the lie there, as he was trying to earn trust through common ground. Something that wasn't going to work this time, as Keira was only using this as a reference to make her point, not to try and get to know him better like he assumed.

"Good, then you will also know that like Andy Dufresne you don't crawl through 500 yards of shit to get to freedom on the other side, only to then jump back over the wall and hand yourself in. So, if I was to kill myself right now, then that would be exactly what I would be doing...*committing a pointless suicide*. So no, I don't want to kill myself, Doc... all I want to do is get one God damn night's sleep without having a fucking nightmare, and if you can't help me with that, then this meeting is a waste of your time and mine...time I am trying to get back,' she said finishing this by obviously getting out of her chair and heading to the door. Because the next second the doctor wisely says,

'Alright Miss Johnson, I think you have made your point well enough. I will write you a prescription, but you have to come back for another session for the next lot...understood?' She must have nodded here because she said little after this other than thanking him and wishing him a good day after the sound of a paper was being torn from a pad.

So yes, she was a fighter alright. Now it was just time to discover what she had been fighting against in the first place. That and the first chance I got I was ordering a copy of that book and reading that story for myself. I very much wanted to know who this Andy Dufresne was and how he escaped.

A knock at my door shook me from these thoughts enough to sit up straighter and answer,

"Come in...Vincent?" I said my brother's name in question as it was unusual for him to knock. But then I saw his face and realised something was wrong. Meaning I was up and out of my chair, demanding,

"Keira is she...?!"

"The girl is fine Dom, calm yourself," he said stopping me with a raised hand but if that were true then why did he now look so grave?

"Then what is it?" I asked, bracing myself, for I knew my brother well but even then, what he said next surprised me. He released a sigh and informed me,

"Ranka called me." I frowned wondering why she would be calling Vincent when she knew it was me that was expecting her call. It made little sense...well, that was until Vincent continued,

"She didn't tell me anything other than she was getting ready to call you and felt that...how should I put this, that she thought it best you had... *support.*" I jerked back at this strange request asked of my brother, as it was out of character for Ranka. Unless of course, she knew that what she had discovered would be something worse than she believed me capable of coping with? By the Gods, could she be right, could it really be that bad?!

I swear by the time the phone rang only minutes later I flinched unable to help the reaction, now looking down at it vibrating along my desk as if a bomb were ready to go off and opening this would start the timer. In a way, I suppose it was for I had always known this moment would face me. I always knew that once I had discovered her past, then there would be no way to undo what I had learnt.

This was to be my own test.

So, after looking at Vincent briefly and us granting each other the same look, I snatched out, grabbed it and answered it, thus sealing my fate. For the time had come and there was no going back now.

"Tell me," was all I needed to say for her to start talking and once she did, I knew I only lived to regret it, as for the first time in my existence, I discovered that it was possible for a demon to have nightmares.

Nightmares Keira's past had given me.

An hour or so later and I found myself amongst the rubble of what once was my office. And it needed to be noted that this had been the outcome *with* Vincent here to calm me. Making me wonder if he hadn't then would I have now been buried under the crumbling mass of most of our home?

It was safe to say that my demonic rage had hit, and it had hit worse than ever before. Ranka had been right to be cautious when telling me of Keira's past, for it was worse than we could have ever imagined. Which meant that when Keira had told the doctor that she had survived Hell, then she hadn't been exaggerating like I had initially hoped.

Even Vincent had found his rage when hearing of certain details. Yet despite this, he had still helped in reining me back and now sat with me amongst the carnage. Both of us now back to back and panting for breath, with clothes torn and looking more as if we had been in a bar fight.

Thankfully the club had long ago closed, or I think we would have had a hard job trying to convince the locals that there had been an earthquake focused solely under the grounds of Afterlife!

Now the roaring in rage I had no clue how to account for but thankfully, as I said, I didn't have to. Only Sophia had tried to venture in once, but one look at Vincent trying to hold me back from destroying the walls in my other form and Zagan had wisely pulled her from the room, no doubt making sure no one tried to enter it again.

My phone had long ago been damaged and was in pieces among the debris somewhere, for I had reached a point where I could hear no more. I had hit my limit, and Vincent knew this the moment I threw my phone against the wall ahead of me, and it had burst into tiny fragments...*swiftly after this, my desk had followed it.*

After that it had simply been a downward spiral to where we found ourselves now.

"How Vince...? How could she have endured so much and still have so much light inside her?" I asked still holding my head in my hands that were rested against my bent knees. Vincent's body mirrored my own behind me, only he was looking up at the ceiling. And no doubt before I spoke, had been wondering how deep those cracks went and if we were in danger of the next level above coming crashing down on our heads.

"I can't answer that Dom, not even as an angel," he replied in a caring tone and my hands turned to fists in my hair. I felt destroyed. As if I had been ripped apart and put back together again and I had no right to feeling any of it! Because I hadn't been the one to endure one second of its reality.

"I need to see her," I said lifting my head suddenly before finding my feet. I held out a hand for Vincent, who swiftly followed me up after placing his hand on my forearm. I took three steps towards the open arches of my balcony when I paused, to look around the room.

"Go, I will deal with this...go and be where you need to be," he said making me nod. Then before I left, I walked back to him, placed a hand behind his neck and put my forehead to his.

"My brother," I whispered before he too repeated the sentiment. Then I turned and went to the only place on Earth, I knew I would find peace that night. For she may have unknowingly caused my living nightmares, but she was also the only one with the power to take them away again.

So, I went to her, no doubt getting there in record time in my absolute desperation and the irony wasn't lost on me. She had been the one to go through this horrific ordeal two years ago and yet I was the one now needing her for comfort after learning of it.

I just needed to see her, to check that she was alright and not suffering as she had no doubt spent a long time doing. I could barely believe that the Fates would have allowed such a thing to happen to her! I was angry that someone meant for such things wasn't more protected, or at the very least, placed in my path sooner so that I could have protected her at the time. What had the Gods been thinking?!

As a rule with mortal life, the Gods had little say when it came to the decisions made, for their greatest gift bestowed upon them was free will. A reason many of my own kind preferred to live on this plane, to escape such confines and repressed chains of command.

But Keira had been meant for a higher purpose from the moment of her birth, surely that gave them the means of protecting her better?! Oh yes, I was furious with the Gods right now and would have made it more known by cursing all involved. If not the second I made it to her window and saw her, the effect crashed through me like a wave of a stormy ocean lashing against coastal rocks.

The sight of her simply seemed to wash away all my anger, for I had been ready to murder in the name of rage. But just seeing her serene beauty lay there so innocent and pure, knocked the wind from my sails and the breath from my body.

She had never been more beautiful to me as she was in that single moment, one that would forever be branded to my soul like a gift. For no matter how badly mistreated or forsaken the Gods had acted towards her, that was precisely what she was to me and always would be...

A gift from the Gods.

One that was my responsibility to care for from now on and I vowed not to let her down. So, with this in mind, I crept through her window to get closer. I needed to touch her, to connect myself with her that way, just so as I could convince my mind that she was still real. That she was still here. That she hadn't been taken away from me like that bastard had tried to do even before we met. And up until that moment that I could finally reach out and feel the soft skin on her cheek, I had never known what it was like to depend on another living soul in order to keep me breathing. In order to keep me on my feet and my heart beating for such a purpose.

I had never known what it was to be in love.

But that night I knew...*I knew.*

So, as I brushed the hair from her temple, gently touching her injury, I couldn't help but lean down and kiss her there, trying to sooth away the pain of so much more. I wished that it had the power to penetrate through all the bad memories and take them away the moment my lips left her. I wanted to carry the burden of the past so that she no longer had to. I wanted her to be free.

Free of the nightmares.

Free of the pain.

Free even of what the sky looked like on that day they found her bleeding to death on the steps outside of a hospital.

So, I placed a fist either side of her and leaned in close enough so as I could give her my promise, one whispered into her hair and one spoken in my first language. A promise given in my ancient tongue as a Persian King...

"One day my love, I will set you free from all your past memories. Even if it takes me a thousand lifetimes, I will rewrite them all and each with coming of a new sunrise spent together, doing so with only the sweet and pure that you deserve. But first and foremost, I make this vow to do all in my power to protect you from harm. I would sacrifice my life for yours...

For I would die for you."

After this I hushed her back to sleep before she could fully awake and left, knowing that if I didn't then I would only end up giving in to my impulse. One which would mean picking her up and flying back to Afterlife with her in my arms. So, I left, praying for the day that I wouldn't have to. For the day that I would find myself laying her on my bed and sleeping soundly, knowing that she would be there in the morning. That she would be there to welcome the day with me, as she would all other days that came after that.

But unfortunately, this coming sunrise wasn't yet the day for rewriting history. Which was why I soon found myself at that same cliffside clearing, unable to quite make it home. I just needed to be alone, to give myself the last few hours of darkness before that cruel sunrise without her.

For I knew the moment I saw that warm glow start to trespass on the night what the day would signify...*another one without her by my side.*

But more than that, as I had already made the decision that I would have to leave, if only for a short while. As I needed to find out all I could myself about what had been learnt, which meant going to England. After all, I had already crossed the line I told myself I would regret. For I could never undo what I now knew, which meant seeing it through until the end.

And this end included...

A mortal death named Morgan.

DRAVEN

45

DOCTOR AND PATIENT

After seeing through yet another sunrise without her, I got to my feet and flew back to Afterlife, savouring the heat that caressed my feathers, and therefore taking my time in getting there. I landed on the balcony attached to my office and the first sight to greet me was Vincent sat there waiting for me. The room was back to the way it always had been, now with no evidence of the destruction I had caused not long ago. He truly was what one would class as a godsend.

"Unfortunately, Sophia made me fix that gaudy couch," Vincent said making me smirk as even my brother hated that teal sofa.

I nodded my thanks, unable right then to put such gratitude into words, something I knew Vincent would appreciate right now, for I was clearly a man on the edge of barely understanding his own emotions.

"I have taken the liberty of making arrangements. The plane will be ready to leave by this afternoon," he added, proving that he knew me better than anyone and foreseeing my wishes. Of course, I had given a clear indication last night in my rage what I had planned to do to the vile bottom feeding, Gorgon Leech known as Morgan. So, it was unsurprising that he had taken it upon himself to save me a job. My only hope was that when the time came for his own Chosen One to appear, that I could repay him in kind by helping him the way he had helped me.

I even managed to grin again when I sat down at my desk and found a new cell phone there waiting for me. It was the same brand and model as I preferred and no doubt was already charged, complete with a full list of my contacts ready for my use.

"And Sophia?" I asked knowing he would understand the question.

"She has been updated on all that has occurred...*she...*" I frowned when he faltered as if he couldn't believe what he was about to say.

"What?"

"She got very emotional...she cried over the girl, Dom," he said, and soon my disbelief matched that of his own.

"*She cried?*" I asked on a whispered breath knowing this of Sophia was completely unheard of. I think the closest to upset that I had seen her was the loss of an entire wardrobe of recent clothing purchased back in 1937. This was due to a devastating fire at one of our English country estates, named Witley Court. One which at the time had been our main residence while staying in the country.

"She did, and I don't know who it surprised more, Zagan, I or herself, for I didn't think her capable of such emotion," he admitted with a scratch of his head as if he were still trying to understand it. But then I didn't think he would, for he was the only one of us who hadn't really had the chance to meet Keira yet. He hadn't had the chance to form a bond. Something I knew that when he had, then he would fully understand why Sophia had found her tears.

Or why I had spent the night holding back my own.

"Her bond with the girl is strong," I said as my only answer for the time being.

"Oh, I know, as for once, she didn't argue when I requested that she remained behind to watch out for her while we were away...and you do know how much she would consider she was missing out, seeing as we are planning violence." Vincent informed me now making me smirk. Yes, it must have been a strong bond indeed for her to agree to miss out on such a treat as justified murder.

One firmly labelled as... *revenge.*

A little time later and after allowing my girl enough time to rest I located one of the town's doctors, known as Alfred Spencer. Then I took over his vessel, announced to the girl on the desk who manned his practice, that I was leaving to go and see a patient. To which the door swung closed on a very confused voice informing me,

"But you don't do house calls!"

"I do today," I muttered to myself as I got inside the car that was waiting for me. I then took notice of my appearance and knew that it wouldn't do, as I at least wanted to look presentable, even if I wasn't in my own vessel.

For a doctor, Mr Spencer was surprisingly unkempt, and if the rumours were to be believed, he was a social recluse and one house in the wilderness away from becoming a hermit. And quite simply put, he was also known to be a rude bastard. A strange profession for someone with so much disdain for others, when healing them was the sole reason for that job.

So, I decided on this occasion to give him an upgrade on not just his dire choice in clothing, but also his haggard face that looked far older than it should for a man his age. Of course, it wouldn't last, for when my mind left this body, so would my essence along with it. Changing my vessel's appearance didn't take long, doing so was a mere thought and some creativity. So, by the time I arrived at Keira's home, I exited the car ready to present myself to her, wondering now what her own reaction would be.

I already knew that she didn't like hospitals, and for a good reason after the discovery made last night. But I wondered what her attitude would be towards a doctor sent by me? Well, I was about to find out as her sister soon answered the door and allowed me inside after I introduced myself. She looked taken aback at first, but then I didn't miss the small smirk that played at her lips, before saying,

"Well, I'd better go and wake the patient then. Please make yourself comfortable." I nodded my thanks and sat down, doing so for only a moment until she went out of sight, as there was a picture on the mantlepiece that had caught my eye. I picked it up and turned it towards the window so as to catch the sun. Gods, but even her image imprinted and encased behind glass wasn't enough to dull the golden shine of her hair. It was also shorter than it was now, also unlike she ever wore it today, as it was loose around her shoulders making her appear wild and free.

She was stood next to her sister, with some kind of theme park ride in the distance behind them. I couldn't tell how old she was, maybe in her late teens and still as beautiful as she was today. However, the main difference had been the way she was dressed, as she was more carefree in her short skirt and red vest showing off more skin than she obviously dared to now.

Of course, there was also the lack of her usual fingerless gloves, as they weren't needed in her mind, for not a single mark marred her perfect skin. It made me want to see them now, and then gently kiss each scar I knew I would find, proving to her that in my eyes she was still utterly perfect, no matter how she saw herself. Reason now why I found myself running a single fingertip down the length of her image.

A few minutes later her sister came back down to find me where she assumed, I had always been sat. Being that I had made it back to the sofa a second after hearing her shutting Keira's door on the third floor.

"She should be ready in ten minutes, can I get you a drink of anything, tea, coffee?" she asked politely as was obviously customary growing up in the Williams' household. It was strange, now knowing her real name and stranger still on discovering that 'Keira' hadn't been a lie. I had been glad when Ranka had told me this, but that was about the extent of my good news, for after that it had been lashing after lashing of the worst kind.

"No, thank you." I declined the offer and then watched as she smiled before coming to join me.

"So, you work for Mr Draven?" she asked obviously curious after I had introduced myself as such.

"On occasion, yes," I replied taking care of how much information I gave her.

"And administering health care to his waitresses...happen often does it?" She asked making me suppress a smirk, for her and her husband seemed very well suited.

"Not that I can recall, no, I do believe this is a first," I answered making her grin this time.

"Yeah, that's what I thought," she replied obviously like her husband getting the measure of my actions a lot quicker than Keira did, that was for sure.

"And Mr Draven, do you know if he has a girlfriend?" she asked shocking me enough to cough back a laugh, for she was definitely like her husband, in a way that neither of them was what you would call subtle.

"Sorry, I am just curious as to what his intentions are towards my sister, as I am sure you can understand." She said coming to her own defence and letting me know that Frank had kept his word, keeping our conversation last night to himself and thus earning himself a new level of respect for that alone.

"Well, I can't exactly comment much on Mr Draven's personal life, but I think it's at the very least safe to say that to the best of my knowledge, he is single," I replied thinking it best to give her something here, after all, she was only concerned about her sister. And I supposed that after my actions last night, then it was only natural to assume my feelings ran deeper for the girl than those of me as her boss and her as my employee.

"So, never seen him with a couple of supermodel girlfriends draped on his arm then?" she asked, pressing for more. I couldn't help it, this time I laughed.

"As I said, I cannot really speak on his personal life having only been his personal physician in the time I have known him, but I can honestly say that in that time, I have never seen him portrayed as the picture you just painted. He's by no means another Hugh Hefner." She laughed at this and said,

"So, he's gay then?" I swear if I'd taken her offer of a drink, this vessel would find itself choking on it right about now!

"No!" I shouted unable to help myself as most men who weren't gay would. She raised an eyebrow at my sudden outburst, and I cleared my throat before trying more calmly this time.

"What I mean to say is that I sincerely doubt that." She raised both her eyebrows at this but didn't comment, even though I could tell she wanted to. I however, definitely had more pressing matters than having my sexuality questioned when I was in fact in love with her sister and well, basically had been stalking her not long since she barely first stepped foot off the plane.

"I think it's time I go and check on my patient now," I said getting up and thankfully putting an end to this awkward conversation, one no doubt Sophia would have found great pleasure in witnessing.

I made my way up the stairs just as Libby was telling me which room was hers, making me realise my error for not asking in the first place. I suppose I could be forgiven seeing as I still had the question, 'Is he gay?' rattling around my mind.

In fact, by the time I found myself outside her door I was still shaking my head from it. I then listened for her movements, not wanting to walk in on her as she was still dressing, as that was not something, I wanted to do unless seeing it with my own eyes, not a pair belonging to this vessel or any other vessel for that matter! I didn't care how irrational that sounded. She was for my eyes only!

I listened to her as she finished in the bathroom and padded her way across the floor until the creaking of the bed could be heard. This was when I tapped on the door and made my presence known.

"May I come in?" I asked opening the door a little and found her sat on the bed waiting for me. She was wearing a pair of what looked like gym trousers, a maroon red top that I knew would be hugging her curves in that delicious way. One that made me want to frame her waist, before running my palms up her sides taking the material that concealed her with them. Added to this was an oversized zip-up sweater that unfortunately hid most of what I desired to touch and had no doubt been picked to fend off the morning chill this attic room seemed prone to.

I felt my fingers clench at my sides just to stop myself from thinking about it, along with thoughts of warming up that pale skin with my hands and seeing if I couldn't get it to blush.

She also had on a pair of grey gloves, and her hair had been brushed back into an hair band, so as it flowed down her back with only the shorter parts framing her face. I could smell her soap with hints of vanilla mixed with the mint of toothpaste that she had just used to brush her teeth with. A mint flavour I was suddenly intrigued to taste.

"Keira, I presume." She gave me a sceptical look in return making me want to laugh at her obvious aversion to doctors. At least she was looking much better after a good night's rest.

"It's nice to meet you, my dear, I'm Doctor Spencer," I said holding out my hand for her to shake after positioning myself closer to her. She took it, as her politeness wouldn't allow her not to, and the second she made contact, I felt myself enveloped with a peaceful feeling.

"Hi, it's nice to meet you too," she lied in return making me hold back a grin.

"Mr Draven tells me you took a nasty fall in the woods and was feeling some ill effects of it last night," I said placing down the black doctor's case next to the bed and taking a seat opposite her. She didn't respond to this, so I continued,

"Do you mind?" I asked nodding to her injury, and she shrugged her shoulders in return. I wanted to smirk at her odd, nonchalant behaviour but instead, I shifted closer and lifted her hair from the lump on her head. Then I noticed that it made her shiver and I wondered at the reasons for it.

"I'm sorry my hands must be cold. If you could tilt your head back for me, I will take a closer look," I said trying to keep in mind that I wasn't who she thought I was, so needed to keep this as professional as I could. Even though having her head in my gentle hold only made me wish I was doing so with my own hands so as I could claim her lips in such a way.

So, in keeping with the doctor's persona, I took out the things I would need from Spencer's bag after examining her wound. It looked slightly better today, less angry at least. The bruise, however, was making its way through the first set of blues and purple shades.

"That looks nasty. You should really have gone to the hospital and got some stitches." I said chastising her knowing that this was true, for the cut did look deep enough to have benefited from the treatment.

"I know, but I kinda have a thing with hospitals." she said, and instantly I felt guilty for bringing it up. After what I knew now about her, then it was unsurprising why she would do everything in her power to stay away from what she would only ever associate with her nightmares.

"Bad experience I take it?" I said knowing that it would seem off not to respond to such a comment seeing as I was portraying myself as a doctor. I then checked her pupils with my flashlight, seeing for myself there were no problems there.

"Something like that," she answered as I nodded for her to follow my finger to complete checking her Oculomotor and Trochlear nerves.

"Can you describe to me exactly what happened?" I asked curious to know.

"Oh, it was nothing really, I was just taking a walk, tripped and caught my head on a rock…admittedly I'm quite a clumsy person, so let's just say I don't think hiking is my forte and not a hobby I trust myself to take up anytime soon," she told me honestly making me smile at her in return and want to say, 'not unless I am there to catch you, sweetheart'.

"And what about your symptoms last night?"

"Oh, you know the obvious headache, dizzy spells, nausea, stuff like that," she said trying to downplay it, no doubt so I wouldn't recommend a trip to the hospital for a scan.

"And now?" I asked knowing that I would easily be able to detect the lie.

"I feel a lot better today after a good night's sleep," she replied trying to sound almost cheery. No doubt in hopes of getting me to sign her off on good health and fit enough for work. Well, she would soon be disappointed.

"Do you usually have trouble sleeping?" I asked knowing this was an unnecessary question but one I asked anyway as I was curious to see what she would say.

"Yeah sometimes…well I mean lately."

"Do you take any medication for it?" I added, also curious as to what her response would be.

"No," she lied.

"Yes, well let's take your blood pressure," I said taking out the pump before asking her,

"If you could just roll up your sleeves for me." I knew I was pushing her limits here, but I wanted to know what her reason would be for not showing me unless she felt more comfortable exposing them to someone she believed to be a doctor.

But I didn't think so, as knowing how evasive she had been so far, I wasn't surprised when she only rolled up the sleeves of her sweater and top underneath, not the gloves I saw peeking out underneath when first walking in.

"Are you cold?" I asked nodding down at them.

"I suffer from bad circulation, cold feet as well. Do you mind if I keep them on?" she asked before biting her lip.

"It won't be for long," I told her, taking them in a gentle hold and about to peel them back myself. Her reaction didn't surprise me as she pulled them from me and said,

"Look, I'm sorry Doc, but I have this thing with people touching my arms. Let's just put it down to an accident and leave it at that... okay?" After this, I nodded, having now my answer and deciding that was enough pushing for one day.

I had in some way been convinced that if I could get her to take that first step in showing them to a doctor at least, then she would have an easier time when one day showing them to me. But I had been wrong and now felt guilty for pushing her about it. As I could see now that it was something that needed to be handled slowly and with great care.

"Alright, let's measure it on your neck, should we?" I said in a gentle tone, glancing once at her arms before raising a hand to her neck to measure her pulse.

"I appreciate it, and I assume that all this will remain confidential?" She nodded down at her arms, silently asking me not to tell anyone...no, not anyone...it was me she didn't want knowing!

"You mean Mr Draven?" I asked clarifying what I suspected, half annoyed that she didn't want me to know and half gratified that I was the one on her mind. She didn't reply, but then again, she didn't have to, as her look said it all. So, I told her,

"Mr Draven is only concerned and wants to know when you will be fit to go back to work, anything else will go no further than this room." She instantly relaxed upon hearing this and replied with a genuine,

"Thank you." I nodded before then reaching in my bag and getting out the items I had made sure were supplied in there before leaving Spencer's office earlier.

"I am going to re-dress your wound and give you some pills to take that will help reduce the swelling of the lump and help with the pain." She nodded, now looking relieved and much more comfortable around me. She then watched me place things down on her bedside table moving a cold mug of tea out of the way first. I couldn't help but watch her as she got off the bed to pour it down the sink in her small bathroom situated just next to her room.

Of course, I also noticed the way her top had risen up from the way she had been sitting, and she pulled it down as she passed me. Now granting me a fresh wave of her delicious scent to waft under my nose, making me inhale a deep breath. I swear she was intoxicating as the effect almost made me lightheaded. I just wanted to run my nose across her soft belly and wrap her scent around me, wearing it for days.

I didn't know if the reason for feeling like this was because I knew I would have no choice in leaving her for a few days. Especially considering it will be the first time since meeting her that I would be forced to do so. Half of me was already regretting the decision. But I knew that for my own peace of mind, I needed to see this through in person.

So, I had no choice.

She soon walked back to the bed and resumed her previous position, now with a small metal clip in her hand ready to slip into her hair when I looked ready to begin. I first removed the few makeshift stitches of tape and gave it another clean, making her hiss with the sting. Had I been myself I would have no doubt teased her at this point, before offering comfort, in the way of a kiss. It was a strange impulse, seeing as I had never been inclined to be this way with a woman before, so I continued to ask myself, where was it all coming from?

Females had always been for pleasures of the flesh and nothing more to me in the past, for I certainly didn't even find myself engaging in much conversation with one. So, the need to comfort, or to tease, or even to make laugh had never really entered into my mind before.

For it was merely a coupling of the physical sense and nothing more. And now I found myself barely able to hold back all the new impulses she brought out in me. To find myself utterly content just being in her presence was astonishing in itself. For yes, my lust for her was at times at a near frenzy, with my demon wanting to overtake my mind and my body. But for the most parts, my need to have her in my bed came secondary to anything else, even if my straining trousers often said otherwise.

After the area was ready, I took the small lines of medical tape known as steri strips and cut them to the right size before placing them across her wound, doing so with care. Then, once I had finished and was placing things back in the bag, I noticed the old college logo on her zip-up sweater, making a mental note of it in case I needed the information further down the line.

I also knew that this would have been a big clue for me in discovering her name as I had a feeling it had been passed down to her from her father. Seeing as it was too big on her to have been bought by herself I made a mental note of this also, thinking that if there ever came a time when she asked me how I found out the truth of her identity, then I could easily account for this being the reason. Not Frank, who she might have felt betrayed her in some way. No, I would not honour his part in helping me by then laying blame at his feet.

"All done?" she asked making me grin.

"Yes, it looks better today," I said instantly realising my slip up and adding quickly,

"Well, from how Mr Draven had described it." If she picked up on it, she didn't let on, but instead asked in an eager tone,

"So, this means you will tell Mr Draven I'm fit for work?" I almost smirked, very nearly congratulating myself for it seemed as though our encounter last night had a lasting effect on her. Could it be possible that her feelings for me had deepened these last few days when working in the VIP? Unfortunately, I couldn't give this too much thought for she was waiting for her answer.

"Yes, after three days of rest and depending if you're fine in that time and have had no more dizzy spells, then yes I will." Her expression on hearing this was almost comical, as it was clear she was less than happy with the outcome. Something confirmed when she said,

"Aww come on Doc. Look, I feel fine, great even and I don't want to lose my job or anything." Ha! Now, this nearly had me laughing aloud, for she was trying to manipulate me as a doctor into getting her own way.

The little Vixen!

"I very much doubt that would happen and if I find out that you haven't taken my orders on board, then I will ring up Mr Draven and tell him you're not fit for a week," I threatened with a raise of my brow and trying to hold back my grin once more.

"Okay, okay, three days off work," she quickly conceded as I knew she would. However, I also knew that it was too much of a risk for her to continue going to college without being there myself. So, I quickly informed her,

"Not just work, college too." Then I handed her a note I had already in Spencer's bag, one that I had prepared before I came here. I did so knowing that my plans for while I was away were for Keira to remain safely in her home for the duration. Something she now looked utterly horrified at, looking down at the note in her hand as if it was prison sentence handed down by a jury. Again, I wanted to laugh at her reaction and expression to such things.

"I can't. Look you have never met my history teacher! You have to be dying to get away with not turning up for one of his classes." This time I couldn't help but laugh and not for the reasons she most likely thought but from the fact she had wrinkled her nose again.

"I will speak to Mr Draven. I know his sister is in the same class, so I'm sure she could have a word with him for you." I said trying to ease her fears, as there was no way I was going to allow anyone to reprimand her, let alone for reasons of illness. But then even at the very mention of this, she looked utterly perplexed.

"No...! I mean, no thanks, that won't be necessary, I think I have caused more than enough aggravation for Mr Draven without involving him in any more of my problems," she said first shouting out in panic before explaining the reason for her impulsive reactions and making me frown because of it. So much for congratulating myself, I thought wryly, especially if this was how she still thought of me.

"That's not how Mr Draven thinks. I have known him a long time, and he has always taken care of his staff."

"Oh, I have no doubt, but he was very kind to me last night and considering it was only my second shift, I think he has done enough for me to last my lifetime. I wouldn't like to push my luck." I couldn't help my reaction to hearing this as I looked down and whispered,

"Never enough."

"Sorry, did you say something?"

"I said, fair enough," I said quickly before continuing, and she could question my odd behaviour too closely.

"Well, in that case, I will be off to report back to the man in question." After this I offered her my hand, knowing that this was the last time I was to touch her for a few days and some part of me wished I could have made a lasting imprint on her soul as she often did with mine.

"Goodbye Keira, it was a pleasure meeting you and until next time," I said trying to convey so much more into that 'next time' before I forced myself to let go of her hand, severing the connection between us. I had to force myself to leave, knowing that if I didn't do so then, I would soon find myself looking for an excuse not to leave at all.

So, I turned my back to her and walked out of her door. I also found her sister coming up the stairs, obviously to see how Keira was getting on. But before she could speak, I bid her good day, telling her that I could let myself out.

Then I walked down the stairs hearing the last thing on Keira's mind being sighed out dramatically in her room,

"What must he think of me?"

I only wished she had heard my reply...

"If only you knew, Catherine."

Keira

46

OBSESSIONS

Sunday was what I thought was going to be day one, but I learned later that day that the Doctor had told Draven that I should only go back to work on Thursday night. Sophia had phoned to tell me this and asked if I wanted her to come around with any history notes from the lessons I would miss. She had also reassured me that Draven hadn't said much about last night, only that it wasn't an inconvenience and that he hoped I was feeling better. I almost fist bumped the air but doubts soon took over any excitement. Maybe she had just said those things to make me feel better. Although, considering he had sent me a doctor in the first place, surely that was enough proof he cared on some level.

Unfortunately, my obsessing over the whole thing didn't end there. I wanted to speak to Libby about it but didn't know if I could. I finally dragged myself out of bed being lured downstairs by the most amazing smell of pizza. No offense to Libby but I just knew it was take out. I realised that I was starving. I hadn't really eaten much on Saturday and what little I had, I'd thrown up. It was now nearly seven in the evening and I was so hungry my stomach ached as it growled angrily at me.

"See Libs, told ya, once she smelled the food she'd come down...how you feeling kid?" Frank was sat on the couch digging into one of the two pizza boxes grabbing a massive slice and Libby was on his other side eating hers from a plate.

"I'm feeling better thanks and guys, good call on the pizza, I could eat a horse." I sat down and dug in, taking one without anchovies. I couldn't get my head round anchovies on a pizza. In England you never got them as an option and it turned out that I wasn't missing out. But Frank loved them. Actually, there wasn't much Frank didn't eat.

"So honey, I thought now would be the time to...umm...discuss last night." Libby said this in a quiet timid voice as though not to upset me, and I knew she had a right to know, but it was still so fresh in my mind I really didn't want to go into it.

"I don't really know what to say." I said which just so happened to be the truth.

"Well, you could start with why you didn't tell us that you were working up in the VIP." She was trying to keep her voice calm but I could tell she wasn't happy about being kept in the dark.

"I'm sorry I didn't tell you, but I knew how you felt about me working there in the first place and I thought it would just make you worry even more." Frank nodded, as he actually knew what I was talking about, but Libby noticed and punched him on the arm.

"What?! It's true, you have given her a hard time over working there and you would have given her an even harder time if she'd have told you." Frank said sticking up for himself and me.

"Not necessarily." Libby said sulking.

"Come on babe, sorry to say this Kaz but ever since, you know the 'Thing', you have been a bit paranoid over your sister and I can understand why, I really can, but it's time to let her live her life without making things more difficult." Wow! This was the longest speech I had ever heard from Frank and it made me want to get up and kiss him! It was sweet the way he defended me and what he was saying was right, but my sister hadn't always been like this, it was just ever since she nearly lost me and now she was terrified of it happening again.

Libby didn't say anything, she just pouted and I half expected her to start sucking her thumb.

"Look, you know I appreciate everything you guys are doing for me and you were right, this really was the best move for me. And I know that you worry because you love me, I would worry too if ..." I stopped, not being able to carry on. I would never ever be able to imagine if it had been Libby instead of me, so I physically couldn't continue that sentence. Libby looked round at me and saw my emotion, and her features softened.

"What I'm trying to say is that I understand, and I just want to start over. I actually enjoy working at the club and with the amount of security, I'm sure it's one of the safest places on the planet." She smiled, and I knew that her bad mood had passed and the gossip side of her was coming through.

"Sooo, can you explain how on Earth you even got that job? Because I'm not being funny, no one from this town has worked in the VIP." She sat looking at me as if I had achieved some sort of a miracle, when really it was just a case of my being nice to his sister.

"Well, I *am* being funny when I say I am not from this town." She laughed getting my humour and then I went on to tell her the story of when I met Sophia in history and how I had to take some bottles up to the VIP area and that's when she saw me. I told them how she had offered me the job, leaving out the part when Draven was rude to me. That wasn't enough for Libby's appetite for gossip, so she asked me about the night he brought me home.

"What do you want to know?"

"Well for starters, how did it come about, that he would drive you home? I mean, that would be like Alan Sugar driving home his cleaning lady after a tough day!" She was so right, but if I couldn't understand why then how was I going to explain it myself?

"I don't really know, I mean I was outside feeling sick and then he was there."

"What do you mean 'he was there'... you mean he followed you?" Libby said, clearly loving this story.

"No, no, nothing like that, no I mean, why would he follow me? No, he was probably just getting some air." She smiled like she had hit a nerve and then looked at Frank making sure he was still listening. That's when I knew the two of them had obviously been talking about this. She made a gesture with her hand to carry on, so I continued.

"So anyway, he found me and then I don't know, he just decided to bring me home himself." I tried to make it sound light hearted and like it was no big deal, but she wasn't buying it.

"Oh come on, I need details!" Her hair bounced as she shook her head and I rolled my eyes.

"Like what? That was it...he just picked me up and carried me to his garage, we got in his car and he brought me home...end of story." I picked up another slice of pizza, but Frank responded to the magic work of "garage" and turned to get in on the act.

"Garage, you say? Okay, now we're talking, what type of garage? How many cars would you say? Did you recognise any?" Frank had now turned down the volume on the TV to listen to the rest of the story.

"Oh, I don't know...I guess I saw a couple of red ones that could have been Ferraris, but there were loads of them." I said trying to finish off my pizza but Frank was determined to get more information out of me.

"Okay, so you saw Ferraris, what else? And when you say loads, do you mean more than ten?" Libby was rolling her eyes and I tried not to laugh at him. He was, after all, being serious.

"Umm...more like over twenty, they were everywhere, but I don't really remember which ones ...maybe a yellow one...umm, with a logo of a bull. What are they called?" He smiled and shouted the answer as though we were playing a quiz game!

"You mean a Lamborghini?!"

"Yeah, that's it, but really, I don't remember any others apart from one in its own glass room, but I have never seen one like it before and it looked really old." Frank was close to salivating as he leaned over Libby to get closer to me, so he could hear me better that way.

"Man, I would love to have seen that room. I mean that Aston Martin last night, what a machine! What was it like inside? Did he open her up?"

"Open her up...like her bonnet?" I asked teasing.

"It's called a hood and I mean did he put his foot on the gas." I bit my lip mischievously to prevent from laughing as I said,

"Well yeah, he got me home, didn't he?" Libby burst out laughing when Frank threw up his hands thinking I was being serious, so I put him out of his misery.

"Yes Frank, he went fast...thinking about it I think we even went over a hundred." I laughed when his face beamed back at me and I had never seen Frank so enthusiastic.

"Well I don't like the sound of that." Libby said frowning at which Frank and I both burst into raucous laughter.

"What?" Libby demanded.

"This coming from Miss Speed Ticket herself." Frank said, and my mouth dropped open.

"You have speeding tickets?" I asked in shock to which I was met by Libby's sheepish face.

"Only one."

"Two." Frank added before receiving a scowl from his wife.

"I gather mum and dad don't know." I said smirking as now the teasing tables had turned.

"No and if you tell them I will hide the teabags."

"You wouldn't!" I shouted in mock horror.

"Aww, come on girls let's get back to the car, I'm glad I came home early. I asked him what model it was and when he said a One-77 I had never even heard of it, so I did some research on the internet, guess what I found?" He didn't give us time to guess, as he carried on like a stream train.

"Well, there's a reason it's called that! Because there was only 77 of them made! And you'll never guess how much Libs." He nudged her arm and she winked at me and then turned to him saying,

"Oooh honey, how much?" I couldn't help but laugh at her patronizing tone but he didn't notice.

"1.7 million dollars, that's how much was sat on our drive last night! I mean it's a 7.3 litre V12, which means it's got twice as many cylinders as our car!" He looked pleased with himself as Libby whistled at the price.

"Well, that's all double Dutch to me." He frowned obviously wishing we were guys at this very moment. Still, I was a bit in awe of the price. I mean, why bring me home in something that cost so much... It just didn't make any sense.

"You were so lucky, that was like one in a million type thing!" He shook his head as it was obviously wasted on me, but the one in a million thing I did agree on, but just not for the same reason Frank was referring to.

"You mean one in 1.7 million, sweetheart." Libby patted him.

"Anyway, let's get back to the more important things, like how did he smell?" She then turned to me with a wink.

"What! Oh yeah, 'cause that's more important, his body hygiene?" With that Frank turned up the TV and continued to watch football.

"The one thing I do want to know is why he drove you home...I mean, him personally?"

"I don't know Libs, but he is known for taking good care of his staff." Frank laughed when I said this and we both stared at him to elaborate on his outburst.

"Yeah, I bet he is, ha, ha." He chuckled some more, and Libby was shaking her head as though he was some rude naughty little boy.

"Aww come on, isn't it obvious? He has a crush on her!"

"WHAT? I don't think so!" I shouted in disbelief

"Why do you say that?" Libby asked not wanting to hurt my feelings, but she was clearly with me on this one. Frank sighed as though we were both born yesterday.

"Oh no he just makes sure she is the only one picked up and driven home in a freakin' chauffeured car. Then gets promoted after like what...one shift...?"

"But I..." I tried to cut this down but Frank was clearly on a roll and besides it was clear Libby was all ears.

"Then she has a bump to the noggin and he just picks her up into his arms, after she puked in his plant pot I might add and carries her off to his millionaire's car. Drives her back, whisked her up to her bedroom, like some damn knight in shining armour and then called a doctor to make sure she was alright. Oh no, couldn't possibly be sweet on her, no course not... must be Boss of the friggin' Year, that's the only explanation!" Frank laughed again as me and Libby sat in silence, gobsmacked.

Then Libby turned to me and said,

"Maybe he's got a point, Kazzy." Libby said with a huge grin on her face. Frank again seemed pleased with himself at his conclusion, but I was definitely not buying it. What the Hell would a man like that want with someone like me?!

That night I thought that I would never sleep but thanks to the pills, I was out like a light. And again, I had no nightmares and only a few times did I dream. The dreams would be very brief, only lasting for a second when I would open my eyes and see that the bird was back and watching me from the window.

Every morning I would awaken disappointed that I hadn't dreamed of Draven and the days seemed to drag on and on making me more anxious to see him again.

My three days off were all starting to merge into one. By the third, I was slowly going insane with boredom and Saturday night kept crawling its way back into my mind, making me both cringe and swoon every time.

Draven had become like a drug and I was a junky needing another score. This time away felt like my rehab. I was most definitely ready to overdose on my obsession, because there was only one thing that I wanted and it was the one thing that I would never get... Dominic Draven.

But going cold turkey wasn't exactly working for me either. Even his name brought goosebumps to my skin. After that night of being so close to him, I couldn't think of anything else. I replayed the scene over and over like a favourite movie. Only I couldn't decide whether it was a horror or a romance.

I also couldn't keep from thinking about what Frank had said and wondering if he did in fact have a point. But no matter how much you wanted something I knew I would be a fool to get my hopes up for such a thing. People did nice things for others all the time and it was usually the people who read too much into these things that got themselves into trouble.

I spent Monday doing course work for every lesson so at least I would be on top of things when I went back. Libby had rung the college informing them of my accident and they reassured her that they would pass on the message to my tutors. It was just a shame that they couldn't also reassure me about Reed not getting a guillotine ready for my return. I also had Jack call me seeing if everything was alright. I told him about my fall and he insisted on coming over that night to see me, but I made my excuses, telling him I was still feeling groggy.

Tuesday was a clear day with the sun shining, enhancing the colours of the trees, making the autumn leaves look as if they had been made by the sun. I decided to grab a blanket and do something I hadn't done in years. I sat outside in the back garden and painted the view in watercolours, hoping to capture the beauty I saw each day. Painting to me was like riding a bike, a little strange after years of not doing it, but as soon as my hand held the brush it was like being reunited with an old friend.

When I had finished I couldn't help the tears that ran from my eyes. I used to love art, either creating an image from my mind or painting a view like this, capturing the essence of its purity. It was my escapism, one which I thought I'd lost.

That night the doorbell rang and Libby showed the beautiful Sophia to my room. I was surprised to find her wearing jeans and a hooded sports top rather than her usual glamorous attire. But she still pulled it off, looking as though she was just modelling for a different fashion label. She also wore her hair up in a ponytail making her look cute and even more doll like.

"Oh, my brother wasn't kidding when he said it looked bad." The thought of Draven saying anything about me made me smile, one I couldn't hide. Even if it was about how bad I looked.

"How are you feeling now?" She walked over to my bed where I was sat reading 'Sense and Sensibility'. I was always amazed watching her as whenever she moved, she always did so with such grace and elegance. It was more like dancing than walking. I was just glad that my room was still tidy. That had been one of my only saving graces on Saturday. At least he didn't think I was a slob.

"I feel fine, a lot better. You know I could start back to work earlier." She grinned at me, knowing it wasn't going to happen.

"Nope sorry, doctor's orders, and Dom wouldn't allow it." I loved it when she called him that, it made him sound just like an everyday, average guy. And clearly, he was never going to be just that.

"Here you go, the notes like I promised. Oh, and you don't have to worry about Reed, my brother took care of it." The words were like being doused by a bucket of ice.

"Oh no... why did he do that?" She frowned at me as she handed me the pages of notes and printouts.

"Why not? The doctor mentioned you were worried about it and Dom asked me about Reed, so I explained that he could be somewhat difficult. He didn't like the sound of someone giving you hassle and wanted to make sure that didn't happen." She shrugged her shoulders as if it had been no trouble.

"I just don't want to cause any more problems for him, after all, he is my boss and he has done more than enough already. He didn't need to do that as well." I played with the material on my gloves and looked down feeling embarrassed at being the cause of all this fuss.

"Look, you really don't need to worry, he knows you're my friend and well...I don't have many friends, so I guess he's going to be extra protective." Her eyes looked sad and didn't match the smile she put on.

"Well, I don't understand how a lovely girl like you couldn't have many friends, but I'm glad you're mine." I said in reply and her face beamed at the words.

"That means a lot to me. I have moved around so much and everywhere I go people just want to be my friend because of who I am, not what I am, if that makes any sense?"

"Sure, I get it, because of your name." She nodded, and I noticed a slight tinge of something brighter shining in her eyes. But I thought it must have been a trick of the light.

We continued chatting about other stuff for about an hour before she had to leave and again she hugged me before she left. This time I hugged her back feeling my body go warm when I touched her skin. She smelled like her brother, only the girly version replacing the woody earthy smell for ones of flowers and honey. But again, the scent did strange things to my mind, making me want to hold on to it as long as I could.

Wednesday was very much the same as Monday, as in the weather had gone back to wet and stormy. I also had some more work to do for history but thanks to Sophia, her notes held all the answers I needed, so it didn't take me very long. I would have to thank her for that on Thursday. Only one more day of solitude and I would be a free girl again. I couldn't wait to get out of the house. But more than anything I couldn't wait to get back to the club. I didn't know why, but I just felt so safe there as if nothing could ever penetrate those walls, not even my past.

Jack and RJ paid me a visit in the evening and I told them about my new job. RJ's and Jack's reaction to this were very different.

"Oh my God, that is seriously the coolest news! Now tell me everything!" RJ said as Libby brought us some sodas into the Den where we all sat. On the other hand, Jack looked as though he was going to throw up, as if he had something foul in his mouth and had to get rid of it.

"Why, when, how?" RJ continued and I told them how it all started but she clearly showed her disappointment that I hadn't told her sooner.

"I thought I was going to turn the job down." I said in my defence.

"You should have!" Jack said with a cool manner but he was clearly upset.

"And why should she have, sounds like a dream job to me." RJ said backing me up.

"Because, Keira is too nice to be a slave to that asshole King of Sacrifices." He continued as if I wasn't even there and I felt a sudden urge to stick up for Draven. Jack didn't even know him, so what was his big problem?

"What's that supposed to mean?" I said getting defensive. But he turned to me and his features softened as he replied.

"I don't mean to be rude when I say this, but you don't know what we know...well what *I* know. There are strange things that happen up there, things that are ...just...just wrong." This sent a shiver up my spine and he noticed my reaction feeling as though he had relayed a clear message to me. But all he had done was add questions to my mind not answers.

"Well, why don't you fill me in if I'm obviously so clueless." I was getting frustrated now and was losing my patience.

"Look, I don't want to go into it but just trust me on this. If you stay up there you're gonna get hurt." He said this as he placed his hand on my shoulder as though trying to will me to understand his secret meaning, but I was coming up empty.

They left shortly after that, leaving me more confused than ever before. I mean, this was getting ridiculous. I was going to have find out from RJ what happened to make Jack hate them so much because from the way he was acting, it was like I had crossed over and join a fluffy bunny killing cult!

I went to bed still frustrated about what he had said and how I couldn't make sense out of any of it. I was just hoping for the one thing that I really needed right now.

My drug, my obsession and...

My dreams of Draven.

Keira

47

SENTENCE OVER

The next day I woke up after yet another dreamless night, but I was more positive when I realised that today I was finally allowed back to work. I got up earlier than necessary, so it was still dark and misty outside. I pulled on a big thick sweater and went over to sit at the window seat. The fog filled the air, covering the forest like another entity. It looked thick enough to hold in your hands.

I sat there thinking about seeing Draven again and I wondered what would happen. Would he talk to me? Or would he just act the same as he had done before that shift? The way he had been that night was just so out of character, it would be hard to see him go back to treating me as if I didn't belong there.

The thought gave me an ache in my chest and I circled my arms around myself, as if trying to protect my body from what was yet to come. I was in a no-win situation, but I had come too far to turn back now. If only I could just walk away from it then maybe I would have a chance at a semi-normal life. But my heart had fallen and fallen hard, for not just a man, but something more.

I was ready an hour before expecting to hear RJ's comical little car beeping its horn. I was dressed warm, wearing my denim jacket with a zipped hooded sweater underneath as layers were definitely needed today. It seemed as if I had waited ages for today which was why I was eagerly sat by the landing window, looking out and waiting for my friend like a sniper.

And then as if by my will alone there she was.

"Bless you RJ." I said looking up at the gods and blessing them for giving RJ her love for gossip as that was no doubt the reason she was early. I ran down the stairs and flew out the door as her wheels were still turning.

In the car there had been a constant stream of questions and I had to be very careful how I answered them. I didn't want to give too much away and there was no way I was telling her about what really happened that night. She was freaking out as it was, acting as though I was her new idol. She had even told me that her phone had not stopped ringing since the word got out that the new girl in town had landed the job.

She told me about how she was being asked, or better begged, to be introduced to me. When I asked 'why', she had simply replied,

"Because the club is the hottest thing to hit this town for decades and people travel for miles around to go there. And every year people try everything to get a glimpse of the man himself and every year they only get two chances. When he first arrives and when he leaves. This is the first year that they have stayed longer than a couple of weeks."

"How long do you think they'll stay for this time?" I asked as a new fear pierced through me. I hadn't realised that this wasn't a permanent thing and wondered how my obsession would carry on without the power source.

"How the Hell should I know? You work there, remember? But his sister has started college so who knows? Anyway, here's your chance to ask her."

I looked through the door to my next class and saw Sophia already at our usual seats, looking as perfect as ever. It always astounded me whenever I saw her, as her beauty was always breath-taking and as always, I felt self-conscious. Thankfully, Reed had not turned up yet, so we still had time to chat.

As soon as I entered the classroom all eyes were on me like a swarm of bees to the hive. It was only Sophia that looked kindly at me and on a sigh, I walked up to my seat.

"Hello Keira, how are you feeling?" She said softly.

"I'm feeling a lot better thanks, how about you?"

"Can't complain. The bruising has gone down a lot, that's good."

Again, these were the right type of compliments, as the last thing I wanted was for Draven to see me that way again. My cheeks flushed at the thought.

"Yeah, it looks better now and the rest I can hide with my hair at least." I pulled my hair to cover my cheek as evidence and she nodded. I noticed the boy behind her was staring at me and taking in every word I was saying. It looked as though he wasn't himself. I remembered the boy from last time and he was one of those types who kept his head down looking bored, with his hood pulled way over his head to hide the headphones in his ears. But now he was fully alert and had a strange tint to his eyes. Was he on drugs? What was his problem?

Sophia noticed me looking and turned to see my line of sight. When she saw the guy, she pulled a face I didn't understand but whatever it meant, it had taken effect, as the boy turned back to stare at the front. Only every now and again I would notice his eyes looking back at me. Did he know me from the club? Maybe it was due to the gossip about me that RJ had mentioned earlier.

Reed walked in, followed by a lackey student pushing a projector. I sighed in relief at the prospect of an afternoon free from Reed's droning voice.

"Today's class is about the understanding of observation. You are going to watch this documentary on World War 2 and write a paper on your interpretation of the events. I want constructive views on what you think about the issues surrounding the lead up to the breakout of the war."

Everyone in the class relaxed as they thought the same thing. An afternoon off from Dictator Reed! I, on the other hand, had thought of peace way too soon as Reed called my name.

"Miss Johnson, a moment if you please." The rest of the class turned and stared at me once more as though I was part of a freak show. The only one who didn't seem surprised was Sophia. This had been the class that I had been dreading and for good reason.

I got up out of my seat and a hundred eyes followed. I even felt as if I should do a little dance down the steps for all their effort. The film had started and thankfully our conversation would be drowned out by the sounds of fighter pilots and gunships.

"I understand you had an accident?" He said looking unusually uncomfortable.

"Yes, and I'm sorry I had to miss any lectures but the doct..." He cut me off waving his hand saying,

"Yes, yes, I know. I heard all about it and I wanted to say that just because you have been fortunate enough to be in the good graces of the University's Dean and that he asked me to treat you differently..." This time it was me that was to interrupt.

"I'm sorry, but I don't know what you're talking about. I haven't even met the Dean."

"Don't play coy with me Miss Johnson. I know that your employer is the University's benefactor and that you are somewhat of a favourite of his but that does not mean that you will receive instant A's without putting in the work!" I think my mouth actually fell open, as I was stunned!

"I don't know where you have your information from Mr Reed, but I most certainly intend to work in this class and any grades I get I want to have received them fairly and above all, legitimately. Mr Draven had nothing to do with my absence and why he thought it best to speak to the Dean on my behalf without my knowledge, is beyond me. So, if you will please excuse me, I am missing the reason for me being here...to learn!" I stormed off back to my seat shaking with anger. I couldn't believe that Reed had thought I was expecting special treatment and I was furious if Draven had implied as much. What did he care and why go to the effort? My questions were soon going to be answered as I went back to sit next to the very person who could answer them.

"Are you all right? Did he upset you?"

"I'm fine! Well actually I'm not fine. I would like to know why your brother decided it would be a good idea to speak to the Dean about me."

She nodded and looked over her shoulder at the boy behind. What did it have to do with him?

"Sophia?" I said again through gritted teeth, trying to keep my voice down.

"It was my fault, I asked Dominic to speak to him because I knew that Reed would take it out on you if you missed his lectures. I guess he took it the wrong way."

"Yeah, that's a bit of an understatement, he thinks that I should be getting all A's without any work and a pass in each class! Reed was furious at the thought."

"Oh... okay well I'll have it straightened out, but I'm sure that my brother wouldn't have asked for anything like that. The Dean probably has it all wrong." I felt a pang of guilt as I had been ranting like a child at Sophia, who was only trying to help me out.

"I'm sorry and I appreciate you helping me, I really do, it's just I don't want to be treated any differently, just because I'm your friend. I feel bad enough that your brother has gone out of his way for me but he really doesn't need to. I bet he thought life was a lot simpler before I turned up on the scene." I lowered my head in indignity at the thought. I was like a pest, or some virus that was clinging on. No wonder he didn't want me around, look at all the bother I had caused him already.

"I sincerely doubt that." She laughed before carrying on.

"Besides, I like having you around and really my brother doesn't mind, you just need to relax." She nudged my arm and I couldn't help but smile back at her.

"Okay, but no more special treatment. From now on I'm just an everyday friend who doesn't expect anything but regular friendship in return." She laughed and said,

"Regular it is, only in my life, I'm not sure I know what that is exactly."

"You'll be fine, we will take it one day at a time, and it just means I don't expect you to keep doing me favours. I'm going to be your friend regardless."

"Well, I like the sound of that." She said, and I noticed she wasn't the only one smiling, as the boy behind had also found something amusing in our not so secret conversation. Great, was this going to be added to the next lot of gossip?

"So, back to work tonight. Will you be okay?" Sophia asked as we exited the classroom.

"Yeah, as long as nothing else goes wrong and I can refrain from making a fool out of myself for at least one night, then yeah sure thing, piece of cake." We both laughed and the boy that was sat behind Sophia walked past me giving me a wink. I frowned, wondering what to make of it. I mean why wink at me when I was stood next to Sophia, surely that was like preferring a glass of Perry over a vintage champagne.

I said goodbye to Sophia and started to walk over to where I was meeting RJ. She told me earlier she would be busy chasing up a book from the Library, so I said that I would meet her at the car. I walked out the doors and I pulled up my hood and zipped up my sweater due to the cold.

It seemed that I had done this just in time as the heavens opened letting down big drops of heavy rain. I started to walk faster but didn't know why, as there was nowhere to provide shelter. I noticed the boy who had winked at me had now re-joined his friends and they all looked the same. Baggy jeans and hooded tops with rap star logos on the front. I tried to change my route but a large muddied green area was in my way so I had no option but to keep to the path. I walked past keeping my head low when I overheard the same boy talking about Reed's lesson.

"Yeah man, it was weird, I was like totally out of it! Dude what was I smokin' last night?" He looked different than he had done in class and when I finally walked past his eyes spotted me but there was not a hint of reaction, as if he didn't even recognise me. Had I got it wrong? Maybe he winked at someone else.

The rain was getting heavier now, quickly becoming a downpour. The raindrops dripped off my hood onto my nose and I tried to shake them off when I heard footsteps behind me getting faster as though someone was running. I turned to see who it was but bumped into some screaming girls who were worried about their hair and holding books over their heads in a poor attempt to keep dry. I apologised but it fell on deaf ears and I continued along my path. Then I felt a hand grab my shoulder and I screamed in response.

"Whoa, hey Keira, it's only me." Jack stood opposite me wearing a baseball cap that hid most of his face and the hood of his jacket over that for extra protection.

"Oh, hey sorry Jack, guess I'm a bit jumpy." He smiled down at me but I could barely see his eyes. He lifted a hand to my face and brushed my hair off my forehead that was covering the evidence of my fall. I blushed at the feel of his touch and one side of his mouth curved into a smile as he noticed.

"That's looking better every day." He let his hand drop and I shook off the drips that had rolled down my cheek from my hair. He linked his arm around mine and said,

"Let's get out of this rain you'll freeze in that jacket!" He was right, today was not the day to be wearing light weight material, especially one that wasn't waterproof. He led me over to the trees near where RJ had parked and we huddled close under a large overhanging branch that acted like a protective green canopy.

"Look, about the other night, I'm sorry I acted like that I was being a bit of a dick."

"Only a bit?" I teased and lightly punched him playfully on the arm.

"Oh, it's like that is it?" He said, and his long arm reach up above my head and grabbed the branch above as he was about to shake it.

"Oh no, don't you dare!" I reached above trying to grab his arm down before he could soak me, only it backfired. I lost my footing and fell into his arms, making him shake the tree anyway, soaking us both. We giggled like adolescents and his other arm wrapped around my waist steadying me. He leaned his head down and said in a deep smouldering voice,

"Do you know how cute you look all wet like that?" I stepped back and shoved him gently backwards in the stomach.

"Stop teasing me or I will get revenge." I threatened not being able to keep the smile from my lips as I tried to act serious.

"And what might this revenge be... umm?" He said as he took a step closer.

"How about I set RJ on you?" His face changed and I continued,

"Ha, I've got you there because I know that she can beat your ass!" I joked and he held up his hands to then place them on his heart in a dramatic way as though what I said had hurt. I giggled back as he replied,

"That's cold, I mean that hurts Keira. How could you be so mean?" He tried to look like he was about to cry but couldn't keep a straight face and we both surrendered to laughter.

"What did I miss?" RJ's pink head came into sight as she moved an umbrella out of her way, seeing both Jack and I standing there laughing.

"Apparently, Keira here is under the impression that you can kick my ass and she finds the thought heartlessly funny."

"Well, naturally I can take you, but that's common knowledge Bro." He then lunged for her taking her off guard making her drop the umbrella. He got her head in a headlock and started giving her a noogie.

"Say the words!" He said as he dug his knuckles deeper into her head.

"Never!" She said as she squirmed to try and get free.

"Say the words, Little Pink!"

"You're a homo!" She shouted.

"Now that's homophobic RJ and not nice, just say the words and I will let you free."

"Okay, okay ALL HAIL you, Master of the Rock, who can always kick my butt. You happy now Jack-ass?"

"It wasn't your best grovel, but I suppose it will do." He released her and she swung round punching him in the stomach. It was like watching a Punch and Judy show at the beach. The rain had eased off a bit allowing us to get in the car without getting drenched. I waved goodbye to Jack as he winked at me and it seemed to be my day for them.

Once I was home, I started on my assignment for Reed as now I was even more determined to make the point that I didn't require special treatment. No matter who my boss was!

I had made notes in class but considering I had already seen the documentary once before on the Discovery Channel, I already knew what I was going to write about. The notes had been mainly ideas and a few reminders on important dates, so I got to work and before I knew it I was finished.

Shutting down my laptop I looked at my bedside clock to see I had enough time to get ready, starting with something to eat. I examined myself in the mirror and thankfully my hair had survived most of the rain with the exception of a few curly bits around my face. My hair had a habit of going really wavy when wet and it would tend to dry this way if not brushed straight.

I let down my hair giving it the once over with a hair dryer and repositioned it up once more, off of my face. I pushed the clip through, but little bits escaped and hung down curling by my neck. I redid it again and again until I gave up, as it obviously wanted its own way.

I pulled the hair in front of my face hiding the now greenish yellow bruise and a small cut that I was hoping wouldn't scar. My hair looked different, but it did kind of suit me with some tendrils hanging down giving me a softer look. I put on my normal uniform of black trousers and a long sleeved plain black top to which I added black fingerless gloves, thus completing my outfit.

When I made it to the VIP, I decided to walk in-between the other tables trying to delay the inevitable. I now knew where I was going and could get to the bar without having to walk past the top table. Okay, so I knew I was completely chickening out here, but I just couldn't face him yet.

I noticed the other waitresses looking at me and the only one who waved was Rue. I was still dumbfounded that she knew it was me, seeing that she was blind. Maybe it was my smell, but when I had smelled my skin before leaving, checking I didn't smell of B.O from not showering, it had smelled differently because of the rain so I added some of Libby's perfume.

Once past the scarier tables of people that took looking different to a whole new level, I walked up to the bar to meet Karmun. I wondered if he ever took a day off.

"Here she is, back to fight another shift, how's the coconut?" He pointed to his own head as if I needed an indication to where it was but it was sweet just the same.

"Not one you can make a cocktail from..." I gave him a wink and he laughed.

"But seriously, I am fit and healthy and ready to be put to work."

It didn't take me long before I got back into the swing of things and everybody had asked if I was feeling better. Apart from the obvious, the ones that weren't part of my table plan and of course Draven.

I noticed him at his table surrounded by his usual entourage. There was his sister to his left and his brother to his right. I had never really noticed his brother before, only seeing him briefly when they first arrived, as I could never usually get past watching Draven. His brother was very handsome, but that was no shocker there. Their gene pool must have come from one Hell of a mix of handsome DNA.

His eyes were a combination of Sophia's and a bit of his brother's, but I could never imagine anyone in the world having the same eyes as Draven's. He was fair-haired, unlike his sister or his brother. His hair looked like gold and it was cut short in a halo of tight curls giving him a purely angelic look.

Only his eyes suggested otherwise. They looked cold and heartless when the person next to him spoke. He looked bored and un-amused. I shuddered at the glare he gave them. His body was only slightly smaller than his brother's, being leaner but he too looked powerful. He also looked younger with a softer skin covering his face and his chin was not as square as Draven's. However, again his eyes revealed there was nothing soft about him. He was also in a suit but he didn't wear a tie or waistcoat like his brother did. His look was more, smart/casual, whereas Draven's look clearly stated that he was the one in charge.

Sophia once again looked radiant in a black dress that was cut across the shoulders and went down into a pencil skirt around her perfectly shaped legs. The others around the table consisted of a mixture of people.

There was another beautiful young woman with flaming red hair that reminded me of Libby's, only she was very tall and athletic looking. She had a long swan like neck and amazing brown eyes that looked like dark chocolate. Her skin looked as if it had seen a lot of sun as it glowed with a golden hue. She was wearing a red suit as if ready for a day at the office. I felt a pang of jealousy, as though a snake had bitten me and the venom was making its way round my body via the bloodstream. That was the life I would never have, so why did I even bother thinking about it?

I pulled my eyes away from her perfect features and looked at the others. There was a Japanese man who wore a long black and red robe over black trousers. The material looked embroidered with symbols that were encircled twice creating a pattern. He held his hands together in his long sleeves and looked content, not smiling but also not frowning like the others. I counted one more guy and one other woman but they were out of my view, so I couldn't make out any details.

The rest of my night went by without incident or more importantly without any notice from Draven. My tables were cleared of empties and I was just serving the last one before it was time for me to leave. Like before, my night went by so quickly that I thought Karmun was joking when he told me that I only had fifteen minutes left. I went up to the bar to get my last tray of drinks when the blonde waitress, the one called Layla, pushed into me saying,

"MOVE IT!" Her face scowled at me and I could have sworn I had heard her hiss. She grabbed her tray and flicked her hair back as she strutted back to the top table.

"Whoa, what is her problem?"

"Don't you mean what isn't her problem? It would be a shorter list." I laughed at Karmun, who obviously thought the same way about her as I did.

I picked up my tray, but before I could leave with it, Karmun grabbed my hand and said the words that had my chest expanding in a silent gasp.

"Mr Draven wants to see you out on the balcony before you leave." Hearing this, only one thought screamed out in my head...

Oh shit!

Keira

48

UNKNOWN TERRITORY

As soon as Karmun had said the words I found it hard not to bolt. Since Saturday, I had wanted nothing more than to see him again but now I was very tempted to just make my escape. He made me so nervous, just the thought of going out there had my palms sweating.

As I went to deliver the drinks to my last table, I noticed Draven was still at his. Well, at least I could get out there first and get some fresh air. Maybe that would help steady my nerves. I handed out the drinks and as I walked past the bar put down my tray. I pulled my fringe down covering my damaged skin and walked towards the balcony. The last time I had been out there unbelievable things had happened, both shameful and blissfully wonderful.

I opened the doors only to find myself not alone as Draven was already there waiting. He had his back to me and was looking out into the dead of night. I took a step closer trying to remain quiet, but the glass doors closed behind me making a whoosh that gave away my presence. He turned to face me and I couldn't find my voice. Had he always looked this tall or was it just because now I was even more nervous, and it made him look even more imposing?

He took a few steps towards me and I couldn't help my actions as I took one step back. One of his eyebrows raised and he tilted his head slightly as if confused by my wariness.

"Sophia tells me you're feeling better." He said, as yet again he took another step closer, however this time I forced myself not to move. I couldn't say anything, but I managed to nod my head to indicate a yes. He looked as though he was trying very hard not to smile at my behaviour, which just made my annoying blush deepen. What was wrong with me? I would have to say something soon or I would just end up even more embarrassed. He carried on closing the distance between us and with every step he took my heart rate kicked up a notch.

"You're looking well, indeed a lot more colour than last time." His face looked controlled but there was a slight smirk edging its way to his lips. He was so close now that if I were to see his face I would have to look up, as it was I didn't have the nerve.

His hand reached under my chin pushing my face upwards to meet his eyes. They were as black as the night behind him, but they had a softer touch. He then looked away from my eyes and moved his fingers to my cheek. I must have stopped breathing because my chest felt tight, as though I was running out of air.

"Wh....What...are you...?"

"Ssshh, be still," he whispered gently as one of his fingers touched my lips briefly before going back to inspect my injury.

He was looking for my bruise and he pushed the hair hiding it out of his way. My hair fell in between his fingers and I couldn't help but close my eyes. The trace of his warm touch left a heated trail on my skin and I had the strongest urge to put my hand to his. He continued to brush the hair away from my face, so he could follow the red line with his thumb. He moved it over the cut from one end to the other and I bit my lip to hold in a moan. I could feel his eyes staring down at me, but I wouldn't meet his gaze.

Abruptly he dropped his hand and stepped back saying,

"I am satisfied." I didn't understand what he meant by this but when did I ever understand anything in the world of Draven? I knew that I would have to speak, or I would never forgive myself. So, with this in mind I inhaled as much air as my lungs could take and then spoke without trying to sound as nervous as I felt,

"I...I would like to thank you for what you did the other night and I'm sorry that I have been the cause of so much trouble." There, it was out now and there was nothing I could do about it but wait for his reaction.

"Trouble? I don't know about trouble, but it was definitely eventful, wouldn't you say?" I was pretty sure he was teasing me, and I smiled back still chewing my bottom lip.

He turned towards the door and my heart dropped when I realised that this was the end of our little meeting. However, my heart started hammering again in my chest as he stopped next to me.

"You're more than welcome, *Keira.*" He said, saying my name with such passion I thought I would need holding up again. I instinctively bit down so hard on my lip that my teeth nearly went through the skin. He hadn't left yet, and I wondered if he was waiting for me to say something. I only had seconds to find out. He leant down to my ear as if he had forgotten something and looking at my face had just reminded him, so he whispered,

"Oh, yes and Keira...such a shame you're biting your lip again." And with that he left me standing there alone trying to control my thoughts about not passing out. I felt a sudden chill as soon as he left and didn't know whether it was down to the cold night air or the fact that Draven wasn't there anymore. Every time I got close to him the warmth I would feel was like being covered in an electric blanket from head to toe, resulting in the opposite when he left. It was like it was being torn away from me leaving me feeling not only cold but also empty inside.

When I finally composed myself, I went back inside to get the bag that I had left here last time and my jacket ready to leave. I noticed the nasty blonde glaring at me from Draven's table. She only dropped her foul eyes when Draven noticed it too.

Once I was at home, I felt exhausted and my body ached. Not from working but after four days of doing nothing my body had become used to relaxing. No, working at the club was one of the easiest jobs I had ever had, all things considered. I thought about work and why it always seemed to go so fast? I realised it must be down to the fact that I spent most of my time thinking about Draven and what I would do if he spoke to me.

Which was why I found I didn't have any more mental power left to think about what time it was. Being around him was a drug and the longer I was there the more I wanted to stay. I'd only had a four hour shift tonight but that was better than nothing, as I had learnt recently.

I was about to get into bed when the phone rang and Jack was on the other end.

"Sorry to call so late but RJ's come down with something and isn't going in tomorrow." Jack said sounding a bit too pleased about it.

"Oh no, is she alright?"

"Yeah, she'll live. She's only got flu or something, but it hasn't shut her up yet so it's not that serious! But I was wondering, do you want me to pick you up tomorrow?"

"Umm, yeah... I mean that would be great, but only if you don't mind?" He laughed and said,

"Why would I mind? So, I will pick you up at the same time she does."

"Cool, thanks Jack. I will see you tomorrow then." He said good night and hung up the phone sounding a bit too happy about RJ's condition. I went to say goodnight to Libby and Frank before going back to my room to catch an early night.

I was back at the club for some reason, but I didn't know why. Had I forgotten something? I sifted through my thoughts for the explanation but came up empty. I had already walked up the steps to the VIP and was standing outside the door, not knowing what to do next. It was as if I had been in dreamland getting here and now someone had just clicked their fingers and awakened me.

I stood leaning up against the door and placed my forehead against the warm wooden panel. My head felt as though I couldn't stop it from spinning. The muffled noises behind the wood were getting louder and in turn making my head reel faster. I needed to get out but I didn't want to go back downstairs, as it would be no better there.

As soon as the thought had entered my head the door opposite unlocked and opened slightly. I couldn't help but be startled at the sound, as if waiting for something to burst through it at any moment. After staring at the opening for a while, I finally got the guts to go inside. I pushed it open cautiously still half expecting something to jump out from behind it, but there was nothing there. I walked through, knowing I was making the wrong decision but I couldn't help myself, it was as if I was being called... *or summoned.*

The night air hit me as, instead of walking into another room, I had entered a long open balcony. It was part of the house and it had a roof connecting it to the main building. I could make out a door at the other end but I didn't want to go that far yet. I went over to the stone balustrade that rose up in arches connected to the roof, allowing you to lean over the top of the stone wall and see the open space.

There was a massive portion of the house cut out like a giant courtyard. I looked around to find the same balcony on all four sides, which seemed to go on for miles. This wasn't a house it was a bloody castle! I looked down to see in the middle and strangely found a huge domed roof that reminded me of a mosque, sat at the bottom. It glimmered in the moonlight, making it look like polished copper. There was a sculpture at the very top of the dome but I could only make out a pair of wings, so imagined it to be a bird.

I was astonished at what my eyes were seeing and couldn't get over this actually being here. It felt wrong. As though I should be somewhere in Europe, but then looking at the domed section more like the Middle East. None of it made any sense. I felt a sudden chill up my body as though I wasn't welcome here and this was something I shouldn't have seen.

I turned to walk back through the door I had just entered but it had no handle. My hands went up and down the wood searching for something but there was nothing to be found. I pushed with all my body weight but it didn't budge. I was stuck! I was trying not to panic, but I could tell it was coming and soon. I now had no choice but to walk down the rest of the open hall and try the other door. I couldn't help but think about the trouble I was going to get into because of this.

What had I been thinking?

Unfortunately, the moon was going behind a cloud and I was about to be plunged into darkness. My breathing started to get heavier and I couldn't stop my hands from shaking. I walked forward only a few steps when, as if by magic, the lamp on the wall closest to me lit up in a rising ball of fire. I yelped out my shock and then watched as the blaze calmed to smaller flames at the top. I clamped my hands over my own mouth to hold back from screaming out.

The lamps were made of wrought iron cages which came down into long, deadly sharp points at the bottom. The iron twisted up in strips curling round iron bars, which held burnt glass in between the gaps. The flames licked the air as if the oxygen was making them angry.

I continued forward and when I reached the next lamp it did the same thing as though working off a sensor. There were five in total and they all lit one after the other, illuminating my way down the hall until I reached the door. Thankfully this door had a handle and when my hand touched the cold metal, the door opened automatically.

I turned around before entering and saw all the lamps die one by one making a popping, cracking noise followed by the sound of glass falling to the floor. It was as if they were exploding, so before the last one was extinguished and rained deadly shards on top of me, I quickly stepped through the door.

Once inside, I tried to calm my breathing the way the doctor had shown me to control panic attacks. I slid down the door and put my head in between my knees and concentrated on counting my breaths. I hadn't even seen where I was or what room I was in, but from the warm air, I gathered I wasn't outside any more. I finally looked up and once again I was in the dark. I was really frightened now and just wanted to get back to a safe place, one where I wasn't so exposed.

I stood up on shaky legs and heard a door open, but knew it wasn't the one behind me. I freaked out and tried to get back out onto the balcony, as at this point I would take weird exploding lamps over not knowing what was hiding in the dark any day. However, my hands searched in vain as it was identical to the last door... no handle...which meant no escape!

"Who...who's there?" I said trying to control my shaky voice but with the rest of my body trembling I didn't have much hope.

"You shouldn't be here." A surprised deep voice growled from the shadows and I jumped at the words.

"I...I'm lost" I stammered, hoping the voice belonged to someone who would help me.

"Oh no, you're not lost...you've been found." The voice was getting closer and made my skin give way to goosebumps. I was trying to move but something had me frozen to the spot.

Then the harsh voice ordered,

"Hala Olmak" ('Be still' In Turkish) I couldn't even move my arms, hands, or any part of my body apart from my head. I tried to block out whatever it was manipulating my mind and concentrated on pushing out the controlling force that was trying take over me. I tried to think of a way to free myself so started by drawing in my mind an image of me moving. First my fingers wiggled and then one of my arms was set free, it didn't take long before my body was my own again and I quickly shifted to the side.

"How did you do that?!" The voice snapped with what seemed like barely controlled anger. I didn't answer, not wanting to give away my location as I was still edging sideways.

"Here, let me give you some light, we wouldn't want you bumping into anything and hurting yourself again. I know you have a habit of falling down." His voice was smooth but finished with a rough edge. A candle lit somewhere close by and I could only see the space around me. An orange glow spread out, fading into the darkness and my eyes squinted to adapt to the small circle of light. I moved a little bit more, thinking if I could find another door I could then make a run for it. My foot knocked on something, but I steadied myself on the wall behind me.

"Careful, Keira." The voice knew my name? It was definitely a man's voice, as it was far too deep to be a woman's, yet I still didn't recognise its roughness. It moved around the room making it hard to pinpoint a location. I couldn't just wait here for him to get to me even though he obviously knew where I was, as the light was bouncing off my skin making me glow. Another flame lit up my way, but I could only make out the wall and floor. I kept side stepping feeling my way along when the voice spoke, reverberating around the room,

"I wouldn't keep moving that way if I were you." It sounded like a threat, but it didn't stop me. No, I could feel I was getting close to something as the air had changed.

"What do you want?" I said gaining some courage.

"Isn't it obvious...why, the very reason you came here... *back to me.*" I took four large steps away from the voice, but in the dark I couldn't see as the candlelight didn't reach as far as I had travelled. I hit something waist height, nearly falling and was going to tumble over it when a hand reached out and grabbed me, stopping me from falling. Strong hands pulled me back and in one swift movement had me twisted around and pressed solidly up against the wall.

He gently held the back of my head with one hand, so I wouldn't bang it against the stone my body was now pressed against. His body leant in close and his hand slid down from my head to my neck making its way to the front. Now he held his thumb on my throat without applying too much pressure.

It seemed to be calming my breathing as I was panicking on the inside but on the outside my body remained calm. We were still in the dark and I couldn't see the face in front of me, but I felt as though I was outside again. I wondered if the thing I had nearly fallen over was another balcony. If that was the case, whoever was stood opposite me now had just saved my life. I relaxed my muscles and the voice responded.

"That's it, easy now." I responded to this in a negative way.

"I'm not someone you can control, so get your damn hands off me!" I shouted but his other hand held my shoulder back as I tried to wrestle free from his hold. He gripped my shoulder like a vice, but he never once hurt me.

"I can see that." He said dryly.

"I asked you, what do you want with me?" I said trying to sound more angry than scared.

"Don't be frightened Keira, I would never hurt you." I don't know why but I trusted his words. Maybe it was down to the calming effect the movement his thumb was still making on my throat. His hand relaxed on my shoulder and moved down to my waist, but again when I tried to move away his hand flashed to my side holding me still against the wall.

"Be still!" He said with clear frustration in his voice. Then, it seemed as though he was fighting down his anger as he inhaled a deep breath.

"You want to know what it is I want, but first you will answer one of my questions." His face bent down to mine and felt so close I could smell his sweet intoxicating breath invade my senses.

"What...what do you want to know?" I shook my head as I couldn't think of anything I could offer him.

"Why did you come here?" He asked softly. I hesitated and tried to look away, but his hand slid up my top to get to my sides sending sexual sparks up my body. My chest rose heavily with the sensation and I let out a whispered moan, which made him show his teeth. I couldn't help but stare at a perfect white set but with larger canines, ones that had me gulping.

Did he really have fangs?

When I didn't answer he tried harder to provoke one from me and with his other hand he released my neck and stroked my cheek saying,

"Come now little one, tell me." He uttered softly trying to coax it from me. I tried to think of a different answer than the truth, but in the end, I just admitted the reason.

"I came here to find Dominic Draven." I said, and I was sure I could hear him smile at my answer.

"Is that right? Well, lucky for you... *you found him."* I tried one last attempt to move from under him, but he was too quick, and he grabbed my wrist pulling me back to him.

"Oh no, you don't." His voice held a hint of the truth, but I didn't want to believe it!

"You're lying! Draven wouldn't keep me here like this. He wouldn't even..." I trailed off, stopping myself before I said too much.

"He wouldn't what, Keira?" He demanded and when I didn't answer him I received a little shake.

"He..."

"Tell me!" He shouted getting impatient.

"He wouldn't care!" I shouted as I tried to see into his eyes, but the black night behind only enhanced the dark shape in front of me.

"Oh really...you know me that well, do you? Well, have you ever thought there is a reason I care to keep you here like this?" His voice sounded different, anger now mixed with hurt.

"No, why?!" I shouted still trying in vain to get free. When he had finally had enough of trying to prevent me from escaping, he pushed his body flush with mine, shocking me into remaining still. His frame felt solid with his muscles tensed against my smaller frame. His head bent down to my face and he said in earnest,

"I'm trying to keep you safe, as I said before, you shouldn't be here... not alone with me anyway." I heard the desperation in his words and I swallowed hard.

"Then let me go and I will leave," I said on a whisper.

"I'm afraid it's too late for that, I will have to deal with this in a different way." This didn't sound good, so I tried one last plea.

"I'm sorry that I came but please don't..." His hands left my body and grabbed my wrists like lightening as I said this.

"Don't do what... hurt you?" He didn't sound happy.

"Don't get rid of me." I said as a tear started to form in the corner of one eye. He laughed without humour and replied seriously,

"Why would I ever want to get rid of you? What would make you say that to me?" His hands tightened around my wrists. It was as if he was dumbfounded by my admission.

"Because I'm ...*I'm broken.*" I said as the tears got too heavy and fell down my cheeks. He released my wrists suddenly, as if knowing they were the source of my pain. He took a step back as if I had struck him and I took my chance to move.

"*Oh, Keira.*" I heard my name as sweet as a lover's caress against my cheek before I had chance to get in a step. I shook my head, but he stopped this by framing my face with big hands. He then used his thumbs to wipe the tears of pain from my skin.

"Well, if that is the case, then I guess I will just have to fix you..." He said with his forehead bent to my cheek, his voice hoarse as though it pained him to think of me this way. Then something changed. The very air around us seemed thick, too thick to breathe and I knew the reason why when I heard a rumbled moan. I looked up to see him looking down at my body, features still in shadow but there was no mistaking that sound.

The sound of hunger.

His hands left my face and travelled slowly down my neck. They only lingered for a moment before they journeyed further. The size of his hands covered the space of my chest as he palmed my breasts, lingering his thumbs longer on hardened nipples. This sent sparks of liquid desire straight down to the junction of my thighs. I couldn't help throwing my head back and releasing my own moans into the night. Then his hands continued onwards, spanning my lower stomach and holding himself back from dipping further. This was when he spoke,

"...but before I let you go, I owe you an answer to your question." He said stepping away from me, making me want to scream out in protest.

"You asked me what I wanted." He said repeating my earlier question, but I could barely hear him as the moon had come from behind the cloud revealing the wonderful truth, the truth I had known all along.

It was Dominic Draven.

He was removing something from the long jacket he wore, and metal flashed in the moonlight. I froze as he brought the implement closer to my face. I was about to run, but as though reading my thoughts, he grabbed me once more around the waist picking me up with one arm tightly curled around my torso. He lifted me up to the level of his face until our lips were at the same height. He leaned forward until they nearly touched and his mouth moved over mine as he whispered the answer,

"*I only ever wanted you.*"

Then suddenly he stabbed me in the neck, jabbing me so hard that I cried out in pain before everything went blurred and my body went limp in his arms.

Arms that want to keep me.

DRAVEN

49

LIFE AND DEATH AND THE SEXUAL FANTASIES IN BETWEEN.

By the time Thursday night came around it had been four days since I had seen her with my own two eyes. And then being forced to reach out to her only as Ava when the long and lonely nights showed me her sleeping form. In fact, like all the other times, it was the only moment my mind felt peace, something that was well known by my brother come the end of our time in England.

The truth was the trip hadn't been as successful as I had hoped it to be, for let's just say I didn't exactly come away from it with mortal blood on my hands as I had hoped and very much intended. Hence adding to my foul mood.

Ranka had discovered that Keira's real name was actually Catherine Keiran Williams, but for most of her life, she had been known as Keira. However, this wasn't where the story ended, and unfortunately for us both, she decided to go to university in Southampton. This was when her problems began.

It included stalking, kidnapping, murder, abuse and finally a suicide attempt, one that was never mentioned in the newspaper articles Ranka had discovered when researching her name. But I hadn't been interested in these stories written about the little they knew. What I wanted was the facts, the evidence and the details surrounding the case. Meaning what I wanted was the case file and one of the reasons I had gone to England to retrieve this in person.

I suppose you would say, one of the perks of my position and one that had always aided me in doing my job, was knowing important mortals in high places. As not only could you get close enough to them to manipulate their minds, if the need was great enough, but most of the time, money talked, and money got you results.

Which was why getting a case file sent to you when you knew the Commissioner of the Metropolitan police, who was good friends with the Chief Constable of police in Southampton, should have been easy. And usually, it would have been. That was if the investigation at the time hadn't been one big fuck up from the very beginning and evidence of such a cock-up wasn't then ordered to be buried as deep as it could go.

According to one of Ranka's sources in the police department, they had heard rumours that wind of these mistakes had gotten out to Keira's family and as compensation for not going to the press with it, they had wanted only one thing.

Keira wanted a new identity. This was so as she couldn't be traced, hence the unusual request being granted as she was placed under the witness protection program. She wanted a new life and one that could not be found if a certain murdering bastard ever made his way out of the maximum security's mental facility.

Hugo Morgan was at the time believed to be his name, but this poor fool had only ended up being one of his believed first victims. His real name was Douglas Brone, and frustratingly very little could be found on him. But again, this had also been something I had hoped to change if of course, I had received that case file when I had asked. Something that the Commissioner assured me would happen soon.

Yes, it certainly would and only once my lawyers had no doubt drafted up an agreement of confidentiality, assuring them that once I had the file, the first people I wouldn't take it to was the press.

Of course, Ranka had already started to gather up the details of their scandalous fuck up, something I gathered would become more evident in the case file, hence all the fucking red tape!

Understandably I had left this meeting feeling less than pleased and in need of something to destroy with my bare hands. Thank the Gods for my brother being there to smooth things over, that's all I could say.

For I think my sister would have gone for their throats had she heard how they had only seemed concerned for their own asses!

I couldn't even access the information on where in the country they were holding the prisoner, which only meant more time spent on research. But then came the utter outrage in my reaction to finding out that Morgan had been deemed criminally insane and his defence claimed that he was not fit for trial. Therefore, the outcome of this was no doubt that his life was deemed in the hands of the court and he was committed.

It also turned out that there were only three high-security psychiatric hospitals in all of England and Wales and strangely not one housed an inmate by the name of Douglas Brone, or even Hugo Morgan. Someone who he continued to claim to be even after his capture. Or so Ranka's source had told her.

Which in the end only meant that this trip had given me very little and was nothing more than a waste of time away from her. Even if my brother continued to point out that my presence had been needed in that meeting with the Commissioner in order to get him to pull the strings needed in getting me that case file.

Gods, if I just knew where it was stored, then I would have gone down there myself and retrieved it. But as it turns out, when the police decide to bury something, they didn't do so by half measures.

And by all accounts, all because some rookie cop didn't follow protocol and ended up barely even interviewing the kidnapper; some beat cop who had been approached by a woman who claimed that strange sounds were being heard on her neighbour's property. Noises that sounded like a girl's screams.

However, it seemed Morgan had charmed his way out of being checked at all and after only a brief exchange. For the cop didn't even feel it necessary to look up his details, where he would have discovered Morgan worked at the same university that Keira was last seen before being taken. If he had done so, then her imprisonment would have lasted only days, not over the six weeks it had!

This had been the point where I had to leave the office for fear of destroying one that was not my own! To know that she had endured such a time for so long! Well, I didn't know if the thought would bring me to my knees or simply hand over all power and control to my demon. One that would take hold forever and go on a killing spree to find all kidnappers this world had to offer. And in doing so, making every single one pay, just in hopes of coming across the right dark soul someday!

I wanted his blood coating my hands like no other before him. I wanted to watch him die at my feet and beg me for mercy. A mercy I wouldn't have granted him if I'd had another thousand years to consider it!

He needed to die, insane or not! I didn't care, for his death was the only solitude he would find once I started hunting him and find him I soon would. A vow made to myself but witnessed by the Gods! A vow that I also made, for before his death I would also make sure that Lucifer knew his name. And that solitude would be short-lived for the Devil would be there to welcome him personally when this Morgan found himself at the underbelly of Hell!

Yes, it was most certainly a good thing that I was back home, for I knew that one sight of my girl and both myself and my raging demon would be at ease once more.

Sophia had kept me well informed and said that Keira had, in fact, kept her promise and stayed at home. She had also been over there, which in the end had been the only thing powerful enough to get me from killing someone! Especially when listening to what had transpired between the two of them.

I had even managed to grin when she told me that Keira had tried to convince Sophia that she would be well enough to start back work early. Something I might have agreed with myself just so as to see her sooner...had I been in the country at the time of course.

But by the time we arrived back on Thursday morning, I found there was only one place I needed to be. So, despite Sophia's annoyance I took hold of a vessel in her history class, situated directly behind her. And as I knew it would, the moment I saw her, a calm washed over my entire being. It was like being reunited with my drug of choice after being forced to cut myself off completely.

I had listened to Sophia acting her part as the good friend and was actually surprised to see how at ease they both looked with one another, as if Sophia was portraying a side to her I had never seen before and strangely, it didn't seem like an act at all.

"Hello Keira, how are you feeling?" My sister asked the very same question I too was intending on asking later that evening.

"I'm feeling a lot better thanks, how about you?" she answered in a cheery tone, one I still found astounding considering all I had learned that she had been through. To know that she hadn't just given up on life. Even after one small moment of desperation, she had believed placing that sharp implement against her skin had been her only escape from her living Hell. But to look at her now, so happy and indeed still full of life, the life *he* had tried to claim. It made me...well, it made me *proud.*

"Can't complain. The bruising has gone down a lot, that's good." Sophia replied obviously for my benefit as she knew I would be pleased by this.

"Yeah, it looks better now and the rest I can hide with my hair at least," Keira replied showing her and making me want to laugh, for if she believed she was hiding any part of herself away from me, then she would soon learn her lesson from doing such. But then, as if she could sense me staring at her, she looked over her shoulder at the vessel of a boy she perhaps knew. Sophia also noticed and shot me a look, telling me silently to rein it in.

Soon there was little need for concern as the vile creature known as Reed walked in, believing no doubt that he was Master of this little universe he had created. Well, I'd had the means to put him straight, something I'd had done before leaving for England by speaking directly with the Dean.

After hearing of her worries for missing classes, I couldn't help but take it upon myself to intervene, reminding the Dean just how much money I 'donated' to the college. Therefore, I felt within my rights to request that a woman, who was soon to become my fiancée, be granted special liberties. Especially when she finds herself sick with worry over missing but a few classes.

Unsurprisingly he agreed with me promptly and assured me that he would take care of it personally. I left shortly after this and after first being assured that it was to be done discreetly, as Keira had no knowledge of this.

But more importantly, she had no knowledge of my plans to make her my bride, seeing as she would first have to consent to such a commitment. And well, in doing so, she would at the very least have to be made aware of my feelings for her. Meaning that, I was starting to agree with Sophia, that perhaps dinner and flowers were a solid first step in making that happen.

Either way, it was by the by, as during my meeting when asked what my personal connection with her was, I found myself with a choice. I could have said, she is one of 'my waitresses', which I was loathe to say or 'my fiancée' which I chose for obvious reasons.

I then added the embellishment of our first meeting while she worked for me. I wanted her world to know she was mine, even if I was somewhat sceptical about yet announcing such to my own, as there were certain aspects, I wanted to take care of. Like the assurance that she wouldn't run from me the first chance she got and also, that she wasn't taken away from me the first chance anyone else got!

In the end, Reed's droning voice brought me back to the room with an irritating glare cast his way. But then he mentioned my girl's forged identity, and I was on the verge of growling.

Sophia shot me a look the moment Keira started to make her way down to the front. Of course, once Sophia had found out that I had spoken to the Dean she hadn't held back in telling me how she thought it had been a bad idea, expressing such in abundance. But now, well it looked like my next rash decision made was about to come back to bite me.

"I understand you had an accident?" Reed asked in a brisk tone.

"Yes, and I'm sorry I had to miss any lectures but the doct..." Keira started to say before he rudely cut her off with a wave of his hand, a hand I now wanted to break off and hit him with!

"Easy there brother, try to remember that humans aren't used to hearing their peers growling," Sophia whispered back at me, and I looked to my left and right to see that those sat next to me had now started to back away, looking more than a little uncomfortable. I decided to ignore them, along with my sister and instead focusing back on their conversation at the front of the class.

"Yes, yes, I know. I heard all about it, and I wanted to say that just because you have been fortunate enough to be in the good graces of the University's Dean and that he asked me to treat you differently..." This time Keira was the one to interrupt, and she looked...well she looked pissed off!

"I'm sorry, but I don't know what you're talking about. I haven't even met the Dean."

"Don't play coy with me, Miss Johnson. I know that your employer is the University's benefactor and that you are somewhat of a favourite of his, but that does not mean that you will receive instant A's without putting in the work!" He said now making me want to break his neck, not just his hand!

How dare he speak to her that way! It was obvious now that the Dean had decided not to divulge too much into my relationship with her. But still, if this was what he did with the warning given by his boss, then he either didn't care much for his job, or he truly was an arrogant little prick, who never learned anything despite his profession!

"I don't know where you have your information from Mr Reed, but I most certainly intend to work in this class and any grades I get I want to have received them fairly and above all, legitimately. Mr Draven had nothing to do with my absence and why he thought it best to speak to the Dean on my behalf without my knowledge, is beyond me. So, if you will please excuse me, I am missing the reason for me being here...to learn!" This was the longest speech I had ever heard coming from her, and I realised that she obviously knew how to hold her own, for Reed now looked beyond capable of speaking.

However, this hadn't exactly gone well for me either as I hadn't come out of her speech unscathed and now it looked as though Sophia was going to be in the firing line because of it. She quickly shot me a scornful look before Keira got back to her side.

"Are you all right? Did he upset you?" Sophia asked, already knowing that he did.

"I'm fine! Well, actually I'm not fine. I would like to know why your brother decided it would be a good idea to speak to the Dean about me."

Sophia granted me another look of disdain before Keira claimed her attention again.

"Sophia?" My sister released a sigh and decided to do some damage control on my behalf, and I loved her for it.

"It was my fault, I asked Dominic to speak to him because I knew that Reed would take it out on you if you missed his lectures. I guess he took it the wrong way."

"Yeah, that's a bit of an understatement, he thinks that I should be getting all A's without any work and a pass in each class! Reed was furious at the thought." She said making me realise that Sophia had been right yet again and it was very quickly becoming apparent that she knew the girl better than I did. Needless to say, it was a bitter pill to swallow.

"Oh... okay well I'll have it straightened out, but I'm sure that my brother wouldn't have asked for anything like that. The Dean probably has it all wrong," my sister said, again trying to paint me in a better light than I most likely deserved. Especially not considering that this had been exactly what I had been implying when speaking with the Dean.

"I'm sorry, and I appreciate you helping me, I really do, it's just I don't want to be treated any differently, just because I'm your friend. I feel bad enough that your brother has gone out of his way for me, but he really doesn't need to. I bet he thought life was a lot simpler before I turned up on the scene." On hearing this the vessel, I had been using nearly swallowed his own tongue! Well, she had one thing right, life had most definitely been simpler before she turned up, of course, it had also been boring, uneventful, dull, wasteful, predictable and an endless loop of days that merged into years and then on into decades.

So basically... *personally meaningless.*

"I sincerely doubt that," Sophia said on a laugh, for she knew exactly what my thoughts were right now.

"Besides, I like having you around, and really my brother doesn't mind, you just need to relax." She added, nudging her arm and finally bringing back that smile I loved so much.

"Okay, but no more special treatment. From now on I'm just an everyday friend who doesn't expect anything but regular friendship in return." Keira said injecting me with that warmth I always felt around her when witnessing something she did that was sweet and kind natured.

"Regular it is, only in my life, I'm not sure I know what that is exactly," Sophia admitted making me grin, for she was right, regular just wasn't something we could relate to in our family.

"You'll be fine, we will take it one day at a time, and it just means I don't expect you to keep doing me favours. I'm going to be your friend regardless." Keira told her again, keeping the grin on my face and making it grow bigger before she caught me looking at her.

"Well, I like the sound of that," Sophia agreed, no doubt in an effort to save me from being questioned by the girl.

After this, I spent the rest of the lesson watching her and my sister interacting and looking forward to the day that I could do so through my own eyes. I found myself pleased that they had formed a genuine friendship and hoped that one day they felt for each other as sisters.

It also made me realise that my sister hadn't ever really had this type of connection before. Having only one real friendship that I knew of and that was with the Imp named Pipper. Someone she must have missed when loyalties forced them to go their separate ways.

But I never stopped to ask myself how it must have affected her until now. Something I honestly felt a little ashamed of, as she was my sister and therefore worth my time in considering her feelings on the matter. However, I had not, which had been my failing. One now brought to light by the goodness and light that was my Chosen One.

By the time the lesson had ended, and she was walking out with Sophia asking her about tonight, I found myself unable to just let her go without some way of goodbye. Even if it were impossible for her to know that it was me. So, I granted her a wink and walked away, leaving this vessel soon after.

Which brought me back to the night and the moment she arrived for her shift back at the VIP, making the place feel whole once more. But then I noticed that her obvious shyness was back. As instead of walking past my table, which was the more direct route to the bar, she instead weaved in and out of the tables behind, getting there that way.

However, this time instead of getting annoyed or angry at it, I tried first to understand it, now taking the time to see things through her eyes. She believed my actions were those taken for the love of a sister's wishes. She also believed I thought life was easier before she came into it. She believed every gentle moment shared between us was just a dream she created in her mind.

Therefore, she had no idea how I really felt for her or the lengths I had been willing to go to just be with her. Just to see her one more time before the night seized the day, or when the sunrise signalled the need to leave her window. She simply had no idea just how deeply these roots of obsession lay heavily entwined around my heart, crushing it with the weight of emotions I didn't yet fully understand the meaning of.

She was just a girl with a crush on her boss. And I was just a King who had lost his heart to a mortal, one fated to be mine for the rest of eternity. The differences between us were oceans apart, and yet here we were, in the same room fighting for the moment we could crack the layers of doubt holding each other back. I, for her, was just a fantasy, a dream to be had in the safety of her own mind. But in the here and now, I was only a rejection she feared in its place and ironically, one I would never give her.

So, as the night drew to an end for her time here, I slipped passed unseen onto the balcony, nodding to Karmun and telling him silently to inform her I would be waiting. I kept my back to the doors, looking out into the world and for once seeing nothing of its dark beauty. But then there was her, and for a simple moment, I closed my eyes just listening to her take a breath the moment she saw me.

I turned to face her and noticed how she looked so unsure, so fragile. I took a few steps towards her, and her reaction was to take one back in return. I gave her a curious look that only ended up making her blush. Was she that wary around me now, after only four days apart? Or was she simply nervous? I couldn't yet tell, so I said,

"Sophia tells me you're feeling better." I also took another testing step closer, happy that this time she didn't move. But she didn't answer me either but simply nodded. That's when I knew that it was nerves and I felt myself hold back a knowing grin. So, I continued to eliminate the distance between us by getting closer despite her elevated heart rate because of it.

"You're looking well, indeed a lot more colour than last time," I told her teasingly indicating to her blush, one that deepened, and a knowing smirk threatened once more.

But she still wouldn't look at me, and I found myself pushing for just that, so I took the last step needed to put me well beyond her comfort zone, now commanding all of her personal space. Then I reached under her chin and took her options away from her, forcing her gaze to hold my own. She looked close to begging me for something, but she didn't yet know what. Those beseeching eyes, asking so much of me, eyes that pulled at the centre of my soul, stripped my heart bare and still asked for more... and all in a single look.

In the end, I had to force my eyes from her own, for they had too much power over me. They were dangerous and felt as if they would consume me whole. As if one day they would take everything from me and leave me mere flesh and bone and nothing else.

I don't know where these thoughts were coming from, but I wasn't naive enough not to know its name... *fear.*

I looked instead to the reason I was out here now, to check for myself that she was well. So, I gently ran the backs of my fingers over her cheek, and very nearly reminded her to breathe.

"Wh....What...are you...?" She stuttered endearingly, making me place a finger to her lips for but a moment, while I whispered a gentle order down at her,

"Ssshh, be still," Then I went back to her injury, pushing her hair out of the way and a smile played at my lips remembering how she had claimed she was going hide it today to Sophia. I swear just the sight of those soft golden strands falling in between my fingers had me craving to fist a hand in her hair and bruise her lips with the force of my kiss.

Even Keira seemed to need to close her eyes as if she were feeling this deep connection herself. I then tried to concentrate tracing the red line of her cut with my thumb instead of the line of her lips where I wanted them to open before she could suck my thumb inside. And I knew each soft caress I made she felt it in a way only a lover would. And for her pained expression, it was one that spoke only of her lust, one being drawn from her with every touch I made.

But as cruel as it was for both for us, I knew that I had no choice but to let my hand drop, for if I continued this any longer, then there was only one place it would lead...*the point of no return.*

"I am satisfied," I told her meaning so much more than just the healing of her injury. But then she looked for a moment to be fighting with herself on a decision she only just decided to make, first taking a deep breath to do so.

"I...I would like to thank you for what you did the other night, and I'm sorry that I have been the cause of so much trouble." Now hearing this did make me smile, for she was trouble alright, she just didn't know that she was the best kind.

"Trouble? I don't know about trouble, but it was definitely eventful, wouldn't you say?" I teased making her smile back before promptly going back to punishing that bottom lip again.

So, before I stopped her by taking it in my own and showing her just what such an action did to me. I moved to walk back into the VIP, forcing myself to put an end to our encounter before she pushed my limits to breaking point.

Just the scent of her had my demon growling at me to push her slight frame against the wall and claim her against it. To pin her arms above her head, holding her captive there with one hand shackling her delicate wrists, while my other hand explored all those delicious curves of hers with my lips.

By the Gods, I had to leave, for that image alone was enough to cause yet again a certain part of me to stand to attention and take notice. However, I couldn't pass up the temptation to grant her something more after she had so sweetly thanked me. So, I paused next to her and said,

"You're more than welcome, Keira." This made her bite down so hard on her lip, I was surprised when blood didn't pool around her teeth before dripping down her chin. A sight no will in Heaven and Hell would have stopped me from cleaning away with my tongue.

I had never felt the urge to bite a mortal so much in my entire being, and I knew that this desire would cause problems for me when the time came in making her body mine. By the Gods, but just seeing her biting her own lip made me want to do so myself and draw blood from it. So, I asked myself, how little would my own willpower be reduced to when she was spread naked on my bed with all that creamy pale skin on show.

Just the thought of plunging into her tight depths as I took her breast into my awaiting mouth, before biting down around her nipple and sucking in her life's blood, feeding from her as she in turn fed from me by milking from my cock. Gods! But that image would plague my mind until the day I was able to make it a reality!

An image so clear in my mind and one so erotic, I couldn't help but clench a fist at my side, all the while maintaining my cool façade by leaning down to her ear and whispering my last tease,

"Oh, yes and Keira...such a shame you're biting your lip again." Then I walked away, hoping that the last image I left in her mind was my sexual tease from the night I drove her home, telling her that I remembered and so should she.

After all, that Gods be damned lip of hers was imprinted on my mind...

All fucking day!

DRAVEN

50

LURED INTO ANOTHER MAN'S TRAP

After Keira had finished her shift, I vowed on this night not to go to her. It was becoming riskier every time I did so, as her mind, even in that dream-like state, was becoming more of a challenge to control. It was as though she was unknowingly building up greater walls and blocking me out as her only defence while vulnerable.

Something which I found both frustrating and curious at the same time. How she was even managing to achieve such a thing was still far beyond my comprehension. As at least with Jack, I knew the reasons, no matter how much I disagreed with them. Something I would be appealing against in regards to the decision made by the Gods.

But with Keira, then how she had become so powerful without even knowing it herself was not something I could explain. And I was worried that if I pushed too much, too hard, then in that single moment that I needed to access her mind the most, it would be too late, and I would be locked out forever. Hence why I was being cautious now and hence the reason for my foul mood.

Especially seeing as Sophia was throwing one of her 'Play parties' in her own wing of Afterlife. A place that was essentially like a large apartment sectioned off from the rest of the house and one with its own private club attached. I had, of course, spent many a night in one of these parties of hers and twenty-three years earlier would have enjoyed partaking in them with one or two angels for the night. Or if my mood was feeling particular dark at the time, a wild demon in need of taming in the bedroom.

But that had been an age ago and along with it, a different me. For since that dream of finding her took hold of me that night, I had long since lost my taste for such things. And now that I had actually met her, well, I hadn't just lost my taste for it but I found stepping foot in there utterly abhorrent.

Sophia had even asked that once I claimed Keira would I be joining them again, to which my deep resonating growl was answer enough on what I thought of that idea.

However, she simply said,

"Spoilsport!" over her shoulder before leaving to go and get ready for her idea of sexual festivities. Which meant her personal space would be transformed in no time and end up looking like a high-end sex club. Something I most definitely would be keeping Keira far, far away from in the foreseeable future.

Which was why I found myself for once with little to keep my mind occupied, as all business was concluded for the day. The club had closed hours ago, and there had been no progress made with regard to Ranka's investigation as to the whereabouts of the dead man walking *Morgan.*

I was also still waiting for my team of lawyers to draft the right contract, assuring all involved that once that case file was in my possession, it was to stay there and not ever make its way into anyone else's hands again.

Well, there was no worry in regards to that, for once I had scoured every inch of it for my own assessment on the matter, I was then clicking my fingers and setting the whole fucking thing alight!

But right now, that would have to wait, for I'd had enough for the night. So, I pushed back on my office chair and rose, leaving the room in darkness after killing the lights with a thought. Then I walked down the long hallway that led to my own chambers directly ahead, already wondering if there was much point in even trying to find sleep? It also made me wonder if sleep would come easier when having her resting by my side? Or would the temptation become too much to allow such slumber to claim her when I could instead?

I was soon deep in thought, thinking of all the creative ways in which I could wake her if sleep evaded me. Something I suspected it would when having her lying next to me. But this was when a sudden noise distracted me from my happy thoughts.

I frowned wondering why anyone would be where I suspected they were right now unless somehow someone had broken into my home. It was unusual sure, but not impossible if doors had been forgotten to be locked or someone knew the keycode to get inside.

I rolled my eyes, not typically in the mood for such things, but with everyone elsewhere and no doubt losing their minds to lust...something I, unfortunately, couldn't yet claim I thought bitterly, then I decided to investigate. At the very least it may offer some reprieve from my insanity I thought dryly.

So, I walked back into the VIP to see if I could pick up on any mortal life as I suspected to find. However, the very last thing I did expect to find was a scent I knew well...

"Keira?" Just saying her name aloud made the possibility of her being here all the more real. So, I walked to the door at the opposite end to the bar. It was one she would always enter through, ready for her shift, so I opened the door half expecting to find her standing there, for all other doors were always kept locked.

But there was no one but the lingering memory of her. I frowned and shook my head trying to make sense of it because her scent was even stronger now and it would not have been so from leaving hours ago.

So, I tried the doors on the small landing, one that I knew led onto the large open balcony walkway that framed above the centre of Afterlife's core. A place where the Temple roof could be seen in all its golden glory when catching the sunlight, one that strangely under the moonlight took on a reddish tinge making it look more like copper.

However, this door was only usually accessed by Vincent as it was the quickest way to his own wing of Afterlife, but I very much doubted that he would have forgotten to lock it.

Nevertheless, I tried it now to find as expected, it was locked. I shook my head, now feeling foolish and with her scent deeply embedded in my memory, well my mind was obviously playing tricks on me. I turned around and went back into the club, annoyed at myself for even thinking that...but wait, what was that down below?

I jumped off the balcony, landing on my feet to the club below and just shy of where the item was on the floor. I knelt down to pick it up and slowly brought it to my nose, inhaling deep when there.

"Keira," I said her name again, this time with more certainty, and that was when I heard the slamming of a door closing suddenly. It was the one closest to the bar. The side door she knew the code to. The second it did this the next sound to be heard was a woman's faint cry of fright.

"KEIRA!" I shouted her name, released my wings and flew up to the VIP, before looking around in desperation trying to find out where that scream had come from! I then decided I needed to find some perspective of sound so ran out on to the balcony and released my wings once more, taking me up and over my home.

There I landed and could listen out for the next time she made a sound. Only there were no more cries, only...the slamming of a door!

I knew where it had come from, a small reading room not far from the main library and like most rooms, it too had its own balcony. So, I flew over the roof and swooped down, landing gently on the small narrow platform, as this one had a lower line of balustrades making it easier to land on the narrower stone slabs. It was only a small space, just built wide enough for a few seats that were currently inside and nothing more. But its two joining arches mirrored the larger ones in my office, for it too had no doors, just the dark room beyond.

A room that wasn't as empty as it should have been.

I crept inside veiling myself in the shadows the night offered, for no candle had burned in this room for a long time. Which meant that the girl who now got up from the floor on shaky feet wouldn't have been able to see a thing. Let alone that her chance of escape would have been the door opposite her, one I closed gently with my mind just in case.

However, hearing this frightened her further and she turned quickly trying to get back through the door she had been leaning against, making me act quickly. I took away the handle so as she had no means of escape.

No, first I needed to get to the reasons why she was here, as she wasn't exactly dreaming this time, that much was obvious. Had she taken it upon herself to break in? I had to confess it seemed the only explanation. But even then, I just couldn't see it. I couldn't imagine it was something she was brave enough to do and for what reason?

Well, it was time to get to the bottom of it, and to do that I decided to mask my identity for as long as possible. For I knew she wouldn't have trusted herself to speak the truth to her boss, someone she would no doubt associate getting into trouble with. But with someone else, *then maybe.*

Well, it was time to test the theory and maybe get some extra answers alongside it.

"Who...who's there?" she asked with a tremble to her voice that I didn't like hearing.

"You shouldn't be here," I told her, hoping she would explain how or why she came to be, not only in this room, but in my club after closing. Because if there was one thing I knew with absolute certainty and that was she did not get here alone and without a supernatural influence pushing her limits. For the girl was barely brave enough to look me in the eyes, let alone be brave enough to infiltrate my home after dark, knowing the chances of getting caught were more than likely. A discovery that even if not guaranteed by myself, it would most certainly be one to reach my ears the moment she was found.

But she must have known this?

"I...I'm lost," she stammered, and I shook my head despite her not being able to see me do it. Then I informed her,

"Oh no, you're not lost...you've been found," I said, stepping closer to her and when she knew this, she tried to move. But then she sucked in a quick breath and I frowned, for something was off. I closed my eyes a second, concentrating on what it was as I went searching for it. A presence that lingered somewhere. That's when I felt it! Something foreign, something very old had its influence over her!

I needed to stop her moving, so that I could try and detect more of this control that still faintly lingered over her and discover the origins of where it was coming from.

"Hala Olmak" I ordered in a harsh tone, making her mind still in Turkish, knowing she wouldn't know what I had said, but her mind would still respond to the command. I needed to focus on what it was I was sensing and no doubt the reason for how she came to be here. Had something manipulated her mind into coming back to Afterlife and if so, then why...for what gain?

It didn't make sense to bring her to me now?

But as I was asking myself this, my girl was using this time to discover the full capabilities of her own mind and the moment she shifted to the side, I was astounded!

She wasn't just capable of defying me in her dreams when her mind felt vulnerable like I first thought. No, her barriers were something she herself had consciously built up to protect herself...but against what exactly? Was it really possible that there was even more that this girl was keeping from me!?

"How did you do that?!" I found myself snapping, annoyed with myself that I hadn't even given the possibility thought before. But then I focused on where she was trying to get to and knowing how clumsy she was, I was worried about her hurting herself. Especially seeing as how there was enough furniture in here to trip over, let alone her own feet.

"Here, let me give you some light, we wouldn't want you bumping into anything and hurting yourself again. I know you have a habit of falling down," I said unable to help myself. However, I still made sure to keep my voice unrecognisable for the time being and doing so by giving it a rougher edge by letting my demon take more control over our speech.

Then I clicked my fingers making one of the candles closer to her spark to life. The moment the light lit her features I almost gave up the ruse, just so that I could go to her. Gods, but she was painfully beautiful, like a glowing angel commanding my dreams. An image I could easily become lost in.

But then she knocked her foot against something, and all focus became on her wellbeing and right now, that included keeping her upright.

"Careful, Keira," I warned letting her know that I knew her name. She didn't respond to this or ask me how I knew her. She simply continued to slowly move around the room as if searching for something. So, I continued to light her way, dragging more of the shadows around me still keeping myself concealed from her. But the way she was heading was concerning me, which was why I warned her,

"I wouldn't keep moving that way if I were you." Something she didn't take too kindly to, as she continued and also demanded,

"What do you want?"

"Isn't it obvious...why, the very reason you came here..." I said pausing the second she made a run for it, one that would have landed her hurtling off the sheer drop below had I not caught her.

"...back to me," I said as I grabbed her from behind before spinning her around so as I could press her up against the wall. Meaning that parts of my fantasy earlier in the VIP were coming to life. But instead of imprisoning her hands, I instead cupped the back of her head so that she didn't hurt it on the stone she was now pressed against.

Then I took a deep breath, just knowing that I had her in my arms once again and relishing the moment for how right it felt. But while I was finding my calm and peaceful place, she, on the other hand, was starting to panic.

So, I eased my hand from behind her head and gently placed my thumb over her throat without causing harm. Then I focused my mind on her body, getting her now to take much calmer breaths. I could see her mind working its way through what just happened, and I knew the moment she knew I meant her no harm, for why else would I have saved her life.

I knew she still couldn't see me, as it was too dark out here with my back to the small amount of moonlight that was trying to penetrate the clouds. So, with my voice still holding that rough demonic edge to it, she still had no clue as to who held her captive right now. And for the time being, this was how I wanted it to remain.

"That's it, easy now," I said thinking this would calm her further, but I was wrong. She turned into a little firecracker of anger and lashed out suddenly as if I had unknowingly hit a nerve.

"I'm not someone you can control, so get your damn hands off me!" she shouted trying to break free and just as she tried to twist out of my hands, I placed one on her shoulder and applied enough pressure to press her back to the wall where I wanted her.

"I can see that," I said in annoyance, for she was right, I couldn't control her.

"I asked you, what do you want with me?" she asked, once again trying to sound braver than I suspected she was in that moment. Which is why I told her,

"Don't be frightened, Keira, I would never hurt you." I also continued to try and soothe her with my touch, and once assured she was more compliant, I lowered my hand on her shoulder down to her waist. However, the second she took this as an opportunity to try and move from me again, I gripped her tighter and held her immobile, warning her this time,

"Be still!" I found myself having to take another deep breath through my mounting frustration, wishing now we were back in her bedroom where controlling her had been so much easier.

"You want to know what it is I want, but first you will answer one of my questions," I said deciding it was time to discover exactly what was going on here. Especially now that the strange hold on her earlier had vanished the second, I touched her when saving her from going off the side.

I bent my neck, getting closer to her face as I knew this would intimidate her enough to answer me.

"What...what do you want to know?" she asked shaking her head as if unsure of what it was I could possibly want from her...*oh, if only she knew.*

"Why did you come here?" I asked using a gentler tone, one that I hoped to lure the answers from her, along with my touch. So, I made sure to connect my skin to hers by sliding my hand up her sides, bunching the material as I went. I knew she felt it the way I did by the way a breathy moan slipped from her lips and the second I heard it, I couldn't help but grin down at her. I wanted her to know that I had her now and that she was trapped in my hands.

"Come now, little one, tell me," I whispered caressing her cheek and still feeling every shuddered breath taken with my hand spanning the side of her ribs hidden under soft flesh. Just the way it should be for I had no desire to feel bone beneath my fingers, but her supple skin and the shapely curve to her waist pleased me greatly.

But then my wandering hand froze the second she gave me the answer I had been waiting for, only hearing her say my full name for the first time was one I would never forget.

"I came here to find Dominic Draven." I allowed my smile to grow, letting it be known that she had pleased me.

"Is that right? Well, lucky for you..." I paused, moved in closer and whispered,

"...You found him." But as if she found this so unbelievable, she slipped out from beneath my gentle hold and made one last attempt to

run from me. Ah, my silly little waitress, did she not realise who she was dealing with, for a rabbit rarely outruns the wolf?

Proving this, I snapped an arm out so fast, she wouldn't have seen it before she felt my hand shackle her wrist.

"Oh no, you don't," I told her and pulled her back to me with little effort.

"You're lying! Draven wouldn't keep me here like this. He wouldn't even..." she told me, trailing off quickly before she revealed too much, making me frown in question.

"He wouldn't what, Keira?" I asked only when she wouldn't reply. I shook her slightly, bringing her mind back to my question.

"He..." She stopped again, and I growled impatiently,

"Tell me!"

"He wouldn't care!" She suddenly shouted, and the moment she said it I flinched. I wouldn't care? How could she say that to me? After everything I had done to keep her safe, all I had suffered in waiting and all for what...*for her!*

"Oh really...you know me that well, do you? Well, have you ever thought there is a reason I care to keep you here like this?" I asked bitterly, now in two minds on whether I should try and make her understand or simply leave. But I knew even after thinking it that I couldn't just let her go now. Not without first ensuring she was home safe and no doubt believing this was all just another one of her nightmares... *featuring yours truly,* I thought bitterly.

"No, why?!" she shouted back, still struggling against my hold in a useless attempt to be free from me. But I had hit my limit and on more than just her pointless struggles. So, I finally made this known the moment I stepped into her, pressing my whole body against hers and trapping her in completely. I then bent my neck, getting as close to her face as possible with our height difference so I could tell her the truth,

"I'm trying to keep you safe, as I said before, you shouldn't be here... *not alone with me anyway.*" She swallowed hard, and I couldn't say that in that moment I blamed her.

"Then let me go, and I will leave,"

"I'm afraid it's too late for that, I will have to deal with this in a different way," I told her knowing that my options here were limited as there was only going to be one way now to make her fall asleep, for her mind was too strong like this for me to control.

"I'm sorry that I came, but please don't..." hearing this desperate plea from her now was a like receiving a hundred lashes to my heart, and my actions could not have been helped. I grabbed her wrists so quickly even I didn't fully register the move. Then I demanded in an accusing tone,

"Don't do what... hurt you?" She took a moment of shock before looking left and right as if searching for someone...a saviour perhaps. The thought had me near murderous! But then I soon realised I had been wrong. It wasn't a saviour she was looking for... *it was escape from the saviour who held her captive.* It was escape from having to admit her biggest fears. I knew this when she would barely look at me the moment she began to speak once more.

"Don't get rid of me," she said in a small voice, and its meaning was not entirely how it sounded at first. So, I laughed without humour knowing this was the complete opposite to how I felt. And the irony wasn't lost on me, which admittedly made me angry. Especially as all ever wanted was to have her, keeping her by my side for all eternity.

"Why would I ever want to get rid of you? What would make you say that to me?" I demanded tightening my hold to emphasise my point. But then this was when she fully admitted her fear to me, and the second she did all anger washed away with the sight of her tears.

"Because I'm ...*I'm broken,*" she said in a small unsteady voice and just hearing those words nearly broke my own heart along with hers. Suddenly I let go of her and the scars I knew where hidden under her gloves. But she took this as an opportunity to get away from me. However, the action no longer caused me any pain, for I knew now it wasn't me she was truly running from...

It was herself.

"*Oh, Keira,*" I whispered against her cheek the moment I recaptured her for she barely made it a step away from me. She started to shake her head, telling me, no but I would let her, and nor would I listen. Instead, I simply framed her face with my big hands and used my thumbs to wipe away her tears. Then I rested my forehead to her cheek and told her,

"*Well, if that is the case, then I guess I will just have to fix you...*" and doing so the only way I knew how, by loving her the way I did. I just needed the time to prove this to her. Time my willpower around her wasn't allowing for, as like this, being this close and having her in my arms now was a beautiful torture of the likes I had never known.

Because there was no denying how much I wanted her, not just in my bed but in my life. I wanted her like there was a fire in my soul and like this, it was burning out of control.

Which was why after just one breathy moan of hers, one she no doubt didn't even realise she was making, I very nearly snapped. A rough moan of my own rumbled from deep within me, one that couldn't be helped after a single look down at her quivering body, one I wanted to possess with a scorching fever.

My hands left her face of their own accord, trailed first down her delicate neck before crossing my first line by spanning her full breasts.

They fit perfectly in my hands, and the weight of them I couldn't help but test for a moment before moving on and teasing her hardened nipples with my thumbs.

I knew this had hit the spot for her as she threw her head back and released a moan of her own, this time not one she tried to hide. I wanted to spend more time playing with her, testing her limits of pain as I pinched her nipples, enticing and restricting the blood flow to them. But then I knew that would have, in that moment, gone too far. So, I left my bounty, looking forward to the nights and days when I could be free to tease them when naked and begging for my touch.

Instead, I let my hands slip lower under her breasts, down her ribs and down to her lower belly stopping just before I could reach that one place I knew at that moment I couldn't go. Because if I did, then there would be no force alive with enough power to stop me from making her mine completely. So, I told her,

"...but before I let you go, I owe you an answer to your question," I said forcing myself to step away from her and at least satisfied by the little sound of protest coming from her, for she looked even less pleased about me letting her go than I felt.

"You asked me what I wanted." I reminded her just as the moonlight finally became free of the drifting cloud, showing now the truth she had no doubt known all along.

It was me who had kept her captive. The Dominic Draven she had wanted to find here. I could see it in her eyes as the truth was forced upon her. But as distracted as she may have been, she couldn't help but notice what I was doing now, after creating something in my jacket pocket that I really loathed to create. But I had no choice, for her mind had already begun to fight me without her knowledge.

No this was the only way.

So, I brought the injection closer to her and knew the moment that she intended to run from it. So, I grabbed her, banding one of my arms around her waist and lifting her feet from the ground so as she was now level with my face. Then I told her with my lips to hers,

"I only ever wanted you."

Then I plunged the needle into her neck, hating the cry of shock and pain I caused. I knew the drug would take a few moments to take effect. So, I held her tight to me and soothed her as she started to whimper against my shoulder. I hated knowing that I had done this to her, but I hated dealing with her fear of me even more.

Which was why I released a deep sigh after finally feeling her go limp in my arms.

Arms that wanted to keep her forever.

DRAVEN

51

SLEEPING BEAUTY SPEAKS HER MIND

"I...I...feel..."

"I know sweetheart, don't worry, I've got you now," I told her the moment her body went limp in my arms. I had given her a shot of Midazolam which was a sedative that worked by inducing sleepiness, decreasing anxiety but mainly preventing the ability to create new memories. Something I confess, was my main aim here, for I didn't want her to remember this next part.

It wouldn't put her fully under but would certainly make her drowsy and more importantly, *compliant*. I also didn't want her to be afraid, which was why I decided against releasing my wings and flying her home, which granted would have been quicker.

But then again, the longer I had her in my possession, the better. I also knew how long I had before the drugs started to wear off, which was about two hours from the dose I gave her. However, the amnesia effect only lasted anything from twenty minutes up to an hour, so I didn't have all night like I wished.

So, with this in mind, I walked back to the door she had come through, noticing now all the glass on the floor. I frowned before looking to the cause to see that every lamp along this side of the open walkway had blown.

'Vincent, meet me in the VIP, five minutes.' I sent the message in my mind knowing I had no choice but to force the connection, one we only made when classed as important enough. Now telling him to leave the beauties he was currently tying to his bed and come and find me. His pleasures would have to wait, along with theirs.

"This way...I came" Keira's slurred voice told me this, making me smile down at her, especially when she added,

"Nasty lamps...bad lamps." It was somewhat like being drunk I deduced, which was why her semi-coherent thoughts were being spoken aloud.

"Yes, well they can't scare you now," I informed her making her giggle before asking,

"No, bad lamps can't...can't hurt you...but me they didn't like so much" I frowned wondering who had done this to frighten her?

"I wouldn't let them hurt you, Keira," I told her gently making her smile up at me, then her eyes closed, and she uttered a sweet sounding declaration,

'My hero.' I had to admit hearing this claim coming from her lips now had me faltering a step and sucking in a sharp breath. I knew it was only the drugs talking, but I didn't care. I was taking it, and I was claiming it, and I was fucking keeping it forever!

I continued to walk back the way she had obviously taken, only now entering into the VIP area where she obviously hadn't stepped foot into. Once there I made my way over to my table and took my usual seat, settling her comfortably into my lap and marvelling at how nicely she fit there.

I had to say that from that moment on I vowed to have her positioned here like this at any opportunity I could take, for the comfort it brought me was unlike any other I had ever experienced...and granted, there weren't many. But just the feel of her fitting so well in my arms, in the folds of my body and moulding so well into the curves created, I knew I would treasure this moment repeatedly. And a moment I would recreate as many times as I could after I first made her mine of course.

"Mmm...comfy." she confessed making me grin down at her and push some of the hair from her face.

"That it is my love, *that it is.*" I agreed wishing I could have been like this with her always. Then I frowned down at her curiously, to see what she was doing now as I felt a poking at my stomach.

"Problem?" I enquired making her giggle.

"You're not squishy," she informed me just as Vincent arrived to witness the strange evaluation of my anatomy. He coughed out a laugh making me roll my eyes when he said,

"Am I interrupting something?" Making that twice now a sibling of mine had, in fact, been interrupting...well, *something*...what this something was however I was unsure. But then I had called him here so I couldn't be as angry with him as I had been with Sophia that day in the car.

I was about to speak when Keira decided it was a good time to ask me a question, one that came from an innocent mind and was quickly twisted into one far from innocent,

"Are you this hard everywhere?" she asked still poking at me and referring to the muscle she felt there. Vincent then burst out laughing and answered her,

"My guess, sweetheart, is with you on his lap, then that would be definite yes." I shot him a look and growled before standing with her in my arms once more even after she started giggling.

"So is she pissed or..."

"I had no choice but to drug her," I informed him quickly.

"Did she sneak in here?" he asked making her put a finger to her lips and tell him to 'Ssshh' as if it was a secret.

"I was looking for Dominic Draven!" she quickly declared trying to follow our conversation and being adorable at that. Vincent's gaze softened and asked her,

"Is that so?" Then raised his brows at me in question. I was about to speak when suddenly she slapped a hand on my chest and declared loudly,

"Found him!" This made Vincent chuckle before agreeing,

"So, you did, little bird."

"I need to take her home before the Midazolam wears off and she remembers any of this," I told him making him nod.

"What can I do, Dom?" He asked knowing there was more I wasn't saying, no doubt seeing the broken lamps for himself on his way here.

"Something brought her here, I want to know what and who is responsible. She accessed the side door, took off her jacket and walked up the staircase to find the door into our home open. I want to know how. Get Rue and see if she can pick up any remaining trace of a casting, as we know no one could have accessed her mind," I told him making him nod after first looking surprised. I then took my happy little bundle of confusion towards the staircase when Vincent stopped me with a question,

"But why would someone do that?" I turned to look back at him and was about to tell him I didn't know why when the beauty in my arms had her own ideas.

"To meet my hero, of course." I granted her a gentle smile in return and looked back to Vincent who now looked thoughtful.

"You know she may have a point." I frowned in question before demanding,

"Explain."

"Well, if they had meant her harm, then they could have just taken her. But it seems to me as though they were trying to throw her in your path, maybe forcing your hand into acting in claiming her sooner." I thought on this and shook my head a little, before asking,

"But why?"

"Maybe someone is trying to test who she is in our world…what she means to you by being here… after all, you can't hope to get revenge on someone if you kidnap a person they don't care for? That, or one of our own kind was just trying to speed up a process," Vincent offered, not particularly offering any option that I preferred.

"I doubt it but speak to Sophia, see what she knows." Vincent looked as if he wanted to say more but refrained. No doubt about to offer his views on the unlikelihood of it being Sophia after the last time she had intervened, and very nearly seeing herself banished because of it. So, because of this, like Vincent, I doubted her involvement. But I still needed to be sure. As whoever it was, was obviously doing so with a great knowledge of this place and where I would have been.

"Also, get me a list of everyone not at Sophia's playroom." Vincent agreed and then nodded to the now sleeping form of Keira in my arms, who had a fingertip rested at her lip.

"I will do all I can here, you go and get her home, I already informed Fredrick that you would need the car at the ready, so it should be outside waiting for you." My brother said making me nod my thanks. Then, as I started to make my way down the staircase, he called back to me making me pause. I looked over my shoulder, and he said,

"And Dom…"

"…you're right, *she is beautiful.*" I couldn't help but look back down, taking in her beauty for myself and I swear the sight of her resting so peacefully in my arms made my heart swell. Then I looked back at him and simply answered,

"I know, and I am blessed…*for that beauty is all mine.*" The possessive tone of this last statement made my brother chuckle as he walked away, no doubt expecting nothing less of me.

I then walked out of my club, grabbing her jacket on the way before placing her gently in the back of my Rolls Royce Phantom. Then I turned to my driver and said,

"Take it slow, Fredrick." I then folded myself into the back, taking care not to wake her. However, I did reposition her so as she was leaning against me, with her head nestled against my chest and with my arm securely around her. I couldn't help the pleasure I gained from when she pressed herself closer to me, curling her body inwards and bringing up her leg a little against me.

"Mmm...comfy," she murmured and the whole moment had me asking myself... *would this be what it was like?*

To finally have her by my side and in my life, would it be filled with moments like this one? By the Gods, I hoped so, for something as simple as this just felt like my heart, mind, body and soul had all aligned with my demon and angel sides included. Like every fighting force that lived inside me had, after all these centuries simply relaxed and found peace. And all from the power of a mortal who currently looked so small, so fragile, it was barely believable to imagine the strength she held against me.

Unfortunately, the journey came to an end far sooner than I would have liked, no matter how slow Fredrick had driven. So, I untangled her from my side, loving the little moans of protest and the way her hands fisted in my shirt, trying to hold on to me.

"Easy sweetheart, I am not going anywhere," I told her trying to soothe her fears and making my heart ache ready for the time I would have to leave. After that, she trusted my words enough to let me slip out of the car before reaching back inside to lift her out. A feat not easily achieved, supernatural or not. As I also could willingly admit, not something I had ever done before. In fact, I couldn't ever recall carrying a woman so much, or even wanting to for that matter. That was until there was Keira.

"Make sure the car remains out of sight," I said to my driver indicating to the house with a nod, knowing he would understand. The last thing I needed was her sister or Frank being alerted to the fact that I was carrying their sister back into their home for the second time in barely a week. Especially in her drugged state as that would have looked a little suspicious indeed.

I unlocked the door with my mind and opened it. Then I took a step inside and located her family, who were resting upstairs. I then placed a heavier will on their minds, knowing now that they would remain asleep, no matter what they heard next.

After being assured of such, I then walked up the stairs with her, being hit with the welcoming sense of déjà vu I knew the origins of and continued until we were inside her room. I grinned to myself seeing that it was slightly less tidy than it had been the last time I did this, wondering how she would be when living with me. Would she be conscious of leaving her clothes on the floor or simply not care, viewing it how I hoped she would, *as her own home.*

If I was honest with myself, I had never lived with any other but my siblings and even then, we always had our own chambers within our homes. So, sharing my own personal space with someone was something completely foreign to me and therefore not something I could easily imagine.

Would all that I see now be one day boxed up and merged with my own possessions? Or would she just simply accept all I had to give her and the luxuries a privileged life of riches came with? For money was no object, and one day all that was my own would become hers to do with as she pleased, which included my fortune.

But looking down at her now and knowing what I knew of her already, then I couldn't imagine her feeling easy with taking advantage of this new financial situation she would suddenly find herself in. Not when she wouldn't even take advantage of having a chauffeur driven car at her disposal.

"I believe I will find myself having many a discussion with you on financial matters," I said speaking my thoughts aloud and knowing she wouldn't remember.

"You can have my money for a dance, cowboy," she said sleepily as I lay her on her bed and couldn't help myself when I chuckled softly down at her as her playfulness amused me greatly.

"Alright, Sweetheart, you have a deal," I said on a laugh.

"Mmm...you would look good on a horse," she said dreamily making me smirk and in that moment a need to keep her talking.

"I'm glad you think so," I told her brushing back the short pieces of her hair once more as she wriggled her body further into the comforts of her bed, as some nesting creature would.

"I think you would look better with me on that horse," I told her as her eyes were drifting closed. She smiled at first but then frowned when she admitted,

"I don't know...know how to ride... a horse." I smiled at this, then knowing that sleep was pulling her further under, leant down and told her softly,

"Then I will teach you, my love." After this, I kissed her temple, covered her up and walked away but then her whispered question stopped me,

"When?" I looked back at her, knowing she was already asleep, but I felt the deep need in me to answer her anyway, using this as my opportunity to gift her a piece of my inner feelings...

"When I get to keep you for all eternity."

Keira

52

CAT FIGHT

I felt the pain in my neck and cried out, bolting upright nearly falling out of bed. It took me a few minutes to understand what had happened. I was here back in my room but how did I get here? I rubbed my neck where there was a tiny pinprick of pain as though I had been bitten by something. I turned on my lamp and looked around the room, but there was no evidence that I had moved.

It must have been a dream, but surely it couldn't have been? It had felt way too real. The most real dream yet. I could still smell Draven on my skin and around my waist was warm from where he had held me so close. I got up and went into the bathroom. As I turned on the light my eyes stung at the bright light, so it took me a moment to focus on what I was looking for. I faced the mirror and arched my neck finding a little red lump with a tiny red dot in the middle of it. I rubbed it with my thumb trying to understand what I had just experienced.

The next day went by in a daze, as if I was a drone being controlled by another part of me, the part that had to conform. I answered when people spoke to me, with the right yes's and head nods but it was as if this was my dream and last night had been my reality. I played with the red dot on my neck all day, as if checking it was still there.

Jack had asked me a few times when driving me to college if I was alright and I had answered him as though I was on auto pilot. I walked into history like a ghost. I was still aware that I was being whispered about, but the difference today was I just didn't have the energy to care.

I sat down next to Sophia and she looked at me with a worried frown.

"Keira, are you alright, you're very pale and you look tired? Didn't you sleep well?" I couldn't help the reaction I gave as I let out an almighty laugh. I turned to look at her and she frowned as if I was losing it. Maybe she was right.

"I'm sorry, that was rude of me. The truth is I don't really know if I slept last night." Well, if she didn't think I was crazy before she most certainly did now.

"What do you mean, you don't know?" She said but her face held a hint of something more, as if she was worried and not just for me. Then she seemed to notice the red mark on my neck and I was sure I saw her shake her head. Maybe she thought I had turned to injecting drugs into my neck and this was the result. One doped up, nutty ass Keira!

"Never mind, I just had a bad dream or a good one, I can't really explain it, but I'm fine don't worry." She looked sceptical, but she let it go as Reed entered the class.

At the end of the lecture Sophia asked me if I needed a lift home as she had noticed RJ wasn't in today.

"Thanks, but it's okay, I have a lift. Jack picked me up this morning."

"Oh Jack... as in the 'not' boyfriend but wants to be, Jack?" She said this as she looked round to a passing student and he stared back at her with a strange knowing look in his eye. I hadn't noticed the student before, but he was coming out of our class, so maybe it was someone she knew from there.

"Umm, yeah well, I mean he's just a friend."

"You really need a car, don't you? I bet you would love to have the freedom and not to have to rely on other people all the time." She said as we walked outside together.

"Yeah, I would, but I think I will need a few more pay packets before that happens. Besides, I'm just happy that I have a job and a good one at that, so it won't be long." She smiled as though once again I had missed something important. She said something else that sounded like 'We'll see' and left, waving as she got in the huge black beast of a Range Rover. I couldn't help but wonder if Draven was also in there. I lowered my head as memories of last night flooded back to me, making my waist feel warm again from where his arm had wrapped securely around me.

I had regained some normality on the drive home and Jack seemed happier about it. He asked if I was working tonight and when I replied yes, it was obviously not the answer he'd been hoping for. I thanked him for the lift and waved goodbye as he pulled away.

Whilst at work I remained quiet and most of the time unresponsive. I worked the hours that seemed more like minutes and Draven didn't approach me all night and for once I was happy about it. There was a new feeling I now held for him and I didn't want it to show through. I was now a bit afraid of him. I knew I was being stupid, but I couldn't help it. He had been so powerful and commanding in my dream last night and I had felt powerless and weak against him.

I saw his eyes find mine as I walked past his table to go home, but I lowered my face in what must have looked like disappointment. Of course, I still felt as strongly for him, if not more so, but I didn't know if my heart could take much more or my mental health for that matter. I didn't feel like myself any more. Somewhere along the way I had lost control of my thoughts and it was ever since I had first laid eyes on Dominic Draven.

I went outside to wait for Frank's car to come into view and I sat down out of sight of the doormen. The stone wall was cold and I could feel the wet soaking through the material of my trousers, but I didn't care. I needed to get my head straight. I needed to feel like I was in control of my own thoughts and more importantly, my own actions. This dream had been different. There was no one trying to steal it away from me, making it blurry and I didn't know if this was a good thing. I went through so many different accounts of last night and it all kept boiling down to one thing I had said.

I was broken...

I knew that I could never be 'fixed' as he had called it. There was no hope and I couldn't do anything about it, so it was about time that I just accepted it. Surely then, I could move on? Tears were slowly following others and before long my cheeks were wet with salty water. I wiped them off with the back of my hand, angry at myself for being so soft.

"Pull yourself together, Keira." I said out loud. Frank would be here soon and I didn't want him seeing me upset. I was good at hiding my feelings. Hell, I was a pro. I was a terrible liar but through lots of practice I could have won an Oscar for acting as though I was fine.

When Frank turned up, I played my usual trick of asking him about a game I knew he had seen recently. This lasted me all the way home with just having to nod and say the occasional 'Umm' and 'Ah' when it was needed.

I don't know why, but that night I cried myself to sleep.

I felt better the next day after a dreamless night's sleep however I was still worried. My dreams had been getting out of hand and after how much better I felt after that one good night's sleep I decided I had to do something about it. Even though I dreaded seeing them I made the decision to make an appointment and speak to a doctor in order to get some more pills. If I was going to beat this obsession the dreams had to stop!

I kept that frame of mind all day as I helped Libby with housework and we both cooked a pie together for tonight's meal. Well, I say 'we' in the loosest sense of the word, as it was more like I cooked and she talked, keeping me company.

Every now again I did slip up and when Libby asked me what had happened to my neck, I dropped the knife I held in my hand, nearly severing off a couple of toes. I told her what I had first thought it could have been.

"Bug bite." I said passing it off as nothing, which was far from the truth.

For the whole two hours leading up to my next shift, I tried to convince myself that I was a waitress and nothing more and I needed to get this sickness out of my head before it got me into even more trouble. Because primarily, that was what Draven was for me...

Trouble.

Of course, as soon as I walked past his table for the first time on my shift, all my logic went out of my head as though someone had flicked my obsession switch. I scorned myself for not being strong enough to not want him. Damn him! Why couldn't I find the strength? After all the things I had done and been through... this I couldn't do!

I was fighting with my mind and my heart trying to get them to co-operate, but they were rebelling and as a result I wasn't paying attention to what I was doing. I kept making mistakes, taking orders to the wrong tables and bumping into the other waitresses. In the end I told Karmun that I needed five minutes to sort my head out and he threw a bottle of water for me to catch.

Once outside, I nearly downed the whole bottle, as I couldn't get rid of the thirst nagging at my throat like I'd swallowed barbed wire. I needed some sort of pain to bring me back down to the Earth I didn't feel part of. I let the anger course through my veins and build up and up until I broke. I punched one of the trees by the door making it shake under the pressure. I had hit it with everything I had and sharp twigs scratched at my hand and knuckles.

It didn't bleed but it left a mark and I had accomplished my goal, as now I was fully alert to the pain. I knew it wasn't the best idea but it had worked. I now went back to my job without making a pig's ear of it, as my mother would say.

I buzzed around as I was now back in the zone. I cleared all my tables and replenished them all with drinks again, as though I had downed a few espressos. The throbbing in my hand only made me concentrate more and I pulled my glove over my hand to hide my blazing red skin. Okay, so it was going to leave a bruise, but I didn't care.

My shift was soon over and I was saying goodbye to Karmun, when my night changed for the worse. It was like being on a roller-coaster with a constant stream of ups and downs. Okay, so mostly downs at the moment, but considering my foul mood this didn't surprise me.

I had turned too quickly and knocked straight into the blonde... *Layla.* She dropped her tray, which thankfully was empty, looked down at it and then back up at me with fury in her eyes.

I held my hands up saying,

"I'm really sorry," But that would never be good enough for her so instead I started to walk away giving her space.

"Where do you think you're going, vermin?" She hissed at me. I wondered what it was about me that she hated so much. I turned around and said,

"What did you say?" With my outrage brewing and showing its ugly head.

"You heard me, you parasite!" Her lips curved into a sadistic grin.

"Leave it, Layla!" Karmun was now getting in on the act, trying to convert tension into peace.

"Stay out of this, Kokabiel!" I didn't understand what she called him but it had been effective. He left to stand at the other end of the bar, leaving me alone with this nutty girl, who was gladly putting my crazy to shame. She looked down at the tray that was still on the floor. She nodded to it and snapped,

"Pick it up!" Her words slithered through blood red lips and I half expected a snake's tongue to come out of her filthy mouth.

"No!" I said folding my arms, determined that this would be one night that I wouldn't back down.

"Pick it up now!" Her eyes burned, turning red and blood shot.

"I said NO!" I shouted back and was about to walk away from this rude girl's tantrum, but she grabbed my arm and dug in long fingernails, twisting them deeper into my skin. I squinted my eyes as the pain was making them water, but I still couldn't bring myself to pick it up.

"Do it, I know this hurt." She sneered at me curling her lip in pleasure, which was sickening to see. I tried to free my arm, but she twisted more and I could feel her nails digging into my skin piercing the flesh. I couldn't help the moan of pain, but I still managed to say,

"I have felt more pain than your little cat scratch! Now. Let. Go!" I warned, even though I knew what was coming and waited for the pain to increase as I could already feel little drops of blood on my arm soaking into my glove. I made a fist with my other hand and got ready to swing it at her.

She smiled at my reply and the vile bitch looked happy about it. I tensed my face, not wanting to give her the satisfaction of seeing me hurt, when she suddenly dropped her hand to her side. Her face abruptly turned to stone.

"Is there a problem, Layla?" Draven's strong authoritative voice boomed behind me and it was quite clear he was not happy.

"Nn...o...no, my lord." She said as she lowered her head in respect. I rubbed my arm as you could see the imprints on my gloves where her nails had gone through the material. Damn it, another pair of gloves ruined.

"Keira, would you like to add anything to this?" I turned to face him and looked at him with an over emotional face as the anger I felt for them both hadn't yet subsided.

"No, she dropped her tray and that's about the end of it." I said not wanting to make an issue of it. Layla looked at me shocked why I hadn't given her up to Draven. I just figured that there wasn't much point as he didn't look a bit convinced. He soon turned back to her.

"Back to work Lahash, Eu vou tratar con vostede máis tarde!" ('I will deal with you later' in Gaelic) He spoke the words so fluently, but I didn't have a clue to what he had said or even what language he had used.

She understood though, for what he must have said made her cringe and look frightened. I almost felt sorry for her, remembering never to get on the bad side of him. She was about to leave as she backed up, lowering her face like he was some kind of sultan. And what was with the 'My Lord' bit?

She was about to turn when he pointed to the floor at the tray saying,

"Pick it up!" And this time she did so without hesitation. I didn't blame her because compared to Draven, her anger looked like a kitten next to a sabre tooth tiger.

Once we were alone he pulled me to one side, grabbing the arm that she had dug her nails into, so I couldn't help moaning at the feel of pressure. It was also the hand that I hit the tree with, so it didn't look good for me. He let go of my arm once he heard the groan that slipped out. He didn't ask me what was wrong he just lifted my arm and examined it. I pulled it away from him and said,

"It's fine," and held my hand behind my back.

Draven looked furious and I felt scared being there to witness it. I swallowed hard trying to mask my fear with bravery. He turned his head towards the direction Layla had left and gritted his teeth saying,

"Kelba!" ('Bitch' in Maltese) But again, I didn't understand. I wanted to leave but his tall frame blocked my way. I had never seen him so angry and I could have sworn that I saw his eyes flicker to purple but returned quickly to jet-black.

"I'd better be going." I said as I tried to pass him, but he didn't move, and my hands started to shake behind my back.

"Wait," he said in a softer tone, as though my words had pulled him out of his rage.

"Let me see your arm." He asked and when I didn't move he looked down at me meeting my eyes, but I wasn't going to falter. I'd had just about enough of being ordered around tonight and I was tired of it!

"I told you it's fine and if I don't go now I will be late for Frank." I said finishing it with a deep breath only it didn't sound as steady as I had hoped.

"He can wait." He said pushing it further and the smart thing to do would be to give in, but I just couldn't, so I stayed firm and replied,

"But I can't, so if you'll excuse me, *Sir.*" And with that I turned my back on him and left down the main staircase. Only my plan didn't work very well as when I got there I was stopped by two of Draven's huge guards. They stood in my way, but with my blood boiling from all the humiliation my bravery didn't fade.

"Excuse me." I said through gritted teeth and they looked over me to their Master. I turned looking in the same direction to find Draven's eyes burning into me. His gaze stayed on mine for longer than ever before. I was just about to give in and go back to him when he broke away first, nodding to the men that stood like a wall blocking my path.

They parted and let me through, but I had a feeling I was going to pay for this at a later date. I nearly ran down the steps and out of the building that felt as though it was consuming my soul. I was sure I could still feel his eyes staring at me until I was out of the main doors.

I couldn't believe what I just did. What was I trying to prove? I had just disobeyed a man like Draven. I really was crazy.

It was raining, and I ran for the car parked with the engine cut. Frank had been waiting. This time I couldn't fake anything to Frank so instead I turned to him and said,

"I think I just made a big mistake."

"I doubt that, but what happened?" He said giving me far too much credit than I deserved. He started the car and pulled out onto the main road.

"I just really pissed off my boss."

"You mean Mr Draven?" He was serious, but he didn't look as worried as I did.

"The man himself." I said as I held my head up with a fist to my cheek and my elbow on the side window.

"Aww come on, it can't be that bad, he likes you remember?" He said nudging me on my other arm.

"Well if he did, I doubt he does anymore after the show I just put on."

"Christ, you didn't take a swing at him, did you?" He said as he'd just noticed my red fist. I laughed at the thought and his worried face straightened.

"No, but ha ha. I got in an altercation with another waitress, who is a raging bitch I might add…"

"And you hit her?!" Frank said getting excited at the idea of me sticking up for myself.

"I wish as I came close, trust me but then Draven saw it all and intervened."

"Don't tell me he took her side?" Frank asked no longer smirking.

"No, he sent her on her way but when he had asked to see my arm, after what the bitch did with her nails…" I said pausing to show him the holes in my glove before continuing,

"…I then told him no and walked off." He grinned and then his eyes fell to my gloved arms and sadness replaced his smile.

"Well, I'm sure he admired you standing up for yourself, I can't imagine that happens a lot around someone like him."

"No, never more like, but he didn't look happy about it."

"I'm sure he will get over it and Hell, if you tell a man no, then it damn well means no!" Frank was great, a real big brother. He knew what I had been through and felt the pain just like the rest of my family had, so I knew that he meant what he said. He leaned into me and said,

"Well, I have something to cheer you up."

"What's that?"

"Libby's in bed, so you're safe." We both laughed and I was glad that I had confided in Frank, as it felt good and comforting offloading some mental weight.

I sat on my bed and pulled out the clip that held my hair up and ran my fingers through it, feeling the ache of having it up all day. It fell down my back in one big tube from spending the day twisted. I played with it, separating it into smaller pieces until it hung in waves down to my waist.

I examined my hand and a bluish bruise was starting to form at the knuckles. What was I thinking? I had just got rid of one, only to replace it by another. I pulled down my gloves and ran my fingers over four little half-moon shaped bloody cuts. Well, at least they would fit right in with the others.

I barely ever looked at my arms, as when I did I would usually get upset at the memory of how they came to be. I touched the lighter scars at the top first and then moved down to the deeper ones near the wrist. These were larger, thicker and had never really made it back to skin colour. They were deep red as if a reminder of the blood that once poured out of them. I did the same on the other arm and placed the two side by side. What a mess. I counted eight slits on one and six on the other. I looked as though I had been mauled by a lion.

This was the reason I refused to obey Draven. I never wanted anyone to see my scars and I most definitely never wanted to explain how they got there. Well let's face it, as soon as anyone saw them they would make up their own conclusion anyway, so what was the point? They were a reminder for me every day for the rest of my life of what happened. I didn't want that for other people. After all, I had come here to get away from all of that.

Needless to say, I didn't get much sleep that night.

The next day I spent looking after Libby as she had come down with the same bug that RJ had and the way my week had gone, I was just hoping I wouldn't get it next.

"How are you feeling, Libs?" I asked as I sat on the couch opposite her. She looked terrible with her skin all pale, making her red hair look as though it was on fire.

"I'm okay I guess, I just can't seem to keep anything down though."

"Yeah, RJ has the same thing, but she rang earlier and said she was feeling better, so it must only last for a few days. Do you want any soup or anything?" As soon as I mentioned food her face went a greenish colour and she bolted for the bathroom waving her hand at me.

"I'll take that as a 'no' then." I said when she was out of sight. I was just about to go into the kitchen when there was a knock at the door. Maybe Frank was back, but it would be way too early yet. He had gone over to 'The guys' house. The guys being a bunch of mates he went to high school with and they now all watched football together whenever they could. He hadn't wanted to leave at first but Libby and I both convinced him that she would be fine and as I was staying in anyway, there was no point him missing it.

I opened the door to a man wearing a black suit and a black chauffeur's hat. But there wasn't a car in sight. Maybe he had parked round the side, but why would he do that? He held a long black envelope under his arm and asked,

"Miss Johnson?" He was a bit creepy looking, so I stepped back out of the door frame in case I needed to slam the door shut. I know this was an odd response, but I couldn't help but be wary.

"Letter for you." And with that he held out an envelope for me to take and then he promptly left.

"Who was that at the door?" Libby had re-emerged from the downstairs loo and was cocooning herself back in the bedding on the couch.

"Just a letter for me. Do you think you could hold down a cup of tea?" She nodded like a child and continued to watch some cheesy daytime drama.

I walked into the kitchen and placed the letter on the table while I filled the kettle. Once I had clicked it on, I went to sit down and stare at it as though it would bite me if I touched it again. I turned over the black rectangle and saw that it had been sealed by red wax. I looked closer and noticed the seal was the family crest of the Draven's. It was the same as on the doors and the back of Draven's chair at the club.

Maybe this was about my behaviour last night. Oh shit...maybe I was getting sacked!

I couldn't bear it any longer, so I tore open the seal and pulled out the contents. The sound of the kettle boiling hid the small scream that I had just made, and I dropped the paper back on the table.

I just couldn't believe it, what the Hell was going on?

There must have been a mistake!

Was this real?

Keira

53

GIFT OR DEMAND

I stuffed the letter under my armpit as I carried the two mugs into the living room. I passed Libby hers and I sat back down still in shock.

"Good news?" She asked over her mug.

"I... don't... know." I said slowly, as I was still trying to make sense of it.

"What's wrong?"

I handed Libby the envelope and said,

"This is what's wrong." It didn't take her long for her eyes to widen in shock at the wad of cash she held in her hands.

"WOW, where the Hell did you get that from?" I nodded to the letter that was still inside. She pulled it free from the cash and scanned the letter finding the words that stood out.

"That's your wages? $4000 in a month!" She shouted the words and I stared at the pile of green notes in her hand.

"But that's...that's crazy...you are a waitress, right?"

"Of course, I am! What do you think I do there?" I said getting frustrated!

"I don't know, lure them all sacrifices...Kidding, kidding." She said but I didn't laugh. How could I... I mean what was this?

"Well, at least you can get a new car now."

"I'm not going to spend it, there's been a mistake and it's going back!" I hissed, slamming my hand down on the arm of the chair and then picking up my tea, gulping it down and burning my throat.

"Really? You're not going to spend it?" She said in disbelief.

"No, I'm not...in fact...I'm... I'm going to sort this out right now." I said getting up to go back in the kitchen, ignoring Libby as she asked what it was that I was going to do. I picked up the phone, grabbed the number that was on the fridge and called the club. It rang four times before someone picked up.

"Hello, Club Afterlife, Jerry speaking."

"Hi Jerry, its Keira."

"Oh, hi Keira, what's up?" He asked in a wary voice. He must have thought I was calling in sick and maybe he was dreading the thought of telling them upstairs.

"Don't worry, I'm not calling in sick, I just want to know, could you put me through to upstairs?"

"Umm I don't know...can I ask what this is about?" Oh yeah, he was wary all right.

"Well, it's a bit personal and I don't think they would want me disclosing any information to anyone about it so..." That did it! Before I knew it, the phone was ringing again and this time a familiar happy voice answered.

"How can I help you, Keira?" Karmun asked.

"How did you know it was me?"

"Lucky guess. I'm assuming you got your wages?" Ah, so he knew I would call. I started to relax, as they must have realised their mistake.

"Oh, right so you know it was wrong then. It's okay, I will bring it back later and we can sort it out then, but wow I was shocked..." He cut me off when he said,

"Wrong...? Keira, there's been no mistake."

"What!? But I... don't understand I..." I mumbled my words when he said,

"There's someone here who wants to speak to you, hang on." Oh no, this was bad... this was a very bad idea.

"Hi Keira." I let out a sigh of relief when I heard Sophia's voice on the other end. I was just thankful it wasn't her brother's.

"Hey Sophia, I was just telling Karmun that I think there has been a mistake." I was about to explain but like Karmun she already knew.

"No, there's been no mistake, we have just added a bit onto your wages, like an advance, so you can get a car." What!? Was she joking? They were giving me money to buy a car? I couldn't speak. I couldn't think of anything to say. Not even when all I heard on the other end was…

"Keira, are you still there?"

Sophia had told me how she and her brother felt it was important that I had my own transport, as my shifts might be getting later, and they felt it was unfair to ask me to do this if I had to rely on other people. In the end, I had no other option than to agree to keep the money, but I stated that I would pay it back monthly. This was something she didn't fully agree to, but I decided it was best to approach it in person.

It didn't help that Libby's smugness lasted the rest of the day as she had been right in thinking I would spend it. When Frank came in it was the first thing out of her mouth.

"Guess who's buying Kazzy a car?"

"He's not buying me a car! They have loaned me an advance on my wages and I am paying it back!" I said this last half directed back at Libby, with the temptation to stick my tongue out at her.

"Cool, how much are we talking about here?"

"$4000 bucks!" Libby said in a corny American accent. Frank's face lit up and replied,

"Nice, but babe, leave the American to the pros, yeah? So, when do you want to go and spend your hard-earned dough?" He said mocking me, but it was hard to stay in a bad mood with Frank and his huge teddy bear cute smile.

"Does this mean you'll go with me?"

"Of course. I'm not letting you get ripped off, coming back here with a piece of crap like that rusty tin can your friend's got!" He got up and put his jacket back on and I asked,

"What, you want to go now?" He raised his eyebrows and lifted up his hand as if to say, 'Well duh!'

We were in his car and I had put the money in my bag stuffing it down into the bottom, paranoid that it would fall out or that I would lose it.

"You've got your new licence, right?" Frank had already gone over everything that I needed before I left the house.

"Yeah got it, but are you sure this guy is gonna be open? It is a Sunday."

"Trust me, this guy never shuts. You'd better let me do all the talking because this guy…well, let's just say he's a bit of a ball buster." I didn't have any problems with that. I wasn't exactly brimming over with car expertise.

"No problem," I said as we pulled up to a set of traffic lights.

"Sooo... I guess this means you couldn't have pissed him off that much." Frank said, giving me a wink and I shook my head in denial.

"I don't know what you mean." I said rolling my eyes and looking out of the window casually.

"Yeah, sure you don't...well, okay if you want to play it off as nothing then I'm game but you have to know that this isn't the normal behaviour for a boss.... *right?*"Well yeah, of course I knew that, but was there anything normal about Draven? I mean I couldn't imagine he was spending his Sunday 'watching the game and drinking a Bud'! If I thought about it, I couldn't imagine him doing anything average.

Thankfully, he dropped the conversation as we pulled up to an intersection then took a left into 'Bobby's Used Car Lot' as the sign read. Frank parked the car near a guy washing a big pickup truck. He looked about sixteen and there was no meat on him whatsoever. In fact, he resembled a beanpole.

There was a gritty office and a man emerged from behind a door that had seen better days. The man was short and stocky, with the shiniest bald head I had ever seen.

Frank leaned in to me and whispered,

"Man, look at that head. Bowling, anyone?" I nudged him in his ribs and tried not to burst out laughing.

"Now remember, let me do the talking."

"I don't think that's going to be hard." I said swallowing the laugh that was still there.

"Hi there, Bobby Brown at your service, what can I do you for?" He said giving me a wink that made me smile but not for the same reasons he was thinking. I couldn't help it. He was like some comical but slightly slimy uncle from a sitcom. He wore a tweed jacket with a pair of light blue jeans that were too long for him, so they were rolled up at the ankles. He topped off the look with a crooked smile and yellow teeth.

"We're looking for a reliable car for my sister here." Frank said, and I loved the way he never added the 'in law' bit.

"Sister eh...lucky for me then." I nearly choked trying again not to laugh.

"Well, let's go and take a look should we pretty lady?" He said and motioned for us to follow him. Frank frowned at his attentions towards me, but I just found it hilarious. For some reason he had kind eyes that made me want to smile back at him. However, Frank pulled back my arm and whispered in my ear,

"There's something wrong... he's never this nice!" I shrugged and followed him around to the cars.

"So what's the budget?"

"$3000." Frank said before I could speak and I shot him a look.

"$3000 you say...umm, well if that's what you've got, then that's what you got, let's see what I can do." He said as though he didn't believe the amount.

I let him walk ahead then I whispered to Frank,

"Why did you only say $3000?"

"Trust me, this is how the game is played, watch and learn kiddo." He walked on holding his head high as he caught up with Bobby.

"Hey, what about that one, the red Chevy?" Frank said pointing to a sporty coupé.

"What, the Camaro? Dodgy transmission that one." Bobby said scratching his smooth head. He started to walk over to the bigger vehicles when Frank stopped him as he had spotted another one.

"Now here we are, Kaz, this one's perfect! It's a Toyota Starlet, right?" He asked Bobby who didn't seem that interested as he just nodded.

"Go on Kaz, give it a try." Frank said opening the door to a little white hatchback.

"I wouldn't do that if I were you." Bobby leaned into Frank and said,

"Someone died in there you see and....well... we never could get rid of the smell." I pulled a disgusted face and let go of the handle, rubbing my palm down my jean's leg.

"Nice." I said sarcastically, and I saw Bobby looking at me, grinning. Frank pulled me back away from the car as if I would get infected standing so close.

"Okay, what about this VW Golf?"

"Nah, you don't want that one, look over here, I have something perfect for the lady." Bobby said walking back in the direction of the big boys, where a line of pick-ups and 4x4's sat.

"Here we go, the Ford Bronco, now this is your girl, and it's midnight blue to match the pretty girl's eyes." He said giving me another wink and I giggled, not knowing why. From anyone else I would have found this creepy, but there was something strangely familiar about him. Maybe he reminded me of a regular from the pub I worked in back home. They were always flirting with me but it was only banter... plus I got great tips at Christmas!

"Hey, look pal, if you think that by putting us off all the other cars is going to make us pay $6500 then you can think again! Come on Kazzy, let's check out the Mustang over there." Frank started to walk off, but I just walked around the huge blue 4x4, slowly falling in love. Bobby watched me wide-eyed, smiling as though it was a slam-dunk. He opened the door for me adding,

"There we are, *my* lovely." Then winking at me, but there was just something in the way he said 'my', like he really meant it.

"Uh...thanks." I said getting in the driver's seat and holding the wheel.

Frank walked back to the Bronco and stood next to me looking as though I had lost my mind.

"Look, I will do you a deal. I'll let her go for $4000." Frank and I both looked at him in amazement and Frank shouted an animated,

"What?!" While looking back at me. I just shrugged my shoulders and got out walking round it trying to find the damage.

"Are you kidding, what's wrong with it?" Frank asked picking the words out of my head and frowning as if Bobby was trying to sell us something dodgy.

"Nothing at all, she runs great and the lady needs something strong that will protect that pretty little bone structure. She's a 1995, 5.8 v8 engine and she's a beaut. Start her up if ya don't believe me." He handed Frank the keys as though he'd known all along this was the car he would sell me or more astonishingly the one I would want. I didn't say anything as Frank took the keys and started her up, while I stroked the hood like I was in front of a horse.

Frank got out and said,

"I told you we only have $3000." What? I couldn't believe he was still haggling with the guy! He must have thought that there was something wrong with it for that price.

"Ah yes, so you did. Well, I will tell you what, how 'bout I let ya have her for $3000 plus a kiss." He said motioning to his cheek and my mouth dropped open. Frank looked at him as though he had lost his mind.

"What is wrong with you!? Come on Keira, this guy's crazy." And he started to walk away but I smiled and said,

"So, let me get this straight, not only will you drop the price from $6500 but you will knock another $1000 off just for a kiss on the cheek?"

"A kiss by the prettiest girl I have ever seen. So yeah, I'm old and bald...humour me." He said, and I couldn't help but laugh first at his compliment and then his joke. I mean what an old charmer! But I had to admire his spirit. So, I went up to him and kissed him gently on the cheek, seeing something in his eyes that brought back a memory I couldn't explain.

Frank saw this and held up his hands like Bobby wasn't the only one who had lost their mind.

"Ah sweetheart, now that was worth every cent." Bobby said grinning like a Cheshire cat. Frank came up behind him and said,

"Alright Casanova, let's sort out the damn paperwork."

I got in the car after Frank showed me the basics and I started to follow him home. It felt strange driving again, more so because not only did it feel like a tank, but I kept wanting to change gear as I had never driven an automatic before. Also, I had to keep repeating to myself about the most important rule about driving an automatic and that was to only use one foot. So, I kept my left foot tucked firmly away under the seat so that I wouldn't be tempted to use it for the clutch that wasn't there.

I smiled all the way home and if I'd known the town much better I would have gone for a longer drive. There was so much room in this thing, I think I could have moved in and still had room for a sink! Frank, on the other hand, was still expecting it to blow up or something. Well I loved it!

When we got back Libby had disappeared along with her car and Frank got worried, so he rang her mobile, which she didn't answer.

"Maybe she went to the pharmacy." I said trying to be helpful and not panic. He, on the other hand, was imagining things that included the words 'Hospital' and 'Emergency.'

He tried her again on her phone, over and over and as before she didn't answer. Okay, so now I was getting a bit worried. Why hadn't she left a note or just called us back? This wasn't like her, unless her stomach pain had turned more serious and she did in fact go to the hospital. I walked into the kitchen and was just about to tell Frank to call the ER but he was already on the phone and it wasn't to Libby.

"No, okay, well thanks anyway, if you hear anything you got my number." He finished and put back the handset on the wall.

"She's not at the hospital."

"Alright then maybe something at work came up?" I said and he grabbed the phone again punching in the numbers impatiently. But before the phone could register the front door opened.

"Olivia, where have you been?!" Frank said in a relieved but angry tone. Libby looked innocently at our frowning faces and put a plastic bag behind her, Frank didn't notice but I did.

"What, I just popped out for some Peptol Bismal. Jeez, paranoid much." She said as she walked past us and went straight to the bathroom, leaving Frank and I with the same expression.

"Well, I called your cell like a million times, babe and guess what? You didn't answer!" Frank was upset, that much was clear.

"I was driving!" She shouted from inside the bathroom.

"Since when has that ever stopped you?" Frank snapped back.

"Well, aren't you the one who's always telling me to be more careful? And what's with the third degree?" She asked through the door. I had gone into the kitchen to put the kettle on and also to give them some privacy.

"Well I was worried, I mean you're ill, so I just thought that something could've happened...I mean Christ Libs, I called the hospital."

"Oh honey, I'm fine, look I'm sorry if I made you worry." And with that I knew it was over as I could hear the sound of kissing, so I got up and closed the door which made them giggle like teenagers.

I couldn't help but think that Libby was hiding something, as the rest of the night she was acting... well, kind of weird. For starters, she stuffed her face full of the beef stroganoff I made and then she tucked into a tub of Ben and Jerry's Phish food.

"Well, it looks like someone is feeling better," Frank had said as he too dug his spoon into the tub pulling out a lump of brown gooey chocolate. Frank had filled her in about our trip to Bobby's and she laughed until she cried especially when Frank added,

"Yeah, should have seen his shiny head, it looked more like a solar panel for a sex machine! Horny old bastard!" Then we were all in hysterics.

"Well, it looks like Keira is catching everyone's eye." Libby said nudging Frank as they shared a not so private joke. I just rolled my eyes and took my plate back into the kitchen, saying,

"Kids" as I passed them.

The truth was I was still a bit freaked from what I had seen in Bobby's eyes. I just couldn't put my finger on it but there had been something deep and lurking about the way he looked at me. I tried to shake it off as I did with most things these days, but it still remained at the back of my mind. To be honest, ever since I had met Draven, I had felt something in my life had changed. Almost like my mind was being controlled by another entity. It had confused my senses, making me feel like I was being watched by other people. It was making me see things that I couldn't explain and who knows, it could even be controlling my dreams.

I know thinking this was crazy but considering the facts, what else was there?

That it was just all down to me and my imagination? Maybe the fact that I had seen monsters in people since I was seven years old had something to do with it.

Either way I looked at it, the same conclusion always came up...

There was something wrong.

Keira

54

WEEKS GONE BY

Things at the club changed after that Saturday I had walked away from Draven. Weeks had gone by and yet not a word from him. It seemed that he didn't take kindly to being disobeyed and my punishment was being ignored. He didn't even look my way when I went by and the pain of this got worse, not better.

The one time I thought I was close to receiving a reaction was when he walked past me at the end of my shift one night. Only instead of a friendly word, I got a hostile glare, which made my fists clench and my heart pound in my chest. I was very close to screaming at him but thankfully, I was still scared of him and the bravery from that night hadn't lasted.

Apart from my nights of being ignored at the club, my days had found a good routine. I would spend my time juggling college and working, with the occasional night off, spending it with RJ and the rest of the gang. My problem was that the more time I spent with Jack, the clearer he was making his intentions. I tried to talk to RJ, but it fell on deaf ears as she would have liked nothing more than for me and Jack to become an item.

I had soon got used to my new car and loved the new-found freedom that went with it. I took it in turns with RJ driving to college and it didn't take long before my glove compartment was filled with RJ's favourite CD's. Of course, she preferred it when I took my car, as unlike hers, it didn't sound like a lawnmower on crack!

She showed me all around the town and I took her out to eat at a Mexican restaurant to say thanks. It felt good to do this again, making me feel less like a teenager and more of the adult I was. We all went to the movies one night and they all laughed at me when I had called it the flicks. However, Jack's flirting never went unnoticed as he made every effort to be near me.

I felt as though I belonged. A feeling I hadn't felt for a very long time. But at the back of my mind were my own demons inching their way to the surface, never letting me forget the sense of security that I felt when I was near Draven. It would only stop when I was at the club making me feel as though I had come home. A piece of me was empty and that hole would only be filled when I was there. It was like the building itself was one giant entity which fed from my emotions. I felt as if it wanted me there, it needed me there and it used Draven as the key to keep me there.

Then one day everything changed and I was once again thrown into a world I didn't understand. It had started just like any other day, the only difference being that Jack had asked me on a date and this time I couldn't find any more excuses to make so I agreed. I was caught in the middle of a war with my mind and heart. Both wanted different things. My brain convinced me that after two weeks of silence and being ignored, Draven didn't want anything to do with me and no amount of wishing it would make it so. My heart, of course, didn't want to give up, so it hadn't been an easy decision. I just kept telling myself it's only a date, what's the worst that could happen?

We had arranged for Friday night as I had the night off due to the day shift I was going to do on Saturday. I had never worked the club in the day before, so I wasn't really sure what to expect. I wondered if Draven would still be at his table as surely they couldn't just sit there every day and night, could they?

I had two separate friendships with Sophia. There was the usual everyday one in class and the other very different one at the club. She had tried to explain it once, but I told her that she didn't need to explain anything and that I fully understood why this was. She had a position to uphold and couldn't spend the time talking to me when I was working. After all, she was one of my bosses.

It wasn't as if she just wouldn't acknowledge me. She would always wave and occasionally she'd come up and say 'hello', but you could tell it was frowned upon by her brother. In class though we acted like normal friends, laughing and joking about Reed. She would do her usual trick of asking a million and one questions about me but never really revealing anything about herself. She remained a mystery just like her brother. She never once mentioned him and I never asked.

She did, however, ask about Jack the day that he asked me out.

"I noticed you were talking to Jack before class, any development there?" She said as she twisted a black barrel curl around her finger.

"Yeah kind of, he asked me out this Friday night and I finally said yes." She didn't look shocked as if she had been waiting for it, knowing all along what he felt for me.

"Umm that's nice, you're not working then?" There was something off about her tone, but I couldn't put a finger on it.

"No, I have the night off, but I'm in on Saturday." I said trying to figure out her expression.

She quickly dropped the conversation as Reed entered the room. My relationship with Reed had smoothed out after the misunderstanding was rectified and the evidence that my work was always handed in early and above all, always received a good grade. This wasn't only down to the fact that I wanted to prove a point, in truth it was more down to whenever I spent any time alone with myself, my thoughts would be consumed by Draven. The only way to stop this was to set my mind on a different course and as a result, I was ahead in all my classes.

It was Thursday and I was working at the club tonight. I got in from college to find Libby already home and cleaning again. Lately Libby had been acting weird, ever since her stomach bug. She would clean constantly and eat everything in sight.

I didn't understand her behaviour, as she had never been one of those cleaning freaks or one for over-eating. Granted, before I came to live with them there was mainly junk food and a microwaveable meal on every shelf of the freezer, but they were also fitness fanatics. But Libby had stopped doing yoga and gave up her Pilates class at her health club.

I was on my way upstairs after saying 'hello' to the bottom part of her, as her head was stuck in the oven cleaning it like a woman possessed, when it hit me! I ran back down the stairs flinging my body around the corner so fast that I almost slipped and shouted,

"You're pregnant!" Her head emerged from the foamy oven and she smiled.

"I knew it! Why didn't you tell me?!" I shouted not being able to contain my excitement. She got up and pulled off her rubber gloves, throwing them into the sink. I couldn't help running up to her and giving her a big hug.

"Whoa, too tight, too tight!" She said as I squeezed my arms around her.

"Oops sorry, but come on tell me, does Frank know?"

"No and I don't want you to say anything, not yet." She said holding me back by my shoulders, so she could look me in the eyes.

"I won't but why? Is he not ready?" I asked not believing the question. I knew that he was ready to be a dad. Anyone could see that when he was around other people's children, he adored kids.

"It's not that, look there's a reason I haven't said anything about this and you have to promise not to say a word!" She said holding out her hand for the special secret hand shake that we had made up as kids. I placed my hand on hers and did the moves she knew so well ending in a disgusting spit in each palm rubbing them together. Of course, back when we were kids, we would just wipe our hands on our trouser leg but now we both got up and washed our hands at the sink, laughing.

"So come on, spill it."

She took a deep breath and said,

"Frank's got low sperm count." I couldn't help it but I laughed. I knew it was wrong and Libby didn't look happy about my reaction, but I laughed more about the way she said it than the actual meaning behind it.

"I'm sorry, I didn't mean to do that. It's just the way you said it. I half expected you to tell me that Frank's a spy or something." She rolled her eyes and continued.

"Well, I have my first scan next week and I wanted to wait until after then, just to be sure...I don't want to get his hopes up."

I nodded and held her hand saying,

"But when did you find this out and why didn't you tell me?"

"I don't know why I didn't...I wanted to. It's just that I thought I would be jinxing it if it told anyone." She squeezed my hand back before getting up to make tea.

"I found out when you and Frank went out to buy your car, when you left it got me thinking about why I was sick and then I remembered I hadn't had my period for a while, so I had to get a test."

"And that's why you were all weird about it when you got home?"

"Well yeah, I mean I even heard my phone go off in the car and was about to answer it when I thought...no, I have to be extra careful now, as I might be living for two. It even slowed down my driving."

"So, you went to get a test and it was positive?" I said passing her the milk out the fridge.

"No, I bought four tests and they were *all* positive." I couldn't help my eyes welling up at the thought.

"Aww Libs, that's great news. God, mum is going to freak out." She shot me a look and I quickly said,

"Don't worry, my lips are sealed as long as you promise me I can be here when you ring her."

We sat and chatted about baby stuff until Frank walked in and I realised that I would be late for work if I didn't get a move on. I ran upstairs, grabbed my stuff and ran out to my car. I turned up five minutes late but because I was still wearing the stuff I'd had on for college, it made me even later as I had to change in the back room before I could start.

"I'm sorry I'm late, Karmun!" I said as I whizzed past him taking my first tray to my tables. When I came back for my next one he stopped me.

"Umm, sorry honey, but Mr Draven wants to see you." My heart dropped. This had been the last thing I was expecting. I couldn't help but ask,

"What about?"

"I don't know, but he wants you to go over to his table right now." He said it as if he hated being the one to tell me this. Once again, I felt like running. I had never been over to his table before and it was somewhere I never wanted to go. Not only did I have Draven to face but now I had to face a whole table of unfriendly faces! Sophia was the only one I wasn't scared of but against six others, I didn't think it was going to make much of a difference. So, I placed down my tray and took a deep breath feeling as if I was about to be thrown to the lions.

It was like walking towards the electric chair, I couldn't stop from shaking and I could feel my pulse pumping under my scars at what I was about to do. I could see them all as I got closer and their faces became clearer. But my eyes focused on the man who had requested my presence at his table.

I decided that I wasn't going to speak. I would just nod. This was because I didn't think I could have formed the words even if I tried. I walked up the steps to the same level of his table and was stopped by the biggest guy I had ever seen. It was one of Draven's bodyguards, but this guy looked like he ate other bodyguards for breakfast.

It was the same guy who I had seen briefly twice now, once when they first arrived and the second was when Draven had come to my aid in the carpark. His face was scarred and full of potholes, his eyes were small and dark but rimmed with red. His hands looked as though they could have crushed the head of a cow and he reminded me of a Viking warrior. He stood in my way with his arms folded, which looked like hard work considering how big they were.

"Ragnar, let her through!" Draven's voice ordered. I shuddered as I walked past him.

Once I was next to the table, I froze. It was like being in front of a king and his court. His sister looked up and smiled which gave me a bit of courage, but not enough to get me to move or speak. I looked at the other two, whom I had never seen fully, but I didn't hold my eyes to them long as everyone was staring at me as though I was their next meal. It was like being in a confined space with every type of deadly creature and they were all thinking the same thing...

Snack time!

"Why were you late?" Draven said without looking at me and the others raised their eyebrows at the sound of his words. I still couldn't find my voice and Sophia was about to say something to her brother but he held up his hand to stop her. She gave up and turned back around to face the front.

"So, let's have it." He said with no emotion and my heart sank at his coldness. The anger I felt from this replaced a bit of my fear, so I gritted out,

"It's personal." Which wasn't a lie but my angry voice made it sound like one. I bit down on my lip and tasted the blood as it cracked inside.

"Right, well in that case, you *will* work tomorrow night to make up for it." Sophia looked up at me, eyes full of sorrow, but my face must have got the message across that I wasn't happy because she quickly looked away. The way he had emphasised the word 'Will' was a clear indication there was no getting out of it.

"Fine! I could do with the extra shift, so that just great, it's just dandy." I said with my angry take over in the form of sarcasm and the man next to Sophia shot me a disapproving look. He was very serious and the huge scar that went down one cheek wasn't the only thing that added to his frightening look.

All of one side of his face was covered in a strange series of tattoos which snaked around the scar and ran the full length of his face. The black ink passed through the damaged skin, but the ink disappeared when it reached the injured tissue. It made it look as if there were pieces missing from the design.

Apart from this, he had a very serious but handsome face with long platinum blonde hair that fell down under the black hood he wore over his head. He was ice white and scary. He was also the first albino man I had ever seen. So, when I received this look I couldn't help but find my feet with my eyes before braving another glance. Draven shot him a glare and his eyes looked elsewhere. Then Draven spoke again.

"That will be all." And then he picked up a shot glass shaped like a claw that had been defying gravity by staying up on a single point. He shot it back and placed it back on a tray that Layla was holding out to him. Again, the claw stood up, floating as she took it away. Ragnar, the giant, motioned for me to leave and I did gladly, without looking back!

The rest of the night I worked in a red mist of anger. I couldn't believe that ten minutes of being late warranted that! Jack was right, what a stupid rich pompous ass! Who the Hell did he think he was? I just didn't get him. One minute he was acting like the most amazing guy and the next he was some scary bad ass godfather type, getting pissed off because I was all of ten minutes late! It was ridiculous.

I finished my shift and changed back into my normal clothes, as if to make some point when I walked past his table to go home. Okay, so I didn't know what type of point I was trying to make but his eyes followed me all the same. When I got downstairs, I was met by Jack and the rest of the gang. RJ had wanted to catch this band playing that was called 'The Dizzy Bandits' who were a mix of punk and rock.

"Hey, what's wrong with you, you look tense?" Jack said as he joined me at the bar. I looked back at the VIP area and glared in the direction I knew he could see me from up there.

"Yeah, tense is a good word but pissed off is a better" I said as I ordered a coke from Mike and then changed my mind saying,

"Ah Hell, give me a shot of tequila."

"Whoa, aren't you driving?"

"Yeah, but one won't hurt and trust me, I need it!" I said downing it in one without the lemon or salt.

"Wow, you're hardcore baby!" He said giving my chin an affectionate little squeeze. Then, I don't know why, but I did something so out of character that I shocked myself, as I went on my tiptoes and kissed Jack on the cheek, not being able to help the look towards Draven as I did this.

"Well, the band might be crap, but it was definitely worth coming tonight. But I have to ask, what was that for?" He said with the biggest smile on his face.

"For being sweet and cheering me up." I said as I ordered a more sensible coke.

"So, come on, what happened... leader of the vamp pack been throwing his weight around?" He said as we walked back to the others.

"Something like that, yeah! But hey, I'm really sorry I'm going to have to cancel our date."

"What? Well that sucks! But it's nice to see you all worked up about it. What can I say? I bring out the fighting spirit in every girl." He laughed, leaving me feeling guilty. I excused myself and went to the ladies to compose my thoughts. Of course, it didn't help that I felt like I was being watched everywhere I went.

I looked in the mirror back at my reflection and didn't like what I saw there. I shouldn't have used Jack to get to Draven. I mean, why would it even affect him anyway? He had made it perfectly clear on his feelings for me and if not by treating me like a leper for the past couple of weeks, then most certainly tonight's humiliating torture.

It had felt like 40 lashes to my heart and I hated that I still felt the same for him. I was like a magnet for the worst type of men, they would dig their claws in and I couldn't escape their clutches. Only with Draven, he would suck me in again and again and then spit me back out whenever it suited him.

I splashed some cold water on my face and rubbed the back of my neck with my hands. What a fool I was. Here was Jack, who thought that I was angry because I couldn't go on a date with him and secretly I had been relieved. There was nowhere I would rather be than at the club. The reason I was so angry was the way Draven had spoken to me. His coldness, his disrespect and disregard for anyone else's feelings just because he was angry was excruciating and completely unacceptable!

I stayed later than I had expected to, but I knew that if I had gone early I would have just spent the time in my room stewing over 'Lord Draven'. So, only when the band finished and RJ had flirted with every member including the sound technician, we said our goodbyes and I walked to my car.

It was one of the only ones left in the shadowy car park and it made my truck look sinister. I fumbled with the keys in my bag trying to get into the safety of my 'tank'. I found them but only to drop them on the wet ground, which I could barely see. I bent down, feeling around for them as they had gone a bit under the truck. I felt the cold metal and grasped my fingers round them. I straightened back up and tried the lock but when I looked through my window I noticed I wasn't alone.

Staring straight back at me was the bird perched on the top of the next car. Its eyes were glowing purple and it spread its wings as though ready for flight. It made a high-pitched screech and put its head down making its razor-sharp beak shine in the moonlight. I screamed at the noise, dropping my keys again.

Damn it! I bent down again quickly and whipped them from the gravel floor as they had fallen by my foot. I came up like a shot and rammed the keys in the lock. I looked to check the bird hadn't moved closer but it had gone. I didn't wait around for it to reappear, so I jumped in my car, locking the doors and turning the ignition. I drove out of there like a bat out of Hell!

When I got home all the lights were off and I knew Frank and Libby would be in bed. I sat in my car for a while, still feeling too freaked to move. The bird was the one thing I knew wasn't in my head because Jack had seen it too. I sat there tapping my hand on the wheel trying to pluck up the courage to walk the short distance to the front door. I mean, it was only a bird, what was I so frightened about?

Okay, so it was the scariest, biggest most demonic looking bird on the planet and it looked like it could rip out my jugular with one swipe but hey, apart from that! I counted to three and bolted out of the door not even bothering to lock it. I ran to the door with my key already in hand and shoved it in the keyhole. I pushed open the door and slammed it shut forgetting about Frank and Libby in bed. I listened but there wasn't a sound, so I gathered they hadn't heard.

I just wanted this night to end, as it had been one thing after another. I walked over to the liquor cabinet and poured myself a drink of whisky and then I went into the kitchen to get some ice from the dispenser. I just needed a drink to calm my nerves and seeing as I hadn't yet made an appointment to see a therapist it was the next best thing to sleeping pills.

I took my drink upstairs and the first thing I did was close the blind above my window seat. Knowing that the bird was out there somewhere and seemed to have a tendency to keep finding me, I thought it best to hide. I knew I would never sleep right away so I took myself and my glass over to my desk and pulled out the drawing pad that I kept my secret demons in. I tore out a page and began to sketch.

I woke the next morning to find Draven's face staring back at me. I didn't remember at first that I had sketched a picture of him, so I was shocked to see the perfect features that I had burned to a memory slot in my brain. It was his deep-set eyes, his strong jaw line, even down to his stubble and his shoulder length hair styled back off his face. I had captured every bit of him as though I had copied a photograph.

Just looking at it gave me goosebumps and I quickly put it away in my desk drawer, hiding his cold glare. I had drawn him the way he looked last night and the memory made me close my eyes and push it back into the far corners of my mind, next to the other bad stuff I stored there.

I got to college early, as RJ wasn't in today due to a hangover she called 'study day'. I went to the library to kill time and to get out a few books on American History, as it was the one subject I was going to be in the dark about. Of course, when it was time for British history then I would be back in the game but for now, seeing as pretty much everyone in the class except me was taught it in school, I was going to need to learn it all from scratch. By the time I found the section I only had time to grab one book and run to my first class.

While I was in history Sophia had apologised for her brother's 'bad mood' and asked me if everything was all right at home? I explained that everything was fine, not wanting to disclose any details. I thanked her for her concern and lied about being okay with what happened last night.

"Sometimes, I don't understand Dom's reasoning, but let's just say he likes things the way he likes them, if that makes any sense?" She explained and I nodded but I really wanted to say, 'Well actually, it makes no sense whatsoever but hey... I guess cryptic clues must run in the family.' Instead I just stuck to,

"Don't worry about it." She dropped the subject, not mentioning her brother again.

Before she went, she told me that I could start at eight instead of seven if I wanted but I didn't want to add more fuel to the fire, so told her seven was fine. I didn't want to give him the satisfaction of another showdown.

When I got back, Libby reminded me that she and Frank were going to Frank's parents for dinner and were staying the night, so not to worry when I returned to an empty house. It was going to be the first time I stayed there alone and the idea didn't have me jumping around in excitement shouting 'Party'... if anything Freddy Kruger came to mind.

I had a feeling that this would be one of those nights and the dread washed over me like sticky black tar. With these thoughts, I had a shower and it helped but even Libby's honey milk shower gel didn't make me feel clean. I dried the top part of my hair putting up the rest that remained damp. I put on a black vest over my black underwear that I only wore when I needed to do some more washing.

I pulled out a pair of black long-sleeved gloves and slipped them over my scars, placing my thumb through the hole. I put on my black shirt that did up with a few hooks at the front and tied at the back as it wrapped round my waist. It showed my curves as the material clung to my skin. I added a Gothic black and purple tie that RJ had given me as I was sick of being the only one that didn't make an effort on weekends. I even decided to add a tiny amount of mascara that I had borrowed from Libby. She looked as shocked as Frank when I asked her for it.

"What's brought this on?" She said as she handed me three different types, getting overexcited to see me making an effort again.

"Nothing, it's just most of the waitresses dress smarter at the weekend, so I didn't want to stand out."

"Well you look great, really smart with the whole tie thing." She said waiting for me to pick a stick to use.

"I only needed one."

"Yeah, but what do you want to go for, length, fullness or curl?"

"What?"

"Here, go with this one, you already have the length and fullness, you lucky cow!" She said handing me the one with a blue lid that had the words curl and waterproof written down one side. Well, I guess that was good considering the amount of strange shit that had happened to me while working the VIP, tears seemed to be an everyday occurrence...well, at least I wouldn't look like a panda if anything else went wrong tonight.

"Thanks and you're sure I don't look...well, I don't want to stand out and look like a plonker," She shook her head saying,

"Kazzy, if anything you will stand out for being beautiful, you look great...and look at that skin...flawless." She said laughing when I cringed at the compliment.

I applied the mascara making my lashes even blacker and curl upwards slightly. I examined myself, pulled my shorter bits of hair down over my face, putting them to one side and looked at myself in the mirror.

I felt different…

I felt *exposed.*

DRAVEN

55

THE WEEKS IN BETWEEN

"What do you mean she is going on a date?!" I roared looking up from my desk after Sophia had dropped this knowledge on my lap.

"What do you think I mean, she has no doubt lost all hope and patience in waiting for you to ask her on one and decided to give the boy a chance...*one who never gave up like you thought.*" She replied not giving a shit about the caution our brother had no doubt advised her on taking.

Weeks had gone by since the night she turned up at Afterlife, and I was no closer to her than before. If anything, it felt as though I was running backwards and away from her image as she simply waved me goodbye. At least this had been the cruel depiction that had been plaguing my dreams these past few nights.

We were also yet to discover who or what had brought her here at that time, as Rue had been unable to detect the foreign essence of power that had lingered when I first discovered her. It was deduced, however, that whoever had cast such control over her, had only had enough strength to do so in getting her here and not far beyond.

This was frustrating, to say the least and didn't go down well with my descending mood. But then, this seemed to be the start of all the shit 'there after's' to come.

The first being her next night working, where she seemed to be in a daze for most of it, and if there were such a thing as waitress autopilot, then Keira had most definitely engaged hers. It seemed that even though she clearly didn't remember the details of the night before, whatever she had remembered, was obviously taking its toll and affecting her.

However, one of the worst moments was seeing her after work, sat outside against the wall and out of sight, waiting for Frank to arrive. The doormen were there, but still, I would have reprimanded her for not being in their line of vision if I hadn't first seen the reason why.

I had been stood on the balcony at the time when I found her wiping away her tears with her sleeve and trying to get control of herself when I heard her say,

'Pull yourself together, Keira'.

This was when I realised that due to a combination of events, I had pushed her too far. And my punishment for this was being forced to listen to her gently cry herself to sleep that night. Punished for the fact that I couldn't do one thing to stop it and two, was because...*I had been the cause.*

After this, the decision was wisely made to give her some space, despite Sophia and Vincent disagreeing. However, they didn't fully understand my reasons for doing this, as neither had been forced to bear witness to the lost feeling of utter confusion she was obviously going through.

It also became apparent that after gaining a lift from that cretin Jack, that even Sophia had to concede with me when I declared,

"That's it, she is getting a car!" Sophia didn't disagree, but she did still argue against me just giving her one of my own. Soon making the point that knowing Keira as well as she did, she therefore knew for a fact that she wouldn't ever accept such a thing.

However, she did come up with an alternative, and I had to admit, that her creative solution had given me a chance to at least have some fun at the time...

Weeks earlier...

Sitting here waiting in this piece of shit office wasn't my idea of a typical Sunday afternoon, but then again, I didn't really have a typical anything. Making me wonder what 'typical' days Keira and I would have together.

Sundays were often classed as the 'lazy days' for most mortals who didn't work at the weekends, and I had to say, it was an appealing idea to me. As having any excuse for keeping Keira in bed with me for longer than whatever we would soon deem 'usual' was a thought powerful enough to soon have me grinning.

In fact, I often found myself musing on these simple questions, asking myself everything from her favourite foods to hobbies she would enjoy, having now learnt of her once love of painting and art.

I had even picked out the perfect spot for an art room for her, should the desire be one she chose to pick up again. One I confess, I would take great pleasure in seeing for myself.

Maybe then our 'typical' dates could be at art galleries I could take her to, or museums, considering her love of history. I would often grin wondering if she would hang on to my every word when telling her the real stories of history I myself had lived through.

In truth, these constant thoughts were simply endless. And it was becoming even harder as the days went on just waiting for this time together to start.

But then I saw Frank's car pull up and it put a stop to my constant stream of unanswered questions. As I knew it was show time!

I would, of course preferred a more reputable dealer in my choice but knew that with only the measly 4000 dollars I had 'loaned her', a price that was agreed and bargained down to by Sophia, then I knew there was only one piece of shit dealer in town with those sorts of prices. Hence me now looking at myself in the small, lopsided mirror and outwardly cringing at the sight. Unlike with the doctor's vessel I had taken over, then I very much doubted there was much to be done about 'Bobby, the car guy'.

Keeping it brief, he was short, fat and had quite possibly the world's shiniest bald head I had ever seen on a human. Making me tempted to open up a few drawers of his desk and see if the guy indeed used the same wax on his head that he made the string bean outside washing cars use on the paint jobs. But then again, after first meeting Keira, I doubted anything would shock me these days!

So, that being said, there was little to be done about Bobby's appearance and not even a hat in sight. Bobby had also decided to unknowingly torture me with his dire choice of clothing that morning. As he had decided on a hideous yellow toned tweed jacket, light blue trousers that could have been denim. But really who knew, as I couldn't get past the fact that he had turned up the ends to accommodate his shorter stature. He also had the worst dental care I had ever experienced in a vessel. Which meant that all I had to work with was my charm.

Starting now.

"Hi there, Bobby Brown at your service, what can I do you for?" I said granting Keira a wink and a crooked smile that even made me want to wince when remembering what it must look like.

"We're looking for a reliable car for my sister here," Frank said, taking on the role of big brother and not taking any salesman shit. If it hadn't been said before then, it needed to be said now…I liked Frank.

"Sister, eh…lucky for me then," I said wagging my bushy eyebrows at her and making her cough back a laugh. I swear the sight of her smile alone was worth my time spent in this sleazy vessel.

"Well, let's go and take a look should we, pretty lady?" I said nodding to the lot where there was a vast selection of utter shit!

In fact, I was starting to question my sanity in letting my girl drive anything on this forecourt! But then Sophia had argued that if this was to be an advance on her wages, then it couldn't be something she would consider as taking ten years to pay back.

Not that I ever intended on letting her pay back anything. But as Sophia argued, for the time being, the ruse had to be maintained or she would never have gone for it. And as she had predicted, once receiving the letter this morning, the first thing Keira did was ring up the club and try to give it back.

Vincent had laughed at the time, slapping me on the back and saying,

"What are the odds of the wealthiest man alive finding out that his Chosen One is a person who doesn't even like money! Good luck with that one, brother!" A groan and a roll of my eyes were his only response in return.

But in the end, Sophia had been right yet again, which meant that there would have been no way to get Keira to accept anything more. Which also meant me turning up here a while ago and going through every piece of shit car he had here and trying to find the best of a shitty bunch! One I was currently trying to lead them to now.

"There's something wrong… he's never this nice!" I heard Frank express his concern to Keira now and decided to cut straight to it, putting an end to his suspicions…*for now anyway.*

"So, what's the budget?" I asked, already knowing. However Frank threw what they would say, a spanner in the works.

"$3000." I frowned knowing that I had given her more but unable to argue that without it seeming odd.

"$3000 you say…umm, well if that's what you've got, then that's what you got, let's see what I can do," I said in a way that I knew Keira would pick up on and no doubt be feeling guilty. Which was why she pulled Frank back and whispered,

"Why did you only say $3000?"

"Trust me, this is how the game is played, watch and learn kiddo," was Frank's reply and I had to say, he was right. Never show your upper hand until you needed to, which was the same in battle. However, what he didn't realise was he had just made this slightly more complicated for me. As they were about to find out that Bobby must have been having an off day, that or he had temporarily gone insane and no longer cared about money.

"Hey, what about that one, the red Chevy?" Frank said pointing to a coupé with a terrible safety rating.

"What, the Camaro? Dodgy transmission that one." I said knowing this was going to be the first excuse of many.

"Now here we are, Kaz, this one's perfect! It's a Toyota Starlet, right?" I nodded at Frank's question but didn't start my sales pitch about it, which Keira noticed.

"Go on Kaz, give it a try." But then Frank opened the door for her, and I didn't want her to get attached to one, especially not a hatchback. Gods, I wanted her in a fucking tank truth be told, but I wasn't about to get my wish with that one, so I found the next best thing! Meaning I had to think fast and quickly said,

"I wouldn't do that if I were you." Then I leaned in closer to Frank and informed him in a dire tone,

"Someone died in there you see and....well... we never could get rid of the smell." Keira's reaction to this was a comical one as she instantly let go of the handle. Then she stepped away slowly as if it still had that dead body inside before she wiped her hand down her jeans.

"Nice," she commented making me grin at her little quip.

"Okay, what about this VW Golf?" Frank tried again.

"Nah, you don't want that one, look over here, I have something perfect for the lady," I stated walking towards the larger vehicles and basically anything that would offer her more protection than a fucking little hatchback! It was bad enough being forced to watch her being driven around in that rusty VW her friend drove, but I would be damned at her ever owning something like that!

I walked straight over to the only car I had in mind for her, and the one whose engine had recently been checked by a mechanic, hence the higher asking price written on the windshield.

"Here we go, the Ford Bronco, now this is your girl, and it's midnight blue to match the pretty girl's eyes," I said winking at her again, and this time she giggled, obviously finding me amusing.

"Hey, look pal, if you think that by putting us off all the other cars is going to make us pay $6500 then you can think again! Come on Kazzy, let's check out the Mustang over there," Frank said wisely seeing through my bullshit but unbeknown to him, I was planning on letting it go for whatever she wanted to pay for it. As I was adamant, she was not leaving here in anything else.

So, I ignored Frank and opened the door for Keira, giving her another grin and saying,

"There we are, my lovely." Again, unable to help myself when winking at her and trying to entice another smile or even that adorable little giggle of hers.

"Uh...thanks," she said, slightly unsure and giving me a quizzical look in return. Frank rolled his eyes the second he spotted her in the Bronco and then came back over to me, knowing that it was time to bargain.

"Look, I will do you a deal. I'll let it go for $4000." I said making them both look shocked.

"What?!" Frank said in disbelief before looking back at Keira as if asking what my deal was. She just shrugged her shoulders, got out of the car and started looking for flaws. Oh, there were plenty of flaws alright, the fact that it hadn't just rolled out of the factory and was brand new for one! But as far as the engine went, and well, for her age, it was the best out of a bad bunch.

"Are you kidding, what's wrong with it?" Frank asked being blunt and up front, something I liked in business.

"Nothing at all, she runs great, and the lady needs something strong that will protect that pretty little bone structure," I said this time making her giggle again, and before I had a chance to fully enjoy it, Frank's sigh of frustration forced me to carry on with my salesman pitch.

"She's a 1995, 5.8 v8 engine and she's a beaut. Start her up if ya don't believe me." I threw him the keys I had kept in my pocket, something they didn't question as being odd.

Frank then did as suggested and started the engine up, and I suddenly went through what most car salesmen must have gone through in that moment, where I was silently praying to the Gods for the engine not to suddenly blow.

Meanwhile, Keira was obviously falling in love for she had that soft expression on her face as she stroked the hood as if she was trying to tame a wild animal. It was an incredibly endearing sight to behold.

"I told you we only have $3000," Frank said after switching off the engine and Keira shot him a look of disbelief. However, she didn't argue, as she obviously trusted his judgement. But it also reminded me never to let her loose in a casino by herself, for she had a terrible poker face! But then again, I wasn't surprised as her lying skills were utterly abysmal. A fact I was more than pleased about.

But getting back to Frank's own lie, meaning I now had to get a little creative,

"Ah yes, so you did. Well, I will tell you what, how 'bout I let ya have her for $3000 plus a kiss." I challenged tapping my cheek so she wouldn't think it was anything more. As to be honest, I wouldn't have put her through such a trauma as kissing someone with such appalling dental care. Not when the memory alone was enough to put a person off the act for life, and I had very clear plans about kissing Keira in my future...*for it would be long and often.*

"What is wrong with you!? Come on, Keira, this guy's crazy," Frank said walking away and expecting her to follow. However, she noted my smile and said,

"So, let me get this straight, not only will you drop the price from $6500 but you will knock another $1000 off just for a kiss on the cheek?" So, I told her the truth.

"A kiss by the prettiest girl I have ever seen. So yeah, I'm old and bald...humour me." I added this last part tempted to add ugly and resembled a well-known English dog breed, but I didn't want her sympathy wasted on Bobby.

I watched as she thought a moment on what I had said and then shrugged her shoulders before coming up to me and kissing me on the cheek. I ignored Frank's dramatic response and told her honestly,

"Ah, sweetheart, now that was worth every cent."

So, as it turned out, definitely not your typical Sunday, but I would take it!

Even if the first thing I did when getting back to my own vessel that day was to take a shower and brush my teeth...*twice.*

But despite becoming Bobby for the day and leaving him to wake up and question why one of his cars was missing and he was 7000 dollars richer, I had still kept to my promise to myself in giving her space. I knew after that night in seeing her crying that I was doing more damage than good. And until I could declare my feelings and make her mine, then in reality, by 'having my cake and eating it too' was in truth, only hurting her.

This became even more apparent the next night she worked after crying herself to sleep. She had just been coming to the end of her shift and at the time I had been caught up in a phone call with Ranka explaining that all parties involved were now happy to finally release the case file into my custody.

I had checked my watch, knowing that I wanted to see her before she left, and at the very least ask her if everything was alright. When I walked back out into the VIP to see an altercation between her and another waitress named Layla or Lahash, as she was known to other demons.

I didn't really know much about her as Karmun had recommended her as returning a favour and other than getting her work done, the only other thing I knew about her was that it seemed she was disliked by most. And I could very much see why when I walked out of my home and was met with the sight that made my demonic blood boil!

I stormed over there with the wrath of Lucifer and the moment Lahash saw me, she dropped her hold on Keira's arm, and her face registered her guilty actions.

"Is there a problem, Layla?" I asked in a stern tone I tried to rein back into not sounding quite so murderous.

"Nn...o...no, my Lord," was her response, annoying me further by calling me 'My Lord' something I had asked all my staff not to do when Keira was around, for I knew she would question it.

"Keira, would you like to add anything to this?" I asked hoping that she had plenty to say on the matter and expecting it from the furious look on her face. However, she surprised me yet again, as instead of getting her revenge and sealing Layla's fate, she said,

"No, she dropped her tray, and that's about the end of it." I gave her a look that said I didn't believe this for a second but let it go for now, thinking I would get to the bottom of it once we were alone. So, I turned my attention back to the one who would soon be punished for the offence of touching what was mine.

"Back to work Lahash, Eu vou tratar con vostede máis tarde!" I commanded speaking Gaelic and granting her a warning of what was to come. She winced before moving away, no doubt resigned to the outcome of her actions and what it would mean for her future in working here. A look I didn't give a shit about, and I made it clear when I harshly demanded,

"Pick it up!" This was in reference to the tray that was still on the floor and one that must have been in dispute between the two before I got there. She did so without delay and quickly left. I then took Keira by the arm and started to pull her off to one side. But the second I heard her moan of pain, I let go, having no idea Layla had actually gone as far as hurting her and thus sealing her fate even more.

I lifted up her arm to examine it, needing to see for myself the damage and feeling my rage growing to dangerous levels. However, Keira had other ideas and defied me by pulling away from my hold and making me near close to growling because of it.

"It's fine," she claimed, keeping her arm behind her back as if ashamed. A reaction that made me furious at the bitch that had done this to her. Now making me turn my head in the direction she had left and hiss the curse in Maltese.

"Kelba!"

"I'd better be going." Keira said trying now to get around me, but I refused to move and unfortunately, I was too far gone in my own rage to notice her own. Which was when I knew I needed to take a deep breath and try and calm down before I started to scare her.

"*Wait,*" I demanded softly, before requesting to see her arm, knowing she wouldn't like it, but she needed to start trusting me.

"Let me see your arm."

"I told you it's fine and if I don't go now, I will be late for Frank." Was her weak excuse and one that made me frown before telling her more sternly this time,

"He can wait."

"But I can't, so if you'll excuse me, Sir," she replied with her own stern words of defiance, and I was utterly shocked! Especially when she swiftly turned her back to me and decided that if I weren't to move out of her way, then she would simply take another route.

However, she hadn't been planning on encountering one of my guards who had no intention of moving unless I commanded him to do so, and right now I was in two minds.

"*Excuse me.*" I heard her hiss through gritted teeth and my guard looked to me silently asking what I wished of him. Keira turned to look back at me also, and this was the exact moment I knew, she had hit her limit. I nodded for him to let her through and watched as she almost ran down the staircase and out of my club.

A sight that pained me greatly.

Since then things had changed in both of us. I had no longer the will to push her, and she no longer had the need to gain my attention, for she didn't even once try. Seeing her at the club was becoming a bitter torture I found myself counting the hours waiting for.

I had punished Layla that night, stripping her of her powers at the next Temple Moon, but before then putting a ban on her ever entering my club again. Until her punishment could be carried out, she was to remain locked in my prison, in a room that was reserved for the less dangerous inmates.

However, this didn't last, as Sophia pointed out how suspicious it may seem to Keira that Layla wasn't seen again. Which meant the last thing I needed right now was her thinking I could have done something untoward to the waitress.

So, I agreed for Layla to continue working there for the time being, only under strict rules that she was to go nowhere near Keira and would be watched at all times.

I didn't like it but felt that with the warning, combined with the threat of an even firmer sentence that there was little danger in allowing it.

Oh, how wrong I turned out to be.

DRAVEN

56

HUMANITY LIVES

The moment I heard Keira had a date I had to confess... *I lost it!*

All this time that I had been giving her the space I thought she needed, and it had all been for nothing! Time wasted and all in vain, as for not one moment did I think it would be time spent in growing closer to the boy!

For weeks she'd been driving her car and benefiting from the independence it gave her, as I too had been benefiting knowing that she no longer required lifts off of her 'friends'.

But after Sophia informed me of her date, I found my rage once more. Which also meant doing something rash and deciding to take this 'boss persona' to the next level. I couldn't in that moment think about the consequences of my actions. As I was blinded by hatred for the boy and it was one I knew I was taking out on her the second I saw her approach my table.

"Dom, please I am pleading with you, don't do this! It will only lead..." I put up a hand silencing my sister's logic and no doubt confirming her mistake in telling me.

I think at the time Sophia had been hoping it would prompt me into making my move and put a stop to this time I was giving her.

Well, she had been wrong, for just the thought of this 'date' had me seething and blinded by a mist of red and therefore doing everything in my power to stop it. A reason she thankfully gave me by being late for her shift.

Now if she could have just made it by thirty minutes at least, then that would have given me a better excuse. But by ten minutes, then I really was about to look like the biggest bastard I was about to become!

"Ragnar, let her through!" I ordered the moment she stepped up to the raised dais where my table was situated. The moment I saw her standing there frozen on the spot as if awaiting her sentence, I nearly let go of this insane madness that had overwhelmed me. But then I wondered as to why she had been late in the first place...had she been with him? Had they been chatting on the phone and she had lost track of time?

Which was why I snapped,

"Why were you late?" I asked deciding not to look, for her presence would only cloud me with guilt and I was too angry in that moment to back down. Sophia was about to intervene, no doubt wishing to save her friend the embarrassment, but I held up a hand warning against such.

"So, let's have it," I said, prompting her to continue and silently pleading with her for it to be something important, or anything for that matter that didn't include that boy. Hell, she could have been washing her hair for I cared, as long as she wasn't doing it for anyone else's benefit other than my own!

But then she gritted out,

"It's personal." Which sent me very nearly over the edge. I knew it! I fucking knew it! She had been seeing the boy! Fuck! FUCK!

"Right, well, in that case, you *will* work tomorrow night to make up for it," I said daring her to disagree with me. I swear if she had told me she had plans, I would have vaulted over this table, grabbed her, thrown her over my shoulder and taken her into my office to then ravish those lips that seemed intent in torturing me so!

I would have made her scream my name for hours until she forgot all memory of this parasite that wanted what was mine! But then her brazen reply brought me out of the strange mixture of rage and lust induced haze that had afflicted me.

"Fine! I could do with the extra shift, so that's just great, it's just dandy," she said making me question, who the fuck ever said dandy!

Dandy!

I swear the girl was being adorable even when I was angry at her! Gods be damned, but if she didn't get out of here right now I was going to cross another fucking line, and it started with that sweet, smart mouth of hers! And afterwards, maybe that fine, shapely behind of hers that I currently want to see naked and baring the imprint of my hand before kissing the sting away with my tongue.

Damn it, what the fuck was this girl doing to me!?

"That will be all," I said knowing that I needed her out of here before I gave my demon the green light to do whatever he wanted to do right then. Asking myself, what would have come first, fucking the girl senseless or bathing in the blood of her 'date'?

All reasons why I picked up the nearest drink to me and downed it, wishing it burnt like the fires of Hell just for something else to focus on other than the hurt in her eyes. I felt like a bastard the second she walked away and for the rest of the night onwards. Sophia was furious with me, but I could care little, for she wasn't the only one.

Keira seemed to spend the rest of her shift stewing over my harsh treatment of her, and by the end of it, I couldn't say that I blamed her! What the fuck was I doing!? I was just pushing her away; that's what, but I couldn't seem to help myself.

Just one thought about her with anyone else, and I lost all my sanity! I just wasn't used to all these new emotions, guilt, jealousy, the blind lust that threatened to take over completely! It all fought against each other and made me act out, in a wild, uncontrollable manner. Making reckless decisions, without doing as my siblings suggested and taking the time to process these thoughts before acting on them.

It was true I was known for my quick temper and murderous rage when the time presented itself. But this was something else! This was almost beyond control and if truth be told, enduring such a trait wasn't fair on Keira. For how could I expect her to want to live with such a hardship when even I didn't want to!? I needed to get a grip on it before I ended up going too far and doing more damage than I could ever hope to repair.

For the price was too important to pay, and I was to find this out the hard way when the end of her shift soon came around. And there was one thing I could be certain of...

Payback was a bitch named self-loathing.

By the time Keira had finished her shift, she had gone into the back room, and I had made my move to stand when Sophia hissed so as the others couldn't hear,

"I think you have done enough damage!" I frowned down at her but remained seated, thinking that on this one occasion it was wise to take her advice. For upon reflection, I didn't think it looked as though Keira was inclined to listen to anything I had to say right now.

So, I was forced to watch as she left, walking past my table now wearing the same clothes she had come rushing in here wearing. Then she marched straight downstairs, to the bar and ordered herself a shot of tequila. That's when I knew how much I had truly fucked up this time!

I decided the second I saw her, and the boy stood there conversing at the bar that I couldn't be trusted to watch this any longer. So, I got up and stormed into my office before I yet again did something rash. Of course, Sophia followed me.

"Just what the fuck was that?!" she demanded, slamming the door behind her. I seriously didn't have the strength for it anymore so instead of finding my rage, I found my humility, something that felt like in that moment had been beaten into me!

"A mistake," I told her bluntly as I deflated onto the sofa and held my head in my hands. She had just been about to say more, obviously planning for this outburst of hers, when she stopped mid-flow.

"Uh...come again?" she asked clearly in shock that I would admit such a thing so easily.

"I am not so blind as to not know when I have committed the offence, Sophia, I am fully aware of my actions as I am when paying for them, as I am right now with my guilt," I said admitting the way I felt and thus taking the wind out of her sails. She released a big sigh and lowered herself next to me on the sofa I hated.

"It was pretty shitty," she said making me groan and grumble still with my head in my hands,

"Not helping, Sophia." She chuckled then and patted me on the back before telling me,

"If it helps, I was a total bitch to Zagan when we first met." I rolled my eyes, a motion she couldn't see, for I remembered the time well. Which was why I told her,

"Yes, I do recall."

"Yes, well did you ever wonder why?" she asked now making me raise my head up and lean back, readying myself to no doubt learn something new about my sister.

"Why?"

"Because I finally found my humanity." She replied making me frown in question, so she continued.

"I had finally found that part of me, part of my vessel's history that it had been holding on to, that taught me what it was like to finally feel...well...*human,*" she said shocking me for I had no idea.

"So, I understand what you're going through and how difficult it is to process all these new emotions. Especially when we are often ruled by our demons. Because before they entered our lives, we felt ourselves so in control of all aspects of life, but then when you fall in love, the scariest thing happens and that is having no choice but to let go of that control and entrust it onto another." I had to confess that I was dumbfounded, for she had just described how I had been feeling since meeting Keira.

"I remembered all the anger I felt towards him at first, thinking how dare he have this hold over me? How dare he be able to stir all these emotions, this jealousy, this guilt, this seemingly senseless reason of worry or concern I felt for him! I couldn't understand any of it but then in the end, do you know what he told me?" She paused and waited for me to acknowledge this part of her story, so I nodded for her to continue.

"He told me I wasn't supposed to understand it, I was just supposed to feel it and let it happen and then one day when I least expected it...it would just, *all make sense.*" I thought about her profound words and realised that it was true.

We weren't born to know these things or were even destined to learn them. We were just simply given the means to accept them one day and discover for ourselves the true meaning of love. If, of course, we were lucky enough to find it.

After this Sophia got up, obviously knowing that what I needed right now was time. The time I should have taken when finding out something I didn't like hearing before acting irrationally because of it.

But then just before she left, I couldn't help but wonder about the end of her story. Which was why I asked her,

"And did it...all make sense one day?" She smiled at this and answered me just before she left,

"Yes, it did...as it was the day, he died for me."

Keira

57

DANGEROUSLY EXPOSED

got to the club with plenty of time to spare, knowing I would never make the mistake of being late again. I walked through the main doors after my usual head nods to Cameron and Jo but I couldn't shake the feeling that something was going to go very wrong this evening.

I crossed the massive hall, snaking in and out of the early arrivals for the band that was going to be playing. It was one of the better known bands but no matter how many times RJ had told me, I just couldn't remember the name of them. I noticed my friends sat ready at their usual table and they waved when they saw me. Jack looked shocked at the sight of me and I suddenly felt self-conscious. I should have just stuck with my regular look.

I ran up the stairs before I chickened out and pushed open the door. For some reason it seemed busier tonight than any other night I had worked. I was about to walk round the back out of view when Akako the Japanese waitress stopped me and said,

"Sorry no go, no go, walk round." She said and then dipped her head leaving me feeling less than happy about it. I had already taken my jacket off and had it over the strap of my bag, so I would look strange putting it back on when I was already here. Some of the scarier clientele were starting to stare at me, so that made me move my feet in the direction of Draven's table.

I purposely remembered how mad he had made me last night, which made me hold my head high instead of letting it hang down pathetically. So, when I walked past, I finally looked as though I had some balls. However, I couldn't help looking at Draven for a split second but it was enough to catch the different look he was giving me. I had never seen this look and I had to say, *I liked it.*

It was a mixture of surprise and shock with the smile adding a different edge to his eyes. The look he gave me made me feel...well, kind of sexy. But as soon as I passed, so did the feeling.

"Umm, hi Keira, you're looking...good." Karmun said clearing his throat. I felt my face get hot and I wished I had changed before leaving the house dressed like this.

"Thanks." I said as I walked past going to put my bag in the little room. I dumped it on the chair and threw my jacket, not caring where it landed. I just wanted to check the mirror, worried that there was something else on my face apart from mascara. But there was nothing but my pale skin with the hint of red cheeks and very dark blue eyes that were now framed with thick lashes. I could see that there was something different about me and it wasn't just down to the lashes, but I couldn't figure out what. Giving up, I went out there and started my shift.

Sophia was waiting for me when I walked out and she too did a double take at me, which made me blush even more.

"Keira, you're..." I interrupted her saying,

"Yeah I know I'm early." I said in a loud voice and unbelievably Draven shot me a look as though he'd heard.

"That's not what I was going to say but yes, you are and it hasn't gone unnoticed, along with *other things.*" She said looking me up and down. By this time, I was the colour of a cherry.

"I would like to invite you to join us for a drink at our table after work." She said as Layla walked past looking as though she was swallowing her own tongue.

"Umm thanks, but I don't know if that's a good idea." I said as now I probably looked as shocked as Layla had only it was making it hard for me to swallow!

"It was at my brother's request, he feels as though he was a little hard on you last night and would like to make up for it, if you'll let him of course." She said smiling, as though she'd had something to do with this.

"Well, that's very kind but I don't think..."

"Come now, surely you wouldn't deny him this?" She said in a very persistent tone.

"I guess not." I replied, only realising that I had agreed to it when she clapped her hands together saying,

"Excellent! Till later then." She said with glee, leaving before I had time to recall the 'yes' I had sort of said. Great, now I was going to spend the rest of the night worrying about spending social time with the Dravens!

There I was again, more confused than ever. One minute he hates me the next he wants me to join them? What the Hell was going on?! This wasn't right and if I went over there at the end of my shift, then I would most definitely be playing with fire.

I spent the rest of my time serving drinks and picking up empties feeling as though I wasn't the only one who knew about this strange twist of events. It seemed they were all waiting for this to play out. Of course, the end of my shift was coming along quicker than I had hoped for and with only ten minutes to go I was starting to panic big time. So much so in fact that when a fight broke out, it took me more time to register what was going on.

One guy in a black military jacket was flinging another guy across the table, smashing glass all over the floor which spread as far as my feet. It wasn't in my section but the one next along, so this put me in the firing line. I stepped back to move out of the way. Although, little did I know I was moving in the way of someone else...

Someone who hated me.

Layla had been stood against the bar with a tray of slim vile looking glasses that reminded me of test tubes. She was looking straight at me with even more hate in her cruel eyes and I instinctively took a step back from her. But in turn she took a step closer to me with a murderous look that twisted her features and made her eyes blood red. This terrified me as I knew the awful truth.

I was seeing her in demon form!

I didn't have time to react and all the other eyes were on the fight that was still going on. I was trapped in front of this crazy, evil bitch and one thing was clear without having to hear her speak...she wanted me dead and gone.

Before I had time to turn, she closed the gap pushing her hand into my side sending a searing pain through my body that spread like a plague eating my flesh. She leant her face down next to my ear and whispered,

"Good luck with that one, Elegido!" She spat out and this was one language I knew well. She had called me 'Chosen One' in Spanish.

She walked away smiling, leaving me standing there in the worst agony I had ever felt. I staggered about and looked down to find that she had stabbed me with one of the thin glasses she had held on her tray. Only this one was metal and looked more like a round hollow knife. I couldn't scream, even though I tried, but my voice was lost in the crowd that was still trying to stop the fight.

I put my hand to my side but the metal was in the way. I looked back at my hand and my skin had been replaced by the colour of the blood that now poured freely from my body. It was warm and thick, reminding me of the last time I had seen this much blood on my hands. I could feel acid in my mouth and my knees gave way as I tried to move away from the bar.

I fell putting my hands out to save myself, but one slipped with the blood on it and flew into the glass that covered the floor. It dug into my palm as though my skin had been made from tissue paper. I tried to pull out the razor shards with my other hand but I couldn't focus on where my other hand was. Things were going blurry as I heard someone shouting my name.

"Keira...! Keira, look at me!" A strong voice was shouting in a controlled yet desperate voice.

"I... my side I can't..." I said trying to make sense but the words wouldn't come out right.

A hand went to my side and I heard what sounded like a growl when he obviously found the problem.

"Keira, can you hear me? You're going to be fine, just don't close your eyes. Okay...Keira look at me!" I opened my eyes at the voice and saw Draven leaning over me. He had a mixture of fury and pain in his eyes as he barked out commands in a different language I couldn't understand.

"Find her, I want her alive!" He said to the figure standing behind him, who looked like one of the men from his table. I kept feeling this stabbing pain as I moved, so my hands went to the cause as I tried to pull it out, but hands found mine before I could get there.

"Oh no, don't touch that little one. You have to leave it, or you will bleed out. I promise it will be gone soon." His voice was smooth, and it had a calming effect on my mind. But the pain was overtaking it and I wanted him to talk to me more. I could feel myself being lifted as an arm slid under my legs and another arm went under the upper part of my body.

"Keira, stay awake and talk to me." He said blowing more scent my way and I breathed deeply letting it take the pain away for a brief time.

"I don't want to go..." I said hoping it made sense. His hands gripped me closer to his hard chest.

"You don't want to go where?" He said trying to get me to keep talking.

"Hospital." I mouthed the word and the glass in my hand pinched as I moved it, forgetting there were shards still embedded in my skin.

"Don't worry I'm not taking you to hospital."

"Why?" I said wondering if that wouldn't be the smart thing to do.

"Because there isn't any time and because I can help you now." He said, and I was sure I could feel him running.

"Doctor?" I said meaning to add the 'Are you' at the front of that question but he understood.

"Something like that...oh no, come on Keira, open your eyes for me." He gave me a quick shake to get me to respond. I opened my eyes but it was getting harder as I felt as though I was falling.

"Nearly there, come on, keep with me now!" He said and it felt as though we were flying, he must have been running that fast. My eyes couldn't focus. It was like driving at death speeds and watching it all go past in a blurry vision. Amazingly, I managed to find some humour in the situation,

"You said that last time." He let out a tense laugh and said,

"So I did."

We were slowing down now and I heard a pair of big doors opening.

"Have you got everything ready?" He snapped out and I didn't like the sound of the word 'everything'.

"What everything?" I said wondering if he was asking me but then another voice spoke and I knew the answer.

"Yes, Master." A woman's voice said in a quiet timid way.

I opened my eyes and saw that we were in a large room but my mind switched back to the pain consuming my every function and I screamed as I was put down on what seemed to be a couch.

"Ssshh you're ok, I know it hurts but it won't for much longer." He said standing up and taking off his suit jacket.

"You promise?" I said and the back of his hand caressed down my cheek as he replied,

"Yes, Keira, I promise." He then demanded,

"Leave us!" To the girl who was still in the room. He pulled up a chair right next to me and pulled a small table closer to him that held lots of things I couldn't yet make out.

"Now, I'm going to pull you up slightly, but it will hurt... you ready?" He got closer to me and held both hands under my arms to pull me up.

"No but do it anyway." I said waiting for the pain to come. And boy did it come.

"AHHH AHH! Ouch, okay...okay, now that hurt!" I said trying to not cry but my cheeks were wet, so I think it was a little late for that wish.

"I know. I know it did, but you won't have to do that again." He moved to the table and now I could see a green bottle that I knew well. He then picked what looked like a sugar cube out of a glass jar with some silver tongs and placed it onto a strange slotted spoon, which had a design of wings cut out of it. This was then placed over a glass with a fancy silver bottom that curled up like a thorn vine overtaking clear glass.

He took out a tiny glass bottle and popped off the lid, then dripped some strange red liquid onto the sugar. Then, picking up the green bottle, he poured it over the sugar until the liquid ran over it into the glass below. He filled the glass then dripped some more red liquid onto the sugar before making me jump slightly as he set it alight. I didn't even see how he did this, as there was no lighter or a match in his hand.

After the sugar bubbled and caramelized he dropped it in the glass making the mixture turn from green to red. He stirred it before passing it to me, but he must have added yet something else to it as it was now black. Or did he just blow into it and it changed colour? My mind couldn't control what was real and what wasn't.

"I need you to drink this, but careful, it's hot." He said as he pressed it to my lips.

"What is it?" I asked, pausing before the glass.

"It's absinthe and it will help with the pain... drink." His voice took on a more authoritative tone making me obey. The liquid burned my throat but not because of the temperature. It felt like acid tickling its way down inside me. But within seconds of it hitting my stomach the pain started to change into a numb ache more than the stabbing, ripping feeling I was used to.

"Better?" He said as if feeling it too.

I nodded and automatically my hand went down to grab the implement that was still embedded in my side. He stopped me again just like the last time.

"Oh no you don't, let's not get too hasty. I need to stop the bleeding first, you're still losing a lot of blood." His hand let go of my wrist and moved to where the metal was sticking out of my skin.

"How come I can't feel the pain anymore?" I said and his eyes flicked to me, looking up from my side.

"Because I didn't like seeing you in pain, however, you will feel the side effects soon enough."

"Side effects?" I looked at him with wide eyes and a worried frown.

"Hold very still...okay?" He said gently, ignoring my question. He placed his hand down on my stomach, stopping me from moving suddenly, while his other hand was positioned around the metal ready to extract it.

"Will this hurt?"

"Do you really want to know that?" He said as he yanked it hard away from my body, not giving me chance to answer. My question was answered as my body arched upwards from the agony and I screamed once more. His hand pushed down on my stomach and won the fight with my body's reaction. I was flat to the couch and panting from pain.

"Good girl...Ssshh... It's alright now, that's the worst bit over with." He said as he smoothed my hair back from my wet forehead and then slid his hand down to wipe the tears from my cheeks. It took me a moment to come back from that one. I remained silent trying to catch the breath that his quick action had stolen from me. He turned back to the table and grabbed a piece of white material holding it down on the now open wound.

He had examined the weapon for a moment with a dangerous glint in his eyes before crushing it into thin shards. It shattered in his hand and he threw the evidence away in an angry gesture. I looked on in amazement but still didn't speak. The white material had turned red but thankfully the pain hadn't returned.

"I need you to stand." His face was soft and full of tenderness. His hand went under my body again and he lifted me with ease. I was soon upright and in a pair of arms so strong I felt safely caged in iron girders. I stood facing him and my blood was on fire from being so close. His hands were coming up around my neck and I didn't understand why.

"What...what are you doing?" I said flinching backwards. However, he just took a step into me, moving closer and I could hear my breath hitch as though trying to play catch up with my erratic heart. His hands started on removing my tie from around my neck.

"I have to get to the wound. Do you have anything on under your shirt?" He asked, and I thought I would pass out and not from extreme blood loss. He wanted to undress me?

"Umm...yes... why?" I said timidly.

"Because I need to take this off." He said as he put his hands around my back closing the space between us completely. My head only came up to the top of his chest and he bent his head down slightly looking over my shoulder. His hands found the knot of material where my wrap shirt was tied behind my back. I couldn't look into his eyes even though they were obviously scanning mine. His arms encircled my body and I had never felt so protected. His body being this close did strange things to my senses, making me want to touch his skin in the places his clothes concealed. The sexual tension emanating from us both was clogging the air, making me tremble with need.

When he had untied my shirt he lingered there for a moment before removing the rest of it, peeling it away from my skin and exposing my bare shoulders. His touch was soft and gentle as though any sudden movement would scare me. He threw it to one side as if it should never have been there in the first place. Then he moved back picking up a long red velvet scarf and came towards me with it held out as if he was about to put it round my head.

"What are you going to do with that?" I asked, stepping back.

"Don't you trust me?" He said cocking his head to one side as though trying to read my thoughts. When I didn't reply he stepped towards me and placed the velvet around my eyes, knotting it at the back of my head.

"The drink I gave you will start the after effects soon and I don't want it to frighten you." He said smoothing out the material over my eyes with gentle thumbs, making sure that I couldn't see.

"Frighten me?"

"It will make you see things that aren't there...it acts as a hallucinogenic."

My eyes were no longer a sense I could use and my heart started hammering out a beat at the raw power he had over me. I heard him moving and then I jumped when his hands touched my waist.

"We both agree that your top is ruined, right?" He said as his hands stopped moving.

"I guess." I said not getting the question. Then his hands grabbed a handful of the black cotton and ripped it open just under my bra, so my stomach was exposed. Again, I jumped at the noise and also the air that hit my skin. His hands were back over my stomach and it felt like his head was level with my navel. Maybe he had sat down but because I couldn't see, I didn't know anything other than his touch.

Then something strange took place. He placed his palm to my wound and held it very still. I was about to move as I didn't understand what was happening, but his other hand caught me, holding me in place by my side. He then gently applied enough pressure to secure me from moving backwards. I was quickly being pulled closer to his body before he spoke,

"Now be still." His hand released its tension on my side, but I was still unable to move.

Then it happened.

A wave of fire entered my body and coursed through my blood stream making me convulse. It felt like someone had injected me with a mixture of morphine and a burning aphrodisiac. The remainder of pain was being washed away but leaving behind the sands of desire. My body lit up like every sexual switch was being flicked at once and nothing could stop the moan coming from deep within. I felt the evidence of such scorching need dampen my thighs and sizzle along my nerves as though Draven's fingertips were right there at the core. I gasped for breath just as my knees gave out.

"Draven!" The plea broke out before I could grasp it back to the safety of unknown yearnings.

"I've got you... I've got you now, Keira." Draven hummed softly in my ear just after he caught my body from caving in on itself. I shook and then the storm of fiery passion calmed, turning into a deep feeling of euphoria. One only found after the sweetest sexual release.

Now, every fibre and molecule felt strong, as if another energy had entered my body making me feel reborn. A metallic taste filled my mouth as if I had been struck by lightning and my eyes filled with tears but not from pain. It was as if my body couldn't contain the sensations without producing evidence on how magical it had been. My muscles tensed as I felt them grow powerful. I felt strong, as though I had been genetically altered.

His hand felt my body respond to whatever he had done to me because he whispered,

"Easy there." He held me still for a moment before making sure I was steady.

"Now, let's take care of that hand." He took hold of the palm that still had glass embedded in my skin. I had forgotten about it, as the pain had long gone. Although, now my hand shook in his as another fear hit me.

"Are you still in pain?" My other hand went to my wrist stopping him from removing my glove.

"No, but I don't... I mean...oh God, please don't!" I said spluttering out the words, wishing I could see his face. I lowered my head and I could feel the material go damp from tears that started to form as my old fears became too much to handle.

"I won't remove your glove Keira, just the thumb...okay?" His voice sounded sympathetic and I continued to hang my head in shame.

He knew.

He pulled the hole over my thumb and peeled it back, folding it over the wrist. I bit my lip as my nervous tension gave me away. I had to control the urge not to yank my hand from his. It didn't take long as I could barely feel the glass being picked out. If anything, it felt as though he just moved his hand over mine and the glass all came out at once. Like metal filings to a magnet, leaving me with a tingling on my skin.

"Are you alright?" I started when I felt his breath brush my cheek, not registering when his large presence was standing once again. I nodded, biting my lip, thanks to what his close proximity was doing to my mental state.

"Good, now raise your arms for me." Okay, so if I was biting my lip before, now I was close to tearing the damn thing off!

"Wh...what?"

"I know you heard me, Keira" He said whilst fingers lightly peeled a strand of hair from my forehead.

"But... why?" My stunned voice stammered again, to which he merely responded with a short command,

"Now Keira." So with the voice of my boss turning hard, my arms shot upwards with little thought.

"Good girl, now place them firmly behind my neck while I lift you." I couldn't help the little sigh I released as a result of both the endearment and order I received.

He must have bent his head down for me to reach him, as my fingers grazed the cords of his tensed neck. I swallowed the hard lump in my throat, one I named 'this is crazy' and wrapped my arms tighter for a better hold. Once this happened he lifted his head, momentarily taking my body with him as I clung on. I yelped at the sudden shift, but then his arms swept out and took my legs from beneath me.

"What happened?" I asked on a whisper, referring more to everything that had happened in the last hour.

"That was me saving your life." He simply stated.

"And now?" I asked as he started to walk with me tucked away safely to his chest.

"And now, I am going to clean you up."

"Clean me…you're going to…"

"Yes Keira, do you like being covered in blood?" He asked in a new voice that I was fast leaning was Draven being amused.

"No, of course not." I said quickly and I heard a quick short rumble of laughter.

"No, I thought not." He replied with a smile in his voice. I decided to remain quiet at this point so as not to embarrass myself any further.

I felt him walk just a few steps before I heard a door being opened. Then sadly, I felt myself being lowered from his arms, arms that I felt far too comfortable in. He positioned me so that my back was pulled in tightly to his front and I felt the hard rim of a sink at my belly.

Without saying a word his arms came around me to turn on the water and they remained that way, trapping me to his frame.

"Tell me Keira, what is your full name?" His question caught me off guard and this wasn't helped when his hands circled my wrists. He pulled my hands from gripping the edge of the sink and plunged them into soothing heated water. Meanwhile, my mind went into full panic mode…did he know? God I hoped not!

"My full name?" I asked trying to gauge his reaction.

"Yes Keira, your full name." He repeated directly in my ear making it hard not to shudder, especially when his hands were scrubbing gently in between my fingers.

"Well you…um, you know my name." I tried to say but it was getting harder to think when he started rubbing our hands together now washing them as one.

"That might be true, but I'd like to hear you say it all the same." He insisted again not moving his lips from my ear. I wondered where his mind was at with this question and I just prayed it wasn't anywhere near the truth.

"Keira...John... it's Keira Johnson." I said more forcefully the second time, after clearing my throat and his hands tightened their hold on top of mine for a moment.

"I see. Very well Keira Johnson, let's get you clean." He repeated my name like the lie it felt and I was just happy that I was facing away from him and my eyes couldn't see what my lie did to him. I tried to keep my breathing even as his hands continued to wash away the night's horror from them. I just knew that if it hadn't been for the bloody water I imagined running off my skin, this would have been one of the most erotic moments of my life.

"I need to get to your injury now." His voice sounded thick with some emotion I prayed to God to be shameless erotic hunger. He lifted my hands from the water and gave them a little drip shake, which should have woken me from this mindless addiction. That was until his hands started to rip what was left of my vest top, exposing me to just my bra. His fast action wasn't enough to miss the feel of him brushing against my breasts and I inhaled sharply.

"Easy now, I won't hurt you. I just needed it out of the way. Be brave for me a little longer, okay?" His fingertips danced little circles across my ribs in a soothing manner and I nodded as my voice had left me. Well, that's not exactly true it didn't leave me, more like it was put on lock down. One so I didn't end up sighing his name on a carnal whisper.

"That's it, just relax into me and let me take care of you now." Oh my God! That one thought slammed into me thanks to his delicious words skimming across my skin, mirroring the very fingers belonging to my dream man.

"Yes." This one word slipped past my barrier and came out as I turned my head against the neck I found there. I felt a moment when his body grew tense at hearing this escaped word but then I relaxed back into him, causing him to do the same. I felt as though this was *our* moment. No dreams, no nightmares, no balconies and no social status between us. It felt like I had made a crack in the hard shell which my Draven was locked deep inside. And I wanted just a moment, a second in time to stop the world spinning and hold on to this feeling.

And oh my God, didn't it just feel so freaking good!

Draven seemed to understand my needed moment as we both remained still just breathing in sync, bringing us closer together with every fill of our lungs. I could swear I felt him whisper something into my neck but its understanding was lost on me. Then things started to move along and if I felt good before, then now I really felt the fire!

His hands stretched across my skin so that he held as much of me as possible.

"Arms up, sweetheart." His words barely penetrated my euphoric state and because of this he had to physically take control. He held my gloved arms and lifted them up and back to hold on to him behind me. This new move caused my body to bow outwards, thrusting an already heaving chest further on display.

"*By the Gods.*" I thought I heard him mutter, or it could have just been in the hope that he was feeling anything close to the Heaven I was rising to. His palms ran along my upstretched arms and then continued down the length of my body, brushing along my sides in a torturing way.

I decided then and there that his hands were pure magic that I was starting to seriously need over every inch of me. I could barely think, even as he started to use what must have been a cloth to wash me. All my mind would sing was the chorus of us being skin to skin. Anything else was mute at this beautiful point as I was now dependent on his touch to keep my body singing. Obsessions of the mind now being super charged by obsessions of the body.

I don't know how long it lasted but I knew without question it was over far too soon. Hell, I could have died in his arms of old age and it still wouldn't have been long enough!

"You're all clean." He said and was it my imagination that his voice now sounded strained and hoarse? I reluctantly lowered my arms and not feeling the ache, told me it definitely hadn't lasted long enough.

"Uh...thanks." I said shyly thanks to the aftermath of a hot as Holy Hell moment with my fantasy guy.

"You're welcome, Keira. Now turn around while I bandage you up." He had manoeuvred me further in the room using his hands to guide me at my waist. He remained a constant strength around me and even now when he was once again sitting in front of me. Then he starting wrapping strips of material around my waist and his hands worked with skill as if he had done this many times. I mean, who was this guy, a doctor in another life?

Once this was done I let out a short squeal when I felt my body being lifted again and then swiftly carried back out of the bathroom. I tried to get my reactions to his touch to calm down now that our moment was over, but this was proving difficult when he kept sweeping me up and holding me impossibly close.

He moved me over to the side telling me to sit down, once letting go of my legs and allowing my body to slide slowly down the hard length of him. I did as I was told but I had the biggest urge reach up and find his lips with my fingers, swiftly followed by my mouth. I wondered what he tasted like, how his tongue would feel duelling against my own in one of the most glorious battles between two people lost to lust.

But this was where that thought process took another turn, as now instead of pure sexual hunger powering my body, another essence filled my veins making me feel strong. As in 'bitten by radioactive spider' strong!

"What did you do? I feel... different."

"I gave you a drug to help heal you, so you will feel a little more... *energetic."* He said with a smile in his voice.

"A little? I feel like I could take on the heavyweight champion!" I said still feeling the buzz of the drug.

"Well, you did beat the crap out of my tree, so I wouldn't put it past you." He said laughing. I had never heard him fully laugh and I wished I could have taken off my blindfold to see it.

"How did you...? Oh, forget it. There's nothing you don't know about, is there?" I said letting my defences down and being completely honest.

"There are...*some things."* He said with both concern and regret lacing his words.

"Do you need to call your sister to explain why you won't be home?" His voice felt closer to my face, as he ran his fingertips a trail down my cheek to the tip of my chin. And once there he used his thumb to silently extract my bottom lip from my teeth. Teeth that found my bottom lip because of the question he had asked.

"No, there's no one home tonight, they won't be back until tomorrow...but why, what... do you mean I won't be home?"

"You need to rest before I let you go anywhere tonight." He said before I could hear him doing something else but was at a loss to know what. I had to admit to myself how much I relished hearing him say this and gave into the little chills of happiness assaulting me as a result.

"I feel fine now." I said so he didn't see me as weak.

"You say that a lot, don't you? Keira, you were just stabbed and nearly bled to death, I think the least you can do is sleep for a few hours." His voice held a hint of humour mixed with disbelief.

"But I ..." He cut me off saying,

"I'm just going to give you a shot and it will help..."

"No, don't!" I said putting my hand out to stop him. My hand had found his shoulder and I could feel his soft skin over solid muscle twitch with the contact. Where was his shirt? I moved my hand slowly up toward his neck and could feel some material from what must have been a vest. This was the first time my skin had found this much of him and I bit my lip at the feel of his strong frame under my fingertips. I couldn't help my actions as I traced them right up to his jaw line.

His body had gone rigid under the feel of my touch but then after what seemed like minutes of us both being still, his hand grabbed mine pulling me closer to him. I could feel his face so close now and like so many times before I stopped breathing. I was now destroying my bottom lip again with good reason and I swallowed hard.

"Why are you so nervous, Keira?" His soft voice invaded my concentration and I couldn't answer at first. I just loved the sound of my name from his lips and right then wished he had said another name, one that was long forgotten and left behind. I finally shook my head slowly and lied,

"I'm... not nervous." But my broken voice proved otherwise.

"Then tell me Keira, why are you biting your lip again?" He said in a smouldering voice that contradicted the sharp pain that shot in my arm. I knew then it had all been a ploy to inject me all along when I wasn't paying enough attention.

"Ouch, that wasn't fair!" I said pulling back and rubbing my arm.

"Would you have let me do it any other way?" He sounded amused and I didn't answer. The effects of the drugs were already making my head feel heavy and I tried to fight it by pulling the scarf from my eyes.

What I saw in front of me must have been from the drugs in my system as there was no other way to explain it.

Draven was glowing and the vast space behind him was taken up with an impossible image...

Wings.

DRAVEN

58

KILLER JEALOUSY

hat night I only saw Keira one more time, and that was to check she made it safety to her car. However, even then I made the mistake of doing so as Ava and scaring her. At the very least I was satisfied to see that she was alone and not with Jack.

Who, I had learnt from Sophia, she had made a point of spending time with for the rest of the night she was in my club. I was mad, this is true, but I was no longer mad at her but more so at myself for being the cause.

It just felt that, despite all my good intentions, I hadn't ended up doing right by her as I had convinced myself I had been. For all my choices had been based around that knowledge and now it looked as if it had been done in vain.

Well, it was time to make amends, and I was starting on her next shift, the one I had forced her to work. I told Sophia of my plans and wanted her to ask Keira to join us for a drink after work. Now determined to give her a better opinion of my council table than the one I had forced her to endure the night before. Needless to say, that Sophia was ecstatic by this change in me and I swear she was already secretly planning our wedding!

Well, as long as Keira agreed then Sophia could plan whatever she wanted to, for all I wanted now was a chance to prove I could be anything but the bastard I had portrayed myself to be... and shamefully, on more than on one occasion.

But I swear that night as she walked in ready for her shift it was as if she had picked that moment to torture me with the knowledge of how beautiful she was. For I quickly found myself unable to help the look I gave her as she walked past my table. I swear it felt as if I was stripping her bare with the strength of my lust, one emitting from me like a crashing wave and her crimson blush told me that she knew it.

She was wearing something new tonight and I most certainly approved. She now wore a tight black shirt that crossed over her body, creating that delicious V-shape at the front and gifting me with the hint of her ample cleavage, one she tried to tame with the vest she wore beneath it. But having experienced those handfuls of soft flesh myself, I knew that she was hiding nothing from me.

The shirt continued to wrap around her and tie at the back, accentuating her curves thanks to being pulled tight at the waist. With this she wore her usual black trousers, only now thanks to this new shirt she wore, it allowed me unrestricted access to enjoy the sight of her behind encased in the tight black material. But it was her choice of accessories that really surprised me, and I found my mind leading me down a dark sexual path just when looking at it, wondering how I could tease her about it later.

She now wore a black and purple striped tie, and I naturally approved of the colour choice. However, now I was just wondering how such a thing would look tight against her skin when I finally managed to tie her to my bed with it.

Her hair looked different too as it was slightly damp and therefore had waves hanging down that had slipped free from its clip and were bouncing around her shoulders and down her back as she walked. She even decided on a subtle amount of makeup, as her eyes looked wider and even more curious than usual, now being framed by even longer lashes. She looked both completely fuckable and utterly adorable at the same time. Making me now wonder at the combination and what would transpire from such a look once bound to my bed with that tie of hers and screaming my name, begging me to stop after hours of forced pleasure on her.

Gods help me!

Sophia chuckled next to me when she heard my groan for mercy and watched the rest of my drink go down in one... *like this would have helped!*

"I believe someone is trying to make a point," Sophia commented while sipping her drink and looking pleased.

"Then consider it fucking made!" I almost snarled insight of my lust for her and thus making Sophia laugh.

"Don't you have a mission to complete," I reminded her after watching Keira now putting her bag away in the back room, one solely reserved for her. Sophia smirked and said,

"Why yes, I believe I do." Then she got up, and I watched as she glided over to the bar to wait for Keira to emerge. I swear my heart was trying to pound its way out of my fucking chest! Nervous once more! I shook my head and asked the Gods yet again for sanity.

"Keira, you're..." Sophia started to say, but Keira interrupted her and granted me a look the second she said it,

"Yeah, I know I'm early." She then looked surprised to find me watching her, and I raised my brow in question, letting her know that I had heard.

"That's not what I was going to say but yes, you are, and it hasn't gone unnoticed, along with other things," Sophia replied looking her up and down smirking, and I was glad when she let it be known how her new appearance was also on my radar. But of course, she blushed at this as I knew she would.

"I would like to invite you to join us for a drink at our table after work," Sophia added, and Keira frowned as if this was the very last thing she wanted to do. For a moment I wondered if I should intervene, forcing the issue and demanding she have a drink with me, maybe even going so far as to doing so alone and stating that it was a date.

"Umm thanks, but I don't know if that's a good idea," she confessed glancing my way again.

"It was at my brother's request, he feels as though he was a little hard on you last night and would like to make up for it, if you'll let him of course," Sophia said turning the persuasion up a notch this time and I was thankful for it.

"Well, that's very kind, but I don't think..."

"Come now, surely you wouldn't deny him this?" Sophia added not taking no for an answer as I had insisted she not.

"I guess not," Keira said sounding unsure but conceding all the same.

"Excellent! Until later then." Sophia said with a clap of her hands knowing that she had won a round for me. I just hoped this didn't mean the purchase of another car, for that was usually Sophia's price.

The rest of her shift was painfully slow as I found myself restless and impatient to call an end to her night and have her seated next to me, where I intended for her to sit. Now with only ten minutes left I quickly ordered that another chair to be brought over when something happened.

Something I confess was unusual in the VIP but not solely unheard of. However, it was something that angered me all the same.

A heated debated was quickly getting out of hand, and from the bare bones of it, it sounded like an accusation had been made that one of my waitresses had slipped something foul into one of my enforcer's drinks. I knew this wouldn't have been the case, for it was Candra's section and someone who had been a reliable employee of mine for this past three hundred years or so.

Of course, one of her regulars in her section didn't take too kindly to the insult and decided to intervene. This resulted in a fight breaking out before my guards could get there. I was on my feet in seconds, dealing with the pair myself just after my enforcer had found himself being thrown across the table, causing an explosion of glass to scatter across the floor.

I grabbed a hold of his military style jacket by the collar and yanked him first to me, so that he could see who it was that had hold of him and then forced him to his knees, demanding in my demonic tone,

"Yield!" He did the second he saw who faced him now and dropped from my hold, lowering himself further in a show of submission. Then I looked to Candra who was off to one side and demanded,

"What is the meaning of this?!"

"I don't know what he is talking about, My Lord, but his claims are false, for I would never..." I raised a hand and then watched as my men picked my enforcer off the floor, as I, in turn, picked up a piece of glass from the floor before bringing it to my nose. I turned my head the second I caught a whiff of its stench.

"Rafflesia arnoldii." I growled making Candra look shocked, for I knew she wouldn't have done this. His drink had indeed been laced with something known as the corpse lily. It was also known as the largest individual flower grown on Earth and had a distinct decaying flesh odour, hence its name. It was also used in our world for creating elixirs and was known to have some side effects on certain demons for causing paranoia. Which would explain why my usually calm enforcer was now acting this way.

But I couldn't understand who in my club would do this and more importantly, would risk doing so under my nose, knowing how much they would have to lose...

Unless of course, they already felt as if they had lost everything...
Fuck!

"Keira! KEIRA!" I shouted suddenly looking to the bar and finding the one thing I feared the most! For there she stood, now looking dazed and confused, but I trailed her own gaze down to her side where she had her hand until she brought it closer to her face for inspection.

That's when I saw it...*Blood.*

"Keira!" I shouted running to her and throwing anyone in my way off to the side, no longer caring that seeing such strength would be questioned. For nothing else mattered than getting to her. I watched as she collapsed to the floor, trying to save herself as she fell into the scattered glass. I was too late to stop her from falling, and I cursed myself knowing it.

I skidded to the floor, coming to her side and lifting her head up slightly, demanding with urgency,

"Keira...! Keira, look at me!"

"I... my side I can't..." she said slurring her sentence as if she was still trying to make sense of what was happening. I looked down at her injuries and growled the second I saw the very fucking shot glass I had not long been drinking from now sticking out of her side as blood poured from around the wound.

Lahash was a dead woman!

I couldn't help but release a deadly growl, half of me wishing I could release Keira's care to my sister or my brother and go on the hunt myself...my demon half that was. But I knew I would never leave her, not when my girl, my Chosen One was bleeding in my arms!

"Keira, can you hear me? You're going to be fine, just don't close your eyes. Okay...Keira look at me!" I told her making sure that she stayed conscious. I also didn't want her going into shock, so needed to keep her focused.

"Find her, I want her alive!" I demanded to Ragnar, Zagan and Takeshi, who I trusted would find her, especially with my brother and sister leading the hunt. I barked out more orders, some to Lauren another waitress and taking care that as Keira was listening, so doing so in another language.

But then Keira must have wondered why the implement was still embedded in her side, as I felt her moving, no doubt trying to take it out herself. I quickly took her hands, moving them away and told her gently,

"Oh no, don't touch that, little one. You have to leave it, or you will bleed out. I promise it will be gone soon." I also allowed my voice the power to flow over her mind as much as this new turbulent situation would allow, but it was enough that it no doubt took away some of her pain.

I decided then to move her and take her back to my chamber to heal her, for I didn't want to do such with an audience. So, I took her into my arms, being mindful of her injury and doing so with care. Then I looked down and saw her eyes were starting to close.

"Keira, stay awake and talk to me," I said in a desperate tone and sending yet another wave of control to her mind trying to take away the pain. Thankfully, it let me.

"I don't want to go..." she started to say, almost whispering the words through the fog of confusion.

"You don't want to go where?" I asked already knowing the answer but also knowing the question was one way to keep her talking.

"Hospital." She only mouthed the word this time and winced straight after, telling me the pain was slipping through my control.

"Don't worry I'm not taking you to hospital," I told her, knowing I never would put her through that, not when I could heal her far better than any doctor could. And after seeing her like this, then it was damn the consequences, for I would decide on the aftermath of my actions later.

"Why?" she asked obviously now concerned for her wellbeing, and I would have rolled my eyes and muttered 'finally' if the situation hadn't been so serious.

"Because there isn't any time and because I can help you now," I told her, now running down my hallway wishing I could do so at blinding speeds, but I also knew this would only end up frightening her.

"Doctor?" she questioned, and I would have laughed had the circumstances been different. I couldn't imagine telling her that I was a doctor would have gone down too well, considering her aversion to anyone in the profession due to her past. So, all I offered her was a vague,

"Something like that...oh no, come on Keira, open your eyes for me." I quickly added the demand the second I saw her eyes closing again, so I shook her a little, knowing the small jolt of pain would do the trick.

It didn't.

She closed her eyes fully, and my panic was easy to hear when I shouted down at her,

"Nearly there, come on, keep with me now!" Oh fuck it! I finally gave in to my urges and practically flew down the rest of the hallway, getting to my door a second later.

"You said that last time," she reminded me still with her eyes closed and I let out a strained laugh, agreeing,

"So, I did." Then I walked through into my chamber seeing Lauren there after I had instructed her to get what I needed when barking out my orders earlier.

"Have you got everything ready?" I demanded looking around my personal space and seeing now that she had put the things I requested on a small side table by the largest sofa.

"What everything?" Keira asked in a small voice, thinking I was asking this of her.

"Yes, Master," Lauren replied and watched with wide eyes full of concern as I carried Keira over to the sofa. Then I laid her down as gently as I could, but it wasn't enough to save her from the pain. The sounds of her screams cut through me like a knife!

"Ssshh you're ok, I know it hurts but it won't for much longer," I told her trying to soothe her fears and get her through the difficult part, which was...*trusting me.* I then took off my jacket, throwing it to one side and rolling up the sleeves of my shirt. However, her small, vulnerable voice stopped me mid-action.

"You promise?" she asked, and that simple request nearly brought me to my knees for how much it affected me. So, I ran the back of my hand down her cheek and told her in earnest,

"Yes, Keira, I promise." Then I turned back to Lauren, remembering we weren't yet alone, as I hadn't yet dismissed her.

"Leave us!" She nodded respectfully and left the room, leaving me to my patient. I watched as Keira tried to focus on what it was I was doing, as I commandeered a single chair pulling it next to the sofa, along with the side table.

"Now, I'm going to pull you up slightly, but it will hurt... you ready?" I asked knowing I needed her in a different position than the one she had sunk down to after first placing her there. I hated that it was going to hurt her and was ready to send another wave of control to her mind, but her panic was making it difficult, as she had already begun to shut me out as she usually did.

"No, but do it anyway," she said being brave and I didn't prolong the wait, doing it swiftly after and making her scream out because of it.

"AHHH AHH! Ouch, okay...okay, now that hurt!" she said holding her eyes shut tight as if still working through the pain, meaning I could see the tears escaping from underneath her lids.

"I know. I know it did, but you won't have to do that again," I assured her before sitting down and going back to making her a drink I knew would help in making her more...*compliant.*

I could have used the drug Midazolam once more, but after the effect it had on her for days later, I vowed not to use it again. So, I had asked Rue some while ago to mix me up something to help make her mind relax enough for me to control certain elements of it. After first having no choice but to divulge the reasons why.

In the end she had simply nodded, vowed her silence and wished me congratulations. When I had then enquired as to why she was congratulating me on such, she then replied,

'I maybe be blind My Lord, but I am not without eyes.' Telling me, she could sense my feelings for Keira no doubt from day one. I had to admit, I respected her level of loyalty and thanked her for also making Keira feel so welcome, as Rue had always gone to great efforts to do so.

And now I knew why.

So, with a practised art in preparing Absinth, I went to work mixing her drink, adding the something extra Rue had given me days earlier. A mixture I admittedly kept in case I ever had a repeat of that night I had found Keira wandering my halls unexpectedly. I confess I didn't expect it to be used so soon or for this grave reason, I found myself dealing with now.

I soon had it ready, and after providing a little aid to the elixir, Rue had made, heating it so as it would mix well with a slight flame, and then blowing on it, turning it to black.

"I need you to drink this, but careful, it's hot," I told her, pressing the glass to her lips.

"What is it?" she questioned and rightly so seeing as it didn't look like any drink she had encountered before.

"It's absinthe, and it will help with the pain... drink," I told her knowing the moment it hit her system I would have more control over her mind, like being able to cease the pain as much as I could, one I knew would only worsen once her adrenaline had run dry.

She did as she was told, and I could see the burn of liquid make her eyes water, but she held back the urge to cough, and seconds later she looked up at me in shock.

"Better?" I asked knowing I had finally achieved my goal, in taking away most of her pain. However, after she nodded, she then tried to remove the crude weapon from her side, something I put a stop to instantly.

"Oh no you don't, let's not get too hasty. I need to stop the bleeding first, you're still losing a lot of blood." I told her, going to the offending item myself and repressing a growl.

"How come I can't feel the pain anymore?" she asked, and I looked up at her from where I was leaning over her torso, preparing to take it out.

"Because I didn't like seeing you in pain, however, you will feel the side effects soon enough," I informed her trying to prepare her for what I knew would be a strange experience for her once I started the healing process.

"Side effects?" she asked looking worried, but I ignored this question for the moment and concentrated on getting this fucking thing out of her.

"Hold very still...okay?" I warned her gently, now placing a hand on her stomach and anchoring her to the seat so that she didn't move, and no more damage was caused in the process.

"Will this hurt?" she asked in a quiet, vulnerable voice that made me want to kiss that question away.

"Do you really want to know that?" I asked at the same time pulling it from her, so not giving her mind a chance to dwell on the fear. She screamed again, this time fighting my hold as she doubled up from the sofa.

I held her firm until she was once again flat and I could get closer to her. I quickly gave in to the urge to comfort her, brushing back her damp hair and, wiping away her tears with my thumbs.

"Good girl...Ssshh... It's alright now, that's the worst bit over with." I told her gently knowing that it was true and trying to soothe her through her panting in trying to reclaim her breath. I then left her sweet face and grabbed a piece of gauze to cover her wound to slow down the bleeding until I could begin healing her.

I looked down at the blood coated metal shot glass in my hand, one that was shaped like a talon and crushed it the second my rage got the better of me. I didn't want to scare her with my actions so calmed my demon from letting go of that rage, telling him that soon we would have our revenge. For she was dead, one way or another. Lahash would pay dearly for this!

I took note that she was watching me with curiosity, no doubt asking how I had managed to crush metal so easily in my palm. Which was why I needed to gain back control and starting with that open wound.

"I need you to stand," I told her tenderly, knowing now the pain of doing so would be gone, thanks to the drink taking its full effect.

Meaning that I could now scoop her up in my arms and lift her with ease without hurting her. I soon found myself stood facing her with my arms around her and for the moment I couldn't help but bask in the simple feel of holding her.

I could even hear her erratic little heart pounding in her chest from being this close to me. Because right here and now, there was no questioning this as being her dreams or reality. There were no uncertainties between us.

It was just us with nothing in between.

Well, other than blood-stained clothes I thought wryly, knowing it was about time I rectify that. So, I reached up and started to remove her tie, knowing that it was something I would be keeping for the foreseeable future.

"What...what are you doing?" she asked me in an unsure tone, taking a cautious step back. However, I wasn't going to allow that for long, and took a step into her, telling her without words that she was going nowhere. Then I continued to remove her tie before wrapping my arms back around her.

"I have to get to the wound. Do you have anything on under your shirt?" I asked knowing that she did but asking so as to warn her what was about to happen.

"Umm...yes... why?" She asked me nervously, and I swear her pulse was hammering against the delicate parts of her skin, you could almost hear it beating like a drum.

"Because I need to take this off," I told her, reclosing the space she had created when speaking with me, as she had to look up and to do so, meant taking a step back. One I reclaimed meaning she now had no choice but to stare at my chest, as I started to untie the knot at her back from her wrap around shirt...something I confessed to have been thinking about doing all night.

"Easy." I cooed, but I don't think she heard me for her body was near shuddering against me for she could feel it to. This sexual heat between us that was burning us both up the closer and longer we remained like this. A sexual tension I only knew would get stronger the second I started to peel away her shirt, which was why I gave myself a moment before taking that next step.

I swear just the sight of unravelling that creamy pale skin was almost more than I could bear. But I wanted to take care with my fragile girl, who trembled in my arms. Which was why instead of ripping it from her body the way I wanted to, I slowly removed it and threw the offending item away. Then I did what I had no choice but to do, as the moment I had healed her, then she would be forced to see me as I truly was. For there was no hiding my true nature after I had forced a part of my essence inside her body, giving her the ability to see my kind.

So, I stepped away from her just long enough to retrieve one of the other items I had required from Lauren. A long red velvet scarf that I wanted as soft as possible against her quivering skin.

"What are you going to do with that?" she asked now taking a cautious step back, and I couldn't say that I blamed her, for trusting me to blindfold her was a huge step forward. Which was why I asked her,

"Don't you trust me?" When she didn't reply I tested her by taking a step closer, knowing that I'd been granted my answer the moment she remained still.

"The drink I gave you will start the after effects soon, and I don't want it to frighten you," I told her knowing it was a lie, as what she would see wouldn't have been anything her mind had conjured up or from any drink for that matter.

I smoothed my thumbs over her eyes gently after securing the thick band of material around her head, taking care not to cover too much of her nose.

"Frighten me?" she asked curiously.

"It will make you see things that aren't there...it acts as a hallucinogenic," I said and then watched as she turned her head as if trying to use her other senses to tell her what was happening now, which was why she flinched when my hands found her waist.

"We both agree that your top is ruined, right?" I said knowing it was and again subtly telling her what was going to happen next.

"I guess." she said in a small unsure tone and the grin I gave her in return, well, I was glad she couldn't see it for it belonged solely to my demon.

Although I had to be honest, he wasn't the only part of me satisfied that I could finally rip her clothes off her and see for myself her unhidden body. Something I had been dreaming about for far too long. So, I gripped handfuls of it and tore it up the centre as easily as if it had been made from paper. The act enticed a little 'yelp' from her that again had me grinning.

I then used my mind to move the chair over to where we were now stood and sat down so that her soft stomach was just below my head height. Now with the access I needed, I place my hand over her wound. Then just when I felt her about to move away from me, I quickly held her in place with my other hand gripping firmly at her side, quickly pulling her back to where I wanted her.

Then I warned her,

"Now be still." For unbeknown to her, something magical was about to take place. Because finally, I was about to tie her to me in ways she would never understand the depths of.

As it was to be...

My first Claiming.

DRAVEN

59

BLOOD ON MY HANDS

The moment I forced my essence to fuse with hers I knew what she would experience, for it was only natural. I had never done this before, but every single supernatural being knew how it was done. But if I were to describe it, then I would say it was a little like feeding from someone only in reverse. Instead of taking that energy, you were gifting it back to another, so instead of taking a piece of them inside you, you were letting a piece of yourself go.

But for me, it wasn't supposed to be a sexual experience, however looking at Keira now, then I would have to conclude that it had been a great misconception. Because watching her now, writhing in my hold as she felt the first waves of the sexual current coursing through her body, then I can honestly say there was nothing else like it.

The long deep moans coming from her were like feeling her nails along my back, begging me for more, even though her hands were kept fisted by her sides. I wanted to pick her up, throw her to my bed and show her the real thing. Soon enticing those sounds with my hands and my mouth, not just the feel of my essence merging with hers. But then when her whole body began to tremble, I knew she was near to her sexual release, and just before her legs gave out, she cried out my name,

"Draven!" I caught her in my arms, holding her through the convulsing of her body, closing my eyes as the emotions overwhelmed me. To feel her quivering against me just after I had done that to her...after I had given her that pleasure, well, it was a bittersweet moment. One made sweeter had I finally be allowed to hold her in my bed for the rest of the night but a bitterness from knowing that I couldn't.

"I've got you... I've got you now, Keira." I soothed in her ear, holding her tight. But then her body tensed as the aftermath hit, no doubt making her feel stronger, now her body was trying to adjust to the intense physical change I had forced upon her.

"Easy there," I warned knowing that she needed time. I then looked down at her to see how she was doing. Her side had healed nicely, now showing no trace of ever being hurt other than the blood still clinging to her skin. Something I would shortly be taking care of. But this was when I remembered her injured hand, for I was sure she must have cut it on the glass when falling.

"Now, let's take care of that hand," I told her sitting once more and taking her hand in mine. I felt her tense, and at first the reasons for such didn't register with me.

"Are you still in pain?" I asked knowing that she shouldn't be, not after healing her. But then when her hand shot out over her wrist, stopping me from removing her glove, this was when I realised. I had forgotten about her scars, and now the panic in her tense reactions became clear.

"No, but I don't... I mean...oh God, please don't!" She said quickly blurting out her plea before looking down at her feet even though she couldn't see them. I knew she was getting upset with herself and my heart ached for her inner turmoil.

"I won't remove your glove Keira, just the thumb...okay?" I told her tenderly, making sure she knew she didn't have anything to fear with me. She bit her lip but otherwise nodded a little for me to continue.

I frowned the second I saw that there was actually still pieces of glass embedded there, cursing myself for missing it earlier. So, I simply ran a hand over her injured palm, absorbing all the tiny glass shards into my own before dropping them onto the floor, crushing them in annoyance under my shoe. Then I watched as the tiny bloody cuts started to heal as I knew they would.

"Are you alright?" I asked when standing and getting close enough that she startled a little when I spoke. She nodded, and I decided it was time to get her clean.

"Good, now raise your arms for me," I asked knowing that with her extreme shyness around me that she would struggle with my next series of demands.

"Wh...what?"

"I know you heard me, Keira," I told her whilst removing the damp strands of hair that clung to her brow.

"But... why?" she stammered out, but I was in no mood to explain myself. However I was in the mood for being obeyed.

"Now, Keira," the second the command was made, her hands shot up when hearing this new tone and it made me grin, for she had pleased me.

"Good girl, now place them firmly behind my neck while I lift you." She released a breathy little sigh when hearing this and I didn't know whether it was from my endearment or the act itself.

So, I bent my head lower for her to achieve what I had asked and closed my eyes a moment when first feeling her touch against my skin. Then I raised myself from bowing my head and took her with me, making her yelp as I swept her legs from under her.

"What happened?" she asked on a whisper as if only now needing the time since being here to clarify what she was clearly questioning as a possible dream. Which prompted me to answer,

"That was me saving your life."

"And now?" she asked making me grin for the treat I was soon in for.

"And now, I am going to clean you up."

"Clean me...you're going to..." Again, my grin belonged solely to my demon.

"Yes, Keira, do you like being covered in blood?" I asked allowing amusement to lace my tone.

"No, of course not."

"No, I thought not," I replied in response to her haughty and embarrassed answer, still grinning from it.

I walked the short distance into my bathroom, first moving aside the tapestry that concealed the door with a flick of my head. Then once inside I let her legs go so that she was now stood trapped between my frame and the sink in front of her. Then without giving her warning, as once again being cruel enough not to, purely so as I could entice those surprised little sounds from her, I wrapped my arms around her, so as to get to the sink.

I filled it up with warm water, however, this time not being cruel enough to use the cold so that she wouldn't cry out in shock. But I decided to take advantage of her vulnerable position, as I could hear for myself the rapid beating of her nervous heart.

"Tell me Keira, what is your full name?" My question obviously took her by surprise and combined with this when I decided to take firm hold of her wrists, an action I knew would quickly have her out of her comfort zone. I then pried her hands from the edge of the sink and placed them into the water, caring little for her gloves.

"My full name?" she asked repeating my question and no doubt giving herself extra time to think about it.

"Yes Keira, *your full name.*" I too repeated this, only now doing so right against her ear, making her flinch. Then I went back to entwining my fingers with hers as I lathered up the soap between our hands.

"Well, you...um, you know my name." she informed me making me grin as I looked down at her from behind, seeing as she swallowed back the hard lump known as lies.

"That might be true, but I'd like to hear you say it all the same," I whispered, still keeping my hold on her and my lips at her ear, so she was utterly surrounded by my presence.

"Keira...John... it's Keira Johnson." She said after clearing her throat, and my grip tightened its hold on her hands as they had started to shake.

Lies.

"I see. Very well Keira Johnson, let's get you clean," I said repeating her new name as if it was acid on my tongue. For all I wanted to do was wipe that fake name away from her ever needing it again, just as I washed away her blood from our joint hands now.

"I need to get to your injury now," I told her, lifting her hands out of the crimson water and shaking the droplets off her delicate fingers. They looked so small in comparison to my own and the colour in skin tone was like milk and honey. A combination that was surprisingly scented on her skin. And I would know, for I'd had my nose near buried against her neck for this whole time I washed her hands.

But now it was time to take it to the next level, for I needed to get to her waist and to do that I wanted nothing in my way.

So, without giving her warning this time, I simply tore what was left of her vest, now gifting me the irresistible sight of her just wearing her bra. I even found myself raising a brow at her sexy choice in underwear, for it looked far from innocent as I would have imagined it to be and instead looking nothing short of sinful.

Oh, my little Vixen.

I suddenly found myself with the urge to look lower and see if the panties matched, but then she inhaled sharply now, feeling the air invade her naked skin and my arm brushing against her lace cupped breasts. I feared she might have been concerned by my intentions which I fully admit were anything but honourable. Especially considering what I wanted to do to her right now. But despite this, I still told her,

"Easy now, I won't hurt you. I just needed it out of the way. Be brave for me a little longer, okay?" I found myself saying this while caressing the skin on her sides, doing so until she relaxed back into me.

"That's it, just relax into me and let me take care of you now."

"Yes." The moment her breathy little plea slipped past her lips I swear I nearly gave up this hoax at playing the gentleman! By the Gods, but if this wasn't what you called a test of will, then I didn't know what one was! Especially when she bared her neck to me, turning her head in that deliciously submissive way. Now quickly causing my fangs to lengthen at the sight and just waiting for the moment we could sink them into her tender flesh and feed like the animal we were.

Fuck demon, yield to me!

I commanded the second that darker side of me started to take hold by planting these dark erotic images once more in my mind. Although to give him his due, she hadn't helped matters by offering herself to me.

I found myself needing time to push past this, taking in deep breaths and muttering for the Gods to give me strength against the tempting curve of her neck.

My hands held onto her waist not letting her move for fear it would only entice my demon, should she start to struggle against me. I was thankful, however, when she remained relaxed in my hold, having no clue just how far she had come in calling forth the demon to take control.

"Arms up, sweetheart." I finally spoke, lifting her arms up now, to secure them up on my shoulders so I could get to her side to clean. However, doing so only made her body more accessible as now her breasts were pushed forward and offering me the stunning view of her stretched out against me.

"By the Gods." The whispered prayer was one that couldn't be contained as the sight was nearly causing my hands to shake. I had to touch her, to run my own hands up her arms, wishing no material concealed them as they did. Then bringing them down again to her waist, showing her the gentle side I didn't know myself capable of right now.

Then I produced a cloth and refilled the sink, before using the clean water to wipe away the blood at her abdomen. I continued with my task trying now to focus on that and not the way she kept moaning in response to my touch.

"You're all clean," I said in a voice that didn't sound like my own, for it was strained and dry like the sight had robbed me the simple task of speaking.

"Uh...thanks." she muttered in a shy tone, as it was obvious our erotic time together was coming to an end.

'Only for the moment sweetheart, only for the moment' I vowed in my mind.

"You're welcome, Keira. Now turn around while I bandage you up." I told her now letting her go and hating the loss. I moved her closer to where I could sit, having nowhere else but the toilet seat as I was careful to shift her body with my hands firmly at her hips.

Then I started to wrap her waist in the bandage I had at the ready, doing so now only so as to keep up the ruse of injury, as now there was nothing there but smooth, unbroken skin.

Then the moment I was done with this useless task I swept her back into my arms, making her squeak in fright, for she was still without her eyes.

I walked from the bathroom and over to my bed, now telling her to sit down, once I had let go of her legs, letting her body slide purposely down my own. She did as she was told, but the moment I saw her tense I knew the after effects of having my essence being merged with hers was once again doing strange things to her body.

"What did you do? I feel... *different,*" she asked confirming my suspicions.

"I gave you a drug to help heal you, so you will feel a little more... energetic," I said smirking and knowing that what I wanted to say was that you feel a sexual need unlike any other.

"A little? I feel like I could take on the heavyweight champion!" she said making me laugh and tell her,

"Well, you did beat the crap out of my tree, so I wouldn't put it past you," I said referring to the night she refused me when requesting to look at her hand. And then indeed finding out from Ava's memories that she punched one of the trees on the balcony in obvious anger and frustration. Something that had shocked me at the time and only ended up adding to my many reasons in giving her time.

"How did you...? Oh, forget it. There's nothing you don't know about, is there?" she said getting frustrated now and being open and honest. Which is why my response was also the same.

"There are...*some things.*" Then after a few moments of silence, I asked,

"Do you need to call your sister to explain why you won't be home?" This was said leaning into her so as I could freely run a fingertip gently down her cheek to her perfectly shaped chin, doing so now so as I could extract that abused bottom lip from her teeth.

"No, there's no one home tonight, they won't be back until tomorrow...but why, what... do you mean I won't be home?" She asked as the meaning of this question finally dawned on her.

"You need to rest before I let you go anywhere tonight," I informed her knowing that once again I would have no choice but to try and get her unconscious, hoping this time she would be more cooperative.

"I feel fine now," she argued making me roll my eyes at her and grin, for I had been waiting for this response.

"You say that a lot, don't you? Keira, you were just stabbed and nearly bled to death, I think the least you can do is sleep for a few hours," I told her with a disbelieving shake of my head.

"But I ..."

"I'm just going to give you a shot, and it will help..." Suddenly she cut me off, shouting,

"No, don't!" Then she blindly put a hand out to stop me. I had rid myself of my shirt back in the bathroom, simply making it disappear when needing to feel closer to her. And now only wore a plain white vest I occasionally did under my shirts. But now I wished my torso as naked as hers for her soft hands started to explore my body making me tense. I was holding myself ridged for fear of reaching out and yanking her to me, as the feel of her hands on my body became almost too much to bear.

But then the moment she found my face, cupping my jaw I knew I couldn't let her touch go on for much longer. So, I suddenly grabbed her hand and before she thought it was so I could put a stop to this, I yanked her to me, so that my face was now a hairsbreadth away from her own.

The second I did she sucked in a startled breath before she swallowed hard and started to torment that bottom lip again, tormenting me right along with it.

"Why are you so nervous, Keira?" I asked gently, luring her in with my voice. Because it was as I feared, for she wouldn't ever willingly let me put her to sleep, as I had no choice to do.

So, this was the only way and seeing as she was still blindfolded, I prepared the right drug that I knew would do this. Knowing I also had to inject her in the right place for it to take quick effect.

Something I would only be able to achieve when she was unaware. Of course, being supernatural helped in locating the right place for I could feel her blood travelling all around her body when concentrating hard enough. So, I knew my moment when she whispered her lie, one I called her on.

"I'm... not nervous." I gripped her arm in the right place knowing she hadn't even registered the move on my part, giving me the chance to hold her steady. It also gave me the chance to push her glove down a little just below her elbow where it had already started to slip. But again, she was too far gone under my spell to notice. Then I asked her,

"Then tell me Keira, why are you biting your lip again?" After this I injected her intravenously straight into her vein, knowing it would only take about thirty seconds to take effect.

"Ouch, that wasn't fair!" she said yanking her arm from me and rubbing over the sting. I had the sudden urge to tease her by calling her a baby and kissing away the hurt. But instead, I simply asked,

"Would you have let me do it any other way?" In the end, she didn't answer me as she started to sway, making me catch her shoulders.

"Easy now, I have you, sweetheart," I told her, not even sure she was listening, as the first and last thing she did before going under was to yank the scarf free from her eyes, now seeing me the way I was never meant to be seen this night...

As a demon with an angels Wings.

Keira

60

THE FRIGHTENING TRUTH

I woke up surprised to find I wasn't in my own bed and it took me a minute to remember what had happened. My head ached as I sat up in what was the biggest bed I had ever seen. I was covered in black satin covers and I seemed very high up as though the bed was on a platform. I looked around and there were thick brocade curtains all around with a tiny amount of light coming through the cracks. It didn't take PhD to realise that I was sat in an enormous four-poster bed and the curtains were drawn.

I sat there, afraid to move as the drugs had now worn off and I was fully awake. But then I felt down to my side which was still bandaged and there was no pain. I decided that I was going to get up, as I was stupid being scared. What was I afraid of? Draven had clearly saved my life.

I moved back the curtains expecting someone to be behind them. I was faced with semi-darkness, lit only by a few candles and the moonlight that poured through glass doors opposite the bed. My eyes had already adapted to the light and I noticed that the bed was indeed on a higher section of the floor. It reminded me of the way Draven's table was in the club.

It had three steps around the platform and I swung my legs over the side ready to get down. I stopped, checking I was alone before moving. The room was in shadows showing furniture but not allowing the details to be seen. There was a candle lit on a small table that was closest to the bed. The candle illuminated a small space around it but stopped me from seeing further into the room. I stepped down off the bed and held on to the frame to steady myself. My legs felt like runny eggs and my muscles ached as though I had recently run a marathon.

I turned to look back at the bed where I had just been sleeping and was amazed to see it looked even bigger. It was a huge wooden four-poster and the posts looked more like tree trunks, being massive carved spindles holding a wooden roof that looked as if it had been carved by Da Vinci himself!

From there hung luxurious fabric that matched the gothic bedding. I pulled them back revealing more of the bed, which could in its own right, have been an American state.

I turned to the table and noticed a glass filled with the same liquid that Draven had made me drink and there were two pills next to it. I picked up the paper that was next to them both and read the words that looked as though they had been written in calligraphy,

Keira, take these when you awaken.
D

And that was all it said. I decided that wouldn't be a good idea, so I left them there and walked further into the room. The room was long and from what I could see, which wasn't much, it was split into two sections. The first part was like a living room/office and the other was clearly a bedroom. From what I remember about it, it had been very grand, with old antique furniture. But my memory of what had happened was unsurprisingly vague. I had only really remembered the way I felt being so close to Draven. Or maybe that was all my mind chose to hang onto and rightly so.

I took the clip out of my hair, letting it fall down in a mass of waves. It was still slightly damp and smelled of forest fruits, thanks to Libby's expensive shampoo. I rubbed my head where it ached from being slept on. I looked down, expecting to see blood stained trousers but all I was wearing was my black underwear set. This certainly brought colour to my cheeks, not only knowing he had seen me like this but to know he had been the one to undress me.

Thankfully, I still had my gloves on but I was still too exposed.

I examined the bandaged area expecting to find blood, but there wasn't any. Come to think of it, what had Draven actually done to it? I only remembered him placing his hand across it, but there had been no sealing of the wound, no anaesthetic and certainly no stitches. So how had he stopped the bleeding?

And then I remembered something...What Draven had looked like when I had removed my blindfold. Draven had told me that I would see things, but I had never expected anything like that. It was strange to have seen Draven as anything but his usual perfection, so I had to keep telling myself it had to have been the drugs.

It was deadly still and silent in the room with only the flicker of the candlelight. Someone had removed my shoes before putting me in bed and only my socks remained. My heart started to skip a beat at the thought that it might have been Draven to once again carry me to a bed...

This time his bed.

I looked around and noticed something black and folded at the bottom of the bed. I discovered my black trousers that had obviously been washed and a woman's black t-shirt that I had never seen before. My first thought was that it was Sophia's but either way I was just glad the next time I faced Draven I wasn't only dressed in my underwear.

My feet were soundless as I moved over the stone floor, making my way to the glass doors. There was no handle and when my hand went out to push them as soon as my fingertips touched the glass the doors disappeared into the stone wall. I jumped at the sound and waited to gather my senses. But as I hesitated, they slowly crept their way back, concealing the entrance once again. Now I knew what to expect, I touched the glass again and walked through on to another huge balcony.

The balcony was very similar to the one outside the VIP, only on a grander scale. It held the same marble pillars, but the difference was it didn't have marble balustrades in between. Instead it had wrought iron railings in a black and gold design. Metal vines intertwined through the bars with huge black roses and deadly black claw shaped thorns.

There were also two large trees up both sides of the doors in massive Japanese pots that reached my hips. My eyes took in the rest of the space and I noticed a staircase to one side. It looked as though it went up to the roof as it spiralled round a stone turret. This place was definitely more like a castle or a monastery than a house or a nightclub for that matter!

I walked a few steps closer to the edge and the full moon lit up the surrounding view of the forest. But as I stepped even closer I noticed that we were higher up than I had first thought and the closer I got, the more I realised that we were hanging over a cliff face. The valley opened up like a crater below, as though the land had been struck by God himself. As soon as I realised the immense drop below I stepped back, as I wasn't the best when it came to heights. Okay correction, they terrified the living shit out of me!

I heard a noise behind me and automatically hid behind one of the trees. The noise came from the room and I was about to step out, but I stopped when I heard a voice I didn't recognise. I could barely see as I peeked around through the foliage, but I could hear a man's voice and it wasn't Draven's.

"Where is the girl?" The man's voice said.

"She was here a moment ago, I can still feel her and the doors won't open for her. She couldn't have gone far." Sophia's voice answered the man but it was different to how she normally sounded. Her voice was strained as though angry or upset. I couldn't help but peek my head round to take a look but as soon as I did, I wished more than anything that I hadn't. What I saw was petrifying on a whole new level!

Sophia's face had changed into a monstrous sight, her skin was cracked as though made from hard desert sand under the hot blazing sun. It was grey and lifeless as though she was a living corpse. Her eyes were all milky white, like they had been burnt and she was now blind, but there was a black substance oozing from cracks in her eyelids. Her mouth looked like a pair of knives had slit it on either side, making it wider and more of the black liquid was holding it together.

I couldn't believe what I was seeing. My body was shaking and I held my hands over my mouth, locking my scream securely inside my body. My eyes filled with tears, as the fear overtook my mind. I pulled my head back out of sight, hiding from this horror. How could something so beautiful have turned into something that nightmares were bred from? I tried to stay quiet as I could still hear them in the room.

"My brother must be informed...go!" She snapped, and I heard the two separate doors close. I waited for any sound to be heard but the room was now empty. I peeked round again to confirm this and my breath calmed slightly when it was clear. I was still clutching onto the tree like it was a lifeline.

This could not be happening. It just couldn't! Not Sophia, I just couldn't grasp onto reality. Maybe it was still the drugs in my system, as Draven had said it would have strange side effects. But deep down I knew the truth. After all, I had seen this type of thing most of my life and what I had seen in Sophia was purely demonic!

My demons had come home.

I was just trying to compose myself when another fear threw me. I was missing in their eyes and they were trying to find me. The last thing Sophia had commanded in true Draven style was 'my brother must be informed', which meant something more terrifying than the sight I had just seen.

Draven would soon find me and what if the last thing I had seen in him hadn't been down to the drugs?! Oh God, this couldn't be happening! I was still behind the tree with my mind racing on ideas on how to escape. Surely, I wasn't a prisoner? This whole thing had just been one huge mistake. Once again, a dreamlike experience with Draven had turned drastically into my own personal terror. I was about to go back into the room when something very dangerous caught my eye, now making this nightmare a very real one indeed.

The bird was back and flying past, gliding in the moonlit air as though it owned the night. And it too had changed just like Sophia had. The bird's feathers had turned to solid black rock and the ends of them looked like rows of daggers. Its body was producing a flaming red energy that was moving like lava throughout its veins, leaving a slipstream of power in the sky.

I ducked as it flew over my head missing me by inches and I couldn't stop the little scream that erupted. I watched as it swooped down, landing on a smaller lower balcony and it made its usual ear-shattering screech into the night. I couldn't take my eyes off the bird as if it was drawing me in, which meant I saw what it wanted me to see. The cry was intended to alert its Master, who had now walked into view.

Draven came out onto the balcony and approached the bird as though it was a pet of his. I hid yet again and I watched as Draven extended his hand out to the bird and stroked his fingers down its hard body. But the bird no longer held my stunned gaze, as it wasn't the only one that had changed.

Draven looked as though possessed by something crawling around his body under the skin, making him glow a powerful deep purple colour. It was as if his veins were pumping it around every organ and therefore taking over. But even this wasn't the most striking difference. No, the real change was what followed behind him, following his every move as though very much a part of his body.

Draven indeed had wings.

I looked on, slowly getting closer as I tried to see more of what I couldn't explain. I could taste the same acid in my mouth as I always did when witnessing the impossible things that I saw, but this was like no other. It was terrifying as much as it was excruciatingly painful to witness.

The tears rolled down my cheeks, as I didn't want to believe my eyes...my cruel, cruel eyes. Why was this happening to me? What had I done to deserve repeatedly getting my dreams shattered in the most horrific ways? This wasn't reality! This was me...it had to be all me...I had to be the one making this happen...it had to be my own madness showing me all this...

Draven and his pet were no longer alone, as someone I couldn't see clearly approached. I knew then that my time in hiding was soon to be up as they must have told him about my disappearance. The person left as Draven's hand went up in what looked like fury. The bird was about to give me up as Draven's eyes followed the direction the bird's head moved to. They were now both looking directly at me and my first impulse kicked in, as my mind shouted one command...

Run!

I turned, and my legs found the staircase that led to the roof. I hadn't realised that the Heavens had opened and it was now pouring down with rain making the stone floor slippery and I struggled to keep upright. My body was wet through and my cold skin was fighting the urge to shiver. I didn't know what was happening behind me, but my shaking body wasn't about to stop to look.

The steps seemed to go on forever as they went around the wet stone wall that wasn't adding much support. My hands slipped from it again and again, but I kept going. My hair hung wet and limp around my waist clinging onto my skin as though it was also afraid. I finally made it to the top as it opened out in front of me. The large flat roof was surrounded by an impenetrable stone wall that looked as though it had trapped me in.

The moon was providing the only light but the clouds that had filled the skies had dampened its power and my eyes tried to focus on any means of escape. After what seemed like a crushing eternity they eventually found a door. My stocking feet slapped their way across the wet floor and I ran until the pain in my chest grew tighter. Then I heard it, the sound of giant wings moving in the air above me.

I flung my body round to face the man who was controlling them. Draven was in the air flying down with such speed that my eyes barely registered the sight. He landed hard knelt on one knee, dark wings spread wide with his hands fisted to the ground beneath him.

The floor shook under me at the power and his head snapped up to meet my frightened face. I saw the roof had cracked and crumbled under the pressure of his landing and it rippled out like veins. My head moved, looking towards the door then back at him, trying to judge the space between us. I thought that I could make it, but he must have thought differently, as he shook his head from side to side telling me a clear no!

I looked one more time into those blazing eyes that seeped through the curtain of wet black hair covering part of his face. I swallowed hard, mentally counted to three and turned to run for it but when I did my body found his instead, blocking my way. I didn't know how he'd got to me so damn fast, but I knew my need to get away was now.

His face was so close, his purple eyes burned into me and the light coming from his skin reflected the water off my own. His dripping hair was as black as the stormy night above and it was now all pushed back behind his ears making his face look even more serious. He looked at me as though he wanted to rattle me to death and my reaction of terror showed in response.

I didn't wait for him to move instead I ducked under and around surprising myself at my quick reactions. I gave every ounce of energy I had left, directing it to my legs and making them run towards the door, faster than I had ever moved before. The door came closer and I knew I was going to make it. I had to make it because this was it...I had nothing left in me!

I grabbed the door handle and prayed that it would open and when it did I let out a premature breath of relief. Draven's hand then came out from behind me, slamming the wood back against its frame, making it shake under his extreme strength.

"Oh no you don't!" He said in controlled anger. I stared at the wood unable to turn my eyes to him, but his voice again filled the night with a daunting order.

"Turn around and look at me!"

I turned with my head down both hiding my tears and horrified face. However, this wasn't good enough for him,

"Keira, look at me. Now." His voice was softer but it was still clear that this was not a request.

My head arched up to his face and my back pushed itself against the door as my fear was too much and I needed the space between us. I wasn't safe and this was my instinct following through.

"Wha...what are...yyy...you?" I stammered, wishing I could replace my fear with anger. His hand came out towards me and I screamed,

"DON'T TOUCH ME!" And I ran to one side trying to get past him.

There was a loud whoosh in the air as one of his wings came rushing forward from his body so fast, blocking my path with a wall of black feathers. I turned to escape the other side and he did the same thing cocooning me in this small space with my back against the door. My heart felt as though it would burst through my rib cage and I panted to try and regain some control.

"Calm down and please...*do not try that again.*" He said frustrated at my defiance. My face was wet, not only from the rain but mainly from the tears that were now flowing freely.

"What do you want with me?" I bravely asked.

"What I wanted was for you to have stayed asleep until the effects had worn off." He said remaining calm. This, however, had the opposite effect on me.

"EFFECTS! This isn't from any drugs, this ...what I am seeing... is real!" I shouted as my hands motioned towards his body, which was fully exposed as he wore nothing but trousers. His defined chest and stomach showed the muscles of a body builder, only made more by nature. Whatever Draven was, he was clearly different, and his body screamed out those differences in abundance. The veins housed the energy that flowed showing purple under his skin. I realised that I had been wrong, he wasn't possessed...this was him. It had been all along!

"What are you?" I demanded, still holding on to my bravery as though it was the only thing keeping me alive.

"It's complicated and you are not ready."

"Complicated! Is that a joke? You're telling me it's complicated and here you stand with bloody wings on your back and purple blood running through your veins! And all I get from you is 'It's complicated'!" I was shaking, I was so angry, and his purple eyes fed from my anger. His wings still held me captive, cutting off all the light from the moon making Draven the only light source in this dark situation.

"What do you want from me?!" He shouted back, scaring me but it didn't show as I shouted back in return.

"The *truth* would be nice!"

"As I said, you're not ready." He said shaking his head making the light move quicker under his skin fuelled by his emotion.

"Well, you have to give me something because I'm *not* going to put this down to me being crazy...no! No way...not this time Draven!" I spat out the words like venom.

"I'm afraid you have left me no choice in this, Keira." He said my name and for the first time it made the reality seem all that more real. It was me that was here, it wasn't the dream part of me. This was real. This wasn't an illness sucking me under. A madness consuming my mind and warping a truth into horrors of the underworld.

This. Was. Real.

"Why... what are you going to do to me?" I asked as my voice clearly spelled the words panic.

"I would never hurt you, I have told you this, but you have to understand...*this*...this you have seen, it is not a good thing for either of us and I have to resolve it before it gets any more out of hand and if I don't, trust me...*you* will get hurt!" His warning was as clear as the water that continued to fall from the sky. So, this was it, this was to be my end? Question was, was it to be by the hand of the man I was clearly falling in love with or the demon that faced me now? I couldn't help my response as I started to cry my despair.

He leaned in closer to me, placing a hand either side of my head on the door. His face came so close I could feel the warmth from the energy that coursed through him. My body couldn't help but still yearn for him the way it had always done. I wanted him and no matter how scared I was, the yearning was still there…I needed him.

"Hush now, don't cry little one." His mouth came to the level of mine so that the words were said over my quivering lips. Then he moved slightly to capture a falling tear in a kiss on my skin, tasting my fear for himself. His body was leant in, consuming the rest of the space between us and closing his eyes he inhaled deeply as though trying to take in my scent. He let out a groan and his eyes looked into mine with such intensity, I couldn't breathe.

"Keira, you just don't understand what it is you do to me. Pr Rios y le diabolic comp mi testing, Ella sere ma!" ('By God and the Devil as my witness, she will be mine!' In Spanish) He said with such passion and my mind tried to translate the words, but it wouldn't work, it would only allow my senses to react to how he made me feel.

He looked me up and down as though he wanted to devour me with his touch and my body trembled at the thought of his hands finding my wet skin. So, instead of trying to run, I did something very stupid. My hands moved up slowly, first to his wide strong shoulders then they moved down his large biceps feeling the raw power move under my hand.

I bit my lip ready for him to pull away from my touch but instead his eyes closed, and he looked as though he had to concentrate very hard not to react.

"Only you, Keira." He spoke in what sounded like pain and his closed eyes tightened with the force of such pain.

"I…Draven." His eyes flashed open at hearing his name coming from my lips and the intensity I saw there was soul consuming. Then a hand cupped my jaw and he lowered his forehead to mine. I didn't know what he was or what he was going to do to me, but at that moment I saw it for what it truly was.

Heartbreakingly beautiful.

Then I broke the spell when my hand dropped at the noise behind us waking me from this trance I was locked in. It seemed as though the bird had found us, and his face turned towards the sound, as if seeing it through his own wings.

"I'm sorry Keira, but it is time." He said as if answering an unsaid question. I didn't like the sound of that, knowing that this would end. I wasn't ready to let go yet so I stepped into him eliminating the last shred of space between us. I put my arms around him pulling our bodies together and pressing myself up against him. He reacted in the way I hoped and held me tight, wrapping his strong arms around me. He took my breath away and his wings wrapped around the both of us fully so all I could see was Draven's face. He looked down into my eyes and said,

"Goodbye, my sweet Keira, until it is our time." And then, before I could protest, his lips found mine, kissing me tenderly as his mouth opened letting the air that had passed through him now enter me.

It whirled around my mind, making me feel dizzy. I tried so hard to focus on bringing myself back to this perfect moment, but I was falling into an abyss of darkness.

It sucked me in until I couldn't feel my body any more, until I couldn't feel Draven's body anymore and until the only thing I could feel was death...

Again.

DRAVEN

61

THE LAST OF OUR TIME

Once I was assured she was asleep, I positioned her more comfortably on my bed and took the moment I needed to simply lie next to her. Now surrounding her body with my own, by taking her in my arms and covering her with one of my wings. I then took a deep breath, smelling the scent of honey and milk again, only this time with a hint of berried fruits, coming from her hair. The combination was almost intoxicating. In fact, I was currently getting so lost in the feel of her wrapped safely within my body's frame that I knew I could have quite easily fallen asleep peacefully.

However, that peace was to be shattered because I felt my brother's presence at my door.

"Come in, Vincent," I told him after shifting my arm from under her and covering her body in black satin. I then folded my wings back and shifted so that I was now sitting next to her sleeping frame.

"How is she?" he asked stepping closer to us both.

"She is well, and now resting as she should be...did you find my next victim?" I asked hardening my tone the moment I had finished speaking of my girl.

"I regret not." he informed me making me growl low, still keeping in mind my sleeping Electus.

"It seems she had this planned for a while, and no doubt had help with her escape," Vincent said making me close my eyes and work through the rage. Then I laid a hand on Keira's bare shoulder, and I instantly found that this helped.

"Witnesses?"

"There were, and I have gathered them in the dining room for you to speak with, but I am thinking that can wait." Vincent surmised seeing as there was only one place I wanted to be tonight.

"No, I will be there in a moment. This can't wait, for the longer she is being hunted, the more danger Keira will be in. She must be found tonight," I said even though I was loathed to leave her, I knew this was more important, as Keira's safety came first.

It always did.

"Then I will give you a moment." I waited for him to leave before removing the sheet from her body and the view once more made me simply want to lay down next to her. But I had a job to do, and this time, it was an execution I could freely commit.

So, I removed her shoes, leaving her socks for I had seen her sleeping with them on before and wondered if this was because she indeed got cold feet like she claimed. Then came the next line to cross, but one I no longer cared crossing, for the girl was mine. Just as this body was mine and right now, I wanted it as comfortable as possible.

Which was why I rolled her to her back and unbuttoned the front clasp of her trousers, before peeling them down her silky smooth legs. Thus quickly noting that my earlier question had been answered, her panties did match her lace black bra. Once they were completely removed and she now lay in just her underwear, I simply stood back and took the time to admire the breathtaking sight, for she was utter perfection.

By the Gods, but there were no other words for it! Meaning I couldn't then help but lean down and whisper into her hair,

"My little Vixen pleases me greatly." Then after granting her a gentle kiss, I moved back and covered up the exquisite temptation lay out before me, doing so with the sheet once more before I could resist taking advantage of the sight any longer. Then I added an extra layer to her protection against myself and pulled the curtains around the bed.

After this and in case she awoke, something she shouldn't do for many hours yet, I wrote her a simple note leaving it next to some pills for her to take, should she wake in any discomfort. I also made sure not to leave her in the dark, so lit some candles around the room, casting a warm glow instead of her finding the pitch black of night.

Then I walked away, ready to do what I was born to do...*deliver justice.*

"I want you to check on the girl," I told Sophia after my council meeting had finished and finding out that Lahash did indeed have this planned all along. Which we were all starting to believe could account for our traitor, for it seemed now that she could even be linked to Lucius.

However, I doubted his plans included trying to kill Keira for that would not serve his gain at all. Now using her as a tool to get from me the one thing I knew he wanted the most, then yes, that was the more likely outcome. Which then begged the question as to why she would disobey orders from her master?

It also became apparent that she had help in escaping but was still being hunted and my men were confident that they would capture her by the end of the night, for they were closing in.

"Of course, the last time I checked, Keira was still sleeping soundly," Sophia replied smiling and no doubt happy that my Chosen One was finally in my bed.

"Did you leave the clothes as I requested?"

"Yes, and like you said, nothing fancy, I had her trousers cleaned from blood and left a simple black top for her in case she wakes," she replied as knowing Sophia she needed reining in when asked such a task. I had feared to find poor Keira waking up and finding nothing but a ballgown to wear.

"Good, inform me the moment she wakes. I am going to investigate the evidence Lahash left behind." I informed her of where I would be once she had checked on Keira. I had no idea how long the drugs would work on Keira's mind, but at least I knew her sister wasn't at home waiting for her, thanks to being informed of such earlier, with her telling me that no one was home tonight. It was fortunate then that she could stay as long as her rest allowed, for I was in no rush to have her leave me.

However, it looked as though Keira had other ideas as no more than fifteen minutes later one of my enforcers entered the room I was using. I had been on the balcony after hearing Ava calling me out there, and I was soon to find out why.

"My Lord, your sister wanted me to inform you that the girl is missing." At this, I turned around slowly, now taking in the poor soul who had been asked to deliver this unfortunate news. In fact, my rage was just about to erupt to new levels with the rise of my hand when Ava squawked, gaining my attention.

I quickly dismissed him with a deadly growl and turned back to my pet, knowing now what she wanted to tell me. She motioned her head over towards the balcony just off my private chambers, and I was utterly shocked at what I found.

For there, shivering in fear was Keira, trying in vain to hide from view but spying on us all the same. But this wasn't what shocked me.

No, it was the fact that she had been able to get out there at all, for I had ensured all doors were locked to prevent this from happening in the first place. So how then did she managed to open up those glass doors?

But then the second she saw me something in her must have snapped and it wasn't just the sight of me with Ava. No, now she didn't just look frightened, she looked beyond fucking terrified!

That was when the full horror of my new situation hit me. Her mind, the drugs, the merging of my essence with hers, it all led to one thing…she could now see me in my true form, along with Ava's. And even possibly, Sophia's!

Fuck!

"FUCK!" I roared, this time aloud, the second I saw her start running for the narrow staircase. One that spiralled around the turret above my chambers and up onto the walled rooftop above. I then cursed the Heavens and the second I did they responded. A storm came out of nowhere causing a downpour and no doubt making the precarious steps slippery. I had no choice but to take to the skies, just in case she fell, and I could be ready to catch her should she fall.

I watched, now keeping my distance so as not to frighten her into making any wrong moves, for she was already unstable enough on her wet socks. Then the second she made it to the top, I made my move, and with it, my presence known for there was no point in hiding myself any longer.

It was time for her to face the truth, one I knew I would never be able to hide, for the chances of convincing her that this was all a dream were long gone…I knew that now.

This was the point of no return.

I saw the moment she made it and found the door that led back down into my home. But right now, I needed to keep her contained, for it wasn't safe for her back inside yet. Not when her mind was now wide open to see all the things she could encounter, most of which would no doubt terrify her even more than what she was now.

I swooped lower, and the second she heard me coming from above, she spun around just as I had started my descent. I was falling quickly and landed hard on one knee, cracking the stone beneath me on impact. Then with my fists still to the ground and my wings stretched out wide I looked up at her to see her wide eyes in both fear and astonishment.

But I let her look for as long as she dared to before she then looked back at the door. I knew what she was doing, which was why I shook my head at her, telling her no. Telling her not to chance trying to make the distance for she wouldn't get far and my demon…well in truth,

He liked the chase.

But what he liked especially was the type of prey we would soon catch, for it would only take a blink of an eye to do so and she would soon be ours for the taking. I took a deep breath the moment she ran, trying once again to get my demon to back down, for she was only making it harder on herself by provoking him.

Then I ran a frustrated hand through my wet hair pushing it back before making my move.

Unsurprisingly, she only made it a few feet, before she ran straight into my body, for I had moved quicker than her eyes would have ever been powerful enough to follow. However, I think my fury was easy to see, and one I was hoping was enough to get her to back down and submit to me like she had done many times in the past.

However, as I kept learning, my little vixen didn't feel like playing nice and instead dodged my larger frame by ducking under my arm. She had no idea she only managed such a thing because her body still benefited from my essence, making her slightly stronger and faster than usual.

I growled the second I saw her make it to the door and just as she pulled down the handle and made the slightest of cracks, I was quickly there behind her. I hammered my hand down on the door, making it slam shut and out of her hands.

"Oh no, you don't!" I warned as the frame rattled from the force of my anger. I was furious that after everything I had done, everything I had proved she would still run from me this way. Even in my other form, which I knew must have come as a shock, but I had still foolishly hoped her reaction wasn't what I feared it would be. But the devastating truth was...

It was worse.

So, it was time to face her fate as it was mine. For I needed her to see me, the real me, just as I needed to see for myself her reaction to it.

"Turn around and look at me!" However, the moment I saw her wince and the tears fall down her cheeks I took pity on her, this time easing my tone and forcing back my demon. Then, still making a firm demand and one she thankfully took seriously I said,

"Keira, look at me. Now." The moment she did her reaction was like having my heart ripped out and shown to me as it stopped beating. For the utter terror there now was a bitterness I could almost taste. She even ended up slamming her body back against the door, just to put some space between us.

"Wha...what are...yyy...you?" She started to stammer, and because of her distress I couldn't help but reach out to her, making her scream in fright before trying to run away once more.

"DON'T TOUCH ME!"

I felt that scream rip through me just as I commanded my wings forward putting a more gentle stop to her escape...one done so, without touching her, I thought with a bitter shake of my head. Then after taking a deep breath, I warned her,

"Calm down and please...*do not try that again.*"

"What do you want with me?" she suddenly demanded, and I swear I nearly said the ability to go back in time.

"What I wanted was for you to have stayed asleep until the effects had worn off," I said calmly hoping it would induce her to do the same. However it did not, and it seemed her rage was quickly winning out against her fear. Good, rage I could deal with...her being terrified of me, I could not!

"EFFECTS! This isn't from any drugs, this ...what I am seeing... is real!" she shouted motioning at the demonic and angelic energy that flowed freely through my veins, lighting them up as if they travelled through my body on the flames of my abilities. Flames that had long ago burnt away my vest when my own rage hit. But thankfully, I'd had the foresight to stop before it consumed all of me, and she now found me stood here naked. As I really didn't think that would have helped my case.

"What are you?" she asked making me tense, for now, was not the time for that conversation. Hell, but looking at her reaction to me now, and I was starting to wonder if there ever would be a right time!

"It's complicated, and you are not ready," I replied knowing this was most definitely true. However, she obviously didn't agree.

"Complicated! Is that a joke? You're telling me it's complicated and here you stand with bloody wings on your back and purple blood running through your veins! And all I get from you is 'it's complicated'!" she shouted almost shaking from her anger and again, I preferred it far more than her fear, even if seeing it only managed to spike my own now making me shout back,

"What do you want from me?!"

"The truth would be nice!" she snapped making me shake my head and tell her plainly,

"As I said, you're not ready."

"Well, you have to give me something because I'm not going to put this down to me being crazy...no! No way...not this time, Draven!" She threw at me, and I knew in that moment why she hated doctors as much as she did. It wasn't that she feared them, she just feared that they believed she was crazy...but why? Why would she think that, for surely it couldn't have anything to do with what happened to her? For no doctor in their right mind would accuse her of such after knowing what she had been through.

In the end, I had no choice but to shake these questions from my thoughts and focus on the problem at hand. That being my scared little Chosen One.

"I'm afraid you have left me no choice in this, Keira," I told her, knowing that once and for all, I was going to have to force her mind to bend to my will and I now had to do so by any means possible. Even if it meant using my one and only chance left to do it.

"Why... what are you going to do to me?" she asked no longer angry but now in panic, and once again the insinuation stung.

"I would never hurt you, I have told you this, but you have to understand...this...this you have seen, it is not a good thing for either of us, and I have to resolve it before it gets any more out of hand and if I don't, trust me...you will get hurt!" I told her trying now to convey the severity of her situation and mine, for if I let this continue, then all I would be asking myself would be when was the next attack coming to take her life from me. No, I needed to stick to my original plan and just hope that when the time eventually came, then it wouldn't be too late and through my own actions,

I hadn't lost her forever.

But hearing this now and her response was a heartbreaking one as she started to cry. And I couldn't bear it! So, I placed a hand either side of her head, just hoping that there was a shred of feeling left inside her, one I knew that she had once felt for me.

"Hush now, don't cry little one," I told her tenderly, over her trembling lips, then noticing a tear falling in the corner of my sight, I kissed it, tasting it for myself and very near shaking from the force of it. I then inhaled deep, her scent seemingly more enhanced due to the rain and making me groan before confessing,

"Keira, you just don't understand what it is you do to me... *By God and the Devil as my witness, she will be mine!*" I added this vow in Spanish as a fever named Keira was trying once again to overtake my senses, and like always, she had not one fucking clue!

I swear looking down at her wet little body now, all I wanted to do was show her with my own just how much I wanted her. Just how much I wanted to worship every fucking inch of her! But then, as if a question were being answered by the Gods of hope, she started to slowly raise up her hand, as if about to touch an untamed beast.

I froze, for fear of frightening her with any sudden movements, not wanting this moment to end. Not wanting to have the gift she was about to give me taken away. Then her fingertips finally found me, and she slowly started to explore the new appearance to my skin. She then started to bite her lip nervously, and I found I had to close my eyes against the sight before I took her up against this door and fucked my world into her, forcing her to see it all!

"Only you, Keira," I whispered in promise making her suck in a startled breath at hearing such a confession.

"I...*Draven.*" The second she said my name my eyes flashed open and I took hold of her jaw, holding it still so that I could place my forehead to hers needing the deeper connection between us.

And it was in that moment...

Heartbreakingly beautiful.

But then like most beautiful moments, this one had no choice but to come to an end. For I heard Ava in the background alerting me to her hunting call, for Lahash had been found. Meaning that our time here was at an end.

Something I told her softly.

"I'm sorry Keira, but it is time." But this was when she surprised me the most and more than she ever had before. Because instead of cowering in fear that I half expected or the lash of anger to strike me, what she did do was simple...

Tame the Beast in me.

For she stepped into me, eliminating the last inches of space and claiming it by putting her arms around me, and pulling me in close. It took me less than half a second to react before wrapping her in my arms and holding her in return. Then I enveloped us both in my wings, allowing the power from my skin to light up her beautiful features, making her look so ethereal that in that moment I even questioned if she were real or not.

She really did take my breath away. But it was as I said before, our time was at an end, which meant only one thing for us,

A bittersweet goodbye.

"Goodbye, my sweet Keira, until it is our time." Then I finally allowed myself a piece of her, as I lowered my head, placed my lips to hers to kiss her for the very first time. The second she gasped and opened up to me I took the opportunity I needed, deepening the kiss. And in doing so, betraying her in the worst way possible. As now, like this, I was finally,

Able to take hold of her mind.

The second I had her in my grasp I turned her world into a spinning abyss of darkness, taking everything I could from this night away from her. I had no idea if such a thing would work, but it was enough for her to finally fall limp into my arms.

For I was right, after what had happened here then I had no choice left.

It was time to say goodbye, and after being shown the last image of love she felt for me, then I knew now there was only truly one way to do that.

I had to break her heart...

And with it, my own.

DRAVEN

62

1867 FICTIONAL DREAMS

J looked out of the salon window as I often did, taking in the East Parterre and Flora Fountain, barely listening to the tedious sounds of snobbery at its finest. This was after Sophia had planned yet another social gathering in an attempt at what she considered to be neighbourly conduct, an act I could barely abide. But unfortunately, it was a necessary evil in some cases, for contact with influential humans seemed to be in more frequent need as the years went by.

Things were certainly easier back when I was King of a conquering nation, even if acting human was a heavy part to play. But as my sister often reminded me, everyone had their role to play in society and if I were to continue to rule my own world in this one, with humans as the living majority, then it meant life would continue in their presence, whether I deemed it necessary or not. And although I did my best to surround myself with my own kind, I knew that doing that of a scullery maid wasn't a chore a powerful demon or angel would kindly look upon.

Which was precisely who I was observing now as she made her way around the side of my home in what soon became obvious was a precarious manner. Her body language alone suggested she was hiding from someone, and knowing the hard labour involved, it was no doubt the cook. Mrs Weathers was known as somewhat of a tyrant in the kitchen. Although, her pies alone were of legendary status in all of Worcestershire and worth any hassle that may arise in trying to maintain a peaceful household at Witley Court.

I was, however, thankful that this was only one of many homes I owned, not only throughout England but throughout the world. Which meant that for a few weeks each year I could indulge in culinary delights at the expense of only a slight fuss made upon our return. Ah yes, country life was a damn sight more peaceful than town, and a chance for my wings to be rid of the suffocating smog of London.

But that all seemed inconsequential right now as I became fascinated by the delightful creature sneaking past the east wing of the house.

"And how was town, Lady Draven? I hear the fashions there have once again changed from our simple country style. However, Henry just recently bought me a delightful bonnet back from town that..." I heard one of our guests speaking to Sophia who didn't look half as bored as I or my brother did, and the half empty decanter of brandy was testament to it.

"And as to what has caught your attention so intently brother, for I regret to tell you that escaping through that window will only brand you as a mad man, not a suicidal one being that we are on ground level and therefore would do little damage," Vincent said with a playful smirk gracing his lips as he joined me. I didn't bite as I usually would have, as

I was far more inclined to allow my eyes to follow the actions of this strange girl, one who seemed to pull me closer with every step she took.

What was it about her?

My brother must have seen the object of my interest for he chuckled,

"Ah, a new maid for Mrs Weathers to torture no less, and a beautiful one at that." I frowned not caring for the way my brother spoke of her beauty, for strangely it felt like my right to do so and my right alone.

"Who is she?" I asked, speaking for the first time in what felt like the hour the sun had been slowly giving way to dusk before night consumed the day. Naturally my brother first frowned at the question, for it must have been the first time throughout our many lifetimes together that I had shown interest in not simply a maid, but a human one at that. But instead of conveying this confusion in a question returned, he simply replied,

"I do not know, but it was mentioned that some new staff were obtained after illness took the lives of some unfortunates that once worked for us, so I gather she is one of the replacements," he answered just as her near stumbling on the uneven gravel path peaked my interest enough to take action, for I felt my steps mirror her own. I even found myself almost reaching out to try and grab her in a fruitless attempt at preventing her fall. My actions didn't go unnoticed as my brother continued to give me a quizzical stare, one that was soon joined by Sophia's from across the room. For she could no doubt hear our conversation just as clearly as if she had been stood within our circle.

But little did I care, for the second she went out of sight I found my hand making a fist in annoyance.

"Is it to be believed she is who I think she is?" Vincent's question suddenly jolted me into tearing my gaze from the last place I had seen her form before she disappeared from sight. For now my mind was solely tormented with the depth of his words...for could it be...*finally,*

My Electus had found me?

Just this single unspoken question had me suddenly leaving the room, escaping the confines of my class and no doubt polluting my family name through acting in such an abrupt manner that social decorum would deem unacceptable in a gentleman. But little did I care for such things, for what possibly stood barely within my grasp had been something I had been searching for in what felt like an endless eternity. And it was one I was not about to let go now for the sake of a chosen name or a bought reputation.

So, I left the Green salon, one that hadn't long been finished for it had been a new project of Sophia's and served as a useful enough room for it was situated next to the grand ballroom. But right in this moment it served even greater purpose, for it was next to a room that would grant me access to outside without travelling through the house to chase after her.

I was now thankful that it had been designed as such, for not only did it offer reprieve from the often stifling conditions that one of Sophia's lavish parties could produce, but it allowed me a way to slip out of the centre doorway and down the stone steps that I knew she had just slipped by.

It made me wonder what my reaction to seeing her would have been had I seen her in a ballroom full of people all trying to prevent me from getting to her so quickly. In these tedious events, I often found myself like the rest, taking solitude in the night air and away from the hundreds of bodies consuming all that they could from their rich hosts before the night ended. But now, with no one in my way, I conquered the steps just in time to see the end of her plain dark cloak flash from behind the corner of the dining room alcove as she continued, remaining close to the building and presumably trying to stay out of sight.

I could have caught up to her very easily, even without the aid of supernatural means, for she seemed considerably smaller than my taller frame. This meaning that my legs would easily have cut the distance between us with little effort on my part. And I confess, that given my first instincts this had been my original plan. However now, I found myself curious as to where she was going and what she was up to, for as Lord of this grand court, it may play into my hands if I was the one to catch her in a suspicious act.

So, like the predator who stalks his prey, I veiled my presence and watched her from a short distance as she made her way past the corner of the building, keeping out of sight of the drawing room windows.

She then continued along the south portico, where sweeping grand stone steps and an entrance awaited her next move, for this was at the back of the house that faced the impressive fountains of Perseus and Andromeda. Of course, unbeknown to humans and also to many of my own kind, this was one of few secret entrances into the Janus Temple. It was also the very reason I had the house commissioned to be built here back in 1655 on the site of a former medieval manor house. After that, Witley Court has continued to grow and change, mainly thanks to Sophia and her predictable boredom.

Which made me question what my flighty little bird thought of Witley Court when first coming here and finding it her new home? This also begged the question who was she and when did she find herself in my employment? Questions I would soon discover the answers to, I was certain. But first, I let my unsavory actions concur as I continued to follow her unseen, all the while never really getting a clear enough view of her face. A face that right now she hid the entirety of by the large hood of her cloak, one that seemed to drown her slight frame.

I wondered then what she would look like dressed in the finest of silks and draped in the riches I had always reserved for one such as my Electus. But then these thoughts were quickly overturned by one more erotic. For seeing her naked in my bed was a sight I hungered far more for. Now to see what it was indeed the Gods had truly gifted me with, for what a treat that would be for me to unwrap, but first I had to capture it.

I watched as she paused at the bottom of the steps by the great white lion sculptures that were situated on plinths and were symbolically watching over the entrance to the Temple of Janus, our God of Time. Once there she peaked around the corner and looked up at the house, no doubt in order to assess her current situation and ascertain whether her chances of continuing unseen were good or not. Little did she know she was being stalked and by the Lord of her small world.

I too looked towards the house and saw in between the large pillars, servants serving their purpose. So, with a slight thought sent their way I cleared her path so that I could continue to discover her motives. I even found myself grinning to myself when I detected the audible sigh of relief she took before continuing on with her mission.

She continued towards one of the newest editions Sophia had made, which was the grand conservatory my sister had found great joy in showing off to her new guests only earlier this summer's eve. Of course, she hadn't been entirely up front as to where she had obtained such a large collection of exotic plants or the fact that most of them would die, withering away to obscurity the moment she left the room.

However, I found myself grinning once more as the girl paused just outside the large windows, unsurprisingly unable to resist taking a peek inside, no doubt seeing very little due to the lack of light from both sides. This meaning that she gave up on this pretty quickly and half of me wondered had this been her only reason for being out here and if so, it hardly warranted hiding one's actions. Although it had been noted that the heads of the household certainly maintained a regimented work ethic where duties of the house were concerned, especially no doubt when its master was in residence.

But seconds later and this proved only an added bonus in her plans, as she carried on past Louis XVI court and on towards the coach yard, suddenly making me fearful she was in fact trying to leave the estate. Well, I wasn't about to let that happen or for her to steal a horse as it looked now to be her plan all along. For she managed to sneak past the west gatehouse and into the stable yard.

I found myself frowning at her actions, questioning why she would try to leave here. A considerable and sought after employment in her lower social standing and one not easily come by unless you could be recommended. I watched as indeed my fears were being proven correct, for she waited for the stable hand, John, to finish his duties before slipping inside the south stables. So, I followed her and found myself near astounded when instead of heading towards where the saddles were kept, she walked straight to a certain stall. She then started cooing to one of the tame mares we had there, a grey dapple I had recently purchased solely for the reason that she was a beautiful horse. And so it would seem I wasn't the only one who thought this to be the case.

"Hello again, my friend, I told you I would be back," she whispered into the stall before the horse stuck its head out to greet her warm invitation. The girl then made a delightful sound the moment the horse nudged the side of her head, prompting her to raise a hand and stroke the soft velvet of her nose and muzzle.

I had to say that the sight had me transfixed, especially when the sudden actions from the horse made the hood of her cloak fall back and finally award me with a beauty that simply took my breath away.

By the Gods, I was enraptured by it!

It was a little like looking directly into the sunrise only being able to marvel in its splendor a few moments before its power overwhelmed your senses. She was a goddess, even in her plain attire, which was the standard black dress with starched white apron pinned to the front. But even so it was not enough to hide all the curves of her body from me, making me itch and flex my fingers in and out of a fist just to help contain the temptation to touch her. One that in that moment would have no doubt been a startling and distressing situation to find herself in.

So, with this firmly set in mind, I continued to watch as she remained lost in her own world of beauty when faced with the reason she had sneaked in here.

"And look what I brought you but shush, don't tell anyone as it could get me into trouble." She told the horse then looked around before reaching into her pocket and retrieving the real reason she had been acting guilty. I swear I nearly laughed aloud giving myself away when I saw the sugar cubes in her hands, ones I had brought back specially from Germany as they weren't yet available in this country to buy, being invented only a short time ago. And yet another way for Sophia to show off our wealth with the neighbors, I thought with a mindful roll of my eyes.

But upon seeing this and knowing myself the sweet tooth of a horse, I decided now was the perfect time to let myself be known and introduce this poor innocent girl to her new Master. So, I first exited the stables before removing the veil and then re-entered acting as if I were enquiring after our new dapple.

"Ah John, I was just in mind to ask after our new...oh." I had meant to say more but the second she looked directly at me my mind stumbled for the sight was like a thunder bolt had sent a current through the wave that just crashed into my soul. For I even found my hand gripped tight against a beam so as to hold my body immobile.

For it was her!

It was truly her and as if up until that moment all I had was hope in my heart, one the Gods quickly allowed me to morph into truth. For now, I had the proof of such and the sight of her was all I would ever need. But I wasn't the only one who looked physically affected, for she too took a step back and seemed to need the use of something structural to stop herself from falling.

And what, I wondered, was it that she saw in me now? Dressed in black and as any gentleman of wealth would for dinner. But without my long jacket and gloves, I hardly looked fit for the walk I had proclaimed to have been taking. But I cared not for such things. Let her believe what she wanted, for she would soon know the truth of the matter in which her life was about to change.

I knew I needed to speak and soon before she really did flee this time, something she looked a few seconds away from doing. I also noticed how she had instinctively hidden her hand behind her back, one I knew contained the guilty reason of her crime. I had to hide my knowing smirk as in that moment it seemed as if I held all the power of the situation...ironic then, of the power she held with a single look in return. Power, that at just the sight of her staring back at me all wide-eyed and blushing had over me, for I swear such a look could have brought this King to his knees for the first time in an eternity.

But just then my own steed, sensing my presence, let his be known for he was as wild as I needed him to be. Samson was a black Shire and stood at seven feet two inches tall, which many considered an incredible height, for he was quite literally a beast of his kind. He was also extremely loyal and therefore made it quite impossible to be ridden by any, other than myself. He was also thought to be quite unruly which was why he kicked out suddenly at his stable, one that had to be reinforced many times.

"Ahh!" The girl screamed naturally at the sound and jumped in fright.

"Assez!" I shouted commanding 'enough' in French so that Samson would calm at my command. However, the girl now looked even more terrified and stepped back further, lowering her head in submission. I took a deep breath knowing I had done more damage to her frayed nerves than my horse. So, after a moment, I decided to try again now that my steed was calm once more.

"I don't believe we have met?" I said, thinking this was a better way as any to introduce oneself to their intended soulmate. I stepped closer and she instinctively took one back, making me frown down at the sight of her fearful actions. It was utterly abhorrent to me to believe she viewed me in such a way but then again, how else would she view the man who currently held her future employment in their hands. No doubt she had heard of me and knew of my arrogance and quick temper, being that of Lord of Witley Court and its firm but fair master.

I had expected her to speak by now but instead, when I raised a brow in question, she simply shook her head in small erratic movements. Oh yes, she was most certainly afraid of me.

"What is your name, girl?" I asked trying to keep my voice even and unthreatening, despite my growing annoyance at seeing her so cautious around me, even if her reaction to such was warranted.

"I...I...erm...well, I am sorry, Sir...My Lord, I meant to say..." She started stumbling for her sentence and I had to admit, it was the first time I had ever seen a sight so adorable in all my years. The way she started to bite her bottom lip in a nervous habit in between her little clusters of words. The way her eyes would dart around me, trying to focus not on my face alone, for it was obvious that my unwitting intimidation was preventing such. It was all the most endearing sight I had seen in all the years that my memory would allow me to travel back.

I decided to take a closer step, seeing as she had nowhere else to go with her back firmly against the side of the stable door. So I was assured at least in the knowledge that if she were to remove her being completely, she would need to bypass me bodily to do so...something I wasn't about to let happen. So, I pressed on with my plan and continued to close the distance between us, making her appear more nervous with each booted step I took.

"What is it you have there?" I asked, once again keeping my tone non-threatening but finding it impossible not to take the opportunity to tease her, seeing as I already knew what it was. Once again, I almost laughed at her wide-eyed reaction wishing to have seen such a sight in the daylight to detect the true blue colour in her eyes.

"I...I...well, I can explain," she started to say but obviously contradicted that fact by not explaining at all, which was when I decided to take pity on her.

"I see," I said, this time walking to the stall and clicking my tongue on the roof of my mouth to get the dapple to come and say hello once more after Samson had startled her, just like the other skittish creature currently occupying the same space and now seemingly frozen in fear by my side.

"She is a beautiful creature is she not?" I asked, trying to draw her closer and into a conversation with me. I looked down and slightly to one side taking note of her reaction to seeing me take the mare's head in my hold and gently stroking where she once had.

"She is indeed, my Lord," she agreed granting me a slight lilt to her tone, indicating she definitely had a soft spot for this horse. Well, if that were so, she would soon find it being gifted to her. But first, I needed to know the essentials, like her name.

"And am I to know the name of the girl under my employ who likes to sneak in here just to see such beauty?" I asked still seemingly keeping my attention on the horse and not on the far rarer beauty next to me who had me secretly captivated. I hid a grin when she first had to clear her throat before answering who was essentially her master and therefore one she knew she could not get away with refusing twice.

"Uh...oh yes, I am sorry, my Lord, forgive my..." I waved off her apologies and told her,

"There is a simple solution to most mistakes made and in this case an answer given will suffice just fine," I told her, this time in a tone that spoke of my intention of finding out the information I sought.

"Yes, but of course, my name is Miss Williams," she replied making me turn to her and smirk, for I knew she had purposely given me her family name so as not to implicate herself fully in being here. For I knew there were a few others that worked for me with the same family name meaning, as suspected, she had been recommended by one of them.

"And am I to know your first name, Miss Williams?" I asked making her roll her lips inward once as a sign she really didn't want to grant me this personal information.

"How about I make this easier on you, Miss Williams. We will make a bargain, you and I."

"We will?" she questioned, making me grin again as you could almost see the worry ticking around her mind like a clock readying itself to chime.

"I will make you a promise not to tell anyone of your little expedition in finding beauty, if you grant me with a name to add to my own discovery in finding the same," I said now being as bold as I wished, which meant leaving the mare to retreat back inside her stable for my sights were firmly set elsewhere. I heard her sharp intake of breath, no doubt asking herself now if she had heard me correctly and its double meaning. Well, from the sight of her deepening blush, I think my answer was as clear as the natural rouge developing on her pale skin.

I watched as she looked down at her feet as if trying to hide from me and it was only when I cleared my throat did she resist the urge to continue the offence. For it wasn't an action I would abide, no matter if such was born from her shy nature.

But then she granted me her own gift when she finally told me her name, one she had no true comprehension that I had waited an eternity for…

"Keira, my Lord, my name is Keira."

DRAVEN

63

A DREAM THIEF

"Keira, my Lord, my name is Keira," she told me and I absorbed the name as if an elixir of light were being consumed, for I had never heard of the name before. Which was why I couldn't help but take the last step between us until her back was now flush against the panelled wood.

"And do you know who I am?" I asked wanting such confirmed. She nodded sharply making me do the same just the once. Then I slowly started to raise my hand, making her fearful eyes follow it a little before she could no longer help herself but question my actions.

"Wh...what are you...?"

"Ssshh, be still, for I will not hurt you, girl." I told her gently before finally severing the cord of time between us and touching her for the first time. I did so by tenderly running the backs of my fingers down her cheek, making her inhale a shuddered breath and close her eyes. Eyes hidden, which now cast shadows on the apples of her cheeks thanks to her long thick lashes.

"Exquisite," I told her making her eyes snap open in surprise. A reaction that considering her obvious beauty, was a curious thing indeed. But I found my eyes travelling once again to that tortured lip of hers and wondered at the pleasure gained from such an act, one I wished in that moment I had the freedom to explore myself.

But I was still considered a gentleman and right now I wasn't exactly behaving as such. So, instead of focusing on her lips and allowing my mind the free will to indulge in what it was I wanted to do to them, I reached down and wedged a hand between her back and the wooden frame. Doing so now so that I could take hold of the hand she continued to hide from me.

She was still seemingly in a trance from my brazen encounter with her soft creamy skin for she only put up slight resistance when she realised her hand was clasped firmly in mine and was now being brought around to the front of her.

"Now what is it you are hiding from me I wonder?" I asked and suddenly I was transported into another time when I asked her a similar question. However, instead of wood behind her there was a wall of stone and it wasn't cubed sugar in her hand but a small capped container. I shook my head gaining back my thoughts and ridding myself of what seemed like another point in time trying to merge with my own.

"No I...please...I can explain!" She started to panic as she held her hand in a tighter fist. But I simply started to peel back her fingers, assuring her,

"Calm yourself and worry not, for you will not be in trouble...trust me, *Keira.*" I said almost feeling myself purring her name for the first time and letting it be voiced from my lips like a prayer to the Gods to be allowed to keep it forever. After this, something in my voice must have convinced her of my words and I was happy in the knowledge that I hadn't yet needed to exert my will upon her, finding myself uneager to do so. She slowly started to allow me to open her hand more freely and I couldn't help but smile down at the three sugar cubes I found there.

Her reaction to such meager takings, one would have thought she had stolen pieces of the finest silver or come across Sophia's pearl earrings! But no, she had taken a few lumps of sugar to feed my new horse because she thought the treat was worth the crime. I don't know what she read in my gaze, but it clearly wasn't what I was thinking, for she started to speak, doing so quickly in her defense.

"I am so, so sorry, my Lord, I knew it was wrong to do so but the moment I saw them and your new horse, well then I didn't think a few would be missed...of course that's no excuse for stealing and I beg of you, please let me keep my employ, for I promise this will never happen again!" Hearing now the way she begged for my mercy left a bad taste in my mouth and I frowned, without thinking upon how it may appear and the reasons for such an action that would be conjured up in her fearful mind.

She recoiled from such and acted as if I held a whip in my hand readying myself to brand her skin for the offence, when in actual fact I felt like laughing because of it. For if she only knew what riches I held in store for her. As I could quite easily believe myself buying the sugar factory in which the cubes were made, just so that she could fatten every horse I owned for her own amusement. Although, it had to be noted, that Samson's preferred choice of treat would have been an apple. But thankfully there were orchards on my lands so that was one problem solved.

These random thoughts however didn't aid me in trying to prevent the impudent laugh that wouldn't have exactly spoke well of the moment. As laughing in sight of her discomfort wasn't going to grant me in her favour any time soon. So instead, I decided to show her my thoughts on what she classed as her unforgivable thievery.

"Come." I said the single word then took her hand in a firm hold and started to pull her over to my own horse, one I knew would behave in my presence despite the given chance to intimidate another as Samson often enjoyed doing.

"But where are you...?"

"There is one you forgot to indulge," I told her and the moment she saw which stable we were now heading towards I felt her resistance as she pulled her body back in a futile attempt at preventing me from getting my way. Well, she would soon learn, I thought with a hidden grin, for I wasn't known to yield to any powers that prevented me from getting what I wanted.

"You favour one of God's creatures in sight of another that equally deserves your attention?" I asked knowing this would guilt her into the act but then she surprised me with her honesty when she said,

"I would not likely be seen stroking a lion after doing so first with a kitten for fear of losing my hand in the act, one you deem as equal, whereas I most certainly do not." I swear if my wits had not been with me just then I would have lost the battle in allowing my shock to show with the unsightly view of my jaw dropping. For if anyone were to walk in here now then it would have looked as if she had struck me with a weighted glove after receiving such a brazen and truthful reply.

Instead, however, I raised a brow at her in question for not just the bold manner in which it was delivered, but in which such strong opinion had been so easily given. A fact I liked very much indeed, for she would one day be classed as my equal.

However, today was not yet that day and her deepened blush confirmed as much. Also, it had to be said that she now looked regretful in her reply. So, before she could take it back, I grasped her hand tighter in my own before using the hold to yank her firmly forward, making her stumble purposely into me. Then before allowing her time to fully assess her shock at the act, I whispered down at her,

"And I most certainly would not allow such a thing to happen, for fear not little maid, I am here to protect you and your hand." I then finished such a statement by giving her hand a squeeze before pulling her the rest of the way, something she now allowed. The reason being that she now trusted me or that her mind was busy questioning itself on my last comment. Either way I managed to position her in front of me, trapping her slight frame between my chest and the stable door.

I felt her tense against me, and I couldn't help but lean down placing my lips close to her ear so that I could rid her of her fears,

"Easy now, girl, for no harm will come to you, my fearful little maid," I whispered making her shudder against me, no doubt at being referred to as my own. Something she would soon find herself having no choice in getting used to, for nothing could take her from me now that I had finally found her.

She didn't speak but I could feel her increased heart rate through my fingertips still held at her wrist.

"Now be still, for there is someone I wish for you to meet and holds a dangerous beauty like no other."... '*Other than you*', I wished to have added after speaking such.

"Dangerous?" She whispered back in question, one I did not answer. No, instead I called forth my steed the way I usually did, with a clicking sound made at the side of my mouth. Samson's heavy weighted hooves pounded on the floor as he approached from the shadows of his larger stall. The second the dark looming silhouette of such a mighty beast began to be seen I grinned at her reaction. One that involuntarily brought her closer to me as she took a fearful step back meeting only with the tensed muscles of my chest.

"It is often thought that the most beautiful creatures on earth are the ones too dangerous to touch for fear of what may befall us should we seek to tame such beauty," I told her placing a hand at her waist and unable to help myself when applying pressure, thus giving action to my words. I also allowed my voice to lull her under my command just enough to free her of her fear and give way to her curiosity.

"But fear is a cage we cannot see or feel standing in our way of obtaining the things we truly want," I said as I lifted her hand slowly as Samson stepped closer still and her gasp at the sight of such a large and impressive creature was a sound I anticipated, along with her reluctance.

"That same cage of fear can also be a misconception of the truth standing right in front of you, should you choose to take the chance to reach for the key to free yourself," I told her just as I left her side and used both my hands in front of her, encasing her almost entirely in the wide stretch of my arms. Like this, our size difference was a startling realization of the power I easily held over her, for once again she trembled in my hold. I knew that I intimidated her, as I did most people in my company and this wasn't solely down to extreme wealth and the top of the social tower I stood firmly upon because of it.

It was down to my dark presence and the larger size of my being. Even my immense wealth wasn't enough for most ladies to try and make a claim for my hand in marriage. One that would have been pointless to try if their bravery did warrant the effort, for it was an endeavor never to come to fruition. Not when none other than my Chosen One would ever draw me into tying myself that way to another soul, no matter how the image of a bachelor was a strange one. Not when there were so many female suiters out there in need of a rich husband. But I had never been interested in gaining a wife just to keep up the human appearances, for I cared little for such cause for gossip.

But now, for this little bird in my arms readying herself for flight at the first opportunity, I knew it was different. For she *would* be my wife, she simply didn't know it yet.

However, she was beginning to understand how I selfishly liked to be granted my way for she let me peel her fingers back with both hands holding only one of hers before revealing the sugar. Then I extended her arm out to my horse knowing that there was no real danger but using this moment to build trust in the act.

Samson, as I knew he would, lowered his head, sniffing at the air in a curious manner. But when he took a step closer, she flinched, turning her head to the side and closing her eyes as if readying herself for the bite that would never come.

Ironic then that the only one with teeth that wished to bite into her flesh and taste the essence of her soul was the demon at her back whose fangs had extended. Something that happened involuntarily, as it was triggered by a mixture of her scent, the sight of her fear and the pounding of her blood pumping in her neck. One that was now extended to the side as though she was unknowingly offering her crimson bounty to me.

I closed my eyes against the tempting and erotic sight of her submitting and forced my fangs to go back to those belonging to a normal man. Then I whispered down at her,

"Trust me, for you will come to no harm in my arms," I told her despite the despicable acts I wished to do to her. Acts which included making her scream my name in pleasure, proclaiming me as the Lord who owns her body to do with as I wished... *especially whilst being tied to my bed.*

However, my words of encouragement worked for when I told her to open her eyes she did as was instructed just before feeling the soft velvet muzzle of Samson munching happily on the cubes. She then made a surprised sound and I looked down at her side on to see she was now smiling. Her smile, along with the enchanting glistening of surprise in her eyes, was a sight I would never forget for she was utterly captivating.

So much so that I found myself unable to tear myself from the view and in order to continue such a look of wonder gracing her face, I moved her hand to stroke down his head, encouraging her to do so on her own. I also made sure to hold him steady with my other hand so that he was discouraged from making any sudden movements, for my touch would always calm him.

"He is so handsome," she said making me grin in return, hoping she found his owner to be the same.

"Do you ride?" I found myself asking her but instead of gaining the gift of her words she simply shook her head, telling me as I suspected.

She didn't ride.

It was not unusual, for unless she happened to grow up on a farm, then it was unlikely she would have been given the opportunity to learn the required skills to do so. This knowledge pleased me, for it meant an opportunity gained on my part for I would have the pleasure to teach her myself.

"Then you must be allowed to learn, for I see you take great pleasure in time spent with such an animal. But I assure you, that this is but a small taste compared to being able to ride one," I told her making her now look back at me in shock.

"I...but I, well my Lord that is very kind of you to offer such, but I fear I could not," she argued making me raise a brow at her.

"And why not, may I enquire, for I know it is not through fear, for I saw no such manner when you were with my dapple?" I said giving way to the fact that I had been watching her freely before entering, a fact I saw her mind start to focus on before answering me.

"It...well, it wouldn't be right...proper even, for you to grant me such favours when others above my rank are not awarded so." Her answer gave me cause to grin. However, I refrained and instead waved a hand in the air as if batting away her reasons like you would an annoying fly in the hot summer months.

"Then I ask of you this, am I not Lord of this Court?" The moment I voiced such a question I could see her panic set in, for she knew where such a conversation was heading.

I knew this when she quickly looked one way before the other trying to escape my expectant gaze.

"I...well, yes but of course you are, my Lord," she answered simply because she had no other choice. And once again I found being the cat in this scenario playing with the mouse in front of me was granting me no end of pleasure, something severely lacking in my life of late.

This is when I decided to heighten the game and I did so by motioning with my head that Samson was finished with gaining her attention. For right now it was my turn and mine alone. It took little willpower sent his way for him to heed my command and she watched with fascination as he did so without my having to speak a word.

But then her attention soon snapped back to me for when she turned fully to face me, I placed both hands against the edge of the door behind her, gripping the wood and trapping her in the space I commanded.

"Then by the rights of authority within my own household do I not possess the status to sanction such a decision?" I asked her, whilst lowering my head enough to catch her eyes, ones that continually tried in vain to elude me.

"Well, yes of course, my Lord, you have the right to command your subjects..." I stopped her there for what I gave her now was no command.

"This is not an order given, Keira, but a kindness I wish to see accepted when granted by one's Master." I answered making her visibly gulp.

"But of course, and...well...I did not mean to offend, for the offer is a lovely and most generous one, my Lord," she said making me grin for she was a sweet girl indeed, one I would enjoy spoiling. I was just close to confessing as much when John walked in on our conversation making me want to growl back at him.

"And what do you think you two are...? Oh, my Lord, forgive me, I did not know you had...Keira, is that...?" The second John said her name something in me snapped. Of course, her reaction didn't help in calming my dark mood for she quickly raised her hood and looked off to the side in hopes of hiding herself away before being recognised.

She then blushed as if she was ashamed to be seen as such and my anger nearly exploded, for the wood in my hands cracked under the strain I put it through.

"I will be with you shortly, wait for me outside!" I snapped, needing to be rid of him and quickly before my rage allowed way for my demon to show through. But the girl misunderstood, for whilst still looking at her feet she muttered,

"Yes, of course, my Lord." Then she began to walk around me jarring me from my annoyance and setting me on course for new reasons to be vexed. I instinctively put out my hand to stop her, placing a flat palm at her belly and igniting a gasp from her at the abrupt contact.

"John, leave us." I corrected without looking at him but knowing I would find the shock in his features there regardless.

But I cared little for the opinions of others, especially when they were trying to stand in the way of obtaining my Chosen One. In fact, I wished in that moment I could have cast rightful decorum into Hell and taken what I wanted right then and there. I would have simply thrown the now trembling girl over my shoulder and carried her to my bedchamber where she would have remained until she realised what it was she meant to me.

Oh yes, I most certainly missed being the King of Persia for that was precisely what I would have done and not a single subject would have batted an eyelid in concern.

Once we were alone again, I reached up and pulled the hood from her, making her flinch as if I had been ready to strike her down. This only managed to anger me further, which was why I demanded harshly,

"Why did you hide yourself?!" Her eyes shot to my own before lowering once more just as quickly.

"My Lord, I..."

"Answer the question!" I snapped quickly losing my patience with such wasteful formalities. She jumped at the loss of my soft and tender words, no doubt witnessing this new side of me and finding she now had reason to be cautious. The realisation of such just annoyed me further.

"Your reputation, my Lord, I did not want it sullied by being seen conversing with me, for your offered kindness to me deserves kindness in return and giving cause for unfounded gossip amongst your servants was not a way to repay such sentiments," she said and suddenly all of the anger left me as if being drawn out through an open window in the middle of a storm.

I released a sigh and couldn't help but raise a hand to cup her cheek, making her once again grant me with a wide-eyed doe look, as if asking me silently what it was I wanted from her.

"Oh, my sweet girl, for you know not how little I care for the foolish prattle of others when my name is in question, for I answer to no one. Which includes conversing with whomever I choose."

"But My Lord, I am but a simple scullery maid and I have barely even been here longer than one and twenty days, I fear I do not deserve such favour, nor such kindness." I allowed the side of my lip to raise before enquiring,

"So, let me see if I am correct, are you saying because you haven't been long under my employment that you don't deserve my kindness?" I watched as she contemplated her reply and when I saw the slight smile hidden there just waiting to be allowed to fulfill its purpose, I pushed her for it.

"I see you have thoughts on this, please enlighten me with them."

"It's just that I haven't yet been here long enough to even break a nail in my duties, let alone deserve your attention for anything but being branded as a thief, seeing as that is the role in which I must own up to this eve." I couldn't help it but upon hearing her reply I actually started laughing and I had to admit, hearing it even sounded foreign to me! And I wasn't the only one, for she looked shocked at witnessing the sudden reaction and she couldn't have known what a rarity the act was.

"Alright then, my little thief, if you truly wish to make amends, then you will meet me here tomorrow at noon for your first lesson…yes?" I added the answer I wanted to hear and caught sight of her eyes so that she could not escape my chosen look of intimidation, for I would have my way on this matter.

As once I finally got her on my horse and far from the sight of her responsibilities, then I hoped she would feel more inclined to open up and act on impulse rather than what she believed was the correct standing for her social class.

After all, I wasn't looking for a slave or servant to share my bed, but in fact, that of a queen. One I already considered her to be after first laying my eyes on her. Now all I needed to do was get her to believe the same.

"I asked a question, Miss Williams," I said using her family name this time to strengthen the sound of my determination. I knew it worked when her eyes quickly sought mine and her answer this time was immediate.

"Yes, my lord," she said, but in a way as if she had little choice in a matter I had already deemed settled. But was she really that reluctant to spend time with me? Well, I guess only time would tell and that time would start tomorrow. But for tonight I found I couldn't let her leave without one last unspoken promise made. So, I leaned down getting closer to her ear before telling her softly,

"Then I will bid you goodnight…*my little sugar thief.*" I heard the sharp inhale of breath and grinned whilst my lips were still out of sight knowing how I was able to affect her the way I hoped.

I knew this when she murmured a whispered goodbye before rushing from the stables the moment I moved out of her way, so that she could flee. Running from what she no doubt considered an intense first encounter with her master.

Well, if she thought that had been so, then she needn't wait long for the next, for tomorrow would bring me one step closer to achieving my goal.

For tomorrow...

I would finally make her mine.

DRAVEN

64

DEATH OF A DREAM

"**W**here is she?!" I roared after waiting too long for her in the stable yard by the east gatehouse. John looked at me in concern for he could see I was a man on the edge of his temper and no doubt didn't want to be around when I finally gave way to it.

When leaving her last night, I had started to make my plans, telling first my sister and brother of my discovery. Both had expressed their happiness, as I knew they would. And Sophia even went as far as ensuring that one of her riding habits be sent to the girl's room so that she had the right attire to wear for our lesson.

Now all I needed was the girl in question to arrive and all would once more be calm, for patience was not an accomplishment I could claim, and neither could my demon.

For he was currently clawing at my skin to go and tear through the house looking for her.

In fact, I was just about to go and do this when I saw Sophia walking towards me looking grave. Then I noticed what she had bunched in her arms and I frowned in anger...*her riding habit.*

"I am afraid, brother, that the next time you wish to make plans with your Chosen One, that you do so first by proclaiming her as your future bride to the rest of the staff."

"Why, what happened?!" I snapped making Sophia first snarl back at the direction she had just come from before telling me the shocking truth.

"She is about to be punished, for when they found my riding habit in her room, they branded her a thief and a liar as they would not believe her claims of a riding lesson with the master of the house," she told me making me growl low in my throat, a threat that spoke for itself. Then I demanded,

"Where is she?" Sophia pointed towards the kitchen court and said,

"I believe she is being kept in the wine cellars for now whilst awaiting her punishment after George speaks with you on the matter." I released a sigh of relief at least knowing no harm would come to her until I had spoken with my steward, but still, just the idea of her being down there no doubt frightened and unsure of what would happen to her next was bad enough.

"Then call for George and have him meet me there, for I will not have her down there a second longer!" I barked before pounding through the servant's area and past the kitchen where I saw a few maids looking fearful. But there was no cook to be seen which gave me a bad feeling that chilled my spine.

"Where is Mrs Weathers?" I asked in a sharp tone. A girl curtsied before speaking,

"Forgive me, my Lord, but I believe she has taken it upon herself to...well...to..." The young girl looked nervously to her friend before I snapped,

"Speak up, girl!"

"She is punishing the new scullery maid herself, my Lord." Hearing this I very nearly lost my ability to hide my true nature, for it was ready to burst free of my vessel at any moment. I even found myself first gripping onto the door frame before leaving the room to run down to the cellars that were thankfully close to the kitchen.

I could just hear the girls telling Sophia how Mrs Weathers had for some reason taken a disliking to Keira and was particularly hard on her, making her do most, if not all of the worst chores in the entire household.

I had to close my eyes against the thought of her on her knees scrubbing the floors or ankle deep in mud and animal waste. But then I heard a muffled sound of a girl's scream and with little care for others, used my supernatural side to get me there quicker. I swear I managed the steps down in only three quick movements before I was able to round the corner into the main cellar space. This was done just in time as I saw the cook raising her hand again and the riding crop she grasped was unmistakable.

At seeing this I swear I very nearly snapped her neck but instead put myself in front of my Chosen One, taking the blow on my arm so that she didn't receive it. But then, the second it made contact with my skin, a strange vision took hold and suddenly I was back in Persia. I looked down at my arm seeing now the coil of a whip and one look up told me where I was. It was my harem and I was the King of Persia once more.

But who was it that was at my back this time? I turned around to look and couldn't believe my eyes when I saw her...*it was my Chosen One.*

She too had looked transported there through time and I had to say that even given the grave circumstances she looked as breathtakingly beautiful as ever! But then, the second I heard a scream, one coming from a woman ahead of me I looked and saw the vision disappearing, making way for the depths of my own reality.

I then grabbed the outstretched crop and snapped it in two with one hand, making Mrs Weathers gasp, covering her mouth with both hands.

"My Lord, I..."

"SILENCE!" I roared at her in fury making the girl now at my back flinch and whimper also. Then my steward, George, entered and with him my sister who along with myself, focused accusing eyes at the cook and was no doubt ready for murder.

"By God woman, have you lost your mind, what is the meaning of this!?" My steward demanded accusingly at Mrs Weathers who was standing aside looking horrified, no doubt now worrying over her own fate.

"I...I...well she was a thief and..." she said trying to justify her actions and I snarled at her but catching myself in time before I could let the beast of my demon do more. This was thanks to Sophia shaking her head at me warning me of such actions.

So instead, I took care of my Chosen One, who was trembling at my back.

"No, she isn't. You were wrong and far too hasty in your actions for Miss Draven here has just informed me she was the one to give Miss Williams her riding habit as I first suspected, and because of my suspicions the very reason I told you not to take action until I had spoken with Mr Draven myself on the matter!" My Steward said in a harsh tone, but I had heard enough.

"Get out!" I suddenly shouted the second I turned to see that the girl's dress had been torn open to reveal the entirety of her back and thankfully I could only detect one strike of the crop, that had begun to welt. However, for my murderous temper it was one too many and I was far too close to tearing one of Mrs Weather's limbs from its socket and sending her to Hell burdened with it!

"My Lord, I..." the cook tried to say but I roared,

"GET OUT NOW, ALL OF YOU!" This time I was obeyed, and it was just as well for the girl suddenly burst into tears and was close to falling to the floor. She had been tied by the wrists to a hook on the wall that was used to hoist full barrels onto their brackets, only this section of the wall was empty after last year's harvest had encountered a devastating early frost.

I decided I needed her free far more quickly than my patience would allow, so instead of untying her, I simply yanked at the metal hook and ended up tearing the thing from the wall. But I didn't care that she saw such an impossible feat of nature, for her wellbeing right now was my only concern.

After this I then gathered her up into my arms, being mindful of her injury and swept her legs from beneath her before they could give way entirely. She let out a yelp of surprise and once more I found myself seeing the same actions being done, only from a different time.

But this time it seemed a lot more serious for she was bleeding at her side. I shook my head trying to rid myself the horrifying sight of her blood seeping into the material of her strange attire and of me running towards a door at the end of a long corridor.

Then she spoke and at first, I heard her say, 'Doctor' but then it morphed into the sweetest sound of my name coming from her lips for the first time spoken,

"Draven" There had been no Mr or Lord in front of it and strangely coming from her lips, it felt more like a given name. Well, it was one she could have for I swear it gave me a comfort unlike any other. So, in return I held her tighter to me as I carried her from the bitter memory of this place. Then I made my way up to my own private rooms using the staircase the servants used as it was closer and would get me there quicker.

Once there I placed her down on my bed wishing that the first time in committing such a profound act had been under better circumstances. In fact, she looked to have fallen asleep in my arms on the way up here, for the second I placed her down she seemed to jar awake.

"Ssshh, calm now, for no one will harm you again," I told her gently making her still as I rolled her over to her front so that I could assess her injury. However, this must have started to make her feel uncomfortable as she was still bound and being in my presence, she tried to cover herself mumbling little excuses and apologies. I moved to the front of her and bent a knee to the floor, putting me at the right height so that I could untie her from the ring bracket. Then, as I let my fingers loosen the knot in the rope, I told her.

"No, it is not anything for you to be sorry for, as you hold no fault, for it falls solely at my feet," I said taking that burden as I knew it was true. On hearing this she looked up at me with wide eyes before she did something surprising. She grabbed my hand in her smaller one, putting a stop to my actions a moment and squeezed before telling me sternly,

"No, the only one to blame is the actions of a bitter old woman who was looking for any excuse to inflict cruelty." I nodded once knowing that she was right as much as she was wrong. Because, as much as I was the Lord of this house, it seemed that the root of its problems never reached me as they should. For I doubted that Keira was the first victim of cruelty by the hand of Mrs Weathers.

"Speaking of which, lie flat so that I can see what she did to you." I ordered once she was free of her restraints, but when she didn't move, I silently questioned it with a look.

"Be assured, my Lord, she inflicted little damage...*thanks to you rescuing me.*" She added this last part as barely above a whisper and added to it was a blush to match the shy tone in which it was spoken.

"And that is as I hoped to find it...after I have seen for myself that is." I said adding this last part as an unspoken demand and it was one she didn't miss. Which was the reason it was no surprise to me when she rolled to her front once more, baring her back to me for inspection.

There was a single red line in the middle of her shoulder blades and at its center, the place that it impacted the hardest, the skin had started to welt. I was just glad she hadn't torn the skin, for I didn't think my rage would have been prevented if it had.

Which reminded me, Mrs Weathers needed to be punished for what she did and being stripped of her job was only one of them, for once I was through, I would see to it that she never worked in another grand house again!

"Does it hurt?" I asked and knew she was being brave when she shook her head telling me no.

"I will have my sister bring me a balm so that I can wrap it in muslin to prevent infection spreading...stay here and rest a moment," I told her, wishing that right now I could have forgone the pretense of who I portrayed myself to be and just healed her the way I wanted to. However, leaving her for a short time would at the very least give me chance to issue some orders.

Or should I say...*punishments.*

A little time later and I found myself with the conflicting task of cleaning her wound. Conflicting because on the one hand, it gave me the perfect excuse to touch her skin, whilst gifting me the opportunity to prove to her that I could be gentle with her. Especially in case she still feared me and my imposing size. But then on the other hand, just seeing the proof of brutality set against her and I wished my punishment on Mrs Weathers had been far more than one lash of the same crop and banishment from my home.

Of course, she tried to argue her case and thankfully had the acute foresight to do so to my steward, not to me directly. For there would have been no saying what I would have done if she had.

But after discovering the true the amount of complaints set against her, well, it turned out that Mrs Weathers wasn't just a hard woman with unrealistic expectations of those that worked under her. She was in fact also an unnecessarily cruel woman who used her role as a way to inflict her own version of punishments on those she deemed unworthy of working here.

Thankfully, I had learned that Keira had first started working as a maid, instructed by my steward George, until the cook started to complain at him that she needed more staff, for yet another girl had walked out. Now we knew why.

But when I happened upon meeting Keira for the first time, it turned out that it had only been her second day working under Mrs Weather's instructions. Of course, given Keira's natural beauty, apparently, according to the other scullery maids, Mrs Weathers had taken an instant dislike to her. Meaning this afternoon's incident would have no doubt only ended up one of many had I not intervened when I did.

Of course, Mrs Weathers denied all claims, but it was of little consequence for her fate had been sealed. Primarily, when I forbade my steward from offering any kind of reference in her name making it near impossible for her to obtain another position like it, no matter how far she travelled to seek one out.

Needless to say, she had been furious, especially when I had her forcibly removed from Witley Court without even being allowed to retrieve her things. Items I shortly had my men gather and throw into the streets of the village she was soon to be residing in. She also was refused her wages and was told that they would be distributed as compensation for all those she had terrorized since working here.

But it was a meagre amount, so I would no doubt be adding to it, for now after seeing the way Keira had been treated after only two days, I felt somewhat responsible for not being made aware of the situation sooner. The Gods only knew what horrors she had inflicted on others during her eight years employment under this roof.

Which was why I currently had my steward compiling a list of names that could be potential victims of hers, so that in some small way I could make amends for her crimes. I was also hoping that with enough witnesses that came forward maybe some charges could be made against her, for that had been the outcome I had really been hoping for.

"Sssss," the sound of Keira sucking air through her teeth brought me back to my task at hand, as I had just been running a cold cloth over her back that had started to bruise.

"Forgive me, for I am afraid it is necessary," I told her in what I hoped was a soothing tone.

"It's alright, I understand," she said and it reminded me of what the damage could have been had I not arrived in time. For it may have only been the one blow, but by the looks of it, then many more and such action would have rendered her unconscious and unable to move for days. Not surprising as Mrs Weathers was not slight of frame but considered more of the stature of a man than any woman one would consider feminine.

"Now I am going to apply the balm, hold still," I told her so as not to startle her when she felt it cold against her skin. She nodded and did as she was told, holding perfectly still the entire time.

"Good girl," I praised as my fingers coated her skin with the balm infused with chamomile, an effective plant in helping prevent any infection on the skin from spreading.

I also tried to make the most of having her lay on my bed. A reason why, once I had finished wrapping strips of muslin over her back, I informed her she was going nowhere the moment she tried to move.

"But...I...well I can't stay here, my Lord," she stuttered in utter shock.

"And why not, for it is my bed and therefore I have sole right over any other to proclaim who should or should not be allowed to lie in it," I told her making her gasp at my brazen reply.

"But I could easily make it to my own bed and that way you would not be..."

"No! I will not hear of it, now you are to rest after I have had food sent up here for you...do you understand?" I asked her once she had turned on her side to try and look at me. No doubt finding out for herself that I could not be moved in my decision.

Unsurprisingly she nodded her head giving in to my demands. Then, before I left her to rest, I couldn't help but grant her a small slice of what I had in store for her, no doubt giving her much to think about whilst I was gone.

So, with this in mind, I placed my weight to the bed next to her and leaned into her space before placing my lips at her ear. My actions made her tense as if unsure what to expect from me next.

"Have no fear, little maid of mine, for I will get you on the back of my horse soon enough."

Then I was gone.

I slipped back into my bed chamber once night had fallen and I was assured she would be asleep. If I were being honest with myself, her need to rest after such an injury was unnecessary. But just to have the excuse to keep her in my bed was enough to exert my overbearing hand and take advantage of being Lord of this house, commanding all who live within it. And now, looking down at the beauty that lay sleeping soundly in my bed, then no, I couldn't be sorry for the events that had brought her to me.

However, if there had been a way to achieve such without the cause of pain to her body then I would have chosen it in a heartbeat. Now all I needed was the excuse to keep her in it for the rest of eternity and I would be a happy and contented King indeed.

But for now, instead of joining her like I wished I was free to do, I decided to simply watch over her. Which meant I fisted a hand at my side to prevent myself from reaching out to her as I wanted, for fear of waking her.

One day. One day very soon and I would be granted that right, for I may have had permission from the Gods to take her, but I was yet to have permission from her own heart. And that was the only blessing I would wait for, as nothing more could stop me from making her mine.

So, I stepped away from the bed and drew the curtains around her to ward off the night's chill. Then I removed my jacket and waistcoat and yanked impatiently at my cravat, undoing the top buttons of my shirt. I left everything else in case she woke for I did not want to alarm her by being in an unfit state of dress and giving the wrong idea as to my intentions.

Then I slipped into my dressing room and donned a long dressing gown that was thick black brocade with satin quilted collar and cuffs, a gift from my sister who knew I spent long hours of the evening brooding as she called it.

I was just about to tie the cord around my waist as I walked back into the dark room, having no need for a candle to do so as a human would. The second I heard the rain battering against the window, I looked first to the paned glass and then back to the bed to check the sound hadn't disturbed her. However, as I did lightening cracked through the sky and lit up the room long enough for me to see the silhouette inside the curtained bed.

At first I thought my eyes were deceiving me, something I grant you, had never happened before. But right now, if a guess were ventured then I would say disbelief would have played a large part in questioning myself. For the second I saw the shadow of a knife held above a sleeping form I didn't want to believe what was happening next.

"NO!" I roared at the same time my body took flight. I crashed through the curtains around the bed and into the body that had been crouched over a sleeping Keira. I took the body with me to the other side as we both landed on the floor. Then I took hold of the hand that still held the knife, one currently being used in an attempt to wound me. I lifted the wrist and snapped it like a charred kindling, shattering the bones. A woman screamed out in pain as the knife scattered along the floor but the moment I smelled the blood, I knew I had been too late.

This was when I lost all control over my demon side and allowed him to fully emerge for the first time in over two thousand years. In fact, the last time was when fighting

Pertinax, a Persian Devil that wanted to take my place as King of the supernatural world.

But back then there had been good reason to allow my demon freedom for his strength had been needed...but now? Well, I could have quite easily have sought revenge against the mortal beneath me with a mere thought or the barest flick of my hand.

However, my demon didn't want that. No, it wanted Hell's fire to burn flesh to bone and bone to ash. It wanted the agony of death to be remembered long into the Afterlife. It wanted the screams of pain to be heard in Hell long after the life drew in its last breath.

It wanted its soul tortured for all eternity!

Which was why I wasn't surprised the second I felt my wings erupt and my horns push past my vessel's skull, merging the human body with one that had the power to rule legions in Hell. My skin changed to not that of a man but of a beast adapted to emerging from the heart of a volcano. I could have walked through the fires of Hell and emerged unscathed like this.

The criminal beneath my weight screamed the second she saw the wrath of a demonic God above her but her scream wasn't the only one. I quickly placed a clawed hand around the throat of one Mrs Weathers cutting off the sound quickly. A deadly action that took less than a second before I then slowly turned my head to find the horrified face of Keira sitting up in the bed with the torn curtains framing her trembling features.

She looked beyond terrified!

I then scanned the rest of her and saw her hand at her side with blood seeping beneath the white nightgown she had been given. She was panting heavily no doubt through the pain of being stabbed and the sight of seeing me this way.

Time seemed to stand still for both of us and the second I felt the resistance beneath my hand I couldn't prevent my demon from snarling down at her. I had only turned my attention away for a mere heartbeat, but it was long enough that by the time I looked back to the bed...

She was gone.

I quickly and without a shred of remorse snapped the neck of Mrs Weathers. However, the moment I did this she quickly morphed into that of another demon I felt as if I knew...*but how?* For I had never seen this creature before, I was almost certain of the fact.

But if that were so, then how did I find myself hissing the likely name through my extended fangs,

"Lahash."

I frowned trying to make sense of what I was seeing before realisation took hold of my actions. As right now, there was nothing more important than getting to Keira. Just the thought of her blood being spilled had me roaring up at the ceiling before I jumped from the now limp body and ran from the room.

I did so now following both the scent and sight of blood as it led a trail towards the bedroom situated in the west tower. One that faced the north side of the house and main entrance. I ran inside the unused room, one usually reserved for guests and a quick sweep of the room showed me no life. Only white dust sheets that covered the furnishings and stood guard like phantom sentinels. But that's when I noticed a bloody hand print imprinted against the top of a covered chest and next to it a panel in the wall was ajar. So, it seemed as though my secret staircase up to the roof of the tower wasn't as secret as I liked to believe.

In all likelihood it was a secret she had been shown by one of the other maids who had grown up here knowing of the house's secrets. Not surprising really as all one would have taken when discovering it was a brief stumble against the wall and it would have simply clicked open. Thankfully however, the only secrets it held was a great view of the county and for me personally ease of access for those times I was restless in the night and needed to take flight.

But now was not one of those times, for I took the narrow staircase seeing for myself the heavy blood trail along the way, knowing that she was losing far too much. I needed to get to her and fast before she lost consciousness and did so too close to the edge.

I also knew I needed to banish my other side back to a controllable level, so that when I emerged on the roof she wasn't simply faced with the face of a demon. A sight she would not yet understand. So, with extreme control, I bowed over double with the strength it took to get him back to submitting to me.

"She needs us!" I told him on a painful hiss as he fought me for the control he wanted to sustain. I gripped onto the stone wall and felt it crumble in my hands as it too lacked the strength it took to overpower this side of myself.

"Fucking submit to me, you bastard!" I roared this time throwing my head back and grabbing onto my horns in anger, ready to rip them from my fucking skull if need be! Then I fell to my knees and whispered my last plea as my demon roared back at me.

"She will die." The second I said this, realisation overpowered him. That and a deeply rooted fear we had never experienced before. The second I felt him give in to me I resumed my vessel's appearance and ran with unnatural speed to the rooftop, where I burst from the door, taking it from its hinges when I did.

And once there, I found her looking like a ghost of the future. I couldn't understand it or who it was I was looking at now. One moment she was the girl I knew wearing that of a white gown plastered to her skin. So wet, it looked as though it was made from paper. So thin I could see every naked inch of her, making it look like milk was dripping from her every curve. Added to this was the startling contrast of crimson soaking her side and painted the entire length of her as her wound still bled heavily.

But then I would blink and staring back at me was a Keira from a different time standing on a different rooftop wearing black. Wet golden hair flowing down around her, reminding me of the sands of Persia after the storm. Was what I experienced now a clue to the future or was I currently trapped in dreams of a past that in fact never happened?

I didn't know anymore what was real and what wasn't! And I cared not, for right now all I could see was the same fear in her eyes no matter which version I beheld. Both of them made the same steps backwards towards the edge and I frowned in confusion. For surely, she could not be about to do what I feared the most?

"Keira?" I said her name in question and for some reason found myself now unable to move an inch towards her. It was as though the Gods had struck me with an unbreakable power and I was forced to live out my own nightmares as some sort of punishment to some unknown crime.

I saw her turn to face the small battlements of the tower, a low wall that I suddenly wished I'd had built up ten feet tall!

"Keira, what are you doing?!" I shouted in anger and fear, both of which were merging my voice into a strained version of its usual self. Then she looked back at me over her shoulder and the second she gave me her answer I was once again free to move.

Only it was too late.

"Time for me to die..." She only mouthed the words, words first said as my frightened angel dressed in white and then those of my future Chosen One who quickly took her from me,

A beautiful demon dressed in black...

"Goodbye, Draven."

And then both of them fell as one.

"NO!" I roared, releasing my wings and flying from the tower down into a shadowed abyss of endless darkness. But all I could see was a pale hand held out towards me ready for me to catch. I pushed myself harder than I ever had before, knowing I couldn't give up on her. Knowing I had to catch her. I had to get to her in time!

I couldn't lose her now!

I couldn't let her die.

"Keira!" I whispered her name just as my fingertips grazed her outstretched fingers, but it wasn't enough…

I saw the realisation in her face as she saw the desperation in mine. It was the very moment I realised I wouldn't make it in time. I curled my middle finger, bending it just as hers did the same so that our only connection was an inch of skin to skin.

An inch was all I was granted as we landed together. Dying with only a whispered plea spoken back to me just before,

Dying as one…

"Look for my demons, Draven."

Keira

65

GOODBYE DRAVEN

Slowly my eyes opened as I regained consciousness. A blurry white light brought me round and I blinked a few times in order to gain focus. Certain things started to become clearer and the first was the sight of a window seat with cushions askew.

Sitting bolt upright when too many things became familiar, I was confused at how I was now back in my own room. I jumped up and ran to the mirror on wobbly legs to examine myself. My clothes were all still intact, there was no ripped vest, no bloody trousers and even weirder, I had no bandages. I looked for a scar or a mark, anything to indicate what had happened last night but there was nothing. I lifted my hand turning it over and over, but it too was just as clear as it had been the day before.

"No! It...it can't be!" I shook my head in disbelief. This was not happening! There was no way that what had happened last night was a dream. Not this time! However, there were still things that backed my theory. Okay they were small, but they mattered. My black shirt and tie were missing. My hair was still damp and loose from running around in the rain. And most importantly, I could still smell Draven imprinted on my skin.

No, this was not a dream!

I begrudgingly had a shower, washing away the last traces of last night from my body and after drying myself I got dressed. I noticed it was 10:30am and I was due to start my next shift at twelve. It was when I had finished in the shower that I realised I was ravenous. I could have eaten a bloody horse and its rider! I went downstairs into the kitchen and was about to shout out to Libby or Frank when I remembered that they weren't back yet. It made me wonder who had brought me home...or how for that matter. I ran to the window and my mouth dropped open as I saw my car sat there as if I had parked it myself.

Once I had raided the kitchen cupboards for anything I could get my hands on, I only had just enough time to get ready for work and this was one day that I would be determined to speak to Draven about the truth!

It was as though my body and mind had hit a limit to how many different emotions I could feel all at once. The more I replayed the night's events over and over in my head there was no doubt in my mind that it had happened. He must have brought me back here and tried to cover up last night, hoping I would just put it all down to a bloody dream. Well, this time he wasn't getting away with it. I would demand the truth.

Hell, I wouldn't leave until I got an explanation and not just for last night. No, now after what I had witnessed it only convinced me more that none of them had been dreams. Something was going on here and I had a right to know.

Draven had been coming into my room at night, of this I now had no doubts left. All that was left were the reasons why.

As soon as I stormed into the club, I got a weird sense that it didn't want me there anymore. As though the pull it once had over me had been put into reverse, making me feel unsure and unwelcome. It was strange to see the club this way, like a deserted old Wild West town that had lost its sheriff. There was no security at the stairs like there usually was and it was deadly silent.

I took a deep breath and made for the main staircase trying to retain my annoyed state. I would not let him intimidate me, not this time! Once upstairs, I noticed that most of it was now empty with only one waitress, Rue, and with about five tables occupied. Draven's table wasn't one of them. I walked over to the bar where Karmun, as always, was working. He noticed me and for a split second I thought I saw a nervous glint in his eyes. But it was quickly replaced with an even friendlier smile than I normally received.

"Hey Keira, I think you're needed mainly downstairs today." He said as he was wiping down the bar with a wet cloth.

"Karmun, did you see what happened last night?" I said coming straight out with it. He looked uncomfortable again and I knew the answer, but he remained calm and said,

"Umm... I'm sorry Keira, I'm not allowed to talk about it." He said trying to palm me off with the no gossip rule, but I wasn't having any of it.

"And why not? Considering it had something to do with me, I think I'm entitled to the facts!" I said getting irate quicker than I thought I would. He held up his hands about to say something else when I gave up saying,

"Okay then fine, I want to speak to Draven about it!" I couldn't believe where all this bravery was coming from, but I just hoped it lasted until I was in front of the man himself.

"Are you sure that's a good idea?"

"It's a damn good idea considering I think it's the only way that I will get the answers that I am looking for." I snapped holding my head high.

"As you wish...I will tell him. Why don't you wait on the balcony for him to arrive?" He said, probably shocked at anyone demanding such a thing. I nodded in return and stamped angrily out on to the balcony. Being back here brought back a flood of memories from last night. What was it with this place and balconies anyway? Everything seemed to happen on them.

The cool air nipped at my skin as I pulled my long black jacket closer to my neck, zipping it up the whole way. It was the one with a big hood and also had a big neck which acted like a scarf. The thought of a scarf also brought me back to last night, before things had turned darker and more surreal. I let my mind drift in and out of last night's events, so when Draven finally did arrive I wasn't as prepared as I had been.

"Keira, you wanted to see me?" He said the words in a hard tone and my pulse went up a couple of notches as usual. He stood back from me, unlike all the other times we had been brought together. Now though, it was clearly going to be different as his face said as much.

He was wearing black trousers with a black suit jacket only underneath he wore a more casual faded grey t-shirt that once again showed his washboard stomach, one that I had seen so intimately last night. However, this more casual look didn't reflect his mood.

"Yes...I wanted to talk to you about last night." I said trying to remain strong, only he didn't even look bothered that I wanted to speak to him. It must have been an act surely?

"Ah yes, well, it was an unfortunate accident and I'm glad to see you're feeling better after your fall." He replied changing back to his usual 'boss' routine.

"What fall?" I asked shaking my head feeling the warmth invade my cheeks.

"You must not remember. Well, that's understandable, you went out like a light. I do apologise for what happened and I assure you, I do not tolerate fighting in my club. But well, this is what is expected when drugs are involved. Trust me when I say the matter has been dealt with." *Trust him?* How could I ever trust this man who now stood in front of me? I didn't even know him! He was cold, and my heart froze from its bitter aftershock. This wasn't Draven...This wasn't my Draven! The anger came back, building up inside of me like a firecracker ready to burst.

"That's....That's bullshit! Don't lie to me!" I shouted feeling myself shake with emotion.

"Excuse me?" His voice sounded shocked and also very pissed, but I no longer cared! So, I carried on,

"That didn't happen...Goddamn it, I didn't fall!" I yelled the words and his cold heart reflected in his expression, looking at me as though I was no-one...I was back to being *a no one.* Well I don't think so, I wasn't having it!

"And what is it that you believe to have happened exactly?" He crossed his arms, making his scepticism all the clearer. So, I did it. I did what I had come here to do, and I wasn't about to back down now. I didn't care how much my mind screamed no, I wasn't going to lose this fight.

"Fine, play it like that! We both know what happened last night, but considering you're playing it down as though it was nothing but a 'bump to the head' then you go ahead and do that! But I will never, and I repeat *never* believe that and no matter how much you try to trick me...I'm here telling you now, it won't work!" I said, and the tears welled up but didn't betray me as they stayed firmly in place. I had to tense my fists when I said this so as not to shake with hurt.

He stood glaring, his black eyes holding no shred of the passion that I had seen flow so freely last night.

Then the doors opened and the beautiful red head who sat at his table glided in. She stopped next to him and there was something different about her that I hadn't seen before. But no matter what I braced myself for, what I saw next would crush my heart and every hope I had ever foolishly allowed myself to feel.

She curled her body around him and his arms embraced her, returning the affection. She then looked at me as though I had been made of invisible matter.

"Oh, you must be Keira, the waitress who got knocked down due to the fight, how's your head feeling today?" She said in a voice that sang with the same beauty that radiated off her. I had to use every last breath in my body to answer without showing the tears that just wanted to run freely out of my fragile body.

"I'm fine, thank you." I said and Draven for some reason, probably in disgust, turned his face away.

"That's good. Well I'm sorry Dominic, I will leave you to finish and trouble you with wedding plans later." As she spoke these cruel words I was sure you could actually hear the sound of my heart being ripped apart. I wanted to look away. Hell, I wanted to run and never look back, but I was trapped like a bird in a glass room. I was being blinded by the light and couldn't find my way out of my own personal cage of nightmares.

She lifted herself to the height of his face and kissed him. This was enough to unleash the tears from my eyes, leaving behind a salty road for others to follow. I looked away and wiped them off my skin in vain.

I didn't notice when she left, but to be honest my mind was a blur, consumed with the pain of self-pity. I just want to drown in it.

"I'm sorry, that was rude. I didn't introduce you to my fiancée. That was Celina." He said still holding on to his unemotional countenance and I had lost all of mine. I couldn't speak fearing what I would say in reply. Then, when I thought the pain couldn't get any worse than knowing he was getting married to one of the most perfect creatures this world had ever seen...he spoke.

"I understand there has been a misjudged account of affections that do not exist. Perhaps this was partly my doing as well, as a young overactive imagination can sometimes twist the truth. In light of your clear feelings, I would think it best for you if you no longer work up here in the VIP." He finished this sentence, thus sealing my fate into a pit of misery. He could see the tears and yet his arrogance was still stronger than ever. We were miles apart and the difference was that he didn't care and all the time I was fighting my way to get back.

"Right...you're right, clearly... what a stupid mistake to have made!" I said this out loud not realising, as nothing made sense, but nothing ever does when you're lost.

"I think you're a hard worker and..."

"Stop, just stop!"

"Keira, I..." He said my name and even though this time it was softer I had already lost it. So, I interrupted him with my final decision,

"I quit." I heard him sigh and utter something I didn't catch under his breath.

"There is no need for you to quit."

"Oh, I think there are more than enough reasons for me to quit...don't you?" I shot back making him frown.

"No, I don't. Not considering I know how much it will upset my sister."

"Sophia." I uttered her name under my breath forgetting how she would feel about all this. It didn't matter to me how I had seen her last night, all I could think about was the friend I had made and didn't want to lose.

"She thinks very highly of your friendship and has been good to you, are you really willing to repay her kindness by quitting because of unreciprocated feelings?" This felt like an arrow to the heart and he saw me wince when he delivered the final blow.

"Don't...! Just don't." After everything that had happened between us I couldn't stand here and continue to listen to his lies.

"Fine. I will continue downstairs for Sophia's sake, but only until I have paid off this car..."

"Keira that's not necessary." Draven said but I held up my hand and then spat with venom,

"Oh, but it is as I want *nothing* from you!" This time he winced but I carried on,

"Don't worry I will never be stupid enough to set foot up here again or be foolish to show any of my *young overactive imagination* towards you ever again. I can promise you that!" I said as my last attempt at saving my face. When I said this, there was the first tiniest bit of emotion I saw in his soulless eyes, but I looked away from it, knowing that if I saw anything that would give me hope, I would fight for him...and clearly it was a one-sided battle. One I could never win.

I walked past him to the door and something made me stop. I turned to face his back, as his eyes did not follow and swallowed back the sob saving it for when I was out of this Hell!

"Oh and congratulations.....*My Lord!*" I managed to say before my voice completely broke down.

"Keira wait, I just..." I heard behind me, but I didn't wait around to hear the rest. Just being in the same space with him was torturous enough. So, these were the last words I heard before I ran from the balcony, down the stairs, out of the building and across the car park, as fast as my legs could carry me.

Once I got to my truck, I couldn't even wait until I was in the safety of its metal frame. My body sank against it and I cried till every part of me hurt. I don't even remember getting into my car or stupidly starting the engine. But my body's need to feel safe again was greater than the risks. I could barely even see the road ahead but somehow, as if another body had taken hold of me, it made me drive. I couldn't even feel like I was moving, as my body was numb. I should have been shaking uncontrollably but my limbs just kept going until I reached my home.

Once in the drive, my possessed hand cut the engine and then that was it, I was back to me again and it hurt all over. My body convulsed and I sobbed so much that I couldn't breathe. I gasped for the air in hiccups to fill my lungs but it was proving hard as the tears wouldn't let up and trying to do both was difficult.

I don't know how long I sat there, but the pain continued to overwhelm every part of me and I only realised it must have been hours as it was now dark. Luckily, Libby and Frank had still not come back, and I finally gathered my senses long enough to make it into the house. I noticed there were two messages on the machine and I reluctantly pressed play.

"Hey Kazzy, hope you're having fun with the house all to yourself as me and Frank are staying another night. Be back tomorrow around noon, love you!" Libby's happy voice filled the air and tears rolled out of my tired, sore eyes as the word 'fun' had been painful to hear. The other message made it ten times worse as it was Jerry confirming my new shifts and how Draven had spoken to him telling him that I wasn't needed today and wouldn't be for a few days, so I was to start back on Wednesday. This had me falling to my knees in a crumpled pile on the floor and I cried so hard that I must have passed out.

I definitely exhausted myself as the next time I woke, dawn was breaking outside. So, I dragged my heartbroken body to my bedroom and I fell into bed, covering my head never wanting to see the light of day. I wanted to stay in my safe little cocoon where no-one could ever hurt me again.

How could I have let this happen? How could I have allowed myself to believe such things? Draven had never wanted me. He had never cared and all those nights that it had seemed as if he did were all a terrible lie my mind had created. I had seen things that weren't there. I was swept away by a man who had never really existed, and the result of my mistake was the broken shell of who I was.

My mind had deceived me.

I got up, not being able to sleep, even though I was utterly drained. I wished that I could have just got in my car and kept driving until I came to an end. That end being when the hurting inside finally stopped. Coming here had been a big mistake. I was stupid to believe I could ever have belonged here! I didn't belong anywhere. I just left an aftermath of destruction in my path... I was poison!

In the end, I rang RJ telling her I wasn't feeling good and that if I felt better then I might make it in later for History. She had asked what was wrong and with the sound of my broken voice I got away with telling her it was flu. Of course, after looking at myself in the mirror, my voice wasn't the only evidence of it. I had no colour to my skin, only the red blotches that remained around my eyes making it look as if I had lost the fight. Which was right in more ways than one.

My eyes were the scariest thing as they had no whites left, having been replaced by blood shot lines. My nose hurt around the edges from being rubbed so frequently that not much skin was left there. My lips were cracked through the constant biting, making them bleed. This was so that some of my pain was directed to the outside of my body, therefore relieving some from the inside.

In the end I couldn't face college as seeing Sophia again was going to be too much to bear. The wound that Draven had inflicted was still too fresh and exposed. I finally got out of bed and dressed only without looking at the clock I had no idea how long I had just sat there thinking about what a fool I was.

Once I was dressed, things started to get clearer and I needed to make a change to get past this. After all, I had come back from worse than this, hadn't I? It didn't feel like it. I might have the scars from my past that showed on the outside, but Draven had also left his scars and they ran deep inside to my core.

So, what was worse...? I knew the answer to that question.

I pulled on my father's old college football sweater and grabbed two things before leaving. One was my car keys and the other was the picture I had drawn of Draven.

I got in my car, driving faster than I should have been. I let the sound of the engine drown out most of my self-pitying thoughts. Jack had told me about a place and I drove in the direction that, thankfully, was far from Afterlife. That name...was that what it meant? That Draven would steal my heart and my soul, and this was to be my Afterlife?

Thinking about the pain didn't bring tears any more as if there was nothing left in me. He had taken everything and all I could do was try and resurrect myself to how I was before I had ever seen him. I had to be re-born and there was only one way I knew how to do this, and it was going to be hard. A lot harder than last time...

I found the dirt road after the warning signs for cliff faces and I knew where this would lead me to. I thought of Jack for a moment, wondering how this would have all gone if I had seen him first and he had been the one in my dreams.

The road came to an end in a big semi-circle where the cars usually parked. I turned off the engine and got out. The cold hit me, and the wind whipped round my face as I realised how high up I was. The cold was a good thing.

It kept things clearer and I had my goal firmly set in my mind. As scared as I was of the drop below me, I walked to the edge. After all, what did I have to fear any more when they had all come true in my life? One after another I had been used and thrown away when I was no longer needed...but this time I would change it all. I would never go back to that...*never!* And this was my proof, no matter how small an action it seemed.

The trees swayed around the forest and I knew this was a perfect place to finish this obsession once and for all.

I pulled the picture of Draven out of my back pocket and sat down crossing my legs, getting close enough to the edge to be able to get rid of the problem. I took one long hard look at the pencilled sketch, knowing that I had already seen the last of its original. So now my re-birth would begin by getting rid of every last bit of him, including any of my thoughts about him.

I had the mental capability to cast my demons from my mind by drawing them, locking them into the page thus banishing them from entering my mind again. But I had always kept the pictures and I never really understood why I did this. So, it got me thinking, maybe the only way to get him out of my mind completely was to remove him from my memory. With this in mind, I kissed my hand placing it gently on his face. Then, before I could back out, I began tearing into it with so much fiery passion, that before long it was in tiny pieces in my hands. Then I waited for the reason I had come here.

I closed my eyes remaining still trying to judge the air around me feeling it coming closer and thinking, if this could help once before then maybe I would have a chance. Even if it just got a little better, then that could be enough to get me through this, making the most horrific pain I had ever felt turn into a mind-numbing existence. So, I sat waiting patiently for the exact moment when it felt right to let go of him forever.

It came over me, blowing my hair up around my head and I lifted my hands, opening my palms, feeling the pain being taken away with the pieces I had left of Draven. They blew upwards, carried into the sky where they belonged...*where he belonged.*

I watched as they blew into the green abyss of the forest and my eyes strained as I waited until every last piece was out of sight.

Now, I could move on and finally...

Say goodbye.

DRAVEN

66

HEARTBREAK DECISIONS

"*Look for my demons, Draven.*"

The second I hit the ground my eyes snapped open to find the sleeping form of Keira underneath me. I was fully on top of her with my wings wrapped securely around her, enveloping her in my feathers. My hands were fisted in the pillow either side of her head with my claws out and embedded in the torn sheets. I quickly moved myself from her in fear of hurting her without even knowing I was capable of such a thing.

I had been dreaming of my past and somehow merging it with that of the future. I didn't know how my mind had managed such detail, but I certainly didn't miss the reason why.

It had been a warning.

One that rang loud and clear, for I knew what I had to do next. For now,

I had to let her go.

It was becoming blindingly clear she wouldn't accept me or my world so easily and last night was testament to that, just as it had been in my dream of the past

To her I was nothing more than a monster to be feared and run from. And in truth, for someone who had clearly been put through enough horrors in her life, how could I expect her to accept yet one more?

One of my own people had just stabbed her right in front of me and in my own club for fuck sake! If I couldn't even protect her in a situation like that, then how could I when she hadn't yet scratched the surface of my world?

By the Gods, but just thinking of the list of potential enemies I had, that I knew would make a play in obtaining her, well, it had my blood racing. For the ransom they would hold over me would bear the weight of my entire kingdom as I knew there was no price I would not have paid in getting her back. Which begged the question, just how far was I willing to go to keep her safe. Just how much was I willing to sacrifice of that of my people for my own selfish gain? The truth didn't exactly make me the noble King I had once arrogantly viewed myself as. For the answer was simple...

There was only one sacrifice I would not make and that was her life. And as I sat back on my knees and looked down at my hands now, I could almost see her blood soaked there. I could almost see the hands of a demon after they had just gone too far.

I had just woken from a dream and found claws embedded inches away from her beautiful face for fuck sake! And all from a dream. So, what was to stop me from losing those precious inches the next time and waking to find them embedded in her flesh?

I tore a hand through my hair almost ripping it from my scalp as I held it back clasped in a fist amidst my frustration. I wanted to roar so loud the fucking earth would split open and swallow my problems whole! I didn't want to make this decision or put her through what I knew I had no choice but to do.

I didn't want to break her fucking heart!

I got up from the bed and with a single thought clothes materialized over my body for fear that if I used my hands, I would only tear them in anger. I looked to the doors and saw that dawn wasn't long in coming, knowing I didn't have long left with her. Time I would have to spend on getting her home and setting the first scene in my lie.

So, with a thought, I remembered what clothes she had been wearing last night before a bloody reminder of what my kind could do to a mortal body had rid her of most of them. Then I did as I had done to my own and made them materialize over her, covering the tempting sight and preventing me once more from changing my mind. Something I couldn't afford to do.

Then, before I gave my mind freedom to even start thinking of the different possibilities, I gathered her sleeping form up in my arms and commanded the door open with a thought. Then I ran for the edge, hating the bitter taste in doing so, one that the dream had left me with. For now, I could not rid myself of seeing Keira's face as she fell further from my grasp. I didn't know why but the feeling of it being a premonition was too strong to fully ignore.

In fact, if I were being truthful, then without that dream I wasn't sure I would have woken with the strength to carry out my cruel decision to let her go.

We reached her home far sooner than I would have liked and all the while with me gripping her to my chest as if any minute my wings would suddenly fail me. Like Icarus, flying too close to the sun with nothing more but wings made of feathers and wax, I too would burn from trying to reach the impossible.

Fuck, but I felt cursed by the Gods, not blessed!

I let my wings fold, doing so now when a little closer to the ground than I usually would, proof of how much that dream had affected me. I, therefore, had to confess to myself that it had shaken me more than my ego would usually allow to admit, for owning up to one's weakness was never going to come easy to me. Not unless that weakness was named Keira and lay peacefully asleep in my arms right now. For that I would own up to in a heartbeat.

I let myself through her front door, knowing after what she had told me that I was free to do so for there was no one home. I wondered then at what the day would bring for her. Would she gain comfort of solitude after I had followed through with my plans? Or would she need that of comforting arms to embrace her? Should I in fact wait until her family were home before...no! I couldn't look for excuses to prolong the inevitable, not when my intention was to use last night's events as a reason.

This thought made me reach the top floor even quicker than I would have liked for I knew if I stayed here with her any longer, I would only end up convincing myself there was another way. So, I lay her down on her bed after sweeping back the covers with my mind. Then I re-covered her and told myself that this would be the last time, for I could no longer afford to chance coming here. Not with the power her mind had evolved to.

So, with my only chance to say these words to her, I leaned down to kiss her forehead after whispering the only four words I knew I wouldn't be able to give her after today...

"I'm sorry, my love."

After this I left, and a short time later found myself in my office readying myself for what I knew would be the most difficult day I had lived through so far. In truth, I didn't know how she would take my rejection as I was torn in my reasoning. I wanted her tears as much as I didn't. I wanted her cursing my name to Hell as much as I didn't. But most of all, I wanted her heartbreak as much as I was ready to beg the Gods for a different answer.

The second there was a knock on the door my dark and dangerous mood wouldn't allow for much more than a short barked reply,

"Come in!"

I watched as Celina entered the room doing so as she did most things, calmly and precisely. I often wondered about her and how she came to be on my council. The strange dealings she'd had with some human boy had caught my attention due to its forbidden nature. A boy I couldn't remember and one no doubt left heartbroken thanks to the lie that would need to be told in order to protect yet another mortal form the truth. The same lie I myself was in the process of orchestrating by inviting Celina into my office with what would no doubt be an unusual request.

I nodded to the seat in front of me, thinking she deserved that much for what I was about to ask of her. She nodded respectfully and folded herself into the chair I'd had the foresight to place there before I summoned her to my office.

"I have somewhat of an unusual task to ask of you, and one that must be done so with discretion and delicacy." She didn't look in the least bit surprised but instead, as if she had been programmed to do so, she simply nodded once more and answered,

"But of course, anything my King wishes of me." If only it were that simple, I thought with annoyance at looking who would unfortunately play my fiancée for the day.

It was to be a tortured day indeed.

By the time the afternoon arrived I was wound up so tight I felt like a loaded gun ready to fire. I had told Karmun to tell Keira when she arrived for her shift that she wasn't needed up in the VIP today. Then by the end of her working hours my plan was to send for her to come to my office so that I could tell her that her service was no longer needed in the VIP. Doing so by explaining she had been replaced. Then I would simply thank her for her time here and before the end of the meeting, have Celina come in to play her part. And thus, sealing my own fate within Keira's heart, for she would no doubt swiftly move on after that.

That had been the plan anyway. But like most things concerning my Electus, it wasn't to be that way. I knew this when Karmun entered my office shortly after twelve and told me that Keira had not only been asking about what happened last night, but also demanding to speak with me about it personally.

My reply had been nothing more than to release a deep sigh before nodding at him to show her in. He then informed me that she was waiting on the balcony for me and once again I felt far beyond my depths here foreseeing how this was going to go.

I knew that with her just being here that she would not have remembered many of the events from last night. None of which would have been from what happened on the rooftop for I had been sure to take them all from her. Besides, if it hadn't worked then I very much doubted she would have come back here, let alone face me after what she witnessed of me last night.

No, I had no doubt in this, for it would make no logical sense for a terrified girl to return back to the scene of her fear and face the cause of what she considered a threat. Now the parts that would be hazy to her and no doubt were still in question was probably the reason she was here demanding that information. And as for me, well in truth I couldn't be sure just how far the memories I took from her went back from last night.

If I were honest, then I had hoped that I had taken it all, but just her being here and demanding answers from me made that unlikely. So, I issued one command at Karmun and left to face my doomed fate.

"Inform Celina where I am," I told him before he left my office. Then I grabbed my suit jacket, doing so like it was armour and I was about to head into battle, one no doubt, I would never forget!

Upon seeing her again since I lay her down in her bed early this morning, I couldn't help but take the unaware moment as one last gift. She stood on the balcony facing the national park holding herself as if cold, but her big winter jacket suggested otherwise.

She wasn't cold, she was nervous and honestly... *so was I.*

I still had that nagging feeling inside me trying to hold me back. That small inner voice telling me to use what happened last night as an opportunity to tell her everything. A chance to be honest and hope that she understood how important she was to me.

But I had taken those memories for a reason and remembering my dream last night where she had thrown herself from the rooftop after seeing the monster in me, only ended up cementing my reserve for what I was about to do next.

"Keira, you wanted to see me?" I said letting my voice speak for itself and doing so without the warmth in my tone I had granted her last night. She looked taken aback a moment as she quickly scanned my body, doing so now no doubt to access my frosty demeanour and questioning the reason for it.

"Yes...I wanted to talk to you about last night," she said as I suspected she would and I knew now was my time to enter into the act that I had been obsessing about since waking from that wretched dream.

"Ah yes, well, it was an unfortunate accident and I'm glad to see you're feeling better after your fall." I said setting the scene of doubt in her mind. But she shook her head and frowned at me.

"What fall?" she asked, the disbelief clear in her tone.

"You must not remember. Well, that's understandable, you went out like a light. I do apologise for what happened and I assure you, I do not tolerate fighting in my club. But well, this is what is expected when drugs are involved. Trust me when I say the matter has been dealt with." I told her hoping that was all I would need to say on the matter so that I could move on and finish acting out this bastard charade!

However, that was not to happen, and I knew it the moment she flinched as if I had struck her, even going as far as to take a small step back. Then she tore her gaze from me and looking down to the side as if replaying last night's events for herself. After which, unbelievably coming back at me with a venomous reply as her anger built up before it burst from her.

"That's....That's bullshit! Don't lie to me!" She shouted at me, shocking me to my core...she couldn't remember...could she? No, it was impossible!

"Excuse me?" I said letting my surprise coat my tone and hoping my authority in my position helped in calming her temper. Needless to say, this didn't happen for it looked as though she had hit her limit on taking my shit, which was why she argued,

"That didn't happen...Goddamn it, I didn't fall!" I had to say in that moment it was hard to school my features for I was so impressed by her tenacious will, I only wanted to praise her for it. As it was obvious she had some idea of what happened last night and she was sticking by it.

But I couldn't do this. I couldn't do as I wanted. Not this bastard.

"And what is it that you believe to have happened exactly?" I asked crossing my arms and using intimidation to try and get her to back down on the matter. Something only half of me wished to see for her show of bravery in this moment was actually making this harder to bear. For all I wanted to do was cut the distance between us in a heartbeat and take her in my arms so that I could recreate last night's kiss, only this time one that would not be stolen from her!

But then she spoke and when she did the knowledge of her memories rocked me to the core, for the impossible was just made possible.

"Fine, play it like that! We both know what happened last night, but considering you're playing it down as though it was nothing but a 'bump to the head' then you go ahead and do that! But I will never, and I repeat *never* believe that and no matter how much you try to trick me...I'm here telling you now, it won't work!" She shouted with fisted hands at her sides looking as if they were held this way to prevent herself from slapping me. Regrettably there were also tears held prisoner in her eyes, ones that refused to fall. No matter how shaky her shallow breaths were or the trembling of her shoulders, she held on to them like traitorous prisoners.

I very nearly had to tear my head away just to spare myself the sight, for my guilt was building to unbearable amounts. Building to the point where my reserve was a hairsbreadth away from cracking.

Then, just when I didn't think it could get any worse, it was in that moment that Celina entered into our argument and I had to nearly bite my own fucking tongue off to prevent myself from snapping at her to leave us!

But then I remembered my plan and knew that I had no choice. So, I tried not to flinch in repulsion the moment I felt Celina curl herself against my side, playing the part of my 'wife to be' perfectly. But my repulsion doubled the second I knew she wasn't the only one who had to carry out this act. So, trying not to show my true feelings on the matter, I wrapped an arm around her and pulled her closer to me. I tensed, hating the feel of another woman in my arms where there should have only ever been one.

Keira.

But right in this moment she was miles away from me and currently that distance was growing rapidly with every second I forced her to witness this deception.

"Oh, you must be Keira, the waitress who got knocked down due to the fight, how's your head feeling today?" Celina asked sweetly as I knew she would, as I had already instructed her on what to say. But I hadn't been prepared for this crushing feeling in my chest just by being forced to witness the result of my lies in the eyes of the girl I loved. For now, it was like looking for the lighthouse in the darkness of a storm and seeing it for a moment before it slowly died, signalling your own death. Her soul's light was dying behind her eyes. It was in that moment that I realised just how deeply her love for me ran and I was nearly overcome by the knowledge. Which was why I couldn't help but tear my gaze from the sight of the irreparable damage I was inflicting.

"I'm fine, thank you." Was her strained reply and I felt each word like a knife slitting my skin.

"That's good. Well, I'm sorry Dominic, I will leave you to finish and trouble you with wedding plans later," Celina said and then lifted her tall slender frame closer to me, leaning in for the kiss we never spoke of and in doing so hammering home the last nail in my own coffin. One I had built for myself. I barely touched my lips to hers, wanting nothing more than to remove her by force but my body had turned to stone. Instead I let it happen, cursing myself to the flames of Tartarus to burn for the crimes I set against my own heart!

Fuck, I truly was a bastard!

I knew this the second I saw the limit on her bravery as those imprisoned tears finally fell. This was when my own limit snapped, and I snarled down at Celina so that Keira wouldn't hear.

"Leave...now!" It was said as a threat for going too far and her panicked eyes told me she knew it. The moment she left I found myself taking a step closer to Keira but having to stop myself just in time as she was trying to hide her tears from me. Tears I had asked for, just like the pain that gave birth to them. I had done all of this and for it, I had never hated myself so much in all my time living this life.

Which was why I clenched a fist at my side and continued on with the heinous act.

"I'm sorry, that was rude. I didn't introduce you to my fiancée. That was Celina," I told her knowing this time I wasn't just killing a dream, I was potentially killing a prophesied love gifted from the Gods.

But I knew that was better than the alternative...
Killing her.

Because that was my only fear and if breaking both our hearts was what would save her life, then so be it! So, I took a deep breath and drove my point home.

"I understand there has been a misjudged account of affections that do not exist. Perhaps this was partly my doing as well, as a young overactive imagination can sometimes twist the truth. In light of your clear feelings, I would think it best for you if you no longer work up here in the VIP." I then set my features to stone as I lived through my punishment, which was more of her tears she still bravely tried in vain to contain, along with her dignity. By the Gods, what a queen she would have made!

"Right...you're right, clearly... what a stupid mistake to have made!" She snapped bitterly and it prompted me into giving her something more.

"I think you're a hard worker and..."

"Stop, just stop!" she shouted holding out a hand to me, begging me not to say another word and I found myself astounded that this self-inflicted pain could continue to get worse.

"Keira, I..." I started to say in a gentle tone, wanting to apologise for the hurt I had caused, even if I was unable to take it back completely. But unsurprisingly she was having none of it, especially when she declared,

"I quit."

I released a deep sigh and muttered an ancient Persian curse under my breath before telling her,

"There is no need for you to quit."

"Oh, I think there are more than enough reasons for me to quit...don't you?" she fired back and I couldn't help but frown knowing she was right and quickly backing me into a corner. Because in theory that would have been far simpler. For her to quit working here altogether. But even if I was letting her go, there was only so far I was willing to do so. I still needed her. I still needed to have her close enough to see each day. I knew it was wrong and it was selfish, but I didn't care! I just knew that without getting that little piece of her every day then I would be but a shell of a man after only a few days apart!

I knew this after already pushing my limits when going to England and leaving her for the week. So, I put my decision down to my people needing a functioning King and without her, there would be no such thing! No, I couldn't let her quit! Besides, having her here still enabled me to protect her and that was all that mattered.

So, what did I do, use the one weapon I had left against her, one named...*guilt.*

"No, I don't. Not considering I know how much it will upset my sister," I told her now shamefully playing the part of a manipulative bastard on top of my other crimes.

"Sophia." She uttered my sister's name as if only now thinking of her and hating that she was in the middle of all of this. It also involuntary made me think about my siblings, whom I was still yet to tell of my decision to cut her from my life, especially until I could be assured of her safety.

They had both been given their orders to capture Lahash and were no doubt having far more fun than I was at this moment, for I wished to have been the one conducting the interrogation. But it was true that had I done so after leaving Keira this morning, then I would have no doubt simply gone too far and killed her too quickly.

And if I were honest, if I did so now then it would be no better, for I certainly needed something or someone I could take my mounting temper out on. A temper that was reaching new heights at myself when I continued to force Keira's hand by guilting her into doing as I wanted.

"She thinks very highly of your friendship and has been good to you, are you really willing to repay her kindness by quitting because of unreciprocated feelings?" Once more I had pushed too hard at her limits and in return she lashed out,

"Don't...! Just don't." She warned and I took a shuddered breath of my own, one she was too lost in her own pain to notice.

"Fine. I will continue downstairs for Sophia's sake, but only until I have paid off this car..." This was when I interrupted her, for there was no way I was allowing such.

"Keira, that's not necessary," I told her but this was when I received my first lashing against my heart delivered by her own tongue,

"Oh, but it is as I want *nothing* from you!" I visibly winced, but it was a reaction she understandably didn't care for, as I'd undoubtably gone too far.

I knew this the moment she unknowingly broke my own heart this time by issuing me a promise, one I only hoped she wouldn't hold on to.

"Don't worry I will never be stupid enough to set foot up here again or be foolish to show any of my *young overactive imagination* towards you ever again. I can promise you that!" I swallowed the cold, hard lump of reality, for I had done this. I had brought out this bitterness within her as I had not only shunned her loving me but done so in a way where I had rubbed the foolishness behind it in her face and mocked it!

I didn't know what I doubted more, that she would ever forgive me in time, or that I would be able to forgive myself. Meaning that if she had looked at me in that moment all she would have found was the face of remorse.

But she didn't look. No, instead she firmly walked past me, signalling that this meeting between us was over and I swear it took every ounce of self-control I had in me not to reach out and grab her. For I fear if I had then I would never have been able to let her go again!

But something made her stop by the door and I knew that right then, I couldn't trust myself to look at her. So, I remained like stone as she delivered her final blow,

"Oh, and congratulations...*My Lord!*" This was when my willpower finally broke down entirely,

"Keira wait, I just...this is...*because I love you.*" I whispered this last part to no one as I let my legs give way and landed hard enough on my knees that I cracked the tiles beneath me.

For I hadn't fallen as a man.

I had fallen as an Angel.

My wings were out, and I let my head fall forward displaying my shame openly to the Gods.

That and how...

My ashamed heart now burned.

DRAVEN

67

TORN HEARTS

After this, I only raised my head again when I heard her heart-breaking cries being carried along on the wind. I rose back to my feet and to the edge of the balcony so that I could see for myself the damage I had inflicted. It was like feeling a knife being plunged further into my chest when I saw her. A blade with my own hand around the handle.

For I had done this...*no one else.*

I had never felt the emotion of self-loathing so strongly before, even if I knew that my behaviour in the past towards her at times had been questionable. But this! Well, this was one moment in my life I could finally admit that I had clearly gone too far. Had my ultimate goal really been for her to hate me? Had it really been to twist the love she once held for me into something so warped, it was now quickly becoming a shameful memory for her?

Seeing for myself now her crumbled form leaning against her truck as she cried uncontrollably, then in my opinion she had every right to hate me! For I clearly deserved nothing less.

Now, I knew that there was at least one thing I could do for her and that was to get her home safely. A place where she could at least find peace in the knowledge that her grieving actions weren't being witnessed by any other. Something she would no doubt later on feel shameful of.

If I were honest, I was utterly dumbfounded to see that my rejection had caused such a reaction within her, for it was only proof of how much she cared. I had naïvely believed myself to be the only one that held the weight of love and solely doing so in secret.

Did I believe the girl had hidden feelings for me? Yes, for I wasn't an idiot. But did I ever imagine this level of feeling? No, I confess I had not. The sceptical half of me wondered if she felt this way because she was born for loving me.

But then the same could be said about myself and I knew that the depth of my feelings for her didn't root from any prophecy or deemed so by the Fates. I didn't care what argument to the fact was lay at my feet, for I would dispute it until my dying day. No one had the power to make me feel this way. To make me feel this strongly for her or lose my head to an obsession I knew was far beyond the realms of fancy.

This love for her consumed my soul enough to make decisions based not on obtaining my own happiness but that of hers. I wanted her to live. And I wanted her to do so without fear, pain or suffering, all of which, from the looks of things, I had monumentally failed at achieving. And all because I had underestimated her love for me in return. Believing I was the only one who could feel such sentiments as strongly as I did.

But now, well it truly looked as though I had broken the girl's heart and all for what, in the hope that I can protect her. Not just from my enemies but…well from herself, for just looking at those gloved arms and I knew what she was capable of doing just to escape what she feared was a lifetime of imprisonment from a demon.

The very meaning of my dreams last night showed as much, as she had willingly thrown herself from that rooftop and all so that she could escape *me*.

Which was where my biggest fear lay, the rejection of love because of who I truly was and my demon's reaction to such, for could I really be certain that I wouldn't ever hurt her?

The fear alone in her eyes last night was enough to have me questioning my future with her. For how was something like that to be ignored?

Fuck I just didn't know anymore!

"Fuck!" I shouted before veiling myself and jumping from the balcony, before determined footsteps took me to Keira's hunched form. There I took control of her fragile mind, finding that like this it wasn't half as strong as it usually was. A thought that brought me little pleasure and only ended up doubling my guilt!

But right now, I could do little but exploit it for Keira's sake, as it was clear she was beyond function and I needed to get her home. So, exerting my will on her mind and taking the telling effort to do so, I masked the sight of myself crouching before her. Then I tried to calm her mind a little so that I wouldn't startle a scream from her when I took her in my arms, before placing her inside her truck. I also knew that if this was going to work then I had no choice but to place her behind the steering wheel for she would have to believe that she drove herself home.

Which meant taking over the functions of her mind that controlled her movements, doing so now so that she could start the engine. Then I got into the passenger side and forced her to drive home, doing so safely and hating myself even more every mile we took. I lost count of the amount of times I wanted to pull the car over and take her in my arms. To offer her comfort and beg her for a forgiveness I didn't deserve.

But instead I kept her going.

I just needed to get her home and then leave. I kept telling myself this like some Hellish mantra that made little sense but to punish me. Which was why I took a moment away from my self-loathing the second we pulled into her drive and used the time to say goodbye the only way I knew how.

I reached over to her hand, lifted it to my lips and lay a kiss upon the back of her palm finally allowing a single tear of my own to fall and seep into her skin.

"Forgive me the cause of our breaking hearts," I whispered before getting out of the truck, slamming the door, veiling myself once more and releasing her mind of my control as I walked away. Doing so now to the bitter sound of her tormented sobs.

A sound that had the power to rip apart my soul.

After that, I didn't go back to check on her, as much as it pained me to stay away, I knew that I had no right to do anything else. So, I left her and the knowledge of what I had done hurt like soulweed had started to knot around my heart. Now squeezing the life from it, for what was the use of it now?

Gods, but listen to me!

Well, if this was what happened the first time emotions such as these were felt, then it was surprising that one survived them! For this feeling of weakness sat inside me like a dead weight I couldn't rid myself of and every movement and thought simply reminded me of it still being there. Of course, this wasn't helped by the fact shortly after returning from Keira's home that I had Sophia to deal with. And let's just say that Keira's wrath had nothing on her new supernatural spokeswoman.

I didn't even flinch when I heard my door slam shut, done so with enough force, it rattled the frame.

"What the fuck have you gone and done this time!?" Sophia bellowed at me, making me slowly put down the paperwork I was reading. It was a proposal for one of my abandoned properties in France to be converted into offices to rent with high class apartments above. In other words, it was anything I could get my hands on so that I wouldn't think about what I really wanted to do and that was check on my Chosen One.

I took a deep breath and told her, trying first for calm,

"I did what was necessary."

"Bullshit!" Sophia roared in reply, holding nothing back like usual.

"Careful Sophia, just because I made a decision it doesn't mean I am not already paying dearly for it, which also means I am in no mood to have my mistakes pointed out to me when they are already unforgettable," I said, once again, trying for calm even given my stern tone.

"So, you admit that it was a mistake?" she snapped folding her arms over her fitted red dress, one that finished just below the knee and made her look ready for an office meeting. I released a sigh and said,

"Sophia haven't you realised it yet, but every fucking thing I do with regards to the girl is a fucking mistake I unwittingly seem to make!" I snapped back in exasperation.

"Then why, brother, do you continue to make them when there is a simple answer to all of this?" she asked now choosing to take pity on me and lower her tone to one less, well…like she wanted to tear her claws into me and bite out my larynx so that it would prevent me from hurting the girl anymore. And to be honest, I couldn't say that I blamed her in the feeling, for after witnessing her reaction today, then I was tempted to do the same!

"Simple!? By the Gods, Sophia where have you been the last month, there is nothing fucking simple about all of this!" I snapped swiping an angry hand through the air. At this she started laughing and shook her head as if all men were imbeciles. I knew I was right the second she muttered to herself,

"Utterly clueless." To which my reply was a noted growl.

"Dom, listen to me now, the girl is in love with you for Gods' sake, what more do you need!?" Well, after today I couldn't argue with her there, however her love for me wasn't going to save her from getting hurt, like Sophia wished to believe.

"That maybe so but that doesn't change what happened to her last night and making our union common knowledge will only end up creating greater risks as, short of locking her in a fucking tower, how else am I to keep her safe from getting stabbed again, or taken, or fucking dragged down to Hell for all I know!" I shouted making Sophia shrug her shoulders before enlightening me,

"Tell me what type of love doesn't come with risks of loss, Dom...? By the Gods, I really don't know what it is you're expecting here, her to come to you from the Gods with a 'no harm shall come to me' guarantee?!" I tore my angry gaze from her simply because I knew that some of what she said was true. I was looking for a guarantee. However, that didn't prevent me from continuing my point,

"I cannot let any harm come to her because of me, don't you understand that, Sophia!?"

"But do you not understand, that by acting the way you are already hurting her."

"A hurt she will never die from, Sophia!" I threw back at her making her frown.

"So, what, that's it then, you finally find your Chosen One after all this time and you just give up on her for fear of losing her...'cause that makes no fucking sense!" She snapped this last part by slapping both hands on my desk, bending her slight frame and getting closer in my face.

"It's called being selfless, Sophia, you may need to look up the term!" I threw back making her growl this time.

"Well, here's a term for you, brother dearest, *equality*, as in making decisions together and asking what it is the other person wants because right now, I very much doubt it's being passed out by the front door after crying herself to sleep because her heart is breaking!" Hearing this felt like a slap powerful enough to have propelled me across the room!

"You have seen her?!" I asked tensing at the description of Keira and hoping it was just an exaggeration.

"Once I heard what you did, then yes, of course I wanted to check on her, at least one of us had to, for what is it you chose to do, sit here conducting business!" she said swiping all my paperwork to the floor in her anger. But I didn't care, for I was out of my seat and moving when Sophia informed me,

"If you're thinking of going over there then it is too late, as I made sure not to leave until she was resting in bed, so you would only be wasting your time..." She then paused, made her way to the door and delivered her parting gift just before leaving, snarling what I already knew was true,

"...Time, you just don't deserve!"

After this account of how Keira was doing from Sophia, who I noted shortly after this refused to speak to me again, I decided for my own peace of mind to have someone keeping watch on her actions for the next few days. Just enough time for her to settle into the new work routine and also find her feet once more. In truth this was all guess work, for I had no clue how Keira was going to deal with what had happened.

It was clear from our meeting that she remembered far more than what I had tried to take from her. Which, upon thinking of it, I found myself questioning if that were the case, then why would she have come back? If she believed all that had happened that night, especially the rooftop, then why by the Gods, would a girl who was clearly terrified of me, why would she then demand speak to me?

And why was I only questioning this now?

No, but it couldn't be as I hoped...that no matter at seeing my other side she did in fact trust me not to hurt her? But the reality of questioning myself now was that how would I ever find out the truth of her feelings, when I had shunned her and already turned her away? It wasn't as if I could go back and ask her exactly what it was she remembered of that night. And once again I was back to where I started. Making irrational and quick decisions before allowing myself the time to reflect on the options, for now I may never know.

My musings on the matter were soon interrupted when my phone started ringing on my desk. I had yet been back to sleep in my own bed and doubted I ever would until the day Keira could be with me there. As it stood, I still had her scent embedded in the sheets and ordered that no one was to enter my chamber, for fear that my sheets would be laundered, for that would have been damage I would not have been able to fix.

I knew her scent wouldn't last indefinitely, which was why I refused to taint it with my own body. Besides, it wasn't as though I would have been able to sleep anyway, not after knowing what it felt like to do so with her wrapped in both my arms and my wings. A gifted moment in time I would never forget.

But of course, I knew my vessel would need the rest at some point, but I had weeks before such was deemed necessary. So, I remained in my office, convincing myself that burying my time in work would help it pass somewhat quicker than it would had I just been obsessing about Keira.

However, in reality, I still reached for my phone, hoping it was news about her, and no amount of work would accomplish such an impossible task in forgetting her.

"Speak," I barked unable to keep my bad mood from lashing out my words.

"My Lord, the girl has left her home but isn't heading to college." This didn't surprise me as I would have been surprised had she shown up there today. But the fact that she left the house at all did have me curious as to where she was now headed.

"Which direction is she travelling?" I asked knowing that Zagan was following her as he was instructed to do should the unlikely event happen...which evidently wasn't as unlikely as I first thought.

"That's just it my Lord, she is heading to the known look out point most popular with the hikers." The second I heard this I had a chill run down my spine like the Devil himself was walking along it! I couldn't help but remember my dream, which was why I was out of my seat and releasing my wings as I spoke,

"Remain out of sight, I will be there in three minutes, intervene only if absolutely necessary...is that understood?!" I ordered knowing he would know what actions taken by her would deem it 'absolutely necessary'. Actions I would openly pray to the Gods was only manifested through my paranoid mind.

"Of course, My Lord," he answered before I hung up, throwing my phone back on the desk before running for the open balcony. I veiled myself the second my foot left the stone balustrades and flew as fast as my wings would carry me to the clearing; one used as a viewing point as it offered the best view of the national park.

I got there to find her truck already parked and a lone figure sat about a metre away from the edge. I landed with no sound and kept my distance, although just the sight of her made doing so difficult. I could see for myself the evidence of her pain in her appearance alone.

She looked...broken.

Her eyes were red, swollen and bloodshot. Her lips looked sore and cracked as if they had been bitten within an inch of their life. And the dark circles under her eyes told the story of someone who found no peace from the personal agony sleep should have granted.

What had I done?

Well, there was little point in questioning my actions now, as the damage had already clearly been done and there was no going back. I located Zagan in the tree line and nodded for him to give us our private moment.

In fact, I was still watching him leave when I noticed her movements pulling me back to her not so private moment. I saw her pull something from her pocket but before I could move to see what it was, I watched as she kissed her hand before placing it to the image, transferring the gesture. Then, as if contradicting her previous tender actions, she violently started to tear it to pieces.

I continued to watch as she took a deep shuddering breath once the picture was no more, but instead grasped the pieces to her heart whilst closing her eyes as if waiting for something.

I didn't have to wait long to find out what it was for the second a gust of wind whipped through the trees and around us, she raised up her hands and let nature take the pieces from her. It was such a serene moment that it almost felt as though I was witnessing some kind of personal ritual to rid her of something. Now all I needed to do was find out what.

She sat there so still as her eyes trailed each piece until it blew beyond her vision. Then, once firmly out of sight, she got up and left the look out. Meanwhile I too had been trailing the pieces in my mind and the second she was gone I brought each one back to me so that by the time they appeared in my hand they were one by one fitting themselves back together again like a rudimentary jigsaw puzzle.

The whole time I did this with my own eyes closed, so as to concentrate on the delicate task of rewinding a single moment's history. Then once I knew the last piece had been located, I opened my eyes slowly, as if afraid of what I would find staring back at me.

But once I did, I then had my answer. It was as I thought. A personal ritual of hers carried out for one sole purpose.

It was a goodbye.

I knew that the moment I looked down and saw a picture of myself looking back at me.

A piece of me, she had now literally...

Torn from her life.

DRAVEN

68
WEEKS OF DISCOVERY

In the weeks that followed, trying to stay away from Keira became ever more difficult, not easier as I had fooled myself into believing it would. So, time was spent both obsessing over her and learning everything there was about her past that I could. And, although now having the case file made this easier, I soon discovered it was far from easy reading it!

I knew the bare bones of the traumatic events that took place, but the details were what made this crime against her truly horrific. Her abduction had been as far from what you could class as a usual case as you could get. His sick and vile obsession with her made my own look like a mere passing fancy, not the deep infatuation and passionate love I felt.

His mental state of health was lost to his madness and quickly showed through his own testimonies of events occurred, that it had been this way for quite some time. My guess was that it stemmed from childhood and was triggered by a single traumatic event.

It was no wonder the court system had deemed him unfit to stand trial. Which mattered little to me, for he was about to receive a more final punishment with what I had in mind. For life in prison wasn't what I called a satisfactory sentence for someone who took a life. An eye for an eye had always been my people's way and would continue to be so until the end of our existence.

But even if it hadn't been, then for the offence of touching my Chosen One, well that was without a doubt punishable by death. Which was precisely why Lahash was currently rotting in the worst cell I could find in my prison, awaiting her own death sentence. All I needed now was the right lunar cycle and a worthy soul petitioning for the rights to a new vessel and she was gone. After all, we knew the worth of acquiring a new vessel, so were never wasteful of the fact.

This was another reason I had also restrained myself from going down there myself and inflicting irreparable damage. Something I knew my temper would force me to do.

Gods, but it would have been so easy, as I had the culprit to my misery within my grasp and wanted nothing more than to take out my wrath on the cause. But then I knew nothing would have the power to prevent my demon from ripping her limb from limb and in the process laying her vessel to utter waste.

However, this I found to be ever more increasingly difficult not to do, especially when I finally allowed myself the time to go through Keira's file, as I knew what awaited me. I could have done this sooner but in truth, I was now fearful of what I may find. I knew it was bad, for I'd had the story told to me already, but seeing the evidence of it for myself, well that was something I had never prepared myself for.

My own personal Hell...

Weeks ago.

I don't know how long I remained standing at the cliff face staring down into the image of what Keira saw in me, but it was long enough to have me second guessing every damn decision I had made since first meeting her!

I didn't know what was right and wrong anymore. I only knew what I wanted in my heart. A heart that didn't fucking deserve her, of that I was certain! Because now here I was, staring down at the sketch of my image knowing that it should be in pieces and scattered throughout a world she'd just walked away from. And I couldn't help but find myself hoping that in her heart she hadn't truly said goodbye. Even if I knew that deep down this was what was best for her. To find closure and move on. Even if I secretly hated the thought, leaving a bitter acid in my mouth for me to choke on.

Which made me question myself...just how far was my new selfish nature willing to stretch for her happiness? Especially when my own was on the line. Well I knew the answer to that for I feared I had stretched it as far as I was ever willing to go. For other than leaving this place and never seeing her again, then I had done everything else to distance myself from her. And leaving...well, that was the last step I knew I couldn't yet take.

The moment it started to rain I knew I had been out here too long searching for answers that would never reach me, for only she held them now...*she just didn't know it.* However, there was one last step I knew I had to take and after last night, had been reluctant to do so as things had changed.

That dream had changed me.

Before that moment, I had done everything in my power to get hold of that damn file and learn the last puzzle pieces that made up the darker years of Keira's life...pieces that I confess, I was now not so eager to learn.

So, I tucked the picture away in my jacket and took flight, heading for my home and enjoying the light rain that seemed to help in clearing my senses. Which meant that by the time I reached my office I could at least think enough to do what was needed. No doubt it was to be my last small reprieve before learning of the agony I knew those files held.

An hour later and for the second time since meeting Keira,

I destroyed my office...*again.*

The files told the story of a twenty year old Keira, who at the time decided to go by her first given name of Catherine. She attended a university in Southampton to study her love of Art. Unfortunately for her, Douglas Brone chose that moment in life to kill another professor and take over his identity, becoming Hugo Morgan.

Swiftly after doing so his new obsession began the second he met my Keira. According to the file, no complaint had been filed against him, so when she went missing it wasn't a natural presumption to have him looked into.

Although later on and as part of the fuck up with this case, one that I could see was handled badly from the start, they had learned through her classmates that they had at least suspected Morgan at one time. Keira had started skipping art classes and even though she didn't speak to people about it, they could tell from his side that his behaviour towards her was too close for comfort.

They even suspected him further after his behaviour changed after kidnapping her for he seemed more relaxed than he had ever been. The complete opposite to how he had been when he found her not in his class that first day she didn't show, as his behaviour then was said to be strangely erratic. One girl even described it as seemingly *unhinged.*

But these testimonies were never fully looked into or given much thought, being regarded as nothing but gossip. Of course, it didn't help Keira's case considering she was being looked into as the main suspect in the death of Tom Robertson, known to be dating Keira at the time. This was when my fist found itself embedded in my wall for the first of many times to follow. Something that marked the beginning of my mounting rage.

However, I pressed on, knowing that I had no choice. I also felt somewhat as if I owed it to Keira to find the strength to do so, for what she had endured in the 43 days she was missing utterly astounded me!

But everyone finds their limit and Keira no doubt found hers the day she tried to end it all. Unknowingly proving that Morgan had been more afraid of losing her than getting caught.

After that the investigation didn't take long to get concluded, as they had everything they needed. However, the one startling part about all this was that other than Keira first trying to convince the hospital staff that she had been kidnapped, she then refused to speak further on the matter. Only giving them one name responsible.

She gave not a single statement to authorities nor had she to this day. At first, I couldn't believe it, but the more I looked, the less I found with regards to her side of the events. There hadn't ever been a single documented account where she spoke about what happened to her to anyone.

In the case file the victim is simply deemed too traumatized to make a statement which had me gripping the pages so hard I almost turned the paper back into pulp! I found myself almost desperate to know why this was. Was it because she knew in the end it wouldn't have been needed? For they certainly found more than enough evidence to tell the story for her back at his house. The multitude of pictures were proof enough of that!

The horrific conditions she was kept in. The bloody scene of where she cut herself with a broken pieces of a mirror found in a music box. A sickening room dedicated to his obsession of her that made me bite my tongue just so that the metallic taste filled my mouth to eradicate the bile that threatened to surface. I closed my eyes against the sight of all personal items taken from her and displayed like a fucking trophy! Some of which even included a bag of worn underwear and a collection of her evident female monthly bleed whilst in captivity.

It was when looking through these pictures that I completely lost my senses to rage and hammered my fists down the centre of my abused desk before upturning the two sides. I think after reading the list of evidence they found in his house was when I had hit my own limits and had to stop myself from reading anymore.

I left the crumbling state of my office just as Vincent appeared in a rush, no doubt from hearing of his brother's madness echoing throughout our home. I told him one thing,

"I suggest if you wish to have the walls of our home still standing, then you find me a long line of fighters willing to bloody themselves and quickly!" I then started to walk away from the personal Hell that belonged to my Chosen One, as I went in search of any other way to relieve my temper.

Vincent nodded without saying a word and walked into my office to discover for himself the reason behind my crazed actions, for it was currently scattered all over my office like dangerous shrapnel of her past.

A past that made me want to rip out Morgan's fucking heart and offer it to Keira on a golden platter for her to set alight!

I wanted to be the one to take his life from this world and cast him down into a Hellish side of my own. I wanted his soul tortured and his body to be burned to a cinder daily. I wanted him to live through his worst nightmares over and over again, before every last inch of his flesh was peeled from his bones and consumed whilst being kept alive long enough to watch it all!

I swear the darkness in which these murderous thoughts consumed me surprised me that I still had any strength left to prevent my demon from taking over, as it had done so in my dreams. A fact my many opponents were also pleased about, seeing as facing my demon's wrath would have meant finding themselves more than just beaten in a fight and their vessels bruised and bleeding.

In fact, it was three hours later and many bloody volunteers defeated, that Vincent came to me in the training room. I think there was even a collective and verbalized sigh of relief the moment he demanded everyone to leave.

"You know I am going to have to start charging you every time I fix your office," Vincent said as I picked up a towel to wipe the blood from my face and prevent it dripping down my bare chest. It was from the few times my opponents had managed to get in some minor damaging blows, and a little blood had been all that was left to show for the lucky jabs.

"You saw it?" I asked ignoring his comment and getting straight to the point. Vincent released a heavy sigh giving me his answer before he spoke,

"I confess, the girl has been through a lot more than any of us could have originally thought," he said rubbing the back of his neck which was one of his own habits when frustrated, something I admitted to doing myself on occasion.

"You can fucking say that again but be advised if you do, for it may set me on another fit of rage," I advised making him raise a brow at me.

"How many did you leave broken?"

"I lost count after twenty," I told him letting him know that those he had asked to leave had only been of the handful I had fought against. Did I feel better for it, yes, I did...did I feel better as a whole? Fuck no! And doubted I would until I had Morgan's severed head in my hands!

Vincent once more released a sigh and said,

"Not that I can blame you, for I confess to adding to the destruction in your office whilst reading her case file for myself...that was before I fixed it of course." I nodded in understanding and had to be honest in the comfort I found no longer being the only one to carry such a burden of knowledge with me alone.

"Then in his death you agree with me?" I asked finishing wiping the blood off my hands with the same towel. My knuckles were the longest part of my vessel to heal, for I gave them little rest from being used in the time that was needed for the split skin to close.

"Fuck yes! The ass end of a Gorgon Leech needs to die, there is no questioning that, but may I suggest at first discovering more about his sickening mind before you act." I frowned as I thought about my brother's reasoning, now taking a seat next to him on one of the benches that framed one side of the training room.

"You believe there could be more to it than the simple lost mind of a mortal?" I asked never considering the possibility of it before.

"All I wonder is if you really were the first of our kind to discover the identity of the Electus or if in fact you were one of many down an unknown list and one of them had latched onto this vile creature because of it." The thought made me growl and clench my fists hard enough the skin once more split before giving it chance to fully heal as they were still trying to do.

"I understand that the thought isn't a comforting one, but I still think it's something we need to look into. After all, the dead are harder to interrogate." I gave him a wry look knowing exactly what he meant by this. For he had said the same to me over the last few days whenever I wanted to give into my dark impulse and interrogate Lahash myself. Because he knew I would only end up going too far and in doing so losing a prisoner that could end up being more useful alive...at least for the time being.

After all, my brother may have been the one to interrogate her, but even he couldn't be certain that she gave him everything. It turned out that she did indeed work for Lucius and was in fact very much in love with him. And to a sickening degree according to Vincent's account of the bloody time he had spent with her.

He even suspected this was the reason she stabbed Keira and not because she was ordered to by Lucius at all. Because both my brother and I agreed, that to order such wouldn't have made any sense.

Lucius wanted only one thing from me and from his reasoning, there would only ever be one way for him to get it. He needed something to bargain with, or should I say more like...

Someone.

He knew of the prophecy as well as I did and was no doubt counting the years as I was until she was finally found. Then, once our fated meeting had happened and my love for her had chance to grow into what it was now, all he would need to do was make his move.

Oh, I had no doubt of this, which was in truth the reason for keeping my distance in the first place. I was trying to discover a way to both have her by my side and keep her safe. And short of locking her in a tower where only I held the key, then I was yet to form a plan on how to accomplish such a monumental feat.

Hence my forever mounting rage and frustrating predicament, something Vincent thankfully understood far more than Sophia did. Someone who thought I should have just killed the Vampire King years ago.

Of course, I took this as idle threats said in anger, for she knew as well as I did that in doing so would mean only one thing. Condemning a whole race of my own kind to death right along with him. In truth, it was one of the greatest lines of defense he held and unfortunately exploited to its fullest!

It was well known that Lucius spent much of his later years collecting powerful Demons and Angels. Along with other races of supernatural beings he deemed useful. He would offer them an enormous increase in power but the price for this was an eternity belonging to him. Swearing him their alliance and tying themselves with his very soul.

Meaning that if he were ever to die then so would their Master's power of life. And seeing that there was only one Vampire alive with the power to change another into his race, then in conclusion, it made him their King. And with it, my only true equal in power for his kingdom was almost as large as mine.

However, there had been a time when Lucius' ambitions had been no more than my own. To see the Kings all band together to form one council and therefore be ready for the prophesied end of days. To have the most powerful beings of each of our races sat at the same table, conquering our problems and ruling our kind as one. Needless to say, this hadn't progressed much farther than a few meetings that hadn't ended in blood shed, something Lucius used to consider a plus.

If I were honest, I often missed having him as my right hand, as his skills alone as an assassin were greatly missed. But that had been a long time ago and even though at the time a second world war was being fought for human kind, for my own, it very nearly started the first.

Given all this to consider, I had to then agree with my brother, as Morgan's death could not be met by my hands until we were sure of all the other factors. It was time to think rationally before acting on impulse, for I couldn't afford to make any more mistakes...not when Keira was involved.

"Very well, find me everything you can on his imprisonment. There should be recorded sessions by his doctors along with notes. Get Ranka to gather everything she can in regards to his medical care, now that we have finally discovered where he is being kept." Something that was also added to the case file, one sent to me by the secondary inspector assigned to Keira's case. A man who had been tasked with sorting through the shit storm of mistakes made from the very beginning.

Inspector Matthews had made it quite known of his personal distaste at trying to sweep his departments 'fuck up' under the carpet but his job had been clear after Keira was found. Go to the scene of the crime and join enough of the dots together to build a case against Morgan and then lose the file.

Of course, I also suspected that somewhere between being told this and his disgust *at being told this*, he let it be leaked to Keira's family. Who then used it against the police officials in charge to get what they wanted in return. Hence the unusual circumstances of Keira's new identity, for this was said to be all she wanted.

The officials at the top of the ladder had been only too happy to help in this as they had no doubt been expecting a large sum of money to be demanded as compensation. So, a visa, a few official documents and a name change ended up being little effort on their part. However, Inspector Matthews apparently being the only official that gave a shit at this time took it upon himself to see to the details personally, giving him her number in case she was ever in trouble.

In fact, Ranka ended up explaining to him who I was, and that Keira was soon to be my wife. And because of this that I wanted to know all the details personally with her safety in mind, should Morgan ever be able to convince the courts he was now sane enough to be released. Something Inspector Matthews was assured I would never allow.

After that he had provided me with everything I needed, being only too happy to help the one man he deemed more than capable at keeping her safe, considering my endless amount of resources. Something he discovered when researching my name and finding that I, in fact, owned my own law firm.

Magically the case file showed up as if the place it had been lost had simply been sitting in Inspector Matthews' desk waiting for someone powerful enough like me to come around in requesting it. Needless to say, I liked this account of Inspector Matthews' personality a great deal, enough that I would shortly be insisting to his superiors that he receive a raise.

"Already done, along with asking her to retrieve any of the hospital's surveillance footage the night Keira was found on their steps and when they apprehended Morgan on his return." I frowned, now turning my body to look at Vincent before asking,

"You believe there is something we missed?"

"Call it a hunch," he replied with a shrug of his shoulders as if it was most likely nothing. However, I knew from experience that when Vincent had a hunch, it was usually for good reason. Which was why I didn't question his decision to do so any further.

"So, does our sister still want to tear you a new asshole and have it stuffed with holy water and crucifixes?" Vincent asked making me huff a laugh.

"I can't find myself to blame her if she did, for I'm close to kicking my own ass for going through with hurting the girl," I admitted making Vincent nod to the many patches of blood on the floor before commenting,

"Well, it may be your only option for it seems none of our men were up to the task."

"No, and nor will they be up for trying again any time soon."

"Was it really that bad?" Vincent asked making me release a sigh as I put my elbows to my knees and grabbed my head in my hands, proving that answer with my body language alone.

"Only as bad as wanting to tear my own fucking eyes out so that I could no longer witness the agony of her tears," I replied making him wince.

"I see... or in your case, hoped not to." I lifted my head enough to give him a wry look before resuming my previous position.

"If I am honest then the worst part of all of this was that I had not realised until breaking her heart just how fully it belonged to me...before I lost it completely that was," I said running both hands through my hair and holding it at the base of my skull as I stared into space ahead of me, once again only seeing the memory of her devastation shadowed on the mats.

"I am afraid that all the brotherly advice I have to give isn't based on experience, for as you know I have none when it comes to foreign sentiments of love. But I do know this..." he paused before standing up and placing a hand at my shoulder so that he could conclude a comforting end to his visit.

"That losing something is never really lost when the other person is the only one who believes his words." I had been secretly clinging on to the same hope that one day, I could somehow make it safe for us to be together. But after witnessing for myself the exact moment my words had stolen the light of her soul from behind her eyes, I knew that my chances at one day righting my wrongs were slim at best.

In fact, it made me want to curse the Gods and Fates and their timing for gifting me my Chosen One. Why not back to a time when keeping her safe would have been so much simpler? Back to when I was King and could have simply took her from her world and claimed as my own in that instant. A time when keeping her safe literally meant locking her away behind my fortress and keeping her there, knowing that she would obey her King as her upbringing would have accustomed her to do so without question.

But unfortunately for my current circumstances society wasn't that way anymore and stealing her away from her independent world was something she would no doubt have found a problem with. Which was precisely why I still had in my possession a key to a certain place. One that was finished weeks ago and had remained locked and sat without its new intended resident occupying it.

But that was one secret I would be keeping as my own, for no one needed to know the true depths of my obsession or how far I was willing to go in keeping her both safe and freely mine.

I spoke of course about her intended new home.
A prisoner in my...

Scottish tower.

69

GRASPING REALITY

After that day, I did get slightly better as I pulled myself together and carried on. The pain never fully went away. Instead, it was replaced with a dull ache, as my mind was usually numb. But I went on with my life as you have to. Sophia never returned to History. I didn't even know whether she dropped out or was ill, but it seemed too much of a coincidence that she disappeared from college life.

No-one was allowed to talk about it and the only one who had been nice to me from the beginning was Jerry. But even this, I think, was staged. I completed my shifts like a machine being controlled by the need more than the want part of me. But the more and more I worked, the less painful it got being there. Then even the others started talking to me again and Mike and I were once again friends. We even flirted with each other on occasion. I finally started to relax.

Nothing happened again, there were no more nice dreams that included him. However, my dreams didn't just stop. No, instead they had taken on a darker turn. I decided that after the fourth time of waking up in the house screaming, I would finally give in and see a counsellor.

I had made my appointment with a Doctor Goff and I was now sat in a waiting room with peach walls and crappy pictures of summer flowers in pots and a little girl playing happily with her dog. If this was supposed to have a calming effect, then it most certainly didn't work. After my nightmares, I had seemed to have taken a gloomier approach to life and I tried desperately to control it. I found nothing fun or good in anything anymore and it was starting to scare me.

The only peace I would find was whenever I went back to the cliff face. I would sit there for hours looking out to the view, thinking about where it all went wrong. I knew this wasn't the best way to think and that everything happened for a reason but when your heart is torn, and your body broken, it is very easy to hate that logic.

The woman behind the desk looked over her thick-rimmed glasses and spoke out my name in a squeaky voice.

"You may go in now."

I walked into a room that had been furnished to try and give a homely feel. As though trying not to intimidate you or make you feel even more uncomfortable about the reasons that had obviously brought you here in the first place. The room had a big couch and a smaller armchair next to it. There was shelving around the room with different 'Self Help' books and a few family photos.

Doctor Goff was a middle-aged man with a full beard that had a mixture of ginger and grey bits in it. He wore small glasses and looked like every other shrink I had ever seen. It was as if when they started to develop into adults, people would turn to them saying 'You know you kind of look like a therapist or a doctor,' and they would reply 'Okay, then that's what I will do'.

He motioned for me to sit, as he himself was sat behind his desk, which held a laptop and piles of paperwork. He didn't look very organised for a professional person.

"Miss Johnson, I am pleased to meet you, sorry for your longer wait but I have found it difficult finding any of your medical history. Where did you say you were from?" He said as he stroked his bushy beard.

"This is the deal, Doc. I don't want anyone to know my background as I left it behind me where I want it to stay. I don't want to bring all my old problems into this because that's not why I am here." I said getting all that I had rehearsed out of the way before I forgot. Shrinks had a crafty way of getting information out of you and I knew if I didn't set the ground rules straight away, then I could slip up.

"Then why are you here?" He asked in a non-aggressive tone.

"I'm here because I can't sleep and when I do sleep I wake up screaming for help from my nightmares." I said not taking a breath.

"Help from whom?"

"Sorry?" I said wondering why he asked me that.

"You said you cry for help, I was just wondering who from?" Again, this question I didn't really understand, and I wasn't about to tell him who exactly I was crying out for. So, I lied and said,

"My sister, or anyone really." He raised an eyebrow as if he didn't believe me but carried on without questioning it.

"Why don't you start by telling me about the dream?"

"Okay well...I'm at a club and I'm about to start my shift as I work there you see..." I was stalling, and I didn't know why but his eyes had turned very dark and intense making me not want to speak any further.

"Go on...what happens at this club?" He urged.

"Well, I go into the back room where I always put my bag and jacket. There's this gilded mirror and I always give myself a once over before starting my shift." I said stopping, but his face got more intense and his hand lifted motioning for me to continue. So, I took a deep breath and explained the rest.

"I'm looking at my face in the mirror and I see someone else instead staring back."

"Who?" He asked, and I repeated the same question back at him.

"Who?

"Yes, who is staring back at you?" He asked, and I didn't want to say.

"Just some guy, but anyway..." He stopped me again.

"Just some guy? Someone you know? Someone you work with or for?" He asked, and I froze as he hit the nail on the head with the last one.

"My boss...so anyway...I turn around quickly to find the room is empty and the door is still closed. So, I turn back to face the mirror and it's me again. Only something is different and very wrong as I don't look the same. I have my hair down which I never do, and I'm wearing different clothes."

"Do you recognise your other self from a different time?" He said looking over his glasses as if to judge my reaction to the question. I wondered if he knew I was lying when I replied,

"No."

"Alright, then please continue." He said as he wrote down some more notes in a red leather bound book.

"So, the girl...well I mean me...she is staring back at me with hate in her eyes and I'm always so scared to look at her. I move my face away but then I hear a tapping on the glass, so I look back to find a broken piece of the mirror in her hand." I almost shuddered thinking back to how haunting the image always was to find.

"I see and it's from the mirror you're looking into?" He asked, and I nodded.

"It's a long piece that's thicker where she holds it and it goes down into a deadly point that she is using to get my attention. I freeze to the spot and scream 'What do you want?' She then mouths the word 'DIE' to me and her arm comes out of the mirror and slashes at my arms over and over, cutting my wrists so that when I look down I am covered in blood again and screaming. That's when I wake up." And there it was. Of course, I knew what the dream was about and didn't need any Doctor telling me his theory of interpretation. All I needed were the pills.

"Ah." He said looking at my arms, finding nothing but my sweater's sleeves.

"Any suicide attempts before?" He asked bluntly, and I coughed, as I couldn't believe what he had just asked. Weren't doctors supposed to be delicate about this type of thing?

"No!" I shouted as I was now clearly upset.

"I'm sorry, did that bother you?"

"No, but it took me by surprise."

"Sorry, but I have to be sure and considering I don't have any records on your medical background, I'm in the dark here. So, you said about seeing the blood on your arms *again,* what do you think that was referring to?" Ah, so that's why he had asked. I had slipped up when telling my story, damn it.

"I don't know why, I must have just made a mistake that's all."

"Of course. So, you said you can't sleep. Has anything traumatic or emotional happened recently?" His eyes looked deep into me as if trying to hook out the lies that he knew were coming from me.

"No, I have a lot on at college and I work nights so maybe I'm just wired from it all, but I need to get some sleep." I said rubbing my tired eyes, hoping this was enough to convince him.

"Okay, so you said you work nights, is this at the club in your dreams?"

"Yes, but that really doesn't have anything to do with it." I said getting defensive and he knew it, so he decided to keep pushing for it.

"You also mentioned your boss in the dream. Do you have feelings for him?" Oh, come on! Now he wanted to know about my non-existent sex life.

"He's my boss." I said trying to state the obvious.

"Yes, but things can still happen between an employer and an employee."

"Yes, I know, but nothing happened." I was so close to caving that I could feel the tears coming back for the first time in weeks.

"Umm...I'm not so sure. You say that nothing has happened but whenever I mention the idea, you look upset...I'm here to listen Keira, so please give me that chance." And that was it, the way he said my name reminded me of Draven so much that I could have sworn I was talking to the man himself. A tear rolled down my cheek and I said the words I didn't want to admit.

"Fine, you want the truth then here it is... I fell for my boss and I stupidly mistook that he had some feelings for me too, but I was cruelly exposed to reality and as a result, I am trying my hardest to get over it." I said, and I wiped the tears from my face with the tissue he had handed to me.

"Right well...in that case I will prescribe you with some Benzodiazepines which will help you relax, but this is for a short time only. I don't want you becoming dependant on these and I want you to come and see me once a week for four more sessions, then we will take it from there." He said looking strangely sad from my little outburst.

I got up happy that my time was over. He handed me the prescription and shook my hand giving me a weird feeling when I came into contact with his skin. It was like a familiar memory that I couldn't quite remember.

After meeting with the doctor, I knew that I wouldn't be returning for a second visit. He was very good at analysing my dreams and I knew it wouldn't be long before he got me telling him my sad and gruelling past. Most doctors had a way of digging for the truth as they believed that to face our problems head on was the only way to deal with them. I had already faced 'my problem' head on before and I was not about to do it ever again.

Libby had told Frank the good news about her being pregnant after a scan confirmed what she already knew. Frank had gone crazy with happiness, telling everybody he knew and even some he didn't. As soon as the phone went even sales people would hear all about it. So, unless they were selling baby cribs and strollers, as they call them here, then most of the time they would be the ones to end the call. I had been there when Libby had told our mother and she had cried so much she'd had to put my dad on the phone.

These were the reasons that I hadn't told Libby or Frank about what had happened at the club, or about me seeing any doctor. They just carried on believing that I was still working in the VIP area and they had not seen any change in me. And I wanted to keep it that way. This wasn't too difficult as sometimes people become so absorbed in their own happiness, that they fail to see the truth behind a lie. It wasn't that I thought they wouldn't understand but I had felt so guilty from the last time I was broken, that I never wanted anyone to look at me like that again.

I lied to those who I couldn't hide it from, like RJ and Jack, because they were going to see me working downstairs in the club. I told them that they didn't need me anymore, as the girl who I replaced was now back. This of course wasn't a complete lie as they didn't need me anymore...well painfully more like *he* didn't need me anymore.

Jack had been great, a true friend, whereas RJ didn't let it drop for a while, as every time I saw her she would bring it up. Jack thankfully intervened one night when we were at the club and my shift had finished.

"RJ give it a rest. Can't you see she's sick of talking about it?" He said fighting my corner.

"Well, I just don't get it!"

"No surprise there!" Jack said being sarcastic. RJ hooked out an ice cube from her glass and threw it in his direction only it missed him and hit some poor girl that was innocently walking past. The girl turned to see who had been the culprit and RJ pointed to Jack keeping a straight face.

As soon as the girl saw Jack's handsome, Brad Pitt look she smiled as if throwing an ice cube at her was a good thing. I couldn't help but laugh. I mean, okay it was cute when you were about ten. A boy that fancied you would then throw stuff to get your attention, but in your twenties, it was a bit pathetic.

"Hey bro, I think you're in there, why don't you ask her to the Halloween Gig?" She said not even lowering her voice. The Halloween Gig was held here at the club, when lots of bands were going to compete. It was a huge night that happened each year and the Goth scene loved it.

"Yeah thanks, but I will pass, Butt Munch!" He said playfully. They were just so different you forgot that they were even related. I left early that night but Jack walked me to my car. I was so relaxed around him that it didn't seem out of character when he would flirt.

Consequently, when he put his arm around me as we walked out of the club, I didn't give it much thought to why people were staring. I guess we looked like a couple but because I had made it clear on my 'no dating' rule, Jack hadn't asked me out again. I just gathered he had got the message. So, when he stopped me from getting in my car I was confused.

"Keira, I've been meaning to ask you something but well I guess that you were going through a tough time regarding why you left the VIP...not that I want to pry." He said as I realised he knew the reason I had given had been a lie. Was Jack the only one that really knew me?

"It's none of my business and I get why you wouldn't want to talk about it...trust me, I know how it feels... more than you think." He said this with sadness in his eyes and I knew that his feelings ran deeper than I realised. He was talking about what happened at the club.

"Jack, you know if you ever want to talk then I'm here, okay. I too don't want to pry either but if you ever need anyone, then I'm a better listener than a talker." We both laughed lightly trying to change the glum mood.

"I know. You're a good friend but I..." He wanted to continue but he couldn't find the words which I now understood he wanted to say. So, I did something so out of character, that I shocked myself when the question came out.

"Jack, will you go to the Halloween Gig with me?" His face dropped in amazement, as if this was the last thing he had been expecting.

"You want to go with me?" He said checking he had heard it right.

"Yeah but hey, I understand if you are going with someone else." I said now, worrying that I had it all wrong.

"Hell no, I was going to ask you all along, but I've been waiting for the right time." He said with the biggest smile across his face.

"But hey, won't you be working?"

"No, I have been given the night off so I'm free as a bird." And this was true, for some strange reason creepy Gary had told me that I wasn't needed, even though it was going to be one of the busiest nights of the year! I didn't understand it, but I wasn't going to argue, although I did double check it with his brother Jerry, just in case.

"So, you will be my bird for the night?" He teased going back to his usual flirty ways. I smirked at him.

"Yeah Jack, I will be your free bird for the night." I teased back granting myself a gorgeous smile from one handsome Jack.

I left the car park after arranging times for Saturday night's date with mixed feelings. Was that the best idea, going on a date with Jack? I mean, of course I liked him, who in their right mind wouldn't? But I couldn't help the fear that I was betraying my own feelings. I clearly was not over Draven, but thinking about it, would I ever be?

Of course, that didn't mean I had to live my life as a nun! I had to move on even though I was now sleeping again and wasn't living my life as a zombie.

By the time I got home I decided that what I had done was for the best. I needed to live my life, not shy away from it. I would now embrace every opportunity and tomorrow night would be my first show off this and one thing was for sure, I was going to dress for the occasion! I was going to knock Jack's socks off...well at least try.

When I got in I was glad when I saw Libby was still awake because there was something important I needed her help with and this was one request that I knew she would most definitely enjoy.

"Hey Libs I've got a huge favour to ask." She raised her head round from leaning it against Frank as they were watching some action movie. I think she had even fallen asleep.

"Yeah what's up?"

"Well, don't go all weird or anything but I kind of have a date tomorrow night and well, I need help with a costume." As soon as I said the magic word "date" she was now wide awake and even Frank was looking at me and leaving Van Damme to his kick boxing.

"Oh, yeah definitely, of course I will but I have to ask...who with?" She said as she was out of her seat coming to face me.

"It's Jack."

"But I thought you've been turning him down ever since you got here?"

"Well yeah, but I sort of asked him." She and Frank shot each other a look as if they thought I had been taken over by pod people.

"Okay...umm... so one other thing, what are you going as?" She said trying to keep the grin to a minimum.

"It's kind of just the usual Gothic theme." I said as she followed me into the kitchen. But as soon as I had said the words, she had clapped her hands scaring me into looking back at her.

"Is that a good thing?" I asked, and I could almost see the cogs turning in her head.

"Oh yeah, I have just the outfit, but I think I will need to change a few things." She said but I wasn't even sure if she was talking to me or herself.

"Why, what are you thinking?" I asked hoping I wouldn't regret it this time tomorrow night.

"Well...I have this old costume from when Frank and I went to this fancy dress party last year, it was a medieval theme and I have this black and purple dress with a corset top." Forget about tomorrow night, I was regretting it now!

"Oh no, no corsets!"

"Oh, come on, you will look great, plus if you dress the way you always do that's not the point of Halloween."

"And what is exactly?" I asked with my arms folded.

"It's the one night that you can get away with being someone else. It wouldn't be you dressing up... it will be the Halloween you."

"That makes absolutely no sense, you know that...right?" She shook her head at me.

"Look, what do you think other people will be wearing? You hate standing out, right? And I can guarantee that if you don't dress up as a sexy Goth then you will be the only one who doesn't...hence *Kazzy standing out."* What she said in a crazy way made sense. So, I gave in and agreed. She had free rein to do whatever she wanted. Which I found out also included makeup and hair. I knew I was making a categorical mistake, but she was just so happy with the idea of playing 'dress up' that I couldn't crush her enthusiasm. So, with that I kissed her goodnight and went to bed.

The next day all hands were on deck as far as Libby was concerned. She started with bringing me tea in the morning, waking me up a lot earlier than I would have liked. She marched me into the bathroom and ordered me to shower. When I started to complain that I was hungry she passed me the soap and said,

"Here eat this," and closed the door leaving me to shower. Once I was inside the cubicle I heard a tapping at the door and had to turn off the water to hear who it was.

"What?" I said shouting through the glass and bathroom door.

"Use the stuff I put in there for you." Libby shouted back through the wooden door as I shivered now the hot water had stopped warming my skin.

"Okay!" I shouted back and continued to shower with the new products that smelled like passion fruit and felt like cream covering my body. It had little seeds in it that exfoliated my skin making it feel soft when I got out and dried myself.

Libby dried my hair while I sat there and ate breakfast and Frank came in grabbing a can from the fridge.

"Having fun ladies?" I tried to turn to say something sarcastic but Libby pulled my head back round with my hair and I complained.

"Oww ...! God Libs, don't go into the beauty business, will you?"

"And why not?" She asked hands on hips, brush still in hand.

"Because I don't want you to get sued!"

"Shut up!" She said in a playful manner that made me smile. Once she'd finished drying my hair she put it in huge curlers until I looked as if I could pick up a radio station.

"What are these for...? I'm not wearing my hair down."

"I know, but when I put it up I want the ends curly, anyway don't you trust me?"

My answer in my head wasn't the one I gave.

"Of course, I do but..."

"No 'buts', leave a master to work please." She said waving the comb round as if it was her magic wand.

After my hair was done I was allowed to leave the torture chamber, which was better known as the kitchen and do what I wanted while she worked on my Gothic attire. She had already taken my measurements, which weren't far out from her own and lucky for me she had the same shoe size so I could borrow some of hers.

To be honest, I didn't have the most productive day, as it was hard to do anything with what felt like a transmitter on my head. The day went by surprisingly quickly and after having my nails done and my eyebrows shaped, I was ready for my make-up. I felt like a big kid's doll as Libby was clearly loving every minute of it. She spent what seemed like ages doing my make-up and my face started to ache from holding it so still.

"What time is Jacky boy picking you up?" She asked as she was applying powder to my pale cheeks.

"We said about eightish... why?" I said in a worried tone.

"No reason, just wanted to know how much time I had."

"Libs it's only six."

"Yeah, but I still have to do your hair and then we have to get you into your dress." I still hadn't seen the dress as she wanted it to be a surprise, but I knew her true motive behind it was, so it would be too late for me to back out of wearing it. She also wouldn't let me look in the mirror once my makeup and hair were done. She hadn't left out a thing, from curling my eyelashes to matching the hair clip with the colour of the dress.

When everything was done I only just had enough time to get into my dress as Jack was now sat downstairs with Frank and from the sounds of it, they were both watching a game. Libby had timed it to a tee, as when I finally had been strapped into my dress, I only had enough time for a quick look in the mirror.

I was speechless. I was completely blown away and Libby looked at me with tears in her eyes and her hands covering her mouth waiting for me to speak. I could barely believe it was still me.

I looked...well...sexy!

I was wearing a tight fitted corset that looked as though it had been moulded to my skin as the black and purple velvet material snaked around my frame, making it curve in all the right places. It was tied with a thick purple ribbon that went all the way down my back touching the cheeks of my behind and to the top part on the skirt. The skirt carried on the design twisting to the front of my leg where a big slit ran up exposing my thigh.

The rest of the skirt ripped down in layers, some bits nearly reaching the floor and others in a net material that gave the skirt body. It moved gracefully around with me when I turned in the mirror. One leg was completely on show while the other was hidden under the multiple layers of black.

But this wasn't the part I was most worried about. No, because the stiff boned corset was creating an eyeful of bust that I usually concealed. I had also been conned into wearing knee high black leather boots with a tall heel, but it wasn't as hard to walk in them as I would have thought.

I had already put the gloves on before Libby helped me into my dress. They were purple velvet to match and they went up all the way past the elbow, which I was more than happy about.

After dragging my eyes away from my dress, I looked at my face seeing someone different staring back at me. I was still pale, but my skin looked like it was made from porcelain with a hint of a blush at my cheeks. At this point, I didn't know whether that was from the make-up or my reaction to seeing myself like this.

My eyes were dark and smoky with a long black line across the eyelid that followed down and flicked out at the end. They were black underneath also giving them a dark and mysterious look. They were framed with long curly lashes that tickled the tops of my eyelids.

I licked my lips, but the dark red colour remained, making them look full and like a cupid's bow. I turned my head looking at my hair and seeing the shine of a soft gold as lighter streaks were caught in the light making them look like silk. It was swept back into a high twist, which overflowed with curls hanging down to my neck. The shorter bits hung down curling around the shape of my face.

"I don't know what to say..." I said very quietly but she just held the biggest grin.

"You don't need to say anything... and well, you don't have time anyway." She was right, as now it was time for the hard part, now I had to face people. But even though I promised myself I wouldn't do it, the one thought slipped in and stuck around the edges of my mind...

Would Draven see me?

DRAVEN

70

An Appointment to Keep

@he moment I heard that Keira had made an appointment to see a local therapist I knew it was time to cross another line. Because even though it was obvious that I should have continued to stay away, I simply told myself my reasons now were done solely so that I could discover how she was coping after the weeks since our last meeting. And only half of my reasons were bullshit for the truth was clear...

I was struggling.

Admitting such a weakness was never something that would have come easy for me and the excuses I made now were evidence to that. But despite this there were also legitimate reasons for seeing her now, as I was also curious as to why now she had chosen to make such an appointment?

Especially when I knew of her distaste for doctors and what they may discover about her past.

Because the reality of Keira's past wasn't just what she had been through. But it was also the unusual way she had chosen to cope with it all. As, from what I could gather, not once had she spoken about what happened during her captivity and I did not just mean to the police.

I found out through her medical records that the only reason she had received sleeping pills the first time was due to the family getting involved and speaking to the doctors on her behalf about the nightmares. They had also showed their concerns for she wasn't speaking to anyone about what happened and had seemingly shut down.

So, the doctors explained for them to give her time and once she was comfortable speaking of her captivity, then for them to arrange for her to speak to someone in the profession.

But it never happened this way.

Because after this, as I already knew how she had chosen to deal with doctors and getting her way with them. She seemed to have developed this no-nonsense attitude that both concerned and impressed me. And I suppose that I was now curious to see how she would play this next meeting with yet another therapist. Asking myself would she do the same as she always did? Would she say very little of her past?

I knew she must have been having trouble sleeping because I had been the one to rid her of her pills in the first place. Something I regretted now, especially knowing how she suffered from her nightmares. A guilt, I was ashamed to say, that had now doubled for I hadn't been there for her to protect those dreams lately as I had promised.

But the simple and cruel reasons why, was that it was simply too risky. Her mind was just too unpredictable and with the strength of her walls she had built around her thoughts, then if she woke, I would be defenseless in making her believe my being there wasn't real.

Which was precisely why I had convinced myself that taking hold of one Doctor Goff right now was justified. I also convinced myself that I was doing it solely for her benefit, for no matter what she said to me in this office, I would be writing a prescription for the sleeping pills. Seeing as it was the very least I could do.

Of course, from a purely selfish point, it was also the first direct contact I would have with her in a few weeks. As at this current time my stalking had been forced down to merely watching her through the eyes of others throughout the day. Followed by simply watching her for the entirety of her shift as myself and then after this I would watch her leave in her truck stood on the VIP's balcony before taking flight so that I could follow her home. Then, whilst veiling myself, I would stand outside her house watching how she spent her evenings.

The line I drew however was when she went to bed as this would be my cue to leave. I knew I could have continued to veil myself whilst I spent the night at her bedside. But in truth, the temptation in these times to reach out and gently brush back the hair from her face or stroke the backs of my fingers down her cheek would have been too much to bear.

Besides, I knew that if I had been there during one of her nightmares, then I wouldn't have been able to intervene like I wanted. Not without her discovering my being there. And holding myself back whilst that happened was not an option either. So, I did the wisest thing and took all temptation out of the equation, torturing myself no matter what decision I made.

But I had to confess, these decisions were getting harder by the day to abide by. I wanted her like a fever infected my blood making my body inch to move in her direction. I would suddenly find whichever vessel I had taken control of at the time reaching out to her without being able to stop it. I would then have to make an excuse on the few occasions I had been powerless to stop the brief connection made.

And in that fleeting moment in time my soul would find itself at ease just by brushing against her. It was as if just the feel of her hair against my skin was enough to calm the growing rage my demon was roaring at me on a daily basis.

In truth, I didn't know how long I could keep this distance for, as I could feel my reserve growing weaker by the day, not stronger as my arrogance had convinced me would happen. Which added a great deal to the reason I was now staring at myself in the reflection of a window as a different vessel. Why I was a middle-aged man with small glasses resting low on my nose and was sporting a full beard, something I hadn't seen on my own face in quite some time.

The moment I heard the receptionist say that my next appointment could go in I found myself clenching my fists and taking a deep breath before turning around to face her.

And all from just the sight of her.

By the Gods, was it really possible that this reaction was natural? Because it felt like some kind of spell had been cast upon my heart and an unbreakable curse whispered in my ear tying every fiber of my being to this unsuspecting creature of beauty. The power she held with just the beating of her own heart could have held me prisoner for eternity.

In fact, it did, for I was daily tortured just to ensure that the same mortal heart continued to beat, even if it was to do so for a single lifetime without me. So yes, I was her prisoner alright, one she had no idea she held imprisoned within the fragile confines of her breakable body and fragile soul.

But then if I were to make her immortal, what then? I had asked myself this many a time and it had started to feature as the main argument against my own mind. How long would it take? How many cycles of the moon would have to pass when making her body mine before I would start to see her body begin to regenerate? When her cells would heal themselves thanks to my essence taking hold of her mortal vessel, morphing it into one of my own kind?

And shamefully the biggest question I asked myself was...

Would she really have to know?

She walked inside the office and scanned the room just as anyone would before her skeptical gaze landed on me. Oh yes, her guards were up alright, to the point it was so obvious, I had to cough to hide the laugh I could feel on the cusp of presenting itself.

Instead I motioned for her to sit down opposite me as I remained behind the desk, not trusting myself to commence in the mortal tradition by shaking her hand. I didn't know what I would do if that type of contact was made, for right now with my conflicting thoughts I wasn't sure I could honestly say I would have been able to let her go.

So instead I began my rehearsed deception.

"Miss Johnson, I am pleased to meet you, sorry for your longer wait but I have found it difficult finding any of your medical history. Where did you say you were from?" I asked curious to know what her reply would be...*she didn't disappoint.*

"This is the deal, Doc. I don't want anyone to know my background as I left it behind me where I want it to stay. I don't want to bring all my old problems into this because that's not why I am here," she said ending what I knew was her own rehearsed speech and again I had to resist the urge to grin.

"Then why are you here?" I asked calmly finding myself slipping back to my old habit and stroking my vessel's beard as I used to do when having one myself for more years than I could count.

"I'm here because I can't sleep and when I do sleep I wake up screaming for help from my nightmares," she replied and suddenly I no longer had to fight myself the grin, but instead now the grimace. I even found my free hand gripping onto the chair's arm I sat in, knowing I was close to snapping the damn thing. It quickly became apparent that this was going to be harder than I first thought.

"Help from whom?" I found myself asking, knowing that the first question in reply would look an odd one. It was confirmed when she wrinkled her nose a little in confusion. Gods, but I had missed that cute and adorable look of puzzlement on her face.

"Sorry?" she said obviously wondering where I was headed with my question, so I told her,

"You said you cry for help... I was just wondering for who?" She frowned this time before shaking her a head a little in a nonchalant way before lying. Once again laying witness to her atrocious display at dishonesty in action was nearly laughable.

"My sister, or anyone really." I couldn't help but give into my natural impulse and raise a disbelieving brow at her before moving on and letting her get away with it for now. Even though I will admit, I had hoped my name would have been mentioned in that reply.

"Why don't you start by telling me about the dream?"

"Okay, well...I'm at a club and I'm about to start my shift as I work there you see..." she said stalling for time and I wondered if she would have done the same with me in person? Most likely, seeing that she was primarily intimidated by me. But one day soon I was hopeful this would not be the case.

"Go on...what happens at this club?" I urged.

"Well, I go into the back room where I always put my bag and jacket. There's this gilded mirror and I always give myself a once over before starting my shift." The moment she started speaking of the VIP I found my body turning ridged. Unable to speak I found myself only able to silently motion for her to continue.

"I'm looking at my face in the mirror and I see someone else instead staring back."

"Who?" I asked trying not to sound as tense as I felt.

"Who?" She repeated back as another stalling tactic; one I wouldn't let her get away with.

"Yes, who is staring back at you?" I asked again, telling her in my tone that it was one she wouldn't be able to skirt over...*or so I thought,*

"Just some guy, but anyway..." Oh Hell's fire, not a chance sweetheart! For I was not ever going to let her view me as just 'Some guy' and I was most certain that the person in her dream had been me. For I could only think of two people she would be reluctant to talk about and I doubted she would have even started explaining the dream had that sick bastard featured in it.

Now of course, if she astonished me now and spoke his name, I didn't know how I would have acted, but thankfully, this didn't happen. Not when I pushed the right buttons in questioning her further,

"Just some guy? Someone you know? Someone you work with *or for?"* The moment I added this last option her wide eyes told me all I needed to know, even if her blasé answer contradicted her reaction.

"My boss...so anyway...I turn around quickly to find the room is empty and the door is still closed. So, I turn back to face the mirror and it's me again. Only something is different and very wrong as I don't look the same. I have my hair down which I never do, and I'm wearing different clothes," she said now reeling off her dream and doing so no doubt so that she could quickly move on from admitting that she had been dreaming of me. Now did that mean that she was ashamed to admit it to a stranger or herself, I wondered?

As much as I wanted to know, I had no grounds for asking this, so moved on to a question more relevant.

"Do you recognise your other self from a different time?" Once again, her reaction was written plainly on her face for I don't think she realised how expressive she was. Which made her lie stand out even more.

"No."

"Alright, then please continue." I let her have her lie and decided to make this session seem real by writing down in the notebook, one she couldn't read from where she was sitting. But then she continued with her dream and I had to say, it was little wonder at her being so terrified from it.

"So, the girl...well I mean me...she is staring back at me with hate in her eyes and I'm always so scared to look at her. I move my face away but then I hear a tapping on the glass, so I look back to find a broken piece of the mirror in her hand." Knowing what happened to her and how she came across her self-inflicted injuries, well then this didn't take a bachelor's degree in psychiatry to understand its meaning.

"I see and it's from the mirror you're looking into?" I asked to prompt her forward. She nodded before explaining,

"It's a long piece that's thicker where she holds it and it goes down into a deadly point that she is using to get my attention. I freeze to the spot and scream 'What do you want?' She then mouths the word 'DIE' at me, and her arm comes out of the mirror and slashes at my arms over and over, cutting my wrists so that when I look down, I am covered in blood again and screaming. That's when I wake up," she said finishing her gruesome tale and giving me cause to once again clench my hand around what felt like far too flimsy piece of wood on the chair. Because all I wanted to do was vault over the only obstacle between us and take her in my arms to comfort her. To beg her forgiveness for not being there for her during this traumatic time and promise her that she would never have to endure something like this alone ever again.

However, my actual response was a simple,

"Ah." Then I couldn't help but look down at her sweater, one I knew covered the evidence of reason behind the nightmares her mind inflicted upon itself.

"Any suicide attempts before?" I asked bluntly, knowing just by asking that it would shock her.

"No!" she shouted after first needing to cough back her surprise and now looking visible shaken by the question.

"I'm sorry, did that bother you?" I asked hoping in some way that she would open up to me, even if it wasn't the vessel I would have chosen for her to do so.

"No, but it took me by surprise," she admitted, her tone reaching a higher pitch and telling me by it that this was an understatement.

"Sorry, but I have to be sure and considering I don't have any records of your medical background, I'm in the dark here. So, you said about seeing the blood on your arms *again,* what do you think that was referring to?" I asked homing in on that little mistake she obviously hadn't realised making and giving me cause as a doctor to ask her about the possible idea of a suicide attempt.

"I don't know, I must have just made a mistake that's all," she said in a small voice, one that made my chest ache for her.

"Of course. So, you said you can't sleep. Has anything traumatic or emotional happened recently?" I asked hoping at the very least she would open up about what had occurred between us weeks ago. I don't know why I couldn't drop it, but I had to be assured that she was alright, or at least discover if she had in fact moved on from it. And like many times before, I wished for this outcome just as much as I did not. As I had no real desire to see that my Chosen One had in fact lost all feeling for me.

"No, I have a lot on at college and I work at night so maybe I'm just wired from it all, but I need to get some sleep," she said laying it on thick by rubbing her eyes, which I had to admit, now had shadows beneath them that did prove her lack of sleep. I knew what would help and be the best cure for this, as exhausting her body was one sure way of ensuring a good night's sleep...something I was more than willing to explore once I finally got her into my bed!

"Okay, so you said you work nights, is this at the club in your dreams?" I decided to ask, still seemingly writing down notes as I would, had I been a real psychiatrist.

"Yes, but that really doesn't have anything to do with it," she said defensively but again, I decided to push for the sole answer I was really searching for here.

"You also mentioned your boss in the dream. Do you have feelings for him?" I seriously would have laughed at her expression had I been free to do so.

"He's my boss," she stated hoping this was enough to appease me by answering further. Of course, needless to say, it didn't.

"Yes, but things can still happen between an employer and an employee."

"Yes, I know, but nothing happened," she argued again making me raise a brow at her in question, for she could quickly see that I was unravelling her lies.

"Umm...I'm not so sure. You say that nothing has happened but whenever I mention the idea, you look upset...I'm here to listen Keira, so please give me that chance." I said, now gently prompting her to open up to me and the second I saw that single tear fall down her cheek, I knew I already had my answer...

She wasn't over me.

And didn't rejoicing in that fact just make me the biggest bastard ever!

"Fine, you want the truth then here it is... I fell for my boss and I stupidly mistook that he had some feelings for me too, but I was cruelly exposed to reality and as a result, I am trying my hardest to get over it," she said now unable to stop as a few more tears followed the first. I nodded my head, knowing that I had indeed gone too far with my questioning and handed her a tissue from a box of them barely seen on the disorganised desk.

Once again, the urge to take her in my arms and comfort her was almost too overwhelming to ignore.

"Right well...in that case I will prescribe you with some Benzodiazepines which will help you relax, but this is for a short time only. I don't want you becoming dependant on these and I want you to come and see me once a week for four more sessions, then we will take it from there," I told her unable to prevent my guilt from coating my tone in a tenderness that would seem odd directed at someone I wasn't supposed to know.

After this, however, she seemed pleased to have accomplished her task in gaining what she wanted from this meeting. And I could tell with her reaction to this that she had absolutely no intention of coming back here. Even though she accepted my terms with a firm nod of her head. Then she got up from her seat, signalling the end of her own time here and watched me as I wrote out the prescription, after I first had to go hunting for the personalised pad in Dr Goff's drawers.

I then handed her the slip of paper and couldn't help but end the meeting by giving in to my desperate need to touch her at least once. So, I held out my hand for her to shake, giving in to the urge to make contact but not going as far as to keep hold without letting go as I wanted.

I knew the second she shivered and gave me those wide questioning eyes of hers that she felt our connection, meaning she wasn't immune to what I was also experiencing. That jolt to my heart was like holding a live wire, only one with the power to calm my inner being not inflict harm. It was a warmth that coursed through my vessel and touched the supernatural nerves that spoke not only to me as a man but to my angelic and demonic sides as well.

And then in a heartbeat it was gone.

But it just wasn't enough, and I had a feeling it never would be, for I couldn't ever see myself reaching a limit of time with her. She gave me a quizzical look back in return but didn't ask what I knew in her heart she wanted to…

'Did she know me?'

Oh, but she knew me alright, just not yet the version of myself I was ready to share with her. But soon…very, very soon for that time was coming and my strength in preventing it from happening was almost at an end.

So, for now I let her go, walking out of the door and doing so with one last look over her shoulder at me, that single question still held firmly in her gaze. However, the second the door closed, I in turn closed a pair of eyes that weren't my own at the same time ripping the single page from the notebook.

It was the only evidence of me being there and after taking hold of the secretary's mind long enough to erase all evidence of Keira being there as well, I reopened my eyes. Doing so this time in my own body and looking down at the only piece of truth now written in my own hand for me to see.

I had brought the page back with me and only two lines were written there. The first being,

'My beautiful little liar'

And the last...

'When will you be mine?'

DRAVEN

71

BLOODY CRUMBS TO FOLLOW

The annual Halloween 'Battle of the Bands' was always a big night for the club and a night I was glad to say we usually missed due to our time here being concluded long before now. But everything had changed...

Now there was her.

A girl who was currently walking through my doors dressed like sin itself and innocently smelling as sweet as any recently untouched, fallen angel would. She may have been sent to me by the Gods above but right now she had been packaged by the Devil himself! For the temptation was too great to be delivered by something so pure.

I swear all I wanted to do was jump from the balcony and claim her in front of her own world, just so they knew that she was mine. I didn't know where she had got that dress from, but I wanted to both tear it from her body for tempting me and worship it whole for it made her look like one of Hell's Goddesses.

Crimson red velvet clung to her torso in a tight bodice that frustratingly provided those around her with a bountiful view of an ample handful of creamy flesh. A deep curved line of her cleavage was a sight just begging for me to bury my fingers into. Then to take hold of one breast before ripping the material down from it so that I could taste its ripe fruit for myself.

I could almost hear the scattering of black beads as they rained down from the torn heart shaped neckline. That same glittering of beads looked like fallen black tears that now clung to the material like morning dew. And the black droplets continued down into a V shape as if pointing the way to other known milky treasures I knew lay hidden beneath layers of a full velvet skirt.

I then found myself smirking to myself at the crown of black tears worn nestled amongst a mane of golden curls, curls that looked as tamed as they did unruly. The crown was made from the same beading clustered on her torso and edging of her ballgown. It was made to look like stalagmites of black ice reaching upwards like seven glittering fingers.

But this little red princess was lost, for her disguise was fooling no one as I knew of her innocent ways. Those shy little glances my way and slips of murmured words spoken in my presence...I knew how I affected her, just as I would tonight when this King made his presence known to his soon to be Queen.

So, I adjusted my demonic mask, one that was matt black and covered most of my face. It was one that had been molded to my features and its folds added to the devilish affect. Especially with its elongated nose and the raised wishbone shape that curved from the centre of my forehead that created its own crudely shaped crown. From this, two curled horns added to the effect along with the two points that reached my chin down either side of my mouth. I even allowed my demon side to blacken my skin around my eyes knowing that it would aid in making my disguise more intimidating.

To my mask I added a period costume; a long black military style jacket. One you would have associated more with a pirate, with black buttons running down each side and each nestled in a bed of thick curled embroidered cord. Large folded cuffs matched the damask material of the accentuated collar. Beneath this I wore a black shirt left open at the neck under a double-breasted damask black waistcoat that matched the jacket. Black trousers, heavy boots and a sabre belt hung slightly to one side from the weight of the weapon that hung there.

I had picked my choice of costume based solely on her for I wanted to ignite those breathy little moans of surprise from her. I wanted to see those submissive eyes sneak their secret glances my way. I wanted to feel her tremble under my touch... and I knew just how to get what I wanted.

Now it was time to put my plan into action and it started off by watching her as she made her way cautiously through my club. It was as if she knew she shouldn't have been there but simply couldn't help herself. And little did she know that she couldn't, not even if she had tried.

For she was drawn to my Afterlife, *my home*. She was drawn to the core of me, as I was to her. So, like a moth to the crimson flame, I allowed myself to walk down the staircase now. And for once relying on the gasps of surprise from the crowd as a back drop to make my entrance known to her.

She turned around slowly, being the last to do so as she watched the master of this demonic domain arrive. Doing so amongst the sea of humans all playing my kind for an evening on the dark side. But little did they know that the real monsters were only ever a hairsbreadth away and often fed from the fears of the unknown.

And speaking of fears, the moment her eyes took in the sight of me I saw her painted red lips part and heard the whispered gasp slip through the air like a secret. One travelling an invisible current straight to me, for that sound belonged to me and to me alone.

The crowd started to part the moment my feet touched the last step and as I knew it would, it led me straight to her. She looked like prey that had been caught with no chance at escape, so the effort in trying wasn't worth it. No, instead she would simply watch as the predator stalked close to her, unknowing of her fate in doing so. I couldn't take my eyes off her, devouring the sight like a man freely displaying his obsession...no, not like a man, but like a demonic King who had finally found his intended Queen!

I continued to keep her captive with my gaze and became immensely satisfied when seeing the blush rising to her cheeks. Then when I was seconds away from her, I commanded to start the music back up so that I would have reason to take her in my arms to lead her into the first dance.

I could see that she wanted to take a cautious step back the second I stopped only inches from her. The way she slowly looked up at me I knew it was coming, so the moment her foot started to move I acted. I reached out and snatched her from completing the act, hauling her tight to my body and igniting another gasp from her.

"This moment is mine!" I all but growled down at her and it was the only warning she would get that she was going nowhere. Her eyes widened in both fear and surprise, a look I fed from, unashamedly absorbing it and coming close to tasting it like a sweetness bursting on my tongue.

A devil's kiss of the soul.

I felt my hands on her flex and had to swallow down the urge to swing her into my arms and carry her back to my chamber. Gods but what I planned to do to this delicious body would take days for the demon in me to be sated nearly enough to function!

However, the second I saw my name being whispered from her lips in question I knew that my actions were startling her. Thankfully, the angel in me intervened. I felt my hands relax and one spanned against her lower back. Then with the other I took her gloved hand in mine and started to lead her around the room in a waltz. A feeling that bloomed inside me and made me feel but one thought...

At Last.

She continued to look up at me as though she could barely believe this was happening and other than whispering my name, she had yet to speak to me. It was as if we were both lost in this silent battle of what was real and what was simply a dream. For surely this couldn't be happening. And as if thinking my own thoughts, she spoke,

"Is this really happening?" she asked me, barely a whisper. One in fact, had I not been of the supernatural kind, would have been lost to the music. I spun her body before pulling her in tight and igniting a breathy moan once more. Then I let her hand go so that I could cup her face to tell her,

"If it's not, then I fear I will wage war on the Gods for their cruelty, for having you in my arms feels like Heaven." She sucked in a startled breath and before she could respond further, I retook her hand and spun her out from my hold intending to bring her back again.

Only the sudden sound of all of the windows smashing had me accidentally letting go. I frowned taking my eyes from her for a mere second to look at what had caused such destruction. However, when I looked all the windows were still intact.

I looked back at Keira expecting to see her standing there waiting for me, but *she was gone.* Instead all I saw was a flash of crimson as she made her way through the crowd. Where did she think she was going? Did she really think that she could run from me?

Well, she was about to learn her first lesson when believing she could deny this King his rightful prize. So, I started the hunt weaving through the crowd but at every turn I made I just managed to catch sight of her dress or golden hair as it flashed through the throng of people. I frowned in annoyance at this game she was playing, so decided to even the odds. Doing so with merely a thought I froze every single body in the room so that I could find her quicker.

Even the music stopped, as I now slipped between the pillars of people with deadly silence...that was until I heard her desperate plea,

"Draven!" It was in this moment that I turned suddenly and saw her outstretched hand between the crowd, reaching out to me. I quickly realised that she wasn't running from me at all, *she was being pulled.*

It wasn't her game she was playing...*but someone else's.*

Her face was there calling for me, desperation in her voice and eyes wide with fear. But then just as quickly, she was gone in an instant. I suddenly roared in anger and the moment I did the lights exploded above me, plunging the room into darkness. I knew this hadn't been my doing and before I could question it further a red glow started to seep through the windows as if a blood moon was suddenly breaching the clouds.

"How is this possible?" I asked myself aloud when that same red glow started to penetrate the darkness enough to see the bloody graveyard in which I now stood. Human bodies all lay mangled on the floor, as if a wave of violence and terror had swept through the room and killed everything with a mortal pulse...*well, not everything.*

"Keira?" I spoke her name the second I saw her standing there opposite me only twenty feet away and also standing amongst the bloody horror my club had become. She was shaking in fear, with her hands curled into fists by her sides as she looked down at all the broken bodies that once resembled the people that she knew.

"No, no, no...NO!" She started off whispering the plea before screaming it, no doubt wishing that this new

nightmare would end. But then we both heard the sadistic laughter coming from behind her and we knew it was far from over.

"Keira, come here!" I ordered with a stern voice, but she wouldn't move, as if she couldn't. So, this time I tried to infiltrate her mind into doing as I commanded, knowing that the presence was getting closer.

"Keira, listen to me now and do as I say...*come to me now!*" I almost roared this last part, screaming it in her mind and trying to cut through her blinding fear. But then the sinister laughter came closer and soon, added to its demonic sound was a shadow approaching her from behind. This was when I finally tried to move, asking myself why I hadn't tried before? But then my question was answered when my legs refused to move and my entire being was now in control by another.

There had only been one other time in my existence that this had ever happened, so it wasn't hard to guess now who was responsible. It was back when a 'once' brother in arms had felt what he believed was a knife imbedded in his back twist by my very hand!

A knife I held and changed history the moment I became his immortal enemy.

I would never forget the look of betrayal upon his face when he realised what it was that I had kept from him all this time. Two thousand years in the making and it all had come to that single point of discovery, one I had hoped he would never find. For in his mind he had been betrayed by the Gods for a second time and by the hand of someone he had pledged his loyalty to...a life he believed I had forsaken for my own gain.

A life sacrificed for a second time.

And now, it was time for his revenge.

"Lucius!" I hissed his name the moment his Vampiric features came into focus as he stepped up behind my Chosen One. Her shaking terrified body now framed by his larger one. And now with his wings hanging down from his massive

horns shadowed behind her head, it ended up creating a trick of light, looking as if they belonged to her. But given their height difference it was merely an added sense of deception. One Lucius had known would play on my mind.

His smirk told me this.

"Keira run...RUN TO ME!" This time I did roar this in her mind, putting all my power of influence into the command, but she didn't move and I soon discovered why.

"Tut, tut old friend, I think you will find that she has a new master of her mind now and it's a shame but there isn't room in there for the both of us," Lucius said as he tapped the side of her forehead, one long black talon growing dangerously as it did.

"Leave her out of this!" I growled making him laugh again.

"Just remember, Dom..." He paused as he now ran that claw down her face at least being careful enough not to break the skin. I watched as Keira closed her eyes unable to do anything else. He then held the tops of her arm tight in his grasp before finishing off his threat to me,

"...You asked for this!" Then he spun her round quickly to face him before wrenching her neck to the side and sinking his fangs into her vulnerable flesh.

"NOOOO!" I roared, powerless to do anything more as he forced me to watch as he took the most important soul to me from this world in the blink of an eye! Then he tore his bloody mouth from her gushing neck once her body now lay limp in his arms.

"Tastes like the fucking sun!" he snarled up at the ceiling before looking back at me with amber fire now lighting up his demonic eyes and said,

"Soon, my friend." Then he dropped her lifeless body to the floor, and I was forced to witness as it fell in slow motion, as if doing so in water. Lucius simply walked away into the darkness to the sound of my demonic hatred behind him, cursing his name to the Gods above and below.

And I was left to run to catch the death of my Chosen One to the sound of his laughter. But the second I caught her she simply turned to ash and I suddenly jolted from this nightmare, taking with me the horrifying image that unfortunately was now...

Scarred to my memory.

"Dom!" I woke with a start the second my name seeped into my conscious mind and I soon found myself at my desk where I had been working. I looked up to find my brother looking down over me, clearly concerned and I soon found out why for he nodded down at my hands. I, too, allowed my gaze to fall on the only evidence left of my nightmare, finding my demonic hands had torn inch deep gouges from the solid wood of my desk. It now looked as though one of Cerberus' Hellbeasts had been here causing the havoc I knew had come from my own desperate hands.

"I...I..." I started to try and explain but in all honestly, I didn't even know where to begin. This was when I felt my brother's hand lay at my shoulder and looking up at him now, I could see the worry there in that crystal blue gaze.

"Did you dream of her?" he asked and when I closed my eyes at the mention of Keira, he had his answer.

"I was too late to save her again," I confessed, still unable to look at him and being instead forced to look once more at the fading eyes of death as they disappeared from sight, silently asking me why I hadn't saved her.

My first dream of her death.

"I think I can assume by the surfacing of your demon that she fell from the roof again?" Vincent said making me wince before standing abruptly from my chair and walking away, needing to put distance between any evidence of the dream.

"You mean jumped, for do not forget that fact here brother. A suicide chosen instead of dealing with the repulsion my true self brought her!" I snapped running a frustrated hand through my hair.

"That may have happened in your nightmares, but shouldn't you be more focused on the reality that proved that dream wrong," Vincent said making the point just as he had when I first told him of it. Doing so by highlighting the fact that Keira had been on a rooftop and even though she may have run from me initially, she had never once tried to jump from the roof and take her own life. But instead of surrendering to his point I chose to ignore it altogether and told him,

"It was not the same dream." Vincent didn't say anything but instead gave me the time I needed to elaborate. Something right now I didn't want to do, almost as much as I knew I needed to. Because if there was one thing I knew about Lucius, it was that the man had proven his extreme will of patience in regard to waiting for my Chosen One. However, as I also knew, there was only so far that patience would stretch, and I personally had long ago almost hit my own limit.

"She was in the club, we danced and then Lucius appeared before snatching her away and killing her before my very eyes." Once I finished, I could tell Vincent was visibly shocked. Because the question was why? Yes, it was common knowledge that he was our enemy and would use any means possible if it meant him getting what he wanted. But killing her? Even I wasn't convinced of that.

"You think he wants to kill her?" he asked, his tone laced with disbelief.

"No, I think it was a warning, Vince," I replied as I knew that with Keira's death it would also mean the end to any chance he might have at bargaining for what he truly wanted...*the other half of the Holy Spear.*

"I think you might be right," Vincent agreed but one look at his face told me that there was more.

"Vince?"

"There was a reason I came to your office, Dom, and it wasn't to wake you from a nightmare," he told me, now walking over to my desk and spinning my laptop to face him.

He tapped on the keyboard to power it into action before clicking on what I assumed were my private emails. I frowned in question and walked closer so that I could see for myself what he now spoke of.

"I heard from Ranka when she could not reach you directly," he told me at the same time searching for what he was looking for, his halo of blonde curls nearly glowing from the light that suddenly lit up the screen.

"She sent over this footage of the night Keira was found at the hospital," he told me and I could see from where I was stood the exact moment they captured Morgan. This was after first setting a trap for him by having one of their detectives dressed as a member of the hospital staff, so they could send him into the wrong room. In there they had over a dozen police offices ready to take him down, which they did quickly. And it would seem, that it was one of the only things in this case they did with any efficiency. Other than when it was time to gather evidence, after the crime had been laid out for them, to make of it what was plain to see despite merely having bloody crumbs to follow.

So, they had their victim, their perpetrator and a house full of evidence to convict him all in one night. I knew this thanks to the case file, so what I was seeing now was of little cause for urgency. This was why I looked to Vincent with a questioning brow raised.

"Okay, so we know this was the time he was arrested but look what happens next," he said nodded for me to focus back at the footage. It was the same camera angle of the hallway and included a section of the reception desk belonging to the ward Keira was being treated in. The same one I had moments ago just seen a team full of police walking down as they escorted a cuffed Morgan along the hallway until out of sight.

But time seemed to skip forward as if someone had increased the pace of the footage. Then a hooded figure was seen walking down the hall but didn't look up, nor did he acknowledge the woman at the desk. I knew instantly he was one of our kind, for with a slight movement of his head he controlled the lady sat at the desk who had obviously asked him who he was.

"Who was it?" I asked, but instead of answering my question he nodded back to the screen and told me,

"Keep watching, brother." So I did as instructed, seeing once again time being fast forwarded and taking note of the date displayed in the righthand corner. It was only two days after she had been found and after Morgan's capture. Then exactly one hour after the hooded figure was seen walking down the hallway towards Keira's room, he was seen again, only this time heading away from it.

I was once again about to ask who it was and no doubt in a tone that was evident to my mounting frustration when suddenly the hooded figure turned and looked directly up at the camera. It was as if he wanted to be seen, and I quickly discovered why.

He pulled back the hood and revealed himself as who I feared it to be...

"Lucius!"

I hissed his name with the same venom of hatred I could taste in my dream and was forced to watch as two years ago, before I even knew her name, Lucius had found her. He had planted himself there knowing that in time I would find this footage and one day be forced to realise that he had found my Chosen One long before I had.

But not only that, for he wanted me to know that once I finally did find her, that I would have to live with the knowledge he could have taken her, right then and there and there wouldn't have been one damn thing I could have done about it!

Vincent was right, this was a warning. A two-year-old warning.

And just like in my nightmare, he tapped on his watch and mouthed up at the camera the same thing he had said to me just after he had torn into her neck before dropping her lifeless body to the floor.

Before he had destroyed me...

'Soon, my friend.'

To be continued
In King of Kings
Book 2

fUTURE Books...

Afterlife Spin-off series

The Kings of Afterlife Book 1 – Vincent's Curse.

Sigurd
Jared
Seth

Lucius series:
Transfusion Book 2 – Due October 2019

The Beasts of Afterlife:

Adam (and Pip)
Leivic
Orthrus
Ragnar

Afterlife's Masters of Hell:

Lucifer
Asmodeus

Afterlife's Young Adult Series

The Afterlife Chronicles:

The Glass Dagger- book 1 (Available on Kindle and Paperback)
The Hells Ring – Coming soon.

The Transfusion Chronicles and Hell Beast Chronicles also coming soon.

Other Afterlife Books

The Forbidden Chapters - Book/Part 2

Afterlife's Short Stories

Other

'Devil in Me'
        By
Stephanie Hudson and Blake Hudson.
(Coming Soon)

Keep updated with all Afterlife News...

Check out my ALL NEW website for everything
Afterlife Saga at... www.afterlifesaga.com
(Including exciting Official Afterlife Merchandise!)

And for keeping updated on all Afterlife related news
and upcoming events, please join my mailing list on the
website to receive regular Newsletters.

Or you can follow me on Afterlife saga on
Twitter: @afterlifesaga
Facebook: Afterlife saga page

Also, please feel free to join myself and other
Dravenites on any of the groups below...

The Official private fan groups (Afterlife's Crave the
Drave & Afterlife Saga Official Fan page) on Facebook to
interact with me and other fans. Can't wait to see you
there!

Or feel free to email me with any questions or
comments you may have about the Afterlife saga at
stephaniehudson@afterlifesaga.com

Acknowledgments

Well first and foremost my love goes out to all the people who deserve the most thanks and are the wonderful people that keep me going day to day. But most importantly they are the ones that allow me to continue living out my dreams and keep writing my stories for the world to hopefully enjoy... These people are of course YOU! Words will never be able to express the full amount of love I have for you guys. Your support is never ending. Your trust in me and the story is never failing. But more than that, your love for me and all who you consider your 'Afterlife family' is to be commended, treasured and admired. Thank you just doesn't seem enough, so one day I hope to meet you all and buy you all a drink! ;)

To my family... To my amazing mother, who has believed in me from the very beginning and doesn't believe that something great should be hidden from the world. I would like to thank you for all the hard work you put into my books and the endless hours spent caring about my words and making sure it is the best it can be for everyone to enjoy. You make Afterlife shine. To my wonderful crazy father who is and always has been my hero in life. Your strength astonishes me, even to this day and the love and care you hold for your family is a gift you give to the Hudson name. And last but not least, to the man that I consider my soul mate. The man who taught me about real love and makes me not only want to be a better person but makes me feel I am too. The amount of support you have given me since we met has been incredible and the greatest feeling was finding out you wanted to spend the rest of your life with me when you asked me to marry you.

All my love to my dear husband and my own personal Draven... Mr Blake Hudson.

Another personal thank you goes to my dear friend Caroline Fairbairn and her wonderful family that have embraced my brand of crazy into their lives and given it a hug when most needed.
For their friendship I will forever be eternally grateful.

I would also like to mention Claire Boyle my wonderful PA, who without a doubt, keeps me sane and constantly smiling through all the chaos which is my life ;) And a loving mention goes to Lisa Jane for always giving me a giggle and scaring me to death with all her count down pictures lol ;)
Thank you for all your hard work and devotion to the saga and myself. And always going that extra mile, pushing Afterlife into the spotlight you think it deserves. Basically helping me achieve my secret goal of world domination one day...evil laugh time... Mwahaha! Joking of course ;)
As before, a big shout has to go to all my wonderful fans who make it their mission to spread the Afterlife word and always go the extra mile. I love you all x

Made in the USA
Columbia, SC
04 June 2021

39052438R00426